THE SYME PAPERS

Benjamin Markovits is twenty-nine, and *The Syme Papers* is his first
novel. Originally from Texas, he now lives in London and writes
for the *London Review of Books* and the *Times Literary Supplement*.

BENJAMIN MARKOVITS

·The·Syme·Papers·

A Novel

faber and faber

First published in 2004
by Faber and Faber Limited
3 Queen Square London WC1N 3AU
This paperback edition published in 2005

Typeset by Faber and Faber Ltd
Printed in England by Mackays of Chatham plc, Chatham, Kent

A CIP record for this book
is available from the British Library

ISBN 0–571–21791–5

2 4 6 8 10 9 7 5 3 1

To Caroline

·The ·Syme · Papers ·

Mrs R.:

Impatience, my dear, I may tell you, will never make you a good Geologist; and we must go through a great many facts and conjectures, before we come to the history of the shells, besides some pretty romances which are called Theories of the earth, and tell us how the world was made.

Christina:

Then I am sure I shall like it, for I delight in romances; and whenever I hear the word, I think of the Happy Valley in 'Rasselas', Robinson Crusoe's Island, or the Enchanted Gardens of Armida; but I always thought there were no romances in philosophy.

Mrs R.:

You mean, perhaps, that there should be none; but philosophers, if they have much imagination, are apt to let it loose as well as other people, and in such cases are sometimes led to mistake a fancy for a fact. Geologists, in particular, have very frequently amused themselves in this way, and it is not a little amusing to follow them in their fancies and their waking dreams. Geology, indeed, in this view, may be called a romantic science.

Conversations on Geology; comprising a familiar explanation of the Huttonian and Wernerian systems; the Mosaic Geology, as explained by **Mr Granville Penn**; and the late discoveries of Professor Loomis, Eaton, Syme, and others, 1828.

a series of improbabilities founded upon inaccuracies, and the rest of it plagiarized, I regret to say. A great shame, for Pitt is a genial little goblin, and I wish him well . . .

Excerpt from a memo by Dr Sal Bunyon to the Promotion and Tenure Committee, Department of History, University of Texas at Austin, regarding 'The Syme Papers'.

PART I

·The·Discovery·

I WASN'T LOOKING FOR SYME (my lucky number, my jackpot, my undiscovered genius). I was looking for *anything*, at my wits' end, or rather my *grant's* end, holed up in a studio in King's Cross – part of a flat brown block looking over the skips and lorries of the Caledonian Road. The grant was running dry and so was I, sending beer money back home to the wife-and-two in Austin, Texas. I was supposed to be writing (on a Fulbright as it happens, toot my own horn) in order to (one . . . two . . . three): finish the book, publish (publish!), scoot home, win tenure, and start building the (rather expensive) picket fence. *Writing*, hunched over the schoolboy desk I pinched from one of the aforementioned skips and pushed against the squat window (which, sealed at the sill by paint, locked by a smear of paint over the what-d'you-call-it, jig, hitch, thingum, clasp, *bolt*, had clammed up – stuck fast, unbudgeable, *unopenable*, as the days got longer, hotter and thicker with the dust of lorries and skips on the Caledonian Road). Writing *Fire and Ice: a history of the Plutonist–Neptunist debate on the composition of the Earth's crust and its evolution into modern geology*. A good, a breathless title, no? as Phidy would say. One of my forebears in the long tradition of academic *scroungers*. But you don't know Phidy yet. You hardly know me.

Dr Douglas Pitt, BA Geology and Geophysics UC San Diego; M.Phil. History Oxford, Merton College; Ph.D. History NYU. I have travelled, as I like to tell my . . . my colleagues (as I hope to call them soon) from the glories of sunshine, to the glories of tradition, to the glories of metropolis. I have eschewed San Diego, a border town (all ports are border towns) twice over, the land of my birth – under that synthetic sky, a creation of God's akin to an architect's model, clean, unchipped, constructed for tiny men. Then Oxford and my private renaissance. I *breathed*, for the first time, and recognized that I was born for the company of greatness (the company only). The possession of leisure is indeed a wonderful opportunity. But the letters in that dignified list that produced the greatest pleasure: NY. A wonderful town for scroungers, for men of shabby elbows, who like to look at their feet, and see what they step in. Since those days, and the first blush of my perpetual youth – for I bear the kind of doggedness that never ages, a bright pink face, hanging arms, sweating forehead, the awkwardness of adolescence enduring into middle age – my career has been, in James's phrase, a succession of stops and starts.

I wander between two worlds – the 'two cultures', as C.P. Snow dubbed them – ever at each other's throat, united only in their suspicion of men like me. The *historians* don't trust me, think I'm up to my neck in scientific hocus-pocus, and an amateur of textual integrity. The *scientists* won't touch me, a lightweight of fact and proof, a pedlar of assumptions and interpretations. I have made it the business of my academic life to trace the course of *great mistakes*, and the fruits of them, the errors of science, redeemed by their place in history. Which brings me to *Fire and Ice* (or Fire and Water, more properly speaking – but I could not help adding a touch of Frost). To the clash, now dead two hundred years and mostly forgotten, between Hutton, a mountaineering Scot, and Werner, an old Bavarian gentleman, over a patch of intellectual ground as wide as the world itself – to determine whether our quaint earth was born out of Sea (precipitating from a vast ocean) or Rock (cast up in a great fire). Of course, the question before me was to examine how such curious views could have *precipitated* or *cast up* our own modern picture of the Crust, nearly as miraculous a transformation, it seemed to me, as the prime creation itself. Which brings me to the Fulbright Fellowship and the studio in King's Cross, researching the likes of Hutton, Fairplay, and Cartographical Smith. Which brought me, in the end, to Syme.

Write, Pitt! Write! I said, squeezing my legs under the boy's desk and banging my elbow on the table. Write. The legs weren't the problem, as it happens, for I *compress* with age, grow heavier and squatter, and my underpinnings slipped easily under the oak, from which I had scraped the dried gum with the back of my pen.

But I am a boy no longer (he sighed). The thatch on my head has gone, leaving two fistfuls above my ears and a bony shiny pate between. Pushing forty, they call it; I'm pushing forty, though forty seems to be doing most of the pushing. And my time for tenure, the seal and badge of the academic aristocracy, was slipping, slipping from me. I had begun to try the patience – I have always been good at trying patience – of my peers, my superiors, I should say, as they had become. This was my last shot. Publish or bust.

So write, Pitt, why don't you write? (I believe my name was a great inhibitor of growth, a low ceiling on my evolution. There is only *so far* a Mr Douglas Pitt may hope to rise – so be it.) But I *did* write: over breakfast, dipping those really rather excellent Portuguese custard tarts into my morning coffee (fattening, no doubt, but full of *oomph*); covering note cards, front and back, with ink, stained by the greasy newspaper of my lunchtime fish and chips. All through the dusty afternoons: stuffing the pockets of my tweed jacket with notes and references, titbits, quotations, connections, sudden bursts of wonderful illumination condensed to a black puddle of illegible scribble. I wrote even on the tags of tea bags, rescued from styrofoam cups on my brillig strolls among the builders and the traffic of King's Cross. How I wrote, till my cramped room was cluttered with a thousand inspirations, sticky and half-formed, barnacles on a post left rotting in deserted waters. My dear, my *dears*, I wrote. As I had assured *Missy* Pitt herself, the wife in question, over a course of mostly miserable telephone calls through the depth of a long, wet English year. (Susannah by name, dubbed Missy by me. I should like at some point to undertake a history of the nickname, of the combinations of affection and hatred, and suitability, that *fix* them; particularly, of the qualities necessary to become *the* Great – as I plan soon to transform Syme himself into *a* Great.) Missy worries greatly, she worries *assiduously*, on my behalf; as if, almost, the exhaustion of her concern might push my fortunes a little along their way. And, to be fair to her, my fortunes need a push or two, a jumpstart; and *hers* are likely to suffer soon, should *mine* fail.

9

For Dr Bunyon – the Dean of History at the University of Texas, the Dean of Shambling Geniality, a tall, blinking man of enormous brows – mutters against me; 'concerned', of course. (There must be some root of *sham* in shambling, so often the two limp together, an earnest of false vulnerability from a man in power.) The *Toymaker* and I – and here Pitt gestures widely with his hands, one each way – are like *this*. Dr Bunyon, as the English have it, is not 'on board' – though he sits on a great many boards, and chairs the committee on tenure. His assurance of which prompted the mortgage of a house we could not, quite, afford. His subsequent genial, bluff, insidious attempts to poison me among my colleagues I cannot *comprehend*. (He coined the phrase 'unscrupulous scrupulosity' to describe my research methods, and then refused to explain it or himself to me.) But his insinuations of professional neglect, under a veil of good intentions, to my wife I cannot, and will not, *forget*.

'He must *write*,' he mutters at her, smiling into his left cheek, 'if he hopes to *stick*, my dear.' And she mutters his echoes at me (a foul noise from such pretty lips), until my assurances themselves grow shrill with repetition: I write, I write, I write.

Till first my right fist gave way to strain and weariness, clawed up – like a blasted sapling says the hump-backed prince. And then my left, shadowing its brother, retracted to a perpetual flinch. The fist of Doug Pitt, flinching! After five hours in the waiting room at Middlesex Hospital – the noble NHS, symbol of democracy indeed, that the rich shall grow ill in the squalor of the poor, bless Orwell – a young Pakistani gentleman in a blue sports coat informed me (before rushing off to catch a tee-time or teatime, I could not determine which) that I suffered from carpal tunnel syndrome. What does that mean? I asked, in plain English. To speak plainly, he said, it means that your hands look like *that*: these talons, curled upon themselves, in an animal clutch. (I have been told there is a surprising touch of the animal about me, for a cerebral gentleman – a true *physical* presence.) What can you do for me? I said.

This has always been my cry. 'What can you do for me?' my

father taught – he was the foreman of a business that manufactured poles for scaffolding. (I have also, in my way, concerned myself over scaffolding.) Ask, he said, and you shall get on. And so I *have*, and so I *did*. But people, as I have found to my dismay, grow – how shall I put it? – tired of their own goodness. There have been promises made, positions offered, assurances given – enough said. Dr Bunyon, tall, sloping, *genial* soul, stooping towards his lesser fellows, has proffered *chairs* before (that pinnacle of academic ambition, a *seat*) and withdrawn them as his guests sat down. I am not the first victim of his *concerns*. Generosity, like inspiration, runs dry – the former rather sooner than the latter. You all have met me in your day. I am familiar, no doubt. The kind of under-dog nobody wants to root for, that's me. But my desperate days are almost over. My name will be secure – and in the meanwhile, I have scrounged.

What can you do for me? I asked the elegant doctor. Nothing, he said, in his perfect, precise, clipped English. We are only beginning to understand your condition. What have you understood? I asked. This much – he answered – that it is called carpal tunnel syndrome.

They fitted me with two braces, strapped over wrist and palm through the arch of the thumb. And there I stood, kitted like a champion fighter looking for a prize fight. I have a boxer's build, too: thick in the chest and shoulders, a bulldog's build, a Pitt-bull. But I could not write. The very organs of my enterprise lodged with me useless, my hands, scarce able to clasp the delicate loop of a teacup, mutton-fisted, and serve their mouth its needful.

So read, Pitt! Read! I said. The world is full of men smarter than you; history records them. Scrounge! As Dr Bunyon explained, looking down, you are somewhat short . . . on imagination, in your work, Pitt. (We shall see.) And so every morning I walked up the Caledonian Road, away from the stink of the canal, into the stink of King's Cross Station. Ducked through the arc of traffic around the tracks, the rumble shivering through the soles of my boots from the workmen blocking the road, drilling for pipes in the asphalt with their jackhammers. Across that, into the relative quiet of hotels and big business; up Pancras Road, slipping off to the courtyard of the British Library, that bright brick supermarket of the written word; into the silence and the air-conditioned softness of the reading room. Read, Pitt, read!

My enemies – I mean, my critics – like to believe that I am *thorough*. That is their greatest compliment, the pith of their condescension. Pitt, they like to say, is thorough. Trust Pitt to come up with a good list, a useful bibliography. Pitt, they say, does Good Work; people know it, respect him for it. They don't look for inspiration from Pitt; they look for facts. Wrangling over a quotation or a date, they come to me. 'Ask Pitt,' Dr Bunyon says. 'He rolls up his shirt-sleeves, does the dirty work. I often think', he used to add, in his tremulous, gentlemanly quaver, warbling, 'that Pitt is on to something, with all his digging. That's where the real work is; only' – there is always an only! – 'I don't have the stomach for it.' Giving to understand, you see, that a real high-class brain *wouldn't* have the stomach for it.

All right, Pitt, I said, dig, that's what you're good at, Pitt. 'The overdevelopment of memory', Bunyon calls me behind my back (he is rich with the coins of phrase), 'an evolutionary curiosity'. The species produces people like me, once in a while, to *hoard* history; so that people like Bunyon can pick at it. I like to touch everything as I go by, only I find it hard to set down afterwards. I write *everything*, regardless of starts and stops, or rather, consumed by them. I don't think in *stories*, I think in *seas*, following wave after wave of curiosity. I lack imagination, or suffer from the surfeit of it; I lack *shape*, the gift of sudden freezing, that allows one to tinker with the ice.

Of course, *what matters in the end is what's remembered*. I don't say it's fair. The process of memory isn't fair; nor is the process of getting noticed in the first place. I know enough about that. But there is always hope for the *elephantine*, for memorable cultures, that is, cultures able to remember. The slightest gesture may survive. As Syme has survived, conjuring with a wave of his hand a man's thoughts a century later, and transforming *them* into a vision of the world we have not shaken from us yet, and may never shake.

What Bunyon doesn't reckon on is that *we* hold the keys to the kingdom. Me and people like me – the diggers.

And then there's Syme, a digger of a very different feather.

I wasn't looking for Syme; I was looking for anything. A break-through or a break-*in* to the process of genius that produced ALFRED WEGENER, gentleman of many parts, and the first man to set forth in sober theory the notion *that Africa and the Americas had belonged to a single body of land, that the earth itself had split, drifted and lay slipping and slipping, even as we stand upon it.* He was an adventurer of science, a balloonist of unusual skill, a mountaineer; and not the only man in this story to have died pursuing his convictions, like Dr Frankenstein, in a waste of ice chasing his imagination.

But his great leap of faith and fact, from rock to rock, as it were, or floe to floe, begged and beggared explanation: a thought so plain a child could grasp it, clicking the pieces in place like the cut edges of a puzzle. *Of course*, the shoulder of South America once nestled in the nook of Africa, lovingly land-locked. Look at them thus, a heart broken on the map, the split halves drifting, *of course*. Some terrible divorce had taken place, driven by the enormous powers of separation. And yet, this was a thought so strange no soul had uttered it in a thousand generations of speculative men; a thought as tremendous as the notion that the earth turned into its own dawn and away at twilight, that the sun did not rise above the lip of the horizon simply to please us. (And yet it moves, Galileo muttered, as he left the court; and so it does, WEGENER answered him, the continents on which we stand as shockingly dislodged from their centre as Galileo's spinning planet.) Memory, I reasoned, must have played its part in such a bridge of the imagination – but memory of what, of whom?

I overreach myself. Let me begin at the beginning; which in my business so often means the end, the last leaf remaining, stuck in gutter or garden, from a forgotten Fall. We shall see if we can trace to their bed the slender roots of Inspiration. As Wegener himself declared of his task in 1915:

We are like a judge confronted by a defendant who declines to answer, and we must determine the truth from the circumstantial evidence. All the proofs we can muster have the deceptive character of this type of evidence. How would we assess a judge who based his decision on part of the available data only?

Let us begin with the circumstantial evidence, then, and judge the truth as we may. For Wegener, our honourable defendant, has long been dead, frozen in his sleeping sack between the upright sticks of his skis thrust in the ice of Greenland to mark his resting-place. A last venture, to prove beyond doubt that the continents shift beneath us, measured in the drift of Greenland, *proved* only fatal in the end. A miscalculation, common as a neglected gas-tank, forced the adventurer to turn back – too late in the event. He cannot answer us now. And who can say, if he stood before us, that even he could account for the accumulation of fact and theory, history and observation, precedents and prescience, that erupted at last in so powerful a revolution of ideas? As William Swainson remarked in 1834, 'the revolutions of science are almost as frequent, and often more extraordinary, than those of political institutions' (though our story will touch on those as well before the end).

These are the circumstances. ALFRED LOTHAR WEGENER was born on 1 November 1880, the fifth child of the theologian and linguist Franz Richard Wegener, whose brother Peter, inventor and magician (the black sheep of a family of priests), plays some role in this story (as we shall see) and bequeathed, among other things, a sense of adventure to his nephew. Alfred grew up in a tall, squeezed house on Friedrichsgracht in Berlin, overlooking the canal. The small boy must have grown used to the illusion, looking out of his bedroom window, of the world shifting by him, quite unfussed, through the still waters.

The Wegener family was well known in its way. Alfred's great-grandfather had been a companion of Alexander von Humboldt (the famous explorer) at the University of Frankfurt a century before. An older cousin starred on the stages of Berlin – making a particular sensation in an adaptation of *Werther*, whose yellow-trousered costume found its way into the Wegener household, to be trotted out in the amateur theatricals performed by Alfred and his brother Kurt. It was above all an *intellectual* household and bore the character of Alfred's father: a pious, yet liberal and curious man, consultant to the Kaiser on religious matters, and a keen botanist and gentleman scientist on the side. He cultivated an extensive library, in which the young Alfred used to while away the wet days after school.

Unfortunately, the Wegener home was bombed during Allied raids in 1942. The windows and walls collapsed into the canals, and most of the books that were not drowned with them perished in the fires that followed. We can now no longer wander through the leathery gloom that excited the young scientist, nor trace the infant steps of his education. But one book did survive the fire and water (an interesting escape, between Pluto and Neptune!): a heavy, copper-bound ledger, recording in the father's meticulous hand the date and entry of every volume in his prized collection.

This book was retrieved by the scientist's nephew (Dr Erich Wegener), who occupied the family home during the war. He carried it with him after 'the tumult and the shouting died' – a strange, a heavy burden, a reminder of the gentility of his grandfather's house. The book travelled with Erich to England in 1949, upon his marriage to a young English nurse who served with the Allied forces in the clear-up of Berlin. The family adopted her name, Bilston, to mediate anti-German feeling; and a Dr Eric Bilston maintained a small but prosperous family practice in the neighbourhood of Tunbridge Wells until his death in 1972. Thereupon his puzzled English children donated the heavy tome to the British Library, a record of their famous great-uncle Alfred, mostly unintelligible: lists of foreign titles and strange names and long-ago dates.

And this I turned to, one hot, desperate day last June, clutching the heavy volume between the palms of my strapped fists, *for Pitt is a digger, you know; a roll-up-the-sleeves fellow, a thorough scholar, in his way.*

If I could begin my career from scratch, with a fresh slate, I should return as a *bibliographer*, a historian of the collections of books. What stories might not be told through the libraries of this world? Records of childhood and old age, of generations, of the cloudy atmosphere of solitude and words in which our mind grows tall. What better bed in which to trace the roots of our slightest thoughts than the libraries, the books, we burrowed in as children? And here before me, spread out in page after page, in the thin, knuckly hand of his father, marking title and date, I read through the circumstances surrounding the birth of Alfred's genius. 'I hereby commence', he wrote, 'this inventory of the library on Friedrichsgracht, this new year, 1880. May all future acquisitions be recorded herein.'

The catalogue was arranged according to shelves. I could dimly picture the dark galleries above the canal by the lists of scribbled titles, *feel* the comfortable solitude at a corner, where one row finished and another began, *see* the young Wegener propping his back against a handful of volumes, pushing them flush with the board; just as here or there a run of scribbled book-names leans against the margin of the page, as his father's hand grew weary or the room grew dark in that long-ago new year. Then there is the first thrill of recognition, a title familiar, perhaps even the contents contained within: Schleiermacher, Fichte, Schelling, the Schlegel brothers; *Tales of my Landlord*, 1st Series, 2nd Series; *Headlong Hall*, *Die Leiden des Jungen Werthers* . . .

The moment of discovery is often a gap between two other things. 'Most ideas', Syme once said, 'begin as the answer to an unimportant problem, soon forgotten, a stone washed away once the stream is crossed . . . So true it is that we are at the mercy of our own . . . inspiration – that is too grand a word, which means nothing more than the ability to begin in idleness and end in faith.' And out of an idle, dozy day I stumbled upon my faith.

I believe the first name to wake my attention in the heavy volume was that of Robert Jameson, a prolific geognosist and noted Neptunian, a follower of WERNER (not Wegener, Alfred, his descendant, but *Werner*, Gottlob, an older, even stranger fish in the kettle of German geology). I had come at last to the very corner of the library I sought. I pictured a row of books squeezed into a bottom shelf, away from the window and the door, a dark, crouching, peaceful nook – but we shall never know, for all such nooks were tumbled into the canal below. Here the geologists and geognosists lived in their leather neighbourhood, a familiar company.

In that dark corner, where the young, breathing Alfred might have slept to escape some distasteful chore, the dead and dusty Werner himself lay ensconced, both his early *On the External Characters of Minerals* (entered into the library in June 1884) and *A New Theory on the Birth of Veins* (also June 1884). Werner rubbed elbows with *Transactions of the Royal Society of Edinburgh* (entered September 1884), containing in the first volume as I knew James Hutton's *Theory of the Earth; or an Investigation of the Laws Observable in the Composition, Dissolution, and Restoration of Land upon the Globe* (we live in a world of breathless titles, no?). Between them, Werner (elegant and slender) and Hutton (thick and obscure, supported by a mass of royal correspondence) divided the field into their camps, the NEPTUNISTS and PLUTONISTS (more of *them* later). Charles Lyell's *Principles of Geology* (February 1885) danced cheek by jowl with Richard Owen's *Key to the Geology of the Globe* (January 1886, a surprising inclusion). And there, between Richard Owen of Indiana, and the Reverend Osmond Fisher, Rector of Harleton, England, and author of *Physics of the Earth's Crust* (entered December 1881), I discovered Syme.

The name of SAMUEL HIGHGATE SYME was a puzzle, of course, for a number of reasons. The first being that his was the only unfamiliar book along the shelf; the remainder belonged to more or less eminent geologists of the late eighteenth and nineteenth centuries. Even the title annexed to the name rang oddly beside the others: the *New Platonist*, a brisk appellation beside its windy fellows, and one that smacked little of their earthy company.

And yet it was a strangeness still slighter that made the greatest impression upon me at the time. Most of the books entered the library between the years of 1884 and 1886, when the botanical interests of Alfred's clerical father drew him briefly into questions of mineralogy. Alfred had just entered boyhood at the time. And he recalled much later, in the diaries he kept on the last and fatal Greenland expedition, how he and his father used to hunt for quartz and shale on the long northern summer days in the nearby Grunewald, following dark veins of rock off the forest paths and charting their progress through the overlay of vegetation.

Alfred's father, however, came to suspect the *geognosists* of tampering with biblical fact to reach their conclusions. Though in typical German fashion he kept their blasphemies in good order on his library shelf, he admitted no geological entry after 1886 – except for Syme's *New Platonist*, which found its way to the library nearly a decade later (November 1895), when young Alfred had just turned fifteen. As Alfred's wife Else faithfully recorded in an account of her husband ('a world-altering explorer, and good-natured, humorous man'): 'young Alfred did not like going to the local Gymnasium, as the resources of his own home offered greater scope for a curious mind'.

Perhaps, I considered, the *New Platonist* was a birthday gift from a relenting father.

I spent the next week trawling through Richard Owen's *Key to the Geology of the Globe*, looking for a clue. But Syme's name caught in my thoughts, a teasing puzzle, what the Germans have so delightfully nicknamed an *ear-worm*, pestering its way to the front of my consciousness. If only because I wondered who the hell he was. What was the *New Platonist*, who were the New Platonists? And when at last Owen had exhausted my patience, I turned, almost as an afterthought, to the man who will make my name, as I *his*.

Some of the facts discovered themselves quickly enough. Samuel Highgate Syme was the son, born in Baltimore in 1794, of one Edward Syme, an Englishman, himself the younger son of Theophilus, a manufacturer of *jimbles* (the sturdy anti-corrosive bolts used in the wooden hulls of ships) and prominent MP, predictably, you have guessed it, in the neighbourhood of Highgate, then a village outside London. *Edward*, Sam's father, attended Harrow and Oxford, graduating Master of Arts 'as Hells and Clubs proclaim', in 1788; deeply in debt and quite unprepared for the assumption of anything like what his father would call a profession.

Unfortunately for Edward, 1788 was the year in which *Bonnie Prince Charlie* sank under full sail in a five-knot breeze at a royal display off the Isle of Wight. A parliamentary inquiry was launched, the manufacturers accused, corruption discovered, and public disgrace followed for Theophilus, who soon had no funds to set his son on his feet, nor influence to launch him on a career. (This much could be traced in records of the parliamentary minutes.) Shortly after, Edward joined the Agropolis, a society of young Oxford men determined to establish an idyllic community of Nature on the banks of the Potomac River in Virginia. Their plan, much ridiculed in the daily press, was *to farm.* 'A mere two hours a day in the field', their leader, young Benedict Smythe, declared, 'would provide for their Earthly necessities!'

The society was funded by the purse of Smythe, or rather, Smythe's father, Lord Burkehead, who offered to clear all debts of the young gentlemen of good standing willing to pursue his son's Utopian scheme. (Young Benedict being a noble thorn in his side, and the good Lord willing to support anyone accompanying its removal.) Edward enlisted at once and set sail for the New World.

News of the Syme family, within a great stash of papers, came easily to hand by a stroke of rare good fortune. Before his *annus horribilis* in 1788, Theophilus, Sam's grandfather, had built a house on a plot of land just above what we now call Highgate Ponds. Coverdale Place, named after the farmer who sold his field on what was becoming an increasingly crowded patch, survived the proceedings against Theophilus. Edward's older brother inherited the estate, and upon *his* death Edward returned home from the New World in which he had spent his manhood and buried both his son (the great Sam Syme, the proper business of my study) and his wife. He brought with him a sea-chest full of papers – the title,

'American Notes, &c.' etched in the oak lid – including old love letters, bearers of bad tidings, fatherly advice, and newspaper clippings, of his Utopian venture and his son's fame, each tenderly preserved in a separate album.

My good fortune lay, however, less in Edward's *accumulating* habits than in the idleness and the durability of the man who purchased the estate on Edward's death, a Mr Mackintosh James. He had made what came to be called 'a killing' in a refinement of steam locomotion that redirected the heat of the engine into the process by which the engine was fuelled. At the age of thirty-three, young James was 'set for life', another phrase just coming into vogue – and proceeded to do absolutely nothing with the surplus of years before him. He lived to the ripe old age of a hundred and three, and died childless, after one world war and before another, just in time to avoid the Great Crash.

James left a number of worthless shares, and the house itself, now known as Mackintosh Place, to the newly formed Hampstead & Highgate Preservation Trust. In the century and a half of its existence, two families had dwelt there – and none have followed since its conversion to a museum (of village life and changing times), as I found it. The box of 'American Notes, &c.' was discovered untouched by Mackintosh James, pushed against the brick wall of the chimney shaft in the attic. The oak was scorched and blackened, the papers curled with heat and thick with dust, but the ink remained dry and, above all, readable.

A brief account of the house, written by Edmund Blunden, no less (among his clutch of lyrical historical pastoral pieces), and published by the Trust, had found its way into the British Library; where I discovered it, and news of the cache of 'old and cluttered papers, relating the dead and cluttered lives, of the Syme family'. To Mackintosh House, accordingly, I bent my steps – or rather the soot-caked wheels of the rackety Tube, burrowing its way along the Northern Line, to Highgate, still half a village, perched on its wooded hill.

And there I sat, in a side office of the museum reserved for the curator, cluttered with filing cases, a kettle caked in mineral scum, and a tiny fridge (containing only a carton of old cream and a single hotel mini-bottle of gin). The windows looked over the front garden, so I bent a rustling slat of the French blinds to peer out on the milky sunny day. A slope of grass; then, half-hidden by willows, the quiet stretch of asphalt road poured down long after Mr Coverdale first sold this corner of his farm; and between the loose hair of the trees, the glitter of Highgate Ponds undimmed below. I put the album of the great (so I had determined to make him) Sam Syme to one side – a treat reserved – and forced my ham fists and sleepy brain to turn over the wrinkled letters and journals of his father, Edward, set forth for America over two hundred years before.

Edward's Agropolis was *not* a success, though the travelling experiment docked at last in high spirits: 'With what joy, my father,' wrote Edward on his arrival, 'did I leap to this shore of Liberty! I was weary of that great bore, the sea, a tedious fellow, forever and everywhere at my elbow; and the sight of trees, of towns, and even of Men!, offered delicious refreshment for fatigued eyes. I have flown a rotten country and entered upon a new land, busy with its own youth. How I enjoyed the activity of the merchants, the artisans, and the sailors, especially as it was not my own! It was not the noisy Vortex of London; it was not the unquiet, eager mien of my countrymen; it was the simple, dignified air of men, who were conscious of liberty, and who see in all men their brothers and their equals . . . though I dare say I am delirious with Terra Firma, and would praise the meanest Hovel simply for not swaying in that abominable manner . . .'

Thus they began in great good hope and some good faith; though Edward's letters soon qualified his enthusiasm. 'We get on tolerably,' he wrote his beleaguered father. 'The gentlemen *moan* somewhat at the delightful pleasures of our Idyll, and insist, with wonderful generosity, that each of the other Agropols enjoy his share of the blisses of Rural Life. Our Hands, by this time, are well chapped, and we look like nothing else but what we are: *Farmers*, sound of limb, black with Sun, dreadfully occupied by seeding and improvements upon the Plough and the malignities of the

Weather. Yet even the *sorriest* among us delights in the glorious Scope this country offers, the cloud-like expansion of Valley and Hill, the profligate wastefulness of our Lord on these rude Shores. As I say, we *get on*; and trust, dear Father, you do no worse.'

Their downfall in the end lay not in hard work; as far as that went, Edward was right, the sorriest among them bent their backs to it and *got on*. Nor were the malignities of weather to blame, though they suffered a brutal first winter, in which three of their horses died and the first young son of the Agropolis, the child of Edward, entered the cold world white and out of breath. The true serpent of their paradise, as always, lay in the hearts of the men involved, and the accommodations they made for their sexual loves.

Benedict Smythe, Viscount Burkehead, was in his way a true original. Though his scheme preceded the Pantisocrats, his Utopian ambition surpassed theirs: among the pleasures of the natural life to be held in common by his fellows were the *joys of family*, as their strangely coy deed of *township* dubbed them. There were to be none of the mealy-mouthed 'brotherly' betrothals to sister and sister, practised by Coleridge and Southey. A shared world for Benedict meant just that, and the Agropols, men and women, held one another in equal and often competing love. Eve had entered the garden.

Edward Syme had always been a gentleman of precocious appetite, as the records of his Oxford career attest; and no doubt Benedict's liberal sexual philosophies at one point formed the chief attraction of his schemes. But when Benedict pursued the still-recovering mother of his dead child, Edward, a gentleman of some niceness, revolted. The rift in their small brotherhood – for, despite Benedict's noblest aspirations for equality between the sexes, the Agropolis remained from first to last a *brother*hood – widened and deepened over the following year. Edward must have guessed from the first that in such a contest he was bound to suffer most. Benedict's father held the purse strings of the venture, and unless he watched himself very closely indeed, Edward would be out in the considerable cold of a North American winter.

So he watched himself, displaying even then his talent for the deflection of grief which he would pass so unhappily on to his son. There were rumblings in the little farmstead, as Edward's allies (for, despite the noblest of communal intentions, when have we not separated ourselves, by choice, into pockets of men?) made some mischief for the Viscount – spoiling a field with stones on one memorable and pyrotechnical flare-up between the factions. But Edward calmed them, and the breach in his friendship with Benedict never broke into open war.

The following spring, Edward began to busy himself outside the Agropolis, lending a hand at the local schoolhouse near Baltimore. 'I have decided', Edward wrote in the consolation of his journal, 'to break free of this Bubble, and set myself up, on two feet, as a Gentleman Scholar, among a people who cannot mark the Difference.' The old schoolmaster, Willard Barnes, a veteran of the war and a great believer in the new country, found himself sadly short-handed in the education of its sons. So he took on a young English 'gentleman' fresh from Oxford, engaged on some business, some farming speculation (Barnes never guessed what), who seemed to know his way around a book – not that there were many of them about to be getting on with, now that you mention it. Barnes had two daughters, including a young beauty, famous as far as Richmond and shy as a hedgehog – Anne.

Edward married her before the year was out, shifted his lodgings from the idyll of communal life, and lived in the attic of old Barnes's farmhouse, a sprawled, lopsided, barn-like building beside the school, amid ten acres of its own pasturage.

The character of his new wife is difficult to determine. She wrote little, and the best record we have of the mother of the young geologist, who would set the world on its ears and was already kicking in her womb by the winter of 1793, comes from a rather extraordinary letter Edward wrote to her before their engagement. Willard Barnes appears to have been a strict master and a stricter father – only Edward's connection to the business of the school seems to have permitted him the company of Willard's daughter, and eventually won him her hand in marriage. And Anne must have embraced her new husband with something of the blindness of a first passion, for this is what Edward wrote, and he kept no secrets from her, though he promised many to come.

(There I sat, looking over the gardens of Mackintosh House, the blinds pulled high and the window opened, after a considerable groan and a great scraping of paint, while a file of old papers stood at my side, breathing a dusty cloud into the sunshine; and these tempestuous lives fluttered beneath my hand.)

My dear Anne . . .

Some years ago, and in sore Want of money, after a University career which did not redound entirely to my honour, I fell in with an old college friend, Viscount Burkehead, who offered prospects I could not at the time dismiss entirely from my thoughts. 'I have recently discovered', he wrote to me, 'a tract of Land in the New World, on the banks of the glorious Potomac, offered for Sale; once its limits have been ascertained, its suitability determined, why could it not be prepared, in all circumstances, for a Republic of our own making, in the same manner as you prepare a house for your friends?' Benedict's plan, formed partly under the Inspiration of Dr Priestley and the less noble fumes of a draft of Porter, was to establish an ideal community in this new world, a community of equal friends, in which all property, of life and love, was held in common.

Young as I was, I suspected even then that an old and intractable Leaven in our Nature would effectually frustrate these airy schemes of happiness. And I expect such Dreams will excite in you no more than an innocent Smile, at the extravagance of a youthful and ardent mind. Yet if such only were our folly, doubtless I would yet linger on the Shores of that river among my former Friends. In the course of the first winter, our Common life precipitated a common course, and one of the sisters of our community was laid to bed, with the promise of an Addition to our Venture. I confess myself concerned in her Predicament, and when the child peeped forth at the New World with a blank eye and stopped Heart, much of my own Heart for the Enterprise died with him.

That I venture at all over these painful Scenes lies in my desire that you should be acquainted with the manner of man who clamours at your Heart. Such I have been; and by the force of Nature, such I shall always be; among the catalogue of my weaknesses shall never be reckoned an Ignorance of them. I offer what I have, a fond though wandering heart; a history tainted more by Folly than Guilt; and a stout, enduring Love for thee, though I am a poor, and erring Lover.

Believe me, thine,
Edward Syme

All that we know of Anne is that she accepted such a curious proposal. Perhaps she hoped to reform him – this has been known. From such a union, and such a father, within a year, came Samuel Highgate Syme, whose own airy schemes, after a century of neglect, would bubble up from the depths of his hollow earth, to fuel the fire of Alfred Wegener's imagination.

Perhaps I have overreached myself again, and I must step back. Look around, Pitt, look around, and climb out of your hole for once and quit digging. Professor Bunyon would no doubt warn me to 'take stock' at this point, and so, for once, I shall. I shall begin at the beginning, if I can find it. (Of course, there are in fact no beginnings; only pauses and resumptions.)

In 1915, Alfred Wegener, shot in the neck during a raid in the Great War, returned home to convalesce. In that delicious idleness of a keen, healthy mind and a slack, recovering body, Wegener revisited some earlier speculations regarding what came to be called the *theory of continental drift* – the notion that a single body of land had split, wrenched apart by separate internal plates, to form the spread of continents familiar to us now. In that year he published a slim paperback on cheap paper titled *The Origin of Continents and Oceans*. Wegener presented his idea, in the words of Ursula Marvin, 'not for the first time perhaps but for the first time boldly'. It is this 'perhaps' that I had set out to investigate.

Wegener himself announced his discovery anxious of his influences. In the opening Historical Introduction, he takes pains to point out that the *'first* concept of continental drift first came to me as far back as 1910, when considering the map of the world, under the direct impression produced by the congruence of the coastlines on either side of the Atlantic'. (We shall see Syme lost in that very consideration almost a century before him.) The following fall, a study offering palaeontological support for the idea of a land bridge between Brazil and Africa, convinced Wegener to pursue the matter further; and he first delivered his conclusions on 6 January 1912 (a date distinctly recorded) to the Geological Association in Frankfurt.

Wegener's innovations were twofold and both easily named. In the first place, he posited the existence of an earlier, single body of land of which the continents were parts. Second, he named the internal force that split them apart. In *The Origin of Continents and Oceans*, he carefully dissociates himself from his intellectual forebears, citing one by one those who could lay some claim to either of his discoveries and distancing himself in turn. Of the first innovation: 'It was pointed out to me in correspondence that Coxworthy, in a book which appeared after 1890, put forward the hypothesis that today's continents are the disrupted parts of a once-coherent mass. I have had no opportunity to examine the book.' And of the second: 'Rotation of the *whole* crust, whose components were supposed *not* to alter their relative positions – has already been assumed by several writers (beside many inanities), particularly among our American colleagues' – and here he appends a footnote – 'and found support closer to home in Loeffelholz von Colberg and Kreichgauer, among others.'

He also gives some credit where it is due: 'I have discovered ideas very similar to my own in a work of F.B. Taylor's which appeared in 1910.' Yet he qualifies even this: 'however, I have received the impression when reading Taylor that his main object was to find a formative principle for the arrangement of the large mountain chains . . . [and] continental drift in our sense played only a subsidiary role and was given only a very cursory explanation'. In short, Wegener had struck gold, knew he had hit the motherlode, and could not bear the thought that any of the other prospectors, digging the same bend in the river, might have sifted something of similar ore through their brain-pans. (If only I had looked more closely then, the real clue would have shone through the grit he spread around it, but I dug it up in time.) He was staking a claim to an idea so magnificent and simple, he could not quite believe that no one would pinch it from him.

In fact, the opposite occurred: no one listened. The world had busied itself about a very different geographical split; and even when the First World War ended and the troops went home, a prejudice against German scholarship, as Faul points out, delayed even further the reception of his ideas. Not until the publication of the third edition, in 1922, and its translation into English and French, did Wegener's theories enter the public debate, only to receive, at best, a muted support (Faul again). Wegener, like Syme before him, faltered at the starting-post: he could not account for the Prime Mover, the original force that drove the continents apart.

And so he set forth for Greenland, a fourth and final time, to offer, as Syme had attempted to do, dramatic evidence of the justice of his theories. If only he could prove, demonstrably, that Greenland itself had drifted, almost a furlong, since 1922, no one could doubt him any longer. His mission ended in a more *fatal*, though no less *final*, disaster than Syme's a century before; and he died, in a drift of ice, tracking backwards for supplies.

Track backwards, Pitt! Go over every step! And there I found him at last, buried in a footnote, the echo of that worry in my ear: Samuel Highgate Syme. Wegener could not abuse his native honesty, and in that catalogue of distinctions he recorded faithfully, in footnote sixty-three (out of all sequence), the exception among his 'American colleagues': 'As far back as 1826,' Wegener writes, 'Syme spoke of "segments of the earth's crust which float on the revolving core" .' And there we have the critical connection: a split in the crust, and the drift ensuing. But we have come no closer to Syme.

*

I must step back now and begin at another beginning; *Find the shape, Pitt,* I hear Bunyon rumbling, *and stick to it.* There is a shape, of course; there are too many shapes, and they dissolve into one another and reform, like shards of ice on a bright winter day, or the continents themselves, on their endless drift from unity. Once we belonged to a single shape, but no longer. And so I begin again, or rather, offer another starting-point after an interruption.

One year before the American Revolution, a young German, Abraham Gottlob Werner, last of a long line of Saxon metalworkers, was called to the new Technical University in Freiberg to teach mineral science. He was just twenty-five. By the time of his death in 1817, he had established the Freiberg Academy as one of the foremost institutions in geological science, and along the way revolutionized our picture of the birth of the world. And for the most part, he had got it entirely wrong.

Imagine an age in which no Pole has been reached, no sky breached, no ocean fathomed, no earthquake plumbed. By some trick of human nature, mankind had directed its great powers of intellectual enquiry skywards; and the secrets of the stars were solved long before the mysteries of the earth. Galileo had proved at last the centrality of the sun amid the revolutions of the planet; Newton had established the pull of gravity. We are all of us in the gutter, Wilde once said; yet *most* of us are looking at the stars. The rare man is he who rummages about him in the muck. Werner was that man. With the great problems of the heavens solved, at last we turned our questing down and in, and began to dig. And Werner had his audience.

By all accounts he was a remarkable teacher. He brought three successive generations into the study of geology, or, as he dubbed his new discipline, geognosy; including, very late in life, the young Friedrich Müller, whom we shall come to in time (almost too late for me). Werner's excellence lay in the field. He wrote a mineralogy guidebook at the age of twenty-four, which landed him the job in Freiberg in the first place. In it, he established his own categories for identifying rocks: clear, simple, structured. The chief feature of his mind was its *lucidity*. Unlike

28

Doug Pitt, he had mastered the art of beginnings. He guessed what he could not know and imposed the clear order of his thought upon the world before him. The muddle of matter that would not fit was swept away.

His was a revolution not of discovery, nor insight, but of order – a classic of German innovation. He convinced not by logic but by clarity. He reduced a confusing jumble of rock and rift, of mines and mountains, into a plain system, ship-shape; all the world seemed present and correct. He *tidied up*, reduced, cut out what would not fit, and persuaded.

Werner's views ran briefly as follows. He accounted for the various formations of rock observable at different layers of landscape as the deposits of a former ocean covering the globe. In fact, most shockingly of all, *the globe was an ocean*, a ball of water held trembling together like the drop at the end of a tap. Rock precipitated out of this oceanic solution to form the crust of the earth as we now know it. Owing to the fact, Werner argued, that deep waters run *still* and are thus incapable of inducing precipitates, this original ocean must have fallen and risen (diminished and swelled) to produce the present landscape, each drop in the water level yielding a harvest of rock formations as the accompanying turbulence released basalt from solution.

His system of classification simply referred each rock to the fall in water that produced it. There were *Primitive* rocks, formed in the bosom of the original universal ocean; they included granite, mica, clay, porphyry, etc. Next came *Transition* rocks, layered upon the primitive rocks as the ocean dipped below the crust. These numbered limestone and flint among them, and contained the beginnings of organic remains. *Floetz* rocks followed, after a brief rise in oceanic levels and the ensuing dip; these were rarely found at a great height, as the universal ocean had subsided below the peaks by this time. Where discrepancies occurred, Werner simply ignored them *as discrepancies*, and moved on – to *Alluvial* and *Volcanic* rocks, variations on the previous three. Five kinds of rock, Werner thought, was a good number to be going on with. The genius of his system was its simplicity. Every discovery could be referred to these original formations, exceptions noted, debated, classified, *recorded*. But the world, I fear, is run according to the lucid, the Bunyons and Werners, no matter the absurdities they tumble us into.

Werner was a tiny man, tiny and tidy; bowlegged like a blacksmith, possessing a sharp cleft chin, sharp nose, and sharp wisp of beard, never quite full enough to persuade. He moved with a quivering, restless energy, burning up like the filaments inside a glass bulb, gesturing endlessly, stepping and stopping, with the fever of enthusiasm. He wrote rarely, preferring to *talk* and *influence*. There seemed so little to set down; the world was plain enough, after all. Paper had this tricky way of drawing out and leading on, involving him in a thousand complexities, which a simple demonstration, or personal assurance, could pass over in a minute. He lived on in the memories of his students, and their more patient pens; they returned, again and again, to hear him lecture. I cannot help but think of that old line: 'somehow they were never the same to him/When they were married and brought their wives.'

He died childless in 1817, lecturing until the end, *married* only to the college whose rise he had overseen. Yet Werner's most famous student – his successor at Freiberg, Friedrich Mohs, inventor of degrees of hardness, both geological and psychological – fled at the first opportunity for Vienna and greener pastures; and the Freiberg Academy suffered a long decline through the nineteenth century.

One notable student remained truer to his master. Werner's theories have been ably set down by Robert Jameson, the Scottish son of a soap-boiler, who was inspired by the tale of Robinson Crusoe to follow a career in geology, and who journeyed to Freiburg to effect an initiation. Jameson left this testament to Werner's example and the nature of the discipline the great man left behind him.

> We now come to the consideration of Geognosy, regarding the Internal Structure of the earth, and the peculiar province of the celebrated WERNER.

At first sight the solid mass of the earth appears to be a confused assemblage of rocky masses piled on each other without order or regularity: to the superficial observer, Nature appears, in the apparently rude matter of the inorganic kingdom, as presenting us only with a picture of *chaos*.

Our knowledge of the internal structure of the earth remained a great time very limited and confused. Although observations had been made in very distant countries, and similar rocks discovered in a variety of the most widely distant situations, no successful attempt had been made to generalize these appearances, so as to discover the general structure of the earth, and its mode of formation. The attention of Geology was too much occupied with particular and local appearances, to effect what has been since so fully accomplished by the comprehensive mind of WERNER. *(My own sin that – attention too much occupied with particular and local appearances.)*

That illustrious mineralogist, to whom we owe almost every thing that is truly valuable in this important branch of knowledge, after the most arduous and long-continued investigations, conducted with the most consummate address, discovered the general structure of the crust of the globe, and pointed out the true mode of examining and ascertaining those great relations, which it is one of the principal objects of Geognosy to investigate.

We should form a very false conception of the Wernerian Geognosy were we to believe it to have any resemblance to those *monstrosities* known under the name of *Theories of the Earth*. Almost all the compositions of this kind are idle speculations, contrived in the *closet*, and having no kind of resemblance to any thing in nature. Place one of these speculators in the full storm and terror of *the living world*, and you will immediately discover the nature of his information. He himself will find that he knows *nothing*; that he has been wandering in the mazes of error; and that, however *easily* he may have been able to explain the formation of this globe, and of the whole universe from *his study window*, he cannot, standing upright in the winds of Heaven, give a rational or satisfactory account of *a single mountain*.

Indeed, our researches on the surface of the earth often lead us among the grandest and most sublime works of nature; and amid Alpine groups, the geognosist is, as it were, conducted nearer to the scene of those great operations, which it is his business to explore. In the midst of such scenes, he feels his mind *invigorated*; the magnitude of the appearances before him extinguishes all the little and contracted notions he may have formed from *books*. And he learns that it is only by visiting and studying *these stupendous works* that he can form an adequate conception of the *crust* of the globe, and of its *mode of formation*; unless, of course, he turns to that true prophet of the Mountain Top, Abraham Gottlob Werner.

We always praise the mind that leads us out of *chaos*, no matter the route taken, nor the country reached. But Werner, of course, had his disagreements. His greatest rival to the title of the Father of Modern Geology was another Scot, Dr James Hutton, a dour, meticulous, incomprehensible man, whose theories required an interpreter in his own tongue to be understood. That interpreter was a man named Playfair – if only we all had such interpreters, Dr Bunyon notwithstanding – a lucid, elegant writer whose simplifications allowed Hutton's theory to challenge even the order of Werner's categories. But I am an old obscurantist, a stickler for sticky phrases and muddy texts, and turn for once to the original, Hutton's perhaps mockingly titled *Theory of the Earth*.

Hutton's genius lay in his understanding of *accumulation*. He sensed that the process of life involves an almost endless series of revisions, the making and unmaking and remaking of Matter, which itself is the result of an age of minor transformations. He declared that it was 'in vain to look for anything higher in the origin of the earth than the *continuation of some earlier process*; the result, therefore, of our present inquiry is that we find no vestige of a beginning – no prospect of an end'.

He argued that the earth's crust was the product of sedimentation transfused by heat into new matter. He placed great faith in the strength of fire, a faith he felt no need to justify by experiment. The world around us, he argued, has overflowed from a great furnace, a continual power, an endless shifting. The rocks we see bear the brunt of their fusion. *We come burning hither, caught in the fire of some transformation;* he simply recorded the process, as accurately as he could. He had little interest in marking the genesis of *anything* – contenting himself with an account of how *everything* had undergone some modification. He acknowledged no beginnings and no ends, only the steadiness of change. By some trick of fate his masterpiece, *The Theory of the Earth*, survived him unfinished. Playfair unaccountably never tidied up the remains; and only a century later were those dormant manuscripts, beginning characteristically on chapter four, offered to the public.

These two between them divided the field. The NEPTUNISTS followed Werner and placed their faith in the sea. The PLUTONISTS drew their authority from Hutton and believed in fire. The clergy distrusted Hutton. He took no account of the Bible; and his theories surrendered little space for the suddenness of Divine Creation. His world took shape in an endless moiling and broiling and left no breath for the lightness of instant Light. The Neptunists, for their part, ridiculed his faith in fire. Jameson declared simply (always the virtue of their kind!):

> The spheroidal figure of the earth is a proof of its original fluidity. This important conclusion was never disputed; the only question has been, Whether this fluidity was the effect of Fire or Water.
>
> Rocks which have been formed or altered by the action of Heat are most distinctly different from those that constitute the great mass of the crust of the globe; consequently this fluidity cannot be attributed to the agency of heat.

The Church favoured Werner; and the muddle left behind by Hutton's obscurities dissuaded interest. Jameson's eloquence also had its effect. He founded the Wernerian Society and became himself a respected teacher, numbering among his students both Robert Stephenson, perfecter of the locomotive, and Charles Darwin, who needs no elucidation. Hutton, always patient with earthly processes, bided his time.

Eventually, in 1830 another Scotsman, Charles Lyell, declared the hand of the geologists. His *Principles of Geology*, a work of magnificently cultured summary, announced at last the incompatibility of geologic research with biblical interpretation. The geologists breathed again. And though Lyell – the forerunner of a modern academic, possessed of an excellent breadth of acquaintance, and a mind naturally formed to simplify, reconcile and sum up – never matched in original science the significance of his geologic manifesto, the floodgates had been opened. So true it is that a man of a certain temperament in a certain time can make a name for himself simply by declaring in public what in private everyone else has long known to be fact.

The work surged forward. Lord Kelvin, freed of biblical constraint, attacked the question of the *age* of the earth, by measuring the exhaust of power in the burning of the sun. Again, though his conclusions bore not a particle of truth, the fat had reached the fire, and a great heat and crackling of intellectual fervour ensued. We learn by error first *what the question is*, and then the means for correcting the method of corroboration. Eventually, geologists stumbled upon *radioactivity*; and learned to measure, by the fury of decay, the age of the earth, and questioned again the manner of its birth and the composition of its core.

We now have before us a map of the interior Globe as Sam Syme would have found it, when (as I eventually learned by these strange fits and starts) Syme himself came to blossom and cast his thoughts by a capricious wind to the fertile mind of Alfred Wegener, initiating the great intellectual harvest he brought about.

America, at this point in its history, stood frozen in a strange perplexity. It possessed a giant treasure of scientific wealth, a landscape rich and various and unexplored, a broadsheet of continent scribbled over and over in geologic fact. And yet, as de Tocqueville remarked as late as 1837: 'it must be acknowledged that in few of the civilized nations of our time have the sciences made less progress than in the United States'. The young country resembled the Ancient Mariner, surrounded on all sides by water, but incapable of drink.

Yet such solitude produced in the end the genius of Samuel Syme. And we must remember – as we look more closely at his contributions – the nature of his company. There is a peculiar freshness to the productions of genius in isolation; their minds have not learned the well-travelled grooves of an established culture. Their slightest insight bears the mark of a sudden and new eruption of the understanding. They handle each idea, as it were, with bare hands, unprotected by the thick gloves of familiarity. They make mistakes, naturally; they have never been taught what to dismiss out of hand. Yet they often venture on questions a more cultivated intellect would shrink from. This above all: they cannot distinguish among their thoughts, nor separate the absurd and the simply commonplace from the miraculous and the inspired. Nor can their countrymen, bound in the conventions of their own mediocrity, recognize the 'pearls' among them, worth in *lux* and *veritas* all their tribe.

Nevertheless, there were virtues to the American method. The young republicans, like Pitt himself, were a dogged people, determined to make up in industry what they lacked in insight. There was a new world to be scoured, and the Americans scoured it. In 1809 William Maclure produced the first geologic map in American history, covering the territory east of the Mississippi, and earning him the cartographic honour of being dubbed the William Smith of the United States. Eight years later Parker Cleaveland coloured in the gaps left blank by Maclure, extending the range of geologic examination as far north as Maine.

Yet the Americans, for the most part, were strangely loath to speculate on the raw material before them; they trusted their eyes and hands, but not their heads. They prided themselves on being loyal followers of Bacon and Newton; they spurned, in Newton's words, 'hypothesis as the ignis fatuus by which we are led astray'. (Sam, for his part, was a great, drunken follower of all lights, from sudden flares, to abiding constellations.) They eschewed conclusions (so they said), declaring that nothing could be assumed beyond the sum of the phenomena until an adequate first cause became *palpable* to their understanding.

They compiled fantastic *lists*; the list was the height of their ambition, the pinnacle of pure science. The great cataloguer of the American landscape, F.E. Loomis, personally established, over the course of a lifetime, a map of magnetic readings, covering the entire Potomac watershed, testing each result (a laborious process, involving cold hands and muddy knees) over a hundred and fifty times. He published these 'maps' every decade or so, correcting the measurements in the intervening years, and refining his methods, until he hoped by the end to have established, once and for all, the *perfect* list – complete, indisputable, unerring – the final monument of his scientific fame. (By a single sleight of thought, Syme transformed this dry book of numbers into a keyhole, opening on to the very heart of the earth's core. But his *theories* fell on deaf ears, until Wegener heard the echo of their reverberations.)

'At the present day,' declared Edward Everett, lecturer in geology at William and Mary ('the ninny of Virginny', as Syme tagged him), in 1823, 'as is well known, the Baconian philosophy has become synonymous with the *true* philosophy.' And yet some very odd notions were propounded under its flag. Dr John Esten Cooke, convinced that he reported nothing but the plain facts, determined that all sickness stemmed from an *excess* of blood, and that a healthy human body should contain no more than two pints of the liquid to 'moisten' the internal organs. On taking cold one day, to prove a point, he promptly bled himself to death – neither the first nor the most tragic example in this story of a man who died according to his theories.

Despite these shortcomings, the *business* of geology flourished in America. Construction of the Erie Canal was completed in 1825, establishing Buffalo as a port city; and the young geologist Amos Eaton was hired to survey the exposed strata. Americans dug for coal, for iron and for gold; and they paid even amateurs in the 'new science' to map out the land. Syme himself earned a tidy wage exploring the hills of Virginia for 'bitumen' deposits before deciding on a theoretical career. He invented the 'fluvial lantern', so important to his later work, in order to test the soil for carbon traces; and even constructed the first seismograph, to detect instabilities in the strata (evidence, he believed, of leaking iron in the crust) long before Robert Mallet explored the physics of earthtremors in the 1850s.

The new science offered great scope to an ambitious mind, regardless of education. When 'Sober' Ben Silliman graduated with a degree in Law from Yale in 1802 (despite kicking a football into the Bishop's yard one late night), the president of the college – Dr Dwight, a friend of General Silliman, the young man's father – approached him with a curious offer.

> I recall, [Sober Ben recorded in his memoirs, sixty years later,] one hot-house morning in July, when I was surprised from an idle hour under the college elms, by the steps of my father's old friend, President Dwight, a figure who had always filled me with equal degrees of admiration and terror. Dr Dwight was a great bear of a man, nearly six feet in height, owning hands that could pluck watermelons from the vine. His voice, however, by some quirk of divine humour, was as soft and simpering as a woman's, and seemed to trickle out of his mouth in a faint stream. 'Ben,' he whispered to me, stretching his great hand forth, 'I have a proposition for you. The Corporation have agreed; it wants only your approval. They have elected you the first Professor of Chemistry and Geology in the history of the college. How's that strike ye now?' he added, cradling his thumbs and grinning broadly.

I felt as if a great weight had descended on my shoulders, and struck the wind from me. 'Sir,' I said at last, 'you have mistook me, I'm afraid. I have not so much as overturned a stone nor trawled a stream since boyhood. I am engaged to the law.'

'The law don't want you, Ben,' he replied. 'Oh come now, we've lawyers enough already. You may get on there, but you won't shine. The country needs Science. In the profession I proffer to you, there will be no rival. The field will be all your own. Look about you man,' and he gestured East and West towards the red rocks bordering the fair Elm city, 'Treasure, nothing but Treasure, ripe for the digging. It's a public service, Ben, a duty; a chance to link your name to the reputation of our country and pull it up with you.'

When I persisted speechless, he took me gently by the arm and leaned forward. 'Ben,' he whispered, 'as to the *Science* of it, I'm not particular. We're not in any hurry; take two years and look around you, get the lie of the land. Come back and begin your course of instruction; never underrate, Ben, the ignorance of students. Give it thought, a night or so. Damn this heat.'

And so we emerged from under the shade of those noble elms, and I retired, thoughtful and pensive, to my chamber. And in the morning arose, to begin a career I had not dreamed of till the previous day.

After a two-year stint in Philadelphia, where he pursued the best American education in the sciences to be had at the time, and drank, by all accounts (his own included), more 'porter and strong beer' than was quite in keeping with his nickname, he was both 'on a fair way to gout' and ready to begin his lectures in New Haven. And so, at the ripe old age of twenty-four, Ben Silliman opened the study of Chemistry and Geology to the grand old institution of Yale College.

It is astonishing how much of American geology passed through the hands, in one way or another, of Sober Ben Silliman in the sixty years to come, a lesson, perhaps, in nothing else than the extent to which history is made by *connections of acquaintance*. (Take the lesson to heart, Pitt, and fear these men at the nub of the web, these Sillimans and Bunyons.) From Edward Hitchcock, a former assistant, who became Professor of Science at Amherst College; to Chester Dewey, later of Williams College; to Amos Eaton, the great theoretical geologist, imprisoned for fraud, and later released, by special interdiction of the Governor of New York, to found the Rensselaer School of Geologic Study, for the education, among other things, of the Governor's *son*; to Samuel Highgate Syme himself, though their connection was surprisingly brief, and in the end bitter.

Apart from the influence of his personal instruction, Silliman exercised an enormous power over American geology through the journal he founded in 1818 and conducted until his death in 1864: The American Journal of Science (see overleaf).

This was not the first public forum for American science – being preceded by, among others, the *Transactions of the American Philosophical Society*, the *Memoirs of the American Academy of Arts and Science* and the *New York Medical Repository* – but it became the most important, owing to the breadth of Silliman's interests. He had created a journal that, after a few lean early years, not only supported itself, but did so through its *popular appeal*. Though Silliman published the only public account of Syme's theories I have discovered (apart from a certain novel, a protracted spoof I will come to later), his essay 'The Theory of Concentric Spheres' in 1818, the two fell out over the 'democratic *dilution*' of Silliman's journal – a split that persuaded Syme to try his own hand at a geologic journal, the famous *New Platonist*, discovered a century later in the library of Alfred Wegener.

For the time has come for me to talk of Samuel Highgate Syme himself. To return to Mackintosh House, on a much cloudier, thicker day, amid the clutter of the little office overlooking the ponds; and to open at last that precious album, *Records of My Son*.

The

AMERICAN
JOURNAL OF SCIENCE

more especially of
MINERALOGY, GEOLOGY

and the
OTHER BRANCHES OF NATURAL HISTORY

including also
AGRICULTURE

and the
ORNAMENTAL AS WELL AS USEFUL
ARTS

conducted by

✣ **Benjamin Silliman** ✣

Professor of Chemistry, Mineralogy, etc. in Yale College:
author of Travels in England, Scotland, etc.

VOL. I
NEW YORK
1818

There were letters, of course, tied in ribbon, and wedged into the pocket of the heavy book. Among them, little Samuel's earliest experiment in penmanship, 7 July 1799. 'Pleas to receiv me, Annie says, and my Mother particklerly begs you for a dozzen Eggs – I can bring them long myself – for a great Cake, in honour of my sister's birthday, being one. Excus this, Aunt Bethy, seeing its my first.' The long-ago summer day returns to me; the boy, proud and perplexed over his great creation (a three-line letter), refusing to speak, lest it dim the effect, taps his foot impatiently on the porch, while Aunt Bethy reads it, commends it, flits inside to fetch what's required. And for the space of a minute the boy stands alone, in sudden terror at the path he sees before him now, manhood upon him (the trial of penmanship being past), the inevitable progress towards honour and accomplishment weighing on his heart, tearing him from these familiar scenes – the space of garden in front of his grandfather's farmhouse, the dust rising from the road. And then his aunt returns, with the delicate burden muffled in cloth in a basket, and Sam races back into the anonymous summer day towards the prospect of a 'great Cake'.

Sam's sister, baby Barbara (soon nicknamed Bubbles in all the family chatter), was born in the small house on Terence Lane to which the young schoolmaster, Edward, had brought his bride after a year of marriage and parsimony in her father's house. There Sam grew up. The window above his bed opened on to a thick high field, sloping downhill to the beck that trickled at the bottom, through mud and dead leaf in winter and in sudden breakneck burst after a summer rain. This was Sam's haven, his consolation from the stormy scenes of his parents' curious union, as another letter, this time in Annie's hand, revealed.

Dear Beth, – I write in haste only to relieve you; the silly boy is found – please assure our Father – he is sound and fit and only very sleepy, and moreover, that I myself am happy and easy, now we have recovered him. It was an awful night, as you know, full of rain and crash (though thankfully for my boy, quite warm and thick). Sam overheard some foolish dispute between his father and myself, raised by necessity over the clamour of the storm, and took fright at the violence of the *voices*, never mind the mildness of the *words*. We heard the clatter of his window, and never thought twice, till I ventured in to kiss him at last, and found the empty bed.

All is past now and over, thank God. Bubbles discovered him at last, sound asleep at the foot of the stream that runs along the bottom of the field in wet months; indeed, if anything, the boy was cross and perplexed to be shaken from a very soothing dream, occasioned no doubt by the babble of water, and though Bubbles wept to find him safe, he proceeded to recompose himself and attempt a second slumber, despite the glow of sunrise then piercing through the trees. But Bubbles, brave girl, would not have it, and pulled the poor truant to his distressed mother, who now writes to assure her sister that all is well . . .

There was another curious account in Annie's hand, addressed to a Mr Thomas Jenkyns, of the *Southern Courier*, many years later (we shall meet this Mr Jenkyns again). He appeared to have requested information regarding her son's 'sports and curiosities and other youthful presages of geologic genius', to which Annie made the following reply:

Dear Mr Jenkyns – I have never had a great head for my son's pursuits, and as far as 'youthful sports' and such and presages of 'geologic genius' are concerned, I cannot deny he was a very muddy child and forever falling into things and requiring a great scrub. More than that is perhaps beyond me to say. Our house sits square on the slope of a field, and Sam used to wriggle out of the window above his bed when work wanted doing, and me clamouring up and down the house for help. As far as that went, I consider he displayed a love of nature, and would sneak past us and into the woods at the bottom. Once I recall we found him sleeping at the foot of a low stream which used to spring up now and then when the rains came. He spent all night wriggling under the stars – it was a thick, close evening – and he woke in a perfectly vicious temper at the interruption of a dream, but the sun coming up already, he was forced to retire to his bed; and, recollecting properly, that affair had less to do with presages and more with an untimely matter that doesn't pertain. I never recall in him a great affection for schooling; but again, that could lie in the awkward circumstance for a young boy, of learning under the eyes of his father and grandfather; enough, I believe, to turn any child from his books, and set him loose among the trees. If a mother may have her say, I always reckoned my son more than anything distinguished for a *brave heart*. That, Mr Jenkyns, is my son.

A curious account from a curious mother. Anne seemed a jealous creature, close with her son and husband – the two often blent in her accounts, a single example of masculine pig-headedness and vital force, indifferent to circumstance and particularity, though Sam occasionally distinguished himself for his faith and attachment to her. Perhaps she envied Edward's power over their son; for the father directed Sam's schooling from an early age and appears to have impressed the young boy with considerable awe – at least at first. A handful of brisk notes fluttered to the desk and stuck in the thick, close summer air, unrelieved by the window opened over the garden.

I read over these old school reports, surprised into a familiar tingle of apprehension, as if I myself, at the age of eight or ten, stood open to my father's evaluation – so closely had I identified my task of discovery with Samuel himself and his fortunes. 'The boy possesses', I read, in Edward's quaint, left-handed script, the letters sloping against the grain, 'a keen memory, and the capacity to Improve, upon Application. I believe that much of the haste and Confusion in his work, lies not [only] in a native indolence – a restless Desire to turn his thoughts to everything BUT the task at hand, an Eye drawn to the slightest sign of life without the window, from blue-jay to Maid, a Temper as happy to destroy as to construct – but also in a natural lightness of the Intellect, which steps as easily from First Causes to Conclusions, where a more muddling Mind might plod over the intervening Arguments. Yet for all that he is a careless child and often o'erleaps himself.'

In a later report, Edward offers a more particular account of his son's studies.

> Acquaintance with the Grammar, including prosody, of both the Greek & Latin tongues: middling to indifferent. Knowledge of Caesar's commentaries, Sallust, selected parts of Ovid's *Metamorphoses*: extensive, owing to a natural inclination. Interest in and facility for Virgil, Horace, Catullus: dull and dull and dull, the boy shies from Poetry like a kitten from the Bath. Aptitude for the Orations of Cicero (contained in the volume in Usum delphini): considerable; he takes naturally to Speeches, and from an early age has always cast about him for an Audience; most of these he has gotten by heart and will recite 'em to all and any who dare approach him in the Vein. In general, the boy takes well to what *strikes* him, and not at all to what *don't*; but moreover, I discern a kind of Pernicious Element in him, which, even where his interest lies, seeks to up-end and Disfigure the very Learning on which he has set his Thoughts. The boy knows that two and two make four – and will prove it too if required – but if by any sort of process he can convert 2 & 2 into *five* it gives him much greater pleasure.

Edward maintained to the end of his days a great respect for the arts and culture he had neglected at university and a stubborn indifference to the advancing sciences. His American father-in-law, though a stiff-hearted, pious Puritan, was a great believer in the manly and American application of *hand* and *head* to any task. He disliked 'literary affectations'. The Agropolis, the visionary scheme that brought his future son-in-law to Virginia, had he known of it, must have aroused in him the deepest contempt. And the old farmer and schoolmaster took a keen interest in the new geological work being done in the young country. In the end, the grandfather seems to have won the contest over the direction of the young man's genius.

Besides which, 1809 saw the publication of William Maclure's *Observations on the Geology of the United States*. Maclure, a Scotsman and disciple via Jameson of the theories of Werner, had come to America on business and never left, choosing instead to pursue Wernerian theories across the new continent, 'hammer in hand' (Fulton and Thompson). His book proved a sensation, and young Sam, then fifteen years old, was caught in its spell. (It is perhaps worthy of note that Syme's introduction to the new science was Neptunist in origin.) Exercising a connection to the Silliman family, Willard Barnes secured his grandson a place on the new course in Geology at Yale College, being taught by 'Sober Ben'.

Accordingly, Samuel set off by coach for New Haven, Connecticut, at the age of seventeen, with a 'chest of clothes, chemical devices, etc. a writing box, and his portmanteau filled to bursting with my own Shortbread', as Anne described his departure in a letter to her sister.

He seemed quite affected by the Separation – more than myself, in fact, to our great amusement – though he recovered his spirits in the efforts to shake Bubbles from his leg, who clung there, like a dog with its teeth around a precious bone, it would not part with for its life. Only that evening was I struck for the first time by the great path rolling out before my Son, and the lengths to which his Prospects might remove him from his Home. Our house seemed lonelier than before, less for his Absence than the echoes of his Presence. Bubbles would speak to no one, burying her red eyes in a novel; and even Edward seemed strangely affected and cast-down. No doubt apple-dumplings will cheer them both – I have never known a soul unaffected by apple-dumplings . . .

A strange mother, loving no doubt, but curiously removed, by the miseries of her family, from her own reflections. She could not guess then how quickly her son would return, nor how much of Sam's career would be spent within a day's journey of Baltimore.

I'd wager Barnes had not accounted for the 'visionary' purposes to which Sam would eventually put his education (in the manner of his father, after all), nor how brief that education would be. Yet in his own volcanic fashion, Sam deployed his new learning to instant and profitable use. America had just caught the craze for 'natural waters' that swept Europe at the turn of the century. Priestley had demonstrated as early as 1772 that the 'blinking bubbles' in a spring's gush were nothing other than 'fixed air', and manufacturers had struggled to duplicate the effects of mineral water, which had become a fashionable addition to many drinks. Syme perfected his own process, and by the end of his first semester marketed the results in a private way. We find this early letter to his father.

Sir, – I recall that you and Grandfather were in the habit of retaining the bottles, jars, etc. consumed at the schoolhouse; and wondered if I might avail myself of a portion of them. I seem to have acquired a little business in the manufacture of soda water, much sought-after by thirsty scholars, and cannot procure any glass bottles which will not burst, nor any stone ones impervious to the fixed air. After succeeding perfectly in the construction of a complicated, difficult and delicate apparatus for the production of mineral gases, I have been thus far *completely foiled* by the very defective bottles supplied by the potters hitherto. They will not hold the fluid under such a pressure but weep copiously – and I am bound to join them, in competing Streams. Recollecting however the store of excellent vessels in the backroom of the school, and reflecting on the superiority of Southern manufacture, I resolved to apply to you, as I do now, for a Shipment of them.

Your faithful, etc. son,
Sam

His studies, as a rule, were more '"honoured in the breach than the observance"; he was forever pursuing some fresh impossible scheme, which, impossibly, *came off* – and his nights he spent sleeping crooked in the hall-way at the foot of the stairs in a kind of divan he had erected for the purpose, ready on all occasions, to satisfy any sleepless desire for a game at Cards, at which he lost greatly and consistently and with great good Humour, determined, by some faith in the "Mathematics of Fortune", that his *luck* would turn. . .'

Edward Syme also retained his own strange letter to his son at college, which may give another indication of how Sam's time was spent, if we are to believe the insinuations of a father.

We are all anticipating your return – Bubbles particularly clamours for her brother. I am afraid your Mother and I offer dreary company to a lively girl and I myself have been much occupied of late, by the Schoolhouse & sundry considerations. We expect you to instruct us all this Summer on the composition of the 'philosopher's stone' &c. or rather, where it might be *found*. For my own part, I am so grossly ignorant respecting Chemistry and such like, that I hardly know what it *cannot* effect, and should not be surprised to find you Descend upon us from the Moon, after a relatively simple Operation involving no doubt a great many Explanations . . .

As for this business, of *Analysing*, I hear it sometimes makes Bad Work. If you confine yourself to the laboratory at College, you will do well, avoiding at all cost the *Laboratories* of some Connecticut *ladies*. But I fear the *particles* of which you are composed, and those of some fine Lasses there, are sufficiently *homogeneous* to possess in a great degree the attraction of *affinity*. (Is that how you speak it?) If so, I am convinced that on near approach they would cause such a *Fermentation* as would produce a *Composition* . . . 'Conception is a fine thing no doubt, but as their daughters may conceive, look to it . . .'

Your loving Father, Sam, who misses you,
E.

If only the physician had healed himself.

But I could not guess at the time what revolution in his circumstances drew Sam home, for a far greater term than a single summer, and prevented his return. The next mention of his name, in official records, occurs not at the college induction in the fall of 1813, in the allied courses of Geology, Chemistry, Mineralogy, etc. There Sam is conspicuous by his absence; but he appears again, in the spring of 1814, enlisted in the 53rd Infantry, stationed in Richmond, under the sponsorship of one Benedict Smythe. He had turned with his customary short-lived explosion of enthusiasm to a new task entirely.

His regiment was promptly called north to prosecute the war with Britain; and Sam, after only three months in the service, found himself at the heart of the battle of Lundy's Lane on 25 July, where he conducted himself 'with great honour'. On 17 September Syme volunteered for a sortie against one of the British batteries surrounding Fort Erie and not only led the charge over the entrenchments, but with his own hand 'spiked the first cannon', in a raid that took the British completely by surprise, and effected their eventual retreat. On the recommendation of Captain Miller, Syme was forthwith promoted to lieutenant, for 'his almost total disregard for personal well-being in his Deprivation of the enemy and attentions to his Comrades in the field'. He had been a soldier less than a year – his courage smacked somewhat of the recklessness of a young man not unwilling to die.

That recklessness was undiminished by peacetime. On his return to Richmond, Syme immediately became entangled in a duel with the chief surgeon of the company, 'Dr John Fowles, who', as Sam informed his mother, 'insinuated that I had acted dishonourably in giving him a furlough, claiming that I had myself assumed the emoluments of his office while caring for the sick he left behind him. I immediately declared his allegation false, demanding satisfaction on the field of honour – trusting that his skill with the pistol could not improve much on his infelicity with the surgeon's knife. (In which faith, I was completely vindicated.)'

Sam had of course tailored this account to appease the palpitations of his mother. His messmate, Tippy Adams, recalls a clumsier and messier affair, more miserable on the whole and touched with despair.

> That day I mounted guard with him, and Sam informed me, in the tedium of our watch, that he planned to fall in with Dr Fowles and 'wring his nose'. I laughed at the time, for Sam jested often in such fashion, being full of a kind of vengeful humour, neither entirely angry nor at ease, but a something in between, restless, and disposed to ranting. He personified, as he himself declared to me, the 'mock-heroic, as my father would say'. Accordingly, after our watch, I turned to a brief sleep, believing his boasts to be nothing more than the savageness of an idle hour.
>
> I was awakened shortly after by a commotion, and, dressing quickly, discovered a small gathering in the street outside our barracks. Sam paraded grandly, puffing his chest, and aping the air of the doctor – who, to speak plainly, was a foolish fellow, delighting greatly in a false erudition Sam constantly put to shame. At length, stirred by some remark I could not hear to a livelier anger, Sam, taking a step backward, cried involuntarily, 'Draw, and defend yourself'. The doctor did not answer the challenge directly, but strode toward him, hoping no doubt to grapple his adversary, being a much larger fellow than the lieutenant, and strong as a bear. Sam interrupted his intentions by holding his sword between them, until the Doctor retreated and demanded the affair be prosecuted in an orderly fashion, convening at the Gallery as soon as possible in the presence of seconds.
>
> To this Sam assented at once, and *glided* – I can use no better word – to his quarters to prepare, like a man intoxicated with some pleasurable passion. In fact, I asked him if he had taken wine, and when he assured me that he had not, I consented to be his second.

We met at the appointed time, and, at a distance of ten paces, standing sideways, the duellists awaited the word. I called out, *Are you ready?* and they, at the same instant, answered yes. I then said, *Fire?* and they raised their arms together deliberately, from a hanging position. Sam appeared to aim at the Doctor's hip, and consequently fired first, striking him squarely in the leg and upsetting the motion of the Doctor's hand, who directed his shot at Sam's breast. The bullet whistled by, piercing only the corner of his shirt tail and pantaloons. Sam, unhurt, asked if the Doctor desired a second shot, and being informed in the negative, retired to his room – with the air of a man, I thought, whose blood had soared, more at the prospect of his own death than that of his adversary.

This affair seemed to have doused the fire in him. At least, Sam spent the rest of his time at the 53rd peacefully enough, rising no further in the ranks, and engaging, as much as possible, in the fieldwork and cartography that exercised a portion of the peacetime army. He grew in the meantime from an angry young man into an *ambitious* one; but, like most internal revolutions of our spirit, the transformation left no indication of itself until it was complete.

In 1818, Syme entered upon the career that would occupy him for the rest of his life, and published his first geological essay, in the journal of his old professor, Sober Ben Silliman, the founder and editor of the *American Journal of Science*. This success convinced him to quit the army and pursue full time the theories he had thereby announced to the world. I was getting warmer.

The essay itself, entitled 'A Theory of Concentric Spheres', took up the suggestions of Loomis's catalogue of magnetic variation in the state of Virginia and offered an ingenious if somewhat improbable explanation:

> The Fact of a moving magnetic First Cause is difficult, if not impossible, to be reconciled with a solid Globe. Yet *that* the magnetic needle *does* vary, not only with latitude

but the passage of Time, *and according to a regular and predictable pattern*, is confirmed beyond all doubt by Loomis' excellent Map of magnetic Readings in Virginia. Still, no one, I believe (certainly not Loomis himself), has urged the *variableness* of the magnetic Cause against the possibility of a solid globe; neither the Neptunists nor the Plutonists address this *fundamental* Evidence of the consistency of the Earth's core. We have been given a keyhole to the inner Chamber, but we avert our eyes, and refuse to look.

According to the doctrine of *Hollow Spheres* this whole Mystery of the variation of the compass can be satisfactorily explained . . .

There follows an intricate model of the internal globe, an onion of concentred metallic spheres, whose revolutions combine with astonishing complexity to produce the readings Loomis recorded in Virginia. At this stage in his thinking, Syme seems to have converted from his early Neptunism into the adoption of some at least of the tenets of *Plutonism*, the doctrine of Hutton – who argues the existence of a molten core and an endlessly evolving geological process, *sans* beginning, *sans* end, an eternal fire. Syme's great innovation is to posit a *conclusion* of the Plutonist process, in which the molten core cooled and separated according to the composition of its metals. As the metals hardened, the rotation of the globe spun them into distinct spheres, compressing a *socket* (Syme's word) of gaseous fluid between each one. These sockets allowed the spheres themselves to rotate freely in the whirl of the world, accounting, in their variations, for the movement of a compass needle over time and space.

A mouthful of a theory, and, as they say in the charming lingo of this island, *mad as a box of spiders* at first glance. And yet, and yet, there was *something* in it, as Sober Ben Silliman must have spotted himself when he published it – an attention to detail (for Syme was nothing if not meticulous), but more than that, a *genius of connection*. Nobody before Syme had explored the question of magnetic variation as a means of determining the composition of the core – an obvious step, it might seem today, but Syme was the first to take it. Nobody had adopted the Plutonist account in order to press it to a conclusion. Hutton himself insisted that all journeys (no matter how speculative) to the beginning or end of World and Time were *fruitless*. The best you could do was discover the process of modification along the way; and, for the most part, his followers accepted this restriction. Syme did not.

Yet there was no mention, not the slightest hint, of those 'segments of the earth's crust which float on the revolving core' that would inspire Wegener a century on. Dig, Pitt, dig! I cried, and wrung the venerable pages of the *American Journal of Science*, March 1818, for the last drop of madness, astonishing the stooped and silent readers in the Rare Books and Music chamber of the British Library by the agony of my researches. Dig and dig, to the bottom of this thing, the liquid, shifting core!

But there was nothing there, no hint as yet of the theory that *begot* the theory that changed our world, no sign. And soon a hushed voice, issuing from a balding curly-haired young man, bearing the proud badge of 'BL Staff' swinging about his neck, above a cracked black T-shirt sporting the ensign Metal Head in agonized italics, asked me 'not to *badger* the books so much, I was upsetting the readers'.

So I forbore to badger and read over (in commendable quietude) Syme's magnificent conclusion, which began to frighten me for its very plausibility:

> That a disposition to hollow cylinders *does* exist in nature, we think must be admitted; and that a similar principle exists in the planetary system, at least in some degree, appears to us certain. Every person has seen or heard of Saturn and his rings. At certain periods of time the appearance of this Planet, viewed through a stout telescope, represents him to be surrounded with two luminous Rings or Loops of matter, concentric with each other, and with the body of the planet. These rings nowhere adhere to that Body, but float distinct and sepa-

rate, some considerable distance from him, and from each other, leaving a portion of vacant Space, through which we see the fixed stars beyond.

The appearance of Saturn, we conceive, establishes the *Fact*, that the principle of concentric spheres, or Hollow Planets, does exist, at least in one instance, in the solar system. And if the fact be established in one case, is it not fair, nay, is it not almost a certain and necessary consequence, that the same Laws of Matter which formed a *part* of the Universe have operated upon the Whole?

I began to wonder if I had gone too deep to look around me, having lost the light of common sense above, left only with those far dimmer guides – the intellect on one hand and my own ambition on the other – to feel my way through these deep passages of history, of cause and effect, error and inspiration. Yet I had ventured too far to turn back; the end of my grant stood before me, like the glow of an oncoming train, and I had nothing to show for a busy year as yet. All I could do was rush, as quickly as possible, through the darkness of the tunnel.

I found little record of Sam's four years in the army. He seems to have enjoyed the routine; the early rising benefited his health, and the exercise composed his sleep without too great a burden of dreams. Though Syme possessed a robust physique, a barrel-chested, rosy-cheeked bravado of the constitution (somewhat, I flatter myself, after the fashion of his humble biographer), he suffered from a peculiar susceptibility of the imagination, which could grow sick at a suggestion – a liability which, owing to his ordinary vigour, rendered his periods of debilitation particularly painful. We often find in specimens of great natural good health a proportional rebellion of the constitution, as if their native strength were thrust upon them, and their psyches were too weak to bear the mass of so much vitality.

But the routines of army life assuaged this susceptibility, and the four years appear to have passed, after the violence of his initiation, in a general contentment, if the silence of this period is anything to go by. (Silence, in my experience, being a great indicator of happiness. A restless spirit writes, confronts, obstructs, composes, entangles, and trails in its wake a thousand marks of its tumultuous passage; a happy nature passes smoothly over the years, barely touching the surface and leaving no mark as it glides.) The fury of whatever decision drove him from Yale College to the 53rd Infantry abated; the winds calmed, and Syme seemed bent on the course of an ordinary prosperity.

Yet out of this prosperous calm was born his strange fixation on the 'theory of concentric spheres'. We have no record of the circumstances that precipitated such an eruption, of the moment of inspiration, of the mounting degrees of his obsession. The essay was published in the March issue of the *Journal of American Science*; Syme effected his discharge from the army two months later, wandering from the well-trod path before him into such impressionable ground that history still bears the prints of his diversions. I could only *guess* – hunched over the mottled paper of the *Journal*, turning the delicate leaves with my ham fists, still strapped, and bound and forbidden the use of a pen – the *tyranny* of inspiration that drove Syme, from the comfortable progress of a fashionable career to such strange prospects: a life of disappointment and betrayal, and an early, desired death.

But a century of winds dispersed his theories, until, like a piece of grit (as I hoped to prove), one stuck in the thoughts of Alfred Wegener and produced a pearl. A pearl that eventually cost the German scientist his life, a pearl whose perfect brilliance drove me, *another* century on, to carve within it and discover the source of the original infection. We are at the mercy of our own inspiration and helpless to prevent the spread of a faith, once started, even in ourselves. Who can say where or when the notion will strike?

I pursued my researches now at the Newspaper Library in Colindale, a noble Victorian red-brick building in the middle of suburban nowhere – in a loose field protected by a sagging fence, a set of football posts kneeling in the high grass beside a pile of cement rubble littered with Coke cans. I sat at the top, looking over the green wasteland, while a single fan, perched in the crack of a tall window, blew the hot air around and around the high room.

A tall young man with a pinched nose and a racking sneeze pushed the squeaking trolley towards me and lifted out the book of old Baltimore papers, bound together but surprisingly light, as if the news had thinned with age. 'That's what we've got,' he said, pinching his pinched nose and twisting it to the side to sniff, 'I don't know what it is, but it's what's left. Try not to smudge it, will you?' And then, like an ailing Charon, he steered the trolley back to the comfort of the other shore, among the air conditioning and the forgotten papers.

The pages of the *Baltimore Patriot and Mercantile Advertiser* (1818–20) were less *yellowed* with age than cast into the burnished hue of a dusty summer cloud, the paper thick and softening at the edges, and blotched occasionally with a deeper yellow, like the smear of fat or oil. It was slow work, trawling through the advertisements for 'Cohen's lottery' and the offer of a reward for an 'eloped Negroe – of fine upright carriage, rather thin in figure than otherwise'. There were accounts of the spread of hydrophobia and the death of a young schoolboy; there was the shipping news, arrivals and departures; stories of sea-monsters discovered; records of the sessions in the Senate. More advertisements, for ointments, liniments, potions, pipsissiway (a root that cured cancer). An account of a man reputed to be a hundred and thirty years old, who had seen with his own eyes the coronation of Queen Anne. And then, with a growing palpitation of the heart, and an extra stickiness of the stubborn thumbs, I discovered the following:

> Pactaw – we have been favoured by an account of a remark-able new Science practiced in the humblest of our districts, by our own American Lavoisier, and a *southern gentleman* at that. The letter comes to us from Mr Topliff, apothecary and post-master in Pactaw, Virginia, via the *Richmond Intelligencer*.

'There, in the back-room of my shop, attended by a host of the eager and the sceptical, Lt Samuel Syme, lately of Yale College, offered the following remarkable demonstration of the actions of the interior of the earth. Into an admixture of gray slop, containing, among other things, a sprinkling of sugar! Mr Syme administered a single drop of sulfuric acid and immediately leapt into the cranny of the side-door. His audience had no such recourse, and with what astonishment, delight, discomfort and, I confess, terror, we observed the result.

I think the flame must have gone up to the ceiling, casting a black shadow against the paintwork which remains to this day, a towering inferno of living smoldering ash and fire. The room became intolerable with heat and fume, and though the application of an opened window somewhat diminished the torpor of its effect, none among us but covered our mouths with the hem of our shirts in an effort to prevent from choking. The air positively swam with small lumps of half-burned charcoal and a surprising and overpowering smell of *caramel*. After the initial shock, the gathering issued abruptly through the side-door whence Mr Syme himself had fled, others effecting a more instantaneous exit through the opened window.

This little demonstration has consumed our thoughts and tongues the remaining week, engendering a great variety of opinions and consequent *discussions*, between those that consider his display the actions of a conjurer and a charlatan and those who believe we have stumbled across our very own Newton, or at the least, an American Mr Jameson, and a grand geognosist, as Lt Syme insists on calling himself. Regardless of these debates, no one disputes that Lt Syme has offered us a most convincing picture of *Hell-fires*, and effected more for our virtue in this brief experiment than the Priest has accomplished through a whole season of sermons.'

After the initial excitement of my discovery, I confess I was troubled by a certain *lightness* suggested by the tone of Syme's demonstration. Tippy Adams remarked on a 'kind of vengeful humour' in Sam, and though the volcanic experiment seemed rather teasing than angry, nevertheless it displayed a sense of trickery, the delight of the charlatan, a word broached by the humble apothecary himself. Naturally, the chemistry involved was *old hat* to a man of Sam's education (Silliman impressed his first-year students with such demonstrations); and no doubt Sam revelled in the ignorance of his parochial neighbours. Still, this very desire to *impress* what must have been a collection of farmers with the rudiments of his art embarrassed me. It did not indicate a 'mute, inglorious' Newton buried in small-town life, but a somewhat shabby gentleman playing upon the superstitions of his boorish friends. At best, he appeared a tease; at worst, a sham, desperate for the meanest of admiration. In all likelihood, he was something of both. This did not augur well, I thought, for the role I had in mind for Syme.

I stared out at the waste-green field, falling away from the stretches of suburban neighbourhoods towards London, and wondered if after all I had been barking up the wrong tree, or, worse still, barking where there was no tree. There is a peculiar loneliness to historical research. One acquires a taste, a distinct taste, for *footprints*, the intimate evidence of past lives, marks left in newspaper and letter, even in the items of a will. I had almost forgotten the touch of ordinary days, almost forgotten the courtesies of ignorance – accustomed as I was, by a lonely year away from wife and boys, to rummaging rudely through old lives, stepping on this and that and taking what I could. I missed my home; my wife had scarcely practised the trick of love – for it *is* a trick, a sleight of hand, a gift of eloquence – over the phone in two weeks, that particular intimacy of mouth and ear across oceans of air, conveyed by the warm oily plastic of the telephone. We talked but the heart was gone in us – she harboured some obscure resentment, which expressed itself in politeness and concern. Much has been made in the literature of the past century of the animal within us, unabated by ages of civility. In my experience, even our basest appetites need constant replenishment, they die for want of nourishment, flaring up only now and again in a kind of weak fever. I have known more harm done out of simple human *dryness* than out of any passion or taint in the blood. And there I sat, in the Colindale Newspaper Library, unearthing the life of a dead man who suddenly seemed to me better left buried. I was homesick, and the thick air dampened the splint between my thumb and forefinger till it stank; and I stared out of the window, hoping the rain would come soon.

Once more into the breach, I thought, when the fellow with the pinched nose delivered, sniffing greatly, a little box of microfilm to my table. '*Norfolk Weekly Intelligencer,*' he said. 'I don't know what you've got there; 1821, I *shouldn't* imagine. The dates are all in a muddle. That's what we have, I'm afraid; the rest is buggered.' And he sniffed his way back to his desk.

The Microfilm Chamber adjoined the reading room through an old arched set of double doors that at first appeared to be locked, until I read the proud notice across it: THESE DOORS ARE NOW AUTOMATIC. I waited, counting the slow beat of blood in my ears from the hot day; peered along the crack down the middle of the doors. Nothing happened. Perhaps their stiffness, their silence, their immobility were automatic, unconscious, requiring no particular effort of the will. They stayed put automatically, unblinkingly, unflinchingly. I lowered a shoulder against them; a bruise upon the nub of bone persuaded in me a grudging admiration for them. These doors knew what they did well; in true English fashion, they *remained unmoved*. As I remained, unmoved, before them, staring them out. The timeless silence of a hot day in an old library passed over me. I let it pass, in utter absence of mind, the blankness that follows the first leg swung over the edge of a bed in the morning, and precedes the second sudden brisk step towards the bathroom. I was almost spent, barred from a cave of treasures I suspected in that weak hour of containing fool's gold.

I stood on the casual verge of turning back (by such threads do the secrets even of our own dispositions hang) when I perceived that, far from being locked, the doors had begun to open of themselves and at their own pace – *automatically* and incrementally slowly. They wheezed slightly as they shuddered outwards, as if they had yet to enjoy the first cigarette of the day to clear their lungs. So I waited, until the ancient portals like old men on canes inched away from the middle, and I could squeeze my thick frame between them into the coldest room I have ever encountered in a lifetime of air-conditioned academic chambers.

Once more into the breach, I muttered, braver than before. I seemed to have travelled from the Plutonist fires to the frozen waters of Neptunian theory. Hunched and huddled men stared at the flicker of the microfilms in a darkened room, like cavemen around a fire, rubbing their bare arms, roughened with goose pimples, to thaw the red blood in them and ease the flow. Nobody spoke, only the occasional clatter and whirl of a reel rewinding broke the white hum of the monitors. I had entered the ice-box of history, where the most delicate ephemera are frozen in photographic amber, revealed for an instant by a whizzing electric light, then cast into darkness again. Our memories are at the mercy of chance both ways, I reflected; the luck of what's left behind and the luck of the eye that falls upon them. For as brief as the window of time that preserves us can be the passage of the single gaze that may light upon us later, and remember us to the world. As I flicked through the pages of the *Norfolk Weekly Intelligencer*, racing across the glow of the white screen, I thought not only of the footprints I hoped to find, but the tracks I was sure to miss.

The *Intelligencer* was a collection of clippings from around the country, selected and printed by Bishop Perkins of Norfolk, for the 'curious and pious Mind, which delights in all the works of the Lord'. Each issue opened with a half-dozen pages of ecclesiastical notes, interpretations of scripture, records of sermons; there followed a brief section titled 'Arts & Science & Culture', and finally a page of 'Remarkable Occurrences', such as the interrupted interment of a woman presumed dead, until a tumble occasioned by a clumsy undertaker opened a cut in her forearm, which 'bled freshly to general astonishment'. After a consultation of doctors, and the several applications of a scalpel to her skin, each resulting in a renewed flow, she was pronounced dead again 'on account of the absence of breath' and buried at last. It was not among these phenomena, thank God, but in the previous section that I discovered at last the following news of my 'undiscovered genius', recorded by a Mr Thomas Jenkyns, and picked up from the *Southern Courier*, October 1819:

> We yesterday afternoon witnessed a very ingenious and interesting experiment made by Lt Syme of Pactaw, Virginia, by which the fact is completely demonstrated that water is compressible and also *elastic*, contrary to the hitherto received opinions of Philosophers upon that subject. The experiment was made with a hollow brass Cylinder 36 inches in length, divided in 1000 equal parts and filled with water. A Piston so fitted as to be perfectly watertight was introduced, and by means of a Force ingeniously applied, equal to the pressure of about forty atmospheres, the column of water within was reduced in height by thirty parts out of the thousand, or 3 percent. The utmost degree of compression hitherto ascertained we believe to be about the *thirtieth* part of one thousandth, or the third part of 1 percent.
>
> Lt Syme has undertaken this experiment, in the hopes of proving the effect of compression, not on Water at last, but upon *Air*, believing that sufficient force could liquefy even our own exhalations, reducing them, as it were, to no more than a trickle of Tears. Such liquefaction is vital to a theory of the internal Earth upon which Lt Syme, lately of Yale College, is engaged, following the suggestions of no less than Benjamin Franklin upon the subject of a compressed gas, as the natural Lubricant of the mechanism of the Planet.
>
> Lt Syme expects so to improve and perfect his Apparatus as to be able to apply a pressure equal to that of *100 atmospheres*, the result of which, should he succeed, of

> which we have little doubt, we shall be curious to know,
> and prompt to announce to the public.

My hands shivered as I read, both from the extreme refrigeration of the Microfilm Chamber, and from a kind of *relief*, inseparable from excitement. Syme was no simple charlatan, no village trickster, I was sure. Here at last was proof of the weight of his convictions – the laborious machinery of his theories, each wheel meticulously constructed, patiently articulated into the grand design.

Slowly, I felt, I had begun to grasp the *fabric* of the man. The quality I had mistaken for lightness was in fact a profound *restlessness*, an excess, of energy and intellect, a fresh itch continuously scratched. He turned for relief of this innate discomfort – a kind of tightness of his own skin, from which he sought to burst free – to the easy applause of a parochial ignorance, to flatterers and flattery, to the warmth of simple admiration. But only for relief. I felt I knew my man. The time had come when, with a delicate finger, I could feel *his* pulse as my own. How often had I myself wasted an idle hour bullying and persuading ignorant company, simply to preen my own feathers? But beneath his bright vanities lay a far weightier ambition, a heavy sense of purpose, that drove him on, regardless of obscurity, a deep patience. At times, I flattered myself that his patience had found its reward, at last, in my attentions, my rescue, from the sea of time, in which he had almost drowned.

Of course, I could not hide from myself, even then, a certain – what shall I call it? – tendency to *flinch* from good fortune; or perhaps, more precisely considered, a Failure Drive, if I may coin the term. Time and again he seemed to turn, at the last instant, from the light and find himself a comfortable shadow. Embarked on his studies at Yale (studies particularly congenial to the bent of his genius), he fled after a single year for what? The obscurity of a soldier's life. And even then, just as the fortunes of war offered him the chance to make a name (which he took – it must be remembered that Syme was a man who *took* his chances before he neglected them), he fled again, after his discharge, not to Philadelphia or Boston or New York, the hub of his geological ambitions, but to Pactaw, Virginia, a day's drive from Baltimore, to survey a vein of bituminous coal for the Virginia Mining Corporation (the man had to live, after all) and impress, from time to time, the ignorance of the locals.

Perhaps the clue to Syme's character lies in my own bosom. For I began to suspect that the curious flinching that afflicted Syme afflicts *myself*; and I read into his prevarications and procrastinations (and there were more to come, always more to come, for success dogged Syme, nipping at his heels, and he escaped, again and again, before *I* closed upon him) the history of my own self-neglect. For have I not turned and turned again, at the last moment, from triumph? Declined the scholarship to Harvard, a boy of seventeen, to linger in the sunshine of San Diego and the terminal shadow of my mother's sickbed, to which my father displayed a peculiar aversion undiminished by his disappointment at my 'going to State' and eased only in the end by her eventual death at the age of fifty-five from cancer, during the spring of my junior year. Of course, I had right on my side, and kindness, and fealty; but I lack both the generosity of spirit *not* to regret such chances missed and the greatness of spirit to *grasp* them.

The true artist will trample on his mother, his wife, his children, his friends, to pursue the path of his art; well, I am no true artist, though I have done my share of *trampling* in my time, and been trampled upon. Yet there is always the rebound; and I finagled my way to Oxford after Mother's death on a Rotary Fellowship to wander at last among the ancient halls of learning and put on airs. (I confess myself guilty of a cricket jersey at the time; and even, in a weak moment, a boater.) But after every recovery, there is a fresh evasion; and a year before completing my D.Phil., I chased a girl to New York and never caught her and never went back, and ended up teaching Freshman Bio to a collection of the pleasantest and richest teenage Jews (the rich are always *so* pleasant) from the Upper East Side of Manhattan for *five long years of easy, uncounted life*, confronted at every turn by a host of bustling mothers, who could only regret that 'such a nice young man was a *goy*'.

But after every evasion there is a fresh recovery; and I married the pick of the History Department, a plump and pretty Jewess (my eternal *Miss Susie*), built something along my own lines; and dropped out. So we accumulated (there is no other word) ourselves in a two-bedroom railroad apartment on East 89th Street, while she tutored after hours and taught summer school, to support the wriggly young boy on the way, and the wrigglier old boy turning again to his doctorate, starting from scratch, at NYU, for another five long, penniless years until at last I could *make good*.

And here I sit, and I haven't made good yet; hoping to make good that long-ago no-goodnik, Samuel Highgate Syme, whom even the staunchest mother might be forgiven for giving up on. And Mrs Pitt sweats away through a Texan summer, alone with the two boys, suspecting, doubting hopefully, knowing in her heart, that once again there has been an *evasion*, and that Douglas Pitt, up at last for tenure, unpublished, unsupported by the Dean, betrayed even by his own hands (in stiff rebellion, the channels of communication blocked, the workers striking), has not written a word (for all his Fulbrights) on the Inspiration of Error, while he chases, once again, another lost cause, another evader, hoping that he proves of a different mettle from his own.

I said that I had begun to grasp the fabric of Syme, feel the *texture* of the man beneath my thumb. There was strength there, sure; a certain roughness, a willingness to *make do*, even with failure (I guessed then, and have since been proven wrong). He could work, there was no doubt of that, had an appetite for exertion, a taste for his own sweat, displayed again and again, in his early reports from college, his courage in war; even the books of the Virginia Mining Corporation proved above all that he could *bend* himself to the task at hand. In his first year with the company he covered an almost impossible stretch of ground, from the Potomac to the Mississippi, by himself; while producing at the same time that astonishing piece of scientific illusionism 'The Theory of

Concentric Spheres', and developing the 'ingenious Force' that powered the piston for his experiments in the compression of water. No doubt he hoped to secure enough funds to open a free space for his own investigations; and this he appears to have accomplished, for after the initial burst his outings with the VMC grow fewer and further between.

But there is something else – and I struggle for the phrase – suggested by these intermittent fragments of his life, powerful and irregular as the illuminations of lightning in a dark landscape. A certain *lack of principle*. There, I have said it; the words sit plump and glowing on the screen and my single banging finger poises above the button for 'delete' to remove all trace of such a questionable libel, and . . . forbears. Syme lacked *principle*; he seemed as willing to delight the ignorance of a handful of farmers as to persuade the comprehension of the finest scientists in the young republic, from Professor Silliman on down. He buried himself in obscurity *either* in the belief that a candle glows brightest in a dark corner *or* in the fear that he could not survive the winds of public dispute. I could see no alternative at the time. Satisfied at last that he was no simple charlatan, I could not dissuade myself *either* of the pettiness of his ambition (the rabble's applause, and a rather tiny rabble at that) *or* of the still less palatable notion *that he was a coward*. (And, by extension, from one personality to the next, that my own failures lay in this very weakness – the fear of exposure, of a final reckoning, the devotion of a life to 'something evermore about to be' and never at hand.)

The next piece of evidence I stumbled upon puzzled me still further. I had returned to the house of Sam's grandfather, the white-chocolate elegance of the eighteenth century and the poky little room looking over the garden and the edge of Highgate Ponds. Rummaging through the chest of papers, I discovered the following curious pair of letters, bound in red ribbon and carefully folded, one within the other. I gently disentangled them, softening their edges with a tender thumb before I unbent them. The shorter letter, composed in a fine if elderly hand, was also the more recent and ran as follows:

Sir – you requested, in memory of your late Son, a copy of his correspondence with me, with which I have obliged you. Lately, clearing away a somewhat rotted Case of Books, a Leaf fluttered out, which I had doubtless laid between two pages in some careless Hurry of the moment. I discovered it to be from your Son, and moreover, marked the last correspondence we ever held (though I saw him after, in person, in Philadelphia, and exchanged a Kindness). I now enclose it to you.

I regret to say, that though I knew him long I knew him *lightly*. He withdrew from the College after a single year. He fell out of my Ken for a time, until he obliged me with his essay on the Theory of Spheres, which I chose to publish, believing at the time there was some Method to his Madness that wanted encouragement. I fear however that the *Madness* outran the Method; and when I declined a second essay (being somewhat opaque even to the learned Eye) and recommended that he bend his Talents to some more *practical* branch of our Philosophy (in which he might have shone, and in which I should have *published* him), he closed all communication with myself and our enterprise in the Letter that follows. I could have wished our acquaintance deepened, trusting that had he been 'put on, he would have proved most royal', though the Bar before him, I am afraid, he fixed himself.

Yours faithfully,
Ben. Silliman

P.S. Rest assured, I bear him no ill will now for the tenor of the following.

This then was 'the tenor of the following', a single folded sheet of paper in the characteristic untidiness of Sam Syme himself, odd words smudged with the heavy fist of their composer.

Sir – I could write frequently to your Lyceum on the practical Arts of our Philosophy (which you praise so highly), but I see no Object in it. My pieces are all necessarily *Speculative*, owing to what I consider the shameful Ignorance of even our most lauded Geologists of any *System* of Thought according to which they might arrange their no doubt *laborious* Observations. Such a System is of the *first Importance* if our present rapid progress in the Natural Sciences is to be maintained. Well, you publish nothing of such Matter, excepting now and then a piece, entirely for the benefit of the Author's Vanity . . . To be emphatically serious, your Journal of the American Sciences has admitted such puerile wretched Trash, that I am heartily sick of *Periodical* Fame and prefer to bend my bow at an obscurer Distance. In short, you study to please fools.

I have sent you the finest article on Geognosy I ever wrote, which, properly understood, might set the World on its Ears and guide our science to unguessed-of Shores. You have declined, preferring no doubt a long dull mess of trash about Music, or William's toad. I will not write it, Sir.

Believe me, etc.
Samuel Syme

Whatever else might be said of this curious piece of professional suicide, it did not strike me as the work of a *coward* – at least, no coward in the ordinary sense. By this wonderful outburst of sheer arrogance – the 'stuff' in Larkin's phrase 'that dreams are made on' (for I am nothing if not literary, the leading light of our little Blue-stocking Society in Austin, a poetry . . . workshop, I believe is the preferred term, for professors of a literary turn of mind) – Syme brushed aside his only 'friend in high places', the spider at the heart of the web of the new American Science, the great Ben Silliman, the Toymaker of his day. Perched on the little fridge in the Curator's office, my feet on tiptoes, the letter resting lightly on my upturned hands, I stared at the brittle, untidy words *lost in admiration*. A long, slow growl of rain muttered among the trees outside and the sun cast only a grey shadow of light into the cluttered study, but across two centuries of obscurity and neglect, Syme's complete indifference to earthly powers shone undimmed. Here was a man who ventured everything on the coin-toss of his own inspiration, and stood so sure of the gamble that he could neglect almost to look at the result. I, who have scrounged and scratched my way, humbled and begged, stood *breathless* now at the pure *indifference* of this forgotten genius to his earthly fortune. I knew then, tremblingly, as the blood tickled my thin veins on its delicate passage from my heart, that I HAD FOUND MY MAN.

What I had *not* found, however, was my evidence. Where was this 'article on Geognosy', the 'finest' he ever wrote? If only Sober Ben had published the damn thing, I could trace my source, the mouth of the river that flowed at last into Alfred Wegener. But Ben had not, and Wegener (I had no doubt now) had come by his inspiration after a more circuitous journey. Was this article in Geognosy **the** *New Platonist* that lodged at last in the library in Berlin, where the young boy could feed his parched curiosity? Did it carry on its current those all-important 'segments of the earth's crust which float on the revolving core', which found their way to Wegener at last and formed the first bricks of his new world? That would make my name and fortune?

Alas, Sam's father had tenderly hoarded all the tokens of his late son's *life* and neglected all the monuments of his *thought* he might have left behind him. But at last I stumbled upon some proof that others in his time had held him in the same esteem to which I meant to raise him in our own. Another clipping fluttered from the clutter of Edward's collection, and, after a great and slow manoeuvring of strapped thumbs, I managed to lift it to the wooden desk pushed up against the window. My blunt nose almost twitched with expectation, for I realized, after the first word or two, that I was hot on the scent. The date is 1824; the paper once more the *Norfolk Weekly Intelligencer*; and the extract drawn again from the *Southern Courier*.

> We offer the following invitation to a Lecture, delivered by Thomas Jenkyns, esq., the son of Reverend Jenkyns of Richmond, Virginia.
>
> Pactaw – We have amongst us, in the very humblest of our towns, a Divine, a Poet, a Rhetorician, a Scholar, and a

high-bred Gentleman, who, when physical Science did not sway the universal mind as it now promises to do, still saw with a telescopic View both its intrinsic importance and its possible advantages towards the Honour of our Country and the progress of human society.

Mr Syme, lately of Yale College, will address the question of The Future of Science? and reveal his own researches into the Nature of the Poles at the Town Hall in Richmond, the Friday of the 23rd of this Month, at 6 o'clock, for a charge of 50 cents, payable upon entrance. This is not a Chance to be Missed.

Something about this teasing account froze my attention, quite aside from the evidence of Syme's spreading influence that it suggested. I read it repeatedly for a clue, until at last I realized that the faint chime of recognition ringing at my temples originated in the bell of a name, Thomas Jenkyns, the correspondent from the *Southern Courier*. Trawling through my previous researches, I discovered that *his* had been the name to which Sam's mother had addressed her recollections of the 'presages of geologic genius'; *his* had been the eye that witnessed the 'ingenious' compression of water attempted by Lt Syme. The question remained, who was he? And what part did he play in the rise and fall of the Divine, the Poet, the Rhetorician, the Scholar, and the high-bred Gentleman who occupied my researches?

So I returned to the supermarket grandeur of the British Library, butting through the dusty traffic of King's Cross from my lonely studio flat, and entering the cool, distilled air of a space where books are kept, hoping against hope that Thomas Jenkyns had left some trace of a spent life behind him.

In this, at first, I was disappointed. I discovered a variety of Jenkynses – authors, sailors, clergymen, historians, divines – but, by some honest quirk of fate, not a single Thomas among them – as if, though she would deny me my prize, Fate would not tease me with a twin of history, an insignificant Thomas Jenkyns, a Thomas Jenkyns untroubled by the matter at hand. After all, there was no particular reason my *special* Thomas Jenkyns should have left his name to posterity, seeing that the man he trumpeted so grandly to the skies had been dispersed till nothing but scraps remained.

It was the word 'clergyman' that stuck in my throat, and suggested another avenue to my researches. 'Thomas Jenkyns, esq., the son of Reverend Jenkyns, of Richmond, Virginia,' the clipping read, and of *Reverends* Jenkyns I had found a windfall. Jenkynses, it seemed, by some disposition of their last name, some suggestion of benignity perhaps, or a hint of the absurd, had been drawn to the Church like bees to a jam-pot, and I wondered if the good *father* of my obscure Thomas (my predecessor in the art of *puffing* Syme) had left his mark on the world. (More and more this seemed to me, and the deeper I went, a tale of *fathers*.)

Of *Reverends* Jenkyns there was one curious instance, a certain William Jenkyns, whose funeral sermon upon the death of a Mr Seaborn caused a great stir, it seemed, among the American clergy in 1850, occasioning a flurry of correspondence and a distinctly chilly ecclesiastical *air*. The charge levied at this divine Jenkyns was one of heresy, prompted by his eulogy of the said Seaborn, and seemed to have little to do with my own, increasingly dear, Samuel Syme, except for a strange coincidence of dates; for 1850, I recalled, was the year of Sam's death. But this coincidence seemed too remote to require a deeper investigation, and I returned to Mackintosh Place and the Hampstead & Highgate Preservation Trust, the birthplace of Sam's father Edward and the scene of his death, and the storehouse of his effects.

Here a long and excessively dull afternoon of rummaging at length yielded its prize. Again and again, I had to combat the strange faith of the historical researcher (at least, of *this* researcher) in some *fate* involved in his discoveries, whose hand will reveal what has been lost, whose inexorability (I know no better word) will suffer no relevant stone to remain unturned. It is a strange conviction, I confess it, yet perhaps a necessary one, for scholars who, like Newton, stand only on the sea-side of what may be known, and must persuade themselves that no buried, undiscovered fact will disprove the scanty world they have constructed from the few remains. Yet a world of facts stretches wide and deep beyond the corners of our gaze. No assiduity could discover the whole; and so we work by faith, that the *part* explains the *sum*, that the *pattern* holds true – and that the necessary facts *will* reveal themselves to us, by some agency, and that when nothing is revealed, no revelation is at hand. And so on long, dry, fruitless days we battle the conviction, as much as anything else, that there is *nothing* to find; because an important truth *would*, *by now*, have declared itself.

At last, as the sun set against the side of the house and a few stray beams shimmered on the mottled glass, the long-sought clue did reveal itself to me. (You see how *insidious* this strange faith is, how persuasive, that the clue revealed is the *one that matters*, and not that *other* clue, the undiscovered one, the shadow at the end of the light, endlessly retreating and mysterious.) Stuck, by some dampness acting upon the ink, to the back of a coloured sketch (an accomplished piece of work, depicting Sam himself, 'the delicate temples and too big eyes, the face sad, inward, except for the butting, jutting chin, stubborn and strong above the white cravat; the hair thinning over the large forehead'), a letter peeled off, somewhat blotted by its previous adhesion.

The letter was addressed to Sam himself and signed by none other than Thomas Jenkyns, in a curiously feminine hand, clear and distinct, with a hint of flourish here and there. It followed a peculiar tradition of the nineteenth century, of the fan-letter, peculiar less for the letter itself than the warmth that often greeted its reception. This was a century in which an act of admiring homage produced a condescension that often led to friendship, and I guessed at once that some friendship *had* followed this particular display of admiration, remarkable for its *practicality* (despite a kind of blushing effusion), and the faint air, almost of irony, running throughout it:

Dear Sir – I have hesitated some time to approach a gentleman of your eminence upon such slight acquaintance, with a proposition that may prove especially uncongenial to your particular genius, that walks 'with inward glory crowned' and requires it seems no other title. I should deeply regret the air of a *fortune-seeker*, hoping to wed his name to a bright meteor and follow its rise, attend what may upon its descent. Were it not that I believe the *Honor of our country* the true partner of your ambitions, and the *benefit of society*, both intellectual and domestic, its *Aim*, I should have forborne altogether this chance at a – dare I hope it – friendship that would afford me such remarkable pleasure. In short, I believe I can be of use to you; and through you, of use to the World.

I should begin by speaking a little of myself. I am the son of a Minister, and grew up perhaps too much under the shadow of seriousness, in its Groves. My father, however, is a liberal Clergyman, a keen astronomer, and a faithful amateur of the new sciences. I had been brought up to believe that God had made a World for us to discover, not a tablet of Laws for us to con. Upon coming of age, I hoped to pursue a profession that would satisfy (alas, I knew not what I hoped) a long-pent Desire to See the World; and apprenticed myself to one of the flurry of newspapers, which in the modern era have fallen upon the cities of our Republic.

If nothing else, I have my Trade to thank for my Introduction to you, and a knowledge of the Means by which I hope to make myself useful in your Cause. I had been familiar with your Experiments for some time, and broadcast to Virginia your advances in that ingenious matter of the Compression of Water; but I had not till recently grasped the full extent of the scientific Revolution you intended.

When at last my editor summoned me to his desk upon the publication of your estimable book, the *Remarkable Journeys of Mr Seaborn*, and revealed to me the breadth of your ambitions. A radical man, he had said, of tendencies, with certain leanings, he added, leaning his own head to the side knowingly, had recently published, and despite considerations demonstrated – this was emphasized – a brilliant scientific theory, a theory that proved the earth was hollow to the bone, formed of concentered metallic spheres a fathom thick, which could be traveled with nothing more sophisticated than a carriage from one end of the globe to the other, if only the points of entry were known.

'Despite considerations,' reaffirmed my chief. The consequences were enormous, and the Doctores Universita – he said the latter phrase with relish – were only beginning to sniff the possibilities. The Odor had blown even unto our very Congress, which was then considering your appeal for Funds. My editor glowed, he was luminous, his face shone. The application had attracted considerable attention, and the disputes in the senate and church were becoming a Matter of Controversy – a holy phrase.

It is only upon the denial of that Application that I venture to place myself at the Services of a Cause that has grown so dear to my Heart. Rumors had reached me of the extent to which you were dependent on practical researches of a purely commercial nature for the prosecution of your Theories. The Virginia Mining Company is not worthy of you; nor am I, though I make bold to believe that your Theories are worthy of every, even the slightest, Help. There is no Shame I believe attached to this offer of Assistance. A man on his own may Discover the World; but he cannot Conquer it. For that he requires a Legion of lesser men; at whose head I hope you will grant me the role of Lieutenant.

Your humble and obedient servant,
Thomas Jenkyns

What was Tom's cause? – a question that puzzled more than Sam in his day and leads to no satisfactory conclusions. Tom, like Jacob, seems a *smooth* man; his brother-in-science, Sam, a *hairy* one. I confess an inclination to the latter; despite my own shiny pate, I support a harvest of black and golden hairs upon back and breast and leg and forearm, casting a muffled glow over the swell of the muscle and suggesting, by luxuriance of growth, the vitality of the man within, the earthly fertility, the richness in life and love and *projects*, that particular outcrop of the academic soul. A smooth skin offers no purchase to the eye, no rough grip; we glance off them like sunshine off a window and cannot fix them in our sight. They flicker – Tom *flickers*, shaven, odourless, clean, the paradigm of men, the quintessence of dust, scrubbed till the stench of man, the goodness and badness of him, the lust and love, give off only the faintest and sweetest of scents. Tom had that ease of character, happy enough in its own goodness and its harmony with the world, that he need never *lie* or *cheat* to promote his own interests – the truth, by its nature he seemed to believe, would be agreeable to an agreeable man. He saw no need to battle it. Sam, on the other hand, battled and battled and battled – a bulldog, a pit bull, a man after my own heart, like Esau robbed of his inheritance. It took a far different man from Tom to rescue Syme from obscurity in the end (though Tom, to be fair, played his part); a man both more faithful than Tom – at least, hungrier for faith, and in consequence more full of doubt; but I overstep myself, and *Phidy's* time will come.

Yet Tom was a 'liked guy', as the fellow said to Holly Golightly; more than that, a much-loved gentleman, famous among his friends for his kindness and the grace of his affections. In short, a cipher of a man, whose interest in Syme's projects seems the most puzzling thing of all. Yet that he *was* interested is clear; that he promoted Sam's interests is also clear, and worked extremely hard to do so; and that he had some moderate, even great, triumphs in Sam's cause cannot be doubted; nor that he remained faithful to him and kind long after Sam could serve his own or anyone's purpose. The testament to this fact takes me to my next discovery, the death of my object, the funeral scene – the moment from which Syme's *history* began, at which all speculation takes wing, for its perch in *living fact* had snapped, and no resting-place remained.

Another bell had rung and I returned to the strange Reverend Jenkyns and the uproar over his 'heretical eulogy on the death of Mr Seaborn', the same name to which Thomas Jenkyns attributed the account of the 'Remarkable Journeys' that first drew him to Syme. This was perhaps my second piece of great good fortune, after the cache of Sam's memorabilia discovered in the house in Highgate. As the latter had been preserved owing to the *smoothness* of the stream of time – an attic unrummaged, a house allowed gently to decay – the former caught my attention owing to a *ruffle of turbulence* as the flow of history adjusted itself to a slight awkwardness in its path.

The great prize, of course, in Tom Jenkyns's letter was the fact that Sam had written a book, *The Remarkable Journey of Mr Seaborn*, which seemed to bear, at least obliquely, on his scientific work. I could not guess then the casual mistake that had kept this book secret from me for so long, a clerical error, the careless duplication of a letter and a slight slipping into the plural, but I had no doubt of my ability to *rustle up* the precious tome. Indeed, this certainty, or rather the prospect of it, occasioned my delay, as a boy will keep the fattest sausage for the final forkful; and I scraped around the edges of my prize to draw out the delight of its eventual discovery.

Consequently, I turned to explore the strange coincidence of names between the object of Reverend Jenkyns's controversial grief and the protagonist of Syme's literary explorations, with only half my heart – the shore lay ahead, I was certain; I had stopped only to explore a piece of driftwood caught up in the outbound tide. (I could not guess then the disappointment of my actual landing.) But I soon recognized the error of my inattention, or rather the *second* clerical error, that had blinded the library's computer to the connection between the great scientific failure and the ecclesiastical storm surrounding the elegy of a dead man in Virginia in 1850. (If I could begin my academic career from scratch, I should focus my interest in error on the minutiae of mistakes, *the history of the misprint*, rather than the grander miscalculations that occupy me here and elsewhere.) For the dead man lying quietly in the middle of all the fuss was none other than Sam Syme himself – mistaken, by some ecclesiastical printman, for the narrator of his novel, *The Remarkable Journey of Mr Seaborn*, which had caused all the uproar in the first place. I had stumbled by accident upon his funeral.

Most of *The Exchange of Correspondence, first published in the Norfolk Gazette, upon the Charges of Heresy, levied against Mr Jenkyns, on his Elegy at the death of Mr Seaborn, 1850* makes for dry reading. The offended clergy were inspired by the occasion to a long-windedness of biblical proportions. They seemed less anxious to *persuade* their readers than to *exhaust* them, to batter them into submission by the unanswerable logic of *sleep*. Jenkyns's defenders, of whom there were far fewer, while more elegant on the whole, tied their arguments into such knots that the fingers of the brain grew blunt and chafed attempting to undo them, and preferred at last the soothing tedium of his detractors. The reason for this state of affairs was simple and common enough: the stupid ones were right, as far as the argument went; the clever ones were right, as soon as it *ended*, but couldn't let the argument go.

But the argument itself offers a fascinating glimpse of a world whose answers were changing, a shift of templates as powerful as Wegener's tectonic plates, the latter literally earth-shattering, the former figuratively. Sam himself was only the occasion; the dispute was both more public than the event of his death, and indeed more private than the Reverend Jenkyns's elegy upon it. The question at the heart of it was this: whether the Bible could be reconciled to the new sciences. Our own age has answered so vehemently in the *negative* that perhaps we cannot imagine the urgency of the question in its time; but we must remember that the debate was carried out for the most part not between atheist and believer but between Christian and Christian. Another way of putting the question, more relevant to the terms of the original debate, might be: did God understand the world He had made? To answer no required an act of intellectual courage far greater than simple atheism.

Sober Ben Silliman himself fervently believed that geology required no breach with the Church to pursue an understanding of the globe. A *pious* curiosity bound the intellect to faith in a loving marriage. He made sure his journal honoured no adulterous liaisons, investigations outside the wedlock of Church and science. No doubt his faith, as much as his common sense, persuaded him of the 'madness of Syme's methods': Syme's hollow world suggested both scientifically and emblematically that at the heart of things lay an 'appalling gap'. Such prejudice may have played its part in Silliman's rejection of the missing essay on Geognosy, so costly to Sam's career and to the development, I hoped to prove, of geologic theory. How often in my researches have I come across fantastical errors dismissed by 'common sense', where common sense itself stood rooted in fantastical errors.

We come now to Reverend Jenkyns's eulogy of Syme, remarkable not only for the bristles of prejudice it raised in the hackles of the Church but for the story it told of a much more private faith. Printed in pride of place at the front of the *Exchange of Correspondence*, the sermon explains more perhaps of the man who wrote it than of its ostensible object: the life of Sam Syme, whose body lay before him as he spoke. Over eighty years old, possessed of a spare, somewhat hungry figure, a young man's leanness enduring into age, Reverend Jenkyns declared, with 'cheerful *in*efficiency' as he rose to the pulpit, that 'before us lies a man, whose lightest thought bore the marks of a greater Faith than my own; who shall go to his God more hopefully than I to mine'. I imagine the church packed with a crowd of curiosity-seekers, come to see 'the old wizard Syme stove in at last'; I imagine the buzz of *Schadenfreude*, as the common Christians rejoiced in the safety of their own numbers, and the solitude of Sam's belief; I can almost see Tom Jenkyns himself, the Reverend's son, sat at the front by the body of his dead friend Syme, who will descend quite soon into the hollows of the earth at last, on a much longer journey than he hoped for to a far smaller place. And I imagine the sudden hush that followed the Reverend Jenkyns's declaration of the richness of Sam's faith and the poverty of his own. The Reverend continued, as I read over the crinkled lines, the document mottled, the words themselves blotched and peeling like old skin, suggesting, by the age of the paper, how even thoughts and sentiments grow old:

'Nothing in his Life became him like the leaving of it' has been said too often of the vain and the capricious, too rarely of the steadfast and the good; nor do I hope much it shall be said of me. I have my vanities, I confess, but that is not among 'em. But I had rather go hard and bitter to my Lord, than fade as Samuel Syme has faded, in the loving care of my own son, a half-man, and a third-man, and a quarter-man, dying gently as a shadow slips by degrees into a general dimness when a cloud passes before the sun; though in his day he burned as bright as any star. Perhaps in time, a generation among us shall ask, how could we let him fade so easily? I was never curious concerning the questions that occupied Mr Syme and his companions, among them my son; I trusted my doubts far more than my faiths, I'm afraid, a fault of which Mr Syme was never guilty; and perhaps I shall have my reckoning for it in the end, as Syme has suffered for a broken faith if not a broken heart . . .

A rambling speech, from the querulous tongue of a very old man, unfussed by sequence and connection, when all his life spreads before him, year and year, sagging, somewhat loose at the seams.

I might have done more, and questioned more, for we live in a time, I believe – and this is the answer I give to that coming generation, wherever it is – when we have newly acquired the courage of our *questions*, and not yet learned the courage of our *convictions*. Of which failing, I confess myself guilty, always believing, as I have, that Mr Syme, before us, has served the Lord more by the example of his *doubts*, than I by a steady indifference to my own.

I read Mr Seaborn's account of those Remarkable Journeys [no doubt the untidy reference that gave rise to the printer's error] with amusement, and a pleasing modicum of instruction. And the Great Dig, my own son's particular Holy Grail, and on which Syme himself spent the best of his life and indeed a portion of the *last* and *worst*, summoning a lost enthusiasm for the project only a month

before his death, in the pursuit of which, as I had warned
him before, he forgot to keep his eye on the dinner-plate,
and died of a general weakness and agitation – the attempt
to burrow one's way into the heart of the matter, or rather,
the matter of the earth's heart, with great drenching and
plowing, and tunneling, and occasional Explosions – the
great dig, as I say, has a noble ring to it, though I have
always thought of it as the Big Dig, which, I cannot deny,
sounds less well . . .

A rambling, harmless speech, you would have thought, to have
occasioned such an uproar; somewhat doubtful, of course, and
disrespectful, but hardly the teacup in which to brew a great
storm. Yet the Church had been seeking their occasion for some
time, and fastened upon Syme and Jenkyns's eulogy of him as
their chance to win back the ground of debate from their scientific
cousins – believing no doubt that the madness of Syme and the
meander of Jenkyns could only serve their cause. The first letter
opened: 'I have been sometime considering with myself, whether
to return an Answer to those many dis-ingenuous Reflections, and
unhandsome Insinuations, against the present Church, which I
find in a sermon preached by Mr Jenkyns upon occasion of Mr
Syme's death.' Almost six hundred pages of correspondence follow this initial hesitant consideration. And, of course, in the end,
the churchmen were right: the pursuit of science could *not* be reconciled with religious faith, and the advancement of the former
could be won only at the expense of the latter, at the expense of
God. A difficult single battle for the clergy to fight, in that the
proof of their victory was the loss of the war. And yet they fought
it, stubbornly and faithfully, to the end.

   In the event, the *levity* of Reverend Jenkyns's tone – whose sermons had grown increasingly famous for that quality, and the
almost complete absence of religious faith it seemed to suggest –
prepared me in some part for the shocking nonsense of that amusing and instructive book, *The Remarkable Journeys of Mr Seaborn*,
Syme's first and only novel.

I strode on a bright, clear morning in July through the clutter of construction and traffic at King's Cross – the sunshine catching the dust beaten up in its very fine net – full, I confess, of a pleasant, almost overpowering sense of anticipation. The *New Platonist*, the Holy Grail of my quest, still lay beyond my reach; but a *novel*, a *scientific* novel, hundreds of pages of Syme's thought, unmediated, the breath of his mind caught on the page, the very scent of his imagination folded in the flower of a book. The buses came thundering past me from Euston, great red canvases for advertisement – declaring the virtues of Beers and Movies and Shampoos – the heads on the second tier peering out on their way to work, tiny beside the great flat faces slapped on the side of the bus, seen sipping or showering or shouting and beginning to peel. I thought again of the brittleness of bone and paper; the virtue of paper lying in its almost endless powers of rejuvenation, reprinting, translation, rediscovery – for I am, in a sense, a doctor of books, who breathes life in dead ones and mends them as I go, setting bones and patching scars and allowing the fractures to knit, with a freedom and power impossible to practise on the human body. Perhaps, I thought, today, I shall discover the root of Wegener's insight, tiny as the curled thread at the end of a carrot's nose; perhaps, I thought, today, I shall make my name.

The book itself had been easily discovered, under its title, of course, and not the name of its author. The phrase 'remarkable journeys' produced a number of . . . *hits*, I believe, is the term commonly used to count the doses of the biblio addict – but none of them belonged to Mr Syme, nor anything like him. Mr 'Seaborn' proved luckier, and there, fifth in the column, humming in the delicate green jargon of the computer screen, stood Syme himself, misspelled, the 'm' mirrored, the word pluralized, following a curiously compounded word in the title of his book: *Symmesonia, or the Voyage of Discovery*, by Samuel Highgate Symmes (*sic*). The word, I believe, to be pronounced 'Sym' (after its author) – 'meso' (after Mesopotamia, an original kingdom) – 'nia', a common enough suffix to give a sonorous round to the edge of a word. I called the book in for the following morning, which I have already described, the sun shining, beating up the dust, my own steps brisk, regular, metronomic, the kind of stride instinctively side-stepped by the passer-by, and avoided even by the rags of paper blown from the rush of air under the rumbling buses.

Under the vaulted roof of the Rare Books & Music Room of the British Library, among my fellow moles (the old men in ties and sneakers, the ladies draped in yellow cardigans, occasional students sniffling beside me, all looking forward to their packed lunches, their week-old bananas and pots of yoghurt, their brown-bread sandwiches locked in tiny Tupperware, their cartons of Ribena, their Thermoses of sweet tea), I carried the precious volume to my desk. The book itself, a slim brown volume, left nothing to be desired. The title almost obscured by time, leather roughened at the spine to the colour of split wood, a fringe of gold leaf lining the edges and bursting into delicate flower at the rim. The pages – marbled in green and pink, a peacock's *tale*, dormant – fluttered into life as I opened the book, tumbling in rainbow array. I pressed the stippled leather to my square nose, and breathed in the wonderful odour of books: the sweetness of leather; the must of old paper slightly damp with time; a slight edge, almost sharp, as of tobacco. And turned the cover.

After the marbled inside and a few blank pages (smudged at one edge by a thumb overfamiliar with the tip of a pencil), I came upon the title: *Symmesonia, or the Voyage of Discovery*, by (so the pseudonym ran) Captain Adam Seaborn, New York: printed by J. Seymour, 49 John Street; 1820. On the following page, the Southern District of New York approved the copyright and admitted the tome into its office – sealed accordingly by a red crown, stamped by the clerk, a certain, or rather an uncertain, Gilbert Livingston Thompson (thus briefly recalled from the shades of death by his connection to the great man). And then, at the delicate turn of a page, proudly displayed – in pale black lines of ink, stained by the red of old Gilbert's stamp seeping through – appeared a 'Sectional View of the Earth', a map of the interior planet, the Holy Grail of my investigation, Syme's world itself.

Let me describe it. A succession of circles, widening from the centre, interrupted by irregular gaps that allowed free passage from the core to the crust, according to their rotation; two such caesuras conspicuous at the Poles, to which the diagram directed our particular attention by dotted lines. Inside each Pole stood a series of numbers, indicating various stops along the interior of the crust. Just inside the Northern Pole lay a 'place of exile'. Working westward along the interior globe, one 'sailed' upon the 'supposed place of Belzubia'; and thence, to the Southern Pole, the site of Token Island *within* the globe, and Seaborn's Land *without*. It took me perhaps a full minute, counted slowly, breath after hushed breath, to realize that I had stumbled upon the work of a madman.

This realization was only confirmed by the ADVERTISEMENT that followed, a piece of such bravura insanity that almost rekindled, even as it doused, the ashes of my respect for this 'forgotten genius':

> The Author of this Work, and of the Earthly Revolution which it relates, leaves it to his readers to decide whether he excels most as a Navigator or a Writer, and whether he amuses as much as he instructs. If he has any professional vanity, arising from his enterprises upon the Sea, it does not tempt him to conceal that, in the achievements here recorded, he availed himself of all the lights and facilities afforded by the sublime Theory of an Internal World, published by Lt Samuel Highgate Syme, and by the application of Steam to the navigation of vessels, for which the world is indebted to FULTON. Far from coveting what does not belong to himself, he feels, after having discovered and explored a world before unknown, in the very fertile Bowel of our mother Earth, that he can well afford to bestow on others the praise to which they are entitled. He has one consolation, in which he is confident of the Sympathy of those who wish him well; namely, that if the book is not bought and read, it will not be because it is *not*

> an American book, nor an exposition of the *practical*
> Branch of the noble science of Geognosy. He gives notice
> that he has no intention to relinquish his Right to the
> invention of oblique paddles for Steam Ships, though the
> circumstances narrated at the close of the volume hinder
> him from taking out a Patent at present. Adam Seaborn

A wonderful piece, no doubt, of practical lunacy, of humility and arrogance intermixed, but hardly a testimony to the scientific genius of the man who inspired the great Alfred Wegener – a connection whose existence I had greatly begun to doubt.

Have you ever stood in the dust of a dead man's house, opened creaking the closet of his clothes – racked neatly still, the jackets settled loosely over the thin shoulders of the wire hangers, the trousers pressed and dangling in even rows; explored the larder, the tins of uneaten soup, the packets of spaghetti, the undrunk wine; and *then*, slipped on the jacket, and eaten the soup, and drunk the wine, alone, in the quiet of his absence? Have you ever tracked a dead man's thought down the gloomy corridors of the mind, your comprehension lit by the same shower of synapses that illuminated the passages of his brain almost two centuries before, spark for spark? Have you ever done all this, and then *tidied up* what you found?

Our gods have been replaced by our interpreters, our critics, our biographers, our *computer records*, the caretakers of our posterity. We trust not in fifteen minutes of fame, but in the *possibility* that the mass of our recorded lives might be re-edited, rebound, reissued, and some sense made of it all. If only a patient eye could sift through the endless stream of our life, the ore would glitter free, slighter, no doubt, but simpler and shining. And in this faith, we live by *quantities* – quantities of thought and talk, of actions and reactions, of meals eaten and jobs finished and loves exchanged and anger vented and kindness done; and lies told, and hunches followed, and lust pursued, and laziness tolerated, collecting and spreading like pools of rain. All in the faith that a good sieve will sort out the best of it, the shimmer of gold from the mess of grit; all in the hope that if you live long and large enough, the gold will be there. All in the hope of a *good editor*.

And in this faith I had pursued Syme. But what was I to make of this nonsense! Where was the gold in this grit?

The madness of it all, best forgotten! A stench of shame rose up from the grave of Syme's ideas, rotten at birth and festering from two centuries of neglect. Such natural gifts abused over these laboured fantasies, which, like a bad *lie*, stretched on and on, growing where they could not persuade, as though, by overbearing all interruption, they might stimulate, if not belief, then the silence that usually attends it. This was the *thirteenth chime of the clock*, as an old professor once said to me – not only ridiculous in itself, but calling into question the validity of the other twelve. A selection of the chapter summaries alone gives a taste of the nonsense I had stumbled upon.

CHAPTER I

The Author's reasons for undertaking a Voyage of Discovery. – He builds a vessel for his purpose upon a new Plan. – His departure from the United States . . .

CHAPTER II

The Author passes South Georgia, and proceeds in search of Sandwich Island. – States to his officers and men his reasons for believing in the existence of Great Bodies of Land within the antarctic circle, and for the opinion that the Polar Region is subject to *great heat* in summer. – Crew mutiny at the instigation of Mr Slim, third mate. – Happy discovery of a southern Continent, which, at the unanimous and earnest solicitation of officers and men, he names *Seaborn's Land* . . .

CHAPTER V

The Author discovers the south extremity of Seaborn's Land, which he names Cape Worldsend. – The compass becomes useless. – He states the manner in which he obviated the difficulty occasioned thereby. – He enters the internal world: describes the phenomena which occur. Discovers Token Island. – Occurrences at that Island.

All this from a man who had never been to sea; and never further south than Savannah. Oh, Pitt, Pitt, I thought, what hole have you dug yourself now? What mad fool have you chased to his lair? I closed the book before me with a sudden sense of the *inevitability* of posterity. What is good will survive, Pitt, I thought; no use tinkering with memory; this man has been forgotten for a reason. The horror of that line struck me, like a sharp knock against the bone. *We are all forgotten for a reason.* The passage of time *alone* does not obscure us, cover our gravestones, hide us away in old chests and preservation trusts and the vagaries of libraries – but some internal flaw widens with the years, splits us and we burn like cracked wood. We are forgotten because there is no virtue in us to survive the fire of time, no hard truth incorruptible by age and heat; except in the *best* of us, the ones that count, who shine in history, like a diamond polished by a flame, growing clearer and sharper with the years. Wegener had such stuff in him; death revealed him, tore away the clutter of false life till the rock gleamed through. Syme did not; death left no virtue in him, no matter how I pecked and sniffed at his ashes.

And I had no virtue left in me. The summer was half-done; the days shortening – how I hate that inexorable door of day closing into winter! The fellowship had had a dying fall; not a word written, not a fact proved. Wegener still defied all precedent; the *New Platonist* had burned in the fire of his father's house and no one now could regret its loss; Syme himself was burning up. The last fragments of his life caught fire briefly and sparkled in my eyes, until they too puffed away in smoke. Another year of teaching loomed; the question of tenure loomed; and I had nothing to show for myself. Some grinding streak in me demanded failure, pushed me to the ground, like a boat whose sail is drawn too tight and drives it to a standstill. I had the wind behind me and I fought it, like Syme, and failed.

I turned a final time to Syme's little book and read the almost touching introduction.

> In the year 1817, I projected a voyage of discovery, in the hope of finding a Passage to a new and untried World. I flattered myself that I should open the way to new Fields for the enterprise of my Fellow-citizens, supply new sources of Wealth, fresh Food for curiosity, and additional means of Enjoyment; objects of vast importance, since the resources of the known World have been exhausted by research, its wealth monopolized, its Wonders of Curiosity explored, its every Thing investigated and understood!

In the year 2000 (I ruminated) I won a Fulbright for a voyage of recovery, in the hope of finding a passage to an old and neglected genius. I flattered myself that I should open a new way to an old field, and present another frontier for the enterprise of my fellow academics, supply new sources of footnotes, fresh food for lectures and symposia, and additional means of employment; objects of vast importance, since, as I have come to believe, the resources of the known world have been exhausted by research, its wealth used up, its wonders of curiosity expired, its every thing investigated and understood! And so I shut the book, returned it patiently to the young lady in a sari and boot-cut jeans at the desk, and walked out (ignorant, at the time, that the seeds of fresh hope had already blown into my thoughts and wriggled in the earth of my subconscious).

All nature seemed in symphony against me – I could almost feel the beat of the conductor's baton. For that afternoon the flying ants descended on King's Cross, ugly brutes like fistfuls of raisins, scattering and dropping down trousers and crawling up sleeves. I could smack them only with the full fist of my strapped hand, which left the bones tingling like struck tuning-forks, up the cords of my wrist into my elbow.

I could only laugh, therefore, when the cash point, as this whimsical nation insists on calling ATMs, refused not my card but my credit. My account had run dry, or nearly so. Five pounds and sixty-seven pence still trickled through the system, accumulating approximately eleven pence ha'penny interest a year, at which rate I could buy a decent pizza for my supper by the year 2023. In fact, as I soon discovered, I could not even buy one *then*, as the cash point, owing to some laziness of its mechanical spirit, refused to dispense sums under ten pounds. It felt, somehow, that it had not reached its elevated station in life only to dole pennies to paupers; and though I knew, *knew* in my heart of hearts, that somewhere in its electric bowels it contained a 'fiver' and could have coughed it up, had it chosen to, the blinking machine insisted again and again that it *preferred not to*. I had fifteen pence in my pockets.

So I returned to the luxurious quiet of the British Library, blissfully free of winged ants, and called my wife, on the prepaid strength of a calling card. 'Miss,' I said, appealing to the tenderness of a nickname, 'it's over. I give up. I go home.'

'Oh dear,' she said. (She had acquired, vicariously, a delight in

English understatement by my presence in England. She felt free at last to practise the porcelain primness she had seen in the movies. At the least opportunity, she begged me to keep my upper lip stiff, not to fret, old chap, and a thousand other felicities none of which had ever struck my ear on this 'dear little island'.) 'Well,' she added, in case I had missed the accent she had affected – a kind of Georgia peach genetically modified by indelible strains of New York Jewess – 'steady on, old man, and we'll soon see you home and dry.'

'I could use some money in the meanwhile,' I said. 'I'm skint.'

'Oh Jesus, Doug,' she sighed, breaking character. 'Tell me at least you've written *something*.'

'Not a word,' I answered, 'not a drop.' (Though I would soon go in search of the latter, bubbling and cold, and faithful as Syme had never been.)

The humour of disaster had struck me at last, and in romantic desperation I roamed the alleys of green lockers beside the elevators in the hope that some careless scholar (or, rather, some careful scholar and careless gentleman) had forgotten to reclaim the 'returnable' pound coin from its little slot under the key. The lockers ranged in three tiers, and so I walked in a kind of evolution of the species, knuckle-dragging ape to upright man, along the green rows, checking all at once for the glint of a forgotten coin; which I discovered at last, a single pound, rolling in its plastic slot as I pushed past the door at the end of the middle row, to the faint sound of an egg loose upon a table. With some difficulty, I manoeuvred this treasure into the palm of my clutched hand, and strode forth from the cold, luxurious silence of the library into the roar of homeward traffic at King's Cross, down a side-street to a pub I knew, where, during happy hour (named, I trusted, after the *state* it induced rather than the state that induced *it*), a single quid could claim the flowing reward of a pint of London Pride. I tipped my glass to carelessness, to the serendipity of error, to the scholar who forgot his returnable pound, and buried my nose, at last, alas, in the *warm* beer.

*

I awoke the next morning in a muffled glow of happiness; another hot day, somewhat overcast, though the sun *suffused* the white morning and snuck through the bent slats of the blinds by my bed to illuminate the eyelids over my sleeping eyes. Pieces of the night before floated to the surface of my mind, like driftwood after an explosion at sea. The single pound coin had proved insufficient, despite the romance of its discovery. A half-empty bottle of Bombay Sapphire gin, blue as the Mediterranean though sweeter to the taste, awaited my return that night, on top of the little fridge at my elbow – for the British, by some strange pride of race, believe their *refrigerators* should never outgrow their *people*; an extension, I suppose, of the desire to keep all servants in their place. The bottle lay empty now, tipped over, against the wood-style floor of the studio flat, a slight runny nose the only remnant of its busy night. I remember cracking the ice-tray against the counter, and brushing the precious cold shards into my glass (the tray lay dripping now against the lino); I remember pouring; I remember – to an extent – a certain amount of dancing (solo, a bear's dance, as if to the flame of its own warmth on a cold day); of singing also, a modicum. Of drinking, I remember none, not at all, no, not a drop, sir.

And yet, as I awoke, despite the cotton in my head, I sensed a low warm glow – like the sunshine in the heart of a cloud – of happiness. I saw no *cause* for happiness; in a sober, sensible fashion, I could not have *called* myself happy, not as a rational animal. I remembered clearly the disillusion of the day before; I could not avert my eyes from the disarray of the morning after. My head ached, a faint chiming pain – like the echo of a bell, against, not the wall of a church, but the wall of memory after *that* echo has ceased. A slight ache, no more. And yet I could not deny, as one cannot help the sense of having forgotten something going out of the door, despite the slap of pockets and the clutch of brow – I could not deny that I was happy; secure in happiness, anticipating happiness to come, certain, in some strange fashion, that I had misplaced it somewhere and would soon discover it.

I raised the blinds with a clatter – a mistake, for the glare of the looming morning snuck through some crack in my eyes to the back of my tender brain and *pinched* me. I staggered to my feet and gathered my sea-legs. I stumbled to the bathroom and ran the tap, heard it squeal as it left the pipes, fall flush against the porcelain sink, and flow in a steady, hushing stream, hushing and steady, flowing and gushing, a thick wrist of water, dribbling and clanking down the drain; before the dream broke and I stooped and buried my face in the cold wet. I brushed my teeth, meticulously, until the white enamel squeaked with cleanliness and shivered the back of my neck. I padded into the kitchen corner (that is, the corner that *was* a kitchen, not a corner *of* the kitchen), and filled the kettle and clicked it on and waited until I could hear the catch of steam in its throat. Then I walked, slapping from lino to wood-style with bare feet, to bed again, and sat down, heavily, and rummaged my glasses from the sill, and put them on. And discovered, on a scrap of paper torn from the front of my novel – *Aunts Aren't Gentlemen*, by Pelham Grenville Wodehouse – the cause, the fount, of my flow of happiness.

Two words, scribbled in the dark by a clenched fist loosened somewhat by gin, almost illegible, *spreading* over the scrap as though the letters were weeds, entangled in each other: 'Gulliver's Travels'. That is the reflection that woke me scrabbling for a pen in the watches of the night. Hitchcock is said to have awoken with a similar inspiration, the vision of a perfect plot, and found in the morning only the words: 'Boy Meets Girl'. He was right, of course, in his sleepless certainty, just as I was right in mine: *Gulliver's Travels* held the clue to the disaster of *Symmesonia, or a Voyage of Discovery*. *Gulliver's Travels* would rescue my reputation.

Gulliver's Travels, published in London in 1726 (almost a century before *Symmesonia*), described the adventures of Lemuel Gulliver, an innocent in a fool's world. Its author, Jonathan Swift, hoped to expose the particular follies of the time in a series of fantastical adventures: 'to expose the fool and lash the knave'. A storm of protest greeted its publication. The punters (that delightful English version of the consumer) were appalled, less by the exaggeration of Gulliver's faults than by their belief in the *reality* of his adventures. Swift was forced in all subsequent editions to proclaim not the *genius* of his fiction (as he delighted in doing), but the *fictions* of his genius. No one believed him; he had written for a world of Gullivers, of gullibles, of soft touches.

Oh Syme, I thought – even I lacked faith. 'Have you ever tracked a dead man's thought down the gloomy corridors of the mind, your comprehension lit by the same shower of synapses that illuminated the passages of his brain almost two centuries before, spark for spark?' In sheer vanity I believed to have done this. Of course, I had forgotten the vagary of *words*, those blunt hammers on the anvil of the brain; rarely do they strike the same blow twice, yield the same shower of synapses, the same fury of sparks. I had missed not the shape of the iron but the gleam of his irony; after two hundred years Syme had not lost the power to make a fool of me. I returned, weak but clear-headed, to the cool of the library and once more summoned the small leather tome from the depth of its stacks.

Symmesonia was not a 'Voyage of Discovery', but a *satire* of it. In one swift stroke he had *sent up* the entire academy of geologic science, from Werner to Silliman to *himself*, and all geognostic pretenders in between. I read Syme's 'touching' introduction to the book again, this time with tongue pressed firmly in the pocket of the cheek. 'The resources of the known World', Sam declared in a pen heavy with irony, 'have been exhausted by research, its wealth monopolized, its Wonders of Curiosity explored, its every Thing investigated and understood!' And he went on: 'The state of the civilized world, and the *growing evidences of the Perfectibility of the human Mind*, seemed to indicate the necessity of a more extended sphere of action.' Nowhere could you find a more complete picture of the limits of nineteenth-century American science than in the satire of these lines: its tireless surveys, the poverty of its speculative theory, its persuasion that Baconianism (the philosophy of practical science) offered the prospect of scientific perfectibility, whose pinnacle was *the list* (that monument to geological mediocrity).

Nor does Syme spare the Church and its influence over even the best geologic minds of his day (including that of his old enemy, Ben Silliman), an influence that survived Syme by almost a century, and dogged those, like Reverend Jenkyns, who sought to praise him in the grave. Syme writes:

> I reasoned with myself as follows: A bountiful Providence provides Food for the Appetite which it creates; therefore the desire of Mankind for a greater world to *bustle* in, manifested by their Dissatisfaction with the one which they *possess*, is sufficient evidence that the Means of gratification are provided. As we cannot (yet) fly to the moon, Providence must have granted us 'fresh Pastures' in the very heart of the Earth.

Syme was gentle enough, and just enough, to tease himself, and his own ambitions, in the general censure.

Naturally much of the satire, like all good satire, is lost to the ear of posterity. But certain stock figures stand out. 'Seaborn' himself, the supposed author of the piece and captain of the expedition, clearly represents the *Neptunian* philosophy, which argued, after the teachings of Werner, that the earth was 'borne out of the sea'. 'Wherever we stopped,' Seaborn observes, 'we were visited by great Numbers of People, many of whom, to my extreme Mortification, looked upon me with evident Pity, if not Disgust.' The Best Man, ruler of Symmesonia (again, the touch of humility in Syme's satire, the caricature of his own ambitions), appears to be a picture of Sober Ben Silliman himself, ruler, in the external world, of American geology. Seaborn considers the proper etiquette for addressing so divine a Being:

> Whether I must uncover my head as in Europe, or my feet after the manner of the Asiatics? whether I must bow my head to the ground, making a right Angle of my body, and walk backwards on retiring, as in the court of Great Britain, or flounder in flat on my Belly, after the fashion of the Siamese? whether I was to stand or sit? if to sit, whether on

the ground, or cross-legged, or on my haunches like a
Monkey?

Other figures in American geology come in for their share of
abuse, from Mr Slippery, a picture I believe of Amos Eaton, the
great practical geologist, imprisoned for fraud; to Mr Slim, always
interrupted in the act of reciting some worthless list, a picture of
F.E. Loomis, whose endlessly revised magnetic surveys of
Virginia played such an important part in the development of
Syme's theory.

Gulliver's Travels leaves the reader with little hope for
mankind; Symmesonia, after a careful study, leaves one with little
hope for American geology – an absence of faith that presents too
faithful a picture of the century of American geology to come.
(Unless, of course, I could rescue Syme himself from his obscurity.) De Tocqueville's remark about the poverty of American science appeared almost two decades after the publication of
Symmesonia: 'it must be acknowledged that in few of the civilized
nations of our time have the sciences made less progress than in
the United States'. Syme's attempt to 'lash the knave' into refor-
mation had been unsuccessful, unsurprisingly. In its essence, all
satire relies on despair. A more hopeful view would busy itself,
full of energy and empty of humour, about practical improvements – the satirists, once they have reached the age of satire,
have mostly lost faith.

And yet, and yet . . . I felt at last that I was beginning to get the
measure of the man. Syme repeatedly displayed a nimbleness of
sincerity that never quite crossed into hypocrisy. I know no other
phrase to capture his enormous facility for transforming nonsense
into sense and sense into nonsense, and building vast palaces of
vision, constructed of truth and dare endlessly intermixed. Syme
was the classic straight man, who could deal in the sublime and
the absurd with equal aplomb.

For not only did he write Symmesonia, that monument to scientific absurdity, but he applied, on the strength of its fabrications, for
a national grant to explore the book's geological implications. And

he almost got it. Sam played his hand as high as he could, *bluffing* until even *hè* must have blushed, shamed at last by the nonsense of it. And yet, in its way, I discovered no single act more emblematic of the man himself; for he turned everything that fell into his hands to some purpose, either of pleasure or persuasion, and most often both. He was a journeyman tailor, who patched the rags of his idlest moment with the silks of his richest fancy. Everything had its use and he never shied from the clash between faith and folly. He spent all he had.

I had returned to Colindale, on the hottest, bluest day of the year, in which the mass of English faces in the street faded somewhat, like old upholstery, in the unaccustomed light. I sat in the stifling top floor, by the fan in the window-crack blowing hot air, among the high desks, and could not help but feel the obscurity of my mission. On my left a homeless man, enormously tall and fat, like a bathtub on its hind legs, reeked of his unwashed three-piece suit: grey wool tweeds, gratefully broken at the knee to allow a breeze; a grey waistcoat plumed by a dirty handkerchief in the front pocket; a grey jacket, thin with age, sporting a plastic rose, pinched no doubt from the table of some Italian café. He read deeply in *The Times* of 1901, year of Victoria's death, and marked occasional notes in the flap of his tobacco pouch. I wondered if Syme had spent his last days in such mock dignity, such threadbare respectability, such unabated curiosity.

My old friend, the Charon of newspapers, gentleman of the tweaked sniffling nose, the hay-fever sufferer, wheeled at last his aged fare, a heavy black collection of the *Richmond Intelligencer* to my desk; from which I hoped to discover some reaction to Syme's magnificent spoof, that 'Voyage of Discovery'. I discovered not a *reaction*, but a *declaration*, of such hubris that I laughed aloud, as a man will laugh in a great wind, at the silly *power* of it:

PETITION

Light gives light to light discover – ad infinitum.
Pactaw, Virginia, North America
November 10, A.D. 1821

To the United States Congress

I declare, after the courageous demonstration of Mr Seaborn, lately published, that the Earth is hollow and habitable within; containing a number of solid concentric Spheres, one within the other, and that it is open at the Poles twelve or sixteen degrees. I pledge my life in support of this truth, and am ready to explore the Hollow, if the Congress of this great Republic will support and aid me in the undertaking.

Sam Highgate Syme,
Of Virginia, late Lieutenant of Infantry

N.B. – I have ready for the Press a Treatise on the principles of Matter, wherein I show proofs of the above positions, and account for various phenomena.

My terms are the patronage of THIS and the NEW WORLDS, for my issue and my issue's issue.

I select Dr Abraham Gottlob Werner, Sir H. Davy, and Baron Alexander Von Humboldt as my protectors.

– On March 7th, 1822, the above petition was presented to the Senate by Colonel Richard M. Johnson, from Virginia. After a heated discussion on both sides, the petition, owing to its purely scientific nature, was laid on the table.

Oh Sam, I thought, in some wonder; you press the joke too far. You lack respect for the common yet powerful men in whose hands your future lies. You are careless of . . . you are careless of . . . and at last the answer came to me. *You are careless of your posterity.* You sow the tares and the wheat side by side, secure that you can distinguish your best from your worst and indifferent to the fact that someone else must gather the harvest. You had the courage, the very great courage, of *obscurity*; for you had no wish to be sifted, content, as you were, in your own variety. And such a task you have left behind for me, *who mean well by you now*; such a burden you offered those *who meant well by you then*.

And yet, in its way, the petition had its effect. It drew the attention of a young newspaperman, Thomas Jenkyns, who, from motives of the purest ignorance, allied himself to your cause; and such prosperity as you enjoyed in life, you owed to him. This was your *curious* conclusion to *Symmesonia* (I will no longer dare to apply the word 'touching' to any among the protean shifts of your sincerity):

> And now, kind Reader, having transcribed thus much of my Journal, in a manner which, I hope, will not be thought *too derogatory* to the Importance and Dignity of the Subject, I submit it to your Inspection, with an intimation *that I am ready to undertake a second voyage* to Seaborn's Land, at the edge of the great Gulf; or to war-like Belzubia and the Place of Exile; or, by chance and fortune, to gentle Symmesonia, the pleasantest of Pastures, *by a different route*; and greatly daring, by an aerial excursion thence to the Inner Spheres, even of my own Mind – as soon as I am furnished with the Funds necessary to my Escape from my present uncomfortable situation on the *Liberties*, in the garret of that lofty House, where, it being about the middle of dog-days, the Sun exerts its utmost power upon the roof, within eighteen inches of my Head.

A curious conclusion, I say again; and one that played its part, disturbing the next in the series of dominoes, and overtoppling it at last on their great chain through the years to Wegener and to me.

The great courage of obscurity I attributed to you; and yet, to see your name beside Wegener's, I am reminded of a very different and, yes, still greater courage – not of conviction, but of *half-conviction* – the courage that demands proof *of itself*. For Wegener, too, has left behind him the journal of a 'Voyage of Discovery', his attempt to prove beyond doubt the shift of Greenland in its ocean bed: a much slimmer volume, recording a heavier purpose, and a humourless, unironized adventure, as he attempted to set up an observation outpost in the teeth of the polar ice. I offer the following selection, shining against the foil of Syme's ironic reserve:

> 1. April 1930. This morning, at ten o'clock, we set off . . .
> Departure, an entry in the journal, and then – well, yes, the
> thread has been cut. NOW the expedition begins. I have
> somehow the feeling, of having outrun a swarm of bees . . .
> into another nest, I have no doubt.
>
> 4. May. The difficulties begin. In the course of the night we
> sailed into a line of ice, that lies between us and Umanak, our
> goal. So far south already! Our first attempt at breaking into
> the bay has failed. Already we must stray from the plan . . .

And then, after a series of breakthroughs and delays, adventures and misadventures, Wegener continues:

> 9. August. Catastrophe. We have only twenty days of hay
> left! Enough only for five or ten days of *power* feeding . . .
> Juelg is sick – it seems to be his nerves, a bad sign, for
> someone who hopes to survive a winter such as the one
> ahead. Vigfus suffers from rheumatism. Jon is trying to
> break his coffee habit, since we're running low, and the
> Icelanders are mad for it. Even Weike suffers; his muscles
> bruised by weeks in the sled, till he can barely walk. Every
> day delays our setting off; and the days themselves getting
> shorter. I worry only that, without any real obstacle, my
> comrades have drifted into a muddled sense of *time*. Yes,
> the clouds are growing on the horizon of this expedition. I
> think I can manage *myself*, but I cannot manage *by* myself.

How will it all end? That question now is hot as coals.

Another night. We've dried perhaps a few more days of grass for the horses – like drops of water on a hot rock, but vital nonetheless. My mood is still troubled; I hope it's only the lice infecting my disposition. Simple discomfort can make a mountain out of the slightest inconvenience. Those damn lice! That is my hope – that we're better off than I think we are, because of the cold and filth. I need a good sleep, a thorough sleep. If hard follows hard, we'll show our teeth yet.

1. September. Another foot of fresh snow, and not a sigh of wind. That is just what we need, to stick, like a fly in honey. And the petrol running low . . . and the propeller sleds failing; even when they work, the petrol lasts only half the distance we hoped for – a stupid mess of arithmetic, in which to blunder.

We must, regardless of cost, fit out a dog-sled journey of such dimensions that the sled can supply everything we need on its own! Regardless of cost; that is easily said. This is the greatest crisis of our expedition. That we get through with honour seems doubtful; everything depends on the crew of dogs we can put together. God, what sort of fix have we stumbled into! And yet, last night, tucked in the seat of the motor sled, sliding over the waste of snow-dust, in the twilit sky, how wonderful!

And then, in a final letter to his comrade Weike, his last words:

6. October 1930 . . .
   We manage OK; nothing frozen yet, and we hope for a prosperous outcome. In the other event, let me enjoin you: never stray from the path of knowledge. Improve the road signs at least, stick in a few flags on your way!

Best wishes,
Alfred Wegener

He died that winter, on his way west. His comrades found him much later buried in snow, between his upright skis. A courage of a different order altogether from Samuel Syme's, so it seemed to me; for I had found no evidence of such faith, or, rather, such a profound sense of the *obligations of faith*, in my subject. The wit of Syme's ironies rang somewhat hollow now, though they mocked the very certainty that led scientists to such fates. This, from *Symmesonia*:

> Mr Slim, the third mate, expressed some Apprehension, that great Danger might be encountered in high latitudes; that if we found land, the Ice might close upon us and prevent our return to our Country, as it once served a colony in Greenland. I was not much pleased with this. I have no Patience with an officer who suggests Doubt and Difficulties when I have a *Grand Project* in view. I marked him, but at the same time pretended to listen to his observations, as Objections of great Weight, and then proceeded to *remove them* from the minds of the officers and people, by advancing a Tide of Reasons for my belief that the supposition of extreme Cold at the Pole was *altogether gratuitous*.

A good joke, perhaps, at the expense of *scientific certainties*, and prescient, too, given the fate of Wegener; but a rather easy target (I thought at the time) for a scientist who seemed to risk so little on his theories, who scarcely ventured any of them without a ballast of irony to support them. I learned in time, however, that there is more than one way to risk a life. (I, of all people, should have known that.)

I had resurrected Syme, that much at least: brought him to life again, supplied father and mother, childhood, and even the occasion of his death. I had tasted something of his theories, a great deal of his wit; but of that *lightning flash* of insight (those 'segments of the earth's crust which float on the revolving core') that ignited the mind of Alfred Wegener a hundred years on – not a trace, not the least rumour of its distant thunder. I *knew* that notion had come to Syme, split the small night of a man's thought with a wonderful burst of light. But I needed more than hunches, for Dr Bunyon, for my wife, for the approval of the tenure committee at the University of Texas. For Syme himself.

Now, I confess to you that I never *did* find that elusive journal, the *New Platonist*, the Holy Grail of my researches, printed privately, I believe, and discovered, posthumously as it were (after death by fire and water) in a catalogue of the library of Wegener's father. And I exhort all Americans, all owners of attics and forgotten basements, of chests and old wallpaper, to search up and down for that vital missing link between the hollow world and our own. Knock against the plaster of your walls; tap into the hollows of your floors; explore the gloomy reaches of your attics, stooped in the stifling heat, for a slim volume, I suppose, whose cover bears some portion of the following:

The New Platonist

A journal establishing the Revolutionary
American Science

Edited by Professor Samuel Syme

Then, having lifted your prize from the family papers, from beneath the wallpaper, from the lining of an old chest, open the first delicate page, and I believe you may discover a table of these contents:

I. Aristotle and the New Science,
   by Prof. Syme
II. Inventions: The Fluvia and its Uses,
   by Prof. Syme
III. The Inverted Cosmos: A Primer,
   by Prof. Syme
IV. What It Means to Pactaw County:
   Local Predictions, by Prof. Syme
V. The New Medicine: Wax!,
   by Dr Friedrich Müller
VI. Speculations: a curious coincidence

Our special Appreciation to Mr Harcourt, Esq. of
Richmond, Virginia, who may properly be termed the
Medici of the New Science, our Prince and Patron.

Clasp this precious treasure to your bosom; insure it as a 'national
heirloom'; then contact at once myself, Dr Douglas Pitt, at the
Department of the History of Science, University of Texas, Austin,
Texas.

I place all my faith in that sixth item, those 'speculations on a
curious coincidence'; surely, *there*, if anywhere, lies the inspiration
of Wegener, the seed of thought, buried in a century of neglect,
that grew into such a flower. But I find that I have overreached
myself; step back, Pitt, before you step forward! And I must
explain my knowledge of the cover and the table of contents;
above all, the history of that curious character, the doctor of wax,
mein Herr Friedrich Müller, Syme's sole company in the revolutionary American journal – and, by the sounds of him, as 'foreign
as a Frankfurter' at that.

There is scant need to describe the countless false trails I followed
and the gloomy woods into which they led me. I suffered a most particular frustration over that *Humboldt* clue; for Syme had listed
among his mock protectors, in that grand petition to the United
States Congress, the same Alexander von Humboldt with whom
Alfred Wegener's great-grandfather had attended the University of
Frankfurt. But after a lengthy beating of my brows and a still fiercer
beating of my books; after stumbling through a dozen blind alleys,
head first, into the brick walls of history; after a most painful
exhumation of my college *German*, which demanded a tortuous
reconfiguration of the language wires in my brain, from which, to this
day, I have only partly recovered (a fact to which the reader, no
doubt, will testify in court, suffering, as it were, *vicariously* from the
inflammation of my sentences); after all that, I say, I was forced to
conclude, that Alexander von Humboldt was *not guilty* of a connection to Syme, owing only to the insufficiency of the evidence against
him. Perhaps the list of Syme's protectors – from Werner, dead as
Syme wrote, to H. Davy, a chemist at heart, to the Baron Humboldt,

an explorer – was meant to serve as some kind of coda to the satire of *Symmesonia*. In any case, it did not serve *me*, nor connect Syme to Wegener in the end, though it pointed me, at least, in the right direction – towards Germany at last.

I need hardly describe, I say, the countless red herrings and the stench of them; nor, indeed, the battles with Miss Pitt, my tender wife (whose faith in her husband's *sagacity* had long diminished; whose faith in her husband's *assiduity* was beginning to fade). Nor relate the circumstances of my financial embarrassment; my assurances, my *guarantees*, of being 'hot on the trail', the begging to which I was at last reduced, and the *whimsy of despair* that persuaded my wife to dip into her own private funds (secured by the religious suspicion of her father from the depredations of his goyish new son-in-law, so often indeed does the unity of the flesh between man and wife stop short at the unity of the bank account) in order to finance the extension of my researches, and one crucial, final flight.

Tom Stoppard has said (I myself starred as the *Hermit* in an amateur production of *Arcadia*, performed by our little troupe of Austin Blue-stockings in front of a house filled, almost to the second row, with the remaining members of our little troupe of Austin Blue-stockings) that genius is the ability to open a door before the house is built. Syme had that very gift (as I hoped to prove), and opened the door, with the courtesy of the dead, to Alfred Wegener, who built his mansion around it. But genius, alas, is also the ability to fall *out of the window* before the house is built. And Syme took far too many such tumbles.

He spent his working life on *three* great ideas – so far as I could make out from a careful study of the letters in his father's collection, the newspaper reports, and Syme's own publications. One of them, fabulous; one of them, false; one of them, visionary. I will not include in this list the series of devices he invented along the way. These were only means to an end, the *fruits* of idle hours, on which he often wasted the *cream* of his energies: the fluvia, the compression piston and the early seismograph. Nor the various public projects through which he hoped to support his researches:

the lectures, the journey to the Pole (for which *Symmesonia* served as an advertisement), even the *New Platonist* itself began as a temporary solution to financial difficulties, rather than the conduit to his posterity it proved (*I prove*) to be. No, the three ideas on which Syme spent his life were simply these:

1. The Great Dig
2. The Triple Eclipse
3. The 'Revolving Fragments'

The Great, or Big Dig, as Reverend Jenkyns delighted in calling it, involved the 'compression piston' Syme had developed for his experiments in the elasticity of water. Though Syme became broadly Huttonian or Plutonistic in his beliefs (after the early affair with Neptunism alluded to in *Symmesonia*), he disliked the incomprehensible Scotsman's suspicion of *practical proofs*. For all his speculative genius, Syme was an *American*, a great believer in the virtue of eye and hand. He proposed the simplest of solutions to the question of the nature of the earth's core: dig for it. Of course, like most simple solutions, the practical *application* of the Great Dig proved to be far from simple. Syme tinkered with the compression piston to the end of his life; in those last dry years his faith in the scientific value of a massive excavation revived, and he died in the fever of renewed speculation, *on how to dig himself a deeper hole*.

Syme's interest in the 'Triple Eclipse' could indeed be called a corollary of the Great Dig. Essentially, he hoped to let nature provide the hole for him (as she does for us all in the end). Syme believed that the internal spheres of the earth rotated, like a nest of balls, each providing a socket for the sphere within. Occasionally, the holes or cracks in these spheres aligned themselves into what Syme called an 'internal eclipse' – a gust of fluvia (the internal air) usually followed these alignments, the gas catching fire as it fled outwards, accounting for earthquakes and volcanoes and tsunamis in its progress. Syme constructed tables to calculate the 'rising' and 'setting' of these internal cracks; he believed he could predict natural disasters on the strength of them. And he hoped that a local *triple* eclipse, the alignment of cracks in three sequent internal spheres, would provide the groundwork for the Great Dig, creating a fissure in the outer sphere along which he could quarry into the heart of the earth. There is no question that, of all his mad ideas, this one caused him the greatest, the most particular, unhappiness.

I have said that it is the privilege of the biographer to sift the mass of his subject's work for gold. In the process we often find that the *weight* of his life falls away, while the slightest of his curiosities *sticks* in time. So it was with Syme. For the third idea on which he spent his life occupied the least portion of it. The notion of 'Revolving Fragments', which inspired Wegener a century on, almost died stillborn (as I eventually learned on the discovery of a most remarkable cache of Syme's papers), and received in the end only a moment of his distracted attention. A glimpse into the falling of a thought, soft as dew:

I lay on the ottoman reading Waverley, *and bored at length with the hero's irresolution, rose to give Syme some companionship in his solitary labour and stood over his shoulder. Certain figures he had consulted me upon lay scattered over the rough table, lying across a well-thumbed map of the globe.*

'Phidy,' he said in a still small voice, sensing the weight and heat of my presence at his shoulder. I placed my palm in the softness of his hair. He sat staring at the map, spread beneath his hands. 'Have a look at this.' And he traced his fingers along the edge of Africa, lovingly bending with the curve. 'Does nothing strike you?'

'Of course,' I answered. 'An old . . . coincidence, I suppose, is the best word,' as I touched my own thumb lightly along the pregnant swell of Brazil. 'The Americas and Africa might once almost have been lovers, along the lines of Aristophanes' account, of a split self, searching for its dislocated half.'

'Suppose the shell had cracked . . . ', he said, in a voice as quiet as blown dandelions.

'Yes,' I prompted . . .

'Lay floating,' he said, trailing off into the mists of a speculation.

Then Tom asked, looking up, 'Have you prepared the acid of sulphur for the volcano, at tomorrow's lecture?'

Sam remained silent, the butt of his palm banging against his stubborn chin, as if to dislodge an Idea.

'Go on,' I said.

The banging stopped. 'Suppose a great eclipse – along the lines we've discussed – had at some point – inconceivably distant – only suppose . . .' And resumed.

'Have you prepared the acid of sulphur for the volcano,' Tom repeated, 'at tomorrow's lecture?'

'Hush, Tom,' I whispered, mostly to myself. Perhaps he envied my place at Sam's shoulder; but, to do Tom justice, Sam could be most wonderfully slack in his own cause, forgetful of anything that did not serve his present thought, never mind his future honour. While Tom himself laboured in a swarm of minor perplexities, just such niggling considerations – as time and place, engagements, equipment, lodgings, etc. – as Sam delighted to neglect.

'Just so,' Sam said. 'Now, Phidy, give heed. Consider the eclipse – overlapping cracks in the concentric spheres etc.' He took my hand in his and squeezed it, once, as if to relieve the pressure of his thought. 'But suppose now that currents in the fluvia itself – occasioned by these flaws – produced a friction – that in turn . . .' He released it again – I touched the palm, involuntarily, with the tip of my finger – and the banging resumed.

'I am not in the habit', Tom said, in a passion at the edge of tears, 'of being ignored, for this,' he added, sniffing and squinting at once.

Then louder: 'Have you prepared the acid of sulphur for tomorrow's lecture?'

There was to be no more speculation that evening. Syme said nothing, and Tom rose at last to his feet.

'What are you about?' he said in a tight voice. Another storm was brewing, not to be put off by Syme's silence. 'Turn to me when I speak to you. What are you about?'

'What he was about', I would allege, was nothing short of scientific revolution. The *earth* itself, after the century of small discoveries precipitated by this sudden flash, would undergo a change of *heart*. For Syme, in that moment, had had *the* thought – the shadow of a door fell on him from a house yet to be built. 'Fragments' drifted at last over the sea of his speculation into those famous 'segments of the earth's crust which float on the revolving core' to which Wegener himself alluded in that careful introduction to his ground-breaking work *On the Origin of Continents and Oceans*. Syme for an instant suspected the truth: the *outside* sphere was the only one that mattered; it had cracked and pushed the continents with it.

Of course, Syme himself was interrupted in *mid-thought* and spent the rest of his life trying to reach the *other side* of it. I would like at some point to investigate a 'history of the man from Porlock', the history of *interrupted* inspiration, named after the insurance salesman who broke in on Coleridge's dream of Kubla Khan. The history of *suspended* ideas (which so nearly included this research) and their eventual *animation*. 'Tom' (Jenkyns himself, in a rare fit of anger) broke upon the only reverie of Sam pure enough to retain in waking the lucidity of dreams – and for all his good works on Sam's behalf, that must be his final legacy.

By what privilege (you may well ask) have we been permitted this front-row seat at the *framing of a thought*, this keyhole on a room, the three men in it over a century dead, yet breathing still, chatting, the short, strong one at the desk, sleeves rolled up, butting the palm of his fist against his chin, to precipitate, in such violent fashion, the subtlest emanation of the human soul, a *thought* of such power and perplexity that it anticipated a hundred years of geology, of such frailty, that a word could dispel it, blow it away, till only the scent remained, and that scent fading fast? Who stood at Sam's shoulder and laid his hand in Sam's 'soft hair'? Whose record is this?

To answer, I must return to Highgate and the white-chocolate house above the ponds – the poky room with the little fridge, revealing, upon inspection, the soured cream now drunk or drained away, the hotel mini-bottle of gin, sipped and discarded, replaced by a single jar of mustard, crusted at the rim, and half-empty, sitting at an angle in the egg rack. To the *Records of My Son*, collected by Sam's father.

It is a curious fact about the constitution of our minds *that we know when we know, but we don't know when we don't.* Flickers and echoes deceive us, suggest the full force of thunder and lightning. We forget the power of the *Real Thing*; for *it* fades, too, in our memories, decaying into half-truth and equivocation, until we believe there is nothing else but *mitigated revelation.* Until we believe that a faith in the *pure article* belongs among the illusions of youth, for our fading familiarity with *revelation*, or, rather, our growing familiarity with *half-revelation* blinds us to the sudden light of knowledge.

So I scoured the bundles of letters spread over the cup-stained pine of the desk pushed up against the window, scoured them for – nothing in particular – for *revelation*. For the crack in the surface of Sam's life that would lead me to the heart of it. I read the records of his many petitions; for Sam acquired a taste for petitioning, and did not rest after the absurdly near success of his first attempt at suckering, I should say, securing aid, I should say, earning succour from the American Congress. And Tom, drawn to Sam in the first place by the Senate's interest in his theories, prompted him to a dozen fresh petitions.

In December 1822, he forwarded a request to both houses of Congress for the funds necessary 'to prosecute the Great Dig, a geognostic experiment of vital significance, both to the honor and to the commercial prosperity of the United States'. The request was 'laid on the table' and deferred for future consideration (which meant, essentially, until Syme had proved the experiment could pay for itself, through the interest of the mining corporations).

In March 1823 (taking a step back), he petitioned the General Assembly of the State of Virginia, 'praying that body to pass a resolution approbatory of his theory of concentric spheres; and to recommend him to Congress for an outfit suitable to the enterprise of the Great Dig'. This memorial was presented by Micajah T. Williams (a prosperous landowner whose holdings included a variety of mineral deposits), and succeeded in passing both houses of the Virginia legislature. However, on presentation to the national body in the fall of 1823, the Senate determined 'on motion, that the further consideration thereof was indefinitely postponed' – a great blow to Syme and Jenkyns, which essentially defeated any hope they might have nursed of national support. The fact that his petition was not denied *outright* lies in a curiosity of the law. As it stood, Congress could revive Syme's petition, in the event that his enterprise seemed on the point of commercial viability, and through their tardy aid claim some share in his profits. As it turned out, they never had occasion to do so; and Syme and Jenkyns were forced to look further afield for their patron.

In November 1824, Syme noted the following account in the *Richmond Intelligencer*, still preserved in a leaf of his father's album, the paper blotched and browned, the ink itself *fattening* with age:

> Accounts, dated Oct 27th from Copenhagen, state that a violent shock of an Earthquake, which lasted ten minutes, was experienced in Iceland. It was attended with a noise under ground as of a dreadful Cracking, and immediately after there was an eruption from Hecla. The sea was in a state of dreadful commotion. The eruption was preceded by a very striking phenomenon. A noise was heard – the Earth gaped wide – meteors appeared in the direction of the Volcano – a flame soon followed with smoke, from which issued globes of liquid Fire, discharged to a great distance, accumulating at last and flowing out in torrents, hissing and congealing into the Sea.

Syme applied through the American Minister at the Court of Copenhagen for permission to explore the aftermath (the site, Syme believed, of an eruption of internal gas, of fluvia) – a request readily granted by the Chancellor, Count Nichsotieff, who nevertheless refused Syme's bid for a 'proper outfit, of men & machinery' to attempt the expedition; and the want of means prevented Sam in the end from setting forth. (I could not help but wonder – had he flinched again?)

At this point, increasingly desperate, Tom turned his attention to even the slightest of the European states in the hope that an ambitious but insignificant young prince might support a rather 'visionary' expedition in order to make a name for himself and his little kingdom. I discovered among Sam's papers an almost endless stream of denials, both equivocal and unequivocal; interested denials and uninterested denials; formal and informal denials, in pure and broken English; refusing funds, government cooperation, access to records, machinery, venues for lectures and demonstrations, employment, publication – all faithfully preserved by a father who seemed to consider even the proof of rejection as some evidence of the esteem in which his son was held, some indication of the circles in which he moved. I, on the other hand, could not repress a kind of frustration – not unmixed with pity and admiration – at the . . . *stupidity*, I wish to say, but soften it to *insensitivity*, of a man who beats his fist so long against an unanswered door.

Of course, a slight tributary of partial triumphs ran into the stream of his failures: evidence of lectures held, demonstrations attended, fields surveyed. And within this trickle I discovered the following note, written in an elegant if somewhat elaborate hand, the loops of each 'l' and 's' richly curled, the vertebrae of high-backed 'd's austerely straightened, the feet of 'm's and 'n's daintily propped upon the rigid, imagined line:

Dear Dr Syme [it began, a common enough mistake]:

We have received your petition regarding the exploration of the internal globe – the Great Dig as you quaintly call it – and read, with a particular of interest, your account of the nested spheres, a wonderful Invention of Providence, it appears, should the *outer layer* ever offer grounds for Dissolution. Naturally, we should require a modicum of Proof – a word, I know, to which the brotherhood of Geognosy have never attached much Signification – but to which poor Ministers of Finance must bend the knee, before they empty the Purse.

I have broached the matter with our Prince, who professes a particular interest in the Compression Piston, by which you hope to effect the Scale of excavation proposed by your petition;

and following its Steps (or, in the event of its possession of a single Foot or Spade, *Step*), to descend into a more intimate understanding of the Entrails of this Planet. And I write to you, pursuant of His desire, that we should explore the Matter further before concluding, This way or That, the merits of your Case. In accordance with which, we propose to send a gentleman of some geognostic distinction, a student, at one point, of Werner himself, and a professor of Geognosy at our own university (in short, to speak plainly, my own *son*), to evaluate the claims you make on behalf of your Theory, and to judge the extent to which the Machinery of your Practice could eventuate a deeper Understanding of a question so prominent in all our thoughts – the nature of the Earth's core – before committing ourselves to the Experiments you suggest.

We await an answer; should it prove satisfactory, you may expect Dr Friedrich Müller, by the close of the year.

Respectfully,
Ferdinand Müller
First Minister, Kolwitz-Kreminghausen

Even after such long *disuse*, the letter agitated in me a slight tremor of the *joy of acceptance*, the quiet *yes* that, like a cracked bottle, inaugurates a voyage – a borrowed joy, it is true, but one I hoped to turn into my own. I guessed at once the importance of this letter, for not only did it suggest the eventual success of Syme's petition, but it carried him across the waters, to Germany at last, or, rather, at first – a journey from which, I hoped to prove, so much resulted. Surely, I thought, it is reasonable to trace a line from the University of Kolwitz-Kreminghausen (a tiny, long-forgotten principality on the banks of the Elbe upriver from Hamburg) to the University of Marburg eighty years later, to which Wegener was appointed (on his first return from Greenland) as a lecturer in astronomy and meteorology – and at which, he maintained, the thought of continental drift first crossed his mind. I could not, however, guess then the *windfall* this letter would lead to. It is perhaps unsurprising that a memoir was written; it is only surprising that it was written by a young doctor from Kolwitz-Kreminghausen.

The letter from the Finance Minister suggested a number of things, but an unqualified *faith* in Syme's theories was not among them. It was a *suspicious* letter, deeply suspicious, in both senses of the word – proceeding from, and producing in turn, suspicion. Herr Ferdinand Müller implied rather a faith in *possibility* than a faith in Syme; the letter arches its eyebrows several times; it teases; it whispers, at best, only *perhaps*. Perhaps what? I thought, as Syme himself must have done; perhaps the earth is hollow, formed of nested concentric spheres and empty at the core? Or was there some other, more practical doubt (doubt, I mean, as a step *towards*, not away from, belief) that moved Herr Müller to answer the strange, fabulous, petition?

The more I thought of Müller's letter, the curiouser it became. I pressed my thumb to the thought-provoking divot between nose and brow. (My hands meanwhile felt easier than they had in months; each finger separate and alive, the thumb itself rearing freely upon its mound of flesh like a horse shedding its rider.) Why had the Finance Minister answered the petition? And deferred to his prince only towards the end, over the matter of the compression piston? How much could be read into the suggestive fact that the geologist sent to evaluate Syme's theories was himself the son of the minister responsible for the expedition?

I began to form a picture of the *kind* of interest Syme had attracted. There was the strong suggestion of what we call a 'job for the boys'. Believe me, I have known such 'boys' in my day, their skin glowing with healthy bank accounts, their hair coiffed and delicate, in the faith, in the certainty, that no wind or cloud *pertained* to them; ineffectual men, on the whole, who spend the fortunes of their lives *too* easily. (Did I not declare, from the outset, that this seemed to me a story of fathers?) It would not have been the first time a young man was sent across the world on a government mission to investigate, chiefly, his own curiosity; but there was more to it than that. A minister overreaching himself, perhaps? A genuine concern for scientific progress, or, to put it another way, for the honour of a small German state hoping to make a name for itself? Something of each, I suppose, was at work; but the strongest consideration seemed to me, even then, the possibility that the compression piston might make somebody (and particularly the Finance Minister of a small state heavily veined with mineral deposits) *rich*.

You know when you know; and I knew at once the scent was strong – like a curl of cigarette smoke in an empty room, drifting into a question, asking, who was here? Someone was coming to take a look at Syme and opening his wallet as he came. That night, in the 'quiet roar' of my studio flat in King's Cross, the *shackles* came off my wrists, those blue wraps binding thumb and finger in an impotent clutch. Now the prisoned digits stretched free, walked tiptoe over tabletops and window panes, pattered the bubbles of a hot bath, popping like rain – two months of pent-up force released at last. And then the rains themselves came down over the city (outside the window over the tub). A cloud sagging low over the train station gave up the burden of itself at last, just as my hands had – forgetting the constriction of their own strength, easy in themselves again. Stepping out, dripping, on to the sudden cool of bathroom tiles, the air of an English summer evening cold as white wine through the window, a towel bound across rump and belly (distended somewhat by English *ale*) – I realized another shackle had burst, and it was time to write.

You know when you know, I thought, lying down that night in the peculiar sleepiness that dreams already of the morning and the business of the next day. Love and truth declare *themselves*. I was on the trail at last. Only when the first fogs of sleep descended on me did a small thought, like the glow of a torchlight, disturb my peace – for Sam himself, among the clutter of his inspiration, when the single shining truth appeared before him, *had not known*.

In the morning I began to write, slowly at first, punching stubborn fingers against the keyboard, thick, heavy words like the first drops of rain; and then steadily; and then all at once, in a torrent of explanation. Words took me through the day like breaths, like ticks of the clock; I lived by the word; I stepped words and stumbled words; I inhaled them and sighed them; the slightest, least durable of my motions, the flutter of my fingers, trailed a history behind it. I ate words and swallowed them; saying 'fish' to myself as I placed a forkful on the palate, and whispering 'chew' as the teeth ground over the white flesh; and '*digest*', as the dull lump squeezed and slid towards the stomach. I had lost the patience for academic prose; my fingers chased their fancies; the blood in them flowed rich through the veins, kicking with life, as it were, from a dose of sea air.

And as I wrote, I *read*, living two lives, the beginning and the end at once. As the first dim forays of Sam's genius stumbled beneath my pen, the curious history of the principality of Kolwitz-Kreminghausen unfolded before my eyes: a history as strange and wonderful, in its way, as the life of Syme himself, to my great good fortune. This was nearly the last of my strokes of luck – that Ferdinand Müller turned out to be such a *character* after all, involved in a history as remarkable as Sam's, worthy in itself of historical investigation. But when you reckon the extent of my good fortune, consider the world of revelations I might have missed, walking blindly by, in the dark of history . . .

Kolwitz-Kreminghausen had been restored to its rightful, if inconsiderable, place along the Elbe after the defeat of Napoleon in 1815 and the Congress of Vienna – between Holstein (and Hamburg) to the west, and Brandenburg (and Berlin) to the east. The capital was Neuburg – a small market town built around the river, which enjoyed a brief period of prosperity in the Middle Ages, before the expansion of trade to the Indias and Americas rendered its own cosy little spot along the Elbe less advantageous than before. It refused to die out, however, neither growing nor fading; and eventually became the seat of one of the remoter branches of the Hohenzollern family, the Kreminghausens – a connection that probably accounts for the restoration of statehood at the end of the French Revolution, when the Congress reduced the number of German states to thirty-eight.

Naturally, the territorial distribution of the Congress angered many. Aside from the conservative regimes that replaced the

Napoleonic Code (which, despite its parasitical nature, had offered at least a *taste* of republican liberties), the Congress had prevented the formation of a united Germany, the dream of a new breed of German patriot. The Burschenschaften – the student political societies begun in Jena in 1815 – were growing up, and the *Burschen* wished to play some part in German affairs. KK, however, had the advantage of returning to an established family. (Many of the new states had to fabricate a royal history to persuade their people of legitimacy.) Unfortunately, the old prince had died, not in the war, but during its protraction. The new prince had barely turned twelve when the state was restored.

This left KK in the hands of a growing rank of bureaucrats, swelled, increasingly, by members of the nobility themselves. Napoleon had left his mark on Germany. The swiftness with which his armies had overrun the Holy Roman Empire taught the new nations a lesson in efficiency, never mind republicanism. Ambition turned now to the bureaucracy, which reflected a new meritocratic spirit. Which brings us to Kolwitz-Kreminghausen, governed by a young prince and a rising class of political officials. Which brings us, at last, to Ferdinand Müller, an intelligent and ambitious gentleman, of liberal and nationalistic tendencies, who discovered himself suddenly in a position of some (admittedly local) power.

Syme must have caught Müller in a patch of princely sunshine. Müller successfully persuaded the young prince (now growing up quickly) that a scientist such as Syme, if proven correct, could do for Neuburg what Werner had done for Freiberg only twenty years before: put them on the map. The compression piston *alone* could pay for the experiment ten times over, if successfully adapted and applied to the veins of coal recently discovered south of the Elbe. The KK mines, Müller whispered in the princely ear, could yield enough to rival Britain itself (which currently controlled over 90 per cent of the market) in supplying Holstein and Brandenburg with coal. The little princedom would grow rich.

The little princedom was not the only thing growing rich. For the good minister, so zealous for the honour of Kolwitz-Kreminghausen, so assiduous on its behalf – initiating in his tenure dozens of state schemes, from the university to the mines, and setting in progress the miracle of engineering that would eventually produce, almost forty years after his death, the Nord–Ostsee Canal – had begun to lick the fingers stuck in all those pies. Thank God, in a way, that he did. For perhaps I should never have known a thing about Ferdinand Müller had he not hanged himself from 'a hook above his study door' a little over a year after composing the turgid, oddly teasing letter that promised such hope to Syme (and such hope to me).

Why he hanged himself is a difficult question – only slightly connected, I believe, to the business with Syme. I have said that the life of Ferdinand Müller is worthy of its own investigation; so it is. (How many of us can say so much for ourselves, that the eye of history should focus, even for a minute, on us alone?) And it *has* been investigated. A recent paper by Benjamin Karding in *Sozialgeschichte Heute*, titled 'The coup that never was: Ferdinand Müller and the build-up to the July Revolution', attempts to establish Müller's involvement in an underground parliamentary movement, an offshoot of the student Burschenschaften, fixed on similarly liberal and nationalistic goals. Karding argues that Müller did *not* hang himself because he was caught embezzling state money; he hanged himself because of *what the money was for* – the extent of his revolutionary ambitions (in spite of his repeated denials), which prompted the troops from Berlin to march upon Neuburg at last. But then Karding *would* argue that – for Ferdinand Müller was his great-uncle, many times great.

I called Dr Karding at his home, in the small university town of Neuburg, on the banks of the Elbe. Standing in the tiny kitchen of my flat, I explained who I was and what I was looking for. The phone was propped against the bulk of my shoulder, pressing my hot ear, while one hand (mercifully at ease again) fiddled with a pen, and the other bent apart the blinds to expose a man in a suit with his shoes off, sitting on a bench by the road. A flood of – what, fellow feeling? – surprised me, at the interrupted *loneliness* of my researches, the company I had found in an obscure corner of the 1820s. 'Some trace of Syme,' I urged warmly, 'that's all. Your

Müller gave him money in 1825 to look into his theories – strange theories, I confess, about a hollow earth.' How could I explain them without seeming touched by Syme's madness? 'Still, curious things, theories,' I babbled on. 'And I think *his* may have turned up again . . .' A new fear tied my tongue now, of giving up the secret of my prized connection, the line from Wegener to Syme.

'*Samuel* Syme, I believe,' Karding answered, in the pure watery English of the educated German, and my heart stopped. 'And his *theory of concentric spheres*, is it not?' he added, with the satisfied air of a man laying down the ace of trumps. 'Yes, yes,' he went on, the 's's hissing slightly through his teeth; as if he could not, even in a foreign tongue, quite repress his fondness for the simple affirmative, for *ja, ja.* 'I know all about your *Lieutenant* Syme,' he said, spitting out the word with an 'f', after the English fashion. 'Perhaps, indeed, a little bit more than yourself.'

My heart sank into my stomach, a dull weight, like a swallow of tough meat. The phone nearly slipped from my shoulder, and I caught it with a brief twinge in my wrist. A century of Müllers and another, translated into Kardings, had not robbed the family of their particular turgid, teasing tone. I suddenly thought, nearly two hundred years ago, Sam himself was greeted by just such a 'yes', just such a mocking, equivocal *yes*. (I was hot on his heels indeed, if only I could avoid the hole he tumbled in.)

The man in the suit on the bench had finished whatever thought had kept him there, and slowly stooped to pull first one sock, then the other, over his (now dirty) bare feet. 'If you please' was all I said, clutching the phone, 'if you please' – tricked as it were into the propriety of a foreigner's accent.

'*I should be delighted to entertain your curiosity*,' Dr Karding answered in that *sucking* tone of his, enjoying, it seemed, a toothsome private joke, '*if you would have the goodness to come such a long way*.'

Missy Pitt, to speak in the hyperbole of understatement, was not best pleased. 'Only a day or two,' I assured her, covering my voice in velvet to soften its passage to her thoughts. 'I'm flying into Hamburg and taking the train. Dr Karding will collect me at the station. I'll see whatever there is to see – and then I'm coming home.' The word *collect*, carefully chosen to tickle her sense of the English, missed its mark.

'Dr Bunyon stopped by yesterday,' she said, adding '*kindly*' when I sighed – as if Dr Bunyon, like Death, would go to any trouble for a busy friend. (I shudder to think how our little Blue-stocking Society has survived my absence.) 'He said, if nothing came of this year, there wasn't any hope, he said, in the fall. Those were his words; and *he means well*, Douglas. He said he'd have a word with some of the faculty, to let them keep you on, until you found something else. A year at most. "Tell him to write," he said, and shook his head. What can I do?' she added, in those particular soliloquizing tones that suggest someone is calling out from their *wits' end*.

'The breakthrough is near,' I insisted. 'The breakthrough is near.'

My mind was made up, set fast – for once I would not flinch at the brink of success. One cannot struggle through a forest to the gate, and then turn, without attempting the key, without tinkering in the lock, without pushing firmly, pressing the weight of the full soul against the bars. At least, not twice – counting Syme himself as the first instance of our failure, the two of us twinned by a common thought, the agents of a single idea. I would redeem him now.

The breakthrough was very near indeed.

Neuburg was much as I had figured it – a pretty old town in the bend of a river, white roofs in the distance scalloped like the waves of an unsettled sea. The train from Hamburg, a sleek yellow capsule with slanted windows, arrived on the dot – and I stepped out into the nowhere of a platform on a bright July day brimming with light clouds. Dr Karding had informed me that I should recognize him by the fact that he was 'unnecessarily tall' – and so he was, the lengthened shadow of a man, thin and stretched, striding to greet me with his hand reached out. I followed him down the steps and into the car park, a dour, thick bulldog trotting at his heels.

He had not mentioned how *young* he was – a callow, long-nosed fellow who squeezed into his untidy VW Bug with astonishing angularity. A rather severe grey-green face, like the shaved countenance of an El Greco, suggesting also something of the hungry faith of the Old Testament; a nervous wrist, thin and strong, forever tampering with the signal-wires of his fingers. I wondered how much of the blood of Ferdinand Müller was left in him and shuddered at a hint of the noose about his tautened neck, the bulging Adam's apple.

His taste in music, I supposed, was all his own; for he rolled down the window, squeaking and puffing, and flicked the tape into the mouth of the deck. The dull-aching beat of techno blared across the sunny streets, like darkness audible, boom boom boom, scattering the birds from the lindens along the cobbled road. He smiled at me, wrinkling his lips. 'Yes,' he said, answering my thought, for I had not spoken, 'I've only just got my doctorate. On the subject of my great-great-great-uncle, as it happens.'

I began to have second thoughts. And when he lowered the music and enquired after my researches, I voluntereed only the thinnest of sketches; mentioned my interest in scientific false starts, dead ends; the old battles of Neptunists and Plutonists for the heart of the earth; Syme's place among them – avoiding all mention of Wegener, his library, the catalogue of its contents that survived the bombing, 'fetching up' in Tunbridge Wells after the war; those 'segments of the earth's crust which float on the revolving core'.

Dr Karding in turn described something of Ferdinand Müller: his Napoleonic sympathies, curiously transformed after the victory at Leipzig into a German nationalism (a common enough evolution); formation of the Parliamentary Society on 'borrowed' money; its links with other revolutionary groups, from Hamburg to Württemberg; the outbreak of the July Revolution; influence of the Neuburg underground on the disastrous Frankfurter student rebellion of 1834, which adopted much of Müller's secret constitution, a draft of which was discovered in a mass of papers in the basement of their old family house. 'That's where we're headed now. I suppose, though,' he added, arching his brows slightly, as one testing the rustle of a card up his sleeve, 'your *particular of interest* lies in the son, Friedrich.' He paused a minute, waiting for a cab to turn into a cobbled side-street, then continued, '*The one who went.*'

Again, a sudden caesura – stopped breath, heart, a quiet even in the flow of thoughts, the gap where recognition grows. We turned bumping at last into *our* cobbled side-street, off the Promenade along the river – Fischersallee, an elegant alley of eighteenth-century houses, tall and darkening the narrow lane. Dr Karding eased the Bug over the kerb and cut the engine. 'Come now,' he said, unfolding himself like a stepladder and squeezing out of the driver's seat. 'Shall I take you on a historical journey, the only one of its kind?'

The house was cool and damp despite the pleasant light heat of the summer day; swathes of sunshine cut into the entrance hall in a beam of dust. We stepped up a narrow staircase on to a brighter landing, then turned into the first door by the opened window. 'Here he hung,' Dr Karding said, ducking his head beneath the frame. 'They have patched up the hole where the hook dug in. You see, it would not have done for me – being too tall. My feet would scrape. *Friedrich* also was built too long for such a death. But Ferdinand was a *little* gentleman. A delightful study, no? Please, sit down.'

I sat on a prim, high-backed chair by the window, high enough to catch the edge of sun drifting over the tiled roofs, glancing over the shadows of the street. 'Of course, you know something of Friedrich?' Dr Karding said, sat behind the antique desk in an angle of the room, trying to cross his long legs in the cramped nook between the drawers.

'Only', I faltered, oddly ill at ease in front of the young man, 'that he was sent – sent to investigate Syme. Is there more?'

'A great deal,' he said, delicately rubbing his dry hands together, at the nubs of bone in the palm where the fingers begin. 'Have you any idea why he was sent?'

'I assumed', hesitating again, 'that it was – a job for the boys.'

'Something of that. Something of that. Also, it made things a touch easier at first for Ferdinand to take a little off the top. Only at first, as it happened. There was more – a slight contretemps with the Prince gave the *push*. Friedrich tutored the boy for a while, you know. Quite harmless – only Friedrich had certain . . . predilections, I suppose, which, for his part, the Prince seemed to share. To a point.'

Dr Karding considered a minute. There is something *ageless* about the weather in an old house; the sun falls in untouched, it seems, by the century at hand, indifferent to eras and revolutions.

'Of course, Friedrich in his way was *technically* quite brilliant.' (This word being a particular favourite of the Germans, and loosens their tongues astonishingly – they will quite happily attribute a wealth of merits *technically* that would appal them without this curious qualification.) 'Well-suited *intellectually* at least to "borrow" what he could from Syme and carry it home. If there was virtue in it, of course.'

'Just as I suspected,' I muttered, keeping my end up.

'Have you read Friedrich's books? *The Romantic Science*? *The Philosophy of the Senses*?' Dr Karding asked, crossing his legs at last (to a mighty rumble of drawers and the scrape of wooden feet on wooden boards) and leaning back, head propped in the nest of his hands.

My end fell promptly down. No, I had read nothing by the man sent to investigate Syme, not even the suggestively titled *Romantic Science*. 'I had been', as Newton cried, 'a boy playing on the seashore, and diverting myself in now and then finding a smoother pebble or a prettier shell than ordinary, whilst the great ocean of truth lay all undiscovered before me.' Part of the tide was about to come in.

'Friedrich made quite a name for himself in the end,' continued Dr Karding (the very picture of this distant great-uncle as it happens, long and thin, the shadow of a man at sunset), 'in Berlin society, at the salon of Rahel Varnhagen, among others; and later in Paris. Played his part in precipitating what he called "the sensual revolution" – at least, he liked to think so. But I suspect that most of what he found, in Paris at least, was there already. In his way, though, he came out the best of all of them. The best of them all. Now rather neglected, I'm afraid; though perhaps his memoirs might *put that right*, is that not the phrase? They may interest you, I think.'

There, in the little study where Ferdinand hanged himself, his grandson (many times great!) spread over the antique desk – the flowing corners richly curled, the slender legs austerely straight-

ened, the delicate little feet daintily propped on the old floorboards – a sheaf of papers, yellowing, brittle with age, as though
the rough sheets had been lightly *crisped* in the fire of time. Across
the first of them, a flourish of Gothic script, *Erinnerungen an
Syme*, and then a muddle and scribble of dates below, crossed
out, corrected, until the year 1861 proved triumphant (the year
of his death), beside the name, *Friedrich Müller*.

I did not come home in a 'day or two'; in fact, only a scramble and
lay-over in Reykjavik allowed me to beat the start of term in
September. The manuscript was in something of a state, as the
English say, which tends to mean *no state at all*: a hodgepodge of
visions and revisions, corrections and amendments, the tedious
working and reworking of an internal argument Friedrich
thrashed out with himself, incapable of conclusion, only evolution, like a strand of DNA, from generation to generation, or
decade to decade. Dr Karding – *Benyameen*, as I came to know him,
the 'j' gentled, deflected into half a yawn, the 'i' lengthened and
squeezed into sweetness, after the German fashion – and I battled
through the muddle, lifting one thought to the next, much as we
might have stumbled through mud, a leg at a time. I slept on the
sitting-room sofa, an antique orange affair on tender feet, curled
like paws into the rug, my own feet tucked into each other, the
cushions too short to accommodate them. And in some sense this
posture persisted through the days: my brain bent on a continual
thought, too tight to stretch forth on easy limbs and walk free.

The house soon stank of sleep – we all stank of sleep, the odour of
life in stasis, unrefreshed, bent for ever on a single object – an odd
fact, indeed, considering how little we slept. Two round cups of
steaming coffee were required each morning to prop our wedged
eyes open, by some sympathy, it seemed, with the 'O' of the mug's
rim. Our lives had been confined to the prisons of our minds, the
bars formed of the neglected pages of Friedrich's manuscript – only
the key to them could release us at last into the world. And yet, and
yet . . . we both had a sense, Benjamin and I, sleeping on scattered
pages, waking to work at them afresh, breaking off only to spoon

half-heated tins of ravioli into mouths that seemed almost to have forgotten their primary purposes, devoted as they were to the secondary function of language – we both had the sense of life deeply lived, of time burning brightly in the crucible of our skulls, of true vocation. We seemed to shed at last our bodies, useless lumps – or rather, recline upon them idly, as we might on sacks. We lived on the flame, while the dull, hot wax of the candle accumulated at the bottom – upon our bottoms. Even young Dr Karding, ladder of bones that he seemed, developed a derrière – overfed by canned pasta and that peculiarity of the English I had acquired over the year, baked beans on toast, washed down by milky tea.

I almost grew accustomed to Benjamin's techno banging through the house, setting on edge the thin, old glass of the windows till they fairly pinged their displeasure. The aching beat of it suggested after a time the echo of a mechanical heart, in a hollow space, pumping lava blood through rocky arteries. I imagined the iron and nickel crowns of Syme's imagination revolving to such enormous rhythms, the true music of the spheres, vast and technical and indifferent, grindingly ugly and yet alluring, like devastation. And under its spell we worked, pawing and poring over a dead man's memories, comparing, correcting, collating, translating – deepening by our following steps the path of his life, till it broadened into a road, till it led, smoother and plainer by the day, to Alfred Wegener.

The manuscript, as I said, suffered from the confusions of its author's life. (Above all, this is a record of lives lived, not simply thoughts thought.) In the first place, Müller composed 'on the trot' (as the English have it), and his papers bore the marks of makeshift accommodations: spilt ink, coffee stains, even sea stains rendered parts of the text nearly unintelligible. Those final excited scratchings, scribbled overleaf on the last few pages, record his chance meeting with Peter Wegener (uncle of Alfred, a man of many parts, but fewer scruples) and bear evidence of his increasing physical distress. Müller's hand had changed greatly over the years: the free-flowing ink of his youth had hardened into the crabbed joints and messy, irregular lines of sick old age. He suffered, Benjamin believed, from a cancer of the colon – a weakness hereditary to the family – and had travelled in some haste and discomfort from Paris when he ran into Peter. Müller had come home to die.

Peter Wegener himself plays a crucial if *mediate* role in the story (a conduit of history). He was, as Charles Lamb ventured of Coleridge, a great borrower of books; and it is a curious irony of fate that he has left his final mark on the world by *bequeathing* one of them (though pilfered), upon his death, to his brother: the *New Platonist* itself, as Friedrich Müller's manuscript conclusively proves, together with the conjunction of dates that mark its entry into the library on Friedrichsgracht. I should like, at some point, to undertake a history (and this, I promise, shall be the final revision of my academic ambitions) of the *odysseys of manuscripts*: the idle pre-occupation that led T.E. Lawrence to neglect the single copy of *The Seven Pillars of Wisdom* on the seat of a train and the cold night that led Carlyle's *History of the French Revolution* to be fed to the cottage fire. I shall count the wet day that brought Peter Wegener and Friedrich Müller into the comfort of a tavern fire as among the luckier chances of history – an incident in which the cottage fire redeems itself somewhat from its consumption of Carlyle's masterpiece.

Of course, the coincidence is only lucky when seen *back to front*. When Wegener pinched Syme's journal, Alfred still waited his turn at the revolving door of birth, and the thought of continental drift had died stillborn in the press of Syme's other projects. It might never have been revived, in the shape we now know it, but for Peter's light fingers; but at the time, as Müller's misery attests, the theft of Syme's journal, signed by its author, and a token, in its way, of forgiveness, seemed a piece of very bad luck indeed. And who knows what other course the journal might have taken but for Peter; who knows if Alfred would have died to prove Syme's point, between two skis stuck upwards in the ice, to guide those coming after to his body? Peter played his part. As Milton notes – they also serve who only stand and wait; and those who pinch and run serve, too: serve entropy, I suppose, in the end, another word for the *dissemination of ideas*. We shall come to Peter's theft, and Müller's death, in time.

The evidence before you is, of course, circumstantial. I can show that Wegener knew of Syme, quotes him specifically in his introduction to *On the Origin of Continents and Oceans*; I can show that no other published piece of Syme's writing includes the phrase, so suggestive of continental drift, describing those 'segments of the earth's crust which float on the revolving core'; I can show that, rummaging through his father's library, Wegener *might* have stumbled upon that neglected gem of geognostic science, the *New Platonist*, for I can prove that the journal was *there*, even pinpoint its spot upon the shelf – if the library itself had not tumbled into the canal, struck by a bomb in 1942. But I *cannot* prove that the final essay of Syme's *New Platonist*, 'Speculations: a curious coincidence', contains an attempt to account for the coastal alignments of Africa and South America through his theory of a cracked revolving outer sphere – though there is ample suggestion of such a line of thought in the pages of the following memoir. As Wegener himself declared in his introduction to the great theory:

> We are like a judge confronted by a defendant who
> declines to answer, and we must determine the truth from
> the circumstantial evidence. All the proofs we can muster
> have the deceptive character of this type of evidence.

I offer motive, means, and opportunity – even the smoke from the gun, though the gun itself is lost to history. I leave history to decide.

I had misread Syme's arrogance, believing him careless of posterity, cold to contemporary fame. He seemed too far removed from the clamour of the great world (as I, perhaps, am too close) to love it much – both the clamour and the world. Where he sought flattery, the praise of prince and pauper (of Silliman and the village postman) pleased him equally. He lived, I thought, indifferently, in both senses of the word – and suffered for that indifference. It never occurred to me to call him an optimist: something too faithful to life seems suggested by the word, and such conviction as he possessed appeared to lie only in himself, and nearly died with him. But these memoirs shall prove, if nothing else, that his arrogance at heart was both grander and fonder than I had reckoned, more closely tied to the glories of creation, himself an example only of that glory. For Syme lived full of faith, not in his own virtues simply but in the hope that the world would bend, courteous and loving, to his understanding in the end, and honour him, as he had honoured it; for he was an optimist. As am I.

So I set forth for America, as Friedrich Müller had, almost two hundred years before me; caught an hour of sunshine over the runways from the windowed walls of Reykjavik airport, the polar light green and gleaming like the scales of a fish; 'kipped' (how I shall miss the poky jumble of the English tongue, the odd patched furniture of their slang!) in D.C. for an awkward hour, looped under and over three successive seats, my eyes blinded in the nook of my elbow, my ears half-soothed by the murmur of CNN; and turned, bum-weary but light-hearted, towards Austin, Texas, at last, towards the loving comforts of my plump pretty polly and our two chicks – confident and determined to Make a Name, for the dead, the great, the long-forgotten Syme, if not for myself.

PART II

·Arrival·

I glanced in the mirror, the cracked glass hanging just above the canvas basin in the low cabin. Certainly, a refined face, I thought – if not pretty, and on the whole rather sad. Well, I shall make the best of it. I tucked the cream cravat into the neck of my richest red coat – soft wool buttoned to the breast with fat gold buttons, round as mushrooms. Then loosened the clasp (tortoiseshell, inlaid with silver) in my hair and shook the long brown locks out with closed eyes till they tickled my nape. A breath of the sea blew through the opened porthole, and I sighed once, heavily, and again, more lightly; tidied my hair into a smooth flaxen and fixed it once more at my neck. I must prepare myself, I thought, for the dignity of arrival in a rough new world.

Cries of 'helm alee!', 'back sail!' and other spells from the hocus-pocus of nautical nonsense filtered below, followed by a flap and a creak and a tramp of feet above my head. I could feel the turn of the ship by the turn of my stomach. Then the heel of the floor relented and we entered gentler waters. I sensed the loom of the land, a physical presence, like a wall in the dark at the edge of my forehead: an apt image that, of my journey ahead, of my American adventure. I was fair sick of the sea by now and could not repress, for all my Old World weariness, my studied languor, a flutter of excitement at the thought of landfall in this new world, at the thought of my mission – into the depths of the earth, as it were, through the mind's eye.

A ray of the sun, bright and cold with winter, shot through the cabin on this new tack (as I believe they call it); and by some trick of sea-borne light caught a fragment of the looking-glass. I bent to flutter the lines of my cravat – and nearly drew back at the curious shimmering illusion. A rounder, sunnier face peered back at me from the shard: the plump cheeks of my boyhood, the snubbed nose and fair, shining hair of fourteen. And I recalled with sudden tears the words of the great Werner, when I first appeared at the Academy in Freiburg at the front row of the dusty lecture hall, and overheard him, glancing my way – 'what pretty creature is that? I did not know they came to us so young . . .' But a cloud covered the ray and the ship darkened and my older face slid into the shadow: long and thin, split by a long, thin nose; the cheeks hollowed and dry, bright only with a fine snow of powder delicately applied; the hair brown; and that foolishness of a chin, retreating, slight enough to be pinched between thumb and forefinger, still touching. A young man no longer, already twenty-eight, set forth at last out of my father's shadow.

I have not come seeking Syme, whoever he may be, I told myself, for the hundredth time; I have only answered his petition. He is the supplicant; I, the prince. And I puffed my chest and straightened my long back in simulated pride, only to knock the tender top of my head against a tarred cross-beam, supporting the deck; and cursed again a world unfit for a man of any stature to dwell in. I thought of my true prince, the plump, tearing, young Kreminghausen, who had so lately been my chief charge and care; now given over to the ministrations of my father, the First Minister of Kolwitz-Kreminghausen, Herr Doktor Ferdinand Müller. My dear father I should have said, sole author, I must confess, of this expedition, so necessary (as I had urged him) to my spiritual renewal.

A tap at the door, and then a crack, a smudged nose poking round it, purpled from eye to lip with the mark of its birth. 'Captain's compliments; says, if you'd like a look, best come now. Norfolk coming up. Shouldn't trouble myself. Dirty little hole, if you ask me. See more than you like, before you're through.'

'I shall', I uttered, still tripping over the unfamiliar tongue, 'attend directly – as soon as I have completed my toilette, which, as you see . . . involves . . . certain preparations . . .' But the door had shut and a new cry was raised, in lusty sing-song, echoing above my head: 'when we poor sailors/go skipping to the tops . . .' And I reflected, diverted in my thought, for the hundredth time, on the broader preparations that had involved me in this plot.

*

It had pained my father, I knew, when I sought my fortune in geognosy, abandoning politics and his great dream of a German republic. But he relented at last (he has always relented to every wind, a man stiff and proud as a reed) and sent me forth to study at the Freiberg Academy. And then, at the ripe old age of twenty-one, I published that trail-breaking piece 'On the Convexity of the Seas, and Its Relation to the Internal Architecture of the Earth' (a good, a breathless title, no?); on the strength of which my father managed to set me up again – at the new university he had persuaded the young Prince to found in our little capital at Neuburg (upon certain conditions). And there I had settled (subsided, perhaps, is the better word) in a hum-drum, careless fashion, into the pleasures of a life without ambition.

I had resented at first my duties regarding the Prince – a thoughtless scaramouch, plump in face and foot, a swelling, lusty, joyous creature, with flushed red cheeks and an exaggerated chin, bright blue eyes and sandy hair, a child of his appetites, good natured, as far as his appetites directed him to please. 'He has no interest in these matters,' I told my father, who answered with a prim, brief smile and a glint of his lowered spectacles: 'Interest him.' (The First Minister can assume the sternest of countenances, possessing a nose and brow of truly bureaucratic beauty. It is only the first touch, the first breath of dissent, that reveals the softness of the man; but we are cut from the same cloth, my father and I, and I conceded.)

And yet, I confess, the Prince got on – the Prince and I – got on. He was as naturally sharp as he was cheerful, and often picked up lightly what I had once been at great pains to con. My life settled into a pleasing routine. Mornings at the 'court' – a bright pink cake of a house at the tip of a low hill, grand only in the slope and scope of the gardens running to the river below. Afternoons at the newly built university, where I lectured in dozy complacency in front of a handful of dozy young men, while the slow river eased its massive brown bulk along its bed outside the window. Evenings we danced in the Prince's drawing room – from whence the doors opened on to a narrow balcony and the sunset and the glimmer of twilight and the first stars above and the first flickering lights below. We had pushed an old pianoforte into the corner, and Hespe (a sallow, humourless pupil of mine, but clever, particularly with his fingers, which seemed lighter, happier, than himself) rattled out, from time to time, a somewhat cracked but none the less very pleasing waltz. The Prince loved music; but, despite his native ebullience, he lacked companions after the death of his father (from the gout) in the late wars; and I confess that our little balls and my little lectures often revolved around the same cluster of lazy young men.

(How far I am now, I thought, from those gay scenes: such cultivated sunsets and tidy rivers and pleasant valleys, lightly cobbled with pretty streets. The cabin stank of the bilge and old beef, of sodden stockings and cramped sleep. And a rough young beast of a country lay before me.)

Occasionally, on those bright evenings, a note came to call me away on business: I had earned some little renown as a doctor in Neuburg, mostly for the refinement and delicacy of my professional enquiries. The old ladies, in particular, when taken with the stomach-ache from heavy suppers of roast pork and potatoes, required the services of 'der kleine Herr Müller' or the 'little minister' – for though they had no great faith in medicine, they believed in class. And sometimes, I confess, I was not sorry to be called away – preferring the quiet of a princely tête-à-tête to these boisterous occasions. I suffer greatly from the demands of solitude, and to mount my horse in the cool of the hilltop evening and canter briskly down the pebbled road into town offered me a rare pleasure. Even upon my return, properly cold now, the horse breathing clouds of chill vapour lit briefly by the moonlight, I sometimes lingered below the glowing balcony, watched the Prince whirling away in the arms of this bright beauty or that, easily replaced – and marvelled, happily, at his gift for happiness, delighting more in the spectacle at one remove, as it were, than I should have in the heat and clamour of the ballroom itself.

I should have been a good, a useful, doctor, in a small way. Perhaps I should have been content at that. But I was conscious – ever more so – of a hole, growing as it were in the heart of my life, both wonderful and appalling, like a crack in the ice widening with returning spring. Into that breach I have sprung.

When my father first read that absurd and rather wonderful peti-
tion from Virginia signed 'Professor Samuel Highgate Syme', I was
originally no more than charmed. Such vast and greedy promises
seemed out of keeping with the narrow, elegant comforts to which I
had confined myself. So I remarked, in the lightness of the moment,
that these rather 'new-fangled theories' deserved 'a first or second
look. A curious solution', I added carelessly, stooping my head in
my father's study to peer on to the tall, narrow street, 'to the puzzle
of planetary mass – this notion of a hollowed earth, of nested
spheres. And there might be some more practical application to his
"double-compression" piston, I suppose.'

'I suppose there might,' he replied, tickling the grey and pink of
his soft cheek with the feather of his white quill.

'Might I – I beg – retain the copy of this, for a second glance at
leisure?' I asked casually, as a young boy raced a barrowful of
cabbages disastrously along the cobbled street. And there the matter
rested. (How lightly we acquire the passports of our fate.) But the
seed was sown; and in the quiet intervals of my increasingly per-
functory duties I returned to Syme's petition, tended his brazen
thought, nurtured the slight green shoots of envy and ambition they
awoke in me:

> I declare, after the courageous demonstration of Mr Seaborn,
> lately published, that the Earth is hollow and habitable with-
> in; containing a number of solid concentric Spheres, one
> within the other, open at various points along the globe. I
> pledge my life in support of this truth, and am ready to
> explore the Hollow . . .

I have pledged my life in support of so little, I reflected, promenading
along the river towards the tiny grandeur of the university, and
returned sighing Syme's petition to the pocket of my lemon-
coloured coat. The first bright sun of autumn slipped over the
quiet river, glimmering here and there, strangely suggestive of
the cold to come – 'the cold to come', I repeated sourly, ever more
conscious of that growing hollow within my own life, and loath to
spend another constricting winter at home. Perhaps it is time I

explored that hollow, *I thought, rather than veins of dull rock in green hills – and attended to one great thought with the full thrust of the soul. But instead I turned into the lecture hall, woke with a sharp step my slumbrous charges, and glanced once out of the window towards the river (that slow promise of greener pastures elsewhere), before commencing, with half a heart, the morning's discourse. (On the third decline of the universal ocean, and the rocks it precipitated. Perhaps I guessed even then that Werner's great revolution had spent itself, rolled on like dying waves under a still wind.)*

With half a heart – I have done so much with half a heart, consoling myself always with the thought that so copious a vessel may carry a great deal of passion despite being filled only partway with true desire. With half a heart. And as I bowed now beneath the low deck (curious that our physical attitudes impinge so powerfully on their mental equivalents), I promised myself, as I had in Neuburg setting forth, that, should some true cause appear, I would offer it the full stretch of my passion. What I desired above all was Purity. This has always been the brunt of my geognostic explorations, and I have excavated and precipitated and eroded countless innocent quarries and their contents in search of the purest elements, the originary rocks. (I believe now such researches touched only the metaphoric crust, as it were, of the Purity I sought within – and in a sense Syme's hollowed earth offered the final and necessary evolution of my desire, a world whose heart had been refined away to nothing. But all this by the by.) I sought a Cause unalloyed by circumstance or private faction, which I might serve – unshaken by cross-purposes, unpolluted by the least drop of personal considerations. Once called upon, I knew I could offer the noblest sacrifice: of the troubled soul to a greater Sum in which it has no part, which it cannot stain by its own ineradicable sins and confusions. If only such a cause would present itself to me, free me from half-measures, and their leaven of doubt and irony (those terrible corrosions of the soul).

But I believe I must go still further back to explain myself, and account in some part for the mixture of terror and expectation (I

*would almost say hope) that drove me forward now, as powerfully
as the wind backing our sails. A word on the curious creature I was
becoming, had become: more and more, I managed to keep my soul
in place only by the zealous and careful arrangement, as it were, of
cushions. The least upset sent me shivering by the hour, like a
blown leaf. An unpleasant exchange with the Prince, even a
moment's inattention in the course of his studies, appeared to me
the gravest of slights. (How deeply I mourned breaches in our
intimacy so subtle the Prince never noticed them before they were
resolved again and everything wonderful once more.) The disruptions
of my students, joyous, light-hearted, the outbursts of ordinary
youth (as I knew in my heart, as I knew full well), awoke in me such
trembling anger I would turn aside to let the great wave pass, a
flood of blood to my face and hands, ringing in my ears. And then
curse myself inwardly for the mild misery of the countenance I
turned towards them again – for I was a coward, frightened even at
the echo of my own anger.*

*More and more, I relied upon my cushions to ease the tender
weight of my life. Pleasures here or there, loved faces, even familiar
lines: the bend of Fischersallee, street of my birth; the low arc of a
diminishing sun over the line of the hill at sunset; the wrinkles of
familiar hands, and the tendons and knotted veins running over
their backs; the angles of noses (an idiosyncrasy from which I have
always taken peculiar solace, particularly, I confess, from the
plump, veined proboscis, bridged by glinting spectacles, of my
father). The demands of comfort (both to my soul and body) grew
and grew, clamoured like any petitioners for their cause, until I
could scarcely step from the house without a host of fears nipping at
my heels. The least interruption or surprise prompted in me ago-
nies of doubt, as if the course of the earth had faltered in its journey
and not the plans for a picnic in the gardens on a sunny afternoon.
Yet even my comforts, my plump cushions, my pleasures and quiet
moments, had begun to pall. I suffocated in feathers.*

*Since setting forth from Hamburg, on that short, cold day three
weeks ago, the cushions have been removed. Now every step and
glance strike unsoftened ground; here, my every nerve and thought*

seem exposed to the fresh, cold air. I had stepped into the very gap in my nature I had dreaded for so long, and come to look about me.

I am an incurious man, a fearful man. This is a difficult thought to bring into clear relief, for all of us have suffered now and then from a want of spirit, an inclination to turn away. But I suspect myself of something worse, a flaw less human, darker, more criminal – a sin against life and love. Indeed, my association with the Prince (that fount of careless joy, shining and running over with the beauty of its own excess) increasingly tender, increasingly dear to me, had begun to carry with it a growing apprehension by contrast of my own stark deficiency. I fear I cannot make myself clear; and so I begin again, from another vantage.

We are all of us creatures of appetite, prompted at each step by some desire. And I confess to my fair share of pleasures: the tinkle of the piano running down the hillside, as Hespe batters the keys and I linger in the gardens below, observing the glitter of the dancers above; the laughter of my sister Ruth, as I brush the tip of a feather over the soft sole of her foot, and she doubles over with the ache of joy; the roasted honeyed pork, a speciality of our province, at Sunday lunch; a glass now and then of Rhenish; an occasional cigar; the cut of a fine piece of cloth; a new cravat. And yet I cannot conceal from myself an appalling absence where the heart of life should be, which I can dub by no clearer name than incuriosity, though that light word does no justice to the awful void it attempts to suggest.

As a boy I was known as a 'curious child' – my mother in particular complaining of this fact, as my first forays into the long, narrow garden behind our house, its gooseberries and rose-hips, its red- and blackcurrants, plums and dwarf apple trees, its thick, clumped beds of potatoes and cabbages, and the sandy mottled patches of rhubarb, covered my childish frock in stains of every description: blue and black and purple juices, green streaks of leaf and grass, rich black cakes of mud and the dust of lighter soils. And later, after her death, I sought further fields and greener pastures, chased the hillside streams to their rocky sources, filled my pockets with clacking stones: grey pumice, rough granite that left the dry palm red in winter, geometric clusters of quartz, smooth, brown-backed crystals; and, on all-too-rare occasions, that treasure of treasures, the small, blunted, flinty head of some lost medieval arrow. These I cleaned till my hands bled, rinsing them in the bubble of the beck as it dashed towards the river. And I recall delighting particularly in the purity of the crystals, utterly at ease, at home in the flow of clear water, like frozen shards from some forgotten winter. I sorted tirelessly: storing my collection in mis-matched wooden boxes (some rudely cobbled together, some stolen, the chess pieces they once held wickedly discarded) in constantly refreshed arrangements of colour, weight, sharpness and fragility.

And yet – and yet – what drew me chiefly to these delights (and I guessed as much even at the time) was their solitude, the quiet of the hills, the hidden recesses of the turning streams. The play of my school-fellows, their chatter and rough ways, appalled me, over-whelmed me with an enormous sense of some mystery at work, from whose secrets I alone had been excluded; and though I confess the strangeness of my fellow creatures, their violent joys, pleased and tempted me upon occasion to mix in, I refrained always from the satisfaction of these yearnings, preferring instead the familiar com-forts of my own mind and my exploratory excursions, preferring the cold varieties of stone to the growing, breathing, unpredictable spec-imens of humanity around me. So I repeat, these rambles proceeded from an absence of true curiosity, from the fear of it. Gradually, over time, as I grew increasingly accustomed to solitude, the organ (for such I suppose it to be) of fellow-feeling atrophied within me. And I became conscious that some vital appetite had died, some nec-essary joy, leaving behind it, dried and choked, the most indispens-able well-spring of the soul and source of continual replenishment – curiosity in the workings of the human heart.

At the Academy of Freiberg (which I confess I attended too young, this being my first act of courage, my first filial disobedi-ence) I was known, by my fellow students, as 'little Dr Werther', for my melancholy manner and my solitary pursuits in the chem-ical laboratory. It was generally jested (and the joke, believe me, was well kept and cared for) that I concocted in my tireless exper-iments some elixir of passion designed to restore to me the heart of an estranged maiden, thus hoping by the wonder of science to achieve what the sweetness of Goethe's poetry had failed to effect. Indeed, my colleagues' humour revealed more of their own inclinations than of mine – for they spent, it seemed to me, much of their purses and most of their thoughts on this harmless (and I believe often unsuspecting) maid or that, wasting in flowers and poetry the sweat of their brows, neglecting their studies, and consoling themselves only at some tavern through the exchange of ever drunker and more fanciful boasts. And though I desired neither their company nor their lewd confidences, their contempt led me to suspect a deep flaw in my nature – an absence of common humanity perhaps, or some perversion in the course of my youth. Suspicions which – despite the kindly interest of Dr Werner himself, and those tender afternoons when, too ill to teach, he insisted I read to him in his study, from whose window the valley stretched forth, into the thick-wooded hills and tumbling gorges he had done so much to explain – have grown into certainties over the years.

When he died at last, a wisp of a man, quite burned away by the fire of his intelligence and the insistent restlessness of his hand and foot and eye, nothing could console me. The little stack of books I had read to him – a curious collection, of his own choosing, the tales of Grillparzer and of Grimm, travel anecdotes, and books of paternal advice, such as the letters of Lord Shaftesbury to his son – became a kind of shrine to me. I dipped into them, again and again, less for their own sake than the recollection of those afternoons: when a glass of sunshine poured into the window and covered in gold the floorboards and the little rug at his feet, swaddled against the cold of old age in thick green stockings rising up to his knees; when I heard my own voice, high, fluting, almost shrill, echoed by his nods and sighs, the scratching of his whiskered lip with a solitary finger, and the sudden squeezing shut of his eyes when pleasure took him at some particular passage. I have read and reread since the little shelf of books with this proviso: that I never advance beyond the last page I had declaimed to him from Shaftesbury's excellent letters, as if Dr Werner's death had sealed up even those in forgetfulness, like the unwritten tablets of his own wonderful brain.

Nevertheless, his death awoke in me a sense of how far I had strayed from the common paths of my own age-mates. And I determined at last, as far as was possible, to remake myself – if not in their image, then at least in such fashion as to remove my manners and dress from the sphere of their abuse. A single greatcoat – stained variously by the overflow of sulphur and chloride, potash and magnesia, from countless botched experiments; burned here and there by dropped crucibles and sudden flares and fires; reeking from the tireless pursuit, downriver or up-mountain, of this vein of mineral or that – had formed my sole accoutrement since my arrival at the Academy. I vowed to reform myself. And if perhaps I have taken these fancies too far, this owes less to any faith in their cosmetic effects than to the sudden light in which they reveal me to myself – a new suit of clothes, the altered plume of a hat, an adjusted cravat or refreshed buttonhole may surprise in us a stranger's view into our own soul. Narcissus, I am convinced, lingered over his image in the swelling pool less out of love for his own beauty than out of an appalled suspicion that there was some fatal flaw in it.

When at last I set forth for the house of my father, a young doctor in the new science of geognosy, I looked the part of the prodigal returned, in yellow garters, a cream linen suit and a pink cravat; yet my ambitions had fallen into bankruptcy at Werner's death, and only my father's insistence established me at the brand-new university at Neuburg as a lecturer. (I might have tried my fortunes at Berlin or Vienna, but I did not – I scuttled home to my father.) Only his insistence directed me to the education of the young Prince. And, by my father's insistence, I had grown – happy at last, pleasant, elegant, neither idle nor spent, sufficiently at ease in the company of men to assuage the pressing fear of their mysterious ways that still beset me; indeed, almost comfortable in the presence of my Prince, aware for the first time of that curiosity in our fellow creatures that seems to sustain so much of the world. For all of this I had only my father to thank. From all of this I have effectively banished myself, spurred, like a belated traveller, by fear of the darkness rising over his shoulder. Prompted to seek new worlds in whose expanse my deficiences in the old may shrink to insignificance.

My father's house has always been full of young men, and perhaps his grace with them accounts in no small part for my diffidence. Young men: students, soldiers, idle gentlemen, lounging at ease in the front hall, exchanging insults, jests and theories, forever advancing, without stirring an inch from their posteriors, the history of the world one notion at a time. At first I believe my father courted such company and their talk, hoping to soften in some fashion the unbreakable silence in our house that followed my mother's death. But after a time the thing took on a life of its own; and no matter what hour of day or night I stumbled home from my duties, I was sure to find some collection of lounging fellows, tossing apple-cores in the fire, reeking of whiskey and tobacco, engaged with all the fierceness of youth in questions of liberty, literature and whist. 'It's old Müller!' they chanted, whenever I flitted through the door, 'Grandfather Müller!' – for it was their standing joke that I was indeed my father's father, too old and grand to share in their excitements. Their disruptions had driven me increasingly into the company at court; and when at last I determined to press my father for the right to pursue this American's magical theories, I had considerable difficulty in ushering him from the heat of debate into the relative quiet of his study upstairs, where I closed the door behind me, leaning against it for good measure.

I urged my case with a passion that surprised even myself, inspired by my sense of how lightly I could be turned aside. My father sat in the angle of his study, feet propped upon the desk, a quill in his hand idly tickling the pink of his chin.

'I have given some thought to this extraordinary petition, sir,' I began, hoping to convey an air of studied gravity.

'The business with –' he prompted, rocking back on his chair and then swinging his legs to the ground with a brisk thump.

'Yes, the business with – Syme, Professor Syme.' If only I could stand at ease! One leg placed elegantly before the other, my hands loosely content at my sides. Instead of this exhausting restlessness, sudden swoops and perches, against side-tables or window sills, upon a chair (sensibly and briefly), upon the edge of my father's desk, where I leaned now, flourishing Syme's declaration like a poniard.

'The fellow who thought he could get to the bottom of the earth, I believe,' my father queried, lifting his brows until one might have dropped a penny for luck in the horseshoe of wrinkles that furrowed between them.

'Precisely. I have given the matter some thought. These speculations are by no means as whimsical as we had supposed. There is nothing, strictly, in Hutton to discount them – and though Werner won't tally . . . Still, Werner, dear man, has had his day perhaps and I – we – Geognosy – must stagger on as we may without him.'

The feather tickled my father's chin, lightly, pensively, till I almost felt myself the tiny touch of pleasure upon him, endlessly renewed, bristling against his loose soft skin. Yes, the feather whispered, perhaps, perhaps.

'I could not convince the council on the strength of such uncertainties, I fear,' my father ventured, leaning back, extending the operation of the quill to this cheek and that, then to the slight furrow beneath his nose, upon which he sneezed, once, heartily. 'You must appeal to their common sense.'

'Damn the council!' I cried suddenly, as a roar from below greeted some jest or turn of play at cards, and I rattled off my reasons above the clamour. 'And all sober, sensible reservations! The great revolutions of science have all begun in absurdity. When a man talks to me of common sense, I know he is far gone. Our common senses teach us to eat and grow fat and step out of the way in a shower of rain; and, when the day comes, to die without fuss or fame. It is our uncommon senses to which I appeal – our unshakeable conviction that common explanations must fall short of the wonder of Creation. Whatever we understand at a first glance must be wrong. This fellow Syme seems to have the measure of that. And, to do him justice, no one has gone far into the heart of the earth; he is breaking difficult and unfamiliar ground, and his account seems no less likely, to a clear mind, than a hundred others. The great test is this: imagine the impossible to be true, and proceed from there. How quickly does the rest of the world fall into place around it! What could be more natural, in the end, simpler, plainer even to our common sense, than the fact that the ground beneath our feet is hollow, fashioned by a thrifty Creator who lets nothing run to waste? Consider how much of life surrounds an empty core: our very bones, the quill in your hand, are founded upon air.' Upon which, my contentions ran dry of the very matter at their heart, and I was forced to draw breath.

My father looked at me now, sadly I supposed, as if I had confessed to a slighter, more personal emptiness. 'I have only to look at the company I keep,' I said at last, more quietly, 'to know that such a man as I cannot have the measure of the world. Not here. I had rather risk my soul upon a hundred absurdities than on such certainties as I live among now.'

'There are great things to be done, even here,' my father said, almost timidly.

I rise to anger quick and dry, like a handful of loose grass set a-flame, sharp and indeed (to draw the analogy to its improbable conclusion) almost sweet. 'As for that, Father – there are emptier dreams than hollow worlds, madder and more dangerous fancies. A German republic . . .'

'Hush now,' he said. 'Hush.'

So I urged more gently. 'Only imagine, Father – consider if this fellow were right, how great a revolution we should play a part in. I would stand at the side of the Napoleon of a new science and a new world.'

He lifted, with a blind tilt of the head, his spectacles from their resting-place and blinked at me, till I could see the raw pink at the corners of his eyes. He bit the tip of his thumb between pursed lips, and muttered, mostly to himself, 'We have buried you here – I have buried you here, in obscurity.'

'By the by,' I added innocently, in the long pause that followed, broken only by the clamour below, 'the gardener has stumbled across a rather extensive vein of bitumen at the foot of Kolwitz Castle. Running through the heart of the hill.'

My father looked up quickly, looping the spectacles once more across his plump, delicately veined nose.

'There may be some virtue in this "double-compression" piston

Syme mentions,' I continued, 'some profit in it – that may appeal to a more practical mind. To common sense.'

'We have great things ahead, my dear boy,' my father declared, briskly once more, his mind made up. 'Great days ahead . . .' But that brave phrase lured him into some cloudy vision, and his voice trailed away once more, while he tickled the soft pink and grey of his cheek with the feather of his quill. 'Great days ahead . . .'

'Perhaps the Prince will not spare me?' I sniffed, beginning to blink, suddenly fearful of the prospects I had opened before me.

This seemed to settle him. 'He shall,' my father answered, rising and looking up at his son, for my talents, such as they are, have been spread thin and long, and I stand a head above him. 'If I require it. And this is just the thing.' (He kept repeating that phrase, as if to ward off doubts like devils – though 'the thing' was just what my father could never quite put his finger on.) 'This is just the thing. Double-compression piston, I believe you called it? I must draft a letter to the council. Wonderful new device for excavation, along those lines. Swept America, mining at record speed the virgin country. A vein of bitumen, was it, you said, in the princely gardens?' And on the wind of his new conviction, he swept us both downstairs towards luncheon.

A week later, by chance, Syme's story broke in the Hamburger Tagesblatt – 'The Hole in the New World' – and the news travelled to Neuburg. The council were decided; my course was set.

Such hours we used to spend in those wonderful labyrinths, the Prince and I, heads bent to our studies on sunny mornings, when the dew lay thick as rain on the grass. A blackbird drank greedily beside us from a pool in the toes of Aphrodite, who stood dripping and chilly in a loose dress of Portland stone, flecked here and there by calcareous streaks, in a gesture of frozen welcome. The paths fell away before us in such a profusion of lanes and hedgerows, such a confusion of trees – oak, ash and scattered birch – that we seemed never to wander the same way twice. Here, a marbled cave set in the hillside called us into the shade; there a tiny cupola offered a dry spot in a brisk spring shower, from which to observe the slow Elbe white in a misty patter. At the foot of the hill a low cultivated maze, cut from sharp yew – muddy most of the time and gleaming with black rainwater – tempted our wanderings further. And when at last we surrendered hope of ever finding the green core and the quiet bench at the centre, we had only to step high and light, giggling and steadying each other by hand and shoulder, across the prickly barriers; and by this leap of faith surmounting every obscurity of path and purpose straight to the secret heart.

In these gardens, on a bright, cold, sunshiny afternoon, I took my leave of him. Snow had fallen in the night and covered the hedgerows in chilly blossoms. The paths trailed away in softness, which our footsteps pressed into hard white bricks as we walked along. I had determined to continue our lessons, even in this, our farewell interview; and so we rambled wet and dirty to the dancing beck running down the far side of the hill. This was the subject of one of our geological experiments. We had thrust a heavy rock in the flow of the water to observe the results. (The Prince's burgeoning strength had played no small part in this manoeuvre, and I still remember the fine white steam rising off his pink neck after the heat of these exertions.) Now we stood, in the ruins of a checked stream, to mark the changes.

The Prince, a creature of prodigious appetites, had always upon his person some assortment of chocolates or sweetmeats or nuts, mostly collected in the depths of his trouser pockets; and from these he drew forth a continuous supply of treats, which filled the flushed corner of his cheek, and lent to his voice a curious grumbling quality, like the mutterings of a much older man. He seemed, visibly, to sprout before me – such fierce nourishment did he draw from the life around him, in every swallow and breath – and had grown (in his broader, swaggering, big-boned fashion) by the tender age of fifteen till the top of his head almost nudged the tip of my negligible chin. Something had clouded his spirits that day; and he munched in a sullen, ferocious, hungerless fashion, as if he bore the chocolates between his strong white teeth some personal and particular grudge.

'Observe,' I said, perched on a high piece of rock to prevent my shoes from soaking through, 'the effects of long constriction. The choked stream has swelled, outward and downward. The brisk flow now lies stagnant; the sodden soil offers no hope for the new year's seedlings; the ground itself shudders under foot. New streams have formed, to right and left, tiny trickles that dissipate over the unfamiliar ground, leaving only a trail of slickness in the snow. On the far side of the rock the ground remains dry, somewhat firmer underfoot; and here and there a film of ice has formed across the stones, though higher up no frost could sink its teeth into the stream.'

The Prince, usually attentive and eager to please (if not to learn), scarcely looked my way as I spoke; and wandered, heedless of his boots, into the soaked turf, splashing as he went. He spat from time to time a mouthful of pistachio shells, then filled his fist with a fresh handful and cracked and chewed. I fell silent at his inattention, in a cold huff. The short day set in frosty blazon on the far side of the hill; we observed only the shadows lengthen and the chill deepen, and a faint glow, as of coal fires, seeping around the edges of the sky.

'I say,' he said at last, climbing through the middle of the stream to the rock we had taken such pains to shift, 'I shall be quite different when you come back. I have decided. Everything will be quite different.' And he spat again. The dark fell quickly, and soon his crouched figure took on a dusky glow.

'How sharp the cold makes everything you say,' I observed, turning aside from his last remark. A fresh fall of snow had begun, and a hundred chilly kisses alighted upon my face and hands. 'Quite astonishingly clear. I can scarcely see you – perhaps a dozen feet away, a huddled shape – but your voice rings out something astonishing. Even a whisper would carry like a bell.' And my own voice rang across the bleak hillside, into the night.

'As I say,' the Prince persisted, with a thick tongue, 'I have so many plans. All I need is time. Riding, for a start; I've fallen woefully behind. Hespe says a prince who cannot ride is like a woman who cannot dance. There is so much to learn of things that matter, you know. They all say I am growing fat.'

Then with a sudden fierce burst of spirits he bent his back to the great rock he'd sat upon and laboured to shift it from the stream.

'There was . . .' he huffed, 'nothing wrong . . . here,' he grunted, 'until you . . . began to meddle. Come on, Müller, bear a hand.' (There is always a push, as well as a pull, whenever we leave.)

I stepped gingerly through the growing night and the freezing wet. 'You are the worst kind of fool,' I muttered to myself, picking my way, 'a child's plaything – and a muddy one at that.' But as I stood soaked to the ankles and bent my back at the shoulder of my puffing Prince, a sudden and careless elation swelled within me – whether at the prospects before me or the noble youth beside me, I could not judge. Together we heaved the great rock from the sucking mud and sent it tumbling down the darkened hill, only a faint crash here and there to speak of its violent journey. But the loosened stream had lain dormant too long, and no fresh flow sprung up in the sodden turf.

'As I said,' the Prince repeated, as we strode back through the thickening snow, 'everything will be different when you come back. I don't suppose you shall recognize me at all.'

And so I took my leave of him.

And so I had come, in considerable confusion of spirits, upon my journey, three weeks before. I kissed my sister Ruth farewell in the bright doorway in Fischersallee at dawn. She stood, ghostly and light as a cobweb in a white dressing-gown, her anxious twining fingers bloodless in my palm, only her face hot and pink in the cold morning. She swayed a-tiptoe on her left foot, kicking her right leg behind – to balance her chin and lips to my face above her, though I stood on the cobbled street below the doorstep. Dear Ruth, both child and mother to me, for she came bawling into the world through the dark portal of our mother's death. And the terror and cracked misery of her first tender weeks seemed the voice of the mourning which her birth occasioned, as if in those natal corridors she had been privy to the great secrets of chance and fate, whose whispers we spend our lives attending – and these she cried horrible and loud into the world. Now, plump and rosy cheeked at nineteen, long necked, she wet my face with tears, repressing the sniffles of her snub nose with a delicate finger, poked against its tip. 'You shall smudge me,' I whispered, 'see, oh look, the powder has run upon your chin. Be careful of my complexion. You are an armful of damp, of cold and damp.'

'I shall mind your Prince for you,' she promised, her eyes bright with the dew of broken sleep.

'Not too near,' I teased, sobbing freely now in the light bones of her arms. But the knock of my father's stick – clip, clip on the roof of the carriage – and the following crack of the coachman's whip broke the spell of departure. I suffered the lapse of her embrace and fled into the morning.

My father accompanied me to Hamburg, where the snow fell upon the docks and disappeared in the endless thirst of the sea as quick as footsteps vanish behind waltzing feet. We had been silent over much of the long coach-ride, a silence which I attributed on his part to a widower's loneliness – how heavy the absence of his children weighed on him.

'Ruth is blooming, Father – don't you think?' I said once, to turn his thoughts to the child left him.

'Perhaps she shall be married when you return' was all he said.

My silence, I confess, was rooted in fear – at the thought of the scope and reach of the world outside my father's shadow. A sailor had lowered my box into the jolly-boat and his oars slapped against the pier in the swell of the wave, as he waited for his passenger, to row him out to the Leipzig, dipping and kicking in the blow coming over the North Sea.

My father's words to me then rang now in my ears, as I fastened my overstuffed portmanteau (packed with quills and papers, unguents, powders, garments of every nicety and description, a pouch of varied bolus against the sea-sickness, against insomnia, against all manners of discomforts and disquiets) – and waited for landfall, in that empty sleeplessness only a traveller knows.

'Beware of American women,' he said, smiling and looking up, touching me lightly at the elbow. 'And do not be lightly taken in.'

I stooped to him now, with a wet hand against the fat of his cheek – curious, how our bodies teach us pity and love, simply, while our difficult thoughts must scramble to con the lesson – and kissed his

*brow. Then the swiftness of things removed me, after a clumsy,
murky fall, into the bottom of the boat, and the waves receded
against his receding steps, and both bore us away. The large damp
snow did truly glitter in the shine of my weeping eyes, till I hardened my heart anew at the thought of the journey before me – as if
my father had cast me off, and I had not clamoured to be sent. I sat
low and dejected in the boat, nursing with tender hands a bruised
knee, a bruised heart.*

*Well, I thought now, mounting the dank companion ladder upon
legs not so much used to the vicissitudes of the sea as numbed to
them: my father shall see how little good I am to anyone. And I
determined then and there, in the full stubbornness of youthful
inconsistency: to begin afresh in a new world, a new man, unfet-
tered by fathers, and to champion this strange prophet of a hollowed
earth to the ringing skies, never to return.*

*And then, considerably heartsick, and at a loss for misery or hope,
as one may be at a loss for words, I lifted my head into the wind of
the sea, and, stepping on deck, glanced across the confusion of sail
and rigging at America, this New World, up the fat of the
Chesapeake River – bordered by green threshing banks of trees, their
roots crumbling into the muddy waters – towards Norfolk.*

*As we sailed towards the harbour, gently cutting the sleek water
like brown silk on either side of us, I leaned tenderly against the
rigging, so as not to disturb the careful line of my red coat. The
cording was damp, of course, and I quickly withdrew. Lifting a
handkerchief from my breast pocket, I covered my hand and gingerly
clasped a knot of rope to steady myself – then looked towards this
'New World, shining', as our poet has said, 'like the bottom of a
chimpanzee'.*

*Norfolk, as the ship's boy had declared, was a shabby little hole:
the docks stretched hesitantly forth from the shore, as if they did not
quite trust their wooden steps; the few ships themselves looked
rather knocked-about. Most of the craft ducking and shivering in the
brisk morning were fishing smacks, riverboats, jollies. A few small
steamers, curious monsters like floating stoves, shed their black
plumes on the cold air. To be fair, I noted a healthy bustle ashore,*

and stretched my gaze to determine any peculiar dignity
in the activity of these 'free men' – but across the water, the dark
figures, loading and unloading, swabbing, scrubbing, hammering,
binding, barking orders, directions, good wishes, good humour,
declaring their wares and their misfortunes, appeared no bigger to
my eye than the length of my finger, no grander than any men
should be, bent upon their business, in the bleak and the chill of the
winter day.

The stench of the harbour blew across the face of the ship, and I
stood in considerable perplexity, whether to suffer the noxious gale
or loosen my grip upon the rigging, and stand uncertainly, applying
the handkerchief to my nose. At such times I draw on a concoction
of my own preparation, lemon bon-bons dipped in rosewater and a
bath, surprisingly, of parsley. These dainty lozenges, no bigger
between thumb and finger than a single redcurrant, sweeten the
exhalation wonderfully, and drench even the most inadvertent sigh
in balmy melancholy. I keep a small tin upon my person always,
and tapped it tenderly now, in the breast pocket of my red coat. I
consider it also a harmless vanity that the pucker of citron in the
pocket of my cheek lends a contemplative, brooding air to my
slightest expressions, conveys a certain ruminative dignity. I
slipped a hand to the box above my heart and filched a powdered
candy and dropped it upon my tongue, whose secretions produced
a soothing syrup that stilled my fluttered nerves.

A sudden gust – a flurry of white steps across the crests of the
river – tipped the vessel on its heels, and nearly knocked me off my
own. I steadied myself just in time upon the nearest shoulder I could
find, and looked down surprised to see the mottled face of the ship's
boy smiling up at me. And so I clutched him still, as under that
freshened impetus we turned into the breeze, backed sail and cast
anchor in the flowing harbour – reflecting on the great mystery of
propinquity, and how much of our hearts we give to what is at
hand; for I confess the touch of the boy was a great comfort to me as
we rode at anchor in those strange waters. We are never utterly
alone where a touch of man or boy may soothe us. But I had come
thus far to rid myself of comforts.

I released him at last with great reluctance and a groschen of silver – which he accepted swiftly and disappeared. After a considerable and, it seemed to me, quite fruitless fuss, the crew lowered the long-boat against the skittering waves, and into that first our boxes and the packets of mail were deposited, and then ourselves – a handful of passengers, most of them sorry specimens of German manhood, dark-skinned and dirty from the voyage, and reeking of schnapps, singing raucously as the oars beat steadily to the docks. The full ice of my elegance had been necessary to separate myself from them over the long voyage, and I plumed myself at least on the thought that no one could fail to distinguish among us upon arrival. But a fine cold spray blew across our faces from the disturbed and wintry waters, interrupted only by heavier doses when the blades caught the fat of a wave. And by the time I took my turn to clamber awkwardly out of the boat on to the wooden pier, I was soaked through, from the bilge and the spray and the still colder waters of loneliness.

The wind was as chill as bones as I took my first unsteady steps on terra firma. The sun had dipped under a white cloud, and though the air, sharp and clear, promised a suspension from the soft and heavenly assaults of winter, a week's worth of snow lay already on the ground – trampled and muddied by a hundred passing feet. My heart shrank and froze as I thought of the great country before me. The Atlantic is no doubt daunting, but its blank space is a fit canvas for a lonely imagination, and I could murmur Byron and be content. Only when I saw the angles and corners of my destination did I suspect my insignificance. A row of low wooden houses ran along the harbour over an earthen road, foul with refuse caught in perpetual alternation between freeze and thaw. Here, half-eaten joints of meat and rotted vegetables lay caught in a bank of brown ice; there, the passage of horses left a muddy pool of discarded custard for the dogs to lick at. I had reached America.

I held my soiled handkerchief against the nib of my nose to muffle the fetid air, and called for a man, any man, please! any kind soul – bending my tongue with great difficulty to pierce the cold in the unaccustomed words – to help me with my box. This I directed

to be sent by the next mail packet, up the Potomac, to the Dewdrop
Inn, at Pactaw, the home of that 'meteor of American science'
(according, at least, to his petition) the great Professor Syme. And,
having attended to these details, I bent my steps, halting, half-drunk
from long disuse, into the town, such as it was – with my overstuffed portmanteau clutched in the crook of my elbow so that my
delicate hands might stay warm in their thick pockets. 'What has
brought me here?' I murmured, as I dropped another bon-bon upon
my tongue to sweeten the taste of loneliness in my mouth. 'To what
pass have I come?'

Over the course of the long voyage I had dipped into those
delightful Sketches of American Life by the Frenchman de
Crevecoeur – and felt, I confess, considerably cheered by the
prospects he described. 'No sooner', he wrote, 'does a European
arrive, no matter of what condition, than his eyes are opened upon
fair vistas; he hears his language spoke, he retraces many of his own
country manners, he perpetually hears the names of families and
towns with which he is acquainted; he sees happiness and prosperity
in all places disseminated; he meets with hospitality, kindness and
plenty everywhere.' Well, I thought – I have arrived. And I have
met as yet only squalor and obscurity; the marks of enduring labour
and hasty pleasures; houses erected in a week; neighbourhoods cobbled together in a month; roads left to themselves and the seasons in
appalling disrepair; filth everywhere, minded only by loose pigs
grubbing and grunting through the streets, even in the thick of winter; and the people themselves – hearty enough, I suppose, and bearing a rough dignity – dwarfed by the scale of the country in which
they found themselves. Not a word of comfort from my mother
tongue; not a name familar to my ear; and plenty only of snow and
sky and forest and the broad stretch of that enormous river. Little
enough, I found, of the beauties of home.

I discovered myself, in the midst of these musings, at the coach-
house; and, determined to put some part of the way between me and
Pactaw behind me before nightfall, and sick to my heart of the
water, I leapt in at the back of a packed coach and squeezed into a
space on the bench. At first the brisk pace of the carriage and the

comfortable feel of the ground beneath our wheels inspired in me a new hope and I turned, surprised at my own curiosity, to my neighbour – a heavily built farmer, I supposed, by his beefy hands and thick, mud-caked boots, returning from business in town. He wore a squashed hat over his dirty yellow and grey hairs, and crossed his arms comfortably over the protuberance of his considerable belly, as if the stomach had extended for the express purpose of providing a convenient rest for his limbs. In a word (or two), a short, fat man with a broad look of contentment about him.

'Fine country, this,' I ventured in timid experiment upon my unfamiliar tongue. And bitterly cold, I added to myself, as the wind blew about our ears, delighting, it seemed, in the scope of its playing fields.

'So 'tis, so 'tis,' he replied, staring out behind, as the darkening road lost itself in snow and woodland.

'Somewhat large, perhaps?' I queried. The road itself rattled the carriage considerably and ran through forest and broad fields, up and down the low, awkward hills, deep into the vast continent. The sense of profligate space, of excess, of inhuman abundance, almost overwhelmed me; and we often passed several miles before spotting the next glow of a cosy window, or breathing the sweet dry smoke of a chimney fire. The dark had fallen astonishingly swift and full, and there was no moon to light the road, just the glow of the carriage lanterns amid the thousand shuddering shadows that attended them. Only the eerie suggestion of endless snow illuminated the bulk of the land we drove through.

'Room for us all, room for us all,' he repeated, though, in point of fact, he left little for his neighbours to either side of him, squeezed out by the swell of his paunch.

'You haven't', I cried above the rumble of the wheels, getting straight to the point, 'by any chance . . . heard of a fellow . . . by the name of Syme? You see, I've come rather a long way to have a look at him.'

'The Professor?' says he, and my heart leapt – perhaps this American was greater than I knew.

'Yes,' I stammered, 'yes, yes. The exact same.'

'Well, I say Professor,' the fat man continued, 'but I don't know that he's anything like, to be honest. We all call him the Professor, because it pleases him – and there's no harm in a fellow being pleased with himself. So far as I can see. Sometimes I've heard him called better; sometimes worse. The "wizard", for one – though if that's better or worse, I can't say. Then there's "bluebell", on account of that devilish lantern he carries about with him, always digging and burning in fields and what-not. I've had him round my farm a dozen times. A great one for talking on the job, as they say – still, no harm in that, to my way of thinking, and I don't mind taking a sip of whiskey with any man, even if it is my own. Not that I'd trust him an inch with my daughter, or the slaves, for that matter; too clever with words by half, if you ask me. Still, he's clever with his hands, too – I can't deny it. And as I always says, the hands don't lie; any fellow good with his hands got some good in him. It's in the nature of things, you see. And he's done me a good turn or two in the past. Wonderful way with manure, he has – spent a pretty penny on his "experiments", he calls 'em, and I've never been the loser by it. Wonderful stuff – well, as you can imagine, some of his nicknames come from that; but this being mixed company, I won't discuss 'em. Still, I don't mind letting him loose on my land – has a way of finding something I've walked by a hundred times, and, like as not, it'll make me money. And as I say, there's no harm in that . . .' This phrase seemed to be his motto, and carried him through life in amiable if selfish complacency, perfectly content with anything that 'did no harm'.

Well, I cannot say if I was cheered or cast down by this account; but I resolved to question no one else, for fear of the answers I might turn up. The rest of the journey through the white land passed in sleep or a wakefulness so near it that the only difference between them was a dim awareness that the rumbling clatter of the horses gave the rhythm to my dreams. I remember the dreams, too – for they haunted me several days, as dreams do, like shadows following me at every step, dragging behind me, rich and awful shadows thick enough to catch and tangle in my feet.

I saw my father, flushed with wine, turning towards me, caught in some lascivious embrace; and myrmidons and medusas, hags and harlots, sweet pink lasses and glittering ladies flitted before me in awful pageant, each bending their painted lips to my father's face and lingering lewdly in his arms before the dream passed on. His wig had been tugged loosely from his dishevelled grey hairs and lay about his neck; his shirt stained with wine had been torn open to the heart, the buttons scattered; his spectacles (and this in particular struck me as horrible and shameful) were cracked and dangling useless from one ear; and only then did I discern how his bleared eyes blinked miserably into the dark, and turned with fear to the next pale form that folded him in its insistent arms. Then the dream shifted and the women faded like ghosts at dawn and I crawled into his empty bed. When I rolled over to find a patch of warmth under the thick white blankets, I began to sink, and I knew the bed was a white sea, and I fell terribly slowly down until – infinitely gentle – my soft cheek struck the bottom and lay against the hard rock, nodding a little in the echo of the waves that reached the sea-floor, nodding, nodding.

This rock was the farmer's shoulder, which, upon waking, I discovered had cushioned my sleepy head without stirring, on the principle, I suppose, that there was 'no harm done'. I shook myself, suddenly clear-eyed in the sharp, cold air, and thanked him (to which he grunted, as I had expected . . .). In truth, I was glad, for the second time that day, of a human touch, though a brisk application of my handkerchief removed any trace of his dirty collar. How vast the loneliness of an uninhabited country late at night, careless of the tiny creatures who travel through it! We huddle together in towns, puffed up by brick and mortar, towers and minarets and steeples, to shrink the sky above our heads lest we suspect the huge indifference that surrounds us. In the open country there is no mistaking the scale of our pretensions, six feet high in a waste of empty miles. I had a new vision of my mission: the insignificant come to investigate the obscure.

The carriage dragged up a slow hill, bordered by thick brush netted with snow. A line of birch trees, pale as consumption, stretched on either side, and shivered from time to time their powdered necks. A cold wind opened a crack in the clouds and I saw my first stars in the New World: remarkably like the constellations, I must confess, that glittered above the Prince's balcony. I felt them daring me to journey beyond their glance. This seemed perfectly far enough, thank you – though if Professor Syme is in the right, we shall dig to the hollows below and escape them, after all. The snow had stopped; the night had grown almost too cold to breathe in. At last, the sweating horses staggered to the top, snuffing the sharp air in misty snorts; and as I craned my neck round the side of the carriage, a clutter of lights appeared below.

'Not long now,' the farmer muttered, almost tender, strangely softened towards me in my sleep.

'What town is that?' I asked, my tongue stupid with the cold.

'Newton,' he said, in a muffled grunt. And I thought again of de Crevecoeur and his comfortable promise to the European: 'he perpetually hears the names of families and towns with which he is acquainted . . .' Yes, I considered, he is in the right. 'They'll give you a bed at the Grapes,' the fat man continued, 'if you mention my name – O'Day, that is.'

It was then for the first time I realized how easily I could make myself again, in a world of strangers. My every step and word ventured forth without history, declared itself alone, a bright new flag of its author's disposition. The snow itself lay untouched over the barren plains no purer than I – a recent snowfall as it were had covered my rutted lanes and presented a virgin landscape to the eye. For the first time I knew what it meant to have reached America. (Only later considering even Neuburg had once been a new town.)

I discovered the Grapes with little difficulty; indeed, the carriage tumbled us straight into its white lap, a high bank of snow shunted from the roof into the road. Weariness and cold battled in my exhausted frame to determine which should carry the day – the stiffness of the former or the shivers of the latter – and several skirmishes resulted in a divided field. In short, my teeth chattered and my leg slept. I stumbled in a mincing, huddled manner towards the glow within, hugging my portmanteau to my breast. Drawing my watch with clumsy fingers from its fob (a difficult manoeuvre, encumbered as I was), I was astonished to discover the hour had only just turned nine – whereupon a peal of frosty bells rang out from some darkened church, a cheerful and welcome reminder of comfort and home, that saddened me none the less in the wide silence that followed. 'Remember,' called the fat man, doffing his dirty hat and shaking the flakes from it, 'just mention O'Day, no harm in that.' Well, I thought, the Frenchman was right again – they are a hospitable people. (A fact about which I soon had cause for complaint.)

Pushing through the front door, I entered a low room, thick with smoke and cluttered with chairs and tables circled round the central hearth. A broad crackling blaze leapt up from the grate, and an assortment of gentlemanly articles hung from a low fender surrounding it: boots, vests, shawls, coats and even, to my surprise, a single stocking steamed and reeked in the fiery glow. An assortment of gentlemen – I honoured them with the benefit of my doubts – camped around the fender, fluttering their fingers in the grateful warmth: mostly thickset dirty fellows with ham fists and a week's growth of beard. (I confess that the first examples of American manhood I had encountered did not impress me by their native looks or the natural dignities of their freedom. They seemed a squat, dark, bustling race, energetic rather than elegant, gruff not graceful – a plain-spoken people, fashioned for use not beauty.) From time to time, one of the crowd would clasp his burned hands to his knees and let out a hissing sigh of agony and delight as the hot fabric pressed against his skin. They muttered among themselves, though I caught little of their speech, deducing only that they all seemed in business together, of a mechanical nature.

Mr O'Day's name, as promised, assured me of a room for the night. 'We're full up, so it is,' said the matronly creature I had accosted as she bore an empty pitcher to the kitchens, 'but my daughter squeeze into bed with us very happy. One moment, and I prepare her rooms. Sit you down and the good girl bring you your supper so forth.'

The strange turn of her phrases alerted me to her origins, and I addressed her now in our native tongue. 'I have thought it,' she said, 'as soon as you come in. We get no gentleman here, in the old way, you understand.'

Shy of the men huddled about the fire, I asked to take my supper in my rooms, and she assured me she would attend to it herself. 'Their ways are not our ways,' she whispered, touching me on the elbow, 'I understand. But we gets used, you know, we gets used to anything.' So I dripped gently at the fringes of the hearth until I could venture upstairs.

There a small red fire and a large black cat greeted my arrival; and I stripped my dank garments – my fine red coat and soaked cravat – from my shivering limbs and hung them sodden from the edges of the mantle. Setting a three-legged stool in front of the blaze, I perched upon it and summoned the cat with a cold red hand to my lap, where it sat upon my wriggling thawing fingers and fell asleep. I have made a bad start, I thought, in some obscure way, disheartened by my shyness in front of the rough circle of men. My vows to remake myself seemed to have melted already, disappeared as quickly as the caked ice from my boots propped against the grate. I must begin again, I thought, again, again.

The cat had fallen heavily asleep on my leg, and I believe I had joined it, nodding in the grateful warmth – day-dreaming of the many ways in which I might fashion myself from scratch. The extent of the fictions I could practise upon an unsuspecting people spread before me in giddy array – until, in dozy shame, I realized that nothing betrays our true natures so well as the manner in which we hope to fashion ourselves anew. I could do no better than to bide my time – begin in silence and grow gently out of it. The cat himself seemed to concur, purring and stretching his fine limbs towards the shrinking fire, when a sharp rap at the door awoke both of us, with a start on my part and sharp yawl and scratching leap on his.

'Are you ill?' demanded a lanky, hatchet-faced gentleman at the door, tightly packaged in a dirty apron upon which he rubbed the red of his knuckles.

'I beg your pardon?' I answered sleepily.

'Quarantined, perhaps? Or drunk already, and unfit for company?' He batted a fly from his hollow cheek, stippled by pock-marks like a patch of sand in the rain.

157

'Not at all, not at all, I assure you. Quite the contrary. I had only just sat down from a long . . .'

'Then, sir,' he broke in, 'I must tell you that I cannot accommodate you on these terms; we have no private suppers here – you may dine with myself or my guests. We are an open people; our company, I believe, is good enough for ourselves, and quite sufficient for any strangers – so I have been told, at any rate, and see no cause to dispute.'

'I deeply regret causing offence; only you see, the long journey had greatly fatigued me. I confess I was ignorant of the manners of the country, else . . .'

'Our manners, I believe, are very good manners. We don't wish for lessons, thank you. Your supper has been laid out below. I'll ask you not to trouble my wife any more with that mumbo-jumbo you folks like to spit about.'

And so the insistence of mine host accomplished what my own good resolutions could not. After carefully accoutring myself in a sky-blue smoking jacket, still dry, drawn from the depths of my portmanteau, tidying my long hair (my particular pride) and lighting a small cigar in the remains of the fire, I ventured below.

A long table had been laid athwart the hearth, and here the company had assembled, still steaming from their attentions to the fire. I gathered then that the gentlemen I had the honour to dine with belonged to a branch of the Virginia Mining Corporation – which had lately been scouting the valley in whose heart lay Newton itself for coal, manganese and other useful and profitable blessings of the earth. My countrywoman at length brought in quick succession several covered dishes, revealing beautiful red rows of sliced beef, spilling their juices on to the table; these were followed by an equal number of platters containing mashed potatoes and a further cargo of loaves of bread, bending under the weight of their freshness. To all of which the men helped themselves freely, and only my most resolved determination secured for me a portion of the plenty of which I had so lately been dreaming. The company's leader, as I supposed him to be, Mr Mankins – a powerfully built young man with a perfectly pink scalp, somewhat chapped by the cold, a tuft of hair to warm each of his ears, and a muscular jaw, resembling nothing so much as the prow of some mighty ship – addressed himself to the grace. After which, I confess, the silence was general.

At length, the first clamour of hunger had been assuaged, and a low muttered talk passed along the table between mouthfuls: concerning excavations, locations, concentrations and other mysteries of the mining science, not to mention more humorous accounts of pit-falls, floods, snowstorms, collapsed shafts, Indian attacks and such light-hearted tribulations of the trade. To none of which Mr Mankins contributed his views, preferring to confine the operations of his formidable jaws to the nourishment before him. But when at length I plucked up the courage to address the table, I gestured towards his place at the end and raised my voice as loud as I dared.

'Tell me,' I began, gathering breath, 'for I am unfamiliar with the latest American developments in this noble science (forgive me, I could not help overhearing the business you have come upon) – have you ever encountered in your work a device known, I believe, as the "double-compression" piston?'

Mr Mankins brought his masticatory efforts to a slow halt; swallowed slowly; and paused. 'You're looking for Sam, I suppose,' he said at last. The table had fallen quiet.

'In point of fact, I am looking for a certain gentleman; known commonly, I hear, as the Professor.'

'Sam,' Mankins corrected. 'Neither more nor less. Though I won't object to calling him the Lieutenant; which – in point of fact – is what he is.'

'Ach, all that trouble over the steam shovel again,' cried a small, red-faced gentleman at my elbow, while blowing on a fresh hot toddy the landlord had set at his side. 'It's a hoax, I tell ye, from first to last.'

'He's a crank,' came a call.

'A loon,' came another.

'Can't be done!' continued the fellow with the toddy. 'It's a mere question of geometry, so it is. You – Cannot – Build – A – Ting – What'll – Swaller – Itself. Can't be done, gentlemen; God's own law. Simple human nature. And without dat, de device is No Good,

159

to man nor beast. It'll dig a few feet, sure, and do't well; then it goes phtt, and starts diggin' the air. It's a hoax, I tell ye. El Dorado stuff. Geometry's agin it; and you can't fight geometry.'

'Likewise,' Mankins went on, as if there had been no interruption, 'I won't hear a word spoken against him, being, as he is, without doubt, the finest surveyor in the honourable history of the Virginia Mining Corporation, bar none.'

'It's a pipe dream, Mankins,' shouted a gruff, white-bearded old man, 'and what's more, you know it.'

'Don't mind a pipe myself, now and then,' ventured another, a thick-necked, round-armed giant, hunched over his plate, knocking his knees against the table, 'so long as I don't have to break my back for it; which, according to present practice, is just what I do.'

'Seeing,' Mankins continued, unperturbed, 'that if Sam says a thing can be done, it can be done; and, what's more,' he added, raising his voice to drive home the point, 'he'll do it himself. If he says there's coal in that valley, you can bet a dollar to a nickel that what you'll find in that valley is coal, only coal, and nothing but coal, so help you God. If there'd been anything else, Sam would have said so; seeing as he didn't say so, there ain't anything else. If he says –'

'Knock it off, Mankins,' the gruff white-beard declared. 'Let's have a look at this steam shovel of his, if it's so damn'd hot.'

'If he says', Mankins carried on, admitting for the first time by this repetition, however slight, the existence of any interruption, 'he can build a double-compression piston to dig out a vein of rock, then what he'll do is build a double-compression piston. And why will he do it, gentlemen? Only for this: to dig out that vein of rock. If he declares the earth is flat, something'll come and flatten it for him; if he declares the ocean's filled with tea, you may as well get the kettle cooking. Seeing that, without doubt, if he set his mind to it, if he were a feller with any ambitions whatsoever, he could have been the finest miner in the history of the Virginia Mining Corporation. Hands down.'

Whereupon the gentleman with the hot toddy whispered pungently in my ear, 'It's a hoax, God help us. And which of them is the *greater loon – Syme or Mankins? – I don't know. Though, to be fair, that feller had a nose for the land I'd give my eye for.'*

'As it is,' Mankins concluded, mostly to himself, 'God knows what he has become.'

Well, I thought, having retired at last to the comfort of my room – the fire freshly laid, the cat asleep upon my bed – perhaps I shall find out in the morning. There was some consolation in the fact that, whatever his other qualities, Professor Samuel Highgate Syme could not – quite – be charged with obscurity. He had made a name for himself; and who knows, I thought, perhaps I shall make mine, in following him.

This was my first night in America. How enormous the heart of loneliness becomes, swelling as it were into the night, until the darkened country – clicking with snow, gleaming in the lantern light – seems touched by my solitude; and the most casual stranger may enter intimately into my thoughts. Yes, even the unknown gentleman I had heard so much about and come such a long way to find.

I awoke in the morning considerably refreshed and eager to be on my way. A glance in the mirror revealed, so it seemed to me, a brighter eye and ruddier cheek; perhaps today, I thought, I shall forgo a powdered beauty. My coat and cravat both hung dry in front of the dead fire. The cat had kept me warm in the night, and refused now to venture from the bed into the sharp cool of the room, through which odd gusts of wind whistled from the chimney; well, let them whistle, I thought, half in a mind to whistle myself, despite the cold, carpetless floorboards and the chill in my toes. I had a dim sense of such great things to be done – such miles to journey, such fortunes to be made – that I couldn't possibly, not for an instant, consider lingering in bed for another minute.

The room was darkened by paper blinds, of the kind to be rolled up, and fastened by a great perplexity of string to their window frames. These, after a truly philosophical enquiry I at length unbound, and lifted as it were the lid off the morning. A blue sky poured in, whitened only by the puff of my sharp breath and a faint

crumble of clouds in the far air. Such excess of heaven astonished
me; the sky swooped over the low valley, conveying to my impres-
sionable mind an idea of great speed, *as if the stir of the planet*
itself accounted for the whirl of white in its depths. The day was so
clear I could have threaded a long skein through the eye of a pine-
tree needle etched against the blue sky at the top of the bluff.

   In truth, I almost wept at the . . . lust of life that had crept into
my breast, sudden and almost terrifying in its . . . unfamiliarity.
How long had the course of my life run dry?

   I called for a basin of water – and, to the great astonishment of a
boy tending the horses below, threw wide the window and prepared
my toilette in the open air: tossing my hair over my head and run-
ning a dripping (and ice-cold!) hand through the loose locks. The
chill of the morning struck me like a loving blow, a faint ringing
headache ensued, almost pleasant in the delicacy of eye and temple it
suggested; and after fixing the tortoiseshell clasp at the back of my
neck, I turned to the much graver decisions of my dress. A
powder-blue cravat, I thought, would nicely suggest the glory of the
day (this I rustled from the depths of my portmanteau); and I could
do no better, for an air of cheerfulness not unmixed with
gallantry, than the fine red coat hung dry before the fire. (The rich
crimson would soften the eye against the snow, offer a resting-place
from the general brilliance.) Today, after all, I hoped I would meet
Syme.

   Bright and brisk, accordingly, I ventured from my room to the hall
below. The fire blazed in the hearth, a wicked conflagration leaping off
the fresh logs – but the tables were deserted, except for the stacked
remains of a hasty breakfast. The Virginia Mining Corporation had
sped on their way, it appeared, and I was eager to do the same.
Summoning the landlady, I paid the reckoning – studiously avoiding
any suggestion of 'spitting mumbo-jumbo' – and enquired after the
next coach to Pactaw.

   'Oh, my sir!' she cried, in a fluster. 'That's all gone this morning.
Nothing going to Pactaw so late – it's market day, know you, every-
thing's up and gone about. There's a coach coming back, but that's
no good to ye, is it, seen rightly? "Everything always the other

way" – that's my mother's wisdom, know you, and it isn't half-true. Nothing to be done but sitting down and eating the good bread and cold beef; nothing to be done but that. Take a spot by the fire – there now – a thin fellow like you and he thinks he's going forth without a bite to eat!'

I did as I was told and picked forlornly at the plate of cold beef, sipped morosely at the cup of hot tea, and practised a great many other adverbs, beginning in misery and ending nowhere. I have always been – how shall I call it? – a quick fire, given to sudden enthusiasms, flares, that burn out in stink and smoke. The only thing I ever practised in my life with great dedication is solitude (and its associated crafts: chemical experimentations, rambling surveys, mineral collections, and the like) – at this, I seldom flag, and it seemed I would be able to devote another empty afternoon to the fine art. The fire at least practised its chosen profession as resolutely as I, and the two of us, flame and man, gazed at each other, attempting to stare the other out of countenance. The fire, a great advocate of heat, and myself, expert in cold, wrangled and disputed our ground into the afternoon, waxing and waning, thawing and freezing by turns.

But things are never as bad as they first appear, nor good things as good for that matter (a very miserable state of affairs in its own right, I believe); and shortly after one a rather diminutive gentleman, with fair, close-cropped hair and a snub nose, appeared at the door. 'Oh, that'll be Scotch,' the landlady cried, making a great fuss over him, and hastily assembling the materials for a hearty tea: hung beef, chipped up raw (a delicacy much favoured by the Americans, it appeared), and divers sweetmeats of a sugary brown, beside the fresh-brewed pot.

Scotch, if this was his name, blinked his watery blue eyes in gratitude, and lowered himself slowly – and with an air of extreme delicacy and gentlemanly condescension – upon a chair by the fire. 'Perhaps,' he said quietly, 'it wouldn't trouble you to let the air out a bit, Mrs Grapes, before you talk – a deep breath should do – you'll find, I believe, it reduces the bellowing.'

'The thing is,' she whispered to me, in piercing windy tones,

'Scotch from time to time is given to thirst; he suffers greatly from thirst; it is, he says, the curse of his bones, but he bears up, he bears up.'

'I believe the trouble', the little fellow began, turning towards me, in a stiff, very upright sort of way, 'is that I can't get drunk. That, I reckon, is the root of the matter.' He continued in a quite impersonal manner, like a lecturer discoursing on a familiar topic in which he happens to be expert, and whose niceties, even after all this time, continue to interest him. 'I've got nothing against getting drunk, not at all. I believe it can be done – what's more I've seen it done, and have every reason to credit the performances in that line I've had the pleasure to witness. Several of them, I don't mind saying, delivered not far from this spot.' And he pointed, gingerly, at his feet, so I could be in no misapprehension regarding the spot in question.

'You're too good, Mr Scotch,' demurred mine hostess, 'too kind.'

'Not at all, Mrs Grapes, not at all. Much deserved. I'll go further,' he resumed, addressing me again, 'I wouldn't mind – for once – getting drunk myself. A highly pleasurable experience, it appears, enjoyed all round – greatly tending towards the liveliness of discourse, and, as I've heard the poets call it, the free flow of the soul. A consummation – to take up that vein – greatly to be' – he seemed to have lost his way – 'well, greatly to be consumed, to say the least. No, I've got nothing against getting drunk – on principle. Known several highly respectable gentlemen particularly proficient in that area – esteemed gentlemen. No, the trouble, as I see it – to return to my original point – and I believe Mrs Grapes will have the goodness to support my observations –'

'Much too kind, Mr Scotch,' she murmured again.

'Not at all, Mrs Grapes, not at all. Much deserved. The trouble is that I can't do it. There you have it, sir, in a nutshell. And I don't say I haven't tried. Ask anyone about this place – Mrs Grapes'll do – and they'll tell you, with the best will in the world, that I've tried. What's more, they've seen me do it; night after night; but it's my belief, and I don't mind sharing it, that some things can't be learned. There's some things – either you're born to it or you're not,

like poetry, as they say. That's my opinion, anyway. But I keep try-
ing, sir; it's the American way.' Upon which reflection he peered
into the hot mug in his small fist, as if it, too, might choose to fail
him.

It transpired eventually that Mr Scotch, barring his great defi-
ciency, was to have ventured to Pactaw only that morning; and had
no objection to setting forth, belated, as soon as his 'stomach had
settled'.

'The trouble is all this tea about,' he explained to me, as we
eventually piled ourselves into his little trap; and he gestured
vaguely at the heavens above and the snowy fields below to indi-
cate the extent of the problem. 'A terrible affliction to a man's
stomach – most unnatural. I've heard of men who drink nothing
but water – heard of them, only, mind – and fall dead of the dropsy
at thirty-five. Walk on!' he barked sharply, this to the piebald
horse, an aged creature with a long, long-suffering face, who
seemed to share many of the suspicions of his master, and looked
disconsolately at the great road before him, dripping in the bright
sunshine with rutfuls of the offending liquid. Slowly, he bent one
leg, as if to test it – and then the next – and, suitably reassured,
began to experiment with different gaits, a loping stride, a sudden
flailing burst, a limping amble, hoping perhaps to enliven the
journey by way of variety. In this determination, all I can say is
that he succeeded.

Mr Scotch, accustomed doubtless by habit to these experiments,
continued his disquisition unperturbed. 'It's my belief – and I've
read a thing or two along these lines – that if we could only banish
water from our drink, we should feel the benefits at once. Only, you
see, the difficulty is this: water is a sly devil – and slips in when you
least suspect it. Milk, for example, a harmless potation, you
believe?'

I nodded my assent.

'Perfectly filthy with water, I assure you – reeks of it. I never
touch the stuff any more – not a drop. Pure poison – rather drink
wormwood. Or gall,' he added, upon reflection.

These prejudices aside, Mr Scotch (nicknamed after a Scottish uncle who, in point of fact, when pressed, the gentleman conceded to be Irish) was an amusing companion, and an instructive example of his countrymen. He had thought a great deal, he declared to me, of the 'American question'; and as the miles rolled by (shuddered, perhaps, would be a more appropriate term), he touched on several of his views.

In America, he explained, I should encounter almost no ignorance of any kind. The average farmer (a term of praise, he considered, rather than belittlement) read avidly from 'his youth upwards' – a phrase that seemed to include, in Mr Scotch's opinion, no outward limit, but suggested a steady and inexorable and gigantic trajectory of 'self-improvement'. Both boys and girls were seldom seen without a book of some kind in their hands, and were equally ready to discourse upon the arts, the sciences or the latest political matter. 'I should', he furthermore assured me, 'find no evidence either of those sins that beset life in the "old countries", where the lengthy concentration of men in a single place in pursuit of similar objects has produced in the people a kind of – well, if I say ferment, I believe you will understand me.' By these sins he meant: envy, covetousness, shame, pretension, and, in general, all the evils that attend 'getting on'. In America, he explained, 'We get on, as it were, naturally. Our friends congratulate us and themselves, in their choice of friends; our neighbours applaud us, fired by our example to similar ambitions; even our enemies consider, perhaps, they have mistaken our characters, and rejoice. I say all this', he confided in me, 'without prejudice or fear of contradiction – in that I tell you frankly, I have never got on in life, never shall get on in life, never hope to get on in life. I speak impartially upon a subject of common interest.

'Likewise,' he resumed – after a brief and it seemed satisfactory inspection of a small silver flask he kept in his trousers (to discover, I suppose, whether it contained any water or not, in which fear he was gratefully disappointed) – 'we offer in this country none of that abuse heaped upon honest poverty, which is viewed here rather as one stepping-stone (or, in my case, sitting-stone) in a general ascent than as a condition in itself.'

We had reached by this stage the banks of the Potomac and

cantered gently along its side. The prospect afforded that peculiar pleasure in which the best of winter and summer appear to be combined: the clear blue sky and honeyed sun spread sweetly over the sharp browns and glittering whites of February; and now the river multiplied these effects by mingling both equally in its icy bosom. The flow of water – both astonishingly flat and swift – sped against our road and suggested a strangely delightful urgency in Nature contrasted by our own ambling complacence.

Our prospects appeared to inspire my companion to new heights of national eulogy; and I confess I was not unmoved by the picture of American life he proceeded to draw. 'The foreigner, upon his arrival,' he declared, in the jaunty, awkward tones occasioned by his unsteady horse, 'begins to feel the effects of a sort of resurrection. Hitherto, he realizes, he had not lived – only vegetated. Hitherto, he had not breathed – only sighed. Hitherto' – and these mounted in vigour and significance at each step – 'he had not dreamed – only slept. Now, for the first time, he feels himself a man – because he is treated as such. The laws of his own country had overlooked him in his insignificance; the laws of this cover him – cover him' – and he hesitated over the mot juste – 'cover him like a bedspread.'

It was cold and the land about us wild and wide. Yet I confess that, after a brief recourse to Mr Scotch's silver hip-flask (after the careful application of my handkerchief to the nozzle), upon which I performed a similar experiment to his own – as the liquid burned its path to my toes and my fingers' tips – I was not sorry to travel through such scenes with a curious companion who, despite his many failures and vanities, seemed at least conscious of them both. This prompted me to my next question, inspired by the swell of his recent praise.

'And', I said, turning towards him now, this slight man at my elbow, resting the reins in small hands upon his lap, 'is there no serpent in this Paradise, no worm within this apple?'

'Well,' he answered, and then considered again, 'well.' His fair hair shone almost translucent in the winter sun, and he raised his watery blue eyes, both clear and weak, to me. 'Well,' he repeated, 'there may be a certain – there may be a kind of – poverty or scarcity *of – in short – there may be too little – well,' he broke off once more, before finally rousing himself to his confession. 'There may be a dearth of – of – Doubt,' he declared at last. 'There may be too little – Doubt.'*

This admission appeared to loosen his tongue, for he continued now in a kind of steady ramble, looking at the road before him as if entirely consumed by the experiments his horse attempted upon the four-legged gait. 'I believe I myself would benefit now and then from a dose of Doubt.' He spoke the word as a heathen might utter the name of some god, in whom he could summon no faith, yet to whom he did not wish to appear disrespectful. 'Though, as for that, there is little enough in my circumstances to warrant such . . . seeing as I am what I am – a gentleman-farmer come down in the world – living upon what remains of his – inheritance – and his – luck. Some are born . . . idle, I believe, others have it thrust upon them . . . and a few achieve it, after much . . . deliberation.

'No,' he began again, rousing himself. 'There is too little Doubt in this country, though much of what we have achieved is founded upon its absence. You see, sir – we are both a practical people and a faithful people, a powerful combination of attributes, both proceeding from our want of Doubt. The practical fellow has no use for Doubt. He sees a job to be done – knows quite well he can do it – and sets about it. If he don't know how to begin with it, he reckons, he'll figure it out upon the way. A great deal can be managed in this fashion – and, believe me, Mr Müller – we have managed a great deal. (Though I, for my own small part, have done my best to – as you might say – maintain the average.) Likewise, we are a faithful people – great believers in this and that – Gods and galvanism, sir – Progress and Persuasions. We approach the Great and the Small, equally, without Doubt. Only, you see, sir – sometimes between the two – our practicality and our faith – we come a cropper, as the saying is. When our practicality gets tangled up in the legs of faith – and we aim at the moon – upon small steps and – end up in the Mud.'

Indeed, as the sun beat upon the snow crusted in the ruts and the road grew wet and thick with the slop of winter we seemed to have strayed into the very difficulties Mr Scotch described. A fine spray of mud flew from the horse's hoofs to the passengers in his charge; and imagine my despair at the brown mottle of drying flakes that appeared upon the shine of my shoes and the loose hem of my trouser legs. Still, I reckoned (to use Mr Scotch's fine, manly word), for once, that I was a traveller in a far country – and a little mud – now and then, here or there – could only add to my Romantic . . . qualifications.

'The trouble is', Mr Scotch complained, 'that some among us attempt to bring our faith to bear upon our practical affairs. Trusting, as you might say, to luck, and never doubting the upshot of it all. Of – these – am – I,' he confessed slowly, tasting the painful words upon his tongue. 'As you can see, somewhat down-at-heels, perhaps. Idle, yes. Shiftless, yes. Sunk, yes. Never doubting from day-break to day's end . . . the position of my affairs. Quite secure in that knowledge, at least – though I shouldn't mind, from time to time, a dram of Doubt, about This or That – otherwise known as – Hope. Do me good.' And here he unpocketed and unscrewed and, tilting his head, unfilled a dram of something slightly sharper, which likewise seemed to do him – good.

Bucked by new spirit, he proceeded. 'Yet I believe my state of affairs to be downright providential compared with them – that tries to bring their practical talents to bear upon the articles of their faith. That tries to climb, by the skill of their hands, to the stars. That tries to puzzle the way from America to Heaven – just as they might direct a fellow along the best road out of Pactaw, knowing the terrain you see like the back of their hand. For that's the sin of your great American fools – of which we have plenty enough. The prophets and the preachers; the frontier folks; even some of our business tycoons, and the worst kind of soldier. Not knowing what can be solved by a good heart and head – and what can't. The trouble, as I say, all beginning in the lack of Doubt, of one kind or another; though we grow pretty much everything else we can from the old countries, on native soil – and bigger, and better, too.'

Struck, and I confess somewhat downhearted by what seemed to me the aptness of this last remark – given the object of my present *journey* – I observed the first signs of an approaching settlement. The road broadened into fields, covered in snow stippled by the stubble beneath, white and sparkling in the icy sunshine. At the side of the road a heap of rotting vegetables and picked bones, tattered cloth and occasional shoes, strangely sad and softened by their burial in fresh snow, announced the presence of mankind. At length, as my silver watch told three o'clock in the red palm of my hand, we reached a row of scattered houses (which could only loosely be described as a street, a desultory, irregular arrangement) – low wooden dwellings puffing bravely against the winter through their brick snouts. I heard the last shouts of the men as they shut up their wares for the day, bellowing against the cold of the lengthening shadows to keep their hearts and throats warm. And then I saw the market square itself, dirty with many feet and the remains of the day: loose rice and trampled flour, discarded corn-meal loaves, dried strips of beef, and the thick white skins of cheese.

I thanked Mr Scotch for his conveyance, and, clutching my portmanteau, stumbled into the square on bloodless legs. Mr Scotch himself, quickly and quietly, engaged a number of the departing farmers in small talk, pressing this small bottle or that from the little stock he transported in his cart into their frozen and grateful hands. He glanced at me once as I made my way, lifting an eyebrow and a small jar of some warm honey-coloured liquid in the air – as if to say, 'Might I tempt you in a dram of This, or That, otherwise known, I believe, as Hope?' – but I declined his offer, and ventured into Pactaw itself, the home of Professor Samuel Highgate Syme, Napoleon of the New Science, and the end of one long journey, and the beginning of the next.

A bell rang, once, bright and light in the chill air, and I thought how hungry I was. The market lay in a bend of the river, and there were houses scattered along the bank on which I stood in some confusion – here or there as the fancy of the builder took him. Yet they offered a cheerful prospect to the traveller, suggesting solitude and neighbourhood in equal measure. They reminded me of nothing so much as a handful of gulls on a sandbank – an impression conveyed in part by their white wooden walls, and the plumes of grey smoke

that drifted from their chimneys. Across the water, on the verge
almost of the crumbling banks, stood a somewhat larger edifice –
painted brown, boasting several chimneys, and an occasionally elaborated gable, to distinguish it from its fellows across the Potomac. A
narrow bridge stretched and trembled from the market square to its
side; and a low wooden dock broke the water at the foot of the front
porch; a rowing boat, loosely moored, knocked against its post.
Looking up, I saw a perfect fury of smoke pouring from the rooftops
and blowing downriver, tearing into thick strips before it vanished
on the wind.

Idly conjecturing as to the nature of its occupants, I wandered
into the heart of town. There I discovered at last what I took to be
the High Street: a somewhat more orderly row of houses, some few
of which hung from their eaves gaudily painted wooden signs,
ridged by snow and creaking in the wind that swept down the broad
road. These indicated: several general stores ('McSweeney's Foods
etc.', 'Jacks Corner'); an apothecary's; a junk-shop, 'Simmons'; the
offices of at least three lawyers (much to my surprise, each bearing
the wonderfully optimistic motto 'Legal Solutions'); the derelict
windowless shell of what seems to have housed the Pactaw Racing
Times, portrayed by a bright red horse flying over a pot of gold;
and, at last, the Dewdrop Inn, displaying upon its frontispiece a
drop of a very different nature than the example in its name.

To this last I directed my weary steps, and pushed clattering
(beating my snow-crusted shoes against the step) through the front
door into the grateful warmth of the parlour, where the concentrated
heat of an old fire settled and crashed in the grate. A somewhat
elderly gentleman rose from his seat by the blaze, and, leaning upon
a cane, enquired my business.

'Dr Müller,' I replied, 'come from Norfolk. I believe my box has
been sent on.'

Mine host, Mr Barnaby Rusk – a truly fine specimen of old age,
as tall nearly as myself, and though slightly hunched, nevertheless
suggesting, by the breadth of jaw and shoulder, the shadow of a once
powerful physique – insisted upon accompanying me to my room,
and, moreover, bearing my fat portmanteau up the stairs, which, in

combination with his walking stick, made for a very slow journey indeed. His fine pink face, mottled with age and completely hairless (barring the nose), grew bright red at my proffered assistance, and I was forced to succumb to his help. I halted beside him – as he – stepped – and stepped – and banged his stick – and wheezed – and stepped – and banged – up the first flight, though I was by this time eager to be on my way and encounter the object of my enquiry, the great Syme, without delay.

'I was,' Mr Rusk sighed, pausing for a minute on the fourth step, 'you may be surprised to hear, a boxer in my youth – in Camberwell, outside London.'

'Indeed?' I declared, nudging him from behind and shifting the foot of his cane, an inch, towards the next stair.

'Fought – and bested – in the eighty-fourth round,' he grunted, at the landing, 'George Jackson, who died, the next day, from excessive bleeding. Whereupon,' he resumed, after a brief foray down the hall, 'I took flight – and sailed to Virginia. Whereupon, two years later, I fought – and bested – the British at . . .' A fit of coughing, though obscuring the name of the battle, greatly suggested the memory of its violence and the heat of human conflict – upon which description he subsided, and led me on.

At last we had reached my room, a spacious chamber sparsely furnished, containing only the necessary bed, a rude chest of drawers, and a low table, pushed against the window overlooking the main thoroughfare. No fire had been lit, and my breath left little feathers upon the air. My chest stood at the foot of the bed, upon which Mr Barnaby Brawler (as he led me to believe his fighting name had been) deposited, with a sigh, my portmanteau.

'Have you know,' my guide explained, when he had recovered his wind and limped towards the door, 'moved the box up myself. This morning. Fought and bested it, you know – two hours. Don't worry about me,' he grunted, snorting through his thin, bent nose – as if a grave concern for his future had brought me to his doorstep in the first place. Stepping and wheezing and banging down the hallway, he muttered more to himself than his new tenant. 'Don't worry about me, that's all.'

Left to myself at last, I effected a rapid change of dress, donning a cream lace shirt, a rich blue coat and a pair of yellow breeches. The clothes make the man, after all, and I hoped to impress Professor Syme by the refinement of my manners, believing that a touch of the gentleman could persuade even – or rather, particularly – in a society conspicuous for their absence. 'To impress Professor Syme' – the phrase ran through my thoughts inadvertently, and I realized the fever of anticipation that long delay had roused in my blood. I flew through the parlour and into the dripping road, clattering the door behind me.

I took Syme's petition out of my breast pocket and looked it over in the declining light. Two months before, beside another sunny river (now how distant!), I had lifted it from the envelope and marvelled at his braggadocio. Now that I stood in Virginia I read it for the address at its head: the Boathouse, Pactaw. The street stood mostly deserted, aside from the few stray animals that scavenged the rubbish in the snow; and a horse tethered at the door of the apothecary's. A young boy sat on the door-stoop next to the harness post, and I called to him: 'Can you tell me where the Boathouse lies, if you please?'

He looked at me a little queerly and pocketed the coin he had been projecting with his thumb into the air, to the faint ping of glasses chiming.

'Boathouse,' he repeated, ruminating, as if he had heard the name before, liked it sufficient, but was about to think of a better one. 'Boat-house,' he added, emphasizing a world of new meaning in each syllable in case I had missed an ounce of its significance before. 'I'll do one better,' he condescended to explain at last, crossing his legs at the knee. 'I'll give you a piece of advice. I wouldn't bother with the Boathouse.'

'Why ever not?' I declared, exasperated and suddenly heart-sore, having come so far precisely to bother with the Boathouse. Perhaps I should have adopted a brisker tone with the boy, but the worst of being a stranger is this: part of you trusts everyone.

'Why ever not?' he echoed, mincing his words in a horrible fashion, and blowing them, as it were, into the air like bubbles – in some imitation of myself, I supposed. 'I'll tell you why not,' he declared,

173

swinging his leg to the ground and leaning both elbows confidentially upon his knees. 'Because the folks at the Boathouse is all cracked
up, you get me? Because there's always a bang and flash at the
Boathouse, and stinks coming over the river; because the Professor
wanders round town with pistols in his pockets, taking pot-shots at
the trees; because he's got green hands most of the time, and when
they're not green, they're blue; because they say he's diggin' a hole
at the back of his house what'll take him to China; because the river
runs red when it goes by the Boathouse; because some folks say he
can witch yer into thinking anythink he wants yer to think, and,
contrariwise, bring you to disbelieve what you know for a fact to be
true; because he casts spells on young men in particular, till they
don't come home no more, and never gets out of the Boathouse, and
when they do, all the cry is, "The earth is hollow, mind where you
step"; because – and this I seen with my own eye – they keep a metal
dragon back there, clanking and hissing, and ready to swallow whatever come its way; because it's my belief they'll burn the town down
before they through (folks is glad, I can tell you, they live over the
water); because moreover and beyond anything else I've said, it's
gone four o'clock already and you're too late.'

Frankly astonished by the burden of his little speech, nevertheless
I gleaned from this tirade the particulars I desired. Thanking the boy
– who directed his attention once more at projecting a coin off his
thumbnail, while chewing the left portion of his lip – I made my
way (considerably puzzled by the import of his last remark) to the
market square. There the slender footbridge bore me over the icy
flood. I stood at the middle and watched the water hurrying below
me, East towards the Chesapeake and thence into the broad tide of
the Atlantic – in which perhaps, a drop or two might carry even to
Hamburg and lose itself in the spill of the Elbe running cold and
clear from Neuburg. There are few things that suggest . . . regret so
clearly as a fleet river – which can reproach us equally for the places
we have not seen and the distance we have travelled from home. I
was glad, for once, to suffer from the latter reflection; and, dropping
a bon-bon upon my sour tongue, made my way to the brown house
on the far shore.

The bridge ran into a muddy path, considerably trampled and dripping with the remains of the snowfall. Only by clambering up the side (awkwardly, at one point, upon cold hands and knees), where a bank of snow had been packed hard by someone's spade, could I avoid the gleaming puddles. Thus with considerable difficulty I approached unsullied the back of the house, which appeared on closer inspection to be in an advanced state of dilapidation: shutters dangling off the hinge, windows cracked, curtains pressed to the leaking pane, then fluttering free. But a bright glow fell from somewhere on to the snow in the yard and suggested occupation. The porch I mounted (heart beating quick) groaned beneath my steps; the boards had been warped by the damp, and the brown paint covered in a wrinkling spread of mildew. A clatter and bustle were audible inside, and I strained my ear to catch the murmur of voices – low, expectant, the shifting, reverberant hum of a church before the pastor comes. The close heat of a full house seeped through the wooden boards and drew me in. I knocked once, briskly, and waited.

And yet – such is the perversion of the human spirit that I must say, standing there in the cold, I felt some considerable confusion regarding my imminent acquaintance with the object of my long journey. We always hesitate at the door of belief – aware of the great change between the outside and the in. And yes, I knew as I stood there that I had come so far to be persuaded of a new faith – or, rather, for the two go hand in hand, to become a new and less fearful man. Of course, a part of me wished to believe that the obscure and arrogant Professor on the far side of the door, had stumbled upon a great and shining truth, a revolutionary truth, as wonderful as Galileo's vision of the earth – and that I should serve that truth and, perhaps, make a name for myself and my country in the process that would ring through the ages. That such service would entail a more private revolution within me goes without saying. That I should learn to face bravely and, which is the greater skill, with a free and open heart the company of my – yes, my equals; that I should learn never to shrink from the world, never to doubt my place in it, never to give way to that shameful fear of life that had shadowed my youth. Of course, I felt all these things, as I waited at the door.

And yet – I confess that a part of the excitement I felt at the thought of meeting Professor Samuel Highgate Syme was that of – an uncovering, the unveiling of a fraud. Perhaps, I thought, I would shortly discover a man of some irony – a man who lied with exuberance about his theories, with colour, and with that touch of rebellion that makes all his lies seem deeper and truer than the great swarm of mediocrity that comes to prove him wrong. Perhaps I would take him by the shoulder and say, 'Come, come, among equals, you know, there is no need for pretence.' Or better still, I considered, I would marshal the full force of my considerable expertise, hold as it were the mirror up to Syme – in which he would recognize the empty bubble of this hollow world, and turn at last to a more fruitful line of enquiry. Perhaps, then, in some condescension, I would grant him the virtues of the double-compression piston; refine it a little, and bring it home in triumph to my father.

A scramble of steps; a pause, as of a gentleman arranging his attire, catching his breath; and the door, at last, creaked upon its hinges. A thin fellow of medium height with a bird-like cock to his head answered my summons. I noted his features: a broad, high brow above a narrow face, a strong-backed nose and fine, restless lips that sucked upon the stem of a pipe, which stank and smoked, having just gone out. He wore a morning suit, somewhat the worse for wear – covered in gleaming dust, of ash and (unlikely as it sounds) coal, and thin about the knees and elbows. It was also too large for him, and suggested, by this combination of wear and girth, that it may have outgrown him with age, while the gentleman within remained unchanged.

'Professor Syme?' I ventured, somewhat disappointed.

He looked me up and down, and seemed if anything unimpressed by this investigation. He took the pipe from his mouth and smacked his lips. 'You're almost too late,' he declared at last, and slapped his pockets. 'Have you brought fifty cents? Oh, never mind, come in. We'll see about that later. Come on.'

Then I heard a roar from within, a deep, throaty bellow, like a bear in a humour. 'Tom, damn you!' the roar roared. 'Where have you got to? Blast him!' The murmur of voices ceased suddenly; a frightened silence followed, and I could hear the creak of a floorboard where someone nervously shifted upon his feet.

'Damn yourself, Sam!' the gentleman before me called out cheerfully, and, turning to me, lifted the left corner of his lip and the left arch of his eyebrow – as if to say, 'There's more of this smile when you need it.' Then he cried, 'I've brought another. Coming directly.'

'The world's about to stop, that's all,' came the somewhat mollified reply.

Tom, thus appealed to, led me along the dark corridor and then up a short flight of steps. A stout door stood ajar, a beam of flickering light glowing beneath it, whence a thin mist of smoke likewise escaped. Tom turned gracefully upon his heel, and, crooking his elbow behind his back around the edge of the door, whispered to me: 'Don't mind the smoke, sir; we're only making the world from scratch, that's all.' Then he swung into the room and I followed.

Nothing had prepared me for the scene that met my eyes. I entered a large room lit by the cold sunset, which streamed over the river and through the great bay window at the far wall. This space had evidently formed the main tavern of the Boathouse at one stage of its operations, and was a grand chamber still, with a huge hearth great enough to roast a horse at the centre, a fire blazing within it almost as high as a man. A cascade of crystal chandelier hung from the stippled ceiling and reflected the firelight in a thousand flickering ways. The glow trembled like a butterfly, alighting now here, now there, upon this staring countenance or that, among the men and women who massed against the long wall, intent upon the curious operations in the middle of the room.

The heat was palpable, thick to the touch as honey; it pressed against the huddled spectators, whose faces sweated and shone in the firelight. Indeed, a pungent odour of humanity spread outward from the packed bodies, who, to be frank, seemed mostly to belong to the lowest order of men: farmers and labourers, in their heavy boots and work-stained vests, their broad arms crossed, their eyes wide with innocent amazement. Coughs and sneezes and shuffling feet broke the heavy silences, and there were many pinched noses and mopped brows. A pocket of more respectable ladies stood somewhat apart, bonneted and shawled, in a corner of the bay window. I noted in particular the trim figure of a young woman in a blue frock, whose sharp eyes shone despite a complexion alas somewhat ruined by the smallpox; and the more elderly elegance of a lady who had clearly once been a great beauty in her day – and had retained the charms of an ivory forehead and neck, large and trembling blue eyes, and a mouth still full and red, only a little softened by the years.

But the attention of a newcomer fixed immediately upon the fantastical operation under way in the middle of the bare wood floor – a space cleared of the tables, chairs and dresser now heaped together against the wall on my left hand. Tom ushered me towards the mass of men opposite me, an attention I particularly resented; but I drew forth my handkerchief to muffle the stench of the creatures among whom I had been thrust. Crossing my yellow leg behind me, I crouched to the ground, for the twin purposes of obtaining a clearer view of the experiment and ducking beneath the thick of the heavy atmosphere. Tom himself joined the figure in the centre, crying, 'Now what's all this fuss – everything's turning nicely, hey?' To which the Professor – for such I supposed him to be – only grunted before asking him, 'Kindly to quit playing the fool, and give the world another spin, if it wouldn't trouble him too much.'

From my low vantage I had every opportunity to study Tom's associate, sitting no more than half a dozen feet from the tip of my weak chin, propped upon my knee. Allowing for his position, he seemed by no means a tall man. Indeed, he struck me as somewhat below the average height but appeared all the more powerfully built because of that: lantern-jawed, with a brave and stubborn chin, slightly darkened by a day's growth of beard; a straight, strong, unhesitating nose; a thin upper lip bitten between his teeth, above a plump, rosy lower lip; sharp, broad cheeks crackling and shining with animal spirits in the skin drawn tight across them; thick, liver-spotted forearms bared to the elbow, trembling with his exertions; broad shoulders, with a slight hunch like the growl of fur upon a tiger's neck. In short, a muscular creature, utterly at ease in his skin, well suited to the constant struggle of the flesh against the *hard inanity of the world. And yet above his bright cheeks, the finer, more elegant spirit appeared: fair temples, those delicate doors to the brain; a broad and lofty forehead (furrowed in concentration) above the 'O's of his eyes, impossibly blue and large and strangely unhappy – as if they opened too wide upon the miseries of the world. Yes, a handsome gentleman, I confess, and a form worthy of the beauty of his enterprise – a journey through the eye of the mind to the heart of the world. I knew at once I had found my man.*

His dress was coarse and plain, to say the least: loose trousers, much patched and stained; a cotton shirt, filthy with sweat and rolled up to the elbow; a leather jerkin, unbuttoned, and bald in several patches where the fire had caught it; leather sandals upon his feet. It was these that drew our collective attention, and the curious device by which they drove a burning globe madly above his head, spitting fire and smoke like a world reeling free of its orbit.

I will do my best to describe the contraption – I can give it no better name – upon which the Professor, well, perhaps rode *is the only word for it. It appeared at first glance to be a greatly elaborated version of a spinning-wheel. Syme (as I supposed him to be) sat upon a kind of saddle, propped upon a pole – perhaps it* was *a saddle, for the device itself suggested the cobbling together of a dozen common items, rather than the execution of a fresh design. From this vantage, he plied exhaustively the pedal at his feet, beating his sandals up and down – up and down – with such vigour, I half-expected the machine to stand up of its own accord and begin to gallop. This motion accorded his frame a curious recumbent activity, and accounted perhaps for the contradictory suggestions of strain and complacency upon his handsome features. Everyone in the room I am convinced suffered from the powerful illusion that the Professor was – to put it simply – going somewhere impossibly remote and difficult of access – despite the fact that, like the rest of us huddled about him, he had not budged from his spot.*

The spinning-wheel thus driven by his considerable efforts glittered and grinded with speed, and lifted and retracted, lifted and retracted, at great pace a kind of piston or leg, which rose and fell in front of the Professor's face – which suggested somehow the ludicrous expression of a man being dragged from behind by a one-legged horse (though neither horse nor rider of course shifted an inch). I mention this not to demean Syme's unimpeachable dignity (and it requires a wonderfully weighty gravitas indeed not to be unseated by such athletic exertions), nor to introduce an unwarranted note of the comic into this remarkable scene, but to convey, somehow, the joyous quality of the whole. We stared spellbound at the experiment, with the same unconscious pleasure occasioned by a great display of natural power, a flash of lightning or a gust of wind – when some hereditary affinity with the living world moves in us a portion of the delight inseparable from energy of any kind. Yet the wonder of the Professor's invention is to come.

By some arrangement of gears and levers, some confusion of cogs and wheels, the vertical motion of the lifted leg (I'm afraid the device has beggared my scientific vocabulary, and I must appeal to common objects to convey my impressions) had been translated to the circular and horizontal motion of – if I may be forgiven another commonplace – an arm; which held in its hand an enormous burning globe. This it swung in a dizzying circle around and around its – well, the machine had no head, unless it held that in its hands, but – shall we say? – around the absence where a head might have been. The globe itself resembled nothing so much as a smoking (again, it is far from my thoughts to demean the dignity of the experiment, but I wish to set down, as accurately as possible, the physical impression conveyed, for the use of posterity and such experiments in future) colander; for the sphere, composed of some well-fired clay, was holed on all sides like a pricked balloon, and from these cavities issued a thousand streams of black and ashy fume. Upon such clouds, we coughed and choked and spluttered, but held our breath as best we could, to attend to the running commentary issuing from the Professor, who exercised his tongue almost as tirelessly as he pumped his legs.

The most extraordinary part played in these proceedings belonged perhaps to the gentleman referred to (on more than one occasion) as 'Tom, damn you', whose job it was to attend to a slight projection from the revolving globe – a handle, as it were – by which he spun the world as swiftly upon its axis as it whirled along its orbit. He performed this task with great nonchalance, standing idly by in his black suit, only touching from time to time, with the tip of his finger, the flying handle, to send the globe upon another month of imaginary days and nights, a fresh rotation. The effect of these twin motions upon the . . . vines of smoke issuing from the globe was phantasmagoric in the extreme; their soft expanding tendrils entwined and parted, flowered in a thousand sudden springs, and shed their white blossoms in thickening cascades in just as rapid autumns.

Yet the impression of the whole – the revolution of the planet – was indeed far more violent, and, to be blunt, terrifying, than this image suggests. The burning colander whirled no more than a foot above the Professor's head at such pace that the eye grew dizzy chasing it through its arc, whose radius extended perhaps some four or five feet. The pressed body of men leaned forward as it swung away, in an elaborate release of air and wonder – Oh! – and flattened themselves in fear, their breath and bellies retracted, as it hurtled towards them again, almost scraping the hair off their chins as it shot by. A full year passed as swiftly as a man might count to twelve, and encompassed in its revolution an orbit of some thirty feet – which tested the extent of the old tavern, and left few of its corners unlit by the globe's smouldering path. The ladies were glad of their bay window, I can tell you – and stepped deeper and deeper into its darkening recess, as the large winter sun set behind them, and the small world spun before them. Moreover, each touch, no matter how gentle, of Tom's finger sent the smoking planet shuddering and wobbling on its way; fresh gasps of fear attended the perilous launch – it is the only appropriate image – of each new day. In short, all was confusion and terror and delight – and none of us could suppress a powerful sense of imminent and enormous and wonderful disaster, of conflagration and world's end.

The Professor's discourse on the whole tended rather to soothe than excite. He talked as if he had the birth of creation well in hand – as a gentleman might discuss quite calmly, dismissively even, the glories of a picture whose inspiration he has seen for himself. Yes, he seemed to say, this and this is like; this much unlike; this touch falls short, this exceeds the original. In general the effect of his re-creation, he implied, was rather disappointing; there was nothing, after all, like having a look at the real thing. He could recommend it thoroughly, he seemed to say, the next time it came around. Much of his lecture he aimed above the education of his listeners, who belonged, as I mentioned, for the most part to the labouring and agricultural classes. Perhaps he believed their minds would delight as much in the fine words and learning they could not understand as their eyes delighted in the rich display they could not quite believe. I prided myself among that company for following the letter of his demonstration as closely as the burning example he had set before us.

'I will not touch on', the Professor declared, in as measured a tone as the action of his legs permitted him, 'the absurdities of Werner.' (How my heart rose up in protest at this casual slight. I vowed again to challenge so arrogant an upstart.) 'Much to be said for the ocean – author I dare say of a great many fish – very pleasant, too, on sunny days – but hills, no – veins of coal, no – mountains, improbable.'

Here Tom, the fellow in the morning suit gently spinning the world with an idle finger, interrupted him. 'Begin at the beginning, Sam,' he said, 'see how you like it. As in: description of experiment; method; aims.'

'Damn you, Tom,' Syme cried, not for the last time, 'they know quite well what I'm about. Don't you, gentlemen? (Beg pardon, ladies, fully aware, three steps ahead of me at least.) Great sin of your nature, Tom. Can't let a thing speak for itself. Trust the eye and ear, Tom – that's all. Take in much more than the mouth spits out, believe me. Here we are – birth of planet, you see – all the necessaries. Item one: globe, revolving sweetly. (Mind your bonnet, Mrs Simmons, next time she comes round, there we are, lovely red hair you once had, I know, but to colour in this fashion, something painful.) Spinning gently – once a day, Tom, not a month of Sundays at a go, gentle, gentle, as she comes. Where was I? Item one, the world – which we've split down the middle – heaped with coal, burning nicely, hot as hell-fire. Subsequently filled with iron, nickel, manganese, etc., to determine, as she cools, the disposition of the interior.' To be fair, a certain suddenness was unavoidable, given the breathless exercise of his limbs; and Tom, shrugging his shoulders, kept quiet.

'Following Hutton, you see – great man, went far – not far enough. He believed in fire, had a great passion for it – declared it lay at the heart of everything, always burning, never ending. Then his stopped short. Question was: what happens after the fire? As she cools? Question is: are there ends and beginnings, or only a great stretch of middles? (Mixed company – I know, Miss Thomas, don't blush. Speaking geologically, of course.) Is it only repetition, repetition, repetition – or do we get on after a time and come to something else: new beginnings, new ends? As I said, Hutton, old fool, thought not, consigned us for ever to a great moiling and broiling, endless fires and modifications. Very unsettling to the stomach. Nonsense, of course, reasoned thus: anything with a beginning has an end; anything with an end has a beginning.' He paused shortly to let this settle; some of the farmers nodded; this was talking, after all, stood to reason, don't think much about this Hutton fellow.

'Here we plan to have a look at both,' he resumed, still pumping away. 'How are we getting on? Internal fire, wonderful; fluid metallic interior, moiling and broiling, quite delicious, good, good. (Damn me – left out the action of the sun, pulling at the brew. Never mind, never mind, carry on.) Let me tell you what I think we'll find, when tempers cool. In clumsy approximation of the original: the interior separated according to composition: iron, nickel, etc., smooth spheres, rounded by constant revolution like clay at a potter's wheel, ha? Nested in each other, sphere upon sphere, quite hollow, like Russian dolls. If we've spun it fast enough, that is – that's the great thing. The proof of our little experiment lies . . . lies less in my head than my feet – physiognomy of faith, hey? Jog on, jog on, and all that – a merry heart goes all the way . . . There's nothing like creation after all for working at speed.'

This is the best impression I can give of his commentary, ranging as it did, quite democratically, through such broad zones – and

183

appealing, by turns, to the greatest and least of his audience, myself
included. He had a rich, deep voice, somewhat patrician indeed, and
faintly clipped by the edge of – I conjectured – an English accent,
though the breadth of his vowels and the heavy intonation of his
first syllables were patriotically American. He spoke well, I suppose,
if rather abruptly, as one who could summon his thoughts quickly
and dismiss them lightly, willing slaves all. And there was a kind of
intimacy among his conjectures, as if they all got along quite well
together, and managed to survive, through the force of long habit,
with scarce a word said between them. Unfortunately, we did not
share this intimacy; and I often had the sense, then and later, in lis-
tening to Syme, of having stumbled upon a family of thoughts,
brothers, sisters and cousins, among whom I hesitated to address
any of them singly, uncertain of their relations to one another.

He spoke, I must add, with a certain peculiarity, which struck me
sensibly at the time and ever after absorbed my interest: he held his
head as a blind man might, upright, gazing steadily before him, as if
his audience, though plentiful and just at hand, were somehow
beyond him, out of sight – indeed, almost as if he feared to look his
company in the eyes. As if – as if – now for an absurdity of my own
– as if we filled his head and not his house, and he teased only the
creatures of his own imagination, and never the thick flesh and
blood sweating in the room.

At last even his powerful frame appeared to flag; the zest had
gone out of the years, and the world spun gentler now, spilling less
heat and ash upon its way. 'Perhaps,' he gasped, quite red in the
face and sweating freely now, 'I'm not quite up to creation yet, on
my own. Another minute – there – suppose we're all well cooked by
now. I need strength even for the cooling down. (Especially for the
cooling down.) Where are the buckets of ice? Attend to them, Tom.
Shall we, gentlemen, ladies, prepare to observe the end of creation,
the beginning of the world? Mind the smoke, of course.'

Several buckets of snow, largely melted, stood at Tom's side – a
precaution I had supposed against the hot ash flying from the
spinning globe. (Indeed, the black streaks of divers trampled fires
marked the broad floor, where a particularly blazing particle of coal

had fallen from the punctured sphere and burned away.) But I found now that I had been mistaken. Tom gave the globe an almighty thrust as it shot by, and then stooped to one of these buckets at his side – a great slushy composition of ice and water dusted by snow. He lifted it two-handed roughly by the lip and . . . and – what happened next I cannot describe with any precision. I suppose I saw the globe wheel burning towards him; I saw him lift the pail above his head, as the black tail of his suit slid up his rump; and I must have observed the first sudden cascade of ice, delayed an instant as it stuck against the wooden sides, before it came crashing down upon the burning planet.

The ice, I believe, was to blame; not Tom. He had not accounted for the solid block it had become, had hoped, no doubt, to tip a scattering of snow as the world came by, and cool the planet piecemeal, a little each year, as it were. As it was, he might as well have hurled the bucket at the globe and been done with it – not that we could see much of what followed. There was, at first, a tremendous hiss – as if the full ire and venom of the world had been roused to spitting vengeance. The smoke, the cloud that arose, as thick as nightfall, was instantaneous, and filled the room, blinding us all to the catastrophe to come. We heard, of course, the screams; mostly from the direction of the bay window, though I confess, guiltily, to a slight yelp. Each of these echoed and swelled, magnified immensely in our imaginations by the darkness, the stifling darkness – though again, darkness is perhaps an inadequate description of the lurid sightlessness to which we were confined, as the fire blazing in the hearth cast its red and flickering glow through the muffled air.

We all heard the crash; and I dare say most of us guessed at once what it portended, though we could not see the fallen planet at first. But our eyes grew accustomed to the pall, and as the burning entrails of the cracked globe spilt upon the floor, we saw it too, splitting as it rolled towards the mass of men against the long wall, myself included. I suppose, in retrospect, I can say that we had little to fear; one or two of us suffered a slight burn from the scattering of molten ash; nothing more. But by this point our imaginations had been lifted to such a pitch, and our identification of the ball of fired clay with our own planet was so powerful, that we could not suppress a sense of the apocalyptic, in what was, after all, nothing more than a geological experiment gone slightly awry. The globe smouldered and disintegrated as it rolled towards us – both unavoidably, it seemed, and unbearably slowly. It trailed smoke and fire, spilling its red guts with every revolution; it split into jagged fragments that spun as they settled, bearing each one a little dish of white-hot coals; it fell open at last at my feet, spent and cracked to the heart, and died visibly before our eyes, as the thick red blood running from it grew white and then black and then grey.

The first distinct words I can remember hearing, barring the general coughing, screaming, gasping, shouting of the terror-stricken crowd, were – 'Damn you, Tom!' spoken with a compressed power of emotion quite unlike the casual tone of his previous imprecations. Spoken quite quietly, in fact, as the Professor, still pedalling idly from time to time, squeaking a little, sat in his saddle and surveyed the wreckage. Tom, meanwhile, had accomplished the first sensible thing to be done, and opened the broad bay window. How cold and grateful the wintry gust appeared, thinning the cloud of smoke and cooling many an overheated brow! How quickly we became gently cold, then simply cold, then decidedly cold, and then bitterly, achingly cold, as the sweat dried upon us, and the first faint bells of the headache rang between our temples. By this time, Tom, swishing his coat-tails behind him, had scuttled about the room, stomped on the clusters of fire burning away upon the floorboards, and emptied the remainder of those icy buckets over the larger fragments of the shattered globe. Most of which, unfortunately, lay at my feet; which were, along with the legs attached to them and the fine yellow trousers encasing them, well soaked by the icy waters and covered in a curious sooty mixture of coal-ash and leftover snow.

Tom was tireless and, at least to my disgruntled glance, strangely exhilarated by the catastrophe, crying out, as he ushered his assorted guests from the room, 'A proper first-rate show, I believe, ladies and gentlemen, splendid, splendid – the best show for fifty cents from here to Baltimore! A truly scientific disaster, unplanned, unpremeditated, unrehearsed – over and above the

*entertainment offered on the bill. Confidentially, if I had known, I
would have charged a dollar, ladies and gentlemen, two dollars a
head, for a show like that – the best Apocalypse in town, in the State
of Virginia, in the Union itself. As much fire and smoke as you
please – world's end, conflagration, and I don't deny it, a little spice
of fear, mixed in the pot. Mind your step as you go! Let the word go
round – Professor Syme himself, lately of Yale College, by a rare act of
condescension, explains the Universe to Pactaw! Come again!'*

*And then, for I lingered above the smoking globe and heard, still
more quietly, and with a deeper rage, from the slumped figure on the
saddle who had not budged, 'Damn you, Tom.'*

*I confess the recent display had done nothing to alleviate the
confusion under which I laboured; indeed, rather than resolving
me one way or another, the experiment had fuelled equally the
suspicion that I had come upon a charlatan practising a hoax
and the faith that I had discovered a Galileo of Geognosy, a pioneer
of the internal world. So intimately bound are the faculties of
belief that we can often exercise and strengthen both faith and
doubt by a single action of the mind, intensifying both, and the
conflict between them. At least, I have found this to be true with
respect to me.*

*At last the room cleared – two of the ladies in particular (the
pock-marked girl in the blue dress and the aging beauty) hesitated at
the door, and took rather less . . . scientific leave than the others.
'No,' the girl declared, stomping her foot lightly, 'I don't understand it, and I won't understand it. Nothing was proved; a certain
. . . difficulty in creation, that's all; a way of going wrong.' (Did a
quick kiss from Tom persuade her otherwise?) The fading beauty,
moving melodiously in a faint cloud of her own chiffon, remarked
only, 'I have never seen such wonder, Herr Professor; it was – as
if – the stars had become our playthings – you know?' There was a
certain lingering at the door; and then the silence of near companions
alone again. When I had dried, as best I could, my soaked garments at
the blazing hearth, till I fancied my legs glowed like roast pig
beneath their trousers, I ventured to introduce myself to the great
Professor and his assistant.*

They for their part seemed rather surprised to see me, having fancied themselves, I suppose, finally rid of their goggle-eyed guests. Tom, however, recovered his humour quickly, and declared, 'Why, this is white of you. I had forgotten completely – fifty cents at the door, lost in the hurry. Splendid, splendid . . .'

I quickly disabused him, though strangely shy at last of a proper introduction. 'No, I'm afraid, sir, you mistake me. You', and I declared this as grandly as I could, puffing my blue chest and tucking my hands behind my back, 'have sent for me. Dr Friedrich Müller, at your service; come from Kolwitz-Kreminghausen.'

The smile never faltered on Tom's fine-boned face. 'Splendid, splendid,' he repeated, a great favourite of his, I discovered, and variously applied. His use of it, aided by the natural sunniness of his disposition, was curiously persuasive. In short, it rubbed off on one; and, after a time, one could not help but feel rather splendid around him, among splendid people, in a splendid place. (This despite the fact that a vile, damp, chilly smoke lingered in the room; the fire was dying; a cold wind blew off the river through the unclosed window; a muddy soot of trampled ash covered the burned floor, among clay fragments of the world; and I distinctly heard a weary mutter, 'Damn me, never heard of it,' under Syme's breath.)

'Sam, Sam,' Tom cried, lightly at first and then with sudden sharpness, as his colleague warmed himself, slumped, in front of the fire. Sam turned partly round, lifted his head above a lowered shoulder, and smiled a faint smile that died long before it could reach his cold blue eyes. 'Tom Jenkyns,' Tom introduced himself, pushing the sleeve back from his wrist and taking me vigorously by the hand. 'Professor . . . Mooler, I believe, from Neuburg? A protégé of the great Werner himself, unless I'm mistaken,' he continued, drawing me subtly towards his master, until Syme and I had exchanged a similar salute.

The Professor seemed to rouse himself, and asked with a sweeter smile, 'Author of that excellent little paper – somewhat longer title – on the convexity of the seas – internal architecture, etc. – dose of Werner, with a drop of Jameson, no? – wonderful etc. stuff . . .' I remarked again upon the peculiarity in his manner, for he would not catch my eye, but stared, quite happily it seemed, at a fragment of the world that had fallen to my feet.

'Thank you,' I said, not knowing what else to answer. And yet – shall I say it? – strangely pleased, flattered even, by this knowledge, as one may be by the acknowledgement of a – superior. As I stood beside him for the first time, I noted – unless this were my fancy only – a sweet scent about him, like the odour of shaved wood, both slight and powerful at once, and, above all, warm with his recent exertions. I could not help an impish desire simply to catch his eye. But he swung away from me once more, strode briskly towards the window, and shut it against the cold coming over the river.

'Never mind me,' Tom said, as he stepped out of his black coat, hung it gently over the edge of the door, and grasped the handle of a broom hidden behind it. He began to sweep the damp soot into the centre of the room, would bustle swiftly into the dark corners and then, like a dancing wave, move towards me again, scratching, scratching, chatting all the time.

'I have heard such splendid things,' he began improbably, 'of Kolwitz-Kreminghausen. A little state, I believe, on the rise?'

'It suited me, once,' I declared, to my own surprise, wonderfully happy to talk of my home among these strangers. 'A small place only, it is true. A potatoes and candle place, actually. The heart of the North German wax industry: famous for the lightest, the most mysterious and ethereal of candles. And famous too for the best, the earthiest potatoes.'

'Splendid, splendid,' Tom said, sweeping, sweeping, as if I had gratified him deeply by this account and he were much obliged. This was always his way; and I have never known since a gentleman so deft at putting a stranger at his ease. This he accomplished by the wonderful combination of two rare gifts – a natural curiosity and a studied (I can use no better term to describe the care he took with it) sincerity. 'I believe your lot have set up a brand-new university on the – pardon me – Elbe. This is just the thing with us, sir; there is nothing like learning, after all, wouldn't you say? Though perhaps Sam would disagree?'

'Not at all, not at all,' Sam answered, staring darkly at the river with his back towards the room. 'Though I have never favoured what you might call a "factory of education". A thing can only be learned – learned by the root – contra mundum. There is that in the nature of man – which imperceptibly adjusts – even the most original conception – to the general understanding – or rather, the general misunderstanding. What you get is – in short – slush.' Then he turned, smiling broadly, 'What would your poet say, Dr Müller?' Upon which he succumbed to what at first appeared a most painful coughing fit, though, in point of fact, I believe he meant to say: 'Noch so ein Kerl wie ich, und die Welt geht zugrunde?'

'I have got that by heart,' he continued, in his abrupt manner. 'Wonderful man, your Schiller – they put on The Robbers at the Dewdrop last summer – I shouldn't have missed it for the world. So – droll. Barnaby Rusk himself (your host, I believe?) declared – it was like going eighty-four rounds – with George Jackson – only this time – he thought he lost. Lest you despair of me – as a hopeless misanthrope – I should say – I have a great faith in man – particularly your American man (or mine, rather) – though little enough in men, I confess.'

The Professor squatted before the fire, rubbing his hands; then sat down gently on the broad stones in front of the grate. He had a restless frame, I soon discovered, that required constant revisions. Idly, he lifted a fragment of the burning planet that had fallen towards the hearth and studied it, turning it in his palm.

Tom meanwhile had busied himself about the room, and brought it to some degree of order. The table had been pushed into the bay once more, scraping across the boards, an operation which seemed to concern Syme not in the slightest, and for which I had been too shy to proffer any help. Chairs, likewise, were restored to their place, along with the large dresser – and a rather wretched sample of cups and plates returned to its shelves and hooks. Tom picked up the broom again and formed a small heap from the broken shards of the globe in the centre of the floor, which resembled nothing so much as the remains of a great grey egg, from which the chick had escaped. The scrape and swish of broom-straw on the boards seemed to me *wonderfully soothing, and for the first time I felt, standing against the fire – well, I know not myself what I felt – only that, perhaps, something expected had yet to occur.*

'Now,' said Syme quietly, to his own hands, 'what shall we talk about?'

I have such a heavy-handed soul, and could not refrain, despite an underlying wish to the contrary, from entering at once upon an examination of the theories that had brought me so far. And so we talked, beginning with my beloved Werner, and the question of the fluidity of the earth; moving from thence to an account of geological time, succeeding epochs that correspond to the variety of mineral deposits discovered at divers strata of the earth's crust, which I ascribed to distinct precipitates of the universal ocean, he to an igneous origin; turning at last to Hutton's notion of continual mod-ification, the effects of internal heat, and finally, the experiment per-formed that afternoon, which attempted (with such dramatic failure) to discover a possible conclusion to the Plutonic system, which, the Professor confidently maintained, could yield only a hollow earth, composed of distinct metallic spheres, nested within one another.

So we talked; as the day turned black without; and the fire died down within, settling against the grate; and Tom swept. And I could not suppress in myself, growing and swelling in proportion to the diminished blaze, a sense of – a sense of frustrated – a sense of vehement – an utterly righteous sense of – of outrage, at this obscure and cock-sure gentleman before me, who declared with such dismissive ease that the greatest minds of the century had laboured in absurdity and error, while he – and he alone – in this remote corner of a barbarous land – from this dilapidated vantage-point – a run-down old tavern above the Potomac – had hit upon the exact truth – and what's more, would prove it, by a series of practical experiments (presumably, after the spectacular fashion of that after-noon's disaster) that would re-create, in a small way, the birth of time and of the world.

'How dare you?' I spluttered at last, trembling violently, and striking the back of my hand upon my palm. 'How dare you – assert with such – reckless confidence – that the father of geognosy himself

– a gentleman I had the privilege to know, and the honour to revere
– of magnificent intellect and unmatched practical intimacy – I can
use no clearer word – with the workings of the planet – stumbled all
his life in utter darkness, while you – while you . . .' Words failed
me here, a lucky chance perhaps, as who can guess the depth of
insult to which I would have descended? And in spite of everything,
I have prided myself always upon a certain decorum, and the manner of a gentleman.

Syme for his part seemed unconcerned at first by the temper to
which he had worked me. He turned the shard over in his hand, as if
some aspect of it struck him afresh, and observed quietly in his
piecemeal fashion, 'I dare quite simply – thus – certain that the one
fact – indisputably true of every child (and every nation, for that
matter) – at its birth – is this: that all the world is wrong – and I
have come for myself – to see what is right.'

My outrage had spent itself by this point, and indeed, Syme's last
words had strangely mollified me, when Tom began to sweep the
broken shards upon a cloth laid down for the purpose. 'Gentlemen,
gentlemen,' he urged, in a way that suggested to me nevertheless
that he partly delighted in each exchange as a boy delights in fire,
'there is time enough for such disputes, which run all the smoother,
I believe, on a full belly and a pint of porter.' He lifted the cluttered
cloth and tied the ends in a loose knot and made his way towards the
window. 'Might I suggest . . .' he began, when a roar of Syme's
diverted rage interrupted him.

'Stop at once,' he cried. 'What act of ignorance – of wanton waste
and destruction – are you about to commit? Answer me, Tom.
Indeed, there is no fool like a happy fool; and all you can do is stand
there, grinning idly. Give that to me directly.' And he snatched the
parcel from Tom's hand, and spread it over the flagstones before the
hearth, adding the small piece in his palm to the suddenly precious
collection. 'It is not enough', he continued, bitterly, 'that my experiments are botched – by his clumsiness – my studies interrupted by
his circus antics – but that his ignorance – his really rather astonishing ignorance – don't you agree, sir? – must be watched, constantly, like a young dog – lest it foul this or that on its way.'

'Splendid – splendid,' Tom said, standing quite straight and still, his eyes beginning, ever so slightly, to shine. 'Perhaps, Dr Müller, we should resume in the morning? I will take you home.' He set his broom against the wall and lifted his coat from the door. Syme squatted above his broken world and examined each piece of it, carefully and individually, in his hand. And so I – so we – left him, and ventured into the cold.

The snow had set hard with the frost, and we slipped and scrambled along the path towards the slender footbridge. Tom's spirits, naturally buoyant, had risen to the top again. 'It is only his way,' he said, taking me intimately by the elbow. 'Everything must end in upset – it soothes him, you know. There are such great things still undone, a little storm here and there, now and then, I would almost say, reminds him.'

'I have known such gentlemen,' I answered, thinking briefly of my Prince, so vast a stretch of water and wind away. Then, stung into a pettiness, by some concern for Tom himself (or envy of his station at Syme's side?), perhaps a hint of homesickness, I added, 'They rarely end happy.'

'Oh, never fear on that score, Professor Mooler,' Tom replied, untouched by whatever curious whim had moved me. 'Sam will make a grand old man, a grand old man.'

And then he ventured on some particulars of his own history as we walked, still arm in arm, along the empty street. 'I'm a newspaperman, actually,' he confessed, somewhat shame-faced. 'None of your great scientists, like the two of you. Of course, Sam was a very promising – sensation. My editor told me to look into him' – he reckoned slowly through his altered life – 'three years ago this spring: "The Man who Thinks the World is Hollow". I fell in love with the whole thing, and quit my post directly. Sam (the Professor, I should say) wouldn't hear of it at first – but I am a businessman, you see, and Sam isn't anything like one. He needs me a little, at least; and for me, well, there is nothing like working for a true cause.'

Then he stopped and turned to me at the door of the Dewdrop, and addressed me with the discomfiting honesty of the enthusiast. 'You have come a long way,' he said, 'but I believe you have guessed already that you have – found something. I wish to commend you, Professor Mooler (and thank you) for, well, if I say "your faith", you will know what I mean.'

I hoped to disabuse him, gently, of this confidence (though I could not say even then he had not hit the mark). But, strange to tell, a soft light fell instead upon my darkened heart – from, as it were, an opened door.

I returned to my room, now blazing with a cheerful fire, and called for my supper. There was no fuss about country manners and common dining here, and Mr Barnaby Rusk duly arrived bearing a plate of cold beef and cheese, slowly and with great deliberation, as if to assure me that his whole being had been bent upon the task. By this time I was as hungry as a shepherd, and ate with an appetite sharpened for more than the food that lay before me. I had never known such delightful hunger as I knew then, upon my second night in America. And I supposed that I had Syme to thank for that at least, as I called for a dose of rum in my tea.

This I set beside my bed when it arrived at last. Tenderly disrobing, I laid my blue coat across my knees, and combed the lustre back into the fine wool – catching the dirty snow and the ash and even the smoke in the fine teeth of the brush. Then I hung it upon a hook. A similar application succeeded less well with my yellow trousers, whose legs suffered greatly in the planet's drenched decay; but there was nothing to be done, so I draped them across the back of the chair. Slowly the room took on a familiar appearance, and pieces of myself occupied this or that corner. I shook out my hair and put the tortoiseshell clasp on the table, where it gleamed a little when the fire-light caught it. I confess there is great comfort in the embrace of a night-gown; and I was sore in need of comfort, as I looked out of the cold window, over the dirty, snowy, moonlit street.

Perhaps I was only homesick, a green foreigner, confused by fatigue and strangeness – and indeed, I appeared to myself as a thoroughfare, windy with unfamiliar longings. (I find it hard to write the idea I now have in my mind; but I will try.) Perhaps if you understand my homesickness, you may hear part of the call Professor Sam Syme made to me on that first enormous night when *each piece of the traveller's soul wishes to be touched by some native comfort, and shifts and changes, reaches and shrinks back, for consolation. The image of Syme, the picture of Syme bent over the ruin of his grand experiment, declaring that 'The one fact – indisputably true of every child – at its birth – is this: that all the world is wrong – and I have come for myself – to see what is right . . .' moved me, as I lay in a foreign bed, to the notion that I had come and FOUND SOMETHING. Tom was right. Misguided or not, Syme was a man to whom the questions of life* were *questions, which a man desires even when they have no answers, as he desires land, bread, and love. So I turned at last to the tea at my bedside, sipped and lay down, shifting the warming pan from my feet. And I slept with great hopes of the morrow, and the weeks to come; if I was disappointed, it was not a simple disappointment.*

To the Reverend William Jenkyns:
Pactaw, Febr. 1826

My dear Father,

I thought perhaps it might please you to know that our little company has received a significant addition in the past fortnight. A German gentleman, a certain Dr Müller, and once a protégé of the great Werner himself, has arrived to look into the question of Syme's theories, and adapt them it may be to the service and renown of his own country. In truth, he is a curious specimen, long in the neck, and much given I believe to ruffling his feathers; a great dandy, forever preening himself, and admiring his image whenever we pass a window or a glass. But rather in a nervous hopeful manner, than as a confident fellow giving himself airs. The Germans are an odd lot, I declare; one never knows when their humors begin and their philosophies end. But he seems a sharp creature, if a little silent now – a real Werther-faced gentleman, somewhat lovesick looking, as if he left behind a decidedly tender Lottie.

I suppose the only fly in the ointment – or midge perhaps – if at all, is, to be brief, thus: I cannot help feeling somewhat left in the cold when they babble their geologic hocus-pocus and I lag a dozen paces behind. And a time may come – and the better we get along, the sooner that will be – when he has no use for me, and it is such gentlemen as this Dr Müller who keep his company. (Though, as for that, I cannot imagine Müller himself would hold Syme's attention long, vain and silly bird that he is; only *such* as he, you understand me.) Nevertheless, I write in excellent spirits, and on the cusp, I trust, of great things, though you doubt, Father, though you doubt, as is your way, I believe.

Your faithful son,
Tom

EVERYTHING, I'M AFRAID, needs a *reason* to endure rather than the reverse – not a great reason, nor even a good one, but some touch of luck or logic, the most common being this: attachment, by hook or crook (or, in this case, *book*), to genius or fame or riches or God. These are the four great preservatives of memory. There is a fifth, a slighter fifth, a poor country cousin, or pinkie on the hand of memory, and that is love, which grasps little and releases lightly, but must be mentioned nevertheless. Tom's letter got stuck in with God; but this is a later story. Sufficient for the day is the thought, subtly suggested by Tom to his reverend father, that the welcome even of strangers brings some confusion with it, some residue of reluctance – though nothing compared to the welcome of lovers, or husbands, as I discovered, shortly after touching down at Bergstrom Airport on a wide, hot night in Austin, Texas.

Where Miss Susie Pitt would greet me after an absence of almost nine months. She would wait, as I had requested, in the white Volvo stationwagon – which suggests to me always an echo of the soldier-poet's wonderful line, there is some corner of a foreign parking lot that is forever Sweden – under the overpass, beside the carousel. Not at the gate; I never like to be greeted at the gate, for the simple reason that I am pink, and a little ugly, and quite shiny, and I sweat, four facts curiously smudged together like leftover cake by air travel. So as I stepped off the plane and into that rumbling corridor – the rite of passage of modern travel that bears us from jet to terminal, from the incredible to the institutional, to deaden the enormity of arrival – I knew no familiar eye would 'clock' me at the corded lines. Gathering my legs beneath me, I ducked into the first WC and stared at my face in the broad mirror: pink, as I had suspected; sweaty, as I had feared; wide and empty eyed with sleeplessness, as I knew; and yes, hesitant with homecoming, as I had guessed.

A handful across my blinking face of water, and then I pressed the skin beneath my eyes (which seemed to sag with the weight of seeing, an almost palpable burden), thumb and forefinger rubbing down either slope of my thick nose. (The thought occurred to me that we sleep to let our eyes be emptied of junked images, and flow free and spacious again; and that when we cannot sleep, they grow thick with clutter.)

'There is always a push as well as a pull,' Friedrich had written, and in this belief, at least, he was not mistaken. My wife and I had parted, on a bright blue day of Texas winter, on uncertain terms. How much I would give for *certain* terms, a precise knowledge of the rules of intimacy, and the concessions made to thee and me. But no, the terms change, are broken and appealed to in equal measure by differing parties, and require in any case constant renegotiation. 'Why, having won thee, must I woo?' Coventry Patmore enquired, and I echoed him, at a romantic meeting of our little Blue-stocking Society. (A choice, I am proud to say, that produced a flurry of curious requests: Coventry, they cried, who?) But I would ask rather why, having wooed thee, must I win – again and again, the same ground, only to lose it again.

This ground, in point of fact, is plain enough to the casual eye, and the battles pitched upon it, for an inch of land, now here, now there, may be listed, briefly. Viz: she believes she has sacrificed herself for my career, which I squander and refuse to 'make good'; she does not wish to live in Texas. I argue that I have squandered nothing, that 'good' is not easily made, is rare, is precious and fragile, is too strange a thing to be fashioned by a career; that for my stubborn, dogged insistence on the obscure, the unfashionable, the unlikely, she loves me; that what is given freely – her years of teaching, our years of tight living – cannot be retracted sourly; that I conceded to her ambitions, first once, then twice, and though these blessed boys are the boon of my heart, they are the bane of my head and our purse and my untouchable faith that a great, and not simply a good, life lies at my feet if only I stumble upon it. *Our* feet. That regardless, the bones of her contention break upon one another, as tenure at Texas is an honourable end, offers a good life, according to her construction of the phrase; that we cannot live so wide and well in New York; that (and this I dare scarcely whisper, even to myself) she lacked such dreams as I nurse tenderly, she offered no scale of *ambition* to rival my own; that she has sacrificed nothing, but a stertorous bus-ride, along 86th Street and across the park, to her mother's flat.

What truce could we reach, what pax sign? As Auden noted, to ask the hard question is simple. And then the Fulbright came, granting me the time and occasion to study the roots of Wegener's revelation, and trace them to their tender tips; and then I set forth for England, towards the heavy catalogue, miraculously preserved, of Alfred's childhood haunt, the library on Friedrichsgracht split open by Allied bombs and tipped into the canal; and thus I hoped to publish at last and pluck the flower of tenure from this nettle, academe, resolving, at least, the first point of our dispute: those squandered ambitions. But I did not guess then what I would stumble upon, when I kissed her farewell on a clear January day, and she wept so clear, and free for once of anything but love.

Solitude . . . unmakes us, and I had tinkered happily with the pieces, hoping to build myself from scratch, a task required, I believe, every several years, in order to keep the hands busy and the soul new. Until such time, of course, when the study of living architecture reveals to us our final shape, and we construct at last, tenderly and surely, the monument of our lives, trusting it will endure. Such time, I believed, had come for both of us at last. For Syme and me, that is.

I saw her through the shine of the broad windows, a patient figure in the driver's seat, the long car humming around her in a row of humming cars. I knew her at once, but only by the dirt and white of the Volvo, for her face looked straight ahead at the car in front – a run-down Subaru, lifting and jolting as the engine revved. Nevertheless, I waited for my leather case to rumble through the rubber flaps before I went to her. We had lived an ocean apart for half a year, and could endure, quite easy, another half-hour, separated only by the sleepy guard checking the luggage tickets and the automatic doors. It occurred to me then – as I pressed towards the grinding track, empty still, carting only the stickers left over from former bags in tireless circles – that the blood of my father ran in me; my bald, fat father, always covered in dust and paint, who took a job in Mendocino when my mother grew sick, because he could not bear to dwell in unhappiness. I had always thought him the sweetest, most patient of men, almost insipid in his humility; but he left me to attend her dying. I had the stomach for grief, I knew, but could not endure the constant little lies occasioned by lovers' wrangles; the air of inaccuracies, claims and counter-claims, the subtle misrepresentations, and insistence on subjective untruths. Well, some of these cloud even the house of the sick. More of my father's blood, perhaps, ran in me than I guessed.

The first time I saw Miss Susie Wielengrad – no, not the first time I saw her – the first time my eye singled her out from the frazzled mass of bustling men and women (in varying degrees of middle age) who taught at the high school – we sat together at lunch upon a round table of blue plastic in the cafeteria. The great thing about working at a high school is that it makes one terribly youthful and full of hope; youthful and middle-aged at once, you understand. Children scream, gossip, laugh and make love about one, fill their minds with such a jumbled furniture of intellectual history, no cracked Victorian could hope to match or rather mismatch them for eccentricity. Ions and star chambers, Pips and ellipses crowd their thoughts, until the bell goes, when a wind sweeps through them, driving out the clutter, and friendships, fixed or broken or crushing, fill their heads – such friendships as the assembled grown-ups shepherding their charges from room to room know full well they can never hope to suffer again. The second great thing about teaching at a high school is . . . the free lunch.

On one side, a wall of windows looked down the wooded hill towards the broad green of Van Cortland Park. The *empty* green, except for occasional joggers, threading slowly across the expanse, and a few bums spreading out on sunny afternoons; and, of course, on Friday, the cricketers: West Indians in scattered whites standing in the thousand postures of idleness occasioned by the game, apart from the single figure running long-legged up to bowl. Upon the other side a wall of windows looked over the Lilliputians (as one old hand described them) engaged in countless ingenious varieties of consumption, which always managed to put more food upon the table at the end of meals than the beginning. (He called them Lilliputians despite the fact that several among them, lanky, ambling fellows, towered above us, their backpacks slung at the level of our eyes.) I moved to sit down – a textbook pressed awkwardly between my rib and elbow – and bent at the knees to lower an overflowing tray (of smoked turkey, and gravy, and mashed potato and coleslaw, and, in the little square dip in the plastic corner, key lime pie) on to the cluttered table. The textbook fell, of course, painfully upon my foot. And I had begun to sweat and grow pink and – as is my way, when the system overheats – quite loud with opinion and talk.

Six or seven of us sat chewing and chatting, knights all of the round blue plastic. There was a large one, a shy one, an odd one, a wise one, a loud one, a loose one, a sweet one. You may guess for yourselves the role I filled; and perhaps, even, the role of Miss Susie. The great appeal of teaching, I believe, is the antiquity of the job; we belonged, like prostitutes and lawyers and soldiers, to the traditional vocations, and there is some comfort in that, millennia of grievances to call upon. A certain honour attaches to age, regardless of its condition; perhaps even prostitutes flatter themselves of the pedigree of their profession. Well, we flattered ourselves, a little, justly, I believe, and engaged with great heat and passion in the talk of the hour: *Macbeth*, perhaps; or the peculiar difficulties of mathematical instruction vis-à-vis literary, linguistic, scientific and athletic instruction; the particular and rather inventive awfulness of one of our smaller boys, the new depths he had plumbed, new horrors revealed, the inexplicable fascination he held for several of the larger girls; young love, always a little young love; the latest, freshest, most appalling absurdities of the headmaster, an account that included rather lucid and tenderly detailed descriptions of the care home to which he would be best suited; and, as I believe was the case on the afternoon in question, the kind of table necessary for teaching.

I remember, to be honest, little of the discussion, instructive though it must have been. I remember, however, the sweet one, across the table: a slightly plump, very pretty young woman, glowing with natural health and good humour; eyes, surprisingly, blue, given the delicate Semitic fullness of her nose, the richness of her lips, and the light brown curls that hedged her rather perfect white whorled ears. 'It absolutely matters,' she declared more than once, laughing at her own insistence, 'size of table, colour, shape, room for legs, sturdiness when sat or stood upon. It matters absolutely.' Something about the 'lutely' caught my ear, the New York thickness of it, the pure cool quality of the long vowel, suggesting nothing so much as a steady stream of cold water from a tap. 'Absolutely.' She could have said it all afternoon, as far as I was concerned; she very nearly did.

Upon the salad counter in the food court stood a tall wire fruit-basket, filled to the imaginary brim with impossibly large apples – green moon-like Grannies or Reds Delicious shaped like buxom hourglass figures drawn round; mottled pears, hard as wood-chips; and enormous oranges, sitting like winter suns among them. I had never seen anyone pick a single piece of fruit from the basket. I did not know, and frankly doubted, if they were real. Below them, under the sneeze-protective screen, tubs of coleslaw, tuna salad, cherry tomatoes, cottage cheese, loose-leaf spinach, boiled potatoes (somewhat green), boiled eggs (somewhat green), olives, peppers, crumbled Gorgonzola, various dressings (gluti-nous blue cheese, shiny Italian, splatted Thousand Island, etc.) sat in melting ice. From these, liberal and inexact portions had clearly been scooped; the evidence lay all around me, in tainted spoons, impure dressings, wandering and promiscuous tomatoes, pota-toes, olives, eggs. But every day the fruit shone, undiminished, unchanged, fresh as sunrise, impossibly perfect.

The pretty one had an orange. I remember particularly that she had an orange that day. And after completing a healthful and hefty plateful of cottage cheese, celery and bean salad, mopped up by a single heretical piece of garlic bread, she sat back in her chair and began to peel. Her hands, plump-knuckled, had a practised air. (The technique applied to peeling an orange has always seemed to me a great giveaway, a keyhole into childhood, in particular, the habits and humours of the orange-eater's mother: in this case, confident, cheerful, a lady with a nice eye. How I suffer from her now.) The left hand clenched the fruit in its soft palm; the right one, harbouring a Swiss Army knife (a little one, for keys), winched around the turning globe, tearing a single, long, parti-coloured strip from top to bottom. This grew and snaked upon her plate, a pleasing contrast to the white remnants of the cottage cheese it lay among.

I could smell it almost at once, a sudden pungent sweetness on the air, that fizzed in the nose like champagne, and made me sneeze. She seemed to take visibly orange-scented breaths; and the rest of us around the table breathed an enriched, pulpier atmosphere. Her jaw worked squashily as she picked off quarters of the fruit and put them in the pocket of her cheek. She talked on, with a full mouth, in juicier, wetter language. 'Anyone for a quarter?' she said, holding a clump of the fruit up for inspection. 'Quarter? Quarter?' I didn't dare to accept.

(Whenever I think of her, even now, the scent of that orange fills my breath, sharp enough to taste. She sweetens a room simply by her own good health, like the first cut grass of spring; by the proof she offers – in red cheeks and bright eyes – that goodness equals joy, and both are better in abundance.)

'Miss Wielengrad,' she said, introducing herself, taking my thick paw as I got up to go; then added, blushing, 'I mean, Susie.'

'Miss Wielengrad,' I said, stooping to kiss her through the opened window, my leather case propped against my leg.

'Susie,' she answered, turning the obscurest corner of her rich red lips to my pressed mouth. 'Hello again.' She said it in the shadow of my absence, the slight chill cast by nine long months.

'I had forgotten', I declared, brisk and happy, pushing my case along the backseat, and walking the long way round to the passenger door, 'how enormous the nights are here.' (I walked the long way round, past the trunk and the back of the Volvo, to break our loneliness slowly, gently, chiefly for her sake, knowing that even a dozen steps around the car softens the suddenness of reunion. One, two, three, she could count to herself; here he is again.)

'Well,' she said, 'it's been too hot to breathe all week.'

'Wonderful,' I replied, snuffing the evening air rising off the asphalt, smelling the scent of distance across the flat land, the scent I always attribute foolishly to the telephone wires, running along the highway into the horizon. She turned the car away from the overpass, and on to the brand-new stretch of road from the brand-new airport.

'The quicker we travel,' I said, briskly, happily again, looking about me with greedy eyes opened wide by sleeplessness, 'and with an ever more casual air, the greater our need to arrive *in* and depart *from* places that look as much like nowhere as possible – places that won't surprise us – places that suggest, after all, we haven't moved an inch. I believe', I continued, warming to my theme, 'that even highways have been specially designed to create an illusion of motionlessness, of going nowhere fast, of identical space. Just look . . . '– and I felt the yawn rising – 'at this . . . '– through my Adam's apple – 'road.'

I looked. She was looking already. White and long in the half-light of the street-lamps, under a green moon; dry land to right of us; dry land to left of us; billboards, swooping by, in a wedge of half-shadow; shacks, dead cars; a glitter of lights in the distance too far to budge. We seemed to be going nowhere, it is true.

It is my policy, and I believe a good one, always to be brisk and happy in *the shadow*. The shadow, I should make clear, is the patch of dark and cold cast by that stranger her husband over Miss Susie Wielengrad, when she has not seen me in a while. Susie, I know, being warm and full of light, does not cast shadows; at least, I rarely suffer from them, submerging myself immediately, happily, in her presence again, no matter the passage of months. I know for a fact (she has told me) that my shadow is broad and deep, chilly, lengthening over time, difficult to side-step. She feels first grey, then cold, then strangely blurred, unclear, wavering within its edges. The closer I move to touch her, the heavier the shadow becomes, the more she shrinks. Consequently, I touch her as little as I may. I become brisk, happy, unconcerned by shadows, almost . . . cheerful, in a wintry way, it is true.

I cannot dispel the shadow I cast, deflect it, nor warm it; and the alternative, a manner of velvety gloom, to cushion her within it, seems no better. Over time the shadow ceases to afflict her, in the noon of love, as Donne would say. Perhaps I grow translucent to her, and the light of life flows through me once again. Perhaps, unhappy thought, she cannot distinguish my shadow any more in the general darkness – I do not know. Nevertheless, I must bide my time, cheerfully or not, till she emerges. I prefer cheerfully, when I have the faith and strength for it.

'Yes,' Susie answered at last, 'I suppose it all looks alike.'

Love is composed – as Mr Stephen King (a copy of whose *Lawnmower Man* bulged in the pocket of my Harris tweed) declared simply of the novel – of Plot, Dialogue and Description. The plot of love is rather long – despite certain climaxes (now and then) spaced between deserts of unevent – and can end only, if it ends at all, unhappily. The plot accumulates – that is the great thing, it grows and grows. I believe so long as it keeps growing, all is well. Some pleasures make a virtue of simple quantity, and love is among these. It is like stew – anything may go in the pot, so long, that is, as the stew increases.

I remembered, as she drove – in the natural silence of the driver, along IH-35 into Austin – another meal we shared in the blue-tabled cafeteria overlooking Lilliput and Van Cortland Park. Again, a collection of teachers: a tall one, a young one, a motherly one, a beardy one, a loud one, a plump and pretty one. Miss Wielengrad declared, for the tenth time, cheerfully exasperated, resting her elbow on a copy of *Now Let Us Praise Famous Men*, how impossible it had become to find even a decent compatible young Jew for fun/companionship, who loved country walks and books, possessed a GSOH, even a USOH –

'What does USOH stand for?' I asked.

'Unembarrassing Sense Of Humour,' she said, and continued, 'for f/ship or long-term r/ship.'

'Why Jew?' said the beardy one, a Jew himself, chewing a dollop of tuna-fish salad forked into a split roll. He sniffed as he ate, and brushed the crumbs off the grizzled hairs about his lip.

'Don't get me wrong,' she said, 'I'm very much *reform*,' but added, brightening and blushing, 'except I would like a Jewish home.'

'What is this nonsense,' he said, still chewing, 'about Jewish homes; which, as far as that goes, are rarely done up in the best of taste. I would like a French home; that I understand. I wish to marry a Frenchman; I wish to live above a French wine cellar, these are legitimate considerations. But this is the excellent foppery of the world,' he grunted, being an English master, and fond of such things. 'That perfectly respectable young Jewish men and women, sound of mind and limb, constrain themselves by what they know full well to be ancient hocus-pocus in order to keep alive a tradition they have never believed in. I would require, upon every bar mitzvah, a dish of pork chops to be prepared for the new man, so he may take his place in the world clear-headed. The amount of loneliness spent by decent Jews looking for decent Jews so they can raise decent Jews . . .'

He would have gone on, but for the sudden pinkness in her eyes, which closed, as if to keep away the sting of onion, nothing more. Nothing at all that she minded, only – then she stood up quickly. 'I'm sorry,' she said, 'I have to go to', she said, 'the bathroom,' she said.

'I was going to say,' the beardy one added, somewhat subdued, as she left, 'I wish my own daughter – had done her bit – in that way.'

The curious fact, of course, is that it was not one of the four Jews at the table but I who followed her, out the back way and down the steps to the empty drive where the garbage bins stood. I who told her, 'It was only nonsense,' hiding blissfully behind the unspecified pronoun.

To which she answered, 'Most of us live by faiths we don't believe in,' turning her face into her neck, to hide it.

I had found a woman after my heart! – yes – and kissed her among the trash cans, looking over the broad green of Van Cortland Park, where the bums spread out on the grass in the sunny afternoon. Kissed and consoled her, for she was ripe for consolation, took to it naturally, sweetly appeasable, being easy to comfort as only the good are. There, against the back wall, among the black row of bins, over the smooth white cement glaring somewhat on the bright spring day.

'She's fine – she only wanted – the bathroom,' I said, sitting down to eat again.

I had forgotten to list – in the grounds of our dispute – this fact: that I was not Jewish. Nor were we driving towards a Jewish home – if she would give the name of home at all to what we had stumbled upon.

The dialogue of love is difficult to reproduce, being often tedious, repetitious, obscure, occasionally, indeed, quite meaningless – an act less of communication than of delicate chisel and sand, carving the shape of shared life from a block of time. How are the boys? I said; she said the boys are well; did they speak of me? I asked; sometimes, she answered; did you speak of me? I asked; when the mood took me, she said. Are they sleeping? I said; they are sleeping, she answered; I'll wake them, I said; I wish you wouldn't, she said; I missed them, I argued; you left them, she countered; not long, I replied, not long.

Austin had come upon us, snuck up on the harmless highway while we stood still. First, the strip malls, the low restaurants behind their tall signs, bright and big, and, to my mind, irrepressibly confident and cheerful. Look, they cry, even in nowhere I have the heart to shout out. Then the commercial neighbourhoods, the dental practices and outlet warehouses in quiet bays on the side of the road. At last, after a bleak stretch, the highway swung through the heart of the city – and the dark glow of the low skyline, the orange of the college tower and the sweep of the football stadium appeared. I opened the window squeaking and felt the rough of the hot air against my face again and squinted through it. The great thing of growing up in a sunny land is that home is wherever the heat comes carelessly, thoughtlessly, as abundant as grass and garbage. From San Diego to Austin seemed a small step.

We turned off the broad highway into the sudden quiet of the slip road, then swung left over the brow of a hill towards 32nd Street. 'Missy,' I said, to leave the keen encounter of our wits and fall somewhat into a slower pace, 'I've stumbled upon it, as I said I would.'

'Upon what?' she said, hardly heeding, watching the glow of Safeways go by and the empty slots in the parking lot.

'My life's work,' I said. And then my tongue loosened at last, and I told her, of our very own American Galileo, buried under the ruins of his plentiful nonsense and the weight of time; unearthed, at last, by me, a little chipped, perhaps, and missing a feature or two; nevertheless, great and grand enough to stand upon the shoulder of the giant he created himself, Alfred Wegener, inventor, explorer, founder in his scientific way of plate tectonics, the planetary technology that drives our continents and oceans. I shall publish – secure tenure – several chairs and fellowships – an international reputation – countless dinner engagements – but I outrun myself, Missy, and wish, for now, to present my piece of fortune only in its own sweetness, its own natural juices. I have brought – will bring – an old thing shining into the world again; and will make good a dead man's name.

There is a natural disinclination in conjugal life towards . . . revelation, of any kind. The tendency puts me in mind of nothing so much as a three-legged race, a contest in which I have won a certain renown in the father/son category on the burned, hard fields of Robert E. Lee Elementary School, owing largely to the fact that Pitt's little legs are little longer than his son's, but this by the by. In a three-legged race, the great thing is to achieve and maintain an equal rhythm; she presses her right leg against my left, or vice versa; the two are bound together, forming a stronger, more powerful, but slower, clumsier limb; and so we proceed, galumphing, across the years. There are occasional spills and upsets, of course; she insists that I have over- or understrode, that my leg chafes or tangles, that it rubs against her hip, that I leap slow or fast, and cause her to miss her step; that, in short, I am an awkward brute, and she should think twice before ever binding her leg to mine again. I, for my part, make similar claims.

What, on no account, either party in a three-legged race may begin to do is kick out and run.

Revelation is running.

And I understood this, even at the time. I knew (of course I knew) that she would baulk – not long or hard, perhaps, but a little. We always baulk a little at the changes rung in lovers. And yet, I hoped – we *always* hope – and suddenly saw no reason at all why she could not immediately lengthen her stride and keep pace with me, surging ahead in equal rhythm, strengthening my gait as I lifted hers. There seemed no point in lagging stubbornly behind me, as I turned on a fresh path towards what I hoped would be our fortune.

'I don't know anything about it,' she said. 'You'd better talk to Dr Bunyon.' (It irritated me always this insistence on Doctor; a stupid humility on her part, reflecting her own lack of doctorhood; *I* was a doctor; no great trick in being a doctor. Yet she never seemed to believe it in me; as if she had heard, perhaps, that it might be so, but would hold her judgement till she saw the evidence herself.)

'Of course I'll talk to Doc – to Bunyon,' I answered, less briskly and happily, I suppose, than formerly. 'He'll say what I say: wonderful discovery hem hem – revelation hem hem – all that jazz.'

I didn't like the way I said it. It sounded wrong, the way I said it. It had the wrong echo, fell flat across the darkened neighbourhoods, as we drove towards home; barely disturbed the sprinklers in their whispered confidences; could not interrupt the yawning miaow of a garden cat. It didn't sound important – or important enough – among these common and familiar streets. I wanted to say it again in a different voice, the voice of revelation. But I was very deep in sleepiness now, and nothing seemed to matter any more. Not even revelation; particularly not revelation. Suddenly, and for the second time, I began to doubt. An awful infection, doubt – like middle age, not so much ill-health itself as a suspicion of ill-health, a constant watchfulness over aches and sniffs, a tendency towards portentous speculations. What would Bunyon say, what would anyone say, to the mad and wonderful precocity of Syme? What would I say in the morning, at home again, in my old bed? (You must remember the depth of jet-lag; the chiming of 4 a.m upon my biological clock; the way sleep, the desire for sleep, can make nothing seem to matter much any more.)

She had done this before, my wife, turned a celebration sour, a fact that always surprised me, given her capacity for joy. For she was a joyous woman, my Missy, and her trick was this: her own sudden pleasures never lost the power to surprise her. She lived like a woman constantly receiving the surplus of an old inheritance she constantly forgot. She gloried in the new riches, grew wide-eyed at the abundance she had not guessed of about her feet. Alas, disappointment never lost the power to surprise her, either; pain struck her upturned face a fresh blow whenever it fell (reminding her of another old inheritance she had forgotten). She was a natural innocent, and innocence, like poetry, is a skill one must be born with; it cannot be acquired, nor lost, once possessed. And it means no more than this: that the babble of incident running through her life fell untranslated from her tongue; she spoke the language of it already. I lived, as it were, beside a first-hand account. Needless to say, Pitt translates, consults dictionaries and encyclopedias, compares notes and collates inconsistencies, offers a variety of interpretations, themselves appended by a variety of footnotes, to which, if I could, I would attach another sequence of qualifications. Pitt lives in many-legged fashion, a careful caterpillar going over old leaves again, again. Until now – until Pitt, at last – well, we shall see what Pitt has ventured upon; and whether it will fly.

I said, 'You weren't much better pleased when I got the Fulbright, I have to say.' The words tasted sour upon my tongue. That's an ill phrase, a vile phrase; 'much better pleased' is a vile phrase. Peevishness is a terrible pickler of the language . . . and how I despised the purse of my lips as I said it.

'I'm as pleased as you like,' she said. 'Only it's best to let me know next time you change the world, so I can pay particular attention; and notice it. It's a wonderful luxury, isn't it, changing worlds? Meanwhile, some of us have been getting on with the old world, and doing what we could. As for the Fulbright, of course I was pleased to spend a year alone with a full-time job and the boys on hand in a home I hated. Of course I was pleased about that. Knowing full well you'd go away and start some craziness and never write a word and we'd be stuck in the same place when you got back and nothing changed. Pleased as punch.'

'I've written', I said, reflecting how quickly a man may come to feel he's been at home for ages, 'many, many words.' And I sighed into the softer air of the neighbourhoods as she turned right at the post office towards the park. Dark streets of gravelly asphalt, overhung by live-oak and sycamore, broad and quiet enough on Saturdays for the boys to play football on, or leave their bikes spinning by the kerbless front yards. The crickets scraped away, reminding me once more of arthritic violins, while the sprinklers swished their skirts across the grass. 'How wonderful to grow up here,' I muttered, mostly to myself.

'I didn't,' was all she answered.

Nor did I, I countered in my thoughts.

As good as, she responded, also in my thoughts. So I kept silent.

She pulled the car into the drive, the muffler clanking as the poorly laid cement caught it on the tail. A small white house, a square, one-storey high, white-boarded, blue-shuttered, in a square of grass at the edge of Shipe Park – corner of Avenue G and 44th Street. 'You could chuck a ball', my bigger boy once said proudly, 'from our front yard to the swimming pool in Shipe. Well,' and he looked up at me, for I have taught him to be meticulous in his assertions (*do as I say*, I thought, *not as I do*), 'I couldn't.

Nolan Ryan could. We basically *have* a swimming pool,' he added, making up for it.

But we did not. Only a little living room (where, I noticed, pushing through the screen door, no newspapers lined the cushions of the couch for once); a kitchen (sink gleaming, pot dripping clean on the counter), where the lino peeled from the corners to let the ants get under; a master bedroom (cool as cucumbers in the fridge, thoroughly tidied, sheets tucked in), looking over the air-conditioning unit in the backyard; and a second bedroom, built on the end, with a bunk-bed and a carpet furred and patched as an old dog. No dog itself until tenure, Missy maintained.

'I'm going', I whispered, setting my leather suitcase by the couch, 'to have a look at the boys.'

'Don't,' she said. 'It's a school night.'

'Just a look.'

'Don't wake them!' she urged, angry again at my arrival, my right to claim half of what was ours.

So I crept through the door, both of us creaking. The fan itself seemed to be the voice of their sleeping; breathing softly in tireless circles, aching now and then, with a noise like the crickets outside. The floor was neat, Missy saw to that, aside from a scooter tipped over, tired. A hulk of computer cluttered the desk they shared, keyboard in the opened drawer, monitor pushed to the edge, joystick perched on top. The light of the screen-saver, an airplane zooming brightly across the night, bouncing and zooming again, lit the faces of my boys in the ugliness of sleep: eyes squeezed and gummy, lips crumpled, cheeks flushed. I lifted from the other pocket of my Harris tweed the pack of Devonshire toffee I had purchased at the Heathrow Harrods (a world away) – a tiny, vaguely Scottish-looking hole-in-the-wall, much decorated by the plaid of shortbread, and the pink of iced salmon, in the window. Toffee, I thought, was suitably British. They should know toffee.

The wrapper crackled unbearably in my thick fingers; but I picked the sugary blocks away at last. It is rare that the imagination anticipates all the details of a plot, however small. But everything happened as I knew it would. Aaron, the older boy, sleeping on top, a fair-faced, easy child, unlike his stubborn father, quick at games and friends, shifted and peeped out of his corporeal shell. 'Oh,' he said, 'hello,' and I put a piece of the toffee upon his lips, a rich brown chunk that melted at once into his sweetened sleep. 'Thankoo,' he murmured, through a sticky tongue. I could see almost how I would slip into his dreams again.

Ben was awake now and wide-eyed, smaller, almost lost in the corner of his blanket. I noted the crook of his shortened arm against his belly, the muffled woolly shape of it. A great shame this arm, root and emblem of his awkward nature, his patient difficulty with life, though it could appear curiously grown-up, wizened, when propped akimbo at his hip – as if his trouble were not youth but a foretaste of old age. I put a chunk of fudge into his other hand, and let him feel it, and smudge it, and press it into his own mouth – he never took anything as given. 'We'll talk in the morning,' I whispered, tickling into his ear. And left them both to the brown sweet dreams upon their tongues. The sugar might trick them from sleep; but they wouldn't mind, they wouldn't mind, I knew. My own father, bald and shining in the light from the cracked door, had woken me once coming back from a job with a stick of cane sugar – which I chewed and mumbled deep into the night, repeating as it were his presence, again and again, never to be forgotten.

'They were awake already,' I said, stepping into the bedroom, and seeing Susie through the bathroom door. 'They were already awake.'

We have come at last to the *description* of love, which requires, above all, an attention to this and that. Lord Peter Wimsey, I believe, could track his man by the shape and shadow of his back; there is much to be said for this, for the shape of the back, and I am also skilled in these matters, though in other respects I have little enough in common with Lord Peter Wimsey. Susie, naked in the white glare of the bathroom light, did not turn, engaged as she was upon countless spells and their magical ingredients, ranged along the toothpasted shelf above the sink: bottles of lotion, scented and particular soaps, saline solutions for 'her eyes' as she called them, and the little cages in which the fingertip lenses were kept. I knew, of course, that there was some concession in this, that the door was not shut, nor her shoulders draped in the heavy white towel of her robe.

Her hair fell longer now down her neck. A clump of it stuck, brown and glossy at her right ear, where a splash of water caught it when she washed her face. Her shoulders, narrow, half-slumped, always hurt my heart: they suggested so vividly the weight of things borne. I could count the fine ribs breathing down her sides, for the skin covered only lightly the wonderful device in which her clock was kept. A long back, broad-bottomed, pink – a little blue in the chill of the air conditioning. Then the stubbornness of her thighs, the tender ticklish blue veins at the back of her knees, her red ankles wrinkled by socks and her tiny feet, cold on the bathroom tiles, childish, unchanged. 'You'd better have a shower,' she said, turning round.

In class she wore bright flowing frocks from C.P. Shades and, when the Texas sun or Texas air conditioning permitted, sweaters she knitted herself. On weekends and grocery days, cheap Gap blue jeans and plain Nike kicks with the laces tucked in, and a tie-dyed shirt from the rag and bauble market on the Drag. She favoured their heavy and jangly stones as well depending softly from her lobes; necklaces wrapped thrice around and still long and loose enough to tangle in her fingers when she spoke; and a hair-clip, like a tennis sweetheart's, chalk blue, to free her bangs. Occasionally, in her Jewish moods, a woven shawl, bundled about her head; and she looked like a boy then, with her plump, fair cheeks, broad lips and sturdy nose. She had silk pyjamas, which she called 'Sears' finest', for bed and days spent sick at home – for she grew sick easily and utterly and happily.

And these she wore, under a summer duvet – as I stepped out of the shower steaming and into bed, where the cotton clung to me in various patches, and grew dark. I smelled of great warmth, and the thick scent of my skin filled my own nose with the sour breath of soap and water. She lay with her arms at her sides unmoving; her toes delicately suggested by a bump in the comforter; her eyes, blue as bottles, tilted at the ceiling. Quite silent. She did not stir, even when I tugged and shifted, leaned upon my elbow in the bed, and looked at her. And looked at her again, as the bald pink of my pate pricked and tickled with the sweat of the shower.

I said, 'Pitt is clean now.' This was true and unanswerable, so she did not answer; and I dripped and pondered what else to say, to assuage or incite.

I said, 'Pitt has made good for once, poor Pitt, by chance.'

I said, 'Pitt is a great believer in abiding by good luck.'

I said, 'We're OK.'

(Like tossing pennies and wishes in a deep well, waiting for a ripple and echo and answer, receiving none; dropping another coin and listening again.)

I said, 'Pitt apologizes for loneliness. Pitt has suffered greatly from loneliness himself.'

I said, 'Hello.'

I said, 'I have stumbled upon my life's work.'

'Well,' she answered finally, in a dead voice, 'that must be nice.' At which she began to cry, as if all the stillness had leaked from her bones at last, and she could move again. This endured a minute perhaps, but I dared not touch her. Then she turned in bed upon her own elbow and looked at me. We lay there, eye to eye, our elbows nudging.

'I harden my heart against you,' she said.

'Why?'

'Because you're so stubborn,' she said.

'Why?'

'You always do what's wrong, and say it's right,' she said. 'And I'm the one who has to figure it out.'

'No, no,' I promised her, 'not now.'

She did not mention then that she told me as much when we married and she wished to discuss the question of our children and religion, beforehand. Not now, I said. It will come to us, I promised; or them. Perhaps I'll convert, I teased, if we get that far. (We never got that far and I stopped teasing.)

Nor did she refer to the day I decided to finish my Ph.D. and she declared, I know where this will end, and it isn't New York City; and I said, Things will turn out, you'll see. Of course, we were the ones who turned out in the end.

And when we came to Texas and she vowed, I won't move every two years for you, while you get your head on straight, with the boys in school; and I promised, We'll stay here, of course, and set up shop. (I said shop and meant shop; she would have baulked at the word home.) But I am an optimist, you see, as Syme was. The world will turn to us in the end, if we are right.

I did not mention this to her either.

Instead, she pressed against me, and squeezed the curious jig-saw of our legs and arms into a single – puzzle. The shadow that fell between us shrank and disappeared, for a time at least, at such proximity. And still, I noticed, breathing the heat of her cheek, there clung to her – a scent of oranges.

I missed Syme, I confess it. There is a kind of intimacy, of grow-ing intimacy, in biographical research; we feel, because our sub-jects grow clearer to us, that we have advanced, in a similar way, into their hearts, that we are dear to them, become dearer, become – confidants, specially chosen to 'give them to the world aright'. I have known a convocation of biographers – at a conference, in Lausanne, which we had all attended for the seven-course fair – positively *jealous* of one another, like lovers at a funeral, jostling to lay the brightest flower on the grave. (Never mind that the *lover* in question was an extremely corpulent, occasionaly gouty, general-ly rubicund chemist, who suffered, by the by, from the most apoc-alyptic indigestion, and who had grown, presumably, quite damp and musty in his grave over the last hundred years; still, we fussed over him as if he were Marilyn Monroe.) The trouble, of course, is that the end of knowledge is the end of intimacy; when the investigation is suspended, the friendship begins to die. Our subjects, unlike our romances (though perhaps there is an echo of such decline even in ordinary love), cast us off as soon as we cease to find out more about them. They seem almost to snub us.

Well, there was more work to be done with Syme, more trouble to be had; and I awoke with an almost overwhelming sense of excitement, for – I do not wish to appear ridiculous, I do not wish to appear a fool, nevertheless, I will . . . explain myself. The day a biographer undrapes his subject (or rather plops a heap of papers upon his dean's or editor's desk) rivals in sweetness, in shy pride, in nervous fever, the occasion on which a lover confesses openly to the world for the first time his great love, takes her hand in the street. (Is she not beautiful, he cries, anxiously – do you not find her beautiful?)

In short, I had an appointment with Bunyon that morning.

I woke glad to the heart in the rich scent of the conjugal bed. Missy dozed, smudge-faced, beside me, her hot breath percolating through sleep-fat lips. I eyed her widely, and nosed her, until she blinked; whereupon she squeezed her eyes. "Sonly six,' she said, and shut them again. 'I'm getting up,' she added, and fell asleep. (It is always a miracle to me how much of the patois of ordinary love and joy survives in the grand rhetoric of marital *Sturm und Drang*.) I dressed, donned my Harris tweed and shuffled barefoot into a pair of well-oiled loafers, and stepped into the sitting room. A hot, white morning lurked outside, licking grass and tree, and from its damp maw I briefly retrieved the paper. Six-thirty. Jet-lag had propped my eyes wide with invisible pincers, an enormity of world seemed to tip into them, too much for my brain to unjumble. I couldn't possibly go to work at six-thirty.

Glad to the heart, I said, and yet, I was conscious even then of the *gnaw* (I can find no other word for it) of a deeper hunger in my happy appetite for life, an ache of doubt – a worm blindly nudging through an apple, and leaving holes behind it wherever it ate. My palms grew damp at the thought of Bunyon, his magisterial forgetfulness, the bright flag of his attention flapping in a hundred winds at once, and falling as suddenly still. Bloody Bunyon, as the Brits would have it – just the man to look across the Red Sea parted, and observe (with a wonderfully mimicked air of naivety, of grey-headed boyish enthusiasm) an unusual and quite astonishing *shrub* on the sea-bottom to which he wishes to draw our particular attention. Just the man, in short, to miss a miracle in search of a curiosity.

Well, I could not sit still all morning and stew. So I withdrew from my suitcase (lying tumbled at the foot of the sofa, now happily strewn with newspapers, like a full mouth with crumbs after a meal) the precious sheaf, which I had titled, in staccato type, 'the syme papers, a journal kept by dr friedrich müller, including an introduction and explanatory notes by dr douglas pitt' – a good, fat brainchild that woke in me a flush of paternal pride, as if indeed I had given birth to a phonebook. This I slipped (if a phonebook may slip) into my briefcase, a much-battered antique satchel, the gift of my father.

I stepped into the boys' loo, quickly, for I had grown increasingly uncertain with age of my *waterworks* (a Monopoly card for which I would gladly sacrifice several Mayfairs). I peed away happily in a fine gold stream, aiming for the fleck of fecal matter one son had left upon the bowl. The porcelain shone – and, toting my portmanteau, I set forth into the enormity of a Texas morning in September.

A thick, hot drapery of cloud hung over the sycamores and the live-oaks and drooped down, sticky as cobwebs, on to the parked cars and the plastic toymobiles tipped over in the front yards. The sharp prick of sweat opened the pin-holes in my skin, tickling my bald pate, my palms, and the bone along my forearms. I was home, in the heat again, in the intimate air of a tropical country, which always awakes in me a thousand desires and slackens at the same time every muscle needed to attain a single one. Susie, I knew, wanted the Volvo to take the boys to Robert E. Lee and get to McCallum High herself. So I decided to walk, to tire my buzzing nerves and draw out the sweet anticipation of arrival – while the sun burned away the clouds and began to shine off the wide asphalt. And I walked, through the wide and wealthy decay of Hyde Park, along Speedway, past the laundromat, where the bums drank from their paper bags against the kerb (how glorious the vicissitudes of their lives, dawn and sunset and the night stars!), across 30th Street and Dean Keeton, past the little booth (10 m.p.h.!) where the university traffic guard scratched himself in front of a fan, along the creek and under the stretch of trees where the grackle-birds shat, to the tall limestone block in which the History Department roosted.

I confess (again!) that I had begun to . . . perspire by the time I arrived; my bare feet rubbed angry red against their leather heels, browned by old polish; my armpits grew pungent with sweat, little copses of damp (I could not, in all propriety, remove my Harris tweed, had I wished to); my forehead dripped with beads like a watermelon brought out of the fridge. But the great resource of an ivory tower is the . . . air conditioning; and as I stepped into the halls of academe – decorated by fake new-fangled lounges (red, vaguely French, à la Jean-Luc Godard) and fake old-fashioned portraits (including a particularly gruesome replica of Dr Bunyon himself, stuffed into the pomposity of a bad suit, grinning broadly, his teeth, like brick-work in a New York apartment, *exposed*, I believe is the architectural term) – I began to chill, ever so slightly, and then shiver, as I strolled up the stairs to Bunyon's office, top and corner, from which he could look over his little world.

Perhaps I should spend a moment on the battle of Bunyon and Pitt, and the great war of which we are only the soldiers. The study of science is a relatively recent twig on the branch of history; but Bunyon, our dean and leader, has made it his particular care to tend this twig and nurse it to a glowing, if insubstantial, foliage. Now you may be sure that in any discipline with a double-barrelled name the barrels are pointing firmly at each other – and the scientists and the historians engage in a kind of guerrilla warfare unrivalled in academe for the heat of its prosecution. You may suppose that the scientists among us would carry the honours, owing to (well, there is no harm in honest pride) *our* technical expertise – for the truth is often simpler than the varieties of error, and the wonderful convolutions of ancient thought require considerable untwisting. Yet the historians of science for their part consider themselves the proper equals of their brothers in the History Department – they practise, like the rest of them, an ancient craft, and preen themselves rather on the intricacy of their subject, which seems so much more difficult, more technical, more *serious*, than the intrigues of kings and queens, the outcomes of wars, the evolutions of economies and societies. Worse still, they prance about in borrowed robes – white coats, I suppose – and ape the muddle-headed eccentricity of the scientists they suppose themselves sufficiently advanced to condescend to.

I regret to say, by contrast, that the more *scientific* historians suffer somewhat in our own esteem, less from the eminence of our historical than our scientific colleagues, who struggle at the frontiers, while we map the well-travelled roads that led them there. We stand at the elbow of genius, and glimpse only the legs and bottoms of the new men perched on the shoulders.

Of course, the great prize of any historical enquiry lies in *digging up a buried bone and barking over it*. But the trouble is this: the bones of scientists tend to decay rather quickly, splinter and open and crumble into the mud, while the bones of kings and statesmen and poets are picked clean by time and come up gleaming. True scientists, for their part, not only stand upon the shoulders of past giants, but kick them over when they've had a good look through the window, clamber in, and forget about them what brought 'em to the dance. As George Sarton declared in an early specimen of scientific history, 'From Homer to Omar Khayyám': 'The acquisition and systematization of positive knowledge is the only human activity which is truly progressive – which begins, in other words, in the negation of the past.'

Except. Except upon those rare and glorious occasions when the scientists, the modern fellows, looking for new worlds, lose themselves in the forest, stumble into an impenetrable thicket, an unexpected gate, chained fast, a chasm too broad for bridges, and realize, in the words of the gentleman from Maine, that 'you can't get there from here'. When they are forced to double back, tread old roads again, pore over maps that not so long ago appeared hopelessly out of date and which have long been out of print. Times when, as Wegener had discovered a century before, a dead man holds the lantern at the dark threshold of the future, and we creep behind him, follow his glowing shadows.

In the early nineties a gentleman by the name of Robinson Gould made a name for himself in a small academic way by suggesting – as he had been suggesting for decades, in a dusty hall at Yale in his patrician, sleepy tone, in a voice that seemed to carry its own echoes along with it to spare the trouble of walls and ceilings – that Aristotle had much to teach that jumped-up new-fangled craze known as *modern biology*. Mr Robinson Gould – for he lived in the days when a *mister* was plenty respectable enough for any college lectureship – was a classicist by trade and a scientist by hobby, and may indeed stake his claim to having founded our little subdivision of the Department of History by his unflagging – well, I would say zeal, but perhaps we had best leave it at 'unflagging'. Nobody took much notice of him, except his wife, who seemed to like him, for he was a handsome fellow in an old Brahmin way, though he stooped somewhat with the years and bore a remarkably unhappy moustache.

Until Marcus Lipowitz, the hot young biology prof., overheard one of his classes (having been caught in a shower of rain on what the students loosely described as the Hill, and returned to the lecture hall, loath to descend in a downpour), and began to apply Aristotelian notions of causality to various problems in evolutionary theory. (It should be said that the bronchitis he developed from sitting drenched in a draughty pew by the door played its part in the breakthrough – genius, as is well known, being 1 per cent inspiration and 99 per cent prostration.) Aristotelian causality can be described briefly as the belief that the dog wags the tail, and not the other way round, as had been supposed, in one form or another, by several generations of Darwinians.

Lipowitz's breakthrough brought a certain amount of reflected fame both on Mr Robinson Gould and the more technically inclined branch of the history of science. Mr Robinson Gould himself seemed not only *unperturbed* by the uproar surrounding the development and the generous credit accorded him by Dr Lipowitz, but – how shall I say it? – *unawoken*. The suggestion was even mooted, by those unacquainted with the fair Elm City and its rather more eccentric denizens, that Robinson Gould was a fiction invented by Lipowitz, partly as a joke, and partly as a mechanism for describing the indescribable, the moment of inspiration itself.

Regardless, Lipowitz's work ushered in a brief vogue for the kind of historical science I practised myself, during which Dr Bunyon, a dedicated follower of all fashions, hired me and assured me of tenure. Bunyon himself tried his hand at the game and published a much-cited monogram on 'Trinitarian thought and quantum mechanics – on the ancient and modern faith in the inconceivable'. But the fad faded, as fads do (a fate written in their stars, in their *characters* at birth); Robinson Gould died, almost imperceptibly; and Lipowitz moved on to what he called 'the new Social Darwinism' and questions of species evolution (a tendency distinct from, often opposing, the survival of individual genetic codes), by which he accounted for divers phenomena ranging from the 'necessity of homosexuality' to 'the evolutionary inevitability of the Human Genome Project'. He left us behind, and without him, all too soon, the old-fashioned accounts of defunct medical practices, exploded astrological myths and absurdist scientific traditions (alchemy, Mesmerism, phrenology) once more jammed the journals, and squeezed my own particular brand of scientific historical 'revivalism' (as Bunyon once described it, 'affectionately', he added) into the footnotes, then booted them out altogether.

I wish the matter ended there. I wish the trouble with Pitt were that he did not publish enough and beat a dead horse. (Dead horses, you see, are much better to beat than live deans.) With the benefit of hindsight, of course, I can see that the one piece I *did* publish I should have crumpled up and hidden away in old socks. In retrospect I can see that I should not have begun by making puns, I should not have concluded by making puns, and I should have taken all the puns out of the middle. I can see that now. With the benefit of hindsight. Which, as Byron once observed (speaking through the very wrinkled, very rouged lips of Dr Edith Karpenhammer, at a particularly heated meeting of the Bluestocking Society, convened upon the question of 'Learning from Mistakes'): 'Of all experience 'tis the usual price – a sort of income tax laid on by fate.' I have known more cruelty done in the simple cause of *paronomasia* than out of any passion or prejudice, Dr Friedrich Müller might have observed. To which I have nothing else to add, except – I could not help myself.

'Heads as hard as chopping blocks: Bunyon, tall tales, and the question of quantum Scholastics' was published in volume 21, spring issue of the *Harvard Journal of Historical Science*. 'He must *write*,' Dr Bunyon assured my wife, again and again, inviting her (I mean us) to this occasion or that at the synagogue (celebrations of spring, harvest, atonement, death, interfaith roller-hockey, etc.). So I wrote; pointing out (humbly, of course, and with great respect, in almost incomprehensible prose) that Bunyon's ignorance of Trinitarian belief was matched only by his ignorance of quantum mechanics; that, in short, the two subjects had nothing in common except for the fact that they had managed to confuse Bunyon; and that any comparison of the cultural faith placed in each served only to reveal the *poverty* (a favourite word of mine, and somewhat familiar state) of Bunyon's understanding, both of the distinct and unprecedented place in modern society held by scientific theory generally and quantum physics specifically and the role of sectarian religious speculation in medieval Europe. The trouble was, with all my best endeavours, my prose had not become *incomprehensible* enough. Bunyon, of course, read it; Bunyon was displeased; Bunyon reacted as a fellow might when another fellow deliberately steps upon his – but there I go again, and for once I will desist.

The curious upshot of all this, I believe, was that I attracted the notice of Dr Gerald Schulheimer, who had published my piece in the *Harvard Journal*, and who sat, from time to time, on the Fulbright Committee – and who, moreover, was a devoted enemy of Bunyon, for both personal and scholarly reasons. (I could never determine which grievance trumped the other – that Bunyon stole his wife or that Bunyon beat him to the chair at Texas when they taught together at Occidental.)

Well, one way or another I got the Fulbright.

And now I stood at Bunyon's broad oak door (peppered with

old *New Yorker* cartoons, hastily taped on, next to a plastic notice-board that read, 'Please Expound Explanations' beside a dangling felt-tip pen), the fruits of that Fulbright – sweet neglected treasure – in my battered case, knowing full well that before I could make *good*, I would have to make *up*. Knowing full well that what mattered above all was what Bunyon thought of the greatest, almost the *only*, American geologist of the nineteenth century: Samuel Highgate Syme.

I stood, with paw raised, to the heavy oak; and waited.

I could *see* Bunyon, sitting in the green-backed rich pine swivel chair, spinning in the windowed corner. I saw his bony legs, impossibly long, propped upon the antique desk (the particular perk of the History Dean, a relic of the Civil War, reportedly used by Robert E. Lee to accept the Peace of the Union – rich oak, covered in purple leather, gilt edged, stained occasionally by the suggestion of famous cups of coffee). I saw his bony knees, impossibly sharp; the thin cheap slacks riding up them, exposing a hairy stick of ankle. The nylon sports socks rumpled above the foot, and the red ridges left behind by their too-tight tubing. I saw the outlet-mall sneakers, squeakingly brand new, bearing the proud ensign *NB* in glowing red and gold (these he dubbed his Nota Benes, or his Foot-notes). I saw the green Armani jacket, left over from a long-dead suit, hunched about his broad shoulders and rolled up at the elbows. I saw the moist brush of hair across his forehead; his mottled cheeks; the broad grin between wide, thin lips, the exposed brickwork of his teeth. I smelled the faintly boyish air of a morning squash game and a locker-room shower, the sharper, maturer pungency of Ben-Gay. (He always smelled vaguely, implausibly, of Ben-Gay.) I felt his unbreakable cheeriness, the rapid-fire jolts of his random curiosity, sensed his inexhaustible interest in a world he consistently misunderstood, and, consequently, of which he never wearied. I guessed already the condescension he would show me – the kind *concern* of a man who has got on for a man who won't.

I saw too much.

In any case, I reflected – he might not be there.

I lifted my tender prize from my father's briefcase. Laid it at the foot of Bunyon's door. Plucked the felt-tip pen from the notice-board and scribbled, in all humility, under the title, these words:

Bunyon –
just got back last night
English – wonderful people
this – may be – the breakthrough? who knows?
(you?)
love to hear what you have to say
honoured, etc. to be invited to
your son's bar mitzvah
see you there – Pitt

(Believe me, there is a great deal of the dog in the dogged, of the fawning, the licking, even – and this I scarcely dare confess – of the easily heartbroken.) And then, in one of my characteristic evasions, equally insignificant and shameful, I left my little treasured heap at his doorstep, left *them* – Bunyon and dear, dear Syme – alone together to see how they *got on*. While I fled, into the growing morning, while I . . . flinched.

Bunyon's son, Spencer – who, to be fair, seemed an astonishingly pleasant miniature of his father, only a little hairier, slightly more gleaming in the tooth – was bar mitzvahed at the synagogue spread along the creek opposite the Safeways. A synagogue which I referred to only as Temple beth Longhorn (the bovine mascot of this wonderful state, and symbol of the great Texan religion, football), though I believe it originally had some holier association. Susie and I and the boys had . . . visited it, occasionally, for my part reluctantly, and for hers rather miserably indeed, for it reminded her both of the community she had given up and how odd it looked on what she considered foreign soil. She could not imagine the God of Abraham worshipped in such an accent, and spent the car rides home drawling the last ounce of smoked hickory from the 'baruchs', the 'atahs' and the 'adonays', in unhappy mimicry. Miss Susie, I confess, is in her way a snob. I called these moaning sessions the 'Jew's Blues', a cry I am ashamed to say my sons occasionally took up. This did not help.

The temple, which lay in a fair and shaded plot of grass between the car park and the basketball court (whose rims were rather touchingly *un*bent), had been carefully designed to resemble from the outside an airport hangar. On the inside, the architects had aimed at meticulously recreating the effect of a *basement*, and in this they had succeeded wonderfully. It was on the whole an astonishing piece of work, which managed to appear at once inhumanly large and uncomfortably cramped and gloomy. This I supposed was on account of God. I will not mention the stained glass.

Little of note passed in the service. A somewhat shabby gentleman (dressed in rumpled khakis, a denim shirt much too large and much too tucked in, and a threadbare sports jacket) had appeared, shortly before 'the kick-off', as he called it, to enquire (breathlessly, or rather somewhat too *rich* in breath) if indeed a bar mitzvah was 'about to begin'. When answered in the affirmative, he said, 'I love bar mitzvahs,' and began to empty each of his many pockets into a nearby bin – assorted fluff, dirty pennies, sticks of gum, unrelated gum wrappers, sandwich-bag twist-ons and the like – 'just in case' he assured us, and then explained, 'For afters, you know.' We later learned that he had snuck out before the service ended, and filled his pockets from the table of eatables laid in the auditorium – napkinfuls of babka, bagels, cream cheese, watermelon, gerkins, etc. I admit that I admired him – not indeed as I admire Syme – but I admired him none the less.

The rabbi, I believe, fell asleep once, only to insist (on starting suddenly awake) that, no, not at all, he only thought he heard a gunshot in the distance. 'You know,' he explained, 'like when they score a touchdown . . .' But he was gently reassured by Spencer himself, who informed him that the epic football contest (between the Sooners of Oklahoma and the Longhorns of Texas) was not scheduled to begin till later that afternoon. 'It must have been a gunshot, then,' the rabbi muttered, greatly relieved, and began to chant something, which from Susie's grimace I gathered belonged to a different service altogether. I began to enjoy myself. Spencer acquitted himself with both grace and a certain irreverent idiocy native to the Bunyons, and he stormed through the difficult Hebrew of his Torah portion with an obvious and energetic incomprehension. His sermon, however, on the seven-year wait (which he referred to once, apparently by accident, as the seven-year *itch*) of Abraham for Rachel, proved somewhat more difficult terrain, and he stumbled frequently over his handwritten notes, calling out, on one occasion, 'Dad, is that supposed to be a "w"?'

We emerged from the holy gloom into the cafeterial atmosphere of the auditorium – slightly refrigerated air, broad gleaming tiles, blue plastic tables draped with crêpe, cluttered with plates, notice-boards nailed against the walls and plastered with Crayola art. The food, it should be said, looked slightly plundered, and we could trace a trail of dripping watermelon to the double doors, whence the eager gentleman had made off with pockets full. By this time I was in something of a state, and stuffed my maw with bagel and babka to stifle the nervous chatter desperate to babble out. Ben tugged my coat-tail and whispered to me once, 'Don't let her sign me up for dancing,' referring, of course, to my wife and the miniature balls the synagogue occasionally held, to allow the little Jews and Jewesses to get along. But I was too anxious on my own account to pay him any heed . . . Papa Bunyon, at his restless, long-armed, grinning best, bounced around the room like a ticking bomb. *Had* he read the Syme Papers, and what did he *think*?

I never got the chance to talk to him at Temple Longhorn, consoling myself – as we do, strangely, console ourselves with the inevitability of events we wish at all costs to avoid – with the thought of cornering him later, at the evening *do*. The *chosen* ones (among whom I was shamefully proud to number myself) – those invited back to the Bunyon mansion for 'afters', as he said – shuffled off early, jerked off ties and untucked shirts, to ease into the heat of their parked cars. Aaron stripped immediately into his altogether in the backseat of the Volvo, and sunned his upper half in the open window. Ben, for his part, was more accustomed to discomfort and seemed to take a strange pleasure in the tiny formality of the little suit, and the way the sleeve of the blue blazer swallowed the awkwardness of his arm. He never changed for the reception, and appeared at the Bunyons' door that evening neat, unruffled, like a miniature Bond or one of the more dapper, better-educated villains.

Bunyon's kingdom lay on the curve of a hill in a pleasant neighbourhood of streets known as Henderson Park – named for the little green patch at its heart, decorated by a trickling creek, dead and drooping pecan trees, and, on the few occasions I had the pleasure to visit mine host and *mein Herr*, the slowest, oldest jogger it has ever been my privilege to witness. A posh bit of town, as the Brits would say: blue and white houses, paint slightly chipped in the tireless sun; green lawns faithfully and artificially bedewed; the usual assortment of kicked-over bicycles, flattened footballs, old political declarations cluttering the front yard; hoops set up in the driveways. We pulled in (crackling over nuts, twigs, asphalt gravel) under the shade of a sycamore, and stumped out into the softened heat of early evening. Aaron stubbed his finger on the bell.

Tall Bunyon himself answered the front door, wrapped ostentatiously in a dirty apron, the tracks of his own fat, greasy paws evident on the white front. The skull beneath his pink face had begun to grin already, ear to ear, and he spoke, with characteristic peculiarity, without ever closing his lips over his tea-stained teeth – as if the skeleton inside him enjoyed itself too much not to come out of its closet. 'Wonderful, wonderful,' he declared, a great word with him, used to introduce anything from national disaster to his maiden aunt. 'Wonderful,' he repeated (a true Tom Jenkyns in this, hoping to convey splendour by sprinkling the thought about), guiding us through a plush hallway towards the back. 'Excuse the art, I hope; great clutter – only, you know, I can't help myself – love it all, just the thought of art, great believer, you know, in pure *quantity*.'

Ahead of us, the bust of a plentifully naked woman, propped between books on a shelf, seemed to emerge from a sheaf of corn and loom at us. Against the wall, a broad crimson canvas with a single shiny penny stuck in the middle threatened to topple upon

228

us, bearing the title: one red cent. 'Local artist, teaches at the university. Extremely bald fellow, dry-talking – works mostly on what he calls the "mythology of money". Recent pick-up – my wife hates it. What do you think? Terrifically ugly, I believe. Oppressive, no other word. Makes me miserable every time I see it – can't get enough, can't get enough, though. We mustn't have everything in good taste, must we now?'

We emerged into an open kitchen, cluttered with beers and bottles of wine and jars of Claussen pickles, in almost equal number. ('Marian said it was too much,' he whispered to me, 'but I thought – Pickles!')

He steered us through the clacking screen door into a deep garden slowly filling with people. They milled on the concrete patio, spread out on the stepping-stones leading through the grass, leaned against a little gazebo, sat on the edge of a flower bed overrun with weeds, stood in the shade of a heavy pecan tree leaning on its elbow. Bunyon had a way with him – I can't deny it – at once highly plausible and quite improbable. 'Terrible service – never met such an idiot as – my son. Practically illiterate. Only too glad you could make it. All the way from Londondinium, no? (I got your packet, Pitt – later, later.) Terrific country, England, wonderful, *educated* people. (Susie' – another stertorous whisper – 'great to see you, sad to have him back. My bed is always there for you, you know . . .) Just had a letter from Oxford myself today – remind me, Pitt, you must *remind* me to show it to you' – as if I had forgotten these many years – 'just your cup of tea. I maintain a loose affiliation (I believe that is the word) with Balliol College – loose enough that they can scratch my back and not get too deep in my pocket. They offered, for a certain fee, to carve my features on to a gargoyle in a new college block. Extraordinary people, the English, quite unbalanced. That's immortality for you, hey?'

Well, the party began. I accepted a glass from somewhere and drank unlooking and the joyful fizz ran right up my nose; found myself chatting to a rather serene lady, Bunyon's wife, Marian – a sculptress who worked a great deal in asphalt. An unruffled gentlewoman, with broad, leonine cheeks, little cupid-bow lips, dabbed pink, plucked brows, and startled blue eyes gently preserved from wrinkles by a slight plumping over the years. She emitted a soft scent of pancake powder. 'Horrible man,' she whispered to me, unperturbed, gesturing towards her husband. 'Come and talk to me in the shade. I know exactly who you are, by the way. Don't think I don't. We've met dozens of times. Remind me.'

'Pitt,' I said, pushing out a rotted bench on the patio and easing her into it. 'Doug Pitt. I've been away, all year, on a Fulbright as it happens. Toot my own horn, hey? It's big enough, ha, ha.' I confess to you, innocently, happily, how much I love these occasions, and the difficult delicate nonsense they require: the subtle puffing and expanding of our notions and our natures, the broadening, the unbuttoning. Oh, those colourful balloons of conversation we blow up and burst or let loose, to watch them drift above our ordinary lives, pushed this way or that, by the intimate breezes that spring up in a crowd of people.

'And *who* is Doug Pitt?' she said, touching a speck of ash from the swelling curve of her nostril. '*What* is Doug Pitt?'

'A Symist,' I answered without thinking.

'And what is a Symist?'

'Someone who believes', I babbled, Lord knows why, simply because the words tumbled off my tongue, as they do only when the heart is happy and full, 'that the one fact indisputably true of every child (and every nation, for that matter) at its birth is this: that all the world is wrong, and we must look for ourselves to see what is right.' I stopped there, curious to observe the effect of my borrowed speech, curious to discover how an outsider (that is, to speak plainly, anyone other than Friedrich Müller, Tom Jenkyns, Doug Pitt) might be struck by Syme's braggadocio.

(I could see Susie across the yard engaged in earnest talk with Bunyon himself, the two of them partly obscured by the billows of smoke that sprung up whenever Bunyon prodded a piece of meat between the bars of the grill, or dropped his tongs, or spilled his marinade over the coals. He stood with his back to me, hunched slightly to attend my little wife, who touched his elbow as she insisted upon this or that. Her broad bottom wriggled in what I always called her *tennis* skirt – a pleated lavender cotton number that fell just to the sweet plump roll of pink above her knees. I have told her, again and again, that she is the waspiest Jewish mother I know, that she buzzes practically and nests in flowers and swishes her striped behind behind her. But she insists, on the contrary, it is all the rage now on the Upper East Side – worn ironically and complemented by a blue hair-band smoothing out her bangs.)

This was the maiden mention of my great discovery, my first public outing, and I felt a queer flutter of nerves – even our thoughts are debutantes once, and want dressing up, and flattery. Marian seemed to ignore me, in her powdered serenity, remarking instead in a heavy whisper, 'This is the second bar-becue mitzvah I've been to this year. We got the idea from the Heinzelmans. The whole thing started in Atlanta, I believe – two law students at Emory who wanted to make a quick buck.' Then she added, without skipping a beat, 'My father was a Symist, I believe.'

'No, no,' I began to explain, somewhat taken aback, 'by which I mean . . .' This was a great phrase of mine of the moment – I seemed always to be explaining by sub-clauses and exceptions, adding and qualifying. 'By which I mean that the great mass of men quite deliberately aim to fail – we don't fall short, we *aim* short. We are little conscious' – I was however *quite* conscious of the fact that I had risen to my pompous best – 'of the extent to which failure teaches us where to look and when to stop – it is the edge of the page on which we write – often the ruled lines, too. We check our stride, and never know till the end of the day how much – until turning home bone-weary. It is a physical fact' – this seemed to impress me a great deal at the time, and I hoped to impress upon her the depth of my impression – 'that we tire largely because we hold back, inhibit, rein in. A loose, lengthened stride, shook free, travels twice as far. I beg you to make the experiment. A Symist, in other words, is anyone who walks at his full gait.'

'That's just what I mean,' she continued, unperturbed. 'Belonged to a gentleman's club called the Atalantans, which met, suitably, I believe, in a bleak basement off 4th Avenue near Grand Central. Had a view outside of the garbage cans from the Korean restaurant next door. They believed in a series of prehistorical civilizations lost in some great flood, and hoped to prove it, too, diving for ruins off the coast of India – only they never got the chance, it seemed, or the money, and got mostly drunk, instead. They were all men. It seems to me there are a lot of Symists about. What are you in for?'

A slight billow of powdered scent, a gentle settling of the bosoms, a sigh, and she lifted her eyebrows at me to attend.

'I discovered a fellow,' I said, breathing slowly, at what proved to be my first public . . . *admission* of Syme, 'an old army lieutenant from the 1820s making his way through the ranks – till he gave it all up for science. He spent his life on a moment of inspiration – he thought he could prove that the earth was hollow.'

(Susie was listening to Bunyon now, ducking her head from time to time. Yes, yes, she seemed to say, I know, but what can I do? Then they stood silently together – I liked this least of all. A pocket had formed about them, waiting with an expectant air. Bunyon ignored them and resumed, gesturing widely with a burned stick and rubbing his free hand against his apron. Then he looked round suddenly and fell quiet – there was a general laughter. He began to heap paper plates with ribs, brisket, vinegar coleslaw, summoning the masses with a long flailing arm. He always had an air of talking undaunted, unabated, to inattentive crowds.)

'I'm working a great deal in brine right now,' Marian said, in answer to some question I had no doubt forgotten to ask. 'Making wonderful progress. I've always had this idea that people find sea water soothing. Not the sea, you understand – that's the common mistake. Sea *water*. Just the smell of it. I'm thinking in fountains – it seems as good a place to think as any. Asphalt and brine. New and old symbols, archetypes in their way, of the open spaces – freedom, that's the kind of thing.'

I said, 'Can I bring you a plate of something? A beer?'

She said, 'Was he right, this Lieutenant Syme?'

Well, I thought, that's the $64,000 question.

'He had his . . . moments,' I replied. 'One *supreme* moment. Yes,' I added, warming to my theme, rubbing Pitt's palms together locked by thumbs, 'in time, perhaps with your husband's help, I hope to show – I hope to *prove* – yes, that he *was* right.'

Marian wasn't listening much. There was something immovable about her, something grand and immovable, and simple talk couldn't budge her. She had to get somewhere in her own head first.

'I suppose there *are* a lot of Symists about,' she said at last. And then added, quaintly, enormously girlish, 'Please, one beer.'

'Yes,' I said, 'I suppose there are. My own father', I added, considering the matter for the first time, 'had more than a touch of . . . Syme about him. He worked in construction and believed that a great deal of scaffolding was unnecessary, bulky and awkward and beside the point. "Why," he told me repeatedly, "a *rope's* scaffolding, anything's scaffolding, that's all. There's nothing wonderful about scaffolding" – and he hoped, some day, to design a sleeker, lighter, lovelier support for the buildings in the world that needed attention. He devoted himself indeed (at some personal cost) to his private speculations.'

'A beer,' Maid Marian said, primping her lips together, as if to say she didn't mean to insist.

More and more this seemed to me a tale of fathers.

They brought out Chinese lanterns after sunset, until the mosquitoes came in to feast. Someone put on a record and Susie tried to get us all to dance. She was drunk by this time, and whenever she was drunk she became extraordinarily – happy. Bunyon took her up and the two of them trotted through the flickering shadows to great applause. (Susie told me afterwards, 'It can't hurt, can it? I do my bit towards your career. I understand what these things are about – people – personal people.') She had to drop him quite soon, however, when his legs grew dangerous – and I held my ground when she took my hand, and there the dancing ended.

We lost Aaron for a while. He had snuck through the bamboo border into the neighbours' yard and spent all afternoon on their

233

leafy trampoline, flinging himself just above the bamboo tops when the bounce rang true, till he could see the fleeting heads next door, a brief vision swiftly swallowed in the scratchy green leaves. Then it grew dark and the girl who owned the trampoline came back from ballet lessons and discovered him, and the two of them went inside to play computer games. Someone must have given Ben a sip of punch or swig of beer, for he began to tap the larger members of the party on the hip (or whatever piece of their anatomy he could reach) and declare, bright and brisk, 'Look out, tall man, lightning will hit your shoulder.' Utterly ignorant of the source of this peculiar prophecy, I heard him moving through the crowds throughout the evening, bent on his mission. Perhaps a certain worry over height inspired him (Aaron, for one, towered above him), and an intimacy with afflicted limbs. He never varied the message, considering I suppose that it could not be improved upon; and he never tired of it, either, believing his duty to be sacred, and his victims grateful for such practical advice. Nor did he seem to think anyone could ever be told enough. If someone had been warned before, so much the better; perhaps this time they'd pay attention – though, to do him justice, he appeared to be always on the lookout for fresh prey. Only when he tapped Marian Bunyon on her considerable midriff and called out in the ringing tones of utter certainty, 'Look out, tall man, lightning will hit your shoulder,' did Susie (suddenly out of spirits) choose to bring his evening to a close.

I was never easy to wrench away from an academic party, but Susie gathered the boys about her, and, prying me free at last, offered our farewells. 'In the morning,' Bunyon whispered in my ear, confidentially, almost sweetly, though it sent the blood racing to my tingling fingers, 'we'll talk. Stop by my office. In the morning.'

We discovered the rabbi sitting in his car as we stumbled to our own. I tapped on the window to offer my farewells. He lowered it quickly, said, 'Seventeen–seven' – the score, I presumed, of the great contest between the Sooners of Oklahoma and the Longhorns of Texas – and raised it again, staring at the motionless road. Perhaps this was not the first time someone had disturbed him.

I knew Susie would be unhappy when we got home, drunk and unhappy, which is always worse than either state alone. Such reminders of ordinary neighbourly Jewish life always upset her, especially such queer and altered scenes, such estranged familiarity – not to mention the sudden return to the solitude of *us*, the four of *us*. 'Who ever heard', she asked, deliberately slurping her words, letting her insobriety loose at last, after an evening of social restraint, 'of a bar-becue (fucking) mitzvah? Who ever heard of that?' she cried (even in her lightened state, *mouthing* the offensive term), as we stepped out of the car into the driveway and the thick of the evening again.

'Hush,' I said, 'in front of the boys.'

'Do you ever want', Aaron asked, lost in his own considerations, 'to pee for hours? Just to stand there peeing watching the puddle grow?'

'I will not hush,' Susie declared, 'with or without boys.'

'I can,' Ben whispered, to tease his older brother. 'I can pee for as long as I want. I can pee for a whole day.' Ben had a great sense of untruth, which came to him naturally, amused him endlessly by its possibilities. Aaron had a literal mind. The truth never worried him, never seemed to fall short. It was Ben who took after his father.

'Hush, hush, hush,' Susie echoed, mocking. 'Hush, hush.'

'I'll let you watch me, Aaron, if you want to. If you really want to,' Ben offered, scratching a tickle in his neck with his crooked arm.

'You can't, so that's that,' Aaron said. 'Isn't it, Mom?'

Hush, his mother said. Hush, hush.

When we got them to bed at last, I took her hand on the rustling couch while the crickets bowed and bowed outside, sounding like heartache. 'What did he say to you?' I asked. 'What did Bunyon say to you about the Syme Papers? Had he read it?'

Susie was sober again and very tired and somewhat ashamed of herself and took her hand away from me. It was only ten or ten-thirty, but the chime of a hangover rang in her ears already; she suffered the sleeplessness that has missed its bedtime and must wait for another.

'He hasn't finished it. That's not what we talked about.'

'I didn't know how much it meant to me, until today,' I said, beginning again, following another thought. 'How common it is. We are all a little given to mad ideas, *contra mundum* and all that. Anyone, at least,' I added, 'who spends a year alone. Mostly alone.'

'I said I was worried about you; and he said he knew, he was worried about you, that as things stood . . .' The sprinklers came up, and I could hear the sweet hiss in the grass, the gardens whispering to one another. 'I said I didn't want to follow you around and around going from bad jobs to worse.'

'How wonderful,' I said, only half-listening, 'the thought of going anywhere. I got an email, Susie, incidentally, from a gentleman at Barcelona, the University of Barcelona, who said –'

'I don't want to go to Barcelona.'

'Only a thought. Well, it doesn't matter anyway, after Syme, after Bunyon reads Syme. When he finishes it.'

There is a certain gap – often no more than a foot or two, across the dirty pillow of an old couch – that occurs only between two people who have greatly loved each other. It resembles in some respects a gap in *time*, being quite . . . unbridgeable, despite the fact that the other side appears impossibly close and clear. I leaned over and crossed it – or, rather, *seemed* to cross it to an outside eye, crossed it only in shadow, in overlapping shadow – and kissed her. This occupied a little time, and produced occasional noises: of the springs in the couch; a shifted knee; an arched back stretched awkwardly into position; a sigh, of discomfort, like the release of air from a squeezed pillow; curious sucking sounds; the rustle of burrowing creatures; another sigh, like the sharp intake of breath, at a cold day, lungs filled again.

Then she said, '*I've* read it. *I've* finished it.'

I tried to kiss her again but she pushed me away and touched the back of her hand lightly to her lips. She had a way of shrinking, becoming suddenly prim. She sat now with her knees together, and her skirt pushed down and squeezed between them. Her cheeks had flattened somewhat, and lacked their plump perfection; her nose had become sharp. She could look the school-miss properly on occasion. Then I heard her, and stopped short.

'Is it not' – I began, discovering myself through some perfidy of the dirty sofa cushion and the natural humility of the cavalier in front of his ladye-love, upon my (painful) knees, reaching out to her own knees, knocked together – 'beautiful?' I said, in the virgin shyness and delicate pleasure of an author, the body of whose private thought has been undressed at last by a tender hand. 'Those turning mechanical spheres, the grinding pure contraption of the planet – the echoing halls below the world, where a boy might shout, like Syme, to hear his voice come back at him? His great full faith in the virtue of the mind's eye to see into the heart of things, despite the clamour of naysayers and fools, and the utter obscurity in which he worked? Is it not . . .'

(Pitt is fond of a speech in his way. Pitt considers them on the pot and in the car, delaying at times even the hand that draws the seat-belt to its buckle, while he turns out of the drive into the traffic, and concludes a rolling oratorio in the breathless auditorium of his head.)

'No,' said Miss Susie, biting a twist in her lip. She never quite trusted *plain truths* – they seemed a risky speculation to her and liable to bite back – and so she bit her own lip (a tell-tale) sign, to forestall them. But declared herself none the less. 'It – upset me,' she said, quite sober now, or rather in the last fading echo of drunkenness, and very far away from everything. 'Very much so. It seemed so – it made you appear so – no, I mean *you* seemed so – hopeless.'

'Not that,' I replied, still awkwardly crouched and partly, shamefully, delighting in my supplicant role. 'Try the other one. Hopeful. Utterly full of hope.'

'No,' she insisted, ducking her head, shying from the bar I set in front of her, and refusing to clear it. Susie knew when to insist, to dig in her heels, and she insisted now. 'A little desperate. Hopeless I said and mean. Just that – like your father, you know, Pitt – very much like your father. You sounded like a kook, a crank. The worst of it was, I thought you liked Syme best, you

237

liked him just *because*, in fact . . . he was so far wrong. You wanted him to *be* wrong. You liked him for that.'

'No, no, because he was right – because he was wonderfully, prophetically right.'

'I very much believe', she said, 'that if all the world were clever, you'd make yourself stupid, just to stick out, like a sore thumb. Stick out like a sore thumb – to you that's praise, isn't it, Pitt? *Being original*. To you that's flattery.'

'Not just this second, I believe,' I answered, raising myself on my haunches and standing up, to let my legs think and the traffic of my heart run free again. 'Not so very much just this second. But if you mean that I think to be called original is great praise, is rare praise, is, in point of fact, the only *real* praise – you're quite right in that, Miss Susie – spot on. We use the word now to mean personal or unique; we mouth such nonsense as *most* original – and, worse still, we qualify even that. The most original *whatever* of the year. *Whereas*,' I declared, a mouthful and a sentence in itself, bit off in anger. I had found my stride now, literally and figuratively, and paced along the shore of newspaper at the foot of the couch, from the television perched awry upon the phonebook, to Aaron's inflatable baseball bat, yellow and squeaky and shiny, propped in the corner of the front doorway. 'The great thing about being original is that the only year that matters is the *first* one – everything after that is echoes. Original has nothing to say about the personal or the unique. It means simply of beginnings; something begins with me. Across the great colour-coded board of history, one of the lines, no matter how small, starts here.' And Pitt banged his breast. Pitt was tumescent, towering.

'That's not what original means,' Susie declared, cold as cucumbers. 'Original's just the word you use, when you can't think of anything else nice to say. Anyway, you weren't original at all – you borrowed it all from Syme, and you may as well have left it unborrowed.'

'Second hand', I said, slowing down in breath and foot, 'is better than third or fourth or fifth – which is what most people deal in. I believe that second hand is the best I can do. Pitt has a poor mind, but he spends wisely. He hunts for bargains, for *tsatskes*, as your mother would say. You should know.'

'That's another thing,' Susie said, and left it at that.

I stood and she sat in silence. The evening pressed upon us again, like a subtle flood we had neglected to keep at bay – spilling over and running through all our cracks, spreading to a broad expanse of dark and loneliness. I had been back only a week, but the water between us, crossed at first by the sudden bridge of arrival, had become impassable again, at least not without a thorough drenching.

'I know you think I'm stupid,' she said, pressing her hands upon her lap. 'I know you think I'm – unambitious. That I don't care a bit about changing worlds or setting up monuments of Miss Susie Wielengrad for future ages. That I'm quite happy to leave things as I found them. That I take things as they are. But the fact is' – and here the edge of her voice grew sharp, her hands unclasped – 'I Know How To Live. Never mind if it's all fifth hand. I was taught well. I knew what part of town to grow up in – Yorkville, between 2nd Avenue and the East River. I knew the best restaurants, the bagel bakery, the German coffee house to go to. I knew where to shop. I knew what to wear and when to wear it – the fashions, and which of them to follow, which to ignore. I knew who to have over for Sunday brunches and what to talk about and what to think about. The best new books; the bad ones it was OK to read on holiday. The walks to take on sunny mornings along the river, while the men played chess on the cold stone tables. The longer, colder walks in Central Park. That the only time it wasn't tacky to wear my Barnard sweatshirt was jogging on the weekends along the side-streets between 1st and East End Avenue. Yes, I was a snob – I am a snob. We all dressed up for Friday nights at the synagogue on 79th Street, and we looked at the families in the pew behind us as if they were a little further from God. I knew just how much to believe – how much was appropriate – what I should never mind about, and when it was OK to be sentimental. I went to all the best galleries, and wasn't too shy to say I liked art pretty. I never thought to leave my mark on the world – because I knew my place in it, and was never ashamed of simply being happy.

'Even if it was all fifth hand; who cared? But now,' and here she took my hand, roughly, and pulled me towards the door and into the night and we stood on the driveway under a hundred stars (not a thousand or a handful, but a hundred, a compromise between the dull glow of the city and the enormity of the country), 'I step outside and wonder where is the stink, where is the stink, and the beeping of the garbage trucks, and the dirty streets and the doormen watering them and the trash bags heaped on the corners? This isn't home; I wasn't taught how to live here. Where are the shops along the avenues, the bars, restaurants, hardware stores, cafés with cheap tables on the pavement? Where are the tailors and the laundrettes, squeezed into the ground-floor apartment blocks along the side-streets? Where are the girls from Brearly I used to know, and the aunts living ten blocks down, and the kids I taught and ran into Saturday nights at the kosher Italian? There is nothing here for me.' And she sat down and shoved up on the hood of the Volvo, hoping to appease me by unhappiness, by the tenderness of misery, but I was only angry now, Pitt rising and venomous at last.

And I answered that I wasn't taught how to live; that I never knew what to think or how to dress. That my father dropped out of high school to serve in Korea, because that's what a young man did. 'Don't interrupt me, Susie – I know you know this – I've earned the right of repetition.' All that was left of him by the end was too much kindness and a stupid humility and a tinkering obsession with his no-good job that was the only place his smarts had to go. (A certain amateur interest in immortality, an obsession not unlike my own, with the structures supporting the permanent monuments of our civilization – in his case, office blocks; in my own, books – and a firmly held belief that he could simplify the *scaffolding*.) My mother had an *incident* (with a boy and a bottle) in college and came home and never got over it and never talked about it and met my father in night school, where he was trying to get *up* in the world and she was trying to get *back*, and they married and both stopped dead where they were, because all they really wanted to do was avoid fuss. They avoided fuss until she died. Never underestimate the amount that gets done and doesn't get done in the world out of the honest desire to avoid fuss.

So I was never taught how to live or what to think. Pitt had to go about all of that for himself. Pitt had to crib the material first hand. And so I declared to her, in the faint half-chill of summer midnight, to the bow of the crickets and the soft cymbal of the front-yard sprinklers, the words of the great Syme, uttered nearly two centuries before: 'Let me not be among those wealthy men who pay their servants to attend to the tasks they should perform themselves. Let me then be among the servants, if you grant me leave to go over even old ground with a fresh hand, a clear head, and a curious heart.'

'Oh, Pitt,' she cried, tucked up on the hood, 'I wouldn't mind so much, only all this has happened before. And if I hear again how your father nursed secret ambitions to . . . I don't know what – I'll scream.'

'My father is a self-educated man . . .'

'Your father is an *un*educated man . . .'

'Who wishes to better himself – yes, just that, though you flinch at the low-class phrase; *better* himself. And there's nothing more honourable than . . .'

'I can't bear it – all these wasted lies.'

'His book on the history of scaffolding, a *first-hand account*, could make his name in a small way, and that's all he wants, and more, really, than he dreams of . . .'

'You're just the sort of man to come up with some elaborate nonsense to prove what nobody else would bother to boast of even if it were true. You're too enthusiastic – it puts people off. You get these ideas and let them run away with you, that's what Bunyon said; and this isn't the first time. I said to him, Don't get me started. What about that thesis you never finished at Oxford, where you wrote, against the best advice of all your tutors, about the history of *silence* –'

'Only think, Susie,' I interrupted, a fresh vein pricked, a fresh flow of life's blood pouring forth – 'the single language of human thought utterly unchanged by time. Gestures of rebellion or contemplation that never lose their prime – that never require translation. The syntax, the punctuation of our thoughts – arranging them, filling the gaps between every spoken word, as much greater than the words themselves as the sea is greater than the shore. The first, most fundamental right we possess, to remain silent; Cordelia's privilege and Hamlet's final thought. History and literature are filled with the several often contradictory uses to which silence is put: political rebellion, and political punishment, and political consent; spiritual purification, and spiritual condemnation, and spiritual isolation. Silence invites and denies and ignores and distils, protests and represses and leaves us all for dead in the end – the dial tone equally of life and death. Can you think of a nobler subject to pursue?'

I had grown quite overheated by the flame of a former inspiration, quite red in the face, puffing and bedewed – conscious that when the fire went out the cold of misery would surge around again. Susie looked at me, and reminded Pitt suddenly and most improbably of the ham-fisted lawyer in *The Caine Mutiny*, who had prompted a necessary outbreak to prove a point, but disliked the job, and felt sick about it – an unflattering resemblance, I know, that did no justice to the thick bob of her hair, the wonderful little Jewish stubbornness of her nose, the rich, wide mouth and perfect, peach-shaped, apple-coloured, orange-scented cheeks.

'Then why didn't you finish it?' she said, sliding off the Volvo. 'Why did you – give up' (the word Pitt would have chosen is flinch) 'and run to New York?'

My fire was almost spent, my heart more and more choked in its own ash. 'Because,' I sighed, 'on that particular question . . . I ran out of things to say.'

'And this time round,' Susie answered my sighing, breath for breath, 'it's hollow worlds.'

The great stupidity of life lies in the necessary repetitions, and this was an old argument, well grooved, running upon familiar lines. I marvelled (not for the first time) at our terrible, almost noble, even courageous, capacity to repeat and repeat and repeat; and imagined (not for the first time) the impossible spacious sweetness of a life in which everything was said only once. (Perhaps it would be very lonely.)

'What if I were right this time?' I said, quietly, across the little private corridor of evening air between our faces, three feet long, a head wide, above the pebbled cement of the driveway, in the broad expanse of night. 'What if Pitt made good?'

'Maybe,' she answers, quite calm and cold and matter of fact, pushing the loose net of the screen door with the flat of her small hand, and going inside, 'I don't want you to make good this time. I want you to make *bad*. I want to go home and give up. Maybe', she repeats, 'that's what I want this time.'

And yet Pitt is an optimist, as I said before – Pitt is brave, redoubtable, a wonderful word that means nothing less than the ability to suffer doubt and faith in equal replaceable measures, again, again. And as I climbed the ivory tower towards Bunyon's corner office, my heart rose once more at every step. How grand a thing is possibility, simpler and sweeter in its way even than triumph. For triumph brings with it a world of complications and fresh puzzles, but possibility is plain as a die or a coin, sharp-edged, straight-sided, offering the prospect of a single answer: yes. The hint and hope of a yes at every spin or turn. (Or, in my case, laborious submission of a phonebook-thick wedge of manuscript; but the principle, I insist, remains the same.) I had come to revise my opinions of – well, since Susie has broached the word, I may as well follow suit – Syme's hopelessness:

> I discovered among Sam's papers an almost endless stream
> of denials, both equivocal and unequivocal; interested
> denials and uninterested denials; formal and informal
> denials, in pure and broken English; refusing funds, gov-
> ernment cooperation, access to records, machinery,
> venues for lectures and demonstrations, employment,

publication – all faithfully preserved by a father who
seemed to consider even the proof of rejection as some evidence of the esteem in which his son was held, some indication of the circles in which he moved. I, on the other
hand, could not repress a kind of frustration – not unmixed
by pity and admiration – at the . . . *stupidity*, I wish to say,
but soften it to *insensitivity*, of a man who beats his fist so
long against an unanswered door.

The door *I* beat at *was* answered, by a bellowed 'Enter', and I
shouldered my way, briefcase first, into the room. Bunyon sat as I
had imagined him, with his New Balance sneakers propped upon
the desk, left over right, in a leaning tower pointing impossibly
high at the stippled cardboard ceiling. A collared shirt fell unbuttoned at his neck, whence a tuft of grey hairs bristled, suggesting
by some curious association the overwhelming urge of the man to
scratch himself. 'Pitt, my dear Pitt,' he cried, swinging himself to his
feet to impress upon me once again the undeniable fact of his
great, his superior, height, and took me wildly by the hand. 'Have
a seat.'

Pitt looked about him. There were three chairs in the room, and
by some acrobatic feat Bunyon had now managed to occupy two
of them, one by bottom, another by a draped leg. The third, a little
wicker seat, stood across the desk, heaped to its frail arms with
manuscript, whose title page bore the unmistakable blocks of
meaningless lettering that promise such horrible repetition on the
pages beneath. Pitt removed, by delicate operation, these pages.
Pitt perched.

'I have read', Bunyon began, advancing at once into the academic arena, and prowling about, 'your delightful, your exquisite
little account of Captain Syme's *discoveries*. (Is that what we
should call them? I defer. *Captain*, by the by, was his final rank, I
believe, having looked into the matter some time ago myself.) A
terrific piece of historical legerdemain – I congratulate you, Pitt,
warmly, Pitt. A wonderful stroke of luck, this Müller fellow,
though a bit of a limp handshake, I think you'll agree, on his own

terms. Still, a real old-fashioned, stuck-in-the-stove-pipe treasure. Simply, a joy.'

Bunyon had a remarkable ability to damn not by faint but by enthusiastic praise. I knew his way, of course, foresaw the stinger waggling in the tail – yet I could not prevent in myself a slight swelling, out of that pride we all possess, which believes the most exuberant flattery to be in fact the plainest common sense, and wonders more that it should be so rare than that it has come at last. Pitt murmured a little, of course, and blushed – though, to be honest, Pitt struggles both with murmur and blush, the former often exploding into growls, the latter lost in native rosiness. However, Pitt's blushes soon soured, mottled too deep for pleasure; and the growls came naturally.

'A great pity', Bunyon continued, without the least check in his stride, 'that this will never do. No, *it will not do.*'

He lifted a heap of papers from the floor and dropped them heavily and dustily upon the green leather of his Civil War desk. I recognized them at once – even the shapes of paragraphs and the riddle of lettering too small to read grow familiar as a face, as the lines of a face, to an author. Only these were now scored by red ink, squiggled and desperate marks, evidence of a bloody battle. I rather feared that I – that Syme and I and Müller – had been defeated.

'The trouble with you', Bunyon continued, in his affectionate, intimate way, as if I had asked him, in all honesty, out of friendship, to tell me what it was, 'is that you have always been interested in – conception. Conception, I know, is a blessing, but as Pitt conceives – friend, look to it. We, at the Department of History, University of Texas, Sub-department of Science – the little body under my special charge and care – deal in Ideas. By which I mean', he declared, in a rough breath, warming to his theme, and winching his legs heavily to the ground, 'an idea is simply what happens to a conception when the paint dries – until then, I'm afraid, it's off limits. Can't be sat on, leaned against, used or sold – can't be touched, I'm afraid, Pitt. Them's the rules. You have presented me here with a wonderful – if slightly dubious (*you* know it, Pitt, *I* know it – we must be cruel to be kind, even with ourselves, *especially* with ourselves) – *moment of conception*. A fascinating thing, no doubt – when the brush is dipped and touches the blank canvas. But we don't deal in moments of conception, you and I. Wrong trade. We deal in the history of ideas.'

'I don't understand,' said someone, who seemed to have borrowed the voice of Pitt, and made it squeak. (How terrible are the habits of humility, how deep ingrained. Christ has a great deal to answer for in praising the meek. Pitt's mother was meek, by name and nature. Pitt's father dined happily on humble pie, and ate up the crumbs. Pitt in the packed arena of his own skull is a champion equal to a thousand lions; but step for once out of that noble theatre and he flinches and ducks his head. His heart sinks to his boots and he steps on it. How much of misery begins not in true cowardice but the show of it.)

'I don't say it's hopeless,' Bunyon assured me, delighted at his own condescension and general bonhomie. 'I don't say that.'

'But words are things,' Pitt spluttered, roused at last to resistance by a memory of the distinctly *reified* words of Dr Edith Karpenhammer, which she spat out (slightly stained by lipstick) at a meeting of the Blue-stocking Society convened upon the question of 'The Power of Language'. 'And a small drop of ink,' I continued, heartened as always by the fibre of quotation, 'falling like dew upon a thought, produces that which makes thousands – perhaps millions – think.'

'That's just it,' Bunyon said, suddenly brisk, indicating by a change in the weather, a touch of the north in the wind of his speech, that it was time for me to go. 'Exactly so. Show me the *ink*. Show me *evidence* of the revolutionary geognostic theory that inspired Wegener. Show me Syme's conception with the paint dried – the *idea*. Show me, in short – for nothing else will do – a copy of the *New Platonist*.'

'But they have all been burned, Bunyon, *lost*, you know that – in time, *by* time; in moments of frustration, great disappointment, betrayal, theft. In the bombing of the Second World War. All that's left is the moment of conception – *that* hasn't been touched, can't be touched. There isn't anything else.'

He said nothing to this at first, but grinned, in the manner of someone who assumes a nervous air because it makes him seem a little more human. Outside, the leaves trembled in the blue breeze; the fountain rose and fell and shattered and collected again; the students, trailing backpacks over easy shoulders, walked to and fro. And I realized for the first time how great a darkener of life is a book, which shuts out, with paper curtains, the common light of day – of *days*. Ink, I reflected, is black for a reason.

'You remind me', Bunyon declared at last, leaning back and picking at his yellow fingernails, 'of a man who strikes his hands together – not because he *knows* where the damned mosquito is, but because he *wishes* to kill it. Bring me, Pitt, a copy of the *New Platonist* – and we will talk again, Pitt.'

With that mosquito buzzing in my ear, I left him, clutched my (empty) briefcase and descended from the ivory, air-conditioned tower. The fat heat of day was a relief; even the sweat that warmed the cold of my hands was a relief; even the glare and ache of my squinting eyes.

Well, Susie was right.

Perhaps Bunyon was right, in his way.

I had learned the first lesson of the true believer: that acknowledgement is as rare, as wonderful, a thing as the miracle itself. Syme had known something of this, in his day.

Well.

Pitt was bloody, but unbowed.

PART III

·Persuasion·

In the morning, I was awoken by a knock at the door. A clop-clop, a cheerful step, and Tom Jenkyns was in my room, fussing and chuckling over me to get me up. 'I have brought you tea,' he said, bearing a hot dish delicately in his burned fingers. 'I never rise up without it.'

'Thank you,' I answered through a thick tongue, greatly embarrassed at being discovered in considerable undress, hair askew over the pillow, the stink of sleep upon me – a slug-a-bed, when there seemed, in a general way, so much to do (though I could not for the life of me have declared exactly what – in such fashion do our appetites outrun our purposes). Yet I was glad on my first morning in Pactaw to encounter a known face. I sat up to receive my tea, and from that awkward perch could look out of the window. A fresh fall of snow had drifted through the night, and the window steamed with the heat of our bodies and the teapot.

'If you permit me two minutes,' I said to Tom, 'I am your man.'

I dressed before him – with remarkable and quite uncharacteristic haste, urged by his presence to a rapid toilet, while he peered outside with easy unconcern. Indeed, it was only my awkwardness that offered a slight access to intimacy. Tom was above all a fellow's fellow, and never thought twice of a great many things that habitually preyed upon my mind. I put on my lavender shawl, wrapped it thrice around, and generally stuffed myself, till I resembled nothing so much as a taxidermist's bear. Then we stomped out into the world together.

Snowdrifts lay knee-deep along the broad thoroughfare, broken here or there by this leg or that. The fountain of each tree had flung itself upwards, curving to the top, and paused, white and silent. O, they were beautiful! Perfect, as though frozen in the pale amber stone of the early winter morning. Snow had choked the road six weeks before, as I travelled to the port at Hamburg. And the ship lay in the harbour there, the sea muffled with snow. Now it seemed another life.

Tom Jenkyns, like a boy, had no sense of ceremony with the snow. He raced and leapt into the drifts, banged his cold fist against the frozen signs, till they squeaked and squealed and loosened at last – laughing his high, bird-like laughter which rang even thinner on the bright, cold air. I was glad to see such irreverence in the face of great Nature. I had read so much of this New World, and looked on it still with fear and awe. It was a comfort to find the snow there as well as in Neuburg could be moulded by cold hands into balls. Tom caught my scarf by the end, like reins, and we galloped down the street, falling and pushing in turn. I was only twenty-eight, and Tom had the gift of energy. Pleasure flew from him in a shower of sparks and caught and burned in me as well.

Breathless at last, we marched through the broad market square, now deserted, except for a few stray dogs slumped about a pile of rotting potatoes dirty in the snow. We stepped on to the delicate footbridge and stood above that glittering sweep of the Potomac, while the long, cold wind streamed through us from the west and blew away to the ocean behind. I paused here every morning on the way to Sam, meditating each time upon the same reflection – that I stood at a midway point between two ends, loitering on some bridge – before crossing towards the grand and solitary house on the far shore, and slipping along the ill-kept muddy path that led to his door.

Sam had seen us and let us in, shod in his sandals and smoking what I learned to be his customary pipe. The corridor was chill and dark, but a broad fire blazed in the old tap room, and thither we quickly bent our steps. 'I pray you – do not worry – shan't rain,' Sam said, in his customary brisk chatter, waving his hand at the clouds of smoke gathered from pipe and lamp and the steaming sodden logs in the draughty fireplace. A proper breakfast lay on the table, honeyed ham and bread and milk so cold and fresh that shards of white ice still floated in it. We sat down with a click and pushed our chairs, bottomwise, under the table. Then began to eat in a munching silence – that disturbed only me, it appears, for they did not break it.

The silent meal was curiously intimate – there is nothing after all like the animal within to help us rub along together in a genial fashion. Our appetites were conversation enough, though the tacit assumption (as it seemed to me) of my inclusion in their little troupe both flattered and discomfited me. I learned later that Sam relished quiet repasts, and greatly disliked to have any less material business intrude upon the pleasures of the table; and indeed in this slight circumstance there was a strong indication of the sharp divide in his nature between the grossly physical and the purely, wonderfully rational. Tom himself seemed to go along with his master's whims, and on the few occasions I ventured to interrupt, with some pleasantry or other, I received only a grunt from the great geognosist, and a shame-faced little nod from his associate. The two of them, by the by, seemed to have recovered their good humour; and Tom attended Syme's muttered requests for 'another wedge of bread, cut of ham, swallow of good milk' with tender promptitude.

When he pushed away his plate at last, there was some confusion as to how we should proceed – regarding the best means of satisfying my curiosity, and resolving the unusual business that had brought the three of us together. Syme at length decided to 'take me through' those experiments and researches that occupied him at the moment. 'It is always best – I believe,' he said, 'to begin with particulars and – travel outwards – seeing that no matter the journey – we always set forth from and – arrive – at a very small spot.' Generally, he worked in a kind of garret at the top of the ramshackle inn. There he kept no more than a desk pushed up against a tiny window, from whence he could gaze across the glittering Potomac, the untidy network of houses, and the low white hills beyond – this vast expanse confined to a small round of glass no bigger than the bottom of a pot. 'The mind – at least my own –' he said to me, with half a smile, 'is among those elements – that expand – in the cold. But I am not without – mercy. And seeing as the fire is laid on – below – we may get to business – here. Tom,' he added in a sharpened tone.

'Tom', I soon discovered, was less an appellation than a term of command, that could denote anything from 'clear these dishes' to

'fetch my papers from the attic'. And in fact the word possessed such homonymical properties that it usually indicated several distinct ideas at once. All of which, it should be said, Mr Jenkyns seemed to understand; and none of which he hesitated to realize.

And yet – as Professor Syme and I pored over his scattered notes, field logs, records of experiments, journals, speculations, all spread pell-mell across the table in rustling array (the papers beautifully combining sudden scratched phrases, revelations, injunctions, meticulously observed detail, jumbled calculations, and, indeed, some evidence of the paths he had travelled, blue-stained leaves and muddy fingerprints), while he muttered a low commentary that wove together these extraordinary, disparate facts (and disparate kinds of facts) into a glistening, delicately coherent spider's web – I sensed Tom's growing fussing disquiet around us.

He poked at the fire, peered at it, sneezed in the smoking damp, struck a smouldering log a sharp blow till it split, then prodded the green blackening wound in the wood – appearing meanwhile distinctly (and audibly) dissatisfied with some obscure state of affairs to which he alone was privy. Next he turned his attention to a slight draught whistling through a flaw in one of the squares of the wide bay window. He sighed at it, as if to snuff it up altogether; then tapped the pane, listened to it, looked suspiciously outside, as if some deliberate mischief in the broad winter wind had occasioned it. He spent a good ten minutes tearing and rustling and compacting a plug out of a discarded sheet of parchment, which he then applied, with an air of considerable and noisy expertise, to the glass. 'Tom,' the Professor muttered at last, and Tom sat down upon a chair pushed into the bay and stared dismally along the river; then stood up just as suddenly to examine a fragment of the clay world that had escaped his attentions the night before, and lodged itself in a crack of the floorboards. He scraped down upon his hands and knees to determine whether there were other loose shards lurking about, and made a great show of dusting off his trousers when he stood up, as if to say, 'Finito,' with the smack of each palm on his pantaloons. 'TOM,' the Professor repeated, never looking away; and Tom desisted, stood stock still as a deer for an instant, as if struck by some profound and unshakeable conception. I glanced up then and noted his broad, handsome brow, the high, strong nose – only his thin lips, somewhat peevish, effeminate, pursed, displeased. He began to dally with the loose glowing locks of the chandelier above his head.

It occurred to me then, for the first time, that Tom was . . . envious of me, of my new-found place at the Professor's shoulder, of my geognostic eye. It occurred to me then, for the first time, that I was enviable – and, by some natural extension of the logic, that a spot at Syme's side was in itself a place of some distinction – never mind the damp fire smoking into the room and the obscure little corner of the Potomac in which we found ourselves. My subsequent reflection was less happy – for I had always considered myself a conceited young fellow in my way, and to have thus plainly demonstrated the prior absence of any real pretensions to enviability quite shocked – yes, shocked me, there is no other word. I had always possessed a number of certainties regarding myself – in my uncommon intelligence, air of gentility, of grace, etc., etc. – and never known that I was equally certain of the fact that not a soul would exchange his place in the world for mine. Until, for that moment at least, I saw Tom, fretting to peer over my shoulder, and observe the little notes I made on Syme's calculations.

'WILL YOU QUIT FUSSING,' roared the Professor suddenly, when the glass beads began to tinkle and shimmer in Tom's hand, 'and sit STILL. If you can't do that – fetch another log for the fire – make yourself useful – in the small matters that concern you.'

Tom, in a purse-lipped huff, strode out at once, clattering the door behind him; and we soon heard him briskly stomping through the snowdrifts into the yard. Then the biting knock of his angry axe against a stump of wood.

The Professor never said a word.

Regarding the marvellous tale of the planet's birth, Syme unfolded before me a tale of fires and frosts and spinning, intricate, meticulous devices – to say he was not mad would be perhaps the greatest condemnation I could offer, for no sublunar reason could connect the wonderful links of logic Syme forged. So I withheld my judgement, a dangerous postponement, as I suspected even then.

I grew suddenly aware, in Tom's absence, of our physical proxim-ity, my negligible chin propped in the nook of his shoulder, my downward eyes travelling along his powerful, crooked arm to the papers spread across the table. We were alone for the first time. The faint sweet smell of shaved wood filled my breath. And I realized then that the most powerful intimacy of which a man is capable often involves the details of those conjectures, convictions, that seem to touch least of all upon his private affairs. A theory, in short, passionately held, when . . . undressed (as it were) may expose a true maiden shyness, and offer the mental equivalent of that violence of discovery that so startled Diana in the woods.

The Professor seemed to fall into a kind of blushing consternation at the naked spread of his papers across the table, at the sudden reve-lation he conferred upon me. Having sent Tom out of the way, he now harked after him. He attended each stomp of foot and crack of axe with a cocked ear, allowing these wintry concussions to inter-rupt his arguments more and more until their diminished flow slipped through his fingers altogether; and he fell, hunching his shoulders about his neck, perfectly quiet, not so much lost in thought as in the absence of it.

Silence hung like cinnamon in the air, until Tom broke it, pushing a blast of cold through the door and kicking the snow from his boots. The exercise seemed to have restored his pink good humour, as he dropped an armful of fresh split logs beside the hearth. (Tom, as I soon discovered, always recovered easily, dipping and rising again, dry as a feather, like a duck in a pond.) He began to construct a second blaze from the wreck of the first, while the flames spat and hissed at the cold limbs of their new bedfellows.

'We should leave him to his work, Dr Müller,' Tom declared, and I confess I felt at once peevish and grateful for this interruption. Grateful in that the company of men (or I should say of man, in the warm and powerful concentration of the singular) has always ren-dered me . . . uneasy; peevish in that I suspected Tom (already!) of jealously guarding his little 'geognostic treasure' – for all his proud petitions to the world and windy endeavours to broadcast Syme's the-ories beyond the bend in the Potomac River where we found ourselves.

'Yes,' the Professor said, rising briskly, and striding to the bay window, 'to my work.' He lifted to his eye the black shard Tom had discovered that morning, and lost himself in the contemplation of the charred and dusty fragment, which formed a curious contrast to the milk-white ray of the winter sun that fell upon them.

'Why of course,' Tom said, clapping his hands in that sudden joy which was his peculiar gift, 'I know just the thing – a tour of the town. Splendid, splendid.'

Tom and I, like schoolboys released, tramped out into the snow, hugging our shoulders until the heat of beating hearts suffused even our fingertips. We scrambled, wet-footed and wet-handed, back along the trail to the little footbridge that led across this narrow reach of the Potomac to the market square.

'I have something to show you,' said Tom at last, for we had begun in silence, natural enough I suppose in the chill air, almost too cold and dense to breathe – though I suspected already that some unspoken contest between us thickened our tongues. Tom guided me along the central thoroughfare to the old junk shop – indicated by the sign picturing a somewhat blue ship under a rather green sea, and a decidedly elderly mermaid sorting through the wreckage. 'Simmons' was painted broad and red above the door. Various contraptions in various degrees of disrepair graced the front window, leather rubbed black by long use, silver greened and mottled in the sea of time.

Tom led me inside, stamping his snowy shoes in the doorway. A bell tinkled, and a woman in what is gently termed 'her middle ages' – just turned forty, perhaps – rose to greet us. I recognized her at once as the fading beauty present at the great experiment. She wore a wine-red dress, pressed flush against the tender white of neck and bosom, like the plumage of a cardinal against the snow. There was an easy gallantry in her carriage, and she seemed indeed to allow the room to shift around her, rather than exert herself, in moving from here to there. Her figure perhaps revealed a touch of the years – a certain twist of the long dress against her full hips. But in her face was nothing old. The rose of her lips and the ivory of chin and cheek

*had not felt the hand of time – which had brushed instead, lovingly,
against her hair, red-gold and rich once, now thinner and fallen into
the yellow leaf. Tom took her hand and gave it a smacking kiss, as if
deliberately to mock her perfect dignity. 'Mrs Simmons,' he said, 'I
have brought you a countryman.'*

*She nodded at me and clapped her hands together once. 'Was it
not very wonderful?' she said. 'Last evening? (Though you did
make a stew of it, I believe, Mr Jenkyns.) But to think such great
experiments cobbled together from my own – perhaps, Herr Müller'
– and here she turned the great blue of her wide eyes upon me – 'you
could discover for me the English of* Unrat?'

'Rubbish, I think,' I replied, blushing at the tease in her look.

*'Oh, that is unkind, Herr Müller,' she answered, smiling. 'I had
hoped for bric-a-brac, perhaps.'*

*Just then a broad young fellow with chapped hands clattered in
the shop, saving me from further embarrassment. He asked for 'old
horseshoes, which he might', he added, wrinkling and scratching his
nose, 'turn to some account – by boltin' them to a loose door . . .'
And as she attended to him, I had a chance to look about me.*

*The floor was bare wood and there was a great shine of brass in
the shop, glinting off knick-knacks, telescopes, old plaques, spectacles, burnished carriage wheels. I felt as if I stood in a sailor's cabin,
shipwrecked at the bottom of the sea. Mariners' tools collected on the
wood like barnacles. I picked up an old octant and peered through it,
squeezing one eye shut, and allowing the other to roam at will
through the gloom of the shop, until it lit, by chance, upon Mrs
Simmons. She swayed gently in the swish of her dress, a mermaid
past the first blush of youth, yet more elegant in age than the sharp
young ladies I had known, always fretting themselves, and busy
about their looks. I did not guess how long my eye fixed upon her,
until – to my considerable astonishment and confusion – I observed
her, through the thick lens, turn a sly eye upon me, and smile.*

*'She is Bavarian,' Tom whispered in my ear. 'Married an
American merchant captain and came here. Her husband volunteered against the British in 1812; died soon after at Fort McHenry;
not much mourned, far as I can see. The shop is full of things useful*

to Sam. He has a bit of a fancy for her, you know. (The Muses speak to him through her, you know.) I don't.'

This was the first unkind word Tom had uttered, and I guessed then the great delight of Tom's heart – gossip – which, in the largest sense I believe, is what drew him to the Professor in the first place. For Syme, as I had seen myself, gossiped with the gods more lightly than any man I had ever known; and was himself the object of more human curiosity. I guessed something else, as well: that perhaps Tom's envy extended even to the affairs of his master's heart.

Summoning my courage, I ventured a few words to Mrs Simmons in our native tongue, polite and awkward. How quickly the familiar becomes strange! For I felt a greater stranger, conversing in these native phrases, than I had since coming an alien to these shores. I picked up a few things – the hasp of a door, a brass knob – and set them down again.

Mrs Simmons touched me on the elbow, as some people do, with an intimate slight bump. 'How long have you been here?' she asked in grave and gentle English again.

'I arrived only yesterday,' I answered in German once more, determined to overcome my natural shyness – so great as to be palpable, a blush of the brow hot to the touch. I feared that in discoursing thus, in our mother tongue, I had claimed a privilege to which I had no right. But I persisted, and enquired in turn about Professor Syme.

'He has been kind in all ways to me and purchases a number of bits and pieces. For a shop like this is slow work, of course. And a lady needs occupation – I believe they call it.' She looked at me quite mischievously, with the smile that gleams on a glass of wine struck by candlelight.

'I will come again, if I may. It would be a comfort to hear my mother tongue.'

She nodded and we left.

Tom and I walked out into all the whiteness, so different from the precise shop-room shadows, their degrees of darkness and overlap, the shine of the brass, the small feet of the tables, and the gilt of the cloths laid over them. I guessed already the heavy loveliness of Mrs

Simmons, which drowned everything in the honey of her sweetness.

'I thought you might like to meet Sam's mistress,' Tom said, in a flat voice, unlike his customary chirp. Something appeared to have saddened him – perhaps himself.

'I did like it.'

We walked, deep as our boots in snow, down the heart of the road, while the silence spread between us, and the ice of the eaves shone till our eyes smarted.

Tom took me now through the loose and empty streets past a bright brick church and the newspaper office and the racing course. All directions still lay tangled in my mind like a cat's ball of string; and I could not have wound up our path again for love or money. We dined together and the hours rang out three times over our ale. Tom knew the tricks of winning strangers; and he practised them that afternoon. He always had the air of someone imparting confidences – he could make a guilty secret of the weather – and bound men to him by little conspiracies. Only when we split ways and I walked back alone to Mr Barnaby Rusk and my cold room (the fire decayed to dead soft ashes on the bricks) did I wonder suddenly if they supposed I had joined them and become a new member of Syme's salon.

I have accused my homesickness of softening me and leading me into a more mysterious and satisfying view of Syme than I had anticipated on setting forth. That burning planet, spinning, smoking, a device both rough and intricate, brave and disastrous, glittered in my memory. I dreamed of Syme that second night as I had seen him, flushed with the effort of creation, talking, talking, consumed by his thoughts as the globe was by its liquid fire – except that in my dream the words themselves shone and exploded as he spoke, burned away upon the air, and fell in scatterings of ash upon the floor. When I awoke to a brisk knock and heavy tread, it seemed the most natural thing in the world to discover that the Professor himself had entered the room, unbuttoned his greatcoat and draped it over my chair; and stood now, rubbing his brawny arms with either hand.

Syme was never easy at close quarters. He would duck his head and speak into his clasped hands; stride hither and thither, twitch at the curtains, peer out; turn suddenly and briskly the full sun of his attention upon his interlocutor, then darken at once, eclipsed by some cloud of preoccupation. 'Come on, Müller,' he cried, in his rough voice, 'I've been busy since six – upon a new planet – an imaginary planet – formed let us suppose by – erosion – as a pebble in a stream – only consider – for an instant – such a powerful stream.' He sat down at my feet, squeezing them together; and, still half-asleep, I considered this curious proposition for an increasingly uncomfortable minute. Then he rose briskly, leaned upon the splay of both hands against the window sill and stared out, utterly absorbed by the view of a tethered horse slowly scratching clear a foot of snow. 'Never say', he muttered, 'that the animals – are incapable of – concentration.' Then louder, once more, 'Come on.'

He looked at me now and I looked at him, my hair spread out over the pillow, my fingertips pinching the covers closer to my bosom (to expose the least quantity of hand), my eyes dim and blinking with sleep. I could scarcely speak – my English tongue loosened last after waking, and the best I could manage in reply was a grunted, 'Morning.' So deep in dreams had I lain that I suffered a peculiar shock in discovering that Syme could see me – this above all seemed miraculous and strange, that Syme saw me, that I had stepped so far from the haven of my own thoughts as to embark on the sea of his. Slowly the morning hardened around me, and the world grew sensible to my touch, and ceased to shimmer with dreams. Syme turned away and stooped to the ash in the hearth, as I stepped from my bed.

'Wonderfully clean, ash,' he said, as I began to dress, 'far superior – in many respects to – soap.' He lightly rubbed a pinch of the grey dust between thumb and finger, then brushed them clean again. For once, I omitted some of the niceties of my toilet, slung a pink cravat about my neck and left my long hair to tumble freely over my shoulders. Dressed and ready, I declared to his crouched back, 'I am your man.'

Sam rose awkwardly, turned on one leg, and looked at me. 'Good,' he growled. 'Better. You have come such a long way, I must trouble you to come a little farther. Can we offer you a real democratic Sunday roast at my father's table? In Baltimore, I'm afraid. Tom and I leave by coach at eleven.'

I accepted happily and stretched forth my hand to seal the offer. His own was cold and wet to the touch, for he had pressed it against the window pane while looking out.

'It is very close in here,' I said, and moved to let in fresh air.

But he turned to the door, and said more heartily, 'Shall we make a proper visit? A few days at least? Pack your portmanteau, and we can catch the mail together. You shall have the finest guest chamber – the floor will do for Tom. Good, that's settled – at eleven sharp. You will like my father – all strangers do.'

With that he shambled out, in his muscular way – stooping once briskly to examine some irregularity in the floor, then stomping on. Pondering over the unhappy suggestion of Syme's parting word, I began to pack my things.

At eleven accordingly the three of us set off by coach on the road to Baltimore. Tom and I set forth in a flutter of high spirits, and even Syme caught something of our merriment. He held up his briefcase to me. 'I have brought you some of my papers to look over,' he shouted against the clatter of the wheels and the driver's calls. We stopped for lunch at a tavern, the Apple Cart, perched between road and river. Trickles of dripping snow, along breast and back, teased us into shivers as we trudged through wheel ruts to the door. Mugs of steaming cider arrived and we held our hands around them till they seemed to melt away. When the brew burned its sweet cinnamon path down my throat and into the coursing of my blood I knew I had reached a noble land. Syme stood in front of the fire and struggled out of his greatcoat, arising from it like Neptune from the sea, steaming and roaring, as it dripped and drooped to his feet in a cold puddle. For the first time he seemed to belong to our youth. And he talked! How he could talk when the spirit was in him.

'I looked over this morning,' said Syme, 'when I woke early and could not sleep again for the cold, that final and magnificent passage of the Phaedo. You are acquainted with the Phaedo?'

'I confess . . .' I said, blushing, a proper schoolboy.

'I thought, Tom,' the Professor interrupted, raising an enquiring brow at his friend, and thumbing his lips in contemplative fashion, 'he said he was a doctor – a German doctor?'

'I heard him,' Tom replied, ill at ease, checking his pockets, as if the answer might lie there. 'Don't tell me I didn't hear him.'

'Perhaps we have the wrong fellow,' Mr Syme said, relieved at a possible solution. 'Perhaps that's it. Educated gentleman – wasn't he – the one we want?'

'I might have seen one – you know how it is in Pactaw, one minute not a soul in sight, and the next can't squeeze through the road, for doctors.'

'Tall fellow,' Syme asked in his gruff staccato, 'glum face? Looks like he's trying to see the tip of his nose – but can't quite? Determined not to believe a word he hears? Won't trust – the time – if one tells him?'

'Only in translation . . .' I finished at last in a brief pause and puffed a fat cloud at them from one of my occasional cigars. How they fell mum at that, and looked at each other, and glanced at their boots. Perhaps they expected me to laugh or lighten, but I did not – the Greek is a serious matter, and I would not give way to their teasing. (I could hear the eaves drip in the silence, and suddenly saw myself from a vast distance, a speck caught in a corner, that corner itself a speck and so on.)

'Herr Mooler,' Tom said at last, 'don't take on so – we only jest. I beg you not to look so glum, so Teutonically sincere. Our expedition (for it is nothing less) begins in joy.'

I blushed again and said nothing. At last, Mr Syme cleared his throat.

'You recall – the final dream of Socrates – testament in the phrase of your mad poet – Herr Müller – that the wise in the end prefer the beautiful. I am waiting – believe me, gentlemen – for that end. If only beauty would return the preference. In that great dream (long held to be nothing more – yet what more could one wish?) the logic melts – suddenly dissolves – leaks and dries away as our snow will – in a few days – but he teaches – in those final words –' Syme stabbed the air with his pipe, as if to prick the bubble of each phrase as it blew away, 'that the great end of all philosophy – natural and metaphysical

– is the myth of creation. *This has been my text – my Grail. To begin with – Beginnings – and finish with them, too – if I dare.'*

For all his pomp, or perhaps because of it, Syme had a charm no drab witch of common sense could dispel. There was something pathetic in these boasts – the talk (as I knew even then) of the self-educated man, who believes each unfamiliar book to be an undiscovered country, a new world proudly claimed by the possessor. I heard the braggadocio of naivety in his voice, of course I did – I am an educated gentleman, well travelled on the roads of learning. And yet when he asked me, 'Would you like, Phaedon, to hear the tale of creation?' – it was all I could do not to answer, 'Yes, please.'

The sunshine drifted white with winter over the floorboards; I heard the tick of dripping from the lintels. A little pool of snow and dirt had formed about our feet, and Tom scraped the toe of his boot in it while his master spoke. 'We are born in fire – shaped by the death of that fire.' This was a characteristic confusion of Syme's – a conflation of the race and the planet. 'Then worn smooth (I now believe) in the black current of the via lactea – like pebbles in a stream – smooth and round, of course, since the planets spin. Let us perch upon the moon and look down. A brilliant ball lies at our feet – for indeed the very hollows, full of water and mist, present a colour of their own as they shine (a perfect rainbow, indeed, or worldbow, rather). With the hands of Atlas, we stoop and lift its shell – opening up crown upon nested crown of burnished black. (Believe me, all our hearts are black at the core. It is only the shell that shines.) Let me write their names for you.' Syme cried for quill and ink and scribbled them on a piece of old manuscript from his portmanteau: Washington (Syme was a true republican), Caesar, Cassandra, name after curious name, a mad mythology. Syme gave me the slip and went on. 'After the sun cast us off – the fires died slowly within us. We burned away – like silver in a crucible – and cooled into – though this is only speculation – seven layers of metallic crust – separated according to their composition – think of oil and water – over a thousand years or so.'

Did I believe a word of it? I saw it all before me like a schoolboy's alchemy, except that, in Syme's glass vials, earths and suns lay stoppered. I loved nothing so much as the last 'or so', for when Syme erred a thousand years burned away like a fly in the flame, scarcely to be reckoned. 'Though this is only speculation!' – I knew not whether to laugh at the absurdity or the grandeur of him; but Tom was right, there was a kind of joy in it all, a sense of wings stretched at last. 'How are the layers arranged?' I questioned, to prompt him further.

'Like Russian dolls, if you like, growing smaller and smaller – stacked on top of one another. I call them crowns – though they are in point of fact – a sequence of concentric rotating spheres – jointed by a tightly packed metallic gas – known as fluvia. It is found mainly beneath the earth's surface – though it escapes occasionally – through volcanoes, of course – and smaller cracks. It is breathable – eminently breathable, I'd swear my life on it – and allows for the free independent rotation of each of the seven crowns – though there is occasional friction – between Calliope, the second crown, and Cassandra, the first. Strike your hands together with cupped palms – feel the smooth socket of air – keeping the palms apart.'

He did so, I followed him, Tom, too – the three of us laughing openly now, a curious convocation, much admired (I believe is the term) by the common punters. 'That is something like fluvia,' the Professor continued, rubbing his hands now. 'At sea, I believe – sailors see it in the sunset on hot days. The sun sucks it through the ocean – in huge bubbles to the air – where it burns red like gold.'

We all fell silent at the thought, lost in wonder at the strange world shimmering and swelling around us – until the bubbles, one by one, were pricked and dispelled by ordinary day: by the clatter of cups; talk of men; our wet feet. Then Syme said, in a kind of glorious regret, 'We stand on the roof, you see. If only we could discover a crack – on a nearby farm – a village street – under a humble lake – we might climb into the house – down the chimney like a thief into the heart of Nature.'

I could not say a word to this. But he needed no answers, caught in such fine flow; and I would gladly have listened to him talk for days, as I had listened to Werner, in the sweet honesty of awe. For I have always been a listener at heart, and a follower, a natural *admirer of the world, shy of my own steps in it, eager to hear the passage forced by greater men than I.*

'Kepler was the first,' Syme said, 'perhaps till now – the only scientist – in the sense in which the word will be used – in a decade's time perhaps – if we succeed.' (Did not that 'we succeed' ring in my ears and both unsettle and delight me?) 'Because of a discrepancy – eight minutes of arc – between the path of orbit according to accepted theories – and the path of orbit according to the finest observational data of the time – eight minutes, you understand – he overthrew a system of cosmology – that had ruled our thoughts for two thousand years. A nice destruction with so small an instrument! A true scientist. Eight minutes on this earth measures a distance of eight miles – so slight indeed that on a clear day – the errant navigator of a ship – may see by the naked eye the mark he has failed to hit.'

I ventured to interrupt him, anxious now to prove my own abilities, but Sam anticipated me. In truth, I was happy to keep silent, and I swallowed my question in the bitter-sweet dregs of my cup of cider.

'Naturally the term cuts a far greater arc in the more distant sky – but the image serves to illustrate the nicety of the calculations. A faith in precision is the first requisite of the modern scientist – a faith not so distinct from a man's religious faith. Let me explain. The scientist trusts – in the organization of details – despite a world of unexplained phenomena. The Godly man trusts in the Cause – of such organization – despite the mass that is unintelligible and perverse. Both faiths require the fisherman's instinct: beliefs survive only – at certain depths – like fish – they must be left to their natural habitats – if they are to stay active and potent. They should seek neither to rise too high – nor dip too deep – nor consort with other fish – at different plummets. Kepler understood this better – perhaps – than any man.'

The landlord called round for more orders. Tom gave me a canny look. 'Are you thirsty?' he asked. 'Sam will talk us all dry yet.'

'Hush,' I told him, 'you will break the spell. Surely I have found an American Mesmer, a new magnetism.'

'You flatter him,' said Tom, but saw that Sam had fallen dark, as if a cloud passed over him. He took a long draft and turned his back to the fire blazing in the grate.

I asked, 'What do you make of Baconianism?' and sunshine broke upon him again.

'The herd that follow Bacon', he mocked, 'have isolated one of Kepler's gifts – not precision itself but rather – a kind of humility that accompanies precision. A vile and gross, slyly boastful, ignorant, arrogant humility. A kind of wilful American pride in saying – I do not know – I cannot guess. Baconianism has led us directly into the bog – where we now find ourselves – which but for Kepler's braggadocio – we should never know to escape. For Precision is a deep fish, to be sure – but it cannot plumb every depth. In the end we must explain this world – by its causes – not by the measurement of its actions.'

'That is our creed, you see,' said Tom gaily.

'As ever, though, I began myself with a precision: that crack in the universe – nicely measured – that opens upon such vague and powerful depths. It was a question of mass – a simple question of mass.'

He paused. The snow had ceased and the sky cleared. We had not yet passed the midpoint of the shortened afternoon. Light fell through the window and on to the blaze, like a bright ghost. There is no cheer so ethereal as a sunny fire. My thoughts strayed from those deep matters, as indeed did Syme's, for when he spoke again, his tone had softened and his subject changed.

'I have been much plagued lately – by familiar dreams. For some years – a dream has come to me – in different shapes at different times – but saying the same thing. "Syme, you must get to work and compose – music!"' He laughed. 'Formerly I took this to mean what I was already doing; that the dream encouraged me, as fellows cheer – the laggard in a race – that I should continue to practise that particular science I have made my special study.' He smiled, as though he were ashamed of his fancy, and stared at his boots. 'Lately it has occurred to me, however – that the dream means nothing of the kind – and that in fact I should listen more closely – and really do as it says, and compose music. Especially since, in this regard, I have fallen some ways behind.' He stretched his aching arms and hunched his huge shoulders. 'I talk, upon occasion,' he said, 'a great deal of nonsense.'

Tom and I did not answer, stood around him smiling, out of a peculiar sort of . . . shyness, I suppose. A truly famous time, but the coachman, like an evil messenger, summoned us at the door. Sam, his tongue loosened, still bubbled over with talk and could not sit quiet in the coach. The fire of his thought had burned its way into his bones and blood. He crossed and uncrossed his legs, stared out of the window, and then put his hands to his knees to keep them still. His eloquence promised well for our visit, and in that confidence I slept all the way to Baltimore.

The short day had set before we arrived. Syme had long fallen silent and Tom gave me a significant look as we forced open the frozen gate and followed Sam into the front garden of his old home. A shadow passed across a light within, and soon a figure stood in the open doorway. 'I had begun to worry,' a man's voice called out clear in the clear night. 'Sam, my dear.'

Syme nodded and took his father's hand, but soon pushed past him, calling, 'Mother!' and, 'Bubbles!' up the stairs and along the hallway. I heard a rush of steps and the delighted sigh of 'Brother'. Tom shook Mr Syme warmly by the hand. 'I have returned your son to you, you see. Please to keep him, if you will.'

'I would if I could, Tom. But you do it better,' said the father. 'It is good to see you. And the famous . . . Friedrich Müller, I believe, I am glad to meet you. There are some in this godless country, you see, who can speak a civilized tongue. I dare not think of the butchery Tom has practised on your name.'

'Is it not Mooler, then?' said Tom, delighted in some peculiar way by his own ignorance. 'He is already Phidy to us, Mr Syme. I assure you that he is Greek to his heart's blood.' In truth I had never been called Phidy (short for Phaedon, I suppose, the steadfast narrator of Socrates' final days) till that moment, but the name stuck. After that my title in America was always and only Phidy, and the Symes knew me as nothing else.

'It has been such a pleasure to meet your son, Mr Syme,' I said timidly, acutely conscious of my situation. Or rather, ignorant of it – for my particular role regarding the Professor's enterprise wanted a great deal of clarification. I knew not whether I was Syme's supplicant or his executor; and wavered in my dealings with him between a kind of administrative arrogance and the humility of an apprentice.

'Yes,' said the father with an air I could not name, 'I suppose it has.' We had remained standing in the entrance hall, but Mr Syme took our light travelling cases in hand and led us in. 'Anne, my dear,' he called, 'tonight we have with us a true European. One of the old breed.'

A door opened on our left and a woman stood in its light. She looked as much like Sam as a woman may, though older and perhaps less happy. Her figure was nearly as tall and her bones were built for the same strength, though in her case only the frame was completed, and the flesh hung loose off her neck and collarbones as a well-worn dress. 'You must forgive my husband,' she said affectionately, in a voice like old upholstery, both softened and frayed, 'he is a dreadful snob. For my part, I am pleased to welcome you, Mr Müller, simply for your own sake, and as a friend of my son.'

'Say rather my judge, Mother,' called Sam laughingly from behind the door, 'or, should I say, my benefactor – Phidy?' He sat on a low settee beside a fire, infinitely younger he appeared already, and more easily – happy. The uncomfortable heat of his blue eyes had been turned low, and he caught my own eye above his mother's shoulder, without flinching for once. A girl's head, plain and contented, lay on his lap. The head rose quickly and sat upright on top of its body – which appeared somewhat older, more used to things – and both were flustered at having been surprised in so intimate a posture. 'Tom!' she cried, recovering, and flung herself at my . . . friend. Then she stood straight and smoothed out her hair, more childish still in her sudden propriety. 'I beg your pardon, sir,' she said to me. 'Only we are old friends.'

'Bubbles,' Tom interposed, 'meet Phidy.'

'How-do-ye-do,' she said, with a curtsy.

Sam called out, 'You must excuse my sister; she is not accustomed to the ways of gentlemen.'

'Shame, Brother,' she urged, from the side of her wonderful mouth, which seemed to wriggle a hundred ways at once, while the rest of her plain good face kept mum; 'you know better.'

I kissed her hand – 'Such courtesy!' cried Sam – and saw a wedding band on her finger. 'I am a child only for tonight,' she whispered, observing my look, 'to see my brother. Tomorrow I return to my husband.'

That evening was the happiest of my stay thus far. Tom and Sam (I shall call him Sam now, happily and easily at last) and Bubbles rejoiced in my new sobriquet and 'Phidies!' flew across the supper table like bees at a picnic. Only his mother Anne was quiet, quiet and proper, and called me 'Mr Müller' if she passed along the wine. She had what Tom later described to me as a 'face upon a face, like a painted doll's' – a lovely girlish countenance carved within the broader jaw of womanhood and motherhood, yet unfilled, unfleshed by age, out of a curious . . . abstinence, which I observed already. She said little and ate less. When she did speak, the conversation halted like a boy beside an old woman. But after a decorous moment, away we flew again. Sam's father was charming, a natural gentleman. But as the evening wore on and the wine ran low, his eyes drained of colour and his face filled with red; the nose looked pinched and pointed. There was something coarse in his aspect then, as rough as parchment, and his tongue grew sharp. 'Not every son travels to Pactaw to see the world,' he said, laughing heavily.

Sam replied, deep in the wine himself, 'The world shall come to us. Is that not so, Phidy?' and I scarcely knew what to answer.

We sat before the fire after supper. Sam lay at his mother's feet with his head on her lap and his legs stretched along the grate. He adored her, this much was clear already; and should have happily opened the earth and led her by the hand into its wonderful heart for her sake alone, to please her. Even though, as I guessed already, she was the kind of lady who did not suffer the extraordinary gladly, as others dislike fools. Sam for his part wished only to amaze her. Mrs

Syme sat quite straight with her hands on his head, though she did not move them nor stroke his hair.

'You'll burn your boots, fool,' cried Bubbles, and busied herself in pulling them from her brother's feet. She laughed more than he.

'It is always like this,' Tom whispered in my ear. 'For a night, or half of one, he is content to be a child again. But no more. You will know him again in the morning.'

Still, a fire is always companionable, and I contented myself silently by reading in its busy flames the thousand images that had impressed themselves upon me in that long week.

Sam's father excused himself quite early. 'I am afraid I am too old for my children now, Phidy. I must to bed.' The room seemed much emptier after he had gone; Anne's uneasiness grew in proportion and filled his absence. Her eyes had followed him anxiously as he left and fixed themselves on the closed door while her ears traced his light steps up the stairs. She remained stiffly in her seat and could not think for the life of her what to do with Sam's head. But when he shifted to punish some foolishness of Bubbles, she rose quickly and excused herself and bade us good night. That was the general signal and we did not linger long.

I tiptoed upstairs and Sam followed more heavily with a lantern. 'We have given you Bubbles' room,' he said. 'She must make do with the study. Never fear,' he added laughing, 'she is a tough Bubbles.' He opened a door to a cold, fireless room, and I saw shadows and a white bed. 'I am glad you have come, Phidy, good night.' I fell in love then, I think, with the charm of being taken in by a new family in a new world. 'Do not be taken in,' my father had said. The Symes were a curious gallery of characters, and I rolled their pet name for me on my tongue, in each of their various tones and accents. Need I say that Bubbles' voice fell most often on my inward ear? I wondered what manner of man her husband might be and fell asleep to the echo of her teasing 'Phidy'.

The great affair of Sunday afternoon was dinner, after church. A rare patch of sun from her own slight stores of happiness had fallen on Anne Syme's head that day. She had prepared a feast. Her face was red with steam and toil and her hair wrinkled in the kitchen heat. But she was happy for once and did not glance for ever after 'Father'.

There is no beauty like a well-laid table. Anne sat upright at the head and watched her son carve the swelling ham, and she offered the first cut to 'Phidy'. I did not know her well then, nor Sam's father who in time I came to know better. Like Sam, he had his faults, but envy was not among them, and he had that rare grace that can charm equally in the corner or in the light. For Anne shone and Sam shone in her heightened looks.

That Sunday dinner was significant for more than a woman's brief good spirits, however. The talk turned to Sam's 'great theories', as Anne called them, and she wished to hear my opinion of them. 'I confess', she said, 'that I am a little surprised, a gentleman such as yourself, sir, should have come such a long way to see my strange son.'

'He sent us such an extraordinary petition,' I said, 'it would have been churlish to decline. I pledge my life, he declared, I pledge my life; the least I could undertake was a sea voyage.'

'And what do you', she enquired, touching a corner of her lips with a napkin, 'make of Sam?'

'So far we have discussed only the bright surface of his theories. We have not yet ventured inside to the matter of them.'

'Do you mean the papers and all those numbers?' she asked. 'I always quiz Sam for being so close with them. "In time," he says, "in time." But I think nobody can work entirely alone. I know Tom is there, bless you, Tom, but he's not much good with figures, are you? Sam needs somebody else with a head for figures. I was good with them when I was a girl, I suppose that's where Sam acquired the habit. But I haven't kept in practice and I don't know all the new fashions. I cannot understand any of the numbers he tells me and I would have thought anybody could understand a number. But Tom says you are a hot-off-the-press scientist in Germany. I think it is so important to have colleagues.'

'I told you before, Mother,' said Sam. 'He is not my colleague, he is my – judge.'

'That sounds awful,' said Anne. 'You aren't, are you?'

'I am only a curious onlooker,' I said. 'I am his student, I suppose.'

'There, you see,' Bubbles broke in. 'I suppose you are always asking him questions? I bet he doesn't tell you. What do you ask him, perhaps I can help?'

'I should like to ask him what he is investigating at present. What work is there to be done and what do you still hope to learn?'

'I'm sorry, Phidy,' he said, in his curious interrupted manner, a flow of words like a frozen river breaking into ice. 'You have come in the middle of – a barren season. I am looking for a hole or a crack – in the first crown, you see, under Virginia. Something we could poke our noses into. The only clue we have is escaped fluvia – the gas between the crowns. We reckon that if it leaked – it would make its way through earth or water – into plants or the ground or the air. So we test them in the spring – with a lantern-like contraption of my own devising. Fluvia burns blue. But under all this snow, nothing can get out, so we have – little enough to do.'

'What have you discovered so far?'

'Traces here and there, of course. Branches of birch – burning like a blue heaven. Odd ponds with strange plants in them. But nothing yet substantial enough – to suggest a real fissure in the crown.'

'Is there a pattern to them?' I asked. Sam looked puzzled. 'I mean do the traces follow a particular pattern?'

'You understand, Phidy,' Sam said, sighing I suppose over my misdirected curiosity, 'that in theory at least the gases escape through aberrations – random cracks that develop in the first crown, which does not move. Each year the traces should be found over the same cracks – unless a new one develops. But beyond that there need be no – consistency – to our readings.

'Unless,' he continued, then stopped still as a gravestone. 'Unless,' he said again and we all fell silent. 'Not a word for a minute!' he cried, almost angrily, though we had not spoken. We sat foolishly in our chairs and did not dare to eat. Anne coughed. Only Bubbles took a piece of ham to her mouth with a sly look. The ham was arrested in mid-air as Sam spoke again.

'Phidy,' he said at last, looking into his plate (and did not Tom flinch, as if a blow had struck him, when Sam called my name),

273

'suppose there was a pattern. Suppose – the traces in a particular spot – grew weak and strong, not only from season to season, but from year to year. What would you interpret from that fact?'

'Either that the path fluvia followed to the outer air was blocked or irregular, or that the source of fluvia itself was blocked or irregular.' I was in a curious spot, describing a man's madness to himself in terms as crazy as his own. Did I believe it now – him, now?

'Exactly,' he said, scarcely heeding me. 'I had assumed the path – was blocked; but suppose the source itself was irregular – or, rather, that it followed a fluctuating and regular pattern. Then I thought – what could account for those fluctuations? And the answer came as soon as the question. What if not the rotations of the crowns themselves? Suppose again – that the gaps in two crowns overlapped in a kind of negative eclipse – would not the resulting stream of fluvia be doubly powerful? And stronger still for a triple eclipse? Could we not deduce – from the strength of those traces – the motions of the crowns themselves – and even the regions of their imperfections?'

Sam was away, in a flight of fancy as improbable as it was enchanting. Yet was there not some cold, sober good sense to his reasoning, an air of matter of fact? The meal was broken up at once, and I shall not soon forget Anne's delight declaring itself to any who would listen.

'Have I not said, Sam,' she cried, 'Father, you have heard me, that he needs the company of men such as himself? Phidy, I have told him often enough, he needs colleagues.' Poor Tom, I thought. 'No wisdom can grow entirely in loneliness, I have learned that myself. Bubbles, is it not a treat to see your brother thinking before us, reasoning aloud?'

She was always somehow a motionless woman, but now pride sang from her straightened back and could barely be contained by her still hands held against the front of her dress. 'For once, I have you all to witness, and you see that I am not such a fool. I was right, wasn't I, Father?'

'I am sorry, Mrs Syme,' I began, 'to have been the innocent cause of ending such a happy meal . . .'

274

Sam had cleared a space before him, and plates of ham and jugs of ale and a dish of butter and spilled cups and dirty knives lay all in a heap, thrust together and puzzled at one another's company. Sam shouted at Bubbles to bring it all away, and Mr Syme stood aside and said quietly to no one, 'Scientific discovery seems very unsettling to the digestion,' and left. Tom laughed (unhappy and shrill) and spurred Bubbles on with the carving knife.

'Nonsense, Phidy,' Anne said, and Sam took up the word: 'Phidy, we must go into this at once – while the mind is hot, so to speak. We need space, Mother – a tableful of space. Fetch the papers with me, Phidy. Tom, quit fooling for once – see to it that we have some elbow-room to work when we return.'

There was a great deal to be done. Sam and I sat long poring over charts of figures, comparing them, combining them, mapping them on to larger charts until my brain grew numb against the cold obstruction of numbers. Tom drowned among them and stared helplessly out of the window, fighting his feet and hands to keep still, lest he rouse Sam's sharp tongue. In the end, Tom settled on the task of making tea, which he accomplished admirably and miserably and to great honour. The day grew grey without us, and then black. Still we worked, until a bell somewhere tolled eight times and Anne said, absolutely, she must have the table clear for supper. Sam and I looked up, spent, and knew in each other's eyes that after five long hours of calculations, we had discovered that grand thing, a possibility.

I had known Sam Syme for only four days. I had come a great way to . . . have a look at him, and already he had summoned me to fight beside him. He was a great summoner of men. I knew then what had drawn Tom to him, a year or two before, and led him to resign a respectable life at an ordinary newspaper for the hard task of keeping in business a mad genius. Sam had the gift of turning his own affairs into questions of life, and he claimed us as a king would press into his army citizens defending their own small homes. After all, if Sam were right, the world under my feet would be transformed. The world around me was already taking its shape.

In a quiet moment after supper I sought the solitude of their porch, well fed and suffering from that curious loneliness that seems an echo to good humour and company and healthy spirits. Mrs Syme, to my surprise, came to join me, sat down beside me on the steps, hoisting her apron beneath her, and sighing and saying nothing.

'A fine meal,' I ventured at last, to break the silence. 'I believe there is no happiness like the happiness of the . . .' I hesitated over the word 'stomach', fearing it improper, and sought another in some anxiety. 'Table,' I concluded at last, in great relief.

'I am glad you have come and to have met you,' she said quickly, keeping her head down (like her son!), and embarking, it seemed, upon a long thought that had been unravelling for some length in her meditations. Then she looked up at me, and I noted the strange youth of her inner countenance (I can think of no better term), for she had a doll's eyes and nose and lips, upon a broader, heavier head. Half a moon fell over the sharp snow and the path it left led deep and wavering into the beginning of the woods.

A confession: I have always had an indifferent way with mothers. They seem a strange species, and quite unlike the ordinary run of women. Indeed, there seems to me something strangely masculine in the breed, something practical and well worn, even when they preen themselves, as Mrs Syme undoubtedly did, pinching her cheeks, touching her lips, and keeping a weather eye on her figure, whenever her husband stepped in the room. 'It has been', I began, sounding the note of appreciation, and missing the proper pitch (I could hear this myself) by an octave or so, 'a great –' joy, I would have said, but she interrupted me.

'I wished only to say to you,' she broke in, 'again' (blushing slightly, so she looked both younger and older, a girl and a fussing grandmama, depending as the moonlight caught her pale hair and shone yellow or white), 'how pleased I am – to meet you – and see my son in such – fine company – because – because – in short, Phidy' – she stammered at my pet name, quite red-faced now – 'I wish to tell you that I – call it a mother's fancy if nothing better – that I DO NOT TRUST TOM JENKYNS.'

We could see a horse cantering some way up the road, a dark shape shouldering through the cold, with a heavy rider – and then hear him, the hoofs muffled in snow, the sharp and distant breaths. This seemed to spur Mrs Syme to conclude her surprising confidence. 'I beg you, Phidy, not to mistake me and believe that I doubt Mr Tom's good heart or . . . application; but I fear – I fear greatly – that he puffs my son – for his own purposes – puffs him with a great bellows – and my son, Herr Müller, is just the man to be – led on by rumours of his own success – till he – till I fear he will – burst. That's all. I mean to say that I am glad that he is in respectable hands. You seem to me, sir' – and she sought the word her son had used, and found it again, strangely comforted by the term – 'a good judge. That's what Sam said. A good judge. And that's a fine thing, Phidy, I believe.'

I had no time to answer her, for the horse clattered up to the foot of the porch, and Mrs Syme rose quickly beside me, as if discovered in some conspiracy, and seized a broom resting in the doorway, and began to sweep the dust of snow off the steps into the road.

The horseman proved to be Bubbles' husband come to fetch her home. He was a butcher named Reuben, a bluff, sober, successful man, with hands as big as melons, one of which fairly crushed my own poor palm when he shook it. 'I shan't get snow on your fine carpets, Mrs Syme,' he called, standing out in the cold. 'I've only come for Barbara.'

Barbara called for 'a minute, my dear' and flew about the house in a tiny tempest. We gathered on the porch to see her go. She embraced Sam long and cried, 'I am so glad, there is nothing like a geognostic revolution to cheer a Sunday night.' She kissed Tom and then ran to fetch her small bag, then ran out and in again and took me by the hands. She pecked me on the cheek and said, 'Beware of my brother, Phidy.' A blush of warm shame spread over my face, welcome in the cold wind of the clear night. 'I shouldn't listen to a word he says.' She was gone before I could protest, lost in Reuben's great cloak as the horse disappeared into the snow.

That night Tom made me his proposition. We were all tired as dogs and I at least was more than half-asleep. Sam's parents had gone to bed and the three of us sat before the grey end of a fire. I held a brandy in my hand and the flame of our cigars made up for the ebbing warmth of the embers in the grate. Sam smoked on his back, stretched out on the hot tiles beside the fireplace. 'There is a great deal of work to be done,' he said, not for the first time that day. 'We need another man.'

'We need more than that, Sam,' Tom said, a trifle peevish still. 'We need money. That old lantern for testing flu' won't do any more, that's all. It is time to bring in Galileo; we want precision now. This is not the first time the matter has come up, but I think it is the first time, Sam, that you will own I am in the right.'

I sat among them and could not guess whether they spoke thus openly out of indifference to me or because they had assumed my complicity. I did not remain long in silence or in doubt.

Tom turned to me, with a practical air, and said, 'This report you mentioned, Phidy, what goes in it? If you want to get to the bottom of our enterprise, you may have to go with us a little way. We cannot have you along as a free passenger, you see that, Phidy, don't you? We must all carry the weight. Don't that tally with your ideas of the mission?'

I could not tell whose mission he meant. When I said 'yes' to Tom I did not suspect my answer mattered very much. An answer is often the easiest thing to give. I comforted myself with the reflection that most of our decisions have been made by the time the question comes. If we have lingered long enough to hear it, our answer is probably assured. That night by candlelight I composed my first 'report'.

My dear father,

I have arrived safely in America after a somewhat solitary journey, in the course of which I had a great deal of time – and, as the sea swept by us, room – to examine the disposition of my character which has brought me here; and which has, in some measure I know, disappointed you ... My first impressions of this new world can be confined to two words: such distance and *such cheapness! Distances are not considered in this country as in Europe – an American thinks nothing of travelling a hundred miles for a day or two; and indeed, even now, I am writing from Baltimore, under the roof of the Professor's father – though we return to Pactaw, a long day's coach-ride to the south, in the morning. Food there is in plenty, fine meats, and thick cheeses, and sweet ales – indeed, I have dined well in this new world, with a freshened appetite, and begin, I believe, to grow plump. There is plenty of everything, in fact: of dirt and squalor and poverty and riches, of low and high, of broad and narrow, of the genteel and the coarse, the proper and the improper. Plenty of everything, that is, except, as one American put the case to me, of doubts: 'an American doubts of nothing'. I have known a great while that doubts are a kind of infection, and may be caught from one man to the next; but I did not suspect until now that the reverse is also true, and that their absence is equally contagious, and may be passed, from hand to hand.*

A natural gift for doubting, I believe, Father, is among the reasons that I have baulked at those political ideals on which you have spent the capital of your heart. Any Idea (no matter how great or good) that involves the disposition of men is bound to slip into a thousand little errors, growing and compounding each other, until that seed of truth, from which it rose, is strangled and buried in a kind of undergrowth. And yet – I have begun a great many thoughts in my short stay in America with that phrase – and yet, among the attractions this enterprise affords me, the chief of these is the company of the men (or rather man) I have stumbled upon. 'Do not be taken in,' you warned me; well, I confess, I have been taken in, in the kindest fashion, by my hosts; and for the first time in my life, perhaps, begin to feel at ease among my – well, I hardly dare say it now, though I should have been appalled at such humility two months ago – my equals. Before I left home, you desired me to return with something, you did not care what, that should be exclusively American, something which could not be procurable anywhere else. When I saw Sam Syme I longed to pack him up, and direct him, per next packet from Baltimore, to you – for he was the first article I met with that could not by any possibility have been picked up out of the United States.

Such fire as glows and boils within him! I believe the phrase 'fearless in thought' could be construed as damning, the mark of someone hesitant in the field of fact, and brave only in the barracks of his contemplation. And yet how few of us are truly fearless in thought! Syme clambers up the branches of his imagination, certain at each turn, that his foot shall find a limb, his hand a hold, wherever he reaches – and in that certainty I follow; and, it may please you to know, have even guided him once, this very evening, towards his next ascent!

I apologize, dear Father, for the uncharacteristic enthusiasm of this letter – I will endeavour to correct it in future, it is quite unlike me. Only you must consider how cold my chamber is now – the ice glistening against the pane, like the tooth of some winter animal waiting to creep in; the fire dead in the hearth; and the pan cooling in the bed. It is the only warmth left me tonight – but such warmth – the smouldering remnant from the fire of this afternoon's . . . inspiration, which I hope will prove a great, a signal advance, in our discoveries. In short, I wish to say that Syme's theories are by no means as visionary as we supposed; that I believe I have some (and by no means insignificant part) to play in their development; and that, if exploited properly, they could be of rare service and honour to the German nation. Surely, this is what we hoped. To this end, I require a slight addition to the funds we agreed upon. Unfortunately, Syme's experiments are costly and mine in probing his are no less so . . .

Believe me ever, etc. your dutiful son,
Friedrich

I fell asleep in Bubbles' bed, to the sigh and click of the wind in the icicles in the eaves, less lonely than I had ever been since coming to America. Naturally, I took this step fully conscious of my own equivocations. 'Syme's theories are by no means as visionary as we supposed,' I wrote – an interesting choice of words! Of course, I knew that I had joined them after a fashion, but comforted myself with the thought that what fashion remained to be seen. Yet equivocations are subtle and fluid creatures and rarely survive the processes of life.

We returned to Pactaw the following morning. I promptly shifted my slight gear to Syme's house, and ensconced myself in a small box-like room looking over the river and the market square. I explained my change of plans to Mr Barnaby Rusk, as Tom came to help me with my chest. 'I shall lodge', I said, 'with Mr Syme, a gentleman who lives across the river, and with whom I am engaged upon – some business.'

Mr Rusk considered the matter a moment and said, 'The same gentleman, I believe, who came to see you at breakfast the other day? A broad, low fellow with a swagger? Yes, yes,' he added, scratching a lonely loose grey hair that curled from his pink chin. 'I remember him well – he should have been a fine – he should have been a fine' – Barnaby occasionally required several swings at a sentence, just as he needed to rock once or twice to lift himself from a chair – 'pugilist, I believe. I should have been glad to take him on . . . in my day. He could go a few rounds, I think. The chest of a – chaffinch, sir; that's the clue. Never mistake it.'

Tom gave me a sly look, and we giggled shamefully when hauling the chest towards the bridge. 'Hush,' I cried, 'he shall hear us – Mr Rusk sets great store by his dignity.' But this only set off Tom afresh, and I confess that I followed – strangely cheered nevertheless by this surprising confirmation of Sam's . . . endurance.

The house suffered greatly from damp, and my bedchamber was cold as a cow's nose each night, for it had no fireplace and lay far from the kitchen. I needed no other excuse to linger late with Tom and Sam, drinking rum and tea beside the tavern fire and warming our shoes against the grate.

Sam, with his boundless energy for devices large and small, jury-rigged a line on which we might drape our night-gowns every evening without singeing them. 'We shall go to sleep warm at least,' he said, 'though we awake as cold as in our grave-beds.' The hanging garments themselves had the air of the cemetery about them and we often talked deep into the morning in the company of those pale ghosts.

My new role sat uneasily on my conscience, and I reasoned to myself that a man might follow a preacher and not a faith – for I could not yet happily describe myself as 'a believer'. I was enthralled by the man, and it was in his company that I felt the fulfilment of my project.

The snow, however, delayed much of our experimental work, though we had time in abundance to complete the adjustment to Syme's theories begun at that fateful dinner. Sam designed an improvement upon the magic lantern, his first invention, whose small flame was a blue eye peering into the hollows of the earth. It was called the magnesium match, a thin, flammable wire trapped in a crystal prism and suspended from the inside of a glass hood. We held this lantern above a fire of leaves or twigs or the alcohol solution of loose earth or pond water. Then we lit the match and a thin blue spirit of light appeared in the smoke and danced high or low upon the lantern's glass walls. The position of this gay faerie depended on the content of fluvia in the smoke, and we etched a fine web of reckonings against the glass to chart her. We could now measure such niceties of blue as would suffice an angel in tracking the depths of Heaven. Tom playfully named this lantern the flu', and so we called it. But snow still barred us from the Pearly Gates. We ate and wrote and talked and slept under that roof, often days on end without venturing forth. It was Tom's task to keep our bodies and souls together, an ungrateful job – until my father could answer my call for greater funds. For our souls could eat the air, crammed with visions and calculations, but our bodies grew often so chilled they nearly forgot their material selves.

But there were parties, too, and weeks spent free of all thoughts of this hollow earth. An old clap-up piano landed in the shop of Frau Simmons one day, and Sam declared he must have it, though the keys rattled like spit on a hot pan and the pedals squealed at every foot and the back panel bellied forth like a sail in the wind. 'I must compose – music!' he declared, over Tom's high-pitched protestations. We could not lift it across the narrow footbridge, so Sam rigged a pulley to a willow branch and lowered the piano on to the frozen river, with a handful of boys recruited, to steady her as she came. A swarm of townsfolk, like flies, followed everything we did – though in a general way we were disapproved of, and the boys I fear received something of a hiding for lending a hand to 'the cracked wizard across the water', as Sam was sometimes called. How sweetly she slid across the ice, the keys smiling like a mouthful of broken teeth, at the brisk air and the exercise; while Tom chased after her and banged half a song into the cold afternoon along the river – for he was just the sort of fellow to give in with a good heart, and go along with anything when the time came. I can tell you she was not so light to lift again upon the other bank.

When we finally installed her in the tavern room, and Sam had spent a hot week in shirt-sleeves, the fire roaring to fill the hearth, while he repaired her (such a dismal banging and groaning and tinkling as Tom and I endured!), Sam insisted on having a 'musical experiment', as he called it, and invited a handful of the locals across the river to celebrate – often the same fellows who attended the first catastrophic display I had stumbled upon the previous month. The ladies came, of course, wives and widows, and nervous young things, bonneted and blushing, and among the latter two: Frau Simmons in a green dress that glittered silver in the light, till she did indeed resemble the elegant mermaid swimming through the gloom of her shop sign; and Kitty Thomas, the baker's daughter, whose sharp tongue and stubborn insistence on what she knew and did not know greatly amused Tom, who minded neither them nor the pockmarks marring her pretty face. I brewed a special pot of Glühwein over the fire – cheap claret, costly oranges, sticks of cinnamon a finger thick, and brandy – and thought, If only you could see me, Father, and how easy it is to get along when everyone who knows me better and my dour spirit is half a world away. Though I confess to feeling a slight heartache at the imposition of the ladies, and their claims upon my companions' affections.

In the event this mattered little, for Sam spent much of the *evening at the piano, happy and red in his fine face, quite drunk, banging away; and he insisted, definitely, drunkenly, insisted, that I take the hand of 'fair Frau Simmons' (as he said it), while he was thus engaged. And so my compatriot and I . . . exchanged a look . . . and ventured a step, and, whispering a kind of apology – 'I'm afraid,' I murmured, 'Quite so,' she replied, and added,'We must obey him since everyone . . . have you not seen? . . . does as he says' – took each other by the hand. And away we whirled! How happily I cannot say, till I remember thinking, at a hot and breathless pause in the music, Do not glance in a mirror, Phidy, for you shall not recognize the joyful gentleman peering out.*

Sam had a sweet voice, rich and deep and light withal, as if it floated to its own surprise above the ordinary clatter – of footsteps on the floorboards and hurried 'pardons' and scrapes and little squeals and grunts of effort and concentration. I remember one song in particular, as the bells rang out two o'clock across the river, and only a handful of souls remained; sitting mostly on the sill of the bay window or leaning against a wall. He played tirelessly, and even at that late hour could sing out with a kind of mocking and melancholy bravado:

> *In leafy dell or dingle*
> *Where lovers like to mingle*
> *And maids and bachelors single*
> *Walk past them sadly,*
> *There will I roam or rove*
> *For friends the stars above*
> *And if I'm not in love*
> *At least I'm madly.*

And I thought, as he turned to us smiling to see if we twigged, What a talent for happiness he has, for ordinary and wonderful happiness, for easy 'good times', as the old men say, remembering. And I thought, as I took Frau Simmons' soft hand (ever so faintly etched with the fretwork of age) for a final waltz, Perhaps I am learning something of that, too.

In the morning, of course, we faced a different reckoning: hard heads and a heap of empty bottles by the fire; and empty purses and tired hearts. And it was Tom, as usual, who swept the grate, and cleared the room, and dropped the bottles into the first thaw of the river. That afternoon — a bleak, black, lingering, miserable hole of an afternoon, that squeezed us into a corner, and pinched us to mean spirits and sharp words — a letter arrived from my father, answering my . . . answering our request. I sat with a thick head before the fire while the snow dripped off the lintels in the dull thaw; and I read — with a sudden pang at the sight of my father's hand that reminded me how far I had come already, how loath I would be to return — these words:

My dear son,

Ruth stands over my shoulder and begs me to 'leave nothing out', though I scarcely know what to 'put in' our lives are so quiet here, since you've gone. I think she means only that I should 'tell him how much we want him' and then she thinks twice, and pinches the bridge of her nose and squeezes her eyes (as is her way, you well know), and says, 'No, no, he shall miss us and want us himself then, he shall feel low, et cetera, et cetera. Tell him' — she now insists — 'how well we get on, and he shall think we've forgotten him, and come back at once . . .' Well, I have put it all down, and I trust that you shall take her meaning, and understand — and add my own perplexity of joy at your prospects and regret at your absence to the pot, as they say.

In fact, however, I must report that your sister does 'get on' quite shamefully these days, waltzing through a round of sparkling balls that would do honour, I believe, to Vienna, for the Prince has taken a fancy to what he calls 'the old way of doing things' (before you know who and what, he adds, though I doubt very much that he does), and the little parties that used to grace his drawing room have spilled into the hall and the gardens. A fountain is under construction, and heaps of marble lie tumbled in the courtyard, waiting it seems for a giant's hand to set them in place. The pipes, I believe, are proving to be a great nuisance, and horrible trenches are being dug and readied for the summer. He wishes, he says, to 'entertain his people in the grand style' – and sends strange spies, high and low, in quite a comical fashion, to discover specimens of the same suitable for his largesse.

In fact, your old student Hespe with the clever fingers has got in with him lately, and holds his ear, as the saying is (perhaps I have not got it quite right). Hespe is quite changed since you last knew him from the slim and sallow youth who made a great show of being bored and having seen it all before, who wore his ennui like a rose in his button-hole. Apparently this is no longer the rage. For one thing, he is becoming quite fat, and dresses in the most peculiar fashion, which he terms traditional, and puffs his chest out when I mock him, and claims German gear is good enough for such as him . . . He is a foolish soul, but I am fond of him – as, I believe, is your sister – who shrieks now and beats me, and protests, she did but dance with him twice or thrice the other night as there wasn't another gentleman for miles around to be had for love or money, without they suffered from elephant's feet or fearsome beards that stank of their dinners or – but you can imagine the rest, beginning perhaps with her cherry-coloured striped dress, which cost me four marks and three shillings per yard – though she did, I confess, look lovely, a proper little Gretchen.

No, no, the rage, as I was beginning to say (which has crept upon us in quite surprising fashion for a rage) is now for everything old and everything German and everything to do with the people. Of course, it will not surprise you the number of lies that are told in the service of our good old-fashioned – commonsensical – plain as daylight – history. To give you a notion of this, I need only say that Hespe himself sets up now for a historian, as the noblest title a man may claim, and, what is more, a Romantic historian – to distinguish himself from the other charlatans. In this cause, he has constructed an elaborate and wonderful genealogy

*for our Prince, complete with heralds and ancient demesnes, to
prove his ancestral right to govern his (I blush to repeat his word)
children in a manner compliant with their traditions. (We used
to pride ourselves on our philosophers, but even they have
become historians, in these times.) The Prince, bless him, has
begun to give himself airs – according to which, I must learn to
navigate carefully, if we are to reach a free port at last.*

*The truth, of course, is that we have no history – only
histories, which grow narrower and pettier the closer we look.
Since the battle of Leipzig, I feel, we have lost our way – for the
simple reason that it is possible to defend as a people what cannot
be maintained as a people. But we have a future, I trust – and,
what is worth a great deal more, a language, all praise to Luther!
who gave us not only freedom of discussion, but also the instrument of discussion. We Germans are the strongest and wisest of
nations; our royal races furnish princes for all the thrones of
Europe; our Rothschilds rule all the Bourses of the world; our
learned men are pre-eminent in all the sciences (I puff my chest a
little, and think of you, dear boy); we invented gunpowder and
printing, and hazard a journey even now into the heart of the
earth; and yet, if one of us fires a pistol he must pay a fine of three
thalers; and if we so much as christen a ship The Liberty, the
censor grasps his pencil and strikes out the word in the shipping
times.*

*I apologize, my son, for going on at such length; only I wished
to answer in part what I believed to be your doubt, regarding the
hopelessness of what you term Idealism exercised in the realm of
practical politics, in the affairs of men. You concern yourself with
the permanent and unchanging revolutions of the planet itself,
and I honour you for it. But never believe that our – for we are
greater than you suppose, and growing – doing and striving are
mere idle caprice; that out of the store-house of new ideas we
select one for which to speak and do, strive and suffer, somewhat
as our linguists formerly selected each his classic, to the commen-*

tary of which he devoted his whole life. No; we do not lay hold of the idea, but the idea lays hold of us, and enslaves us, and lashes us into the arena that we, like captive gladiators, may battle for it. We are not the masters, but the slaves, of the word. Perhaps you begin to understand something of this yourself now, I believe. I would like to meet this fellow Syme, some day.

Well, Ruth has grown quite tired of me, fretted and sighed over all this nonsense, and departed at last, to see to our lunch (she is a good girl, after all, and has acquired an appetite). The rains come down so heavy today we cannot venture out – the Elbe is vexed by a thousand drops, and the surface resembles nothing so much as a field of brown grass. (I see it from the window in my study.) But I have saved the best for last, as they say, a little nugget to brighten a short afternoon. Whatever its other merits, this new Romantic spirit has induced a great pride in all things German, the more fantastical the better; and the Prince (who tells me, with a wink, that he scarce remembers who you are) has agreed to support your experiments. (I have managed to persuade him that Geognosy is, above all, a Romantic science; invented by Germans and now advanced by Germans to the honour of Germans everywhere, most particularly those resident in the grand principality of Kolwitz-Kreminghausen.) Accordingly, I enclose a draft for twice the sum originally agreed upon; which I trust will see you some way into . . . the heart of the matter, as they say, and bring you out again and home again, soon, soon.

Your loving father,
F.

P.S. I hope, next time you hear from me, to have a more particular and less theoretical account to offer, of my ideas. There is always a quiet before the . . . (He presses a finger to his lips.)

Well, there was something that concerned me in all this, a slight worm nibbling in the apple; and I confess that I shamed myself yet again to reach into my father's pocket just as I strode forth proudly on my own. Moreover, the tidings of home (of my sister particularly, and that fool Hespe) awakened in me a strange, recalcitrant melancholy, that baulked at the very thing that fed it, but would not be satisfied with anything else, and returned again, and again, to these pages to make itself miserable. I did not reveal our good fortune to my companions until at length Tom discovered the bank draft for himself, peering over my shoulder, as I dozed briefly before the fire with the letter spread across my lap. And yet, it is true, that I was somewhat mollified by their happiness, then happy altogether, and then drunk, as we emptied the last of the bottles in my father's honour, and cured our thick heads, as they say, with a hair of the dog that bit us.

'How did we get along,' I whispered to Tom that evening, considerably confused in my ideas but holding fast to the main thought, 'before I came along?'

And he drew himself up at this, and declared with a belch, 'By my wits,' and then lowered his head a little, and confessed, 'By scrounging – experiments, lectures, articles and, worst of all, surveying,' and then dipped it still more and admitted, 'And when nothing else would do, by selling what we owned – look about you – to see how little is left.' It is true: the great house (the fruit, as I discovered, of Sam's mining days) was bare; most of the chambers empty; the windows cracked; the roof leaking; the floors loose; the fields about it barren and ruined by rocks. Then Tom pressed both cheeks in his hands, and widened his eyes and his mouth to 'O's, in a ludicrous demonstration of the happy hopelessness in which we were engaged.

By degrees we grew accustomed to our new-found supply of wealth. Our reports grew more detailed, and I confess that Sam had no small hand in their composition. I recall in my own defence that I did occasionally request an audience with the great 'double-compression piston', part object of my mission in the first place. Sam, for once, would look me in the eyes – an uncomfortable stare, I assure you – and declare, fondly it seemed, that he had half a mind to 'revisit' (this was his word) that wonderful invention, but 'You must – you must ask Tom (it has become his particular concern) – for its

whereabouts – as he had hired it out – on business, I believe – some-
thing of that order – and would know where to find it.' I sensed
indeed that the question awoke a curious resentment against Tom
(of all people), who, when similarly applied to, knocked a knuckle
against his brow, and protested, he had seen it only the other day,
and considered (he said as much to Sam at the moment) it was time
to 'dust it off' (again his phrase) and put it to some particular use,
now that the spring had returned and the earth was ripe again.
Then he would thank me, particularly, for the reminder, and busy
himself about something.

Of course, my suspicions were aroused, but I had little heart
for suspicions at this time (for once in my life), and I recognized also
that my mission had changed – subtly at first, until, as the winter died
in its spring grave, altogether, so that I could scarcely distinguish my
aim from Tom's. We were in the business of . . . revolution, and revo-
lutions always sacrifice a number of doubts along the way. And sud-
denly it seemed we had no other cares but the duties of world
discovery, and very pleasant duties they were. Like an enchanted
cloud, my father never failed to answer our calls in golden rain. By
April the three of us were entirely supported by those regular drafts on
the German bank. We learned to doubt his bounty as little as we feared
that the sun would fail us on the morrow, though I at least did wonder
how it was managed, and worry a little.

Though my own role in that strange crew remained uncertain, I
learned a great deal about the company I kept. The contentment of
others is among my favourite studies, the resource of all solitaries,
misfits and constitutional misanthropes (a role I once took pride in,
though I was rapidly growing to doubt my natural claims). I believe
I have a gift in that way, though I am neither pleasing nor easy in
company, and it is a difficult subject. For I know no deeper nativity
than the way we are happy. It is as recognizable as the way we walk
and as awkward to imitate. Our joy is a country of one. Friends
learn to speak its language as a foreign tongue, but do we not mark
the trace of accent, the hint of translation? No, this is how I live, we
feel like roaring. I love searching for that key in another man's char-
acter that opens on a happiness they would not share or exchange if

they could. I loved looking into Sam's heart, though I envied and feared him, and I asked myself perpetually, Should I trade fates with him if I could?

Syme's contentment was obvious. It resembled hunger. It fed on anything and everything and could live only so long as it was never satisfied. His sensual, intellectual, political, personal appetites demanded not only their food, but his perfect right to it, his superior right. He found it as obvious that his joy was greater than yours, as it was that his arm was stronger than yours. With a quite impersonal belief in the value of mass, he was willing to sacrifice your tastes. A man's friendship with Syme began with the task of rendering palatable his own inferiority. So it was with me, as it was with Tom Jenkyns. We fed on his scraps; but they fell from the plate of so gigantic an ambition that they were richer than the food on another man's table.

Tom Jenkyns knew his ground in our strange fellowship. He kept shop among everyday and business matters, petitioned the government for funds, posted propaganda, wrote to editors and journals, arranged lectures, and, to conclude this worthy list, persuaded me to draw on my father's kindness. He was tireless and painstaking and faithful in Sam's service. He was an able man; and I reasoned that in some secret chamber of his bosom, he must have scorned Syme's weakness. For in his way Tom was an ordinary fellow, just the kind to marry and mock a desperate ambition such as Sam's. I watched him and could not help but wonder, How much does he believe? But Tom's rare flights of the absurd made him an eccentric, and so fitting company for a bird of Sam's feather. This is the manner in which Tom adapted himself to Syme, and under his care Syme grew fatter and fatter among the clouds.

The perfect winter continued to thaw into a miserable spring — endless drizzles and bleak, middling-warm afternoons. The sea of snow retreated, leaving a kind of brown weed behind, draped on brown lawns, the sides of buildings, the edges of streets. Syme's great experimental season had begun. In the mud and damp of a slow spring he saw nothing but golden exhalations and the bare-bosomed earth breathing freely again.

In such a long, hard winter, Sam reckoned, a wealth of escaped fluvia must have gathered in the frozen turf beneath its snowy blankets. For Sam the dank thaw promised an ethereal but tremendous harvest. 'The harvest of a century,' he called it. We burned heaped piles of branches and leaves in lonely forests. Sam approached farmers, and with a charm Mesmer would have envied convinced them that their sodden pasture might contain a rare and refined element, 'the fumes of gold', he said. They often stood at a distance, silent in their heavy boots, while Sam lit bonfires in their fields.

We must have made a romantic picture, huddled in our coats, stooped low to the cold ground, selecting crumbs of earth or a twig or leaf, and carefully marking the specimen and location in our heavy notebooks. We peered down caves and pushed through undergrowth, summoning those enchanted azure sprites wherever we went. Sam dripped a concoction of his own into ordinary street puddles and set fire to them, calling forth their blue ghosts. We were like spirits from The Tempest or Goethe's devil, or the alchemists themselves about their business, searching for that oldest of New Worlds, the earth's core. We left a trail of blackened turf across much of Pactaw County. We were foot-sore, back-weary, hand-chapped and heart-full. We were, as I told myself repeatedly, pioneers of a kind; and we slept easy at night, and woke brisk in the morning.

Of course, just as the crop was ripe and the greatest work to be done, I fell ill. Snifflingly ill at first, so that I trudged beside the eager steps of Tom and Sam, as they chased those magical breaths into the glass flu'. Then well and truly ill, until Tom said (not unhappily, I must say, with a wicked sympathy and exaggerated concern), 'You have discovered quite another flu', Phidy, and should go to bed.'

I spent countless days by my bedside window, watching the slow hours, and the river carry broken ice and driftwood to the south. Sam evinced a particular dread of all illness, being a confessed hypochondriac, though paradoxically indifferent to all physical discomforts in others, which he dismissed as a kind of moral and intellectual weakness. I saw little and less of him; and though Tom for his part proved a skilful, if somewhat enthusiastic, nurse, he

292

insisted always that I must not tire myself (nor, it goes without say-
ing, intrude upon them). In short, they were busy, and I could not
help but suspect that some old order between them had been
restored, as they trooped day after day across the breathing land. I
began to repent my coming. I sneezed at the country, at Syme's the-
ories, at Tom's 'hypocrisies' – I simply sneezed.

My only comfort was the strange Mrs Simmons, the lady from the
nautical shop, and (so Tom insinuated) Sam's mistress. She came
from time to time and sat at the foot of my bed, bringing steaming
pots of lemon soup to smoke and sour the cold out of my eyes and
nose. 'You need light,' she said, 'anything alive needs light, even if it
is only grey and wet and the sun don't show his head.' Then she
looked at me and added coyly, 'Perhaps you are not alive.' But when
I was well enough to be shifted, she bade Sam build a kind of divan
for me in the old tavern room, and once settled there before the fire I
never moved. Our growing acquaintance induced her at last to speak
to me in our native tongue, and we spent many cheerful afternoons
talking of nothing and watching the sun and rain in their spring
duet upon the window. My heart beat more busily when she came,
for she surprised in me a latent longing for home, which had been
buried, like Sam's gases, beneath the beautiful snow.

I had time then to reflect on the strange nature of their attach-
ment. Mrs Simmons must have been a lovely girl once, and she was
lovely still after a fashion, with a curious underwater quality, a
melodious slowness. But she was odd company for a man of Syme's
youth on the one hand and energy on the other. I think her self-
reliance drew him to her in the first place. For though Sam could
concentrate with a fury, he often preferred to spend his strength on
more restless and trivial affairs. The confidence of others attracted
his powers as a bed of earth draws weeds to it. Especially when, as
in Mrs Simmons' case, there seemed so little cause for assurance: a
middle-aged widow in a foreign land, keeping a trinket shop, to put
it unkindly. She had few friends. She once explained to me that
friendship involved too much fudging, and I laughed at first but
puzzled over the word for some time. When Sam began to do
business at her shop, and carped at prices and mishaps and delays,

he must have sensed her poise. She seemed as untouched by his complaints as an underwater swimmer by rain. (An unhappy thought.) Her indifference tempted Sam as a red rag maddens a bull.

That is one account of their odd love. Perhaps I have painted Syme too grand for the second. He possessed an enormous sense of certainty, regardless of the matter at hand. It was undeniable, unavoidable, like a monument. Beside his, an ordinary confidence looked as big as a house at the foot of a palace. Yet in which would you choose to dwell? His confidence was magnificent, true, but it required endless repairs and small jobs. It required more work than common faithlessness and doubt, for Syme was the most faithful of men. It sapped his strength and robbed him of sleep. If he turned to Tom, Tom only pricked him to new efforts. But Mrs Simmons was a natural Penelope, a waiter. She made even homecoming seem unimportant beside her waiting. She accepted Syme to her bed and heart, and refused to worry over him. Even Syme came, as we all do, like a lover to his insignificance.

'Have you ever woken Sam,' Tom once asked me in his wicked way, as he brought me a cup of tea one morning before they set forth, 'so fond of waking men himself? Snuck upon them when he sleeps late in his mistress's bed?' He perched a minute, at the edge of my head, and looked out of the window. 'How he clasps her,' he continued, staring at the river, 'snuggles in the crook of her back, and swallows her with his arms, as if he might fall off should he let go. While she wriggles to escape and cannot and consigns herself to a late morning; until you appear, and she gives you a grateful look, and prods him till he stirs.' But Sam called him then, and Tom left me to another lonely morning, free to ponder what prompted this strange confidence.

Perhaps I have dwelt too long on the strange Mrs Simmons, but I found her a fascinating creature and a keyhole into Sam's heart. She meant the world to him, I fancy, even more than Tom did. When I grew well enough to go out, I visited her in the gleaming shop and she put a chair for me by the window. She called it 'your perch, Phidy'. From there I watched the customers move silently among telescopes and chronometers, their faces reflected brassily at every angle, with distended noses and enormous hats. I watched the sun shine longer and brighter on the street outside. We grew intimate after a fashion – what fashion remained to be seen. She was a most consoling woman. And I grew well, slowly at first, and then well enough; then well altogether, just as summer, like a circus, began to pitch its tents in Virginia.

'This is no season for commerce, Frau Simmons,' I declared one day, proud and preening myself, in a fine red coat and a sky-blue cravat. 'Shut up your shop and come play, for these are the rites of spring!' – taking her hands, you see, and spinning round.

'I am an old fool,' she said, laughing and gasping, 'and you are a young one, Herr Müller.'

There was an awkward moment when we tumbled over a chair, a thin-legged, elderly, mahogany creature on velvet tiptoes. We landed plump on the settee, arm in arm, and her hair fell thick as grapes over my face. We untangled each other, rather slowly, and sat there quite demurely after that, all laughter fled, a presage of the awkwardness to come.

And so I sat on the porch steps one fine afternoon in May, waiting for Tom and Sam to return. On my left, the fields fell away from the river. Even across the water the land lay green again, clothed in woods that surrounded the loose streets, except where the highway cut a muddy brown through their swathe. In the market, ladies strolled in twos and threes under the jaunty haloes of their parasols, dipping their heads now and then, and inspecting. Birds tumbled about the air like boys in a fresh lake, scattering and screaming in the sky. I noted a tremble in my gaze and looked round to see the postman crossing the footbridge – a thin, upright shape bobbing above the river – before he walked up our path with a lengthened stride, knocking his bag against his knees, a tall, sweating gentleman in high boots.

'Sir Postman,' I cried, sunning myself, in gallant spirits. 'Mein Herr Mercury. What bird is that, there in the sycamore, the brown one with the dirty red breast, looking up, as it were, for rain – the gloomy fellow?'

'That', said the postman, an Irishman, intoning his words as a miser counts coins, one by one, 'bird is – a robin!'

'Don't be a fool, man, a robin's a chit of a bird, red as apples, no bigger than thumb and forefinger. That brute could hire blackbirds to polish his beak.'

'If that bird ain't a robin,' said the postman, working out the impossibility of it in his entire body, a contortion that began with his knees and developed alarmingly in his elbows, 'I ain't a postman' – he could think of no greater absurdity – 'and that', he added, throwing a bundle at my feet, 'ain't post!'

'Pity then,' I said, scratching the side of my nose, quietly. 'Robins have always meant bad luck to Müllers – I mean, the German kind.'

So out of a blue sky, the bolt fell.

The postman had not budged, stood above me, casting a long, thin shade. He liked to see his handiwork enjoyed. 'I could do with shade myself, just a spot,' he said, as I broke the seal.

His left arm scratched the small of his back without bending. He wanted a moment to breathe in peace and talked to me as I read, in a soft buzzing brogue like flies in the afternoon sun. 'To think of the long way that's come. A man brought that to the post who don't even speak our language. I doubt he rightly knew where Pactaw was, even if he had heard of Virginny. A thousand such-like passengers rode with that letter to Baltimore to unload in a country that don't understand 'em. Then to find its way here, to a man such as yourself taking his ease on a sunny afternoon. It's a miracle of sorts, a long shot.'

I did not answer, for the shot had found its mark. It was a letter from my father.

My dear son,

I have news to give you that grieves me most in that it touches somewhat on yourself. The Prince, as I believe I mentioned to you, has taken a great fancy for the 'old ways of the court' and begun to build and develop and unearth his little palace, to plant groves where no groves grew, and in short, to commit a thousand foolish amendments to the beauties of nature and of architecture, which were never wanted, and shall be regretted when complete. (To say nothing of the great disfiguring mess in the meantime, when the mud runs over the cobbles and the gaping pits like graves stare out of the once gorgeous gardens.) He prances about on a new Arabian charger (purchased at ruinous expense from the public coffers), dresses in battle-gear for ordinary Mondays, and waves a very sharp and very silly crested blade above his head when the spirit takes him. Moreover, I am informed, by Hespe of all people, who calls himself now Lieutenant (a title I am happy to grant him, as he commands exactly no one and certainly not myself), that the Prince desires an army! To protect I suppose the little ruined hill where a pretty house used to sit, that in great kindness and humility, we used to term his court.

(Ruth I should say protests that I am unkind, and that Hespe has got on wonderfully, and deserves at least our sympathy and respect, if not our blessing, for the lengths he has travelled already to improve his station in life . . . et cetera. I never saw the great merit, by the by, of improving stations when so much else wants mending, but I let it go.) Of course, I have no doubt that the Prussians are somewhere behind this; and that the Prince, who travelled lately to Berlin (with his Lieutenant), has begun to give himself airs to match those of his cousins at court, who are for the most part just as foolish but (and this is far worse) not nearly so ridiculous, and greatly to be feared. They seem to have put some nonsense in his head regarding the liberal menace and such stuff (I wish it weren't nonsense, my son), not to mention the threat from Austria and the confusion over a German nation, and the rival swelling and posturing of what amount to little better than packs of brigands (though perhaps I am being unkind to Vienna, we shall see). As it is, the best of us have little hope for a German people, never mind nation, and I believe that until the former rises, the latter shall remain 'in bits', as they say.

All of which means, I'm afraid, that the public purse has been given over entirely to organizing a military worthy of Kolwitz-

Kreminghausen (as Hespe puts it) – I should have thought a couple of shepherds and an angry goat should do the trick, but I am, of course, no 'soldier' (Hespe once again – who seems to have confused a titular *lieutenancy with a battle-tested decoration). Believe me, steps will be taken – and I trust your humble father will* know where to put his feet. *But in the meantime, you are* recalled, *as the saying is (not to mention* warmly recollected*), at once, and required to return with the plans of this miraculous double-compression piston, which Hespe trusts will open that vein of coal in the hillside, and pour wealth into the public coffers (which means, of course, the Prince's pocket, where Hespe keeps a hand warm). With said wealth he hopes to put Kolwitz-Kreminghausen 'on the map' (he takes the English as a model of mercantile progression, and has begun to ape them in other ways as well, the worst of them* sartorial*). I replied that I had always thought the great virtue of a map was that a town required no special merit to be included upon it – but he brushed this aside as foolish pedantry. (Believe me, Son, that even a foolish pedantry is a kind of safeguard against far greater evils; and the moment the pedant is cast from court, never mind the fool, bad times are at hand.)*

Well, you have guessed the upshot already, I am sure. Among the evil consequences of this, I trust, temporary development is the fact that the funds for your American expedition, which appeared so promising, have been withdrawn. My only comfort lies in the knowledge that, if no other good comes of it all, the Prince's foolishness shall at the least return my son to my side again – where he has been sorely missed.

Your loving father,
F.

P.S. I trust the double-compression piston is practicable?

A cloud flew across the sun and the long nose and dim eyes of the sweating Irishman fell into clear relief. A fly drank from a crack in his cheek and I wished he would go away. 'That's grateful to us,' he said, wiping his brow. 'Not bad, I hope?'

'Pressing,' I answered shortly, without moving.

'It's never as pressing as it seems,' he said, and after a period of rude silence on my part bent his long legs to the road again. An hour passed and I did not shift from my seat, in that empty space around a grieving heart as vast as the sky around the sun. The ink smudged in my damp hands as I read the letter again and again. I knew my father would make light of even the gravest misfortunes; and that this touched him deeper than he let on, and upset certain plans he had nursed, secret even from his son, I also guessed. But, like Tom, he had a head for heights (or so I consoled myself) that was proof against low concerns and swarming irritations. And shall I tell you a most curious notion that lay uppermost in my thoughts as I waited for my companions to return? That somehow I had been caught out, like a schoolboy, for playing truant, and must return now, heavy-hearted, to receive my beating. That the game was up, and had proved little more than a game, after all. The shadows grew great as trees and the tired feet of Tom and Sam, limping beneath their heavy packs, trudged up the path from the fields before I raised my head.

Sam was in a black mood; I could see that at once. Tom put a finger to his lips, a sign of caution more than silence. I presumed the usual causes: the day's tests had gone badly; Tom's patience had stung him; his shoes fitted ill and he was weary of the heat . . . Sam needed no great reason for a rage that would satisfy an army of injustices. I was about to give him ample room for a windy grief.

'A good day's hunt?' I asked, as they left their packs at the foot of the porch and sat beside me. I could taste the sour smack to my voice, like spit on silver or cheer on misery. Sam said nothing, and Tom answered, provoked himself perhaps, 'A perfectly foul bright blue summer day.'

'If you will make a fool of yourself – do it in your own affairs, Tom – if you have any,' Sam replied with warmth. 'And the first trick is this – let a woman come.'

'Kitty, the baker's daughter, is a pretty girl, as you know,' Tom explained to me calmly. 'With a neat hand. As the business was close by, I thought she could meet us with a picnic and ease the time. Even make herself useful, which she did. Sam had the misfortune to spill a cup of cider on her notes, so that the ink ran, and we have to start from scratch in the morning.'

'Only a fool would set a cup in the grass – an inch away from a long day's work.' I guessed his anger had another and deeper fear behind it, perhaps of losing Tom.

'She did not expect elephants to come by, as we are only in Virginia,' Tom said.

'This is not a game for schoolboys and their sweethearts – or picnics in the sunshine. It is my life's work and if you cannot make it yours, Tom, I do not need you. I asked you not to bring her; enough. You know well that if Kitty had not met us – a day's work would not have been lost.'

'A day more or less should not matter,' I broke in at last. 'We are bankrupt.'

Tom, in fact, took the news best, with a heart attentive to my private grief. Perhaps he was glad of it, and wished me gone and Syme to himself again, but the gift of consolation requires a subtle eye as well as a warm hand, and Tom had both. 'You say that your father would never breathe a word if he could help it, Phidy. But he cannot you see. As the case affects us, he must tell us, though it were nothing but a dip in fortune.'

'There is more,' I said, shaking my head, 'and worse, I am sure.'

Sam had stormed off, remarking, 'It needed only that,' in a dry tone. My anger rose against him, until I learned pity from Tom.

'He does not have the stomach for disappointment,' Tom offered by way of apology. 'If he had, we should not love him, though he might love the rest of us the better. To be plain, I have had enough of Sam Syme myself today, but now is not the time to turn from him.'

Sam was in a rage in good earnest that evening. The night was cold under a clear sky, and Tom lit a fire for comfort. Syme drank too much at supper and the fumes of wine and the close hot air inflamed his temper, dry already, and he began to talk. He railed at Tom, at my father, at Kitty and me, at Mrs Simmons. 'Stuck here in this hole – the plaything of a sailor's widow – and not the only one by all accounts.' He railed at himself. I think in every great man there is a kind of underground movement, a seditious sect that clamours for failure like a radical for the government's downfall. It is the trembling of revolution. 'Only this would be a fitting injustice!' he seemed to cry – misery, scorn, imprisonment, betrayal, not the simple disappointment of being stony-broke. These black moods sharpened his sense of life. For Tom and me, they were as good as a high wind. Syme had such powers that even his anger could restore our faith, and his rage pricked my spirits to new life, after the blow they had taken at my father's news.

The two were closeted for over an hour after supper in Sam's bedroom, a broad, bare chamber across the hallway from what we called 'the tavern'. I sat in the latter, listening to Sam shout and Tom (for once) match him word for word. Some of these reached me, muffled by the wall: 'bad luck' several times, and 'useless' too, then 'I'll be the judge of that'; at last from Tom, and this repeated, 'Well, then, you must show him' – show him or tell him, both came up. There is nothing as dreadfully lonely as a great argument in another room. My only comfort at hand lay in the company of those two men, who scarcely thought of me, I suppose. My father was an ocean away and I could only guess the position of his affairs. Sam's predicament surrounded me and his anguish roused my blood.

At ten o'clock, the two entered. Sam's anger was spent, and he sat down quietly as if abashed by his former violence – his eyes seemed thick but with that curiously sleepy look of a victor. 'I would like to call to order a council of war,' Tom began, in a dry voice, as if pressed to a reluctant duty. Nevertheless, my heart thrilled at being included in the debate. 'Phidy, I have a question to put to you, that may touch somewhat near the bone. I am sorry if it does, but this cannot be helped.'

'There is a time for tender feelings later,' I answered proudly. 'Do not consider it.'

'Thank you, Phidy, I am glad. You can guess your father's situation better than we. Is there any chance he will recover his influence soon and restore our funds?'

'As to his influence, I cannot answer for it. But he would not have written unless he had done all in his power to maintain our grant. Only when he had failed finally in that respect would he have informed me of it.'

The plates and glasses of our meal lay unwashed on the table. We had shifted our seats since supper. Sam and I sat by the fire, I on tiptoes with my hands on my knees, Sam slumped in his chair, leaning back and resting it against the arch of the hearth, as if the heat had gone out of his blood and he needed the warm blaze beside him. Tom took up the leftovers of my glass of red wine and drained them.

'Well then,' Tom continued, 'our choices lie at hand. The simplest and easiest is to admit defeat; and perhaps this is also for the best. I have no doubt that Sam's father would employ him in his school. The editor of my old paper, Mr McClanaghan, has assured me that I can return to my former job when I wish. You, Phidy, have a father who needs you. And have perhaps the most pressing and particular reasons for – desisting.'

There was a short silence and I suddenly had the sense of some fate in the making. Most decisions, like fields of grass, grow over time and circumstance, but others have a clean birth, and we have a hand in their first breath. I was filled with the delight of a surgeon peering in at the processes of life, and I was very near to giggling with simple joy at the world around us and the power we have to alter it. Yet my stake in that world had just been withdrawn. My father had summoned me; my mission was over; and my service (or rather, for I must be honest, my father's) to that small band had died at its source.

'I would be sorry to have come all this way to watch over the death of a great scientific revolution,' I answered at last, with a spice of irony I could not measure myself.

'Just as I told you, Tom,' Sam said in reviving good humour with his eyes shut. 'A true – geognosist – could not abandon – such a chase – such a prize.'

'Well, as for that,' Tom began, peevishly, 'he has had little chase in him, these past months, and less geognosy; but let it go. As for the prize, we shall see. Of course, our second road', Tom related, 'is the steep and thorny way to Heaven, but may be just passable – with good legs.' And he gave me a sharp look, then paused to settle his ideas. After a deep breath, he began again, staring at the fire, and listed his thoughts in a bored way, an argument over-rehearsed; but he gradually warmed to his theme, in spite of himself, and his voice rang a little (with some sadness, it should be said) by the end. 'We need money and we need an audience, and both can be won through a – magazine. Here is the plan. We start a publication to broadcast . . . our discoveries to the world, and collect a handful of silver in our way. I have talked to McClanaghan of this before now, and he may grant us the loan of one of his presses, for a sum, of course. If we want it to float, though, we need subscribers. A thousand at least, at three cents an issue. We want names, and the only way to get them is to beg for them, on foot, town by town and even door by door. This is not for the faint of heart – or limb. We are beggars truly and will very soon be homeless when this place is sold to set us up and on our way. We could call the magazine "The New Platonist", or something in that line; a weekly paper covering the science of the times. Your new researches will be delayed, Sam – but there is no help for that. This is a chance to play a hand in public affairs. More than that, it is a chance for fame.'

The last word struck an odd note in my ear and echoed in my thoughts. I had wondered before what drew Tom to Sam's mad enterprise, but should never have guessed the answer was 'fame'. Tom had seemed curiously free of ambitions, happy to suspend his own in a greater cause – and yet . . . But I had lost the thread, and shelved these suppositions to chase down the rest of his speech: they were to begin at once, with as full a purse as they could muster; settle with a steamship company which had long sought a purchase on this reach of the Potomac, and hoped to restore the house to its former uses; then shift to Baltimore and Sam's father before they set off. Tom needed a week or two to arrange their affairs, plan their engagements and lodgings and so forth. As he spoke, I began to wonder for the first time whether they included me in these arrangements. Until Sam broke in at last, and enquired, hooding his eyes in a bemused fashion, 'Will you join us, Phidy?'

Tom glanced up at Sam and bit his finger. I said nothing, while the fire flapped against the hearth, and Sam shut his eyes altogether as if in sleep. I wondered what prompted them to ask me. Tom, I could tell, hoped I would decline, shifted in his seat, crossed and uncrossed his legs, and frowned, in his peculiar way, till little wrinkles ran across his high brow like the ripples of a sandbar. He wanted Sam to himself again, which means it must have been Sam who wanted me. I blushed, bursting to break the silence, not daring to answer.

Perhaps, I reasoned to cool my blood, Sam felt in some way more broadly countenanced by my presence, seeing I'd come straight from the horse's mouth (in a manner of speaking), from Werner himself, the founder of geognosy, regarded even at that late date as one of the leading lights in our field. I mattered to him precisely because I was a scientist, and had not dismissed him at once, out of hand – because I had remained so long at his side – because, while I looked on, he could say to himself that he practised his science not in utter but merely relative obscurity – and there is great consolation, believe me, in the difference. Perhaps . . .

'We have agreed, Sam,' Tom broke in at last, through pinched lips that suppressed a something like delight, 'that – Dr Müller – should not accompany us, without he knows the full . . . state of our affairs, I think they call it, when there is something unpleasant to reveal.'

'Well, Tom,' Sam said, waking up and sighing, 'you made that bed; but regardless, I suppose I must lie in it. Come on, Phidy; I have something to show you.'

And with that he settled in his chair (to a loud bump) and stood up, rubbing his hands against his warm trousers. Tom never stirred, smiling in a thin way, as if his lips had stuck and he could not open them wider. 'Put your coat on, Phidy,' Sam said. 'I suspect we'll both be a little cold, before we're – satisfied.' He lifted a burning twig from the fire, and with it lit the wick of the lantern that hung from a hook above the hearth. The swelling glow caught at once and cast a strange shadow of Sam against the wall, all angles and quavering gestures of mysterious intent. Then we tramped outside.

The night was cold and full of stars, a windy spring evening that blew the last of the winter from the north. Away from the house and the river stood a small barn, which I had supposed gave shelter to such implements as had fallen into disuse with the surrounding fields: ploughs and hooks and harnesses that had come with the place, and not been touched. I had never seen Tom or Sam go in it, though I heard once a great banging late at night, had supposed Sam could not sleep, and had crept outside so as not to wake us, while he tinkered with the flu' or constructed some other intricate device for the creation of the world. I suppose it argues a certain want of curiosity in me, that I had dwelt so long in that house and never looked in. There was a great deal more, of course, that I had never explored – cupboards and closets no one touched, passages that seemed to lead nowhere, and darkened windows observed from without that gave on to rooms I could not quite place within. We dwelt after all in a grand old river-inn, far more extensive than anything we could require. And I had in point of fact given the barn-gate a rattle once, only to discover that, though hanging loose on rusted hinges, it was demonstrably locked, without a key in sight. You may have guessed before now that I am not the sort of gentleman to trouble himself greatly over locked doors, shying as I do even from the open kind.

Sam bade me hold the lantern, and lifted a large brown key from his pocket. After a short struggle we heard the click, and the key turned; but I had to set down the lantern in the grass and bear a hand in lifting the loose door above the mud that had swelled around it through the long winter before we could push it, scraping and squeaking, swinging wide and inwards. A thick smell of rot and dust filled our nostrils. Then Sam took up the lantern himself again and stepped in.

A thousand shadows danced away at once, flickering across the high walls of the barn and losing themselves in the dark corners above the roof-beams. The first thing I noted upon entering was a pile of coal at my feet – a great black heap that spilled a few hard nuggets over the packed earth and sat in a drift of its own soft sable dust. Behind it, rusting slightly, in a dozen pieces and accumulations of pieces, resting awry at every angle, lay what appeared to me like nothing so much as one of those wrecks the imagination leaves behind when the tide of sleep draws out again in the morning. A kind of stove lay at the heart of it, drawn no doubt from some early steam-engine, and choked on the ash of an old coal fire. From this a series of pistons and levers and gears and wheels extended, like a hydra's tentacles from the central head, sprawled across the packed earth of the barn floor and gleaming, here and there, at the joints when the lamplight fell upon them. The most substantial of these limbs terminated in what can best be described as an enormous claw, a seven-pronged shovel whose fingers curved inward and dug, even now, into the dust. This hand (to pursue the analogy) had been entirely severed from the body of the mechanical beast, as if some valiant St George had cut it away in slaying the rusting monster; but it seemed to have maintained a life of its own, and I half-expected it, at any moment, to revive itself, and, with a will of its own, begin to dig. The whole contraption conveyed at once the contradictory impressions of great violence and miserable decay. I felt somehow as if I had stumbled upon a former field of battle, which by its very stillness evoked some measure of the storm that had led to such a calm. At the same time the fantastical device smacked of a more intimate and solitary defeat, suggested in some indescribable fashion the mechanical workings of a most particular imagination, which had overreached itself and become entangled in its own proliferation.

'The trouble, of course,' said Sam, setting the lantern on the floor, 'is that it cannot – swallow itself.'

I had no answer to this; and so we stood there, in the thinning must of the old barn, while the shadows played upwards from the ground and seemed to engulf the ceiling in black flames. I felt strangely sick at heart, though in some respects my admiration, or rather the awe in which I held the gentleman beside me, had only increased. His future, however, or, to put it another way, the result of that experiment he had practised upon his life, seemed at the moment quite clear – and heartbreaking.

'As for the double-compression piston,' Sam continued, in a kind of apologetic and forlorn boastfulness, 'that – section of the machine – there – running from the engine – and fed upon itself: it is, as they say, as good as – advertised. I have achieved – unheard-of compressions, equal to the force of forty atmospheres – and proved beyond doubt – the elasticity of water – by effecting a reduction in volume of thirty parts out of the thousand – many times greater than had been supposed possible by the natural philosophers.'

I said nothing, looked at the wreck before me, and thought, Was it for this I had journeyed so far, to learn its principles, and apply them to that vein of bituminous coal in the princely gardens? Which piece of this extravagant dilapidation should I return with as evidence of Syme's ingenuity? (Though in its way I could think of no more expressive emblem of his genius.) What shall I tell them when I arrive home? That I was deceived? Is there any hope for Sam, beyond such fantastical convolution and ruin? And yet, as I stood beside him in the sweetening chill of a spring evening, my reply to these questions grew only clearer.

'The trouble, as I said,' Sam repeated, lost in his own thoughts, 'is that it cannot – swallow itself. Observe the little – pit, as deep as a grave – dug in the corner of the barn. A moment's work, I assure you, Phidy, what should have taken several men – an hour to perform. The trouble is that at a certain depth – six feet, in fact – the sweeping action of the spade – is starved by its own success. It scrapes the air. What we need', he added, rousing himself, 'is a more direct device – that bores a hole as straight as any plummet – and then, when it comes to an end, as all things must – swallows itself, and begins from – scratch at the new depth. I have not despaired,' he said, his voice ringing shrill in the great barn, 'I promise you that much at least. All of this' – and he gestured widely with his arm, so the shadow raced around the wall – 'is not so hopeless as it seems. We are only a step or a – thought – from triumph – or, rather, the next step and – the next thought.'

Then he stooped and lifted the lantern again, and said, reaching a hand to my shoulder, 'Come, Phidy – I believe you have seen enough.'

Tom wore the same thin smile when we clattered in again; he had shifted his seat to the fire, and spent the time companionably, it seemed, prodding and stirring it to life. He looked up at our entrance, and stretched his lips perhaps, an eighth of an inch on each side, as far as they would go without parting. 'Well?' he said at last, as I hung my coat upon the hook. 'What did you think? Or, rather, what do you think?'

I did not reply, only knelt beside him in front of the fire, and rubbed my hands against the thick heat. Sam stood in the doorway still, neither in nor out, as if he had forgotten something, and could not turn to look for it till he remembered what. We could hear the river, flush with spring, surging past the bay window towards the south and east, into the Chesapeake and thence to the Atlantic, till it met, several thousand miles later, the Elbe again, which ran past my home.

'Well, Phidy,' Tom said again, over the crack of the flames. 'Are you with us?'

'Yes,' I answered, without looking up.

I suppose I should explain myself, but I must confess that I equally would like to hear a lucid account of my motives at this point. To be certain, my faith in Sam – not only in his ingenuity, but in his honesty, for I had come over the course of these months to persuade myself beyond doubt that at the least he was no charlatan – had taken a heavy blow; and perhaps, stunned and robbed of wind, I was too weak to turn from him then, in the same manner that a physical attack (and this felt not unlike) enervates the very faculties that should remove us from a second assault. Yes, this much is true – that my faith in Sam, thus enfeebled, sought strength and consolation in Sam – and I felt obscurely that I must abide by him now. There was also the consideration that my so doing would disappoint Tom, and insinuate me further between them. This thought perhaps played no small part in my decision to stay, though I could cast a kinder light on . . . myself, and argue that I wished only to prove Tom's vague suspicions of me false (which I signally failed to do) and justify Sam's . . . interest in me. Then there was Mrs Syme's confession – that she did not trust Tom Jenkyns – and her consequent delight in my association with her son. I thought of all these things.

And, strange to tell, the wreck of the double-compression piston itself pointed my course forwards, forwards, to follow the road with Tom and Sam. Considered thus: without any prize to return with, I had no cause to return. That rusting creature, the mutilated iron hydra that seemed to have turned upon and slain itself, symbol of the extravagance and futility of Sam's imagination (this above all impressed me in the barn, the fact that Sam's profusion of thought and fancy resolved nothing and led nowhere and could never be untangled), charmed me, indeed, by the very hopelessness of Sam's cause. It is sometimes easier to venture forth with a whole doubt than half a hope. And I believe that in my heart of hearts I had guessed already the upshot of all this . . . speculation.

The fact that my father's fortunes had clearly suffered some reversal; the fact that he called me to his side; the fact that my sister had fallen in with a fool; the fact that my country seemed to be running to ruination, that my once-loved Prince led the way — these likewise persuaded me to remain, for I had no stomach for such contemplations, have always been most particularly discomfited by the vicissitudes visited upon my home. So I tore up my father's account of them, and dropped them in the grate, and watched them singe and flare and crackle and rise in ash and smoke — and then I turned, considerably relieved, expectant almost, to the world before me, and my second home, and my new companions.

I awoke in the morning and straightway wrote a letter to my father. I told him that I would come 'soon, very soon, but not yet'. That I was too deep in the business before me to withdraw at this point, without a clearer reckoning of its possibilities. I told him to write at once, to a cousin of Tom, our only fixed station in the travels ahead. For the rest, I knew no more than himself what bed would hold me from night to night. I was too tired and dull at heart to hear or heed my own words as I wrote them, but the breath of love lay in them, as plain and good as the air that passes our lips despite our notice. I sat on my knees and composed this letter on top of my trunk in a grey, wet dawn that hung over the trees like linen.

Such a bustle and fever I have never known. From that milky dawn through a grey afternoon and into a pale, dank evening that never quite fell to night, we worked. We dismantled our home on the river until a houseful of things had shrunk squarely into three large wooden boxes and two trunks, my own among them. Afterwards, Sam perched on top of one of the boxes with dirty hands and dusty knees and remarked in a rare flight of whimsy, 'It is like sitting on top of a year – a very small year.'

His instruments were a delicate business. The double-compression piston could not be shifted from the barn, but the Potomac Steamboat Company had agreed to let it to us at a reasonable rate. (This, I need hardly say, over Tom's vehement objections; but Sam won out in the end; and housed under its roof, among other curious mementoes – sorting like with like, I suppose – those fragments of the world, left over from the disastrous experiment that introduced him to me.) Tom wrapped the other, slighter, more fragile (that is, less broken) contraptions – the glass flu', for instance – in velvet and then bundled them in linen. 'Take them to Mrs Simmons for safe-keeping,' he said, and Sam listened meek as a child even to such intimate advice. Tom loaded our arms with these rare works, till we were stiff and rich as pharaohs in their tombs, and sent us off. 'I have the papers to attend to,' he said and sat down at the tavern table to write.

A summer shower had fallen. Sam and I walked in slow swathed steps across the river and through the empty market to Mrs Simmons' between puddles that sparkled like sequins in the gloaming. 'I feel I have been an evil omen to you, Sam,' I said.

'Nonsense, Phidy, you came at the end of something,' he answered in what seemed a kindly spirit, 'and now stand in the middle of it.'

We reached the shop. Sam tapped at the window and Mrs Simmons peered at us through the curtains and then drifted slowly to the door. 'Maria,' Sam said as she opened it, and I learned her name for the first time. She had a slow smile that always delighted my heart, for she tried to hide it as if it did not become her. She turned it now on Sam as we walked inside, laden with delicate devices. Maria had a tender hand for such things and set them in cushioned boxes, as sweetly as one would lay a child to sleep. Then she took Sam's hand in her own, rich as wood with age, and I felt a shock of envy that I had no one to bid me 'fare well'.

'You must not take him long, Phidy,' she said, then added, as I slipped embarrassed towards the door, 'and I shall miss you.'

I left them to each other's comforts, but lingered a minute in the dooryard since the rain had come back. I heard Sam say in a tone I did not think he possessed, 'I do not know – if I have the heart for it, Maria.' Then rain or no, I set off and found Tom smiling at my solitary return.

Tom was a wonder. He stayed up much of the night writing letters to book clubs and universities and scientific societies and even to churches. I posted a sackful of them in the morning. He arranged an auction that afternoon for some of the furniture and a few bits and bobs Sam did not want to keep. He stuck a broadsheet to the garden gate: 'The Great Geognosist Opens His Cave!' A townful of people, curious as to Sam's ways and the interior of the decayed mansion across the river, wandered through our bare house in a dusty many-legged tide that left nothing untouched. They seemed surprised to find no cauldrons or magic carpets, but a very decent table, some serviceable chairs, and a number of perfectly acceptable pots. Kitty proved to be the most practical creature among us, and managed to collect a heavy purseful from our possessions.

At last the crowds had gone, having stolen what they did not buy. 'Anything the wizard touched', I heard one old church-going matron declare, as she slipped a silver spoon in the bosom of her dress, 'will cure a cold, or send a ghost.' Kitty and Tom and I sat on the sill of the great bay window (all other perches having flown), with the windows flung wide and the river coursing behind us.

'The gentleman from the steamboat company is coming tomorrow morning for the keys,' Tom said, 'and to settle accounts. The post for Baltimore leaves at noon. It was a foolish house, of course, much too big for us, and given to draughts and damp; but just the sort of thing for Sam to fix upon; and I must say, I won't miss it the less for being impractical.' We sat, the three of us, with our legs hung down like boys fishing. Our thoughts seemed empty as the house, our ears followed the hush and rush of the river, and our tongues said nothing.

'I shall be glad to see the back of you,' Kitty cried at last, when the silence grew unbearable, 'fools on a fool's errand chasing a fool.' Her

311

words had nowhere to turn and rang strangely against the bare cupboards and swept grate.

'That is unkind, Kitty,' Tom answered gently.

'But true,' she said more softly and nuzzled her face in the crook of his arm. 'Do not look at me,' she muttered in his shirt, 'I am an ugly creature and will miss you.'

Once more, I left another man to his farewells.

The next day we shifted our quarters to Sam's childhood home. As the coach turned along the river towards Baltimore and passed the grand old inn (which I did not think to see again), I reflected on the odd fate of a man who takes his leave of no one, as all the company he loves travels with him – barring those that live too far away for farewells. I was glad to have my companions to myself again.

Joy surprised me, as the three of us turned up the road to the familiar farmhouse outside Baltimore where Sam grew up. 'I cannot see it for trees,' I cried, running ahead of them up the path. Summer was kind to Maryland, transformed it into a green palace with chandeliers of leaves hung from the chestnut trees, and thick emerald carpets strewn about our feet. The countryside rang with the noise of life; bird and insect kept up a hidden beat, like the secret whirring motions of a great clock. The air was heavy with green perfume, and every breath of it filled my blood to my eyes. Somehow I had left my father's misfortunes behind me in Pactaw and was embarked afresh on my journeys. I took the hand of Mr Syme with real good fellowship.

I was given my old bed in Bubbles' room and fell asleep that night watching the moon fat against the window. This is a fitting starting-point, I reflected from that misty shore, with a foot each in the waking and the dreaming world. My true partnership in our small band had begun in that house five months before; there could be no better spot from which to set forth.

In the morning, I awoke to an unfamiliar prospect. The view had been white on my first day there, and the window ice to the touch. Now I flung it open upon a warm green sea. The ground rose before me in abundant grass and lost itself in the straggling beginnings of a wood. An uneven brown path ran through it and offered the most delicious promise of a leafy and secret exploration. I knew right well that the woods gave way to another road, and that the path led directly to the schoolhouse. But the image of that brown string lost in a green ball grew fixed in my mind as the symbol of enchanted prospects.

We did not stay long. I believe Tom feared Sam would settle there, and, as soon as he could manage it, he planned our departure. I may as well say here that Sam and I came to rely completely on Tom's directions in the next few months. We slept where he told us and followed where he walked and stopped when he found time to stop. We were as ignorant of our destination as sailors of their captain's course and worried as little about it. The land around us changed almost as often as the sea around a ship, but rather than whistling for a wind, we called for Curiosity, and under its impetus sailed towards the humble treasure of . . . a list of names and promised subscriptions to the magazine. Our only fixed harbour was a lecture at the City Hall in Philadelphia which Tom, by a stroke of fortune, had arranged for Sam. 'That is our Trafalgar,' Tom said. 'We can gather five hundred subscriptions in a day.' For the rest, we trusted ourselves to his guidance and relied on our own companionship. After another busy afternoon spent packing (under Tom's watchful eye and jealous hand), we reduced our belongings at last to a manageable burden. Tom told us we were leaving on the morrow, and soon after a rather quiet supper, we turned to our beds.

Tom woke me early and I stumbled downstairs to the kitchen. 'Have a bite for the long day,' he said, tearing a piece of old bread and dipping it in a jug of milk. 'Sam won't be roused.'

Anne joined us at breakfast in a white gown and sat in straight-backed silence while we ate. She had been out of sorts since we came, complained of the headache and sleepless nights. Edward said it was all puritanical starvation and nerves; regardless of the cause, she looked half a ghost, pinched and gaunt, and I guessed the effort it cost her to see her son off without worrying him. I had no talk in me, my head stuffed full of sleep and my tongue dull and dry; ate as carelessly as I breathed and could barely keep my head from the table.

'Sam was always a grand sleeper,' Anne remarked at last. 'That used to give me some hopes for – for his happiness.'

I stared at her in puzzlement as Tom left to wake Sam (again!) and collect our things. To my surprise, Anne shifted to his chair beside me and began to talk. I thought that she would remind me once more of her suspicions of Tom, and I prepared myself this time to be loyal. But instead she turned to a source, I suppose, of still greater doubt – her son – in the private troubled fashion of the sickbed, when the sufferer, afflicted by some preoccupation, believes that if only this particular worry could be relieved, sleep and health would return.

'He was always blind as a mole,' she said, biting colour into her lips. 'Not in the eyes, you see, but in the head and the heart. I don't mean that he wasn't a very loving boy. Have you ever seen a baby mole? Sam caught one once and brought it to the garden. He called it Breadroll and used to spend hours watching him nose through the grass. Did you know moles have fingers, Phidy? His little hands were already strong as spades, and he dug up whatever fell in his path: rocks and clumps of earth. If he could not dig himself clear he pushed his head against whatever stood in his way, until it rolled him on his back. Then he lay flat wriggling until he wriggled to his feet again and set off in a new direction and ran into another stone or tree. He never got far.'

Too tired to answer or comfort her, I only nodded, nodded; and soon after, Tom and Sam joined us. 'We will miss the Post,' cried Tom, and Sam embraced his mother. The two stood equal in each other's arms, only her hair was longer and fell down Sam's shoulders in a grey heap. Tom called again and I kissed her hand and we left, walking in the first sun of the summer morning. 'My father lies a-bed' was all Sam said, concealing the bitterness he felt. We scrambled on to the New York Post bound for Middletown. I was too sleepy to talk and full of such joy, like a cup delicately brimmed, that does not wish to stir for fear of running over.

OF COURSE, THE REJECTIONS DID NOT END THERE. I kept banging at the door (when I did not run from, flinch from it), and others came, of great variety. Never believe that 'no's look all alike, for they contain such mixtures of 'maybe's and 'never's that no two resemble each other exactly. Indeed, I grew adept at picturing the men (and occasional women) behind the missives, at desks both ancient and modern pushed up against university windows across the country, the clutter of their papers further cluttered by the clutter of my papers, Müller's papers, *Syme's* papers (such a broad, thin snowfall of Syme on academic cities, so vast a winter, which swept even to Canada at times!), not to mention the memoranda of our reviewers.

There were the clipped tones of the grey-haired Brahmin from the old-school presses, of universities Harvard and Yale and Princeton. 'Dear Dr Pitt,' they wrote impeccably on heavy paper with the mark soaked through, 'Thank you for your letter of October 23 and for submitting your manuscript to my consideration. I found it interesting; not interesting enough, I'm afraid.' Then they signed their paper bullets in little squibs (their *marks*) that seemed to indicate both that in a humble fashion they believed themselves to be only servants in the cause of *Lux* and *Veritas*, and that, servants though they were, they shouldn't wish to know Doug Pitt, son of a scaffolder from San Diego, if they passed him in the street (an eventuality they did not consider likely, seeing that Pitt lived in the wilds of Texas).

There were the Californian rejections, most improbable of all from the presses of Santa Cruz and San Jose and Santa Clara (and, dare I confess, San Diego), effusive and frothy and full of sound and favour, signifying nothing. 'How greatly', they said, 'we enjoyed this history of Dr Syme, found it persuasive and elegant and rich, at once scholarly and captivating, timeless and urgently topical, a work both vital to its own academic tradition and more broadly relevant – just the sort of thing, in short, the editors at the press of Santa [Cruz, Clara, etc.] would love to take on! Which makes it all the more painful for us to inform you that we must at this moment regretfully decline your piece for publication . . .'

Then came the ladies, massively, impeccably coiffed, preserved as if in the jelly of an early and enduring middle age. They lived in New York and treasured their independence; they worked for the presses of Columbia and NYU, even, among the lower breeds, for CCNY; and lived in squalid little studios on the Upper East Side, with a high-rise view of the other squalid little studios on the Upper East Side. They adored their windswept, concrete, factory-style balconies, and planted potted oases against the reinforced glass walls, and sat, just at the edge of the sliding door, as far as they dared, when the sun came out and the thin metropolitan air was warm enough to breathe, and they told themselves smugly, fearfully, guiltily that they were enjoying 'a minute's peace', and how happy they were to live alone. They began always in breathless apologies of one kind or another and concluded always in ruthless apologies, and said very little in between.

There were the 'standard' rejections, of course, endlessly duplicated and hastily signed, which proved, on a wider sampling (which, I confess, I . . . undertook), not to be standard at all, containing . . . multitudes of indifference. The ones with ticks pleased me most, suggesting as they did that a simple slip of the hand (so much easier than a painful editorial overhaul) could shift my work from the category 'Unsuitable at this Time' to 'Submitted for Further Evaluation', even (though I scarcely dreamed of this) to 'Accepted for Publication'. (The ticks, I should say, never hesitated, never missed their mark.) There were the uniformly intimate, which began Dear ___ and then jiggled my first name some inch above the line, till Doug became muddled in the date and could never untangle itself. These tended to make a great show of suggesting what I knew and didn't know about my work in particular and the field in general. 'As you are probably aware,' they began, and I could almost hear the Doug in their tone of voice, 'times in academic publishing are hard, particularly in the remoter fields of historical science · · ·' But they concluded soothingly, hopefully. 'Having said this, we are sure there are presses who might feel differently [though only, I suppose, in the free spaces of their ___] and we wish you the best of luck elsewhere . . .'

The worst, I believe, were those who simply returned my own introductory letter, as if, in all honesty, Doug, it contained within it the seeds of its own rejection. To this they appended, in blue felt-tip raided no doubt from their children's school satchels, such sentiments squeezed above the return address as 'I greatly respect your personal journey, Doug, but alas . . .' The best were those that managed to get my name wrong; these never quite hit home, they seemed to apply to a Slavic, more dangerous man, taller perhaps, and more heavily haired, the favourite of my aliases being 'Dr Duglo Pi', a name by which I insisted my family address me for an entire blissfully mysterious and suggestively nefarious week, until Ben twisted the syllables into Dr Du Gloppy, at which point I put a stop to the business altogether.

And then there were the good ones, the ones that meant well by Pitt. Written by just the sort of people who (I hoped) would follow Pitt's thought; and who did, to a point, then stopped short. Observed here or there, an inconsistency, a gap, little stumbling places I had known of some time, but managed, in the homely familiarity of my own mind, to overstep whenever I crossed them, and forget, as soon as I passed them by. These *sympathetic* rebuffs (are there such things?) argued in the end (and most damningly of all) what I suspected by then to be true: that I had offered a quest without a grail, a chase without a beast; that until I could prove not only the *fact* of Syme's conception but the *details* of the idea that persuaded Alfred Wegener (a copy of the *New Platonist* itself?), until I could do *that*, Syme would never step out of the hole into which he had fallen, and Pitt could never climb out of it on his back.

These, I need hardly say, I hated the most.

Susie, for her part, could not bear it.

She used to wake early for class, wriggle and sigh in bed, then sit up demonstrably and sigh again. 'A hug,' she said to a lump of somnolent Pitt, which, once provided, led satisfied Susie to seek the little black bright-buttoned tablet (known to our curious age as the 'remote control') Pitt had discarded at the side of the bed before sleeping. This usually involved some substantial discomfort to Pitt – a quantity of misplaced knees and elbows, of bruised ribs, but Pitt slept on doughtily, until Miss Susie triumphed at last. Then a quick buzz and the breakfast news brightened our bedroom (and woke Pitt) with a *television* morning, dawning sunny with couches and loud with sipped coffee, while Pitt pressed the pillow to his head and tried to sleep again.

Then a succession of pops and sighs – the tiny bubbles of sound Susie blows at all times, so that she crackles with life as a log with fire, stirring and shifting and announcing each stir and shift: as she rises from bed; as she seeks her slippers; as she finds them; as she wraps her cold, goose-pimpled, air-conditioned limbs in a dressing-gown; as she binds the cord about her plump pale waist; as she stops in front of the TV (a little colour box propped on the window ledge beside the AC unit) and allows herself only a 'second's peace'; as she stomps out of the door, to prepare the boys' breakfast and her own, while the TV buzzes on to an empty room, empty of everything except for Pitt, except for Pitt trying to sleep.

'Susie!' – a cry rings out, from Pitt's sleep-clogged lungs.

'Damn you!' – a mutter, from the same source.

Then the noise of Miss Susie waking the boys, equivalent cries, equivalent mutters, like father, like sons.

Then footsteps, rustle of dressing, touch of make-up against the eyelashes and lips (dreamily, daintily imagined by a happy half-sleeping husband, or a half-happy unsleeping husband, depending). Then a pause, of steps, beside the bed, beside the head of Pitt within the bed. A brisk, a disappointed, an uninspired 'good morning'. A moment's wifely pity – a button pressed – the buzz of the television dwindling, dwindling into the centre of the tube, swallowed by grey reflecting glass once more. Footsteps. Door slam. Silence.

Silence.

Almost sleep.

Sleep. A moment or two – a quarter-hour. (At the most.)

Then the dull flap and thud of the mail upon my feet – upon the feather-bed over my feet.

The morning rejections.

Susie and the boys were gone when I arose, showered and shaved, naked and pink in the steaming bathroom, wiping from time to time the fogged glass with my squeaky palm. 'Our joy is a country of one,' Phidy said; and he was right, for how much of my life passes in snatched pleasures, Pitt does not like to say. But our grief is a country of one, too; and I sagged lonely between the cushions of the couch, coffee in hand, among the papers, and read over the almost endless flotsam of denials, both equivocal and unequivocal, that the tide of Susie tossed upon my feet each morning; interested denials and uninterested denials; formal and informal denials, in plain and pedantic English; refusing publication, refusing publication, refusing publication.

Thus uplifted, I walked to work.

The work itself, the teaching itself, went swimmingly enough, with this proviso: that it is *difficult to swim in puddles*. I taught two classes: first, a standard history of science from Plato to Planck, in which I managed to attract (quite remarkably) the fewest students to enrol among any of the three lecturers engaged to teach the subject (among them Bunyon, who considered it a mark of proletarian pride to assume the most basic duties of his faculty, mostly, I believe, because it is the only subject he had truly mastered, broad and shallow enough for him to escape drowning). Second, a seminar of my own devising based largely upon my doctoral thesis, which proposed and comprehensively proved the notion that Newton's alchemical and astrological speculations ran not only side by side but *hand in hand* with the mathematical and physical advances that made him famous – so true it is that the army of reason marches upon its *imagination*, as Napoleon's battalions are said to have marched upon their *stomachs*.

'Newton & Nonsense', I called it: an enquiry into Newton's

unorthodox conjectures. I had two students. The tenure committee was due to meet in the spring. I had only a few months left to make my mark.

Susie had supper on the table when I came home. I left the rejections open for her to see beside the telephone, but they were never touched when I got back (after a snooze stretched out on the piebald carpeting of my office, among the coffee stains and the cigarette stubbings, left over from the days of academic smoking). She was a wonder of organization, and beside our bedroom window had erected an *antique* discovery of mine (from a year when my gifts brought peace): the pine partitioned despatch box of an old telegraph office, discovered in Fredericksburg, a pigeon-holed wall-hanging of a hundred little cubicles, in which she filed (each hole neatly labelled) the bulk of her (I should say, *our*, for they were in fact mostly *mine*) significant papers, from tax returns, to jury summonses, to job applications, to school reports. But she would not touch my rejections, nor slip the cover-notes in the little box marked *Rej* above the slot for *Rel* (which contained a great many pamphlets on mixed marriages, and their results, the decline of faith in modern Judaism, etc., etc., and other paper pills to poison our marriage). The rejections she left to me.

The gift, by the by, had only just smoothed over a most *diluvian* row, occasioned by the disappearance, or, rather, the reappearance of a little, apparently harmless, slip (six pages long, front and back) of a job application – for the position of History Lecturer, with a Special Interest in the Sciences, at Fordham University, located in the Bronx, New York. The date of application had, as dates will (a physical fact of which I could not persuade her), passed by, and no bickering or regret could push the time back, regardless of how much she desired a return to 'the City', as she said, nor how much I disliked such prospects, considering the presence there of both her mother and grandmother, not to mention the significant dip in position, from Texas to Fordham, the move would occasion.

Susie discovered this little packet – the long lines untouched, my name in white, my previous salaries a nought, my education a wide snowfall of blanks – propping up the shortened leg of my bedside table. She said, stooping to retrieve the crumpled wadge, 'How you can live in such mess, I don't know.' She said, 'You wouldn't find something like this at *my* end of the room.' She said, 'Honestly, Pitt, what's this doing down there,' and yanked the bundle, black with dirt and deeply indented, out from under the foot, causing last night's glass of dusty water to wobble and spill and drip steadily on to the mock-Eames bedside table.

'Because it wobbles,' I said, 'otherwise.'

Then she began to read. (This is a great fault in Susie, that she reads things better left unread, like bills, and warranties, and leases, and mortgages, and Christmas cards, etc. There are some games that can only be lost by playing – and the challenge of the daily mail is one of these, as I have told her, again and again.)

'What's this?' she said. 'What's this?'

'And then my water, if it is water,' I added, by way of explanation, 'spills; or tea, if it is tea.'

Susie turns aside too readily from my explanations; she seeks the truth herself; discovers a different version of events from mine (to which she has scarcely attended) and complains. (There are always different versions of *events*, which is why the word carries such an uncertain weight in the world's vocabulary. 'Eventually' suggests only that at some stage, in the future, a thing will probably come to pass, most likely when everyone has ceased to care about it one way or another. The Germans, an exact and subtle race, have whittled away at even this much conviction; and their word '*eventuell*' means only that something may or may not occur, depending on contingencies, an assertion undoubtedly correct.)

The next thing she said was 'But this would be fantastic!' as she twigged the nature of the application, and rifled through the thin pages. At this point, I confess, I felt a certain amount of shame (and that curious flush of tenderness that rises in us when we have done the thing that will upset our loves). 'At Fordham,' she said, 'why that's perfect! You could catch the train to 59th Street and transfer to the Q. It's so sweet to be out of the tunnels and over the river. I could get the yellow bus up 1st Avenue, and leave no later than a quarter till – just as I used to, riding up to school. Oh my dear,' she said, 'oh my dear.' (A strange phenomenon, I believe, how sudden love blooms at even the prospect of being planted in a privately desired patch of real estate.) 'Na-na will be just around the corner from your office. We could all meet up for coffee when class is out.' And she pressed her fingers to one another and then to her lips, as if to kiss the prospect they had caught between them.

A word about this Na-na. I first met Susie's grandmother on a bleak, whistling day in December, before we were married, when school shut because snow had flooded the subway tracks. Susie managed to snaffle a car from the college counsellor and we rode up to the Bronx through a haze of dirty snow and brake-lights. We arrived three hours late for lunch, or three hours early for supper, to a little row house with an old Cadillac in the front yard that hadn't been driven since 1962, and had begun to grow things and resemble a rusted flower box. There is nothing unusual or shameful in this, only it was known as 'the family car', in the sense, I suppose, that all the family benefited equally from it, that is, not at all.

At various points in our history together (this being the first), at the slightest of provocations (such as the bus never came, the sub-way's down, the airport's closed, my back hurts), we were told (or *I* was told, as Susie didn't drive at the time, and we had only just begun to 'go out' and lived apart) to take it, to take it with all bless-ings, to take the family car, and not be silly, it's only sitting there. This much is true – it was only sitting there. This is also true – it *could* only sit there. Regardless, before we left that evening in a blizzard, after a seven-hour supper that involved, it seemed, a sin-gle dish at several stages in its evolution, I was told, by Susie's mother, not to be a fool, to take the family car back to Manhattan, where it could get a run-around, with her blessing, and I should never think twice about it. Only Susie's insistence that our friend, the college counsellor, may be somewhat put out if we left his car in the Bronx and returned with another prevented our pushing that Cadillac across the Triborough Bridge to get it home.

Na-na had come out of the shower to answer the door; she wore in lieu of a bath-robe an old blue overcoat that belonged once to her husband, and now hunched about her wet shoulders with an air of misplaced military bravado. Clumps of thin black hair hung from her skull, revealing the nude pink of her scalp, slightly steaming in the chill of the doorway. Regardless of her ablutions, she smelled of cabbages and onions. She smelled always of cabbages and onions. There are only some things, I should say now, to which the odour of cabbages and onions can be seen as a welcome addition. Such as sausages. Na-na was not sausages.

Much of the first two hours were taken up with a number of variations on the question, 'Na-na, why were you in the shower at three in the afternoon?' We sat down to tea – Na-na, it should be said, still dripping through her overcoat. 'Lovely tea,' Susie would say, 'Na-na, why did you take a shower?' This was followed, at certain points, by 'Was it a nice shower?' and 'Did you dry off?' and 'Do you want me to get you a towel?' and 'Did you manage to use the soap we tied to the shower-head?' But we always returned, faithfully, to the heart of the matter, and 'Why did you take a shower at three in the afternoon?' In its own way, the conversation offered no less scope for variety than your ordinary getting-to-know-you chats; and I was not ungrateful for being given a set theme to work upon.

The only trouble was that Na-na spoke no English. And neither Susie nor her elegant and assimilated and successfully married (in every sense of the phrase) mother Bétte – the busy and trim head of a gallery, painfully slender to Susie's eyes, though more of a sister, etc., than anything else – spoke whatever it was that Na-na *did* speak. Regardless of this circumstance, Na-na is held to be something of an oracle; consulted upon the slightest family decision, her advice religiously followed – if anyone can ever figure out what it is. Pitt should have spent his childhood boning up on Lithuanian; his omission to study this has led to the current impasse in his relations with Na-na, who (Pitt should now confess) is not really called Na-na at all, but Nanna or some such nonsense – it is only Pitt who believes a slight misapprehension of a name can be both humorous and healthful to the subject, and insists upon calling her Na-na, like a goat braying, no, no, no.

Pitt, believe me, is familiar with this *bray*. To do him some justice, he has suffered greatly at Na-na's hands, in that the least decision involving any member of the Wielengrad extended family must first be put to Na-na's incomprehension – or, rather, it is the family's incomprehension to which Na-na's decision must be put. It seems to Pitt more than likely that the ancient oracles were in fact simply cabbage-scented foreigners who never understood their supplicants, and who uttered replies their supplicants never understood (demands, no doubt, for such necessaries as a new overcoat for the shower, or larger onions) – thus manufacturing between them a considerable air of divine mystery. The fact that Na-na *eventually* consented to Susie's coming to Texas belongs to the more miraculous of these mysteries – it is Pitt's belief that only the tickling whisper in her boiled ear of his sly suggestion (unheard by Susie) that they would transport themselves in the 'family car' to the great Southwest 'sealed the deal', as they say, in one of her lucid moments – if lucidity can be defined as that access to understanding that permits the function of a constitutional insanity.

But I digress. (She was *cold*, by the by; that's why she took a shower at three in the afternoon, because her house was so cold the lettuce froze, and she was losing the feeling in her fingers. That's why she wore the overcoat, too.) Then Susie said, 'What was this doing under your goddamn bedside table?'

She had asked the right man, I don't deny that. I could have given several answers to this question, having made a particular study of Aristotelian notions of causation in all their glorious variety. The *efficient* cause was no doubt Pitt himself, who slid what came to hand under the bedside table – prompted, I believe, by a wobble too far, as he set his cup of tea upon a much-loved copy of Palgrave's *Golden Treasury*, and spilled a thin ring of brown over the leather cover. The *final* cause was obvious enough – to steady the mock-Eames bedside table Pitt had purchased only the week before in a moment of solitary antiquing on Burnet Road. The *for-*

mal cause (though here I am liable to muddles) lay no doubt in some predictable flaw in the carpentry that resulted in the shortened leg (just as such a flaw had resulted in my son's abbreviated arm?) and the ensuing wobble – the ideal form of the bedside table being in some abstract fashion satisfied by the addition of a heap of folded papers beneath its foot. The *material* cause – and here I venture on firmer ground – was the application for the position of History Lecturer, with a Special Interest in the Sciences, at Fordham University, located in the Bronx, New York: a sheaf of coloured paper, which Pitt had been using as a bookmark in the copy of *Jurassic Park* he had turned to (he is ashamed to admit) when Palgrave's *Golden Treasury* had begun to . . . pall.

The real trouble with the material cause was that the material was *out of date*. (Now that I come to think of it, there may have been some ambiguity in the *final* cause as well.)

'What's this? What's this?' Susie repeated, frowning and squeezing her eyes, as the penny dropped. And then she gave a large, heartbreaking sigh – a sigh, in the first sweetness of upset, directed more at the vagaries of human nature in general than Pitt's in particular. 'Oh, Doug,' she said, at last. 'Oh, Doug.' (How plump and lovely her cheeks looked then; how brave and miserable!) 'Why?' she asked, now wrinkling her lips into a horrible false smile, a smile of suppressed *distaste*, of stifled condescension. 'Why?' she asked again, all her natural loveliness of temper and feature puckered into anger. 'Why did you not apply for this?'

'Because . . .' Pitt murmured.

'Why did you not *discuss* this job with your *wife*?'

'Because . . .' he managed to breathe at last, 'the date had passed. Because I forgot and the date had passed. Because I am sorry and I forgot and the date had passed. Because I am deeply sorry and the table wobbled and I forgot and the date had passed. Because I am sorry; and it wobbled.'

Susie began to tear the application, with considerable force, and a great red grinding of her jaws and swelling of her cheeks, into little pieces; which she then dropped, effortless and gently (in sharp distinction to the violence of her previous exertions) to the floor, drifting like snow into a scattered heap, while she said nothing.

'I am hopeless,' Pitt freely admitted, believing as always that the best policy is apology, abashed and abased and wholehearted, 'empty-headed; irresponsible and unreliable; wool-gathering and hare-brained; addled and forgetful; scatter- and feather-brained. I am sorry and the date passed and I could not bring myself to bring it up and the table wobbled.'

'You'd have been better off,' she said, in a quite terrifying calm, 'if you had thrown it away.'

'I thought of that,' Pitt said. (Then wished he hadn't.)

'You wish you hadn't said that,' Susie said.

'I simply forgot,' Pitt urged.

'I thought you were many things, Doug: childish and selfish, a little bit crazy and full of junk ideas. I knew you made things up to please yourself, things that wouldn't please anybody else, but they pleased you. I never minded that, much. I used to like it. Pompous, too, if you could be, but you can't be, even when you try, you're just too *odd*, so it doesn't count. But I never thought you were dishonest, not dishonest . . . when it mattered.'

'I simply forgot,' Pitt repeated.

The truth is that I simply do not know whether the week I let slip past before I turned again to Robinson Gould's *The Science of History & the History of Science* (in which wonderful and neglected tome I first stuck the packet and proceeded to neglect it further) resulted from *intention* or *inattention*, the tiny insertion of a harmless preposition ('at') marking, it seems, a world of difference. In Pitt's defence, I should say that I am a great *tagger* of books, scribbler of restaurant phone-numbers, jotter of projected revisions of my academic ambitions, presser of leftover receipts and theatre tickets and sandwich coupons. Any book of Pitt's should scatter an autumn of loose leaves from its hair, when held at the spine and violently *shook*. In my defence, I can honestly say that the sin at least was *characteristic*.

The fact is I did not wish to return to Susie's life and world. And the time passed by . . . conveniently.

In my youth I remember faintly envying the adult capacity for *indecision*-making, which, according to all sophisticated accounts (of which I read whatever I could lay my hands on, Updike, Amis, C.P. Snow, grand tales of *foreign* life), allowed grown and responsible men to act from motives that were not only mysterious to the heroes themselves but cast such ambiguity over their acts that legitimate doubts could arise regarding *what, even on the simplest level, had actually occurred*. Growing up, Pitt committed many dubious but no *doubtable* acts. I knew why I did whatever I did and what I had done. Most of the time, Pitt acted out of hunger – though I am not such a stubborn prole as to limit this hunger to the purely physical appetites. (Of which I had, and still have, plenty, though I also wanted to get up in the world and make a name for myself; and I wanted *class*.) I anticipated, on growing up, experiencing a kind of mild intoxicated pleasure (life enjoyed at one remove) on learning to commit those loose and ambiguous actions that seemed to have not one but many and shifting causes, and not one but various and doubtful effects.

I found this in fact to be the case.

By way of apology, I bought my wife the old telegraphic case of pigeon-holes, as a promise of reform. Pitt would become responsible. Thoughtful; upright; reliable; hopeful and savvy; hawk-eyed and level-headed. (Thesauri are great comforts to Pitt, offer the prospect of advance and evolution by simple association – a phenomenon writ small of the great revival of Syme upon which he is bent.) Not to mention: important, authoritative, powerful and executive. (Nor culpable and full of blame.) Of course, the only things Pitt organized were rejections. Susie still managed the rest.

She used to watch me after work, perched on our bed with her nose in the air to observe my methods – while I sat at the desk and sorted through the heavy Nos that fell on my feet each morning. 'I'd separate those,' she would say; or, 'You don't need a copy of that.' She twitched her lips a little and sniffed, like a mouse, a connoisseur among mice, disapproving of the fashion in which a younger, less experienced mouse busied itself about a piece of (admittedly distasteful) cheese. For Susie, secretly, loved to *sort*, had acquired Pitt himself in this fashion and put him in his proper place. 'I wouldn't keep that,' she said occasionally, when Pitt picked up a particularly nasty review. Pitt, needless to say, kept everything. He did not himself like to take a hand in the forces of oblivion; they are strong enough as it is.

Susie could not bear to stand aside and watch me muddle through them; and she could not bear to involve herself in the muddle. So she flitted and twitched, peered over Pitt's shoulder, and fled to make coffee, then inched her way back into the room, upon some pretext, as Pitt recalled the particulars of the redraft that had been rejected, made a note of them, looked for an envelope or a paper clip, retrieved what he believed to be a superfluous paper clip from another bundle (which promptly disbanded), discovered he had lost his original note, despaired, and stuffed the two disparate rejections into a packet that split at the seams, and could be held together only by squeezing it tightly into a stuffed pigeon-hole for which it was never intended. Susie despaired.

And there was, to be fair, something ghastly in my scrupulous (and hopelessly unsuccessful) retention of failure (as Bunyon himself might have put it). But Pitt is fond of ghasts and ghouls and found some relish in the work, enjoyed in himself the *utterly insignificant bravery* of the crank and the outcast. (This, it occurred to me in my haphazard evolution of the term, is the true mark of a *Symist* – solitary courage, for it does indeed take courage, to fight a long battle against an enemy's *indifference*, a battle that can only be lost, passionately lost.) Something about the brick-like cavities of the pigeon-holes suggested to my mind the awful conclusion of 'The Cask of Amontillado'; and I fancied that Susie felt herself to be a witness to a macabre twist on the plot, in which Fortunato *bricked himself* into his grave among the catacombs – as if each fat rejection slotted into its cubicle was a brick laid in the growing wall around me. (A copy of Poe, needless to say, is never far from Pitt's bedside table.)

It was now midnight, and my task was drawing to a close. I had completed the eighth, the ninth and the tenth tier. I had finished a portion of the last and the eleventh; there remained but a single stone to be fitted and plastered in. I struggled with its weight; I placed it partially in its destined position. But now there came from out the niche a low laugh that erected the hairs upon my head.

Of course, in Pitt's case – and this I believe is the more general phenomenon – the laugh is uttered by the observer *outside* the wall, and not the creature caught within it. It is she who says, 'Let us be gone,' and 'For the love of God'; and the man within who determines to remain, and complete his enclosure.

I should say now that Syme himself was not to blame for our marital impasse. I had been aware for some time of a certain tension between us (between Susie and me, that is, not Syme and Pitt) – a tension which perhaps can best be explained by what Captain Queeg refers to as 'geometric logic'. As follows: Susie and I had discovered one day that we lived upon a single *line*, as it were, stretching away endlessly in either direction. (Pitt naturally conceives of Interstate-15, shall we say, running through the deserts of the West, towards heat and heat both ways. But any line will do: the pool shark will no doubt conjure up an image of his cue; and Phidy, a gentleman dandy, envisioned 'brown string lost in a green ball . . . as the symbol of enchanted prospects'.)

The extent of the line induced a kind of intimacy; such dots as we were huddled together to set us apart from the horizons emptying out on either side. In fact, it was very hard for us to keep our places on the line, recall points of origin, distinguish *here* from *there*, or even *this* way from *that*, as the infinity both sides seemed to render such distinctions pointless, to say the least, and impossible, to say the most. Vaguely we knew that some days, some years, we travelled east (shall we say), some west – and for a time the direction did not matter, since the distances involved were negligible in the sweep of the great line itself, so slight indeed as to appear relative or, at the least, easily reversed.

So we never worried about it, much, Susie and I – despite the fact that we knew, quite well, we must turn towards opposed horizons in the end (in the *ends*, I should say) – despite the fact that we understood (from the first, I believe) that we travelled on the same path differently, and must in time (there seemed no hurry) return to our original courses, and part.

It occurs to me now that a *ray* (I think they call it, a severed line, infinite in only one direction) would be an apter image, for Susie had a fixed foot in mind, a final destination and a way of life: New York. Whereas Pitt travelled always and only outwards towards nowhere and nothing in particular and further still. This, Pitt declares grandly, tucking his thumb into the button-hole of his Harris tweed, is another mark of the Symist, who, as Dante beautifully observed, walks uphill with the fixed foot *behind* him: 'my weary frame after short pause recomforted, again I journeyed on over that lonely steep, the hinder foot still firmer'. (Always walk, *crede Pitt*, with the firmer foot behind you, believe me, friends.)

Pitt admits, however, Susie's claim that it is easier to walk the other way, downhill, towards home.

After short pause recomforted, Pitt determined to begin – once more, from the beginning. (This itself is a mark of the Symist – most people begin again from middles, from ends, from tasks left off or pieces broken away; but the true Symist starts from scratch, and scratches away till he unearths the start again. Pitt is a true Symist; my father was a true Symist, and suffered so many beginnings he wore an air of hesitation many mistook for humility, but he was no humble man, my father at heart, only stuttered a little, naturally, at the start; and stopped again, and started again so often that the stutter appeared his characteristic accent, his native idiom, his way of life. It was not.)

Let me begin in faith: I knew then, as I know now, 'in the thoughtless way one knows vast things, like one's own death', as Phidy put it, that Syme had left some further testament behind him, of the great conception which had moved Wegener a hundred years on, a tag or a strand of hair, to say the least, by which

330

we could know him again. I pored over Müller's account, night after night, bent over the desk while Susie slept or tried to sleep unhappily. She said, come to bed, Pitt, the light is in my eyes; she said, in sleepy murmur, my mother said the trick of good painters is knowing when to stop, and the only way to face it, is admit, it means giving up on whatever it is, you haven't gotten right yet, even though you still might, nevertheless, it is very important sometimes to stop stop stop and turn to something else as your father did didn't he.

But he got nowhere, I said. I think I'll stick. (There are the lessons we learn by imitation; and the lessons we learn by the fear of imitation. Of these, the latter are by far the most powerful, yet the most difficult to con.)

Come to bed.

I knew the clue was there, the final piece of the puzzle, the last brick in the slot – and strangely the two images merged in my head, the bricks of rejection Susie saw me lay atop one another, raising a narrow wall of failure around me, to shut out the world; and the ultimate proof of Syme's greatness (the 'single stone to be fitted and plastered in'), which lay, no doubt, in the heap of left-over bricks at the building site of the written word, where he worked, and where I kicked about.

Come to bed, she said again, asleep already, come to *bad*, through sleep-fat lips.

(And I thought then that the trouble with lessons was this: that they ran *contrary*, and left us to choose, not whether to learn or ignore the homily, but *which* to ignore. For my father, in fact, had shown me the way to the *country of one*, where he lived; and I had discovered my own country – such islands belonging to the family business, *what* business exactly remains to be seen.)

The breakthrough came at last from an old friend. One morning there fell on my feet a package (which Susie for once had misfiled, for it came *cold* from no press, but warm with incipient inspiration), bearing news from Neuburg to Austin, Texas – and not, as I soon found out, *for the first time*. Dark and willowy Benjamin

Karding, the lengthened shadow of a man (who falls, it seems, across the breadth of my discovery), had stumbled upon a curious coincidence while digging into the history of his uncle (many times great) Ferdinand Müller and the failure of his republican ambitions. This set me off on an almost fresh and local trail: beginning at the university libraries (whose collection of nineteenth-century immigrant journals, pamphlets, letters, fliers, receipts, bills and playbills is an outpost of German barnacles in American waters) and ending somewhat further afield, as we shall see.

If I could begin my academic career from scratch, I believe I should devote myself to the history of *immigration* – a history in its way not unlike the history of '*great mistakes*, and the fruits of them, redeemed' in time, upon which I have in fact spent my life. Of course, a history of immigration is nothing less than a history of the world (of the truth of which I have repeatedly failed to convince my wife), and this story is perfectly *autumnal* with those (almost) impossible coincidences of time and place from which the whole of our lives . . . *hang*. Syme grew up outside Baltimore, because his father Edward (a Symist in more than name) had set forth from bankrupt London to the New World 'to establish an Ideal Community . . . of equal friends, in which all property, of life and love, was held in common'.

Declaring, 'I had rather risk my soul upon a hundred absurdities than on such certainties as I live among now,' Phidy discovered Edward's *son* (the great, the geognostic, etc.) outside Baltimore, forty years on, while fleeing the influence of his own father (bent on ideals similar to Mr Syme's, for which he paid rather more dearly). There Syme and Phidy were joined improbably by a third immigrant, Mrs Simmons, a widow carried from Germany to Pactaw by her husband's interest in exploring the commercial possibilities of Virginia's riverways – a woman, by the by, involved in *conjunctions* of time and place that played no small part in the outcome of this story.

This is only the beginning; or the beginnings.

After countless peregrinations, an ailing Phidy returned at last to his childhood home (to shorten the journey between bed and burial), setting off the chain of theft and influence that inspired Wegener, sixty years on, to die between upright skis in a snowstorm, seeking evidence of the *movement of the earth*.

Wegener's grandchildren emigrated to England after a second disastrous war, which destroyed, among other things, the sole recorded copy of Syme's brilliance in fire and water, bombs and canals, but could not burn away the evidence of it in the great library catalogue from Friedrichsgracht. This turned up in the new British Library (a red-tiered supermarket imitation of the gallant St Pancras Station perched above its shoulder), where Pitt discovered it, journeying from America for the purpose.

Wars played their parts, too: the revolution that fixed the father of Syme in his adopted country (until a late and last migration to the family home in Highgate), and set up son Sam as an American, and a great American – the first genius of theoretical science (as Pitt hopes to prove) in the New World; the war of 1812 that offered him the prospects of a military career, in which he shone, briefly, before turning his talents as a surveyor to a more speculative terrain; the French Revolution that gave a scattered people a taste of republican life and suggested to a liberal German middle class the *dream of a united Deutschland*; the battle of Leipzig in 1813, at which the Emperor was defeated, and a country awoken, though only a memory of the dream survived in the patchwork nation the Vienna Congress stitched together – including a most insignificant rag, the Principality of Kolwitz-Kreminghausen, which sent its first ambassador of science, Friedrich Müller, across the water to investigate the commercial and theoretical possibilities of that mad genius, Professor Samuel Highgate Syme, of Pactaw, Virginia.

A dream (of German nationhood) which, by the by, had a habit of recurring in nightmarish variations, among them the first and second world wars; during the former of which a young Alfred Wegener was wounded, allowing him the convalescence to compose that ground-breaking treatise on the heart of the earth, *On the Origin of Continents and Oceans*, inspired by a copy of Syme's *New*

Platonist, which was destroyed in the Allied bombs brought on by the *latter*.

A dream which, in the freshness of its youth, inspired the ambassador's father, Ferdinand Müller, to attempt a rather foolish, insignificant and noble little coup, that briefly established a seventeen-day parliament in the Republic of Kolwitz-Kreminghausen, before the heavies from Berlin restored their silly cousin to his court (in its state of constructional dilapidation, among the unfinished fountains and battlements, looking over Neuburg and the Elbe).

A dream which, after a succession of unsuccessful revolutions through the heart of the nineteenth century, led a German liberal elite to seek their fortunes elsewhere in Europe and the Americas; among the pick of their destinations, the foci of their heavy migrations, being that 'Italy of the New World' –

Texas, of course.

Phidy, after all, had a sister, Ruth; and that sister had a son.

The trouble was natural enough, natural and predictable. Conception is a blessing, I have said, but as your daughter may conceive – Ferdinand, look to it. It seems to have been largely a question of . . . timing. Ruth and Hespe were engaged; father and prospective son-in-law had their little disputes, no doubt, but Ruth believed these to be customary in the circumstances, proof indeed of a kind of intimacy between them, an equivalence of character, that seemed to her, rather than anything else, to justify her choice. Yes, she thought, young Hespe and her father were only *too much* alike.

Her engagement fell on a terribly windy day at the end of May, when the rain drove through a crack in the window and positively soaked her father's papers so that she had to dry them on a line before the hearth; and Hespe, bless him, had the most awful cold and looked absolutely pitiful, huddled before the fire in the barrack room (as Ferdinand called it), quite shrunk in figure and bloated in face. He could barely speak the precious words, for the swelling in his already *fattening* nose (she mustn't tease him so cruelly, but how *plump* he has got, and so *quick*): 'Would you, Ruth? *Might* you, possibly, consent . . .?'

Their son was conceived on the sweet summer night when (a world away) the rains crashed down on the barn-like church in Perkins, Virginia. But only the moonlight splashed across the Elbe, in a corner of which Ruth and Hespe (on a broad calico cloth she had brought along specially and spread, with Hespe's clumsy help, over the grassy bank) first made love. For she was (in the family way) an unconventional girl, and surprised in herself an *insistence* of passion that absolutely astonished poor trembling Hespe, in whom the event reproduced many of the symptoms of that terrible cold: a flushed fever in the face, shaking hands, runny nose, including the sense of mental and physical prostration that induced him to propose to her in the first place. She was, as I said, in the family way; and due to be married that summer.

A week before the wedding, Ferdinand Müller was arrested, on the charge of embezzlement (and suspicion of insurrection) at what turned out to be Hespe's information. He had begged the authorities, it should be said, to delay a fortnight. They never married. Regardless, Hespe profited at the high price such betrayal demands, becoming Primary Assistant Deputy First Minister to the Prince. If only he had shown his colours before Ruth pledged her heart, young Roland Müller (as he came to be known) would never have struggled on to the scene. To be raised – in some embarrassment (or vestige of pity, or shame, or love) – out of the purse of the Prince's new right-hand man. For Ruth, utterly piti-less, and unashamed, and loveless, turned an old flame to her son's account without a second thought. Roland, to do him justice, shared a great many qualities with his grandfather, even a few ambitions, as we shall see. His talent for getting on, however, he must have owed to Hespe.

Ferdinand Müller had once declared to the Parliamentary Society, before Friedrich sailed for Virginia, before Hespe danced with Ruth, at a particularly hopeless stage in the progress of his revolutionary *Gesellschaft* (and a characteristical-ly *enthusiastic* stage of his liberal ambitions), that:

> We must, I regret to say, consider the possibility of a for-

eign Germany as our only chance of achieving a national and liberal state. We must gather a community of people – young of limb, fresh of heart – to establish the best of our youth in the New World, while at the same time providing for a large body of immigrants to follow us annually. And thus we may be able, at least in one of the American territories, to establish a true, a *German* state, which shall itself become a model for the new Republic, and an inspiration to Europe.

Is it kind or cruel of history that twenty years on the Prince who imprisoned him led the way and his grandson followed?

In 1842, Henri Castro (a French speculator) founded the Adelsverein (*'zum Schutze deutscher Einwanderer'* – also known as the Society for the Protection of German Immigrants in Texas) in Biebrich on the Rhine, and could convince nobody but our poor old Prince Carl of Kolwitz-Kreminghausen to serve as its titular head. Castro negotiated with the Texas government to set up a colony of six hundred families on a plot of land he had never seen ('laid out along the Guadalupe River fifteen miles above Seguin') and could scarcely imagine, and then he began to sell. The only trouble was that, unlike Phidy, Kreminghausen suffered on those shores no second spring. 'He appeared', as a fellow pioneer declared, 'to be an amiable fool, aping among log cabins the nonsense of medieval courts. Our manners are a little rough here, but plain and just, and we get the measure of a man pretty quick.' In the course of a year he was laughed out of the country. But he left behind Roland Müller.

Ruth, unsurprisingly, had been against her son's venture from the start, out of personal, that is, and not principled reasons. She did not trust Prince Carl, for one thing; and she doted on her boy for another. She recognized the first as a fair, and the second as an unfair, ground for dissuasion; half-doubting herself, she could not dissuade. Roland, for his part, knew more of his grandfather's politics than of his father; he was tired of life in a narrow principality, as his uncle had been before him; he was tired (it should be said) of his mother. He wished to get on with things; he liked a little grand talk for its own sake, but suspected all the nonsense of a liberal state 'seeded from the best of Germany and potted in Texas soil'. He suspected even the promise of commercial prosperity, but guessed that for a fellow who could figure his way, Texas might be a good bet. So he made it.

Here's an early record of Phidy's nephew, from the diaries of the great pioneer Herman Seele, among the founders of New Braunfels, Texas:

> Another, even slighter incident will serve to illustrate the air of good luck that seemed to follow Herr Müller around. While shifting the bulk of our goods across the river, we set sentries on either side, and alternated the duty of rowing the cargo between them in what proved to be a by-no-means water-tight ferry-boat. Young Roland (typically) had the tiller when a cask of wine, which had slipped and tumbled down the rocky incline, was being brought across the river. Some of the hoops had loosened or broken, and the wine (sherry or port) began to leak more and more rapidly into the bottom of the vessel. Roland spotted immediately how clouded the bilge had become, and stooped to taste the mixture; deciding it tasted good, he began to drink with a will. Never one to stint his friends, he beckoned the ferrymen to stop pulling, and the three of them buried their faces in the scarlet stream that slopped about their feet. The men waiting on the bank, seeing the boatsmen ply themselves with the strange libation, grew excited and shouted and urged them to come ashore. Which they did, at last, upon Roland's insistence, whereupon everyone crowded into the boat, dipping with buckets and hats into the accidental punch, until all had wet their whistles and filled their bellies. The drunken feast that followed became known as Roland's Toast; and he walked in all of our good graces ever after.

He did indeed seem to walk in grace – acquired a fortune in cattle, lost it and began again; won it back ten times over in railway speculations; had a bank named after him in New Braunfels (where he kept his money), and a school (where he sent his only son, born late to him, a child, as it happens, of the French mistress, who never survived his birth). He died, at the well-pickled old age of eighty-eight, just before Wilson sent the boys 'over there' to fight against his beloved homeland, a curious conclusion to his grandfather's dream of establishing 'a true, a *German* state [in North America] which shall itself become a model for the new Republic, and an inspiration to Europe'. (Pitt wonders how his own boys will suffer from Pitt's ambitions. Or carry them forward?) Roland's will was written in German. He bequeathed to his son his fortune (which was squandered), and his home, a relatively humble, white, weatherboard house, with a wind porch for the cool of summer evenings, off Seguin Street in New Braunfels. This remained, and was bequeathed in turn to a single granddaughter.

Why does Roland trouble Pitt and occupy his thoughts? What part, if any, does he play in the business of Samuel Highgate Syme? None, I suppose – except, Pitt says, rubbing the dry of his palms together, for this. Some time after the failed revolutions of '48 and the death of her brother Phidy, and some time before the collapse of her son's first fortune, Ruth Müller left the family home in Fischersallee (in great disarray, taking what she thought of, including a handful of her brother's journals and such letters as seemed to bear on the great question of a trip to the New World, including an edited version, as I discovered, of 'The Syme Papers', titled *Amerikareise*) to a cousin (grandfather of my old friend Benjamin Karding, many times great) and sailed partly (breathe, Pitt, breathe) and partly steamed to TEXAS. Where she lived with her son (and, briefly, her daughter-in-law) in the house between Seguin and Market in New Braunfels, which he saved from ruin while Ruth lived, and kept from affection when Ruth died; and where, to this day, a *Fräulein* by the name of Inge Muller runs a bookshop.

As I said, if I could begin my career from scratch, I would begin with immigrants (if only my wife would follow).

*

Pitt had decided to undertake that experiment known as 'a family outing'. He was tired of the loneliness of his business, *what* business is clear, as huffy Henry would say, 'a cornering'. (This despite the fact that loneliness had tempted him into it in the first place). He wanted company, pitched just right – like the buzz of television and assembled guests in the room next door, loud enough to remind the solitary Pitt of *ordinary happiness*, quiet enough to suggest *they kept him in mind*, and did not wish to disturb what they could not comprehend, his Great Work. He wanted, even, a little understanding. There can be too much understanding, and too little.

Pitt, without doubt, suffered from the latter.

The trick, he knew, was to get Susie on board. Then the boys would follow.

Pitt's father was an *enthusiastic* man, full of schemes and theories, a great reader and rustler of newspapers (of the low kind), quoter of experts, pursuer of private notions, speculator. Despite his great, his natural, his abundant humility, Pitt Snr had *projects*. Of the ordinary American kind: to fix pipes, and tile bathrooms, and clear out garages, mend cars, plan yard sales, sweep gutters, etc. He undertook in the evenings (as they say, a wonderful phrase, suggestive of gas fires and quiet) a history of scaffolding, for which he prepared a series of notes, and wasted a great many hours in the San Diego Public Library. 'I came to the business by chance,' he used to say. 'What counts, Son, is that I stuck to it by choice.' He argued, for instance, as I believe I have mentioned, that scaffolding itself could do with an overhaul, and hoped to provide the theoretical scaffolding (as it were) from which to tinker with the practical. In the course of which he invented a number of curious devices, which he pressed upon his bosses, and then his co-workers, and at last, in an unhappy episode, attempted to sell to the local paper. 'There is always more work to be done,' he said; 'that's what I've learned. The hard part is . . . to do it.' He possessed the kind of enthusiasm that charms where it does not persuade – and this in its way was the tragedy of his life.

Susie, however, like my father a creature of enthusiasms, *persuades*; eminently, easily persuades.

I have puzzled over this difference many times, and come to various conclusions. The first of which is this: that it helps, undoubtedly, to be pretty and pink in the face, rather than heavy and red; to wear skirts that swish, and shoes that click, instead of boots and trousers; to possess stockings, in addition to enthusiasms, which may be pulled up, above the knee; and hair-bands, of pale blue, tucked behind the ears. (I should say now that I do not believe my father would prosper any better with such ploys.) But there is more. My father and I, Pitts both, approach our pleasures as if they were rare and out of the way. 'A little known fact,' he used to say, 'want to hear it?' We take just such delights as we trust have never been taken before, eclectic delights, abstruse, pernickety, uncommon, singular – lonely. A Pitt would shame himself to suffer ordinary joy.

While Susie has the gift of making the strangest pleasures seem common. Her joy is – I can think of no better word – *plain*. She never doubts that the world delights *with* her; and so it seems to, and delights *in* her. She presumes that her good luck is of the standard variety, and consequently *enviable*. (Pitt has never been envied.) What pleases her, she seems to suggest by her high spirits, would please *anybody*; and so, by the power of her conviction, tends to please *everybody*. Her enthusiasms move lightly from private to public. Projects seem never to originate in her; she has only taken them up in her way, and we all follow along in her way.

Pitt, then, must learn to interest his wife.

This proved easier in the event than I had supposed. It was simply a question of fellow-feeling among immigrants.

Hubert G.H. Wilhelm's excellent treatise on 'Organized German settlement and its effects on the frontier of south-central Texas' offers this curious account of the first settlers' attempt to make a home out of the dry country they discovered.

> It must appear as something of a paradox to consider the
> fact that the German settler chose to expand primarily into

the relatively inhospitable environment of the Edwards
Plateau, while holding his spread into the coastal plain to a
minimum. The psychological fact of preference for a hilly
terrain probably was influential.

('Thank God, at least,' said Susie, 'or German paradoxes, that we
live in the hill-country.')

Ruth brought her piano when she came, uncertain of the rough
world her son had made his home. It landed at Indianola among
her other belongings, and was eventually hauled by oxen to New
Braunfels, a hundred and fifty miles from the coast. She was not
the first German lady to come bearing music. Valeska from
Roeder arrived in Texas in 1833, with three brothers and her
father, and a piano to come. She died, however, of starvation in
Cat Spring before it got to her; and her sister Rosa Kleberg inherited the box of sheet music and the little upright that followed
Valeska's funeral. It proved to be a great, if short-lived, success.
There are records of dances held at the Klebergs' home in
Harrisburg in 1835. But the instrument, alas, was burned to ashes
a year later in the Texas Revolution.

Ruth's survived a little longer. Her son had for some time been
trying to set up a German press in New Braunfels, and had spun a
number of schemes to raise the money for the printing press,
including a concert, arranged by Dr Alfred Douia. (Roland did not
believe in spending lightly, until he had tried everything else. A
good thing, too – three years later he was bankrupt.) Nobody
came, and the plans were dropped, until Ruth happened along
and took the thing in hand. Roland proposed another musical pro-
gramme, and advertised his mother, 'The Wonderful Ruth Müller,
Star of the Neuburg Concert Halls', as the chief attraction. The
concert was a great success, and not ten days later the first edition
of the weekly *Neu Braunfelser Zeitung* appeared in the shops.

She had arrived; and had never been so lonely in her life –
despite being in some respects (unwed, for one; a mother, for a
second) an expert in the field of loneliness. The 'enormous
evenings' terrified her, black skies that filled the great bowl of

night, and leaked even to the horizon at the end of a road, or a turn in the river. 'I feel', her quill whispered to the attentive ear of her journal parchment, 'that I could step off the end of the world, at any moment, and nobody would know that I had gone. I know now what *nowhere* looks like: very dry, though the rains come hard when they come; there are occasional trees, which grow in no garden, and mark nothing; a river that passes in a great hurry to get away; a few poor huts, cobbled together from timber and dry stone, littered here and there, as if indeed, at a summer picnic, people had simply sat down when their feet were tired, and they could go no further, and begun to build. Nothing makes any sense, but nobody dares to admit this, so we all carry on, as if home were only a carriage ride away, sing songs, make bread, etc., in the old style.'

She had learned what her brother had discovered forty years before, the terror of landscape: 'How vast the loneliness of an uninhabited country late at night, careless of the tiny creatures who travel through it! . . . In the open country there is no mistaking the scale of our pretensions, six feet high in a waste of empty miles.' And indeed these words may have comforted her, if there is comfort in a dead brother's fellow-feeling – as she sat in her bedroom and looked out of the back of her son's house towards Market Street and the occasional lights, and turned over these papers from home.

But Pitt outruns himself. We are not there yet! Have only turned past the Safeways on to MoPac, with an ice-box knocking about in the back of the Volvo, and a wife beside him, and two boys clambering over each other in the rear. For Susie loves a day-trip, the fuss over maps and roads, the free local advertising pamphlets in unfamiliar gas stations, the bags of ice in metal bins on the pavement outside (only a dollar a pop, 'So much for so little,' she says, 'isn't it? So heavy and crackly and only a buck'), the constantly rebuffed anticipation of arrival. Even a day-trip to the heart of her husband's content (his word) or madness (hers); yes, she'll drive even there for an afternoon in high spirits, being sweeter by nature than Pitt, who has promised her a Texan Yorkville, an old

German town, and a taste of immigrant loneliness at the end. Not to mention bratwurst and beer.

I should say now, Pitt had few great hopes for this expedition (as far as Syme was concerned), and in this (among other things) he was not . . . disappointed. He came out of curiosity; this was satisfied. He came to give his sons a glimpse of the business he was in, for they knew little of their father, and, in the case of Aaron, respected less. Susie once said to me, 'You're not *his* kind of dad' – an absurdity all the more painful for being . . . true. Aaron glowed with brown and Texan health, brushed the sweat that clumped his cowlick to his forehead with the famous air of a boy to whom life comes easy. (Nothing comes easy to Pitt, or Ben.) He boasted long legs and quick hands, and the bony behind of athletic youth. He feared Pitt, I believe, as an image of the potential awkwardness and ugliness within him, just as he feared Ben for the imperfection of his brother's arm. Clumsiness and shyness and inadequacy disgusted him, in the same way that prim old ladies are 'put off' by the 'realism' in TV. He lived in his imagination, and was seldom disappointed. The body of Pitt appalled him, the sweats and rolls of it, the broad hams, and splayed feet, and glistening face. When Pitt used the bathroom I saw him wait, until the lid on which his father had sat cooled down, before he dared to go in, no matter how urgent the demands of nature upon him. Aaron wished for no touch of his father's heat.

This, in a fashion, is exactly what his father wished to give him. So he hauled the boys out of bed on a Saturday morning and set off, on one of those rinsed spring days only the end of a Texan winter can provide: cool enough that the noon sun battled no haze of heat to cut bright through the clear blue air. The highway sparkled as we drove through the 'nowhere' of the Texas hill-country, between the lines of the telephone wires and the low juniper hunched over the rocky soil. 'We followed', Pitt murmured to himself, quoting his researches, 'the fresh wagon tracks, civilization's first imprint in this wind-beaten sea of grass. To our right, nothing but river and desolation' – and, as it happens, a descendant of the railroad line on which Roland Müller built his second fortune.

343

Pitt had small hopes of a second *beginning*, however, and desired mainly an . . . *interlude*, such as belong to the best of life, never mind the misery between. A word, by the by, that signifies not only a gap, but the entrance, of Comedy and Love upon the stage, to break the heavy acts of a morality play. (I had forgotten that *breakthroughs* involve often the slightest of gaps or entrances – half an opening through which the pent-up floods can burst, in wonderful, joyous violence, before they reach the next obstruction, and the waters level then rise again.)

'Schlitterbahn,' Aaron said, waking up. 'I want to go to Schlitterbahn.'

We had passed one of those monuments to the American West, a *billboard*, a particularly prominent and revolting member of which species advertised just such a sluicing and sliding, and eruption of happiness upon the thrust of water, as I desired in its metaphorical sense. Among the scraps of old Germany remnant in the Texas hill-country, the most popular by far and generally known is the word to '*schlitter*' – one of those onomatopoeias that signify nothing so much as the stupid jibber emitted by mind and tongue to match the natural and equivalent clumsiness of the body. The great-great-grandchildren of the Müllers and Klebergs and Ernsts who settled this wild country to 'establish a true, a *German* state, which shall itself become a model for the new Republic, and an inspiration to Europe' had retained little perhaps of their Wilhelm Meister, and their Beethoven, and their Biedermeier, but recalled an old word that meant nothing but 'sliding about in the wet', and put it to new and more elaborate uses.

All of which, by the by, I explained in rising tones to my elder son (who stared across the fleeting strip malls in deliberate, and, as it were, *concentrated* inattention) to indicate, No, we shall not go to Schlitterbahn.

And for once Susie supported my paternal resolve. 'No,' she repeated, frowning and leaning forward in that particular way that means she desires the end of a journey, and the beginning of *arrival,* 'we are on a *treasure* hunt, at least according to your father. Tell them what it's all about,' she said, as if Pitt had talked of anything *but* since coming home.

Pitt began, described the library at Friedrichsgracht, the nook, where he alleges that slim volume of Syme's thought, the *New Platonist*, stood pressed between bigger and lesser works; explained the route by which the great catalogue (a recipe of the ingredients cooked together in young Alfred's mind) arrived at the British Library at last, where Pitt *reheated* the mixture, and – But perhaps I should begin with Wegener himself, buried between upright skis in the ice of Greenland, where he had come to prove a shift in the bleak island no greater than . . . Or the question of mass, that slight discrepancy, into which Syme stuck the razor of his wit and pried, until a glimpse of the earth's core (or so he thought) opened beneath him . . . Or should I list the men (from Wegener to Ferdinand Müller, and Syme, I believe, between) who died in some fashion chasing their fancies, to prove, over the clamour of absurdity, what has since . . .

'*Second* thoughts,' Susie broke in, reconsidering, 'I'll do it, I'll do it better. You'll put in a hundred revelations that have nothing to do with the matter, and leave out the sex and the tragedy and the futility, etc., and how the whole thing boils down to the fact that you shouldn't leave home in the first place. Boys,' she said, rounding in the car, 'let me tell it like it is. This is the story of a nut who thought he could prove *the earth is hollow*; and another nut, who thought he could prove the first one was right. Nut number two is your father. He has staked his professional reputation (and our house) on a man named Sam Syme, who lived a hundred and eighty years ago and went around digging things up and declaring there was nothing there. Everyone would have forgotten about Sam except he looked like Orson Welles or George Clooney [Susie made sure our sons knew each], and the girls and the boys both liked him – including a German gentleman who ran away from his own dad (another nut who argued nothing could be better than Germany united) to investigate Syme's theories.

'The trouble was, of course, that Sam was wrong. And the

German gentleman (named Phidy, whose sister ended up *here*, God help her) knew this, and wrote a great many agonizing pages about it, but never actually *told him*. (As I am telling your father right now.) And then Phidy got a little mixed up about the girls and the boys and eventually . . .'

'No,' Pitt said, red in the face, 'that is not it, that is not it at all.' And left it (he shames himself to admit) at that. Because (shall he confess?) there was some pleasure even in hearing his wife botch the story, as we delight most in the hand that tickles our parts least familiar to the human touch. He guessed then the great misery of the crank and the pedant. Not that no one *listens* to them, for there is always a kind ear or tongue too shy to interrupt – but that they so rarely hear the *echo* of their thoughts against another soul, and they live as it were without walls in the unresponsive space of their imaginations. As my father had lived (in spite of his son's best efforts at a generous hearing), travelling further and further afield. This, too, is a mark of the Symist – except, in the case of the original, for one famous evening at the Zweivierziger Club.

Susie kept mum now, twisting a corner of her lip round to the middle, and biting it – in some perplexity, aware that her good spirits had in the proof betrayed an alloy of bitterness, to say the worst, and anxiety, the least. And yet her blunt, strong nose pressed forward again as she resumed her seat; her shoulder strained the seat-belt at the pulley; she sniffed, as if to say, in the enduring girlhood that never left her, How much longer, how much longer till we get there? For Susie, runs Pitt's theory, had, in spite of herself, developed a taste for that black blood, faded on yellow skin, of the written word, on which Pitt feeds.

'IN NEU BRAUNFELS IST DAS LEBEN SCHOEN' read the banner that greeted us as we turned on to South Seguin (or 'Life is Good Here', a line unlikely to have originated in Miss Ruth). Weatherboard warehouses and restaurants pushed up against the sidewalk; a hardware store advertised its wares in Gothic script; waitresses in red frocks and plumped blouses wheeled trays of heavy beer against their bellies as they negotiated the swinging saloon doors on to the porch. Punters of every variety crowded the sidewalk, in the festive understanding that held the word *German* to be a kind of acknowledged public code for the word *Beer*, just as *French* passes for *Lewd* or *Rude*. One or two lederhosen propped up skinny mustachioed, slightly balding gentlemen, who squeezed their nether parts into them, and practised what they believed to be their culture. 'Our first view of the colony' was, as Herman Seele had declared a hundred and fifty-odd years before, 'expansive'.

Pitt experienced that strange blend of intoxication and sadness that accompanies decay of any kind, whether of grape, grain or town. And he turned in some relief towards the green side-street on which Ruth Müller had spent her last days, and slid the Volvo into the shade of a sycamore outside Inge's Books: Second Hand German.

Stretching and creaking, Pitt emerged, and opened the back door to the boys, who fell out grumpy and wrinkled as if they had been tumbled in the wash of sleep. Susie strode up to the low porch already, her broad bottom plumping the blue corduroy skirt at every step, first one buttock and then the next. She stood impatient outside the screen door, and lifted her hat – Susie believed greatly in hats of all kinds – a Mayan weave of brown straw. Holding this by the dimpling round, she fanned her face so the rose stuck into the brim by its thorns trembled. Susie in Pitt's humble opinion occasionally wanted *taste*, in the manner of the rich and the worldly, who have come out again on the other side, and returned to kitsch – but Pitt, son of San Diego, raised in the business of construction, confesses his humility, and would not dare to comment.

'Come on,' she said, 'come *on*. There is always too much – *delay*.'

Pitt led the way (as was proper), lifted the latch and creaked open by a finger, with that infinite gentility reserved for the elderly, the screen door, and stepped into the gloom and old tobacco scent of books. Aaron, following last, let it clack behind him, clatter, and clack again on the rebound. He glanced around him in the arrogant disinterest of youth, plucked a title from the shelf (Grillparzer, I believe, in the wrought-iron tangle of German

Gothic script), and said, 'Why have we come all this way – to look at books – nobody can read?'

'Germans can read them,' Ben said, stout lad, who took naturally to whatever he did not understand, wherever he did not belong – a habitat I believe to which he was more accustomed than most, and where he felt himself (like the blind in the dark) to be at a certain advantage.

'No they can't,' Aaron replied, in that happy denial of the obvious characteristic of an older brother.

'Weren't you listening in the car?' Susie whispered, in the hushed hiss that set her on a level with the children, and made them love her.

'I was listening,' Aaron replied, '*that* was the problem.'

Corridors walled with books opened here and there; arches appearing unexpectedly led between them or around them, or, in one cramped instance, to an upright coffin of books set against a window where Pitt squeezed (but could scarce unsqueeze) himself. (The view of the yellow yard and the AC unit and the neighbouring weatherboard house proved somehow a gloomier vista than the rows of old and unreadable volumes on either side.) Pitt stumbled once upon a slight door in the wall locked (he tried it) above a stoop; a steady and low drip behind it suggested a kitchen and a sinkful of plates. There was another door somewhere else – or was it some *time* else, and the same door? Pitt felt lost, happily lost, in the accumulated – neglect – and endurance – of second-hand books.

Some of them carried no doubt in boxes, portmanteaus, coat-pockets from the Vaterland, grown old on foreign soil; others born in New Braunfels itself, a second generation of immigrants, self-consciously uttering a mother's or grandmother's tongue. They followed one another, row upon row, stack on stack (as Pitt supposed, in his whimsy) through such a maze of assertions – fictional, historical, biographical, poetical, theatrical, financial, geographical – clauses and sub-clauses, brief conclusions, qualified at once, and later reversed, revived and discarded again (not to mention the endless asides, and unashamed digressions, in parentheses), that I felt I had wandered into a great all-encompassing argument, one Teutonic sentence several generations long, and knew not which way to turn, to reach the beginning, or where to stop, and call it an end.

Susie would say, I suppose, that it was a bookshop, and leave it at that. (But this is Pitt's story, and he shall do as he pleases.)

There was a table – or rather a pine board levelled on stacks of books – in a corner looking over the porch. A TV perching upon it, a black-and-white box, reached its antenna askew to the heavens whence all inspiration flowed. An old woman with a tight white bun on her head and a few loose crackling strands of hair across her face sat with her elbows on the table. She sniffed from time to time, and rubbed a bony thumb against the nib of her nose, to appease the sniff; then sniffed again. She was watching basketball; and the low chatter of crowds filled the shop, the squeak of gym-shoes, the bang of the ball, the dry interruptions of the announcer.

'Give me a minute,' she drawled, when Pitt approached her. Her low sniffs, regular as ticks, continued, pausing only for the brief application of her thumb – now to the bridge of her nose, which she rubbed like a schoolgirl erasing a foolish mistake. 'Back-door,' she muttered at the flickering screen; 'damn kids. Back-door's open all day long. Can't shoot – can't cut. Not much good for anything, are they?' she added, turning towards her customer with a smile that sagged a little after registering eighty-nine years of variegated bemusement. 'Half-time,' she declared, suddenly at attention. 'What can I do for you?'

'I am looking', I said, 'for Inge Muller.'

'You are looking', she said, 'at Inge Muller.' Then added, in a slow-burning drawl dry as juniper, 'Never underestimate a preposition. They move worlds.'

A woman, Pitt recognized, after his own heart.

There was the inevitable stumbling around the question at hand. A certain lengthy digression on a possibly unknown cousin? Name of Karding? Long, dark fellow from the German side of the family? Not unknown at all, thank you – Inge proving a keen genealogist – rubbing the sniff in her nose – brother of Ferdinand Müller ('before this barbaric country took the umlaut out of us') had a boy who bought the house on Fischersallee when Ruth packed up – name of Karl Heinrich, good-looking kid, who fathered only daughters, seven of them, and the oldest married a Karding – noble family, owned a great deal of land in Schleswig – produced in their heyday even a minister of finance at Berlin, before the ordinary falling away as the stock dried up.

We were interrupted at this point by a clatter from the back room, where Ben, through a low door above the step, had disappeared. (Ben was in his way the more fearless of the two, belonging as he did to no conventions – an awkward child, who *wriggled* into thoughts and corners his brother could not, and usually knocked over a great deal on his way. Aaron, golden boy, believed in rules, because he won; and proprieties, because they shone on him; and sat mum beside us, only twisting his neck a little to catch the half-time show on TV.) Inge lifted herself in the brittle weightlessness of old age, and moved to examine; and Susie and I, her hand in mine (the embarrassment of our children always rendered her a little *childish*), followed. (She turned always to me in her shame.)

Ben was discovered raising a small whitish beast by the loose-bunched neck, and trying to balance him on what I suppposed to be a *second* stack of paperbacks against the wall. (He, like his father, was nothing if not persistent, and, having stumbled upon *cats* on the one hand and *books* on the other, could not resist the temptation to – experiment.) 'Ben!' Susie cried, squeezing harder, as if to say, The son of Pitt . . .

But Pitt's attention was elsewhere. He could not help reflecting on the sadness of storerooms – especially this, where once perhaps Ruth Müller had spent her age. A sheet of baking paper had been plastered to the small back window to frustrate prying eyes; it wrinkled in the stuffy chamber and let in only a squeezed grey light. Heaps of dusty books tumbled about us. Some of them boxed and spilling over – redundancies, perhaps, or ballast at an auction, but there needs no special reason for a book to suffer neglect. Some of the boxes three-quarters empty (a strangely hopeful condition), their fellows I supposed already broken free for the border and the opportunities of the showroom. Ben desisted (the cat scrambled off yowling), widened his eyes to 'O's, and wrinkled the ends of his mouth downward – he had learned early a wonderfully adult air of apology. It served him well. 'Only books,' Inge said, accepting. 'Nothing holy about books.' The cat, a dirty creature the colour of old newspaper, had perched on an empty container of fresh water beside a stack of what looked like albums. 'We may as well start here,' Inge continued. 'I suppose you've come about Mutti's papers.'

Susie's soft palm was instantly damp in my own. How wonderful that the machine of man, a device infinitely older than all learning, has adapted itself to register (in the sudden sweet perspiration of animal heat) nervous pleasure at the thought – how shall I describe it? – that a heap of scribbled and dried-out pulp lay at hand, which may offer traces that a gentleman a hundred and fifty years dead had developed his theory of concentric internal spheres to prove (Pitt breathes), etc.! All of this distilled into a fine sweat pressed into the wrinkles of Pitt's palm.

Pitt, of course, was too familiar with such hopes. *Mutti* proved indeed to be Ruth Müller (Inge's great-grandmother), a tough and accomplished lady who would, I suspect, have proved a more useful confidante to Sam Syme than did her brother Phidy. Certain betrayals, of course, are possible only to men among men. A heap of papers, or books rather, neatly and privately bound in calico, had survived their . . . editor Ruth, like bones in a grave. (Are we not all *editors* of those fates and physiques Nature has thrust upon us, amenders, at best, of a set text?) These Inge lifted from an old Sony box, gone at the edges, home once of her little TV – and set down in a cloud of dust on the blue carpet peeling back from the walls. Susie, slipped already to her knees, blew on the covers, and lifted the edge with her finger, as slow as if a butterfly trembled beneath.

'Oh, Pitt,' she breathed, 'it's just as you said.'

What *exactly* she meant by this has never been clear to me. Pitt,

I believe, could be forgiven for taking offence at her tone, which suggested, if nothing better, a former lack of faith. Which suggested more, in fact (and less): *surprise*, that any of Pitt's concerns should have its material echo in the world at large; surprise that Pitt is not imprisoned in his own thoughts, but ranges freely over Things As They Are; surprise, in short, that there is *meat* to Pitt.

And yet Pitt took no offence, for there is something in delight (in *her* delight) that trumps resentment and distrust, something indisputable about delight, and irresistible. Pitt was pleased to watch her, bent above the books, recognizing here or there among the German narrative a familiar name, a 'Phidy', 'Tom' or 'Sam'. She did not question, as Pitt did, the purpose of these several copies. Had Ruth hoped, perhaps, to publish them, and make her brother's posthumous name, in the manner of Fritz Ernst and Herman Seele, whose testimonials of American life had achieved a general currency in the homeland? What labour of love was here? Is that why she strained out all the unhappiness (like pits from a confection), Syme's futility, her brother's faithlessness and bitter departure? For even a quick glance (bent beside his wife, his knees aching slightly against the wall-to-wall and the creaking boards) revealed to Pitt that 'Amerikareise', as Ruth had titled Phidy's memoirs, had bowdlerized (a word eminently suggestive of the *guts* it removes) the Syme Papers, and left behind a travelogue, curious if not happy; indeed, often happy. Wonderful what an *edit* can do, I thought, the natural selection according to which we are all judged in the end. (Unless Pitts come along, and sift.)

Then Pitt thought, Perhaps she needed courage for her own journey.

Venerable Muller broke in above us and declared, in her crackling voice, 'There was a letter in one of them – from Friedrich – unsent. Gone now. Well, not gone strictly. Just lost – and not that, either. I suppose, young man, I should invite you to my . . . bedchamber . . . to explain. You see, I ran short of – paper. Better take the boys with you. You'll need them.'

She led us through the shop again, trailing Pitts of all sizes; up another little stoop, through a low door into what proved indeed to be the kitchen: checkerboard lino, smoked-glass windows where the diminished sun breathed dust into the room, and a wet sink, where a pan of bacon fat stood propped, on which the tap *did* drip. An awkward set of steps rose out of the back into the roof; and these we climbed, Susie following first, her straight, boyish nose bent forward to sniff the possibilities ahead. Boys like corners and attics, and even Aaron galled her mother's kibe as he tumbled after her up the stairs. I heard *her* wonder first. 'Oh, Pitt,' she said, 'oh, Pitt – how beautiful. Oh, Mrs Muller.'

Sunshine fell at a slant into the loft. There was a low bed pushed into the corner, over the wooden boards, bleached the colour of pale ale where the light reached. A white chest of drawers beginning to peel, with postcards Blu-tacked to the sides: of Paris and New York and San Francisco. A red yarn runner thrown the length of the attic, on which the boys slipped about, rumpled it and – forgetting their bad manners in the hushed excitement – even smoothed again with careful feet. Through the narrow dormer windows, I saw mostly the cheerful blank of a blue sky, and the tops of the trees and the television antennas on Market Avenue. But it was the wallpaper we peered at and touched, with the tips of fingers and the backs of hands; and even sniffed.

Her bedroom smelled powerfully of – paper. Perhaps the atmosphere of the shop room had leaked above in the heat of the spring day. Press your nose into the bent spine of a book and you have the snuff of it – rich and sweet, faintly dusty, and redolent of fermented . . . words. I had never before considered the beauty of the human hand, by which I mean the scratch of the pen wielded, and not the paw itself. 'I never looked at Mutti's papers any more,' Inge said. 'They sat in boxes and got dusty. So I called a nephew round to help me plaster them – that's when I could still get on my knees. It took a day, and we used everything we had. The overleafs, I'm sorry to say, were sacrificed. But she kept her journals mostly on one side; and when she didn't – in the letters, for example – we read them out and picked the better one. So this', she added, looking round herself, 'is what there is.'

What struck me most forcefully, in the fields of Ruth's penmanship on either side, was how much like *fields* they appeared: the grasses of her alphabet swaying in the soft breath of her eloquence, always forward, a little forward, as she thought of a new thing to write. Trees and hedgerows grew where a date stood out; names occasionally appeared in capitals, alongside the titles of plays attended, and, as we soon discovered, performed. Little hills rose when she was drunk, I believe: large letters gave scope to her wandering hand, to slip and find its course after all, and a few lines filled the page, and comforted her with the thought that a day had not passed by unreflected upon. Grass in a graveyard was not a more natural crop of human life than the written word. Like a harvest half-finished, her letters were scattered about the walls, bundled into sheafs of words, and laid out to dry. They stretched even into those dark corners where the slant of the roof met the floor; for which, as Inge had predicted, we would need the boys.

'Come on, boss,' Susie declared, setting her hat on the rug, and rolling her stockings in little bundles down to her shoes, 'tell us what we're looking for. (If we may, Frau Muller, if we may.)'

'Mention of *Sam*,' I said, as Ruth kept her journal in German, and only names would do, 'or *Syme*, or the Professor; or Highgate, or Tom, or Jenkyns, or Phidy, or Friedrich; or,' Pitt added, spitting slightly, '*Geognostisch, Wissenschaftlich*, Abraham Gottlob Werner. *Genius*. But mostly Sam Syme, Sam Syme, Sam Syme.'

'Come on, boys,' Susie said, and bent to her knees and pressed her perplexed forehead to the slant of the wall, and began to read; and thus inspired, we did.

We found, of course, mostly red herrings. Herrings, after all, are a plentiful fish. And we learned, naturally, more of Ruth than of Sam. The boys lay on their backs and pushed themselves into the corners; they were covered in dust when they rolled back, their bottoms brown, and the rolls in their socks thick with dirt. There was in general a great deal of sneezing, in which Inge Muller led the field, protesting she always sneezed, she delighted in it, she used to pinch snuff for the pleasure, never to think of it, dears; and she sat on her bed, delighted indeed, and clapped her hands when anyone called out, to 'come, come quick, Dad, and look'. Slowly the walls grew pink and then red indeed, with the sun in setting, before a fine shadow, almost gold, fell across them when it dropped below the trees.

Ruth grew clear. Though the boys and Susie barely understood a word of what they read, they called out from time to time a question, and Inge answered them in that slow-burning drawl, with her eyes closed, and her white-bunned head now propped against the back of the bed. 'The Staatsaengerfest', she intoned, 'was a festival of music, of German music, held in the summer every year at Fredericksburg. I suppose you've found the bill for it, *Thursday to Saturday*, isn't that right? And *fifty cents at the door*? Ruth played piano, until her fingers got too stiff; and then there are two blank years – in her journals, too, she used to fill them with music, and they dried up, when she stopped performing. I would have thought it was the other way around, but no – you need to be a *little* bit happy to write – a little will do. And then she appears again, in the *plays*. Every year the Staatsaengerfest (say it slowly, boys) put on a play and Ruth, as she says herself, took on "*die olle Greisin*", the old hag, whoever she was.'

There were sketches, too. Little pencil drafts of the house we crawled about in now, standing on an emptier road; two or three neighbours scattered among trees until the lights of Market Avenue appeared, glowing in criss-crossed scratches against the page. An outline of a hand (perhaps her own)? A boy in a plump frock (Inge's father)? And the land itself: the swift, slight Campo River at the edge of town, long clear since the red wine spilled and famously drunk by her son, in Roland's Toast; hill-country in spiky flower; broken slabs of rock at the foot of a cliff; and the enormous skies, too big for the page, a cloud stretched wide between two stars that signified how impossible it would be to sketch the entire firmament.

It was Aaron, in the end, who discovered Phidy's letter. He cried out, 'Sam!' but there had been other *Sams* before, and I sighed, as I bent to the floor beside him and rolled over on my back to inspect. He did not flinch from me then, but pressed his finger, across his father's rib, to the spot on the wall where the scribble from a different hand, and life, lined the slanted paper: *Friedrich's*, as I recognized at once.

I sit now at home, in the blow of the air conditioner, under the telegraph slots hung on the bedroom wall. Susie leans upon my shoulder and peers. She has reproached me, as a father and a scientist (these, I believe, were her words), for a *lack of enthusiasm* – in Pitt, of all people, of all things! – at Aaron's discovery, at his *breakthrough*. Merely because I had questioned – I had ventured to question – I had made bold to venture to question – its greater significance to the task at hand. To wit: Syme's revival, founded upon that proof of his genius, the *New Platonist* itself. Because I had questioned *that*, in front of the boy, in the first flush of his excitement, as he stubbed his finger, there, there, upon the wall.

'Write it,' she says, 'write it, put it all in, all of it. The whole *bit*. I'll stand and watch to see you do it.'

She is a lady of passion and great insistence, Miss Pitt. Her round face bright with the heat of her persuasion; her hands, still childish and warm, only the palms, ever so faintly etched with the criss-cross of age, upon Pitt's cheek, in threatening tenderness. 'If you put everything else in,' she says, 'put that in too – for that's the heart of the story, if you ask me, and you don't.'

I have mentioned her boyish nose, thick and straight; her cheeks, broad and pinchable, soft and plump enough to fill thumb and forefinger; her lips, wide and full; and her eyes, blue rings, bright as gas flames in her anger now. And dare a husband say how plain he finds his wife, in the best sense, a face like the beginning of faces, the pattern upon which all other countenances are based, those cluttered corruptions, weakened sophistications, degenerate embellishments upon *her* original – which, Pitt hesitates to say, might serve equally as the foundation of woman or man (as it shall serve for her boys, who grow every day into her beauty), so simple in its lines and rich in various expression, that

356

Pitt feels every visage, stripped to its essence, would resemble her again, and look the better for it.

'Look,' she says, 'what I can't bear is that you get to the heart of the matter, and turn away. What I can't bear is that you take the joy out of it, to prove a point; just when Aaron was about to be happy for you, too. But do what you like,' she says. And leaves him, there, poised above the laptop.

No, Susie, never say Pitt is joyless. Not with fingernails, two days clipped, the shell snug upon the nibs, no longer red or raw, but perfectly formed, to fill the hollow of the keys. Not when the patter of thought runs so happy through his fingers, steps among the perplexity of punctuation, leaps cascading at the edge of paragraphs, to the next bank, a breathtaking inch below, while the faint tip, tip, tip of the key falls and the next black mark appears on the white glow of the screen. Not to mention, most wonderful of all, that breathless caesura before a difficult thought. There is a break in the patter, while the perfect word forms upon his tongue, and Pitt waits, waits, to see it form, like a bead of water at the nose of a tap, and waits, waits, then claps his hands – once, briefly, *thus*, for sheer interrupted joy – to dislodge it, whereupon the flow returns, gushing to the end of sense and sentence, and Pitt is away once more.

Never say that Pitt, short in many things, is short of joy.

But perhaps he shall do as she says and mention Aaron's discovery, Phidy's unfortunate letter (or rather a piece of it), papered to the bedroom wall of his great-great-niece – though Pitt has his reasons (and Syme's) for . . . suppressing it:

> though you are some years dead, since Tom's letter found me
> in that Berlin garret. I was desperately in love with – or, as I
> should say, passionate for – an illiterate Jew girl, with a most
> vulgar faith in sophistication, whom I met once at Varnhagen's
> salon. She loved me for my gentile manners and literary con-
> versation (both of which she borrowed freely) – and how little
> else, I dare not guess, though I persuaded myself – an easy
> convert, always a willing audience to my own arguments –

that I should shoot myself, etc. unless she quit her husband and shared my bed – a piece of logic best contradicted by practical experiment. But I ramble, my dear Sam, and you could never abide anyone's digressions but your own; though you are dead now, though you are dead.

The news of which struck such a blow to my head and heart, I stank of the grief, of the wounds of grief, and scarce crept into the sunlight for a month – demonstrating what you had in a sense devoted your life, both in precept and example, to proving: how much we live in possibility. (In the event the girl mistook my mourning, and came at last, sincerely believing I loved her sincerely, to my darkened bed, where I accepted her chiefly in order to empty my heart of you.) For your death changed little else in my circumstances (a fact unhappy in itself). I had not seen you – in a quarter-century – since those swift sad days at the close. Had not Tom written me directly, the rumour of 'the great Syme's end' should never have reached me, so little greatness remained, and such as had survived confined entirely to your own thoughts and extinguished with them. In the back of my mind, I had never doubted that we should be reconciled at last, yes, with your fame established, and my faithlessness forgiven. (Odd, the convictions we carry with us and never guess that we possess until they are disproved. Well, no one can prove your greatness now; and my forgiveness has run dry at its only source.)

And yet how often I interrupt the past in its progress through my memory! Here and here, crying, hold, an amendment – for an error has slipped into the print-works, and threatens an endless repetition. I should have said – I should have said – a thousand things, but what I said. I should have done – I should have done – a thousand things, but what I did.

To speak plain: I have never loved anyone more than you, Sam Syme. And the great error of my life was not the foolish betrayal (paradoxically vengeful and affectionate) for which you dismissed me at last, but the fact that I never told you, simply this: you are wrong, you are wrong, it is all absurd, you are wrong. Not when I counted your quiet breaths beside me in bed, that long night on the road when Tom lay ill – I should have waked you. Not when you clutched my head in the crook of your elbow, and whispered 'enough' to me, pushing away – I should, for once, have pressed my point, and argued a quite different – sufficiency – that we were better off, happy and young in the ordinary way, than chasing such empty dreams.

'Sam is my only love and a great man, and I would rather be miserable with him than happy with another. He is grand and fine, and everything around him matters wonderfully – the least thing, like me.' But these alas are not my words, and

Phidy was wrong, wrong, wrong himself, Pitt avers, suffering from a different, more loving wound, misdiagnosed as doubt. There is no nonsense like the nonsense of self-justification. Tom and Kitty, to soften the news of Sam's death, bade Phidy to come 'home' to them again – a designation less of place than time, a year of youth in which Phidy lived happy and easy among his highest ambitions, before the inevitable indolence of age wore such furniture down to threadbare shabbiness. And Phidy did indeed mean to revisit them; got as far as Paris, on his way, before succumbing to his usual prevarications and delays, before he *flinched* again; and this shameful letter, addressed perhaps as much to Tom as to Sam, no doubt played the part of his excuses – some low morning, when we go to such lengths to explain *why* we are *where* we are and *what* we are, precisely because we wish to be *somewhere* and *someone* else. But he never sent it; Sam was dead; and Phidy left it out in the grass of his neglect, as Auden says – among his other papers, memoirs and journals, themselves, in their ways, *unsent* letters to the future (till Pitt delivered them). Ruth must have stumbled across it packing up house on her journey west, stuck it in a leaf of 'Amerikareise', where Inge Muller discovered it and pasted it to her bedroom wall. Where my son found it. I publish it now (despite obvious hesitations) to please him, and Susie – a

PART IV

·Heyday·

We arrived that first night, nowhere it seemed, after dark. Tom led us and Sam and I followed in a dull stupor, through which the rhythm of the carriage wheels still rattled like feverish dice. Then Tom stopped at a door and knocked softly and then louder till a woman came wrapped in a green robe. 'Mrs Bevington?' he said.

'That's right.'

'Mr Cooling mentioned you.'

'Of course he did, I'm his aunt. Just go round the back and it's all laid out for you. A little cabin, quite cosy and you can bang about as much as you like.'

I could not guess where we were being led but I found a bed there and lay in it and slept.

The morning promised a hot day. We woke up early, like children, from the heat. It rose in a white mist from the breathing ground and hung in thick vapours round the lamp-posts and the trees, and lay low over the open field outside our window. The air had a sleepy power that barely stirred when the dawn broke, like a lion unconcerned – full, fat and unconcerned – by the approach of a cat. Tom had arranged a lecture for Sam the next day, but in the meantime nothing could be done, and we realized, like children, that the day lay empty before us.

Sam fretted himself into a temper at any idleness, though he loved it too and could not tear himself from the sweet enchantment of a listless hour. 'Hold your cooing at that duck,' Sam snapped once, 'I cannot read – for all your love-making.'

I threw a piece of the bread intended for the bird at him.

'You are going grey in the mouth, Sam, like a dog,' Tom said, laughing. 'Let's go exploring.'

We set off from the back of our cabin through the dry yellow grass. The field fell to a river, thick with the cast-off shells of buds.

They formed a green, starry meadow in the deep black reflection of the water. Syme stepped slowly on bare feet through the hard grass and dry earth, marked with ant tracks like a path of crumbs. Tom and I followed, trailing our shirts over our shoulders. Happiness, that homeless beggar, had come to us in the warm weather.

I remember a trivial incident of that day, less interesting in itself than as a symbol of what was to come. A boat lay moored by the arched foot of a willow tree. The rotting rope hung heavy with weed and wet, draped round the last pole of a small wooden pier. Syme stepped, unexpectedly ginger-footed, to the end of it. 'Hey for a turn at the oars!' cried Tom. 'Climb in.' Sam placed a heavy foot in front of the first cross-bench and fell full-bodied in the boat. He came up, tumble-mad and bruised, and cursed Tom with a real viciousness, whose heavy anger I had learned to ignore. 'Lead your own damn-fool way in future. Get me out of here – get me out of here. Phidy, where's your hand?' But Tom stepped in neatly, 'Nonsense, sit down and be still,' timing his second step with perfect ease to rise to the roll-back of the boat. 'Hey for a turn at the oar,' Sam mocked, recovering his humour and holding up one rotting green pole.

Tom strained the water with his makeshift oar till it caught in the river bed, planted, and gave us a firm foot forward. Tiny green-bladed buds flew away like minnows. We reached the middle of the river, Syme running his hand through the thick water. O easy time. The thick vapours softened the hard sun like cotton round a watch. The boat made its slow path unmarked down the unmoving river.

But I could not remain unmoved, as Tom idly urged our stump-legged gait. Syme sat deep in thought, and I alone was uneasy, deeply aware of those two men as they were not of each other, or, I am sure, of me: Tom's loose-limbed stance, high-rumped, swaying from the hips down like a tall woman, his browned hands active; Syme's heavy shoulders and white-skinned forearms, spotted with unhealthy freckles and odd moles, a pallor that always seems lonely to me, though I could not answer why. And that powerful scent, of shaved wood, breathing from his skin, that tickled my nose and made me shy of him. But for once I was glad of my discomfort, that like a fine skin sensed the very motions in the air. And I must have been sensitive indeed to note the passage of that slow wind.

As I was lost in these thoughts I saw the water rise, over Syme's boot, held in a careless hand, then above his wrist, touching the edge of his sleeve as he dipped it deeper. Tom said in a low, laughing voice, 'We're sinking.'

The rotted vessel wallowed like a waking beast. Water lipped over the edge and lost itself among the loose wooden ribs of the boat's bottom. Gathering strength, it swelled above the cross-benches and would soon submerge us completely. Tom cried, in falsetto bravado, 'We've been struck!' and perched at the head. When he saw it was no use, he leapt into the water, crying, 'Abandon ship!' and 'Death to the King!' I shrank further and further from the rising wet, desperate to keep my white shirt dry. But the boat tilted with the shifting weight as Tom sprang free, and I fell in, disgusted and fearful, knocking my head against a suddenly lifted side. We swam to shore, splashing through the green buds.

Syme sat still in the bottom of the boat, neither moving nor speaking, a very grave look on his face. I wondered briefly if he had a terror of water, though he had the air, I must say, rather of a two-penny prophet, who discovers to his horror that his vision of apocalypse has proved true. A sniff of 'I told you so' wrinkled his nose. The river filled the vessel and swelled gradually above his head.

He is a big-boned man and sank easily, with folded arms – the river swallowed him in a little gasp of bubbles. Tom lay panting and laughing in the earthy grass at the riverside – the laughter subsiding to pants, the pants giving way to caught breath. We peered into the thick green water and saw nothing, waited in growing apprehension, white with a fear that justified itself by its own increase. Tom perched at the edge, prepared to dive. 'Damn him,' Tom said, and then again, 'damn him.' Peace returned to the slow stream. A century of obscurity seemed to flow over Sam's head, a green reflection of the branched sky above. Nothing. And then again, 'Damn him.'

Why does he not dive, I thought, myself frozen to the bank – why does he not leap in? Perhaps because there was nothing but impenetrable quiet to explore, a smug green passage of water that dared us

365

to dispute its innocence. Perhaps because the act of rescue itself proves the moment's desperation. Why did I not stir from the spot, where my elbows made a wet scrape in the steep verge? Surely, it was Tom's place at his side, I thought – as if I had not yet earned the right to protect him! How a thought swells the space of a second, and expands it, across ages, it seems; till time itself loses its elastic virtue and begins to droop, fail. Tom did not jump. I did not jump. We both – looked on – at nothing.

A minute later – I suppose, it seemed like hours, days, years – a grey shape loomed like a fish and then like a shadow that deepened our reflections rising against us in the water; a curious phenomenon, as if he emerged from our own fearful images, staring back at us – and Syme broke the water and clawed at the bank.

'Damn you,' Tom cried again.

'I strode it underwater,' Sam boasted between thick pants. 'A difficult business, I tell ye.' He heaved himself out, leaving deep handprints in the earth, and wiped his paws on his white trousers. 'A lesson, I believe – that the easiest gait – retards us – on certain roads.'

'You are a rare fool,' Tom said, as his fear ebbed into bubbling exasperation, 'and make a great fuss to discover what a child knows full well.'

But Sam hardly listened and lay on his back in the mud, his broad ribs heaving at the good fat air they gulped again. And Tom, having partly recovered his humour – no great trick, given the sight of us – lay down at Sam's side, where the pair of them dried slowly in the fumy sun. (I dared not join them, but crouched, holding my cold feet in dirty hands, at the river's edge.) For an afternoon at least that swift dousing in wet luck lifted our spirits and the three of us talked in better fellowship afterwards. (Tom and I were bound now, lightly, by a guilty secret – that we were content in the end to look on together while Sam . . . well, we shall mark the progress of his burrowing. Yet the incident proved a too faithful emblem of what was to come, if indeed I have read it right.)

The sweet day gave way to a sullen night. Syme sat at the table writing. I lay on the ottoman reading Waverley, and bored at length with the hero's iressolution, rose to give Syme some companionship in his solitary labour and stood over his shoulder. Certain figures he had consulted me upon lay scattered over the rough table, lying across a well-thumbed map of the globe.

'Phidy,' he said in a still small voice, sensing the weight and heat of my presence at his shoulder. I placed my palm in the softness of his hair. He sat staring at the map, spread beneath his hands. 'Have a look at this.' And he traced his fingers along the edge of Africa, lovingly bending with the curve. 'Does nothing strike you?'

'Of course,' I answered. 'An old . . . coincidence, I suppose, is the best word,' as I touched my own thumb lightly along the pregnant swell of Brazil. 'The Americas and Africa might once almost have been lovers, along the lines of Aristophanes' account, of a split self, searching for its dislocated half.'

'Suppose the shell had cracked . . . ' he said, in a voice as quiet as blown dandelions.

'Yes,' I prompted . . .

'Lay floating,' he said, trailing off into the mists of a speculation. Then Tom asked, looking up, 'Have you prepared the acid of sulphur for the volcano – for tomorrow's lecture?'

Sam remained silent, the butt of his palm banging against his stubborn chin, as if to dislodge an Idea.

'Go on,' I said.

The banging stopped. 'Suppose a great eclipse – along the lines we've discussed – had at some point – inconceivably distant – only suppose . . .' And resumed.

'Have you prepared the acid of sulphur for the volcano,' Tom repeated, 'for tomorrow's lecture?'

'Hush, Tom,' I whispered, mostly to myself. Perhaps he envied my place at Sam's shoulder; but, to do Tom justice, Sam could be most wonderfully slack in his own cause, forgetful of anything that did not serve his present thought, never mind his future honour. While Tom himself laboured in a swarm of minor perplexities, just such niggling considerations – as time and place, engagements, equipment, lodgings, etc. – as Sam delighted to neglect.

'Just so,' Sam said. 'Now, Phidy, give heed. Consider the eclipse – overlapping cracks in the concentric spheres, etc.' He took my hand

367

in his and squeezed it, once, as if to relieve the pressure of his thought. 'But suppose now that currents in the fluvia itself – occasioned by these flaws – produced a friction – that in turn . . .' He released it again – I touched the palm, involuntarily, with the tip of my finger – and the banging resumed.

'I am not in the habit', Tom said, in a passion at the edge of tears, 'of being ignored, for this,' he added, sniffing and squinting at me. Then louder: 'Have you prepared the acid of sulphur for tomorrow's lecture?'

There was to be no more speculation that evening.

'No,' Syme said at last, and Tom rose to his feet.

'What are you about?' he asked in a tight voice. Another storm was brewing, not to be put off by Syme's silence. 'Turn to me when I speak to you. What are you about?'

'I need not account – for my every thought, my dear Tom,' Sam answered in a light tone, too weak for its purpose. Then he added more heavily, 'You are here on sufferance only – all of you – on sufferance only.'

'Turn to me when I speak to you!' Tom said again, in a voice I had never heard. Syme turned, somewhat cowed. 'These are only some calculations – Phidy and I sketched between us – concerning an eclipse,' he answered more gently. 'It occurred to me – we could apply a similar logic – to the outer sphere itself, which might explain . . .'

Tom was strangely agitated. 'What right have you to speak to me of sufferance, knowing as you do the daily sacrifices – daily – I make for you in my absence, and all that absence necessitates, from my home?'

'Hush,' I urged again, more boldly now; and I ventured a word between them for the first time. 'I have never heard you speak this way. Do not speak this way to him. Not now, Tom.'

He never so much as glanced at me. Sam turned and said, 'Sit down, Phidy. This does not concern you.' And I sat down.

Tom swayed somewhat on his feet, and his voice had a thin rasp in it, like the rattle of a cracked coin. The first cloud of a fever flew over his head. He continued in a very bitter spirit that overleapt its cause, pricked by some fear I could not see. 'If it pleases you to plot palaces and kingdoms with this weak-kneed calf of a German schoolboy, do not expect my patience. I have come for your triumph, which you *seem so willing to exchange for the easy admiration of children and the dying lust of a sailor's widow. You have a speech to make tomorrow afternoon, a speech attended (through my exertions) by a man named Ezekiel Harcourt, who is in the way of doing you a power of good. If you intend to read a list of numbers at this gathering, you may continue. If not, TURN TO THE WORK AT HAND.'*

Syme did turn, but not towards his desk. 'If you wish to speak – of the easy admiration of schoolboys – how would you call the calf-love of a gullible young journalist – whom I took on at his own request – out of my forbearance?'

'Your salvation. Now turn to the work at hand.'

'No,' Sam said, instantly childish, and flung himself on the ottoman in a heap.

Tom strode towards his bedchamber, and I shuffled aside to let him pass. His coldness stung me deeply ('this', he called me, wrinkling his nose) and I blushed at the recollection, but the rush of blood brought with it a secret joy.

At dawn, in a chill fever, Tom pasted pamphlets advertising Sam's presence around the town, on lamp-posts and public trees. Few were out to see them. Those who were saw the ink smeared in the heavy air and a flaccid sheet of grey paper announcing:

WE ARE STANDING ON HOLLOW GROUND!

Let the renowned SAMUEL SYME
Surgeon of Metaphysics

cut a Path to the Heart of the Earth's Core
and pluck out the Nature of the World we live ON!

Journey with us to the Center of the Earth!

TOWN HALL, FOUR O'CLOCK

FREE ADMITTANCE

REFRESHMENTS

VOLCANOES

The town hall, a cavern of a place, was filled with chairs from the local school, at Tom's arrangement. Naturally, given the subject of Syme's discourse, we could rarely avail ourselves of the church for a platform; but the church came to us, as was not infrequently the case. They formed a solitary battalion. No one else challenged to meet them, except a spreading widow who thought Doomsday was to be preached and a tottering old man with a sparse beard, like grey sticks of straw, and a foul breath, who came for the relative coolness of the great hall and the promise of refreshments.

The local chapter of the Oceanic Society provided red punch on the neighbouring tables. Its chairman, Mr Cooling (the famous nephew), met us in great apology. 'It is too bad. I know it, I feel it strongly, sir, but the truth of the matter is that old Mrs Cumberland cannot venture out in the heat (her doctor wouldn't hear of it), can indeed scarcely lift her feet from basins of water without someone upbraids her, at her age and girth. And she is by way of being the leading light of our little organization. I am, as it were, a lieutenant-commander, on board a vessel where the admiral presides. I have preached and begged, sir – yes sir! – to little effect, for we are no better than schoolchildren when the master is away. And as I said, sir, poor Mrs Cumberland; and to do my poor flock (yes, that's what I call them, between ourselves, sir, and Mrs Cumberland) justice it is a whacking great heat to be going on with. I can scarcely stand myself. Yes, I will take an early dip in the punch if it's all the same. We might as well ladle it out now to keep the congregation happy. It is a great shame, sir, but as you can see we should have a very warm, warm response, ha!, from the Reverend Mr Kirkland's flock. A great shame.' There were nine of us in all.

Mr Cooling bent a long leg and rose to the dusty platform, walked over to the pulpit and began banging it. 'Order, order, the two hundred and sixteenth meeting of the Middletown Chapter of the Oceanic Society is called to order, order.' The fat lady sat up very straight at that, but the Reverend's congregation barely stirred, leaned like horses towards the table of punch. No one had been talking. Tom glanced slyly at me, from his chair on the corner

of the platform, and winked. (An apology?) I sat alone in a row of
otherwise empty chairs.

There was no order or disorder to be called. We were all too hot
for either. Even Mr Cooling was too hot. His notes stuck under
his damp thumbs and his jumbled words fell in the heavy air
almost before they reached us, like dropped sheets of paper: '. . .
rose to the rank of lieutenant in the 53rd, before being called to
God's greater army . . . among the scientists battling . . . if I
might have a drink . . . having found the trapdoor into this little
planet of ours . . . Mr Mooler, if it wouldn't trouble you . . . now
proposes, in short . . . yes, NOW, Mr Mooler, if you please . . .
from a dizzying height of intellect, perhaps I should say depth
[chuckling], perhaps I should say depth indeed . . . thank you very
much, it is a trifle hot . . . proposes to open that door . . . yes, if
you would be so kind . . . MOOLER.'

Here he peers at a note from Tom. 'Oh, I see, open that trapdoor
and descend like a thief into the, yes, into the heat of Nature. Into
the heart. Order Mr Syme a warm round. Samuel Syme.' And he
went to the edge of the platform and lowered a stiff leg and sat down
beside me, whispering, 'Most kind.'

Syme rose from his seat beside Tom and walked to the pulpit. He
drew inward at such shrunken occasions as these. Then he appeared
to me in his plainest dress, in the open, unmarked by grandness or
falseness or failure. Nothing remained but the scars of thought in his
features, the dignity of his figure, and the disappointment in his
address. He was heavy-hearted; still heavy with last night's anger,
though a forgotten weight; heavier still with the heat and the
meagre crowd and the hopelessness of it all. But he was a brave man.
Perhaps more than anything else, he was a brave man. For once he
rose not to but above the occasion. 'Ladies and gentlemen. It is a
pleasure to see such a fine representation of the Middletown elite here
today – despite the heat – particularly Reverend Kirkland himself –
another expert, I believe – in internal fires.' He always began a lecture to a small audience with a dig at the Church, to agitate interest
among them. 'To you,' he continued, in a phrase I had heard a dozen
times before, 'I have a most particular proposition.'

371

It was slow work and he worked on. The sweating widow soon recognized her error, that no damnation was to come, though Sam preached underground flames in abundance. She rose abruptly and left; returned a minute later and ladled a dose of punch into one of the glasses, drank it noisily, set it down noisily, and said noisily, 'I'm sorry to interrupt,' before departing once more. 'Hell-fire; indeed they'll see Hell-fire,' Tom says he heard her mutter.

Syme soldiered on. 'Between the second and the third spheres – no, that is to say (yes, you're quite right, Tom), I was about to mislead you, gentlemen – between the fifth and the sixth spheres – that must have puzzled you for a moment . . .' I ceased to hear him as I shifted to one side, stretched my tired legs and gazed out of the heavy windows into the white summer air. I heard silence surround us like sea-noise, larger than any stir we could muster.

Syme buzzed on. 'Volcanic eruptions – once ascribed to the anger of gods – must now be seen in their true light – free of their hideous mythological drapings – like nothing so much as the costumes of an amateur theatrical society. They must now be seen as the product of gases – released when – in inverted eclipse – two vacuii of the outer crowns overlap. What is at stake, gentlemen? Why have I troubled you on this heavy afternoon – a fly in your midst – buzzing, settling and unsettling, buzzing, ever disturbing? Why can't I rest? Why have I kept you from the cool waters waiting on the table – so generously provided by Mr Cooling – that on a day like this must have drawn more of your glances – and more of mine, I'm afraid . . .'

Here a small boy slithered from his father's lap and dipped a quick cup into the silver bowl, while his father hissed, 'Henry!' only to take a long draught when the boy returned to him, carefully balancing the heavy drink. 'He said there was going to be volcanoes,' the boy announced, to no one in particular, in obscure apology.

Syme had lost his place on the page. 'An omission – my dear boy – entirely of my own neglect, I'm afraid. But to proceed – I will not detain you much longer – indeed, I have said more than I had come to say. My passion carries me with it.' Never to me did a man's passion seem capable of so little weight, and he smiled wearily as he said it. 'The objection to my theories – theories that, if we are to believe them, earnestly, with more than a mere religious faith, would shake the very ground we stand on to its core – the objection that I have heard more than any other is not scientific – as indeed it could not be, since the theories themselves bear no scientific refutation – but psychological, or moral, if you prefer such a term.' He had lost us all by now, though he rose to what followed, and I thought he could never lose me again.

'Churchmen, widows, children, sailors, newspapermen, professors, schoolteachers, wives – all reproach me with one thing. "From what arrogance do you speak?" they ask. "From what high arrogance do you preach – against the thousand-year-old traditions of your people – your universities – and your God? Have you alone seen the truth – where so many great men have been blind?" And I answer them: "From the courage of my two eyes – my thoughts – and the hands He has given me for digging." I ask instead, "With what arrogance dare I refuse? With what arrogance dare I deny the only gifts I am certain of – the gifts of our great God – contenting me with another man's answers – as I rely on the cook to buy the butter or dress a roast?"'

(I should say now that we have never had a cook; have never known a cook; and that Sam for one has never bought the butter, nor dressed a roast. I was charmed, however, at the thought of it.)

'These are not household duties,' he continued, 'accomplished smoothly and cheaply at their best. Our birth is awkward – our lives short – our death unpleasant, too often desired. If in the meantime I look around – let me not belong to those wealthy men who pay their servants to attend to the tasks they should perform themselves. Let me belong to the servants, if you grant me leave to go over even old ground with a fresh hand, a clear head, and a curious heart. I have done so – and this is what I have found.'

A muffled applause, as ten men, myself among them, smote perspiring red hands, swollen with blood in the heat, and shuffled immediately after to the punch table and began drinking silently.

Syme limped to where Tom was sitting and sat down beside him. Tom put an arm around Syme's neck, briefly. He was well pleased,

for he had seen towards the end of Syme's peroration a tall, complacent man enter the back of the large hall to listen silently, slinking
out when the punchbowl was invaded. His name was Ezekiel
Harcourt, and he became an important figure in our lives over the
next year. But Syme had no hope of the good things to come. Nor
did I after such a discouraging day. He turned to Tom only briefly
in his great fatigue. Their anger had not yet dried – how could it in
the soaking air? – and he soon rose to his feet, stepped slowly down
the platform stairs and walked out between the rows of chairs, a solitary, disappointed, but most of all bone-weary figure, turning to his
temporary bed. Mr Cooling did not see him go.

Tom quickly took Sam's place at the pulpit and began banging.
'For those of you who would like to read more of the great Doctor,'
he cried, 'he is producing a pioneering journal, the New Platonist,
for only threepence an issue. My associate, Mr Mooler, is available
at the punchbowl with a list for names and addresses.'

Mr Cooling soon noticed Syme's departure and enquired after
him. He nodded his head in great loops at Tom's apologies. The
churchmen were a stony bunch, no ground for talk. All except
Henry, who tugged at his father's thumb and asked him from time
to time when 'they was going to begin the – Volcanoes'.

There would be no volcanoes, the father explained.

'That's science', the boy said, considering, 'all over.'

Tom had a sickness brewing and could not even summon up a
smile. My heart hurt for Syme. Only the old man had been attentive, mentioned that he had speculated as much, suggested the same
to his wife, God rest her soul – she wouldn't have none. Explained a
great deal: how could a man walk steady with all them crowns
gyrasticating down there below him, and him only with two good
feet? Vacuii, too, that was a thought. All seven of them ever been in
a row? That would give old Widder Thompson her Doomsday, ha!

And my heart rose a little. I remember leaving, looking back at
the bowl of punch. The heavy ladle lay in a shallow pool, could dip
no further. They stood around it with empty cups, none of them
daring to lift the bowl and effect a more complete evacuation. None
of them leaving while there was still punch in the bowl. Three men

signed the list. Henry's father, a Mr Irving, by way of apology, I believe; the old man; and Mr Cooling, by necessity.

Tom and I walked back through the white streets to the cabin behind Mrs Bevington's house. 'His aunt's lodgings were Mr Cooling's springboard to high office in the Oceanic Society,' Tom mocked in a quavering voice. He shook already with fever. He had been calm and assured during Syme's talk, as he needed to be. Now that it was over he was free to wheeze and shiver. The afternoon's speech was a hard event now and could be dislodged. Harder things were to come. We returned to the cabin, whence Syme had preceded us, and I collapsed on a long draped ottoman in the swimming air. I could see Syme through the open door, writing at his desk. Tom, as was his wont after a lecture and despite his overcrowing illness, entered his chamber and leaned his back against the open door. I was shut out for the second time.

And gladly, too. I heard only a few words of Tom's early conversation, including his favourite dictum, 'Simplicity, brevity and Fires.' But I knew that Sam had not spoken. 'Volcanoes' also slipped through the keyhole and made its escape to me. Just in time, too. For by now Sam had risen and I could hear his voice growing and dwindling as he paced from desk to door: 'To be prodded and pricked like . . . come this way to preach at a watering-hole . . . the less intelligent bison . . . Harcourt will promise nothing . . . why did he come do I suppose? . . . a liaison with Mrs Cumberland . . . perhaps Cooling's aunt . . . do not talk to me of . . . what do you suppose my sacrifices have been? . . . to exchange your bed for a baker's fortune . . . with a baker's looks . . . that needs no explanation . . . I am on the verge of great discoveries and you bring me to Middletown . . . I WILL NOT BE BESTED BY ANY MAN.' He stopped there. 'I WILL NOT BE BESTED . . . airs? what airs? I have never given myself – airs . . . Phidy has nothing to do with it . . . nothing to do with us, I should say . . . do not talk to me of my heat or the temper . . . yes, it's true, it's true . . . of course it's a strain, who set the pace? . . . I will not have you pecking around me . . . if I need physic, Phidy will attend to it . . . I am done with you . . . I WILL NOT BE BESTED BY ANY . . .'

I could bear it no longer. Tom's quiet, assured responses, running just too low for me to hear, chilled me as much as Syme's clamour, which hurt me palpably, as if I were a child still who overheard a father's rage. So I fled, into the shimmering streets.

When I returned, Sam sat reading on the ottoman. He looked up and said, 'Tom fainted. I had to carry him to bed. He is properly – soaked. Take a look at him, will you – there's a good Phidy?'

I knocked and entered. Tom lay swathed in sheets like a beast in seaweed. There was no comfort to be found anywhere. His every position seemed to neglect a leg or an arm or the neck. His skin looked chafed and his feet were swollen. But he did not complain, did as I told him; drank deep of the potion I prepared, breathed the spirit of camphor through a laden cloth. As ever he was patient and detached. Nothing could touch him in his fever, neither Syme's anger nor my good offices. He was unreachable, dwindling into the distance like an object seen at the wrong end of a telescope. The nearer I peered, the farther he seemed to perch, a small, neat soul at a great height.

Sam and I spent the remainder of the evening in the adjoining room. Mrs Bevington brought us our supper, chops and potatoes, speaking shrilly and tiptoeing like a shadow (a heavy shadow with a propensity for knocking over cabinets), so as not to disturb 'Dr Phidy Miller's patient, poor dear Tom'. (All ladies 'of a certain age' instantly took to Tom, loved and fretted over him at once.) Sam read and wrote. I thought, happy enough in the summer-loud silence, having ample material for contemplation: the lecture and the mysterious Harcourt; our present plans; Tom's illness, no doubt brought on by yesterday's gentle shipwreck; that more spiritual leak in our little vessel, the rift between Tom and Sam . . . I delighted with the curious inward satisfaction that feeds quite happily on any serious event, sustained equally by fortune and misfortune.

Sam's throat hurt him from the hot weather, the lecture, the argument with Tom and the late night. It had been a filthy day. The air was soaked but no rain came, and the evening did not fall, but stick. On such nights we sprout thoughts and desires, like roots coming out of a broken flowerpot. At last, nightfall brought a more delicious

air. When I saw a curtain shiver, then belly with wind, like a
woman's dress; collapse and sag again, like loose skin; then billow —
my heart rose with it. I removed my jacket and shirt and sat in my
undershirt in the grateful breeze. Syme wore only his pantaloons.
His feet were bare, in easy fellowship with his bare chest and hang-
ing arms. Tom lay ill and feverish in the bedroom next door, for
once the object and not the engine of our cares. But we are never like
our styles in the end, thank God. The lot of sickness should by right
have fallen to me. But I was only hot and hoarse and happy, sitting
beside Sam's work table.

'How could you begin?' I asked, with a rare though over-earnest
pluck. 'What courage you must have needed. Settled in the army,
well placed to satisfy an ordinary ambition. What did your mother
think? How could you desert a solid world and decent prospects for
such bottomless fantasies and a life like this?'

'Most ideas', he said, going over old ground, 'begin as the answer
to an unimportant problem — soon forgotten — a stone washed away
once the stream is crossed. So it was with me. A simple calculation
to occupy an idle hour led me to a quite different question — a ques-
tion of mass and Newton. My breath stopped, as at a blow to
the stomach. *So true it is that we are at the mercy of our own . . .*
inspiration — that is too grand a word, which means nothing more
than the ability to begin in idleness and end in faith.'

He paused and began again — some new thought had teased him
from the repetition. 'I believe greatly in profusion, in . . . You may
wonder at the labour of it — how hard I work at dull connections and
tedious proofs. But, for me, precision is only one kind of
abundance. Such colours, such magnificent explosions! Is not the
magnesium torch glorious? The endless turning of these intricate
spheres? Am I not fertile ground? Was anything ever born without
heat and accident?'

I waited on his word, leg bent over the arm of the chair, long chin
cupped in the heat of my palm. 'There are always a dozen answers
to any question,' he said at last, 'and then the question changes. We
want . . . satiety, more than satisfaction. We wish to be sated from
time to time — to desire nothing. I suppose I began in search of that.

377

I suppose I will find it – that is one consolation. We all do. I earned my dishonourable discharge within the month.

'Tom is a different creature altogether,' Sam added after a short pause, touching my knee lightly and winking his eye at the sick room. How I thrilled at the confidence! 'He has only temperament – a fine thing, certainly, and very useful. But it leaves no room for temptation – and what comes after temptation. You and I have character – a more unhappy gift.'

There were only two beds in the cabin, and Tom and I had shared one the night before. 'You should not disturb the patient, Phidy,' Sam said. 'Come to bed with me.' We undressed together and stepped into the rough cold sheets. I babbled beside him, happy with talk and 'the whispered thoughts of hearts allied'. But Sam soon fell asleep, with that great weariness that can be quenched as readily as thirst. Then I lay restless and awkward at his side deep into the night. I could not turn my thoughts to anything else with Sam so close, and at last, unconsciously, began to count the soft breaths from the still figure beside me.

It was two days before Tom was well enough to travel. Sam and I both nursed him, though he required little. They were significant days to me. One swallow doth not a summer make, they say in this strange tongue; and that night of close companionship in the close air with Tom so close at hand was only the first appearance of the swallow. The next two days ushered in summer. Sam and I delighted in our new freedom. We spent two long days by the cabin, as idle and busy as children. 'What shall we do after breakfast, Sam?' I asked, still awkward in our young intimacy.

'Go to the water,' he said, with a broad smile on his face.

That morning, we dredged the sunk boat from the bottom of the river. Syme stripped completely and dived in with a rope round his waist, while I held the other end from the shore, well hedged in shirt and waistcoat, tie and coat, all white in that white heat. Sam proved a strong swimmer in the event, a second Byron, exuberant in the water, like water itself, a strong fountain leaping and pushing away its own kind in a white shower. Down he went and pulled the boat from where it lay sucking in the mud, a titanic effort, and attached the rope to the cross-benches. He shot up for breath, a suddenly young man, sweeping wet hair from his forehead.

'Pull, you damn fool,' he cried, 'I'm not a fish!'

He disappeared again. The water rippled, shimmered above him, and I could feel the strain on his back as he dug his knees into the river mud and heaved. The boat stirred, lifted, sank, but only skimmed the mud, and then rose. I hauled it to the bank, where it lay pointing at the sky, half-submerged like a dead fish. Sam joined me then, streaked with thick, dark mud, like paint, which rendered him almost decent in a pagan way, and we brought up the damned thing. Its boards lay reeking and drying in the sun. I fetched Sam the white sheet from our bed and, classically draped, he lay beside the river. I secured one corner of the cloth and went so far as to take off my shoes and stockings. I sat coolly and sedately, never quite at peace, but always happy, letting my feet settle below the cool water, stroked by swaying weed from time to time.

But Sam could not sit still. Within a few hours, the excess of his high spirits returns, and he must again be busying himself with something. I marvelled at his fresh forces, wondered at how much they had to do with Tom's prostration, his absent shadow. Now Sam could diffuse his enormous energies over smaller and happier things. I marvelled, but Sam's energy so nearly matched my own inward high spirits, my restless, stirring, ineffectual delight, like the motion of a tree's shadow in the wind, that it seemed but the intoxication of the air, the fine day, and I did not puzzle more over it at the time. I was again sent fetching – to Mrs Bevington for a carpenter's kit.

Sam set to work immediately, tipped the boat on its belly so that the rump stood open to his inspection. He caulked a minor flaw between two boards with a mixture of his own preparation. But he found that it would not do: the weakness was too general and the rot had proceeded too far for such patchwork remedies. We found some old boards in a shed and Mrs Bevington consented that they be translated to a lighter, aqueous bliss.

'I never noticed them till after my husband died, Mr Phidy, and I never could think how they got there, till it hits me once. They was left over from his coffin.'

Mrs Bevington was added to our little gathering and watched the transformation with a somewhat sentimental curiosity. Sam, now dressed and almost decent, was glad of the audience. All afternoon he kept at it, hacking and ripping and sanding and nailing and boarding and a great many other operations, no doubt, all of which he explained to me very thoroughly, though I scarcely heeded him, too happy to sit in the shade with my back against the willow and listen to the companionable unsteady din. By early evening the boat had been repaired, swum light and high, and with two newly fashioned oars we could begin our explorations of the river. Mrs Bevington brought us a bottle of wine for the launch, but we drank it instead and waited for the morning.

Tom rose the next day, late and weak, sipped tea with us under a garden awning. The sky was another perfect blue shell, with that peculiar swept, deserted air of a fine spring morning. But it was high summer, though a little cooler than the day before. We left him sitting warmly wrapped by the bird-bath and took the boat, newly christened Punch, upriver towards Richmond. It was a weary pull. The current was slow but contrary, and the sun lay very hot on the water. My face grew quite red by day's end, a crack-skinned berry. We alternated at the oars and raced for pace. Sam never flagged. His broad, deep strokes brought a fine bow-wave surging past and both our spirits surged with it, stirred to a crest of joy by the simple motion of the blades in the water and the self-made wind tugging our hair and cooling our ears and faces. But the old sticky heat returned late in the afternoon. It settled on us like a fallen cobweb or a glaring cloud, and soon I surrendered my stroke entirely to the indefatigable Sam, who pulled us to a riverside inn.

We sat in the window overlooking the broad current and ordered tall pots of porter. 'Have you ever fought a – duel?' he said to me, as we dipped our noses in the thick brews.

'No.'

He touched a loose hair that had caught on his tongue with his fingertip, looked at it briefly, and rubbed his hands together. 'They make

a curious entertainment. It is a great and common mistake', he con-
tinued, 'to contest them in the morning. Viz: men dragged from their
beds will kill each other through sheer muddle-headed sleepiness –
who might, in brighter moods, render or accept a pardon. Midnight
is no better. Anyone may kill at midnight – darkness has the effect of
strong drink. No, if you wish to avoid a scrape – suggest teatime.
Nothing is easier than to reconcile – at teatime.'

Sam drank deep, rubbed a knuckle against his nose, and said, 'I
fought one once. Just such a filthy day as this. I had been in – a
terrible temper – all afternoon. It seemed the only thing to do.'

He sat back in his seat and lifted the catch of the window, and
pushed open the glass with a squeak and a scrape. A grateful wind
ruffled the river and blew into our faces, and Sam closed his eyes
against it. 'At the time,' he said, returning to his pot of porter, 'I
confess, I shouldn't have minded an – an honourable grave. Only
think what thoughts would have remained – unthought! – had a
plug of iron strayed – an inch inside my tunic! Though there was
in the event little question of that. The chief feature that struck me
about the whole affair (apart from the fact that I felt a hot fool . . .
most of the night, and a chilly fool . . . in the morning) was this:
how little capable we are of – taking a life. Not in the particular, of
course. Nothing could be easier: a click and a spark and a puff of
very pleasing powder, I must say, and there's an end of it. But in
the proper weight and consequence of the act – it is entirely
beyond us. We commit the gravest and the lightest deeds – in the
same spirit – relying as it were on the connections between the
slight and the great – to achieve our ends – between an inch of
iron and this globe of thoughts.' Here he held his own globe in his
two hands, and rubbed these across his eyes till they held his nose,
and he breathed once, deeply, between his palms.

'The trick, by the by,' he added, on a lighter note, 'should you
ever need it, Phidy – is this: aim at the hip as you raise the gun. It
will bear first and throw him off his shot. Fire once in the air after he
misses you, and both sides may retire with honour. There is a lesson
in that – a man with partial objectives will always triumph over a
man with a more – complete sense of purpose. A lesson, it seems,

Phidy, that I have unlearned.' Then he saw my nodding, sunburned countenance and took pity; hauled me up with both hands under my armpits and made his farewells to the clamour of good wishes and invitations that followed him to Punch and echoed long after us down the long, echoing water. We returned to Middletown easily with a lazy surprise: the current must have been stronger than suspected. And Sam rowed us in, gently nosing the small pier just as the sun set, sad and full, and Tom came out to greet us, with a lighter step, dressed, though still a little pale.

We shouldered our packs and departed the next day, whither only Tom knew. The sky was that brown-grey, low-hung miserable drapery of unsettled summer days. But my summer had begun. For if ever I belonged in America, if ever I lent my weight to this enterprise, it was then. Tom's sickness was the beginning; the past two days were the first happy steps. So I left that town with a light step, in fledgling good spirits, though the air hung still around us as if a bell tolled in it.

Even after this respite, our little band had not yet found its gait. I had won a place in Sam's esteem for the first time; but the quarrel between Tom and Sam was postponed and not resolved, had prompted indeed a slight stiffness between Tom and me. I felt as if Sam must 'forgive Tom' before we could prosper, though for what I could not guess, unless it were Sam's own dependence. His spirits had lightened after our dip in Punch, but his heart for the enterprise still lay in the balance. Sam was always happiest when he shied from his own purpose. Tom feared that the dry work in Middletown might turn him from the harvest. After a week of travels our list of subscriptions could be enclosed in the white field of a page. 'He is such a stubborn ass,' Tom told me one night, to breach our awkwardness and deflect his own despair, 'and would make himself miserable out of a philosophical conviction.'

'You cannot follow him when he lags two paces behind,' I answered, half-guiltily, for I often lingered with Sam in the rear. We bided Sam's time, for he held our courage as well as our purpose in his hand.

A week after the Middletown adventure we came to Perkins, a tiny town, with a tiny wooden one-roomed church, whose chaplain was a cousin of Tom's. Tom was at his wits' end and could think of nowhere else to turn, though we had scant hope of an audience in such a place. It was a weary walk. The glass had been rising all day and no coach ran to Perkins. The mail came only once a week, else we would have been among the postman's deliveries. Our only transport was our own six feet, strung out along the road like the legs of some dragging insect, now close together, now staggering apart. We journeyed from Somerville, the nearest town, with our backs bent under all our gear. A heavy, weary walk in the drowning heat. We all felt we must soon go under. I am afraid that Sam and I looked a little unkindly on Tom, as the afternoon wore on through brimming flies and flat, dried cow-pats on the stony road. But Sam said nothing, and Tom and I laboured as much through his silence as through that rain-soaked air.

We arrived at sunset. The cross of the church stood dark as charred wood in the burning light. Like us, the atmosphere seemed oppressed by an intolerable burden, but ours was not so much a burden of weight as of distance, remoteness. Only Syme could maintain a sense of immensity in the face, or, rather, in the corners, of such obscurity, and he had withdrawn. Tom, for all his efficient bustle, lacked the gift of scale; and we both felt little better than tramps, shoes caked in dung, loafing through a village too small to deny us charity. Worse than tramps, indeed, unsupported by their easy purposelessness.

And a barn is what we got when we arrived. After a sustained banging on the door, Tom's cousin greeted us. Jeb was a sour-faced, unpleasant young man, already running to fat, so unlike Tom. He reeked of early intimacy, like an ugly smell that he could not keep to himself. 'I've only got a spare room, I'm sorry to say, Tom. The dogs must make do in the barn. You don't mind that, Phidy? There's just the one bed, and that goes to the wizard. We must have you clean at least, if you speak to the congregation. Not like your fine cities, here, sir. Watch out for them, that's all. Might ruffle your feathers, but won't do any harm, sir, that's my opinion.' And he showed us the barn, thick with the smell of horses, comforting none the less, with their subterranean snufflings and stirrings. We pitched our bags on to the hay and came in to supper.

A comfortless meal, though God knows we had the hunger for it. Syme barely spoke, pinched and withdrawn into reflections like a tight corner. Tom and I picked and gnawed our way through cold beef and old cheese and left a litter of bones and dried fat on the dirty plates. Who could be hungry long in such heat or who could talk? Except for Jeb, who made the most of his stony companions, like a thistle on a rock. Called to the Church by family tradition, he had the worst of its professional airs without the least of its humility or faith. The air rang with the litany of his grievances.

'The Maryland Chapter are a godless people,' he droned between thick mouthfuls. 'The Deacon at Somerville, between the two of us, Tom, never darkened his wife's bed . . . If I were a different man, a word in someone's ear, but it's ever the way, the grasping inherit the . . .' He was just the man to prick Sam's anger in another mood. And he talked on, while the night pressed in around us and the lamplight smeared in the heavy air like fat. Sam kept his peace, though each minute Tom and I expected an eruption. I feared Sam's disposition – his spirits hung drained and limp in that humid obscurity. Perhaps Jeb had his reasons for bitterness, but bitter he was, as rank as meat that has been hung too long.

Sam was to give a lecture that very night. Jeb had arranged for 'the wizard', as he called him, to speak in his little church. A large bill on the tall front doors announced the coming of 'the great Baltimore Geonomist!' I suspected the worst. The great geonomist had barely spoken all evening, was in a niggardly temper that granted nobody a thing. Even if he were in a fine monumental flow of spirits, I little doubted that Jeb's flock would turn at best a deaf ear. At worst, he would have to make his way through a jungle of hard-fibred small-town prejudices and superstitions. There lay my true fear, for, if anything, Sam was in a hacking mood. I did not like to think of him wasting his energy and fury, knees bent in the mud, to pull up such hard, useless roots, probably with so little success. I feared we had the squalor of Middletown to do again.

Perkins, I soon saw, held a very different squalor. The small wooden church was filled with Perkins, Perkins was nowhere if not there, packed tight in that small, high space. The heavy air pressed low the hive of noise: the shuffle of feet on dusty wood, the call for someone's child, the familiar voices of a school hall. It was an occasion. Young girls wore frocks a few years more grown than themselves and kept their hands to their sides and smoothed their fronts, in such an easily broken stiffness that my heart went out to them. Farmers wore their Sunday bests complete with cravats, under dirty, work-easy coats; took their ladies by their arms. Grandfathers sat stiff and proper and straight like the girls; and upset easily, unbent like them too. A few of the younger men grouped together, stuck their long legs under the pews in front, preparing to uphold the town's church and dignity if they were ever questioned. They sat low in their seats, shoulder to shoulder, and glanced at the local girls. I feared them the most. This was too much of an occasion: there were to be no deaf ears turned that night. Syme rose up to speak.

'Ladies and gentlemen, fellow scientists, and brothers *of the Church,' he said with a sly look. Instantly my heart lightened. 'I come to speak to you today with no uncertain purpose.' It was a signal to us that tonight he was not in earnest, that tonight was free and would not be reckoned. 'The ground is splitting, gentlemen, splitting beneath our feet. Can you not hear the yawning maw of Hell?'*

And we did hear it, a terrible cracking at the joint of things, as though a great dog had sunk its teeth into a great bone. 'You have come, no doubt, to hear a madman preach empty bubbles at ye; and indeed I have, for so slight is the shell beneath our feet that the fury of the Lord can shatter it with the touch of His finger's tip. Listen to this fury and have ye doubted? Listen to this vengeance, children, and have ye sinned? Are we not bubbles clustered upon a bubble, and shall a breath destroy us?'

He preached Doomsday in good earnest now, a child's Doomsday filled with an ark of creatures: huge subterranean eagles with wings as big as trees; massive thundering elephants, rearing tusks of heavenly gold moulded into trumpets; giant mice that scratch and paw and poke the earth above them, dislodging loose falls, little more than ash and moss to them, earthquakes and maelstroms to us. Each word solemn and sincere, each gesture of his hand heavy and impassioned, and on he talked and spoke not a word of truth.

The cool air grew suddenly sharp as crystal, and my heart leapt, and the rain fell, down, pounding on the high sloped roofs, till we could scarce believe that outside those four walls there was any air to breathe. Oh the joy of that rain, as it thundered and blasted like Sam's giant elephants. The little church felt tight as a ship surrounded by seas, falling seas. They pounded and pounded at us to get in, and Syme bellowed on. He held us spellbound, as delicately poised as the air before the rains came, and rose to a shout to be heard. 'He shall tear down the walls and embankments we have set against him, batter our barricades – shall we not lie as Jonah lay in the ribs of the whale, shall we not cry out in the hollow of His Heart – for mercy and for faith?'

Goodness knows what it all meant. But Perkins sat stunned. No one knew what to think or say. The rain fell so loud that we half-doubted our ears. The very thought of raising a voice of protest against such combined torrents seemed an impiety. We sat as solemn as old ladies in a bawdy-house. Sam walked calmly through the congregation, through that noise as thick as walls, and with half a raised eyebrow summoned Tom and me to follow. Which we did, gravely, out of the tall wooden door into the unbreathable rain. We raised our coat collars, hunched over together and hooted with a laughter that the wind snatched and the rain drowned. Syme put a wet arm around each of our wet necks and in such a companionable convoy we staggered to Jeb's barn, flung open the door and flung ourselves laughing on a pile of damp hay. Jeb must have been dumbfounded.

We lay catching our breath happily for some time. I was at that pitch of nervous happiness when my love will go out to any manner of thing, so that I scarcely know it when it comes back. Tom said through thick breaths, 'You should not have done that, Sam,' and laughed.

I came in too quick, 'No, that was unwise,' laughing too.

Sam did not answer, but I could feel joy crowding against him like applause for having carried it off. I heard Tom's voice through the grey, cold air. 'They believed every word.'

'Yes,' I chorused. 'That is, they thought you believed every word.'

'Now was that not worth a little mockery, a touch of Symmesonia, perhaps?' Sam asked, knowing our answer.

Sam was content where he was, did not feel the urge for Jeb's spare bed, was happy to sleep among the dogs. The night stretched out before us like a summer day; none of us wanted to sleep. We wanted to talk. Our joy is a country of one, I said. But there is another joy, a traveller's joy, as keen as the first, keener perhaps. I am not a Godly man, but who at such times can doubt that our first thought is love, our first desire understanding, for others and ourselves, a passion shared equally without begrudging? To have stumbled on such a night when Sam was among the company seemed to me as rare a piece of good luck, as undeserved, as seeing a comet or a king pass by.

It was the first time Sam spoke of his family to me – or, rather, in my presence. No, to me, for did I not measure the times his voice sought me and not Tom? No matter, there was enough and to spare that night. 'That was a piece of my father's chicanery,' he said. 'I inherited that much. Symmesonia revisited.'

Tom opened the door to see by. The bright rain fell hard as stones outside. He stuck his face out, upturned, screwed it against the rain as it spattered him. His tongue squirmed out between tight lips, searching for water. He had not a thought for us. Then he came back in and closed the heavy door. The barn was black again, and the snuffling horses seemed suddenly to advance upon our ears. 'You inherited much more,' Tom said, 'and you know it.'

'What else, Tom?' Sam was contented with this talk, leaned back.

'You have a father not a mother tongue.'

'Only when I wish. Tonight could have been one of his flights. I hope we have no cause to regret it.'

Then, as young men will, we began to speak of our fathers.

'Sam never regrets a thing, he says,' Tom began. 'But he does,

387

you know, Phidy, remember that. You regret university, that is, leaving it so soon.'

'I had my reasons,' Sam said.

'Of course, there are always reasons,' Tom mocked, pressing his lips together. A minute passed and he began again. 'Edward used to shower his daughter with gifts. Bubbles, he called her, name fit for a cat, don't you think, not a girl? You don't like it much either, Sam. He wouldn't have her being petted.'

'All those silly presents,' Sam cut in, with fresh irritation, 'bringing home something, sugar cane or gypsy rings, cheap things, you know, but they added up. To nothing, I said. I didn't like the girl being spoiled, when Mother hadn't a stitch to do her justice, gaunt thing that she was. Said so, too, brave boy, when I was fifteen. I WILL NOT HAVE YOU MAKE A POODLE OF MY SISTER. Funny way to say it, sure, but when Mother could barely move at night, what with stiffness and hunger, too. Would you credit it, poor thing? Wouldn't eat. For her to see Bubbles petted over and bound with ribbons – it does the heart no good to think of it. She hated me for it, that's the thing. Anne hated me for it. "POODLE OF MY SISTER," I shouted, "WHEN YOU MAKE A BEAR OF MOTHER." Pater turned his head like a shying horse; wouldn't answer, stood there, head turned. I was in a towering rage.'

'What set it off?'

'A wedding dress. Pretty white lace – the bride died of consumption and her young man didn't want to look at it. Almost gave it away and Pater brought it home for Bubbles. Much too big, of course, then. She looked like someone snowed her in and was beginning to melt, the child. But wasn't it the darling of her heart? And Mother poking through her skin to look lovely and all you ever saw were bones. Not a new stitch to wear in a dozen years, not since Bubbles came out. Who beamed pleased as punch at the gift, while I worked into a towering rage. Then she froze in a corner and Father's head dipped and turned like a horse's, and Mother went purple, didn't say a word, didn't forgive me, either. Till later, but that's another story.'

'What happened then?'

'I went to university . . .'

'Where you belong,' Tom cut in.

Sam ignored him. 'Father got worse – began to get about town. There was nobody left to put the fear in him. Until Bubbles stumbles over him one day in flagrante – the vicar's wife, as it happens. Didn't that break her heart? She wouldn't speak, wouldn't eat for a week, holed up in her room, until I came home and talked her out of it, and when she stepped forth, in a plain dress, her hair poked out cut short and her neck shone bare. She never wore his finery again. Sea change.'

'Your mother blamed you . . .' Tom broke the silence.

'"YOU BROUGHT THIS ON," she said. God knows how; and she hated to see Bubbles petted regardless. Still, it was a shock to see the poor girl – cut back to the quick.'

'Best thing for her, if you ask me,' Tom said. 'Married the butcher, fine man, honest, loving man.'

'Pater raised her above her expectations. But then, he was only born for riches and never had any.'

'You never returned to university?' I asked.

'Couldn't bear to. Never took a degree. Went into the army – Benedict Smythe, old family friend, as they say, paid the commission. But that's another story, bitter too. To spite my father, is the long and the short of it. And it did, I believe, at that.'

The noise of one bell tolling the half-hour made its way through the thick air, and Sam stopped talking. We now heard the runnels, streams and rivers the rain had made. They ran down the barn walls in a throaty burble, into a soapy swelling pool, clanking like heavy things. None of us wanted to sleep. We seemed to stand on tiptoe, anxious to speak – 'May I, may I?' – but too polite, good-intentioned, to proceed, until the silence grew and gave us a spreading sense of the night outside. What could have put us in such childish spirits, that grown men should feel the need to recount the stories of their boyhood and their fathers? Our bed among the horses, like a child's summer quarters? Sam's great irreverence of the evening, that slipped through cracks in the conversation like rain through the loose roof with little squirts of reminded pleasure? The great drumming noise? The sudden chill, which made us huddle in ourselves, solemn and respectful? Respectful of what – of the chance?

Tom broke the silence again. 'You know my father, Sam, what do you think?' Then he turned to me. 'You do not.' Tom had often puzzled me, a patient, secret, playful creature, easily upset and easily consoled – as it turned out, quite unlike his father, who was a preacher; a distant and correct man. 'Jeb followed the family calling; only I strayed,' Tom said, smiling. 'I think my mother minded, but my father did not. He is the happiest man I have ever met.'

'Just so,' Sam answered, smiling. 'He knows the propriety behind each thing – a perfect gentleman. He is spotless. In his manners at table – entertaining a lady – advising wealthy parishioners – conducting himself among the poor. Yet I scarcely know so improper a man. I believe (Tom, is this true?) that he has surrendered all faith in the scriptures – if he ever possessed any. But, like a well-made clock, the mechanism continues faultlessly – the rituals tick and chime at the appropriate moment. He has a watchmaker's delight in these things, I fancy. It is his only approachable delight.'

'There is nothing like him,' Tom agreed.

'And your mother?' I asked.

Sam answered again, 'A perfect dear.'

'She is,' Tom said. 'She was – a farmer's daughter, one of my father's flock.'

I met her later: a large, sensible, happy woman, scarce twenty when she married. She was perpetually puzzled at the good fortune of her match, like a girl who had found a plover's egg and could not guess what it was. Happy and puzzled at once. She had a gift for noisy joy, an easy gait, ran often in the hurry of high spirits, or to catch a child in her arms and swing. Tricks with which Tom delighted me at my arrival, and could still delight me if he chose.

'Have you a sister or brother?' I asked.

'A sister,' Tom said and glanced laughingly at Sam, though I never knew why.

Sam and Tom seemed by then to have regained their ordinary good spirits, thawed, grown merely tired and contented. I had not *and still sat frozen in perfect solemn joy. Or rather, not frozen at all, for I felt it then, yes then as the bell struck three through the thrashing, shredded rain, felt joy well within me, like a spring; swelling and growing clearer and closer from below, till it struck me sharp and I fell back in the hay as at a blow to release its power as it swept past me. I yawned to let its diminishing echoes escape. Who has not felt such intimations, such uncontrolled, almost unwanted, uprisings of delight, when a moment arrives in its full weight: item, a young man (myself), reclined (slightly cold) in a barn in Perkins, with, item two, Tom Jenkyns, now curled beneath his greatcoat with only an ear cocked, to listen to, item three, Sam Syme, perhaps the noblest, highest man I was ever to know; and, item four, youth, and, item five, the recollection of an evening's prank; and, items six through twenty-seven, horses, and, item twenty-eight, splendid hope, and all so far from home. To all of which Tom replied, 'It is late, Phidy. Perhaps we had best sleep.'*

But I was on a nervous edge of happiness and could not have slept for the world. Nor did Sam consent, and in his generosity questioned me concerning my youth: the death of my mother at Ruth's birth; my sister's ripening charms and sly flirtations (alas Sam sighed, smiling); the whims of my Prince, and his little palace on the hill, where I attended such delightful musical evenings to escape the babbling barrack of revolutionary drunks my father kept in the basement (himself how much gentler, richer in true faith than his companions!). The night grew quiet and tiny noises began to emerge like insects in the clear air: the noise of branches unbending beneath their load; the patient hollow echo of wood-doves; the electric twitterings of titmice; and the thousandfold shattering drops of poised beads of water and their endless rebirth. Sam rose from the hay and walked over to the great barn door. Opened it wide and stood in the sudden wind, looking out over the vast grey air and the wet grass-blades, stirring and vibrating like the wires of a swept harp, as wind and water bent and unbent them with mechanical precision. The sky began to crack like a shell with dawn emerging. The horses snuffled, shimmied and neighed as they roused their stiff great bodies. Sam shut the large door, leaving us in a thick grey light. Without another word we all slept.

I awoke before my companions with an almost guilty air, as if a secret had been confessed. There is to my mind something shameful in talk, a crude undressing. But Sam and Tom noticed nothing amiss, as they roused themselves straw-haired and stumbled out under the perfect blue shell of morning. And the air, after that hard summer rain, was so clear and joyous as we set out that we felt we could taste the champagne bubbles on our tongue from the rising sunny atmosphere.

Next we stopped in Golden, Virginia, a small town scarcely bigger than Perkins. Mr Corkney, the local schoolmaster, commissioned Sam to speak for the older pupils at his school. For he instructed children of nearly every age together, from five years onwards till they were fit for the plough, and he feared that he neglected the older students in such a mix. He taught in a one-room cabin built on the sloped edge of his fields, for he was a farmer, too. And he seemed truly delighted to 'entertain the celebrated geonomist', as Sam had begun to call himself, so I took to him at once.

We brought our gear to the barn and dropped it happily in the hay. Sam said, 'I should like a walk – don't follow,' and left with a sheaf of notes stuck under his arm in the humid weather, thick as soup. He often took an hour to himself to gather his thoughts and strength for the coming talk. Perhaps he wished to jostle the two of us together again, for Tom and I had been distant of late. We stood awkwardly now, as silent as a reunion, and I thought how rare had been the spells of our recent good fellowship, or even our solitary company. Sam in a measure had come between us.

Then Tom said, 'Are you thirsty, by chance?'

We found our way to the public house, the Sword and Plough, at the foot of the hill. We sat deep in cracked leather, too low to see anything but the brown clouds of summer through the window, flung wide. 'Good afternoon, sirs,' said the barmaid in a white frock and a voice just gone sharp with her trade, 'what's your pleasure?' She was a brimming miss, scarce fifteen years old, with short straw hair, soft, downward cheeks and upturned bright eyes.

'Two pints of ale.'

She brought us our cups running over, and Tom in his easy way caught her by the hand as she set them down. 'What's your name?' he said, in those fluting bird-like tones that women adored, and let her go.

'Kate,' she answered and then pursed her lips. 'Miss Benton.'

'Kate Benton,' Tom said, pinching his bottom lip, and considering. 'Do you see the gentleman beside me? Look as much as you like, he won't understand us. He don't speak, you see, at least not what we would call language.' Indeed, I was speechless and sat as tongue-tied as a fish. 'He's a prince, though,' Tom went on steadily, 'a German prince.' Kate Benton did stare at me then, but a farmer by the door called to her, and she blushed and fled.

I began to protest loudly at both our treatments, but Tom hushed me to a murmur. 'How can you hope to win her,' he urged, 'if you are not a proper silent German prince?'

And such is my foolish nature that I sat mum, while Tom had the wind of me for the best part of an hour. How he prattled to my mute amusement, speculating over Kate Benton's age, the number and fierceness of her early lovers, and the recommended means of pressing my suit. I could remonstrate only in whispers, or splutter loudly in my mother tongue while he watched me with crinkling eyes. But we laughed shamefully and got on very well. Kate called to me as we left and snuck out of the door behind us, shutting it with her hand behind her back. 'Come here, Your Highness,' she said and kissed me on the chin, then disappeared. O, I was everyone's fool.

We returned to the barn to prepare our couches for the night. Sam had accepted the hospitality of the spare bed, but Tom and I were happy to sleep like dogs in the leftover hay of the schoolmaster's barn. A something lingered in the air that I did not wish to see blown out – a question stood on the tip of my tongue. I feared Tom would slap his thighs and climb into the loft to arrange the thatch before I could ask it. But he lingered too, and answered my question as if the thought grew naturally out of our talk of Kate. Perhaps we had both been dwelling on it. 'Tom,' I said, 'why do you work so hard for Sam? Does it not strike you as a fool's errand?'

Tom sat on the bottom rung of the ladder with his knees tucked into his chin. 'Yes,' he said, 'it is a question.'

'You neglect your own ambitions,' I added, growing braver. 'Even ordinary hopes, you neglect them, too. You know to what I refer, Tom. Your life seems all neglect but for this one man. You seem happy enough, but if he should fail?'

'Do you see, Phidy, that Sam is easily' – and Tom did not hesitate but waited for the word – 'spilled. Do you see that, Phidy? If you do not give him peace, real quiet, he goes everywhere, but to waste. He must be held quite still. And don't smile at me when I say it, Phidy, Phidy-if-I-may, for it's true I think, though you won't credit it, but I am a very . . . still sort of fellow. And I think I do him good.' I did smile, though with a different doubt. Tom went on. 'There is something else. Sam has no head for this world,' and before I could protest, he added, 'Wait till I finish, Phidy. I know you think along a different line.'

He summoned his thoughts for a minute, then continued. 'He has no eye for present fortunes and would not eat unless we fed him. It is my task to keep him fed, but, more than that, I must not let him bury himself too deep in his own purposes. I tell him, "You cannot win eternity until you win the world. And you cannot win the world until you win the admiration of Virginia or Pactaw or something more than the love of a young doctor who misses his father and a down-at-heels newspaperman." He don't see it, and I love him for that, too. For though Sam craves our every thought, and I know he does, he does not reckon our poor respect any lower than Ben Franklin's or the King of England's. He is a true democrat in that. But he must speak from some eminence to be heard. I love him so that I wish every city would raise a statue to him or call their streets after him. But as yet they cannot, for they do not know his name. I have battled him all the way on these travels, as you must have guessed. Now at last he has taken the reins in his own hands. He knows there will be a time for his investigations.'

'I could not keep him from his own task for all the world.'

'Perhaps you might, Phidy. But yours is a different faith.'

There was some puzzle and doubt in those last words that eluded me, but I could not mistake the tone. Tom wished to persuade me of something – of what I could not guess nor to what end. He wished to enlist my belief. And I noted then, as one would mark the face of a tossed coin, that he did not have it, for all my present glowing spirits and enthusiasm. Strange how little it disturbed me, as I stood there idly, and Tom's shadowed face looked up with a curious eye that I could no more answer than water can support a footstep. Or perhaps I misread him?

Sam spoke that night and we took another list of subscriptions for our prospective journal: mostly from young men still ambitious of a city life and a few of their fathers. Afterwards we dined with Mr Corkney, a short, cocky thumb of a man, of Irish stock, with something of an Irish tongue. He was a young man himself, just learning to wear his father's thoughts as his own. 'Excuse me, sir', he said once, not quite attending, for Sam was launched on the seas of one of his speeches, 'but I have always thought a great deal might be done by – digging.'

'Yes,' Sam replied, wrinkling his brows and briefly touching the bridge of his nose with his left forefinger, as though a fly had perched there – a nervous habit. 'Of course, digging is part of the work, a significant part, but there are other things that want attending, such as . . .' And he was nearly away again, sails spread before the wind.

'As a farmer,' Mr Corkney assured him, leaning forward confidentially, and resting his slight weight on his small elbow, 'I can assure you, Professor, that a great deal might be done – in short, a great deal might be achieved – in a new way – by digging.'

But he was ready company and curious, too – a firm, upright man of little weight. Though he was much troubled to consider the matter any further than it involved his great passion for, nay his conviction in, as a farmer, nothing less, well, in short, what might be achieved by . . . Sam in a rare generous temper sat late over his wine, talking to him. Mr Corkney was glad of the talk, come fresh from the university to his father's farm. He had not yet learned the tricks of loneliness.

We had an early start the next day, so Tom and I withdrew. Sam turned towards us as we left, with that characteristic murmur in his

*jowls, to bid us an unintelligible 'good night'. Then he turned back
to the lamp on the table, and I lost his face in the light. The sky had
been low all day, more misty than clouded. But the day cleared at
sunset and the sky soared with evening, and we felt we had a space
for breath again. Tom had a sudden burst of spirits and
hooted like an owl over the fields down the hill. Only the crickets
answered and rubbed his clear fine note to rags between their legs.
Tom clambered up the ladder behind me, nipping my heels, and
wrestled me for the nearest bed, scattering straw. 'You asked me
that question,' Tom said after a sleepless half-hour, lying on his back
and gazing up. 'Why I follow him as I do – and the answer is that,*
wherever he goes, I half-expect the ground to give way and
the world to change.'

Yes, I thought; that is an answer.

*From stagecoach to bed, from bed to stagecoach again; from town to
town; from city hall to college lecture rooms; from inn to aunt to
servants' quarters; from Oceanic Societies to Ladies' Societies for
the Promulgation of Thought to the Star Club, a gentlemen's astro-
nomical organization; from university to university; from atheist
gatherings to Quaker educational meetings to lonely churches with
a renegade pastor. From the first weeks of June to its burning,
drowning end, into a sweet July, cleared of clouds and miasmal airs,
so that each sky and day rose so perfect and pure you felt it would
chime if you rung it.*

*At first my infant intimacy still walked on hesitant steps,
doubting the ground and its young legs. I bounded between Tom
and Sam, now hanging back, now prancing ahead, bubbling with
talk and affectionate spirits, now lagging a pace behind, deferring
with a downcast head under the shadow of my own thoughts. But
even Sam was attuned to these brown studies now, practised at
teasing me from them, generous in his notice. I talked too, brimmed
and fell and rose with talk like a burst lock, after six months of
dammed waters.*

*From time to time I noted the oblique exchange of glances
between Tom and Sam at my high spirits. For once I did not draw*

up at those imaginary lines but swelled on. Instead, Tom withdrew slowly into his endless reserves – I was winning. He barricaded himself in Sam's work, where he remained unapproachable and unapproached. I had never seen him work so hard. He wrote to colleges and clubs, publishers and newspapers; announced our presence in villages and cities; secured engagements and lodgings from night to night. He took us from stagecoach to bed, from bed to stagecoach again; from town to town; from week to week.

But my poor spring of spirits was lost in Sam's great tide. For he was in flood those summer months and overflowed the canal of my excavated happiness like a sea. He carried all waters before him, tributary and river, lake and pond in his endless sweep. He swelled high enough to reach even Tom in his lonely preparations, and he prospered, too. All men rely on the alignment of planets. No matter how we reason our lives, pare them down to their proper agents, and take those agents in hand – the prick of our temperament and action remains obscure and uncrackable, like a seed in its kernel until it decides to come out. We rely on the good luck not of any heavenly constellations but of our own natures: on the setting and rising, the seasons and phases, of internal moons and suns, as powerful and strange to us as those grander burning patterns above. Who has not felt such influences? The evening of talk that like a sudden rain revives a friendship; the unlooked-for confluence of thoughts, an eclipse of sorts, that brings the shape and size of an idea into sharp relief; the day of happiness in an otherwise dry season. Sam's star was ascendant that summer, a full three months of rising fortune. Like the greater man he was, the alignment of his planets brought weather and prosperity to all around him, as if he burned in a much higher sphere.

Such a sweep of America we crossed together, as large as Spain, though it formed but a corner of the New World. What towns and men we saw! Small river villages, clustered like barnacles around a fisherman's post. Farms as great as Berlin, packed with orderly citizens of grain, ruled by a lonely family. Then new cities, with all the big-boned awkwardness of youth, like Baltimore, Richmond, Washington. What pages of names we took! We seemed to pass

through America like recording angels, marking those fit for scientific heaven, at threepence an issue, we thank you. Cooling,
Hutchinson, Marks, the list goes, each stroke of the pen recalling a
line of the face, the slant of an eye, the trick of a tongue. Corkney
from Ireland, Wiseman from Germany, Maclean from the islands of
Scotland, Billingtons from an English hamlet had all ventured
across oceans to find their way to a battered and inky sheet of paper
that promised to provide them with that magnificent pioneering
journal, as it would be, the New Platonist.

Though we were gallant knights, we had no dragons to battle,
only the vast obscurity of our purpose and the ordinary delays of
travellers. I could not have wished to share my insignificance with
two finer men. Of what was our talk? The role of the western
provinces; the appeal of possibility over fact; the progress of
climates; the differing capacities of different men to deal with
extremes of weather; from there to pain; then by way of the French
to the best location for a bakery in a small town – 'Give heed, Tom,
this touches you nearly'; the role of Society in such towns; the way
to wear a cravat; other fundamental differences between nations and
peoples; shared mythologies; the errors of Bonaparte and grounds of
his collapse; the hatred of waiting; necessary developments in transport in a spreading nation; the relation of practical need to the
progress of science; the virtues of democracy (it surprised me in
such an aristocratic temperament, but Syme was a passionate
republican); the importance of newspapers; the relation of thought
to language; the dialect of Golden as distinct from Perkins, Virginia;
local cussedness, stupidity; the benefits of public hangings. He had a
mind like a pack, which swarmed and divided and consumed any
sustenance it found. He took the measure of all things. Of what was
our talk?

The theories of Kuypen; his influence on Kepler; the features of
Galileo; physical causes of mental constitutions; the ugliness of the
members of the Oxford School; the nose of Barnaby, fixed in rain-
swept stone, surviving his beliefs; relation between Barnaby's nose
and Phidy's, on the evidence; Phidy's nose set in stone, as a subject
for contemplation; the deed accomplished, number of pigeons, on

conservative estimate, scientifically calculated, who could perch on said sculpture; the benefits of art . . . the nose of Newton; relations of feature and voice; the accent of Leibniz (here I triumphed); discovery of the calculus; the independence of a man from his time; the dependence; the role of observation in scientific thought; the tower of Pisa; the genius of precision, of doggedness; the longitude question; the story of the chronometer and the hard usage of John Harrison; the genius of complexity and the moons of Saturn; the role of luck in rationality. Of what was our talk?

The bloody heat; the best beer in Virginia; Tom's lechery; youth and beauty; Kate Benton of Golden, Virginia; the Maid of Athens; the Maid of Perkins; sleeping to the noise of horses; Tom's family; Tom as a Man of God; Tom's lechery again; the relation of shaggi-ness and lechery; Phidy's hair; Hölderlin; Germany and madness; the Romantic school; Phidy's nails; Phidy's fledgling beard; Phidy's elongated height; Phidy's pallor; Phidy's trembling shyness before Kate; the love epistles Phidy composed daily to Kate in his spare hours; his fear of sending them; his fear of Mrs Benton; her relation to Mrs Bevington; Phidy's stout denial of all these allegations; Phidy's anger; the colour of Phidy's nose; Phidy's troop of pining lovers left behind in Neuburg; Phidy's constancy; Mrs Simmons; Phidy as Werther; Mrs Simmons; Phidy as 'Lotte; Phidy's grey hairs in spite of Phidy's youth; the burden of Experience; Mrs Simmons; Mrs Simmons; Mrs Simmons; Phidy's desperate retreat behind the flag of Mrs Simmons; the impossibility of embarrassing Syme; Phidy's fascination with Mrs Simmons; Phidy's love for Mrs Simmons; Phidy's inconstancy to Kate Benton; Phidy's retreat, withdrawal, ultimate humiliation.

All men, like a piece of music, have a scale according to which their variations are played. Once they have understood them-selves, they can never be persuaded from their beliefs. How can one scale argue with another? I knew myself in part, but often stared into the distance to avoid the sharp, dismal edges of my convictions. In Germany we call this belonging to 'the Romantic school'. Sam, as no other man I ever met, knew his mind. To talk with Sam was like looking at a night sky and seeing the stars lifted

399

clear into their shining constellations. I had been accustomed to
thinking of the world, at least my particular patch on the sphere,
as a collection of a few lonely objects. These drew me like candles
with their solitary, flickering flames. I loved to fasten my look
upon a thing till it grew misty. So I was the more natural lover,
but I lost my sense of proportion too easily. To me the number one
always seemed much greater than the number two. Three
and four shrank into inconsequence like unwanted children. Sam
knew better than any man that two was twice one, that four was
twice two. How much I learned from him; how little I was able
to teach.

I began to note the changes in the country as we proceeded north.
The cities grew more familiar, the accent quicker. The crops, like a
season, shifted. The labourers, too, of course. Germans began to
appear in patches like clover in a field. At first, I noted only the
churches, the clean, whitewashed chapels, the pastors' names
Ludwigson and Peterson and Roseneck. Then the shops. Strings of
sausages, flecked with clean white bits of fat in their thick dark meat,
hung in the street-windows. The bakers heaped their counters with
big grey sour breads and steaming black breads, soft and yielding as
a hot pudding when they come out of the oven. Then there were the
music-shops. My curious eyes shone in shy reflections from the
upright pianos, standing above tiny covered stools, with the name
Mendelsohn & Son woven in Gothic script into their green velvet.
The beer changed, grew dark, like man with age, and I could taste
the thick, soft liquor of my own native ground upon my tongue
again.

Our tour had taken us as far as New Haven in a roundabout
fashion, past Philadelphia, the site of Sam's crowning lecture-to-be
at Independence Hall. Now our wandering purposes drew to their
source, and we sailed south with fewer tributary excursions. Each
day's journey brought us nearer. Our little band was in earnest
now, and our nerves grew sharp like the air before a storm. Sam felt
the burden of our destination the most, and every night receded
inwards a little deeper. We would set forth in the mornings with a
sunshiny vigour, but by the time we turned to our beds Sam's

anchor had caught in some tangle of his own thoughts. Tom would beckon me to leave him with a finger on his lips. But even from that dim hole, Sam found a trick to lighten our journey; and while he was at it pricked me to question my own doubts, with all the passion we usually reserve for our deepest faith.

In the first week of August we reached New York, bustling with the traffic that poured in from the brand-new aqueous highway, the Erie Canal. We sailed along the Sound at first dusk, that gentle hour when the light calls no envious shadows from the ground. Out of some kindness to me, perhaps, Tom engaged us to speak at the German Club on Amsterdam Avenue. A coach took us to the door, a grand dark building in the sombre Prussian style. I had come home, after a fashion. Like most homecomings, the visit was a test of my affections. Through Sam's chicanery, I gave my 'maiden' speech that night and took my place for ever, sealed by a crowd of witnesses, among the New Platonists.

Die Zweivierziger, the club was called – or the Two-forties, in English. It served as the refuge for German radicals and intellectuals, who wished to breathe the heavy atmosphere of their native tongue and thought, when the lighter, quicker air of their American home failed to sustain them. Travellers, priests, soldiers, statesmen, bankers, philosophers, artists, lecturers, some resident, some itinerant, all heavy-hearted, heavy-winged, heavy-featured, all German. They brought their wives. The club was named after the recent Prussian legislation that required all volumes under the length of 240 pages to be submitted to the knife of the censor, whereas all works that swelled beyond that mystical margin could be published and distributed freely. The name was typical of German radicalism, as I saw it after a year of American vigour. We believed not in true extremism, but in the intellectual daring of Balance. We poised on the edge of the Permitted, neither so coarse as to venture into the passionate Faith beyond it, nor so commonplace as to mix with the middle-class respectability within. A perch from which we could survey everything and claim nothing. The shock of familiarity and then the tang of wilful estrangement drew me towards Tom and

Sam with the force of a fresh decision, as we entered the grand apartments of the wealthy club and began to assess their contents.

The rooms truly were gorgeous. Floor, ceiling and walls seemed carved out of deep, subtly shining wood. Halls opened through arch-ways and via steps upon halls. Heavy, common paintings of com-mon-looking men hung over the marble mantles of fireplaces. I noted their protruding or receding chins, pinched or protuberant noses, flat eyes, awkward mouths, thinning hair. The air was thick with the smoke of cigars – I could scarcely breathe the fat, brown atmosphere, silvered and shining with glassed reflections, from the heavy, wide mirrors hung opposite the gold-framed portraits. Each angle seemed to reveal another recess of room or image, of hall, or the mirrored many-legged crowd. Tom and Sam, neither of whom spoke more than a dozen words of my native tongue, walked arm in arm together, happily mimicking what they perceived to be the ugly, guttural accents of German speech.

'Verstenken sie mit Kraeuterbrunken verkaufter Kinderwurst?' Sam asked.

Tom shook his head gravely and answered, 'Nebel und Dunstbecken kann man nur staunen.'

Perhaps you will not believe it of their dignity, but we were all young men. Even Sam was little past his thirtieth year. It was easy and rich to be light-hearted in that thick gloom.

This was my element, for once – and Tom and Sam had never seen me in it. Suddenly, I seemed presented with a choice, not of word or deed – though those accompanied it – but of loyalties. I observed everything from a certain height. This came naturally to me, who stood a tall head above them all, noting the amused faces of Tom Jenkyns and Sam Syme among my countrymen (milling and muttering around me). I felt that both my German and my American roots lay plucked and clean in my hand, and I must choose which to plant and there abide. Of course, I baulked at the easy mockery, the thoughtless high spirits of my fellow 'pioneers'. They were blind to these people as I could not be and I resented it. But I saw the faults of my countrymen as well, their heavy-winged, weak-clawed intellects. Sam in Reason alone, in massive force, was worth the lot of them: the halls and rich mirrors, the dusty galleries of painted men, the whole Zweivierziger.

I stood under an archway – talking to a man who had known Franklin in Paris – and observed Sam at a distance, as he strolled with Tom in prim, dainty steps, a German sniff to his nose. Ashes scattered from the exaggerations of his pipe. 'Und weltversmetzung kann vogelhaftweise nurnoch exponieren, verstanden?' My heart warmed to him for the first time as an equal, or, rather, from my slightly higher vantage. And I joined them in their mockery. It was a choice of momentary sensibility, nothing else. But such choices are often the flags of our deeper dispositions, and I came to know mine clearly. I walked towards them.

Sam's lecture was not the only occasion. Three papers were to be given that night (in English for the nonce), after dinner in the great low-roofed dining hall. Sam's was the last. I scarcely ate or drank all evening, though plates and drink vanished before me. A lady sat opposite me, an old schoolgirlish dame with dull, iron-rimmed spectacles, and her long silver hair bound by a flowery cotton knot. She talked incessantly of her 'pilgrimages' to Brunswick and the grave of 'Gottie, as I knew him once, sir, when he was my mother's lover. I sat on his lap and he played the piano (Bach, as I grew to know and dimly understand), while my mother wove a flower-crown from a bunch of cut daisies lying in her broad dress. I turned to her and said, piping in my shrill voice, "Mama, it sounds like that creaking gate at the back of the garden!" Mother began to scold me for a dullard, but Gotthold, dear lovely man, said without the least air of condescension, "An honest ear is Nature's noblest work," and shushed my mama quite silent. I have always treasured that remark. You would know him as G.E. Lessing, and recall no doubt his beautiful Emilia. I trust I have not lost the virtue of my ears?'

How could I help but stare? Yet I nodded, and she continued. 'I compose poems, or rather Rosenkränze, woven out of Nature. Is not the chime of words as natural as a creaking door! I am a gatherer, sir, not an artist. And every five years (I measure my life by that season), I return across the sea and lay one at the foot of his dear small tomb.'

She had married a banker, who was now involved in land speculations in the West. She was enormously rich and talked endlessly.
So when Sam, in a spirit of prank and pity, turned to me and whispered, 'You may parade as myself tonight – if you wish to flee the
nymph,' I accepted greedily, before I could reckon the consequences.
He slipped a sheaf of notes to me under the table, and I excused
myself to prepare 'my lecture'.

Public speaking was nothing new to me – especially before so
Teutonic an audience. I recalled morning lectures at the university
in Neuburg, and the handful of sleepy young men who glanced
longingly at the sun on the river whenever I checked my notes.
There is, of course, a little flutter in the fingers, a catch of breath, a
certain constriction about the throat and temples; but I felt my old
German self again as hundreds of white knuckles rapped the table
among dirty napkins and half-empty wineglasses to welcome me.
'Let me begin with a detail,' I announced, and so began. I knew
Sam's lectures too well to falter, even when his notes were unclear,
and I occasionally rendered a knottier passage into its native
German.

An audience is a kind of cave. A voice reverberates in it. We can
tell by the tone sent back whether the matter is good. An interesting
and necessary experiment to test the truth of any proposition is to
speak it out loud, broadcast to a silent group. Indeed, one need not
wait for the echo. The virtue of one's thoughts, their subtlety or
falsehood, grows clear as the very medium bends or baulks at the
message. If the supple air proves pliable to our speech, we sense the
life if not the truth of our words. Nothing can commend an idea that
dies, like a stillborn child, at the touch of air. Some thoughts bruise
themselves on Space. There I stood, addressing the glint
of wine-cups and men's spectacles, the shine of dark wood, the
awkward bored legs of chairs, the angles of elbows rested on the
tables (for I could scarcely distinguish a face or feature in the mass
of listening men), and uttered the theories to which Sam had given
his life, and I – a year. They soared.

At every sentence, Sam's gallant voice ran through my head, as I
had heard it – ages ago, it seemed – on that cold, sunny morning in

404

the Apple Cart: 'would you like, Phaedon, to hear the tale of creation?' That is the tale I told. Werner's innovations and the drenching in which he gave birth to the world. Hutton's theory of fire that dried up the German. The continual modification to which the Scotsman subjected all earthly things – to which Syme posited an end, a burning away, a cooling off, and a polishing. There was such satisfaction in his every thought. The unanswerable quality of his calculations, his dispute not of Newton's laws but the precision of their application; the glory of his Machinery, his glowing crowns, vacuii, fluvia. The confidence with which he stepped from stars to stones, and the delicate shimmering chains of cause and effect by which he bound them. I could not tell you if I believed a word of it. But the air filled and glowed with his thoughts like dust in sunlight, and the applause that met me as I concluded seemed to drown me in hands. It was a peculiar sensation. I felt like an actor given a part to play, as distant to the role, in his way, as the audience. Like the audience, I cheered.

The discussion that followed was warm and mostly laudatory. The only exception came from a short, powerfully built man in his early thirties, sitting beside a grey-haired woman in iron-rimmed spectacles. Sam attacked his own theories with venom. He banged his hand on the table, raised it in one exasperated motion. 'If I may be permitted to speak. Have you all taken leave of your senses? If the lot of you had risen as one man – to denounce the speculations of this Mr Soame – I would willingly, indeed bravely, have added my leaven of commendation – for the undoubted ingenuity of his conjectures. But I will not sit quiet while praise echoes praise – while "still they cried and still the wonder grew, that one small head could harbour all he knew".' Sam aped the tones of a 'practical' man, driven to outraged petulance by a series of absurdities.

'I'm a reasonable man,' he began again, 'but hang me if I see how you can weave a web of such gossamer connections – and call it a science. They look pretty, sir, I grant you that. They are wonderfully symmetric and the dew sits brightly on them. But not one of your reasons will survive the brush of simple COMMON SENSE. Have you got anything to say?'

Trying to catch the tone of superior patience Sam adopted for such occasions, I replied that I 'awaited humbly the substance of his remarks'.

It was an odd contest.

'I could begin where you please,' he said. 'The crowns, for example. Have you conjured them out of thin air? Is this a boy's tale or a theory?'

'It is a piece of both – a model. In other words, an explanation. These crowns are not evident to the sense, no. We lack the sense to observe them. I ask instead: what does my theory have to recommend it? Unlike previous models, it fits established laws: the laws of gravitation (which I trust you will not dispute), according to which the elliptical path of the earth's orbit is the product of the attraction of two balls of mass, the earth's and the sun's. The path is known. The forces are known. The masses should follow. The necessary mass of the earth cannot be accounted for without a porous, if not actually hollow, interior. That is not speculation. It is calculation. If I may be allowed to continue,' I added, as Sam made an impatient gesture.

'A porous interior could not remain stable long. Dismissing for the moment the revolution of the planet itself, the earth's daily rotation would, in the first instance, upset the consistency of any vacuous interior. In the second, it would naturally itself be upset by it. A porous, shifting internal mass would necessarily result in an inconstant gravitational centre, an inconstant rotation, a jagged, uncertain orbit. This will not do. Grooved internal spheres alone can account for the stability of season and day. These grooves must themselves be of a lighter substance than the crowns, else we have the whole business to do again – the problem of mass. Hence, the speculated existence, since verified in laboratory work, of fluvia.

'This model alone matches undisputed physical laws. Thus far conjecture. But I have not rested there. Does the model fit, or seem to fit, ordinary rules of Nature, of motion? The crowns revive an ancient favourite established by the Greeks: circular or spherical motion, inherited as a birthright by every scientist until the modern age. Copernicus swore by it, made it the foundation of his own

revolution in science. Kepler dismissed it only reluctantly, against a weight of observational data. Galileo was the first to discard it, too lightly as it happens. For far too long, the science of the father has been visited on the sons. My theories restore the crown to circular motion, where it belongs.' Again I silenced Sam, who drank, noisily, instead.

'If I may be allowed to finish. Having shown that my theory fits both established facts and traditional natural laws, I enquire at last: does my model offer any new explanations? If true, a host of effects must follow such a cause. Can these crowns account for any as yet unaccounted phenomena? Earthquakes, volcanoes, whirlpools, even atmospheric disturbances such as hurricanes and tornadoes, can be explained by the eclipses of vacuii. Subtler shifts in continents and seas, consistent both with aery legend and hard fossilized deposits, follow likewise, though now I venture into the frontiers of my science, and I hesitate as yet to stake any claims. The number and nature of the crowns and vacuii have been calculated according to well-known eruptions. As with the movement of moon and star, I account for their number and motions by the pattern of their effects. If such a method suffice for the heavenly fields, why should we doubt its more earthly application?' Sam himself might have spoken those last words.

Sensing perhaps that his audience had wearied of the debate, the President of the Zweivierziger, Mr Golding, interceded gently and Germanically. 'I trust now', he said, 'that Mr Soames has answered to their satisfaction even the most fastidious doubts.'

Sam rose and bowed. 'I submit', he answered, 'to the General Madness – not its truth,' and sat down.

Herr Golding, a smooth-faced, stooping, smiling, surprisingly young man, thanked his speakers and closed the meeting of the Zweivierziger Club. 'Those who wish', he added, 'may join me in the Newspaper Room for a less rigorous, more human company over cognac. Members will direct your step, gentlemen.'

A hum followed. A scrape (of chairs) succeeded the hum, and the sea of dim faces grew clear, carried by sharp legs and well-cut suits out of the great-hall door. I joined Sam in a buzz of high spirits, which he shared. 'Wonderful, Phidy,' he said, crooking his arm about my neck. 'You cannot guess the pleasure you have granted me – to hear my own words again – as if they lived outside my thoughts – outside the loneliness of my thoughts.' How strong the arm that bent my neck to his shoulder! Briefly, though long enough for me to catch the thick warmth of him, burning all the hotter I believe for rare joy. Only Tom had a pinched red look about him, like that of a boy who has been left too long in the cold.

I puzzled a great deal over our encounter later. It struck me as odd even then. There I stood, defining and defending with such assurance ideas in which I believed myself to have so little faith. There he sat, attacking with such disrespectful ardour theories in which he had placed all of his. For the first time, I felt a . . . conspirator in their plans. No matter what belief I attached to Sam's work, I had shown at least that I was proficient in it, a suitable apprentice. I could no longer claim the clarity of detached ignorance. Any knowledge involves you in its object, any truly detailed imaginative knowledge. One cannot, quite, know and disbelieve at once. Perhaps Sam suspected something of the sort. His prank may have been directed at my reticence, to smoke it out of hiding. But I was not exposed alone. We had both shown something of our colours. Doubt, too, like a ripe blackberry, cannot be tasted or touched without it stain you. There is always some blood of it left on the fingers. Sam had hunted out my distrust, then turned and watched himself from my corner. The view did not shake him for a moment, but I felt strangely . . . acknowledged. Failure had occurred to him, like any idea.

The sensibility that could record such nice perceptions may seem too precise, too quick an observer, to have played a living role at such a meeting. Ordinarily, I would suspect it myself. Yet it was not so. I have failed to convey the happiness of the whole. The company of my countrymen; my new assurance in such familiar surroundings; the wine of dinner and the cognac afterwards, in whose fumes the pride of my performance glowed. The simple joy of having talked so much and been looked at – all these fed my bluff, blunt good spirits. If I kept a sharp eye for new distinctions, I looked *from the top of happiness on a clear fine night. I felt that I had regained my sharp edges, my curiosity, scope, loose tongue, without losing my admiration for Sam or his protection. And there is nothing so seductive as giving pleasure.*

Tom collected subscriptions for our journal, as Sam and I drank our digestifs, and I read the latest German newspapers. 'We have five hundred,' Tom declared at last, sitting down, with a heaviness rare in him. 'A toast,' he cried, through a pressed and peevish smile, 'to the half of our goal. We turn south tomorrow towards Philadelphia.'

This was the last night we could afford to be light-hearted. President Golding came slowly towards us, stooping from chair to chair. He offered me a cigar (which Sam pinched, brazenly accepting on my 'behalf'), bowed at us all, thanked me again, and smiled in an odd, sweet manner, like a clown smiling behind smiling paint. He asked me a few questions. I answered them. Then he drew out his pocket-watch, a great ticking silver engine of time, and mulled over it. It appeared to satisfy him, and he took his leave, observing, 'The short man in the purple frock, you see, will show you to your chambers. I hope you will be comfortable. Yes, I do hope you will be comfortable.' The last word echoed on like the rumble of wheels. He bowed again, smiled again, bade us good night and left a faint perfume of smiling behind him.

We took our signal and rose to go.

I awoke the next morning clear-headed as a drained glass, wakeful and empty. I have taken my place, I thought. We had early business, though the fair day was still grey outside. Tom and Sam rose sharp as well, and we met in the hall by some common instinct, about to knock on one another's door. After a quick breakfast, in that peculiar silence of early mornings, distended like an image in a spoon, we sought the road, companionably enough if only in the shared concentration of spirits. Philadelphia approached, Tom's crowning engagement of the summer tour. Independence Hall would be filled, professors, publishers and even government representatives promised attendance. Sam had an hour and a half in which to make his fortune.

'I am confident of three hundred subscriptions at the least,' Tom said on the barge from New York. 'You must charm the other two hundred from them. That would tally our thousand, and we could begin our proper business, the magazine.' A summer shower blew us indoors, where we found a large old gentleman looking for a game of whist. Tom loved the water, for it tied him to idleness, and we played deep into the afternoon. Such hands the old man had, big as roots.

He caught me staring, and answered my thought. 'I was a boxer in my youth. Gentleman George, they called me. What have you got there?'

A broadsheet announcing the Philadelphia engagement peeped from Tom's portmanteau. 'Sam Syme, The Illustrious Geonomist, Independence Hall, August 17,' etc. Jackson took it and held it to the sunset cast out to sea.

'There is nothing like a real crowd,' he said, 'and youth.'

Sam turned a green face to him, for he took a sea swell badly. I have kept the placard of that event as well – and hang it proudly in the sitting room, a record of one brief, clear triumph.

The weeks till his great speech turned into counted days. Because of our wandering lives, mail had not reached us for several months. Tom often journeyed a day in advance to fix our schedule, but no post could chase us down. All the news issued from our little band. Sam wrote to Mrs Simmons once a week. Tom wrote to his 'sweet bun' (as Sam called Kitty, the baker's daughter) nearly every day. I wrote to . . . Ruth once, and never to my father.

We reached Pottstown, a village outside Philadelphia, on 14 August. It was an old, poor settlement, not so much a village as a few wide thoroughfares connecting busier towns. We walked down Main Street, a line of dust, broken only by the post office, an apothecary's shop and the tavern. But it lay among riches, like a beggar outside a castle, indifferent to his abode. Pottstown stood in a valley. High straight woods surrounded it, clean and smooth as something built by man, but nothing by man could look so old and free of history. A lake lay a few miles away, the only clear opening in the land, as surprising as blue eyes in a bearded face.

The afternoons held on long in the town. They stretched even longer around the lake, as the water kept the sun. Summer children rowed and splashed late into the light evening, their calls and oars slapping the soft billows and coming to the land like echoes. What wealth the town could boast sat at the shoreline, a few gentlemen's summer cottages, a stone's throw from the bank. Tom's cousin lived in one of these.

'My cousin James', Tom told us, amid the clack and clatter of our steps on the stony footpath, 'is a gentleman, or, rather, he is rich enough for idleness, if nothing more. He is lay-preacher at the white-boarded church to which the main street rises. He writes, too – histories, of Indian traditions, folk tales, the growth and slow decay of the early settlements, like Pottstown. He is a dear man and a good friend.'

Tom approached the cottage eagerly, thinking no doubt of the two months' accumulation of a lover's news (and glad perhaps of a cousin's company to break the increasing closeness of our little band). We walked along the road by the lake, where thick dry roots tore up the parched brown bank to stretch their hot toes in the water's edge. It was a stumbling, up and down amble. We bent our heads down to watch the broken ground and shield our eyes and open nostrils from the swarms of midges that passed in clouds. The evening was already cooling, though the blue sky still fell bright on the lake. We turned from the shore and rose up the pebbled path to the porch. A thick figure sat on the steps, in the loneliness at the end of a lovely afternoon.

James greeted us mopping a wet brow with a wet handkerchief, and extending a newly dried hand. A fine light sweat still pricked from the skin. It had been a hot day. And the evening was still hot inside, though no lamps were lit, nor curtains drawn, and the windows were flung wide. The air was still light, but grey without the sun to watch it. We were very tired. A heap of letters lay on the plain wood dining table, in expectation of our arrival. James brought a jug of lemonade and set it down beside them. He came back with three glasses held in the fingers of one hand and set them down awkwardly. I looked in the other hand and he held a pipe, newly lit.

411

Then I smelled it come like a dog in the thick air. We sat down.

Tom turned to the letters with a quick hand.

Sam said, 'Not tonight, Tom.'

'Let me see who wrote,' said Tom.

'Not tonight.'

Tom stopped looking. Sam had been quiet all day, taut with the prospect of his speech in Philadelphia. It was altogether an affair of a different mass than the other lectures. He braced himself against the weight.

James poured the lemonade, and the three of us sat companionably enough, used to one another's silences. I reflected on the fourth. He was a kindly, sweating man. His hair was always moist and his hand always damp. He ran to fat, too, like Jeb; but James's spreading waist seemed accretions of hesitant contentment, too polite to form actions or words. He was still a young man, though he would not be long. I watched him rise again, return to the kitchen, and bring a glass for himself. He sweated silently.

We turned early to bed. The cottage had two bedrooms and the cousins shared one of them. I heard James laughing through the wall, louder than I would have guessed, with the loose tongue of a young man. They talked deep into the night. Sam and I still said not a word, accustomed to each other's well-worn presence; or, rather, to speak plainly, rendered perhaps a little shy of each other by the cousins' easy fellowship. I listened to our neighbours happily enough, and followed their chatter into sleep. Before I drifted off, I remembered the letters on the dinner table, as one might pause on a staircase some night before knocking on a door. I had a sense of postponement, but postponement of what I could not imagine at the time. The world felt far from me that night. Tom's laughter, ringing through the wooden wall, seemed as alien as the tune of the rubbing insects in the dry grass outside.

I expected to awake with a lighter heart. Sam sat in the dining room, still in his undershirt, when I shook myself out of bed and came in. James was fussing over breakfast. He seemed more cheerful and prated to me with a sudden confidence, a sweet trust, while busying himself with bread, plates, cups and a pail of fat fresh milk from a nearby farm, hauled in a surging unsteadiness through the warm dawn.

He said, 'I have always been an early riser. It is the saviour of an idle man. Tom, as you see, needs no saviour,' he added, laughing.

Tom still lay a-bed, spent with the night's talk and making a sabbath of Sam's preparations. He had done his part. Perhaps he idled now with a wilful luxury to let us know it.

Sam tossed me a pair of letters, neatly bound by James. They were from my father.

My dear boy,

The bailiffs have come today. Ruth was beside herself and I had to hold her from them, whereupon she turned her fury on me. The neighbours stared openly from the window and watched, drinking their coffee. Hespe has been useful enough, in his way, but he skulks about in such shameful fashion, I can't bear to look at him – as if he does not wish to know us any more, and would not, but for Ruth. She adjures me to be kind to him, and says, of all people, I should have no eye for finding fault. This is unfair, but I have no heart to argue the point any more – the old point, or rather cause, on which I have wasted my life, or whatever is left of it, after the sum I have spent on both of you. But now is not the time.

They have rifled your mother's jewels . . .

He stood accused of embezzlement, of a rather moderate sum. The crime was treason in our court, and by law he stood a bankrupt in our country's eyes. Even our house was forfeit to the crown, though as yet he had been spared imprisonment – that would come. I tore open the next letter, dropping the last at my feet.

Well, it has all come out now, as they say, and I confess a part of me is not sorry at the turn of events. Hespe, it seems, has played the spy, and betrayed me to our Prince – first in the trifling matter of our accounts, and now regarding what he calls the 'den of revolutionary brigands' I maintained in our very sitting room! – in short, the rather silly, extremely drunken coterie of discharged soldiers and idle students who used to crash about the parlour, whether I would or no. The best of it is that we are quit of him at last; and Ruth won't speak 'another word to him, as long as he lives' – or of him, it seems, to me.

I must say I am surprised to see how she's taking the news; and sometimes I wonder whether she grieves more over a ruined father or a lost lover – but this is the way of things, I suppose, and I must bear it, consoling myself with the thought of a dear son who shall soon return to me. She says only, in her cryptic way, that there 'are things a father don't know' – and don't wish to, either, I suppose – and in that at least she is in the right.

Bad and worse, I'm afraid, is all I have to tell. They have 'locked me up' until the trial – the Prince, I must say, is proving himself a proper stubborn fool and a willing ear to the wildest improbabilities. It seems I am a regular Karl von Moor, and a threat to civic Peace, and the honour of German womanhood to boot, I make no doubt. Thank God they have granted me paper and a pen, and as far as they go I am happy – and the two, as you know, go far. They have put me, as a matter of state dignity, in the palace wine cellar, mostly because the wine had all been drunk by French soldiers years before, so it was sitting empty. An ordinary prison, it seems, won't do for men as desperate as your father.

Hespe has been declared Primary Assistant Deputy First Minister by way of reward – no one yet has been able to explain to me what that means, except to say that his special duties involve military security (God have mercy upon us), for which he has been promoted to General, second class.

Mostly I wish for the trial to come. (And go.) Till then there is nothing to be done.

Your loving, etc.

Tom came in, wearing his long night's sleep as a young man wears wet hair, coming out after a swim. He began tearing thick pieces of bread and dipping them in the milk jug without sitting down. He glanced over my shoulder. Still chewing, he gathered his pile of letters in one hand and sat down contented in the high-backed rocking chair by the window. Sam did not look up. He had turned to the small heap of correspondence that had gathered through our travels, like a pile of leaves in autumn. He pushed one to me across the table.

I recognized the quaint, archaic script of Edward and skimmed through it.

Dear Son,

Your mother bade me pen a line to you, as she . . . nothing to alarm you, just a sudden weakness, brought on, as I told her it would be, from her excessive spirits of the night before. She wished to dance, you know, with her infirmity and already that evening complained of the Headache . . . She could scarce stand when she awoke, so we brought her a-bed again, and put her feet in bowls of water, for it is damnation hot . . . and you will have guessed the truth, won't you, that it is nothing but heat, for your mother has always taken the heat most fearfully, and worry, for you, my Son, in your long silence. In this I share her Affliction, but trust you are well and thinking kindly of your

loving Mother &
Father

A dust of powdered ink marked the top of the page, shaped after the side of his hand. I recall noting that his father wrote left-handed. Before I had well finished, the next note came, written on small, thick paper from a sharp, thin quill a little choked with the summer heat.

My grief was swallowed by a nearer and stronger grief — but then, everything that happened to Sam seemed greater than my own affairs. I put my letter aside and read on.

Dearest Son,

Your mother continues poorly, though the doctor is hopeful, and indeed she looks almost well today . . . we all think she Mends, except the poor victim herself, who moans as if strapped to Ixion's wheel, in this heat too . . . Bubbles has seen her, and agrees with me entirely, that it is only a Ploy to starve her Figure, by keeping a-bed and refusing even Tea, drinking only boiled water and biscuits . . . though she do seem to suffer hard from her Digestion, which is hardly to be wondered at, and she could not keep down the last real Food we pressed upon her, though the doctor is convinced it is sheer wilfulness . . . but that she desires it, and is grown Implacable in her requests, I would not trouble you, my Son, knowing her ways and your too tender Fears. So consider this note to bring the expected Relief, and know that she herself will compose the next sweet emissary of her recovered Health. Believe me then,

your loving Scribe
(& Father)

The next note came, with a swift rasp, as regular as a clock. The miracle of ink absorbed us, two young men across a table, deep in the world scratched so lightly on the pages before us that a gust of summer wind could scatter it. And yet it was a world, somewhere, as hard and unchangeable as the ground beneath us; indeed, further and harder, frozen as it was by passed time.

Dear etc. . . .

We are all grown quite vext with her. Even Bubbles can scarcely keep her Temper. We believe it is all wilfulness. I think she has begun drinking on the Sly, we can scarce enter the Room for Stink, though she does seem to be in great Pain, poor thing . . . the Doctor has begun to suspect her Liver, and we have already sent Betsy to her mother, for though she was just a girl, she was a smuggler of Liquors as brazen as any on the Cornish Coast . . . she would not confess, but cried a great deal, and desir'd to be excused, which we did, silly child that she was, though she was the only girl as could manage Annie's temper of an evening and now we know Why . . .

And the next came, while Tom looked on, sensing the drama play-
ing out beneath our fingers – yet too far from us, by the space of an
opened doorway, to look on. A purely material gap that a
single stride could mend – but did not; and it grew harder to bridge
when the moment passed without him. I, for an hour at least (but
such an hour!), had taken Tom's place.

> *She continues Obstinate. Her sister Beth has come to us, quite*
> *distress'd at the Change, though we scarce note it now. But*
> *Annie will not hear a word from her, has grown Petulant and if I*
> *ask you to return, soon, my Son, though only if it be convenient,*
> *it is because you have always had a way with her, not because*
> *there is any Cause for Alarm.*

I glanced at the overleaf. This was the first note with scribblings on
the back, scribblings I say, for the hand that wrote told as eloquently
as the thoughts it served the story of the sick-room. Hesitant
scratchings, blotted here and there by a quick hand, the quill chewed
and the fine tip bitten to a rough end, that splayed and spilled over
the page. And so the gestures of grief are often mere sketches, the
full force and colour of misery takes too long to tell.

> *Perhaps I am much to blame, but let not that keep you from her*
> *though it might from Me . . . and if I am to blame, it is you who*
> *have always stood in my Stead, far better than I believed I could,*
> *my Son, so I retreated . . . then, above all Things, you must come*
> *now to serve the Purpose my negligence – true, my sickly Will –*
> *nonetheless has thrust upon You.*

Then another came, joined its white brothers at my elbow, scat-
tered like the feathers of some ominous bird. How small the world of
death seemed, confined to the black bones of ink. And how I was
tempted, with a blot here, an omission there, the simplest of
corrections, to change with a fine penmanship the tale before me,
and alter by the stroke of a pen what no other hand could do.

> *Your Aunt, frail woman, is quite inconsolable. Rages and*
> *Rants and Rends as if she herself were afflicted or possessed.*

Bubbles and I waste all our Energies on quieting the poor thing, so that Annie may sleep a little, and have short Time to attend to her greater Needs . . . but Beth Rages so and has beat me where my bosom is blue and marked red with her finger's ends as I restrained her and her struggles were spent and we both fell quiet sobbing . . . Bubbles is a Tower . . . though she has lost all her Delicate Ways in Reuben's Slaughter-house, she has learned the strength of Ten, and marches about the house like an Army defending all in their Turn and chiefly poor Annie . . . for Bubbles always had a heart for Outrage at the miseries of others and she Tirades at the Doctor – who to speak plainly is a foolish Illusionist, till he does not Trust himself to Come any more nor Retire when he does . . .

We all feel the Need of you greatly, our much-loved Sam, and do all entreat you to Come, though not if it be inconvenient.

Your loving Father Bubbles Aunt

Sam had stopped reading, I could see, like a sprinter who had spent his wind, his shoulders slack over the splay of his elbows, a patch of sweat beneath his arms from the hot summer morning. Had he not galloped over miles and miles of words? But with a new breath, he pushed the latest letter across the sunshine on the breakfast table, and turned himself to the next note in the pile, while I read this:

Indeed now Bubbles has grown Inconsolable, and we can no more support her Grief than we can the loss of her kind offices. It is cruel to say it, my Son, but I think that her long usage to the Slaughter-house has taught her to bear the sight of Blood; and like the digger in Hamlet, she has grown callous to her Employment. She alone has the stomach to nurse your Mother, whom we have begun to Bleed; and when Bubbles loses the Heart for it, there's nothing to be done. The Doctor is an Imbecile and Fool, and Annie flows and groans at the sight of him; but there is no Alternative when Bubbles is in one of her fits; for your Aunt Beth will not enter the Room for Horror; and I dare not touch your mother myself. Indeed it is all Tears and Bedlam at the moment; and Women, and I am scarcely any better . . .

I wished to avoid an Account of Annie's condition, for fear of distressing you, but Bubbles clamours in my Ear and will not rest – 'tell him tell him tell him' till she scarce knows what she says or distinguishes the words or indeed remembers what it is I am to relate. She grows hoarse and insistent as a Parrot, and she frightens me. But perhaps it is best that you know, for you have always been the Pillar of the house, my Son, I know, for which you blame me greatly, but Uphold us now . . .

Mother lies in bed like an Udder or a pricked Waterskin, for the Doctor bleeds her from every vein, and she is so full of evil Blood poor loving heart. She is nothing but Holes and Openings, and is coming out almost before we can stop Her. We have always a fresh basin at hand; but it is only Bubbles as can bring herself to bear the blood away through long Custom as I believe, for the clear Red quite terrifies me it sits so placid in the bowl. Your mother is not placid, is a Volcano; and bleeds even without the Doctor's lancet. This morning Aunt Beth summoned the Courage to sit by her poor Sister, when Shrieks of Alarm brought us all to the bed, where Beth lay swooned quite to the floor – away from Annie, poor thing, for her sensibility – and we saw the abhorred Cause. Her Nose had begun to spout and gush Blood and it ran over her Mouth, where she lacked the Civility to remove it, but she Muttered and Garbled on in the most outlandish tongue, her Tongue itself dabbled with red like Macbeth's Hands, and I could not bear to look on her. We feared she had been drinking again, which Beth denied, confessing that her sister moaned so horrible, she had given her a Bottle of Laudanum at last. This we found under the bed at Beth's feet all run to the floor. Bubbles was a splendid Creature, and staunched the flow with a cold Cloth and cleaned her face, till the skin was quite rough with rubbing and Annie's lips bent indifferent like a babie's Mouth when you wipe it. Beth ran for the Doctor, while Bubbles staunched the blood with cotton wads poked in Annie's nose, and indeed she looks more like a Bandage than a Human Being. Bubbles is splendid, but is beyond her Strength; she shivered and quaked after her exertions, and became so pale that I had to attend to her myself. She lays in bed beside me now while I pen these lines and beseech you, my only Son, to return to us. And I beseech the Gods of Chance and Tiding, Mercury if he still answers to the Name, that this letter reach you in time, for we are all quite Desolate without you, and expect every footstep on the Threshold to be your Own.

Your loving etc.

I became aware of a strange lapse. The events of the sick-room seemed to be acted out before my eyes as I read. But it was not so, I heard only an echo of the tale. I looked up and saw Sam read two or three letters before me. The room was the same clean-boarded wooden summer cottage of an hour before, only the air was loud with the growing morning and the sun fell thicker through the open window. Tom still sat in the rocking chair by the door, though he had ceased to rock. I saw him looking at us, quite still and shrunken in his corner, as if he knew some game was up. James clattered in the kitchen, then came and stood in the doorway. He exchanged a glance with his cousin. Neither moved. Indeed, I heard only an echo's echo, for the first cry rose far from these belated pages. I looked at the heads of the letters, and saw 'June 29, June 30, July 7, the 12th, Tuesday 17' in quick succession. The next note came rasping across the table.

I live in a Mad-house and you will not think me over-nice when I say that I cannot support such Clamour any longer. Bubbles insists on dose after dose of Laudanum to comfort Annie's pain; and the Doctor agrees that there is little else to be done. But though the Laudanum quiets her bloody Rage, the delirium that replaces it is nearly more terrible. Where before she bled, now she Sweats quite calmly, and speaks as matter-of-fact as if she merely directed Nancy to clean the Larder; but the Contents

*of her Dreams are horrible and Cantankerous. And all the while
she grows Thinner and Thinner; though her face is red and her
pores Sweat at every instant, she has quite wasted away to
Girlhood and Loveliness, only Ill, grown very Ill, as I knew her
once, though I cannot reach her now, on her great Mountain of
Hallucinations, and I hear only their Echoes, and cannot bear
their Nonsense. Come come if only to share the burden of her
Mutterings.*

Your desperate, etc.
Father

I looked up. Two more letters lay on the table before me, but the
air seemed heavy and about to break, as it did on that much happier occasion when the rains came down on the tiny church in
Perkins. Sam sobbed, soft as the first drops of rain to prick and
bend the leaves before a shower strikes. Tom simply stared from
his unapproachable distance by the door. James went in the
kitchen and clattered, too cheerfully for my ears. Sam began to
clamour, and his sobs broke now as loud as guffaws in their
upheaval. He was a powerful man, and his grief was as strong as
anger. Tears climbed his high cheekbones and fell towards the
salty corners of his mouth. His face grew puffed and fat. Every
four or five seconds (I was calm enough to note the intervals), his
violent sobbing sucked mightily for air: O, O, O, O. The cry hurt
my chest in sympathy, not with the grief that made it, but the lungs
that shouted it. Then I was up, while Tom sat dumb, and my chair
fell back as I came across the table to hold Sam's shaking shoulders
in my arms.

His head fell towards his chest, and his chin pressed the knuckles
of my hand, and hurt me a touch. His grief cleared like a choked
spring and flowed freely now, without the impediments of social
usage or dry, hardened happiness to keep it back. I remember best
the smell, the odour of grief as I thought, from the chafed blood of
Sam's body, from the wet patches beneath his arms, and the hairy
haft of his neck. Strong as the smell of a horse, as if it came from

421

the hair of our animal parts. The stench of a body's misery.

I stood awkwardly, half-crouched in the legs, for Sam still sat in
his chair, and I had to bend to grapple his neck. My knees ached
above the bone, but still I held him fast, though my eyes had leisure
in his blind, continuing grief to read the note that lay before him on
the table. We seemed alone in the room.

It was a long letter and Sam had come to the second sheet.

. . . all evening . . . and the flowers we laid on her stone that
afternoon were all ripp'd apart by the force of the water, as I saw
for I visited the next day. They lay in strewn heaps; branches had
fallen to the ground among the gravestones and all was untidiness and Confusion, but only of the ordinary kind of a morning
after a storm, to be soon mended, or rak'd away. You must
remember the storm; a real howler. Your Mother has already
found her Mending. The house is much better now that she is
gone and with her the Devils that beset her at the End, poor body.
Beth has returned to her husband, and for once I miss her Clatter
about the house. For God knows I have little Heart in me to cavil
at poverty now or even coarse Manners. Bubbles stays on with
me, for a time at least, at her Husband's forbearance, to such uses
have I fallen Horatio! Come to me now, then, though not if it be
inconvenient. She awaits our convenience now. The first absence
is always of our Duties and I have found that quiet Space . . .

Tom rose, hesitated a moment, then advanced, and (as I seemed
occupied) took the letter from the table. He returned to his chair and
read silently. James had not stirred in the doorway behind me. I saw
him reflected in the opened window by Tom's chair. The cousins
stood together, image and man, equally quiet. All the outside world
called to me under that blue air. Sam had hushed. Though he still
shook lightly, his noise was spent. I felt the relax of his body after
his violent grief. He had been taut for several days with the
approaching lecture, and all his nervous powers collapsed at the
news of his mother's death. She afforded him some relief, at least in
dying. I pressed him hard once and stood up straight,

wiping the thick ichor of misery from his eyes with my palm. I sat beside him and took his hand from between his legs and laid it on the table under my own. He had my every love, then, and all quick perceptions fled from me in the simple contemplation of his loss and my love. Tom at least for a time remained where he was.

Time must be filled though there is nothing but dross to fill it. An hour passed with a hole in it. All our thoughts turned to Sam's great grief and disappeared there. Even the cottage seemed drained of life, as if a sea had receded and surprised us by the objects it left behind: a few chairs, a table, a bright window. I had my own private sorrow to contend with, for I did not tell the others of my father. That thought lay like a looking-glass in the summer cabin. When I chanced upon it, I saw myself in that room and wondered how I had come there.

Sam was the first to raise the matter. 'Tom,' he said, nevertheless twisting his head to look at me, 'I wish to turn home.'

'We shall,' he answered. 'After Philadelphia, there is nothing to keep us.'

'There is nothing to keep me now.'

I stood at his back with a hand on his shoulder, and looked at Tom. I felt the release in his bones. Sam had not the fibre for a contest. Tom picked up the chair I had knocked over, an age ago, and stared at the two of us. This was our second council of war, but now I was at the heart of it, not outside the door.

He said, 'Too much has been ventured to turn from our course now. We hope for too much from this one engagement to sacrifice it for a durable grief . . .'

Sam's force was spent and he sat mum, a mass of silence. Then I spoke, feeling the sad arch of his neck beneath my hands. 'Now is not the time. Another chance will come, Tom. He must give a space to his grief, or it will crowd him later. Who could talk of crowns and vacuii, when all our thoughts turn to another hollow, six feet deep? Bubbles needs a brother and Edward a son.'

'They can wait three days.'

'I have my own reasons for returning,' I said.

'Then go.'

Sam still sat quiet between us, so I spoke for him. 'Mourning is also an occasion and a chance to be missed, Tom. Besides, he does not have the heart for it.'

'Is this what you feared, Tom, in the end?' Sam broke in at last. But I could not guess his meaning, though Tom's answer was clear.

'If you do not attend the great gathering in Independence Hall in three days' time, which lies directly in our route, and for which we have laboured all summer, I have done with you, Sam. You still bear all my love, but my services are over.'

'There is no service left,' Sam said.

'Another chance will come,' I cut between them.

'Without me,' Tom said and left through the kitchen into the garden. We heard the door shut. A fly buzzed and banged in the room, and I turned again to all the loud blue summer air tugging at my heart a stone's throw through the window. It was a heavy question, but suddenly my heavy heart was gone. Sam looked up at me and said, 'It is only Tom's love, you know that. It does not matter now.'

'I will go out to him if you wish.'

'Do. I need an hour to myself.'

I found Tom sitting with James in the glorious afternoon sun, in the wind-shadow of long white sheets hung from the washing-line. James turned shyly away and lay on his side, picking at the grass. He had the trick of inconsequence, and Tom and I did not heed him as we fought over Sam's prospects.

'I am not deaf to his grief,' Tom said, gently at first. 'I wish him the best. But it would have been a rare occasion, Phidy, like the passing of a comet, that holds our attention though nothing follows from it. A last chance, and he could be miserable for eternity and be damned to him. She was not so kind a mother to call him down from such an eminence. Do you not see it? The packed hall, the mayor and his wife, a gallery of scientists, the indescribable heat of half a thousand bodies sitting side by side, and the timbre of a clear voice speaking loudly, to its full dimensions for once, filling the walls around it without fear. I would like to see Sam with such space around him.'

I confess I was moved by Tom's picture. But I was too happy under my rising star. For six months I had waited on them, bending beside them even in my own thoughts. I was not grown to live in such cramped quarters. At last I felt I could walk straight again. And I knew then (in the thoughtless way one knows vast things, like one's own death) that there was no substance to Sam's dream, and that Tom was indeed a shadow's shadow.

'Sam could bring the world to his feet, if he chose,' Tom said.

'Perhaps he does not wish it.'

'Of course he does,' Tom snapped, as though I were a child.

'I will not help you, Tom, I will not tear him from his mother's grave to please your own ambition,' I answered, angry myself. 'Not when my own father needs me.' (Of all my reasons, this had the least virtue in it.) As I stood up to go, James turned over in the grass. I ducked beneath the laundry-line into the house.

If I was cold to Tom, I had the most insidious of serpents to tempt me: the harmony of my own nature. Who can deny the call of their own good health, so innocent a tempter? My thoughts were no longer corrupted by humility. I saw and spoke clearly for the first time. How easy to think such good brings all good with it, when it is only the taste that grows clear, not the food that becomes whole-some.

Sam had not moved from the table, though the sun now fell at his back, casting his hands in shadow. 'I'm afraid I fell asleep, Phidy,' he said. 'Is there anything to eat? For I'm starvation hungry.'

'Of course, Sam.'

'Call Tom.' I stood at the door and shouted, as anyone might on a summer afternoon, into the garden, through the thick, wet sheets. I heard Tom's face against the cotton and then he stepped quietly inside.

'I will come,' Sam said, 'for you, Tom.' He had only postponed the argument, and he was angry. A thin, sharp line had come between them, which cut them the nearer they moved in their ways. I stood between them now.

Towards Philadelphia we journeyed, heavy of heart.

HE WAS ALWAYS BEST AT BEGINNINGS, my father, made a great fist of them. Pitt Snr enrolled in night school in high spirits (his briefcase stuffed to the gills with paper pads, pencils in martial array unsharpened, sharpener, note cards and course catalogues, stapler, hole-punch, one sandwich bag full of paper clips, one sandwich bag smeared with peanut-butter sandwiches, a copy of *Goldfinger* wedged in the buckle for casual access) at the Mesa County Community College to study, of all things, *History*. He had never finished high school, enrolled instead upon another venture, Korea; and settled into construction work when he got back. Then he signed on for MCC; and there he met my mother, Jinny Meeks, making a fresh start herself after an 'unpleasantness at college' in her sophomore year at UC-Davis, involving a boy and a degree of coercion Pitt chooses not to think on. My father made a beginning of her and they both made an end of their education.

My mother was better at endings. They relieved her greatly, partly because, as she declared herself a dozen times a week, in exasperation that never quite lied its way into surprise: 'I just don't have any energy today, dear. I feel – awful – slow.' There was always a check to her free stride. Whenever she got going, something made her . . . flinch; and such weariness these checks induce! Until her right foot never deserted the comfort of her left, and she stood still. (Her characteristic posture: back quite straight, arms limp at her sides, her shoes tucked in together, her eyes blinking. This, she said, was how Mrs Arthurworry, her ballet teacher, had taught her to stand, age seven; and she couldn't unlearn it – the only thing she hadn't unlearned! – since quitting, at seventeen.) Time, of which she used so little, had been kind to her in return; and into her forties she looked like a girl, preserved.

Dance, it seems, had been her only love. And she 'attended' (her

426

word) any production of the San Diego Ballet, whenever 'she got the chance'. 'Going' to the ballet seemed cheap to her. Ballet was a mark of class, she didn't like to make a fuss of it, but the fact was she came from slightly different 'people' to her husband – had 'different pleasures, expectations', in consequence. (Few pleasures, it should be said; fewer expectations.) Yet she taught her son a love of 'culture' – he was greedy for it, heaped his plate regardless of proportion or appetite. This pleased her quietly; and Pitt did not surprise himself when he fell in love with Susie Wielengrad, daughter of the New York Jewish upper classes.

Making an end of something relieved my mother – partly, as I mentioned, for weariness' sake, and partly for honesty's. 'I don't know,' she often said, pursing her thin lips, on returning from an evening out with 'Dad' – dancing, or bowling, or playing Scrabble with 'some *people*, your father knows them' – 'it just wasn't *me*.' *Me*, it should be said, proved a rather exclusive quality, rare in the extreme – few thoughts, or pleasures, or places, seemed to possess it. Every Friday she had supper with her mother across town, and Pitt and son fended for themselves (pizza and the television). She came back brimming with the 'same old wrangles. I try to tell her – I'm not seventeen any more – I can make my own way' – obscurely satisfied, for once, with being clearly in the right; and content to leave the matter at that. Wrangles over motherhood, wifehood, career – she worked as a secretary at UC-SD, in the English Department, for Dr Morgenthal, to whom an old professor at Davis had recommended her, 'until she found her feet'. She had found them, and never left them.

Rooms *grew* in her presence. Her thin figure seemed like an outline of negative space – how vast ceiling and wall stretched around my mother, echoed like halls. She offered a wonderful evocation of exhaustion – so familiar to us that one fatal source of it was hidden in the general malaise, until too late. If she appeared dry of life as a parched ground, then 'Dad' on the other hand danced like rain, danced and danced, and never quite managed to – soften her. They developed a curious language to interrupt the silence between them; and I grew up speaking it like a native tongue. Talk ran backwards among us, away from conclusions. Every statement had its echo in a question. 'Wet day,' Jinny might say, parting a curtain just around her nose to watch rain disappear into the winter-brown lawns. 'I wonder what the weather is?' Dad would answer, rubbing his hands in silly high spirits.

My father, I believe, despite lacking 'class', had the quicker brain and might have got on in life, but for a severe dyslexia (lately diagnosed) that made his love of Scrabble all the more amusing. I can think of no fitter emblem for Pitt Snr than the sight of him poring over an impossibility of letters, broad shoulders slumped, elbows rolled up, his fist in his nose, and that snuffing heavily – while endless combinations of non-words suggested themselves to his scrambled sight, and he leapt at each (half-rising from his seat and licking his finger), then paused, hesitant, abashed, dimly aware of what he called 'his lack of judgement' (spelling), and sat back sighing, before he turned with undiminished pleasure to even greater possibilities that consoled him for his earlier indecision. Crying at last, 'The kid never thinks – the old man has it in him,' whenever he put down a word.

The old man had a great deal in him, Pitt has no doubt, with more proposals at his beck than he had thoughts to put them in, imagination to give them shape, or time to act them in. He wished, he said, in his youth to be a writer, in the manner of such folks as Herman Wouk, a great inspiration; only he lacked imagination. 'I tell you something,' he told me once. 'Whatever I wrote, it all sounded like lies. All I need is – material.' 'Material' was a great word with my father. It suggested to him something that might satisfy his hands – and he had clever hands. It suggested something of which there was a superfluity, spilling over and getting dirty in the overflow. (He liked dirt.) He often came home from work brimming with tales of 'great material' – and these ranged from the banter of his workmates to the buildings he worked upon (never repairing them, only setting the stage for such repairs). He spent his life preserving materials and considering uses.

There were the improvements, of course – those revolutions in the art of scaffolding that would yield lighter, stronger, simpler frames, if only he could solve the trouble of . . . Well, there was always some trouble: such as expense, distribution, spontaneous collapse, etc. Then came the history of scaffolding and scaffolders, for which he spent several months of Sunday nights at the San Diego Public Library, taking notes. He loved notes – beautiful *materials* of his own production. He relished the *heft* of a stack of papers, scribbled over in his own round, flowing hand, as large as a child's. My earliest memories involve fisting crayon sketches on the back of discarded pages, notes towards some never-to-be-finished history or proposal. They lay, bound in rubber band, all over the house.

Young Pitt was a keen cartoonist, and might turn over his creation to discover:

> Scaffolding up to quite recent years has been considered by builders and others concerned, with the exception of the actual workmen, to be a matter of small importance and consequently unworthy of study. Recent legislation (the Workman's Compensation Act, 1967 and the Factory and Workshop Act, 1971), however, has brought it into greater prominence, with the result that more attention has lately been given to it.
>
> The author, in the course of considerable experience in the building trade, has had opportunities of examining a large number of scaffolds throughout the country, affording him exceptional facilities for thoroughly studying the subject, and he has been led to prepare this history, in the belief . . .

The prose suggested to me a curiously adult world – a world, alas, I have come to learn too well – in which distinctions of some perplexity and no conceivable interest are debated in terms as familiar as the weather. For example (discovered lately on the flip-side of a giant tree, from Pitt's purple period, between six and seven):

> Scaffolding is the art of arranging and combining structures in order to enable workmen to proceed with their work, and from which, if required, to lift and carry the

429

material necessary for their purpose. Many definitions of a scaffold have been given by authorities on building construction; some of the best known are as follows:

Mitchel (C.F.): 'Temporary erections constructed to support a number of platforms at different heights, raised for the convenience of workmen to enable them to get at their work and to raise the necessary material for the same.'

Tredghold (Hurst): 'A scaffold as used in building is a temporary structure supporting a platform by means of which the workmen and their materials are brought within reach of their work.'

Rivington: 'Scaffolds are temporary erections of . . .'

My father was a meticulous man. He threw nothing away, including his own thoughts.

(Now the boys use the backs of my proofs for pictures. Turn over any bright, blotted drawing stuck against our fridge, and you will find some fragment of Pitt's research upon them, some fragment of this, perhaps – the bones of my words beneath the skin of their felt-tip colour. For Pitt, like his father, accumulates.)

'Falsework', Dad called his notes. 'Everything you don't end up wanting, afterwards, is only falsework,' he said, and quoted C.J. Wilshere's seminal guide to *Construction Practices*:

Falsework is the temporary structure which enables the permanent structure to be constructed, and which must be retained until the permanent structure is self-supporting.

(I conned this by heart as a child.) If anyone dismissed something as 'false' in his presence, he lifted his stubby forefinger in stubborn pedantry. 'False*work*,' he insisted. 'I guess I should know,' he added. 'I spent my life on it.' (How rare it is, I sigh, that permanent structures grow self-supporting, free of their falsework – as Syme knew all too well.)

According to C.J. Wilshere, 'There are a number of forces which the falsework must resist; it is necessary to consider combinations of these, to make sure all conditions are considered.

But to consider all the worst conditions at the same time may be unrealistic.' In the event, the combination of two forces proved sufficient to overload my father's structures of support. The first was this: that Pitt's blue-eyed boy was leaving for college (only as far as the University of California at San Diego, as it happens – *happened*). The second, it should be said, was less expected.

My father made a great beginning of my mother's cancer. For one thing, he took the day off. He drove her to the clinic on Medical Arts Road, and waited, under the stippled ceilings of the lobby, by the bubbling water dispenser, among the etiolated plants and the bound magazines, for four hours, while my mother waited, in a paper nightie, at the edge of a table-bed a corridor away. My father read slowly, happily and indiscriminately – and worked his way through several back issues of *Home Furnishings*, before he noticed the day had almost gone, and the clouds of dusk had settled over a blue Californian November afternoon. If patience is a virtue, then another gift is its equal – the capacity for such casual, insignificant curiosity as passes the time. My father had both, and could always turn from the trouble at hand to the magazine at hand.

The doctors discovered a dot upon her breast and rang up the next morning with the news. (Nobody told me.) Jinny, having lately finished breakfast, took off her clothes again and went to bed – I remember her, as light as kindling, under the bony sheets. 'She could scarce stand when she awoke, so we brought her a-bed again, and put her feet in bowls of water, for it is damnation hot,' Edward wrote to his travelling son. It was quite cold that day in fact; rags of clouds hung over the sky and dripped from time to time. We clicked on the heat, and dusty breaths coughed from the floor vents. *My* father took off his boots, his jeans, his turtle-neck, and joined Jinny in his Y-fronts and undershirt and socks, and together they watched TV deep into the afternoon. I ran to catch my schoolbus, suspicious, not for the first time, of the world of adults and their imaginary jobs. Your mother is feeling unwell, he said; I thought what he really meant was something to do with sex.

By the time she went in (and under), for a preliminary exploration, I knew the story. My father woke me at five that morning, breakfast set upon the table, the orange in my glass gleaming like a coloured-in photograph. Jinny was forbidden food, and Pitts, plump father and son, ate nothing; even the juice proved too bright and acid for my bitter stomach. I remember coming back at eight – between consultations – to see the light of morning spread over the tablecloth, and a fly sprawled splay-legged in the juice, drunk or drowned or dead at the orange rim against the glass. I picked it out then reconsidered and tipped the juice into the drain and listened to it run away. For once, I thought, according to the obscure logic of grief, I was permitted waste, and a fresh glass.

We drove back at ten to see how she was getting on. That's when the trouble began, I believe. Jinny lay in the high bed too light, almost, to dent the pillow. So thin and dry my mother was, the nurse could find no flowing vein to prick and plug with the sugar drip hanging glossy and glutinous on the rack. She banged once, twice; pinched and slapped, and banged again. Jinny's arm seemed desiccated, nothing but bone and rolls of skin, more likely to crumble like powder between fingers than flow with blood. But then the nurse struck red, and the plug took and the sugar eased into her arm. Father and son looked down, and saw vermilion spilled upon the tiles, her heart's blood, bright as a fire-engine, shining sleekly.

My father lifted the knuckle of his thumb to his mouth and sucked it. Then he sat down. He was a gentle man, could not bear the sight of blood; he possessed too light a temper to support so great a weight.

We sat by her, then went away at noon, and came back at four and sat by her again. The next day I returned to school. Within a week, my father had taken a job in Marin County – we needed cash, he said, but he was gone two weeks and two weeks again, and I delivered and retrieved my mother to and from hospital. Sunday evenings, my father fled to the San Diego Public Library – he said a publisher was interested in the history of scaffolding; it needed only – a few touches. 'A final – kick,' he said. Mostly, I believe, he read the newspapers and fell asleep, exhausted by the prospect of the grief to come.

In January, Pitt received news of his acceptance at the University of Harvard, under a full scholarship; in February, he declined. (This was his first – flinching.) By this point Jinny was in chemo. Her thin, mousy hair became thinner, hung upon her scalp in clumps like a swimmer's bob, exposing the awful shadowless white of the skull. (How intimate a colour *white* is, untouched by the brown of sun! How strange that the common materials of Nature, skull and skin, appear like secrets exposed, secrets of *which* mystery I need not say.)

The other trouble, of course, was her digestion. 'She do seem to suffer hard from her Digestion,' Edward wrote a hundred and sixty years before, 'which is hardly to be wondered at, and she could not keep down the last real Food we pressed upon her, though the Doctor is convinced it is sheer wilfulness.' Now, it was my father who believed in his wife's wilfulness. 'She never ate,' he said. 'Say what you like – but she *never* ate. How do you think she got so thin? Swallow whatever you can, my dear, as the doctor said.' My father had enormous faith in doctors; neglected and trusted them at once, as men treat gods. That summer – one of the hottest in years, burned till the blue sky grew almost black in the sun – I mowed lawns, two a day at fifteen dollars an hour, with Brad Finkelman, who owned the lawnmower and took 60 per cent. I was saving for a second-hand car, so I could live at home and drive to campus, twenty minutes away, at UC-SD.

In the fall of my freshman year, she had her second operation. She died over spring break in my junior year. (Pitt sums up, cuts short.) A studious reader may calculate the space between diagnosis and – my mother always hated words that muddled the clarity of – death. The studious reader may form some conception of years passed, if he measures out a teaspoonful of salt for each day, until a small white hill accumulates on the kitchen table. This should take some time. Death accrued in various amounts; there were shallow days, and heaped days. None were hopeful. By the end, the substance meted out appeared not only bitter, but basic and, in some incontrovertible fashion, necessary – not to mention, immensely desiccating. The sound of the spoon in the grains was intimate, hushed. The sift as they tipped over soft. How quickly time blent and lost itself in the past, obscuring enormous pain – lick your finger, touch the mound and dab your tongue, for a taste of it, slight and endless.

'The first absence', as Edward reminded me, 'is always of our duties.' She died just in time for me to get in on a house for senior year with some fellows majoring in G & G, as we called it – Geology and Geophysics. I had learned from my father's absences – how to repeat them; and he saw little of me before I flew to Oxford. But lately he has enjoyed something of a modern revival in my estimation – I see less dishonour in turning away. Love matters less than the maps we change to put it in the centre. Pitt understands more than he once did about the rights of solitude and the demands of solitary pursuits.

I never wept for Jinny – until lately at a meeting of the Blue-stocking Society convened upon the question of 'Flowers' (over Pitt's protests) at the home of Dr Edith Karpenhammer, a low-roofed dwelling set in a rank garden choked by last year's leaves, the porch sagging, the screen door clawed by cats. The sitting room stank of old potted plants and new varnish. Pitt held his shirt-tails to his nose, breathing, as Peggy Liebowitz (Associate Professor of Comp. Lit., visiting from Sarah Lawrence) chirped prettily these terrible lines:

> And sure as blackthorn bursts with snow
> Cancer in some of us will grow.

And Pitt began to wheeze into the plaid hem of his L.L. Bean. That night he locked the bathroom door, and sat on the pot in his jeans, and blubbed pink and ugly, staring at his streaked face in the mirror. Then he washed his mug, and dried it; flushed; unlocked the door and stepped into the bedroom, bald head shining. Susie never guessed.

*

434

Pitt has never been ashamed of the fact that he lives his life from books. They are the only companions of the self-educated man who do not mock the accent he has acquired or the words he mispronounces. Books are the best of us, infinitely preferable to their flesh-and-blood creators. They allow, among other things, for revision. We live, as it were, in the scribe's ink – every blot tells. We *write* on the snowy pixelated fields of a computer screen, where the least step – may be retraced – deleted. The touch of a finger accomplishes what oceans cannot – wipes slates clean. Each setting forth begins from an eternal, instantly renewable *scratch*. Small wonder Pitt prefers books to those breathing masses of indelible accretion, who compose them. Something sweetens us, as we escape time and dry up – into print.

Pitt, I must confess, stood in need of renewal. Like his father, he had made a great beginning; but there was no end in sight. Even Müller believed, as Aaron discovered, that 'the great error of my life was not the foolish betrayal (paradoxically vengeful and affectionate) for which you dismissed me at last, but the fact that I never told you, simply this: you are wrong, you are wrong, it is all absurd, you are wrong.' Susie for one had no intention of falling into such an error, nor suffering such regrets. She reminded me at every turn of this plain truth (as she called it), until even *my* thoughts stopped short at Syme's absurdity, and refused to budge. A hollow earth, for God's sake! A dead man better left buried.

One end, however, stood in full view: the meeting of the tenure committee, set for 15 March, a date that would decide my academic future, if nothing else.

Susie had already threatened to 'up tents', as she said – she had a muddling way with metaphor – and return to New York, should I fail. I answered only that one *folded* tents, *cut* anchor; possibly upped *sticks* . . . And she looked at me, quite unhappily, and said I took nothing seriously, out of temperament, nothing that mattered, and she had almost given up. I should *listen* to her, and hear how unhappy she was.

I said I *did* listen. I knew nothing to say – to unhappiness. I wish I did.

'Well,' she sighed, 'I suppose it's much easier, and more inter-esting, to prove that the earth is hollow.'

'Be fair,' I said.

'No.'

I thought, but did not say: It is no *easier* at least, believe me, to prove that the earth is hollow.

It was books, in the end, that gave me 'a kick', in my father's phrase. Specificially, another meeting of the Blue-stocking Society, convened upon the question of 'Failure'. We met at the house of Bill Robinson – a law professor, who lived at the edge of the hill-coun-try, in a deep-echoing bungalow built of cement and glass. We sat and bit olives and commented on the new art in the long living room – walled on one side by windows overlooking a gorge, which fell away from the house in a tangle of vines and live-oak. Ben called him always 'Bill Robinson' in a single flowing phrase, never Mister, or Bill – a faintly ironic, more broadly affectionate term, for the ginger-moustached man who used to come round bearing books of verse for the boy, marking a page with his thick thumb for a recitation on greeting.

Spring had come early to Texas; and the crickets creaked through the February evening, spread broad and deep over the hill-country. But there was just enough nip in the air to justify a fire. And Bill Robinson laid one over his stainless-steel hearth, indulging himself in a brief lecture, on the atavistic tendencies of modern man, while he lit the balled newspaper under the log. Then he straightened up, pressed his palms against the butt of his back – he used to be a ball-player of sorts, and suffered for it now – and called the session to order. He picked a slim volume from the pocket of his tweed, held it away from his eyes, squint-ed far-sighted while rolling an olive pit on his tongue.

'A Grammarian's Funeral,' he announced. Bill was no faint-heart in the matter of stress. He gave the big words their weight; and declared in a light, resonant voice, rising to the corners of his sitting room:

That low man seeks a little thing to do,

> Sees it and does it.
> This *high* man, with a *great* thing to pursue,
> Dies ere he knows it.
>
> That low man goes on adding *one* to *one*.
> His hundred's soon hit.
> This high man, aiming at a million,
> Misses an unit.
>
> *That*, has the world *here* – Should he need the *next*,
> Let the *world* mind him!
> *This*, throws himself on *God*, and unperplexed,
> Seeking, shall find him.

A shiver tightened my temple, my forehead, ran along the crooks of my elbows, the heft of my back, my balls, fattened the goose-bumps on my thighs. Pitt knows it well. *That* is Syme, I thought.

I should say now that Bill Robinson keeps an excellent bottle of champagne in the fridge, knowing Pitt's fancy for the tipple; and I had got drunk exceedingly by the time Dr Edith Karpenhammer, blessed and beautiful woman, rose to speak, in her slow-burning drawl. (It would light the old fire under Pitt, again.) She looked like nothing so much as a sheaf of wheat, running sparse. Her 'yaller' hair, as she would say, poked out of her head at all angles; a smudge of fat crimson replaced her puckered lips. Specs as big as moon-eyes perched heavy on her nose, leaving a pink pinch against the bridge. Her husband had run off with a student when she was fifty-five. That was twenty-odd years ago, and she hadn't changed since – a tough, skinny Texan of the old school, with several bones to pick; and she would pick them clean. She was too dry for aging; lacked the moisture Time needed to ferment.

'Come, let me read the oft-read tale again!' she said, in a voice smoked in decades of Gauloise, spitting out the verse as she might a newspaper article:

> The story of the Oxford scholar poor,
> Of pregnant parts and quick inventive brain,

Who, tired of knocking on preferment's door,
One summer morn forsook
His friends, and went to learn the gipsy-lore,
And roamed the world with that wild brotherhood,
And came, as most men deemed, to little good,
But came to Oxford and his friends no more.

But once, years after, in the country lanes,
Two scholars, whom at college erst he knew,
Met him, and of his way of life enquired;
Whereat he answered; that the gipsy-crew,
His mates, had arts to rule as they desired
The workings of men's brains,
And they can bind them to what thoughts they will.
'And I,' he said, 'the secret of their art,
When fully learned, will to the world impart;
But it needs heaven-sent moments for this skill.'
This said, he left them, and returned no more.

She reached over and lifted from the glass table a glass of water, squeaking in the ring of its condensation. She drank loudly, set it down with a bang, and began to address the marvellous gipsy scholar, a Symist after my own heart.

– No, no, thou hast not felt the lapse of hours!
For early didst thou leave the world, with powers
Fresh, undiverted to the world without,
Firm to their mark, not spent on other things;
Free from the sick fatigue, the languid doubt,
Which much to have tried, in much been baffled, brings.
O life unlike to ours!
Who fluctuate idly without term or scope,
Of whom each strives nor knows for what he strives,
And each half lives a hundred different lives;
Who wait like thee, but not, like thee, in hope.

Thou waitest for the spark from heaven! and we,

Light half-believers of our casual creeds,
Who never deeply felt, nor clearly willed,
Whose insight never has borne fruit in deeds,
Whose vague resolves never have been fulfilled;
For whom each year we see
Breeds new beginnings, disappointments new;
Who hesitate and falter life away,
And lose to-morrow the ground won to-day –
Ah! do not we, wanderer, await it too?

The spark from heaven. And just as I began to mourn its absence in my life, steel struck flint and the tinder caught. A flame no greater than a match's burned in my head, illuminating the clutter. I had compiled a record of Syme's life: taped together the scraps he left behind him, collected the memories of his associates, tracked his influence through the disparate generations, traced him even as far as Alfred Wegener, lost in arctic snows. But I had never lifted a single foot in his steps, never followed him an inch along the course he set himself. The time had come for Pitt to experiment: with burning globes – fluvia – double-compression pistons. And I, Pitt thought, the secret of Syme's art, when fully learned, will to the world impart; but it needs heaven-sent moments for this skill.

Dr Edith Karpenhammer read on, interminably dry, while the rest of us picked at the olives and stared at the fire, carefully arranged in the hearth, and the art, carefully arranged upon the walls. Pitt could have kissed her quiet on her powdery mouth.

I talked to a guy I knew in the History Department, Joe Schapiro, a natural Texan, with a pate as bald as Pitt's, and the hands of a football player. He sidelined in what he called 'construction art', and exhibited from time to time in a Tex-Mex café out in Terrytown. Joe was a fellow of infinite and various sneezes; they rolled around his head like thunder in the Colorado mountains (where, incidentally, he kept a cabin) and split from time to time the echoing air. His great hands were never far from his face, kneading cheek and jaw, brow and nose, temple and cortex, to loosen the next fit. Other than that, he was a soft-spoken gentleman, who liked to sculpt things out of rusty scrap.

Joe had this virtue: he wondered at nothing. The variations of Nature, of which he was a keen observer, had prepared him for any of the lesser diversities of men. I approached him with Syme's 'Sketch towards the construction of the magnesium lantern, dubbed by Mr Tom Jenkyns The Flu" alongside Phidy's description:

Sam designed an improvement upon the magic lantern, *his first invention, whose small flame was a blue eye peering into the hollows of the earth. It was called* the magnesium match, *a thin, flammable wire trapped in a crystal prism and suspended from the inside of a glass hood. We held this lantern above a fire of leaves or twigs or the alcohol solution of loose earth or pond water. Then we lit the match and a thin blue spirit of light appeared in the smoke and danced high or low upon the lantern's glass walls. The position of this gay faerie depended on the content of fluvia in the smoke, and we etched a fine web of reckonings against the glass to chart her. We could now measure such niceties of blue as would suffice an angel in tracking the depths of Heaven.*

Joe held the scribbled sketch in the palm of his hand, pinned at the top by the curl of his fingers, and lifted it to the light in his garage studio. His thick arm swelled his college sweatshirt, frayed at cuff and neck through long affection, as he set an impossibly dainty pair of gold specs across his nose, and read over Phidy's account. He stared at it. I stared at him. He stared at me; then unlooped his specs delicately from his pink ears, and pressed his eyes shut.

'I guess it's your business,' he said.

'I guess it is,' I answered. Pitt is an incorrigible mimic, and a great admirer of Men in their Trades, who get to the heart of a matter, then stop. (This has never been Pitt's modus operandi.) Pitt cannot help himself; confesses a sneaking affection for tool-belts, boots and hammers; for drawls; for all things native and unlearned, since Pitt himself belongs best in the world of the *acquired*.

'If these fellas made one,' he answered at last, 'I don't see a reason – I can't.'

How sweet it glinted in the sunshine of Saturday morning when Joe 'brought it round the house', as he said. Susie was gone with the boys, and the drive was empty. I meant to take them to their soccer matches out at Zilker, but then Joe called, so I rustled pink Susie out of her folded sleep. 'Is it Monday yet?' she said, in a languorous, pretty muddle, as I rattled open the curtains, and set a cup of coffee on her bedside book. '*Not* Saturday morning,' she grumped, blinking, suddenly unmuddled, as I tried to rouse her. 'Saturday morning is my morning.'

'Drink that,' I said. 'Joe's coming round. He says it's ready.'

'Joe, joe, joe,' Susie muttered, obscurely mocking, as she swung a leg to the floor. 'Joe joe joe joe joe. Joe. Joe. Joe joe.'

'Joe,' I murmured, an hour later, holding the lantern to the sunshine, and watching the cut glass cut the light. 'Joe.'

'Looks fine,' Joe said, 'I believe.'

A square frame, edged in brass, ran up to a kind of polished steeple. I held the lantern by the 'nod', as Joe called it – from the sketch, he said – a rounded hook that tipped the roof. The magnesium match hung from the underside of it, that 'thin, flammable wire trapped in a crystal prism'. The device had no bottom, so I poked my finger through to touch the match – a rough, curling strip that felt like sandpaper to the tip. 'That'll want replacing,' Joe said, 'time to time.' But the beauty of it all lay in the etchings, which resembled nothing so much as the rays on a child's sun, impossibly particular, burning through the frosted glass. They had been carefully labelled in a loose script that seemed to tumble down the lines: Calliope, Cassandra, Caesar and Washington, and even Maria S., after Mrs Simmons, I supposed. Each glass panel recorded a slightly different concentration of fluvial spirits, which depended on the seasons, and the power of an eclipse.

'To think Sam held this in his hands most of two hundred years ago; and set out with it, to look into the heart of the earth. Such an air of precision, Joe, of careful beauty. Precision, he once said, is only one kind of abundance. Such colours, too – when the green comes off the grass. Is not the magnesium lantern glorious?'

'Well,' Joe said, pressing his palms to his temples in a rather extraordinary fashion, as if to unscrew his head, 'seeing I built it, yes. But what it's good for, that's nothing to do with me.'

'I'll show you. All we need's a Petrie dish and a drop of methanol. Short of that a cornflake bowl and a bottle of gin. Come on, Joe – we'll take it round the park this minute.'

Joe and I looked around the park. The sprinklers had kicked up along the football field and darkened the sheet of mud along the sewage pipe. In one endzone, a man sat on an icebox drinking; another stoked a grill. The toddlers' pool was almost full, of legs and balloons, it seemed; two mothers lay on their bellies with their bikini tops unhooked. The sun stood on the arch of noon and looked down. 'Pitt,' Joe said, squinting, smiling a blind smile, 'I don't think I'm drunk enough.'

I can't tell you what fun it was, at first. By the time Susie and the boys got back Pitt had covered half of the football field down to the creek, and the grass verge of the tennis courts on the other side. His sneakers were soaked through, and stank of sock – the creek, I must say, proved particularly fruitful, rich in curious exhalations of all kinds, not to mention milk cartons, candy wraps, newspapers, orange peels, syringes, bottle tops, beer cans, and the teardrop strips of metal that open them. The knees of his chinos stuck to his skin, then peeled off, as he stretched a leg. Pitt's elbows, likewise, bore evidence of his table manners: the creek-bank where he propped himself; the burred football field; the sprinkled lawn. The rubber tongue of one sole flapped every step, cleft from the shoe above, and chattering idly. When Aaron stepped out of the car in socks, trailing his cleats on a finger over his shoulder, and discerned his father plodding up the drive, he said, 'Mom, who's that bum?'

'What's he done with Dad?' Ben piped.

'Go inside, boys, and get cleaned up,' Susie said, in the Voice That Brooks No Dissent. 'You too, Doug.'

I must confess that I hadn't dreamed at first of *mapping the results* – aiming as I did just to get the measure of Sam's thoughts by following in his steps, not the measure of the fluvial content in Shipe Park, Austin, Texas. (That would be crazy.) It was simply a matter of knowing the way he worked. 'Have you ever tracked a dead man's thought down the gloomy corridors of the mind,' I once wrote, 'your comprehension lit by the same shower of synapses that illuminated the passages of his brain almost two centuries before, spark for spark?' To do that, I needed to know how his hands felt, going about their business, his knees and feet, his back. I wanted to consider the question of a hollow earth from the point of view of a man who had trod, touched, scraped, burned, measured the ground under his feet, and reduced a few acres of countryside in his clever hands to a map of numbers in his clever head.

Naturally, Pitt was – observed. A bearded *dude*, a fellow of houseless head and unfed sides, in looped and windowed raggedness attired, burst sneaks, cut jeans, asked me once what I was 'lighting up'.

'Fluvia,' Pitt replied.

'Is that something new?' the gentleman asked, leaning over me, and sniffing, wrinkling a long, straight nose of unexpected refinement.

'Old,' Pitt said. 'Very old.'

'Used to be', he muttered, ambling off, 'we's all shared what we scored.'

A gang of kids surrounded me once, pointing, when their football tumbled into the creek-bed. I hunched over the edge of the water, lit a dish of earth and scum dosed with gin, then struck the magnesium match, and stood back to observe the blue 'gay faerie' dancing on the cut glass. They said nothing, as I jotted the result in a ringed notepad. Children have a natural respect for the utterly strange, acts without reference, too alien to be assaulted. At last one of their number, obligated by a shadowy moustache, dared to clamber down, pick up the wet ball, and scat. Some of them lingered longer. They looked vaguely saddened by the whole affair, *sobered up*, after the high spirits of their game. It took a few steps into the playing field till the rise of the creek obscured them and their tongues loosened and they cried their tireless boasts and prompts again. 'He burning shit,' they said. 'That man burning some weird shit. Man, he *burning*. You see that?'

I was lucky (I see that now) to attract a cop whose indifference to the vagaries of the world, either natural or professionally acquired, was sufficient for him to accept at face value my rather garbled account of the experiment. 'You see,' I spluttered, drying my hands on my thighs, and rummaging through a stuffed wallet for a university card, 'it is essentially a question of – those – escaped subterranean gases – that groove the internal spheres – whose occasional cracks – overlap, thereby producing an unusual concentration – of – fluvia. Thus far the theory,' Pitt cried, conscious, for the first time, of a desire to dissociate himself from the great Sam Syme. 'I am, in point of fact, a *historian*, properly speaking, bent on a species of archaeological experiment – not a scientist at all, by any means.'

The cop, a light-skinned Latino chewing a toothpick, listened patiently.

'Is that a bottle of gin?' he said at last.

'It is,' Pitt answered. 'Purely *scientific* gin,' he hastened to add.

'That's what I always drink,' the cop said. '*Scientific* gin.'

He lifted the lantern lightly with his pinkie finger, and sniffed it. 'What I like about this job', he muttered through locked teeth, 'is Variety.' He prodded the toe of his boot in the bowl of gin-spiked dirt, then scraped the sole of it carefully against a rock. He spat out his toothpick in the creek. 'Next time,' he said, taking another toothpick from a matchbox in his breast pocket, 'make sure you get a paper bag – for the bottle of gin.'

The best of it all was that it *worked*. Now let no Bunyon wilfully misunderstand me: Pitt gives no credence to concentric spheres, escaped fluvia, eclipses. He is, first and foremost, a historian of error; and has not forgot it. But he has often had occasion to note the brilliance of those devices constructed to establish erroneous theories. Human *ends*, Pitt regrets to say, rarely live up to the sophistication of their *means*. The magnesium lantern was – as

444

good as advertised. 'Then we lit the match', Phidy declared, 'and a thin blue spirit of light appeared in the smoke and danced high or low upon the lantern's glass walls.' That is exactly what happened; and what a beautiful quavering glow it proved to be: composed of light, being itself opaque, free to the flow of the sunshine that shot through it. A blue 'faerie', as Phidy called it, spectral and spidery, spinning a fine web of reckonings against the glass.

Now. Regarding these reckonings. I won't say they made sense. I won't go that far. Doubtless, on the strength of them, I could construct the rumour of some eclipse – under South Lamar, let's say, just short of 7th Street. Before I was done, I'd plotted most of Hyde Park; trooped over Speedway to Hemphill Creek and Adam's Park by the fire station; headed south along Lamar Boulevard, somewhat more patchily, and 'taken a flare' (as, I believe, they used to call it) in the green lot where they sell Christmas trees in the winter (a strong, steady glow); driven to the banks of the Colorado by the old YMCA, and, there among the winos and lovers, among the late-night joggers, drawn my first real crowd, who huddled about the thin blue spirit in such easy, uncomplicated wonder that my heart warmed to the uninitiated world for the first time since undertaking this history; and after that, in a burst of fresh hope, I tracked as far as Zilker and Barton Springs, before calling it quits at last.

I had got Phidy's description almost by heart by the end, translating the cityscape of Austin into his Virginian account, and the we of their companionship into my old solitary passion:

We must have made a romantic picture, huddled in our coats, stooped low to the cold ground, selecting crumbs of earth or a twig or leaf, and carefully marking the specimen and location in our heavy notebooks. We peered down caves and pushed through undergrowth, summoning those enchanted azure sprites wherever we went. Sam dripped a concoction of his own into ordinary street puddles and set fire to them, calling forth their blue ghosts. We were like spirits from The Tempest *or Goethe's devil, or the alchemists themselves about their business, searching for that oldest of New*

Worlds, the earth's core. We left a trail of blackened turf across much of Pactaw County. We were foot-sore, back-weary, hand-chapped and heart-full. We were, as I told myself repeatedly, pioneers of a kind; and we slept easy at night, and woke brisk in the morning.

Only Susie's sleep used to suffer for it, as Pitt crawled in beside her, butting his head against the small of her back, in animal companionship. 'Cold,' she said, in sleepy insistence, cocooning herself in feather-bed. 'Hands and cheeks. Both out. Don't be so much cold.'

Pitt did not, as he says, attach any credence (a curious phrase, I have always felt, involving such a difficult *jointure*) to the map of the internal world he constructed on the strength of these readings – or, rather, to that subsection of onion-layers, cut out under the patch known as Austin, Texas. Nevertheless, such a map proved to be not only conceptually viable but practically feasible, along the lines Syme sketched out, in his first passionate discussion with Phidy, over Sunday dinner. The map *worked* because the magnesium lantern worked, produced a series of various and above all *repeatable* results over a stretch of terrain that did indeed suggest the presence in the soil of diverse concentrations of an unknown gas, of unknown origins. As Pitt discovered the second time he trod over that 'trail of blackened turf' to check his results.

In, it should be said, increasing desperation. For by this time the chase had grown rather tired, the scent stale. Pitt butted his head against the incontrovertible fact that Syme's methods could never get beyond *conceivability*. No, let us be kind, and controvert; let us grant him even *plausibility*, and leave it at that. For there, Pitt grew more and more (and more and more unhappily) convinced, Syme's theories *must be left*. In spite of Phidy's best protestations to the contrary:

The number and nature of the crowns and vacuii have been calculated according to well-known eruptions. Like the movement of moon and star, I account for their number and motions by the pattern of their effects. If such a method suffice for the heavenly fields, why should we doubt its more earthly application?

How, Pitt asked, had Alfred Wegener's (equally powerful) eruption of the understanding resulted from such a *pretty nonsense*? The more I wriggled behind the eyes of Sam Syme, and stretched my fingers into the hands of Sam Syme, the clearer I saw that he did not heed his eyes, and he did not attend his hands. His thoughts ate the air, crammed with visions; you cannot feed theories so. How had such a mind ever conceived that great revolution in geologic science, the notion of a cracked shell and shifting internal plates? Yet from some unhappy compulsion Pitt continued the fluvial experiments, as if increase of appetite had grown by what it fed on – as if, at any moment, the dancing flame might cast a glancing light, not into the depths of the earth, but rather into the remotest recesses of Syme's imagination.

Until one evening I sat, muddy and dispirited, in my own backyard. Or, rather, the rack and ruin of my backyard. Moles, it seemed, had been at it. Cut and tangled grass roots poked out from several heaps of scraped earth. A soft-bellied bag of winter leaves had split against the fence, and spilled over, and stank of rot. The boys' bicycles lay upended in the . . . I should say lawn, but there was little enough of that left, after the winter, and my experiments – their wheels spinning slightly, at a kick of the spring breeze. A bitter-sweet odour of burned vegetation filled the nostril. Little piles of blackened earth, singed and crackling dandelion weeds, charred twigs, littered the yard, as though a bomb had dropped – oh, shall we say, two hundred years ago? – and Nature had never quite . . . recovered. The magic lantern itself was caked in several layers (subtly and variously shaded) of dried mud; the beautiful cut glass tarred by smoke; the magnesium match burned and shrivelled to the wick. I palmed the dirt from the neck, and drank a slug from my bottle of – no longer quite so *scientific* – gin.

As I rose from Pitt's broad and muddy bottom to his haunches, and rolled the ankles of my chinos away from my dirty feet, I glanced into the glow of the opened kitchen window. Ben was staring at me. The doorbell jangled, breaking the silence of my misery, harsh and out of tune.

'That'll be pizza,' Susie said, in the intimate muffle of a conversation from another room. 'Who'd I give the money to?'

Quiet. (How much Pitt loves the joy of looking in, and taking no part!)

'Who'd I give the money to?'

'Oh, me,' Aaron said.

'Go on, then. Be quick. Tell them that's forty minutes and we want the discount. It's after seven, and we called at half-past six. Can you manage that, or should I come?'

'No, I got it.'

'Stays light till six already,' Susie said, mostly to herself, as one door closed and another opened. '*Here*. Imagine that – in February. Doug!' she called, her voice, it seemed, bearing a suggestion of incandescence from the kitchen glow, as it flew into the darkened yard. 'Doug!'

'Mom,' Ben said, still staring. 'Why is Dad burning up the garden?'

He said it, you understand, *without* that dose of irony, habitual to him (his father's son in this); he said it rather out of shame or curiosity – though something matter of fact about the tone suggested sadness, and the former.

'Coming!' Pitt called (standing still), in that echoing fashion of the inward bound that implies excess of weariness and distance travelled. 'Let me just get cleaned up.'

'I don't know,' Susie said. 'It's an experiment.'

'What's he trying to prove?'

'What he's always proving. That everybody's wrong, and he's right.'

As he stood under the shower, Pitt considered how far from the true path he had strayed. How sweet the scrub of the brush against his fingertips, as the water beat him warm again! But it could not scratch the dirt from under his nails, nor bristle his black nubs pink and clean. '*Du mußt dein Leben ändern!*' the poet said; and Pitt spat the words into the rush of water. The magnesium lantern had proved not only a failure in itself, but demonstrated, in terms at once clear and tangible (or, rather, *muddy* and *muddling*), how

448

easily Pitt might be led into the lost worlds of his own thoughts. (Perhaps they had finished supper by now; and he could grab a slice.) Yes, yes: *du mußt dein Leben ändern!* He closed his eyes against the burning stream. *You must change your life!*

I remembered surprising Ben lately in our bedroom – where I found him standing above the opened drawer of my desk; the sort of guilty discovery that would have sent the blood to my cheeks as a boy. My mother's thin bones and girlish figure beside my father's brute mass composed a contrast Pitt's lonely childhood did not like to consider in its intimate union; no boy does, I suppose, but there seemed something particularly awful in the thought of my prim *mother* abandoned to such pleasures in the arms of my cheerful and greedy dad. 'I don't know,' she might have said, 'it was your father's idea; not very *me*.' But Ben never blushed – Susie's easy motherhood must take some credit, along with the boy's unabashed curiosity, and perhaps, even, a tithe of praise is owed to Pitt himself, for the simple friendship of their marriage, in spite of present . . . bickerings is too light a word. It is even possible Ben came in to see if his parents' bedroom offered any clue to their unhappiness; a good place to look first, Pitt concedes, in the usual run of things.

But in fact Ben seemed content to peer into the drawer, holding his shortened arm against the handle. He glanced up at me briefly and looked down again, as if refusing the interruption; and I guessed only then that he had found a copy of the Syme Papers, and they had absorbed his no doubt uncomprehending gaze sufficiently for him to stand, a minute or half-hour perhaps, reading, lifting each sheet as he finished, and laying it face down on my desk. Another minute passed. I did not wish to move or close the door or speak; anything might break the spell; and even tiptoeing backwards from the scene implied that slight burden of expectation a reader baulks at, especially a boy. Yes, I longed for *him* at least to read and understand me – though Ben was too young perhaps, and would acquire my lessons no doubt soon enough, and from a richer, less literary inheritance. Pitt couldn't remember what he'd come in for; and determined to fetch something, anything, from the cupboard, as if that were all, and the kid was too ordinary and insignificant a presence to occasion comment. Say, for example, his Oxford sweatshirt for a blustery Sunday afternoon at the beginning of March. I did not move; he lifted another page and laid it blankly with its fellows on the thin pile.

Every author knows the spell, the crystal delicacy of the silence with which he regards his reader. I am not here, runs the undertone of his incantation, I am not here, I am not here. Pray, by all means, continue. The spell is binding, too, for the writer feels, as if in point of fact he is only fractionally present, while his remainder breathes and thinks, just around the corner of his sight, upon the page in the reader's hand. (Afterwards I looked at the heap on my desk; Sam was taking Phidy, at Tom's insistence, around the barn, where the double-compression piston lay entangled in its own decay.) He turned another page, bending beneath his thumb, whose dirty print (sweating slightly, perhaps?) creased the line 'I had no answer to this; and so we stood there, in the thinning must of the old barn, while the shadows played upwards from the ground and engulfed the ceiling it seemed in black flames . . .'– yes, Pitt looked, and counted too, afterwards, seven pages in all. As Ben turned the last of them, he said, glancing up again, with a trace of irony I could not measure: 'When can we draw on them, Dad?'

Not 'can we draw on them', as he might have asked a year ago, simply eager and indiscriminate, but 'when' – conscious already of the process by which his father's work outlived its always questionable uses and survived as scrap to be recycled and reborn beneath the son's brighter and happier and messier penmanship. (Was it reproach or expectation? Sweet concern for his mother's fate? Acceptance of his father's? Which, I wondered, in sudden silence – having turned off the tap, I stood a minute in the drip of the shower-head.)

Yes, Pitt would begin again, from scratch. (A sadder, wiser Pitt.)

Avoiding such nonsense as the *magnesium lantern*, and those maps of the internal earth, on which he had wasted these impassioned months.

He would go on, as he should have begun. By reproducing, in exact detail, Syme's marvellous experiment of the burning, whirling globe.

Joe Schapiro and I spent six rain-soaked days of the spring recess bent over Phidy's manuscript, from Joe's first cup of tea and cold pizza in the morning to the drop of Laphroaig he knocked back before turning in. Joe was a bachelor, with a certain gentlemanly taste in his graduate students; and on the second morning I caught a glimpse of an oversized T-shirt stretched below a scuttling bottom, as it retreated to the bathroom. By the end of the week, Dr ('not yet, Joe!') Bianca Baumgarten, 'visiting from the University of Hannover', used to sip her coffee, wrapped in a blanket from his army days, while we worked. Mostly in Joe's garage, because I didn't want Susie to see me – 'at it again', she would have said.

He rattled the garage door into the ceiling every morning, to catch the natural light, such as it was – coloured white in the battering of rain that hit the drive each day that week, in drops fat enough for us to pick out not only their individual shapes, but the dozen splintered sparks of water into which they shattered. Mostly, I remember the noise, the trample of a thousand cats and dogs on the tin roof – such intimacy of the sky upon our heads! Joe cleared off a warped ply table, sweeping the sawdust and bent nails into a garbage bag; and we spread the twenty-odd sheets of my translation before us, which recorded Phidy's first encounter with the great geognosist Sam Syme and the wonderful experiment (at fifty cents a head) he was engaged upon: the tale of creation, in a clamour of smoking coal and running ore, spun out before our eyes by a device that seemed, among Sam's other advances, to anticipate the common bicycle: 'I will do my best to describe the contraption – I can give it no better name – upon which the Professor, well, perhaps *rode* is the only word for it . . .'

Well, this was our text; and you may yourselves imagine the difficulties we faced in translating an eyewitness account (a hundred and eighty years old) into a modern and practical reality. Joe was wonderful: unhurried, meticulous, patient equally with his head

451

and hand, as the two strove to match a conception of the experiment and its physical execution with each other. Pitt was all haste and bother, a perfect *volcano* of notions that overflowed as soon as they erupted, and cooled in the very act of forming. He despaired, equally, of any delay, as soon as they encountered it, and any decision, as soon as they settled upon it; but flatters himself, that in his own awkward way he spurred his partner apace, and kept them, as Susie would say, 'at it'.

Even *Doktor* Bianca Baumgarten – as Pitt persisted in calling her, above her blushing, increasingly petulant, protestations that 'we *anticipated* – it is all very much premature – a question, if I may be permitted, of *pre hoc* casting some doubt over the *propter*' – put her very pretty foot in at one point, and demanded to 'look over the original, as I cannot imagine the German language could ever be twisted into such an ugly knot'. (Syme's enthusiasms proved once again infectious; even after two centuries quarantined, as it were, in anonymity. The atmosphere of the garage, heavy with wet, thick with our stale and mingled heats, loud under the banging of the roof, suggested nothing so much as *a great pot on the boil*, lid rattling, the whole brew about to *bubble over* at the excess of internal excitement.)

Pitt ventured to persuade 'the *Fräulein*', as he dubbed her now, that *Doktor* Benjamin Karding, from the University of Neuburg, had corrected these proofs *himself*, and confirmed Pitt in their accuracy.

'Dr Karding is', she stammered, bursting with insult, 'a . . . a very . . . *little man*,' she declared at last, astonishing herself by the vehemence of her persuasion.

'He is a long and willowy gentleman, of great eminence, personal and public,' Pitt assured her.

'I think I know my own tongue,' she snapped.

'Now, fellas,' Joe said, never stirring, running a line across the drafting board.

'Lifted and retracted, for example,' the *Fräulein* declared, glancing over a transcript of the original, 'I find to be a very poor approximation of "*Bein hoch und Bein runter*", a simpler and, I believe, altogether more poetic expression.'

452

How sweet it proved for Pitt, to hear Syme picked over in this fashion! The lift of his leg, long since and eternally retracted, briefly restored by the touch of her quibble, the *huff and puff* of him, the physical expression of his theoretical enthusiasms, tangibly presented to his biographer, in the shape of the *Fräulein Doktor*, poetically raising her leg *hoch* and stamping it *runter*, by way of practical demonstration. Perhaps it was cruel of Pitt to tease her, but he did not rest, until the crescendo of her 'No, no, no' reached such a pitch of exasperation that it broke free of the pristine perfection of her English, and squealed into the native honesty of her *'Nein, nein, nein'* at last.

Pitt, needless to say, enjoyed himself.

Joe enjoyed himself.

The *Fräulein Doktor* also, in her way, enjoyed herself.

We finished a draft of the design by Tuesday evening, and sat drinking Jose Cuervo on Joe's porch while the rain dripped (astonishingly loud) from the eaves, into the fat of the dark green mulberry-hedge leaves. How Pitt loves a blueprint – the mere sketch intimately suggestive of the geometric intricacy that underlies our simplest shapes and acts. By Wednesday, the first awkward legs and arms of the 'spinning wheel' began to kick – clanking baby steps – while Joe, bare-armed in his apron and jeans, lay on his back against the cold cement, observing and greasing and adjusting. Pitt, needless to say, did not keep shtum, and began to suggest things – a great failing of his, as Susie has often pointed out. 'When you know something,' she says, 'you tell us what to do; and when you don't, you suggest. Little niggling suggestions,' she adds in less charitable moods, 'too stupid even to be disobeyed.'

Even *Fräulein Doktor* Bianca Baumgarten had the measure of her man. 'For shit's sake,' she declared at last. 'It is bad enough that you make him build this crazy-thing. It is worse that you help him.'

By Thursday, the 'legs' gleamed under Joe's loving hands; the 'arms' swung through the air with a slugger's easy violence; and Pitt could perch upon the wooden seat, and pedal to his heart's content, flattering himself that his own squat, powerful figure at least faintly resembled the geognostic pioneer who rode that saddle before him:

[L]antern-jawed, with a brave and stubborn chin, slightly darkened by a day's growth of beard; a straight, strong, unhesitating nose; a thin upper lip bitten between his teeth, above a plump, rosy lower lip; sharp, broad cheeks crackling and shining with animal spirits in the skin drawn tight across them; thick, liver-spotted forearms bared to the elbow, trembling with his exertions; broad shoulders, with a slight hunch like the growl of fur upon a tiger's neck. In short, a muscular creature, utterly at ease in his skin, well suited to the constant struggle of the flesh against the hard inanity of the world.

On Friday we sculpted, sloppy in excess of clay, that curious *colander*, split in halves and pricked on all sides, that would form the world (how strange to feel it *slippery* beneath our hands!); and set it to bake overnight, in a great oven Joe had built into the back of his garage for his experiments in pottery. Then, seeing as we'd nudged against week's end, Joe rolled up what he called 'a little bit of happiness' and puffed and passed it round; and Bianca sampled and pinched her eyes at the strength of it, and Pitt himself partook, for once, being short of happiness these days in a general way, and not too proud to borrow a concoction of the stuff, from Joe's private store.

By the time the rains gave over in a stink of heat on Saturday afternoon, the world was ready, and attached to its spinning wheel. We finished the last drop of the Laphroaig in its honour; but I dared not touch the miraculous machine as yet, so perfect it looked (as we all look, before the experiments begin): an elegant device that seemed to suggest, by a curious symbolism, it could fly to the moon and back. Pitt ran his hand over the smooth grey skull of the globe (so soft it seemed!), the wooden perch, oiled by the seat of our pants, the gleaming extensions of leg and arm, *herky-jerky* even in their motionless silence, a presage of the violent force within them. Pitt's palms had already begun to sweat.

454

He apologized to the *Fräulein Doktor* for his nervous needling all week. She ducked her head quickly, and smiled. *'Da knickste sie höflich den höflichsten Knicks,'* she said, gently; and added, 'nodding politely the politest of nods.' Joe had probably told her anyway that on Monday evening (the Ides of March, as it happens), the Promotion and Tenure Committee sat in judgement upon Pitt's professional future and the various futures that depended from it.

Pitt had his reasons, you see, for indulging himself in a spot of needling.

'Tenure,' declared Howard Mumford Jones of Harvard University, 'or the right, after a probationary period, to hold one's professional post until the age of retirement, is the bulwark of academic freedom. It guarantees freedom of teaching, freedom of research, and freedom in extramural activities.' Not to mention the fact that it props up a marriage something wonderful; and allows a good Symist to pursue the proper subject of his intellectual passion. The institution of tenure is one of the more remarkable privileges acquired in the course of American academic history – an acquisition, in its way, *not* unrelated to the liberal struggles that occupied the life, and occasioned the death, of our old friend Ferdinand Müller, the esteemed father of Phidy himself, Syme's impassioned memoirist. 'We have been told many times', Mumford continues, 'that the concept of academic freedom, although some of its components go far back in our history, owes much to the admiration of an intellecutal minority among us for nineteenth-century German liberalism, and its (often competing) concepts of *Lehrfreiheit* – the freedom to teach – and *Lernfreiheit* – the freedom to learn.'

Ferdinand had declared, at a rabbling convocation of the Parliamentary Society in 1819:

> We must *gather* a community of people to establish the
> best of our youth in the New World, while at the same time
> providing for a large body of immigrants to follow us annu-
> ally. And thus we may be able, at least in one of the

American territories, to establish a true, a *German* state, which shall itself become a model for the new Republic, and an inspiration to Europe.

Nearly a hundred years later, in 1915, a Joint Committee on Academic Freedom and Academic Tenure was convened among the frozen fields and falls of Ithaca, New York, upon the following remit:

RESOLVED, That a committee be constituted to examine and report on the present situation in American educational institutions as to liberty of thought, freedom of speech, and security of tenure, seeing that the aim of science is to discover new truth, but every new truth means the disappearance of old error and frequently involves a shock to existing opinion. The shock may be unwelcome but unless there be the fullest freedom in scientific investigation and in the proclaiming of its results, there can be no progress.

A great geognosist once addressed directly the 'shock' occasioned by 'the disappearance of old error' in the 'discovery of truth':

'From what arrogance do you speak?' they ask. 'From what high arrogance do you preach – against the thousand-year-old traditions of your people – your universities – and your God? Have you alone seen the truth – where so many great men have been blind?' And I answer them: 'From the courage of my two eyes – my thoughts – and the hands He has given me for digging.' I ask instead, 'With what arrogance dare I refuse?'

In other words – and hear this, Bunyon – academic tenure had been established precisely in order to grant the Symist 'room to look about him', as Sam said elsewhere. It came too late, of course, for Sam, who suffered mightily from the dull conservatism of Sober Ben Silliman: 'I could write frequently to your Lyceum on the practical Arts of our Philosophy (which you praise so highly), but I see no Object in it. *My* pieces are all necessarily *Speculative* . . . *You* study to please fools.' Pitt would soon discover if the system established in 1915 could benefit Syme's disciple; if the present age was any kinder to the results of 'speculative' work. In short, if the world was kind to Symists.

That weekend – steamy, dispiriting, itchy, miasmal – I turned again to the break-up of that curious band of geognostic brothers, the New Platonists. Müller's account stops short of the inevitable conclusions, their deaths; but there are other sources, a letter from Tom, a letter from Kitty, discovered by Karding among the family papers, which Friedrich brought with him from Paris when he came home to die. There is Phidy's death, too, to be considered; the only experience he would not record, as Woolf says – though he anticipated even that in those final excited scratchings on the back of his youthful memoir, whose pages, drying before a tavern fire (O, the vagaries of tavern fires!) themselves occasioned the final twist of fate, which robbed Phidy (and Pitt!) of the last known copy of the *New Platonist*, which eventually burned in the fires of Friedrichsgracht or drowned among the rubble in the canal (we must always give the Neptunists their due). Pitt was in cloudy and muttering mood, as you see, and waiting for the storm to break. In just the kind of mood to read over other people's bad news.

Phidy, Phidy [Tom wrote in 1850], how many lifetimes has it been since I took your hand? We have heard of your great triumphs, believe me, every one; we take all the German papers now, when we can get them, and, like as not, you've stirred up a bees' nest in one or the other, no matter the bee. How it warms our hearts to hear you go at them! We had all quite mistook you, I'm sure, apart from Kitty, who knew you to be a grand fire-breather from the first, only a little uncertain of yourself, she thought, in a strange land.

Of course, we could not speak your name before Syme, even to the end. The shame of it is, when so many thousand things

fly by us heedless every day, which had best tarry for our life's
sake, that one thing should have caught his ear, which had
best passed by. I mean, of course, that thing, 'The Hole in the
New World', which you wrote, angry I am sure (for that I must
own part of the blame), and such a young man still – we were
all such young men. I must confess it took some time before
the sting of it eased from my heart. And there was no talking
to Sam after that about you.

I said, how many lifetimes have passed, but, in truth, so little
has happened since you left, only the one life, the same life,
slightly diminished. I believe Mrs Simmons has written you,
from time to time, of our vicissitudes – there are so few. Sam has
never left us since that bitter day you saw him last. He would
stay, he said, until you were gone (the last time your name ever
fell from his lips) – and after you sailed, he fell ill, a long, miserable, half-hearted sickness, that never raged openly into fever,
and never quite left skulking in his bones. He has been the companion of our married life, a softened man, brother to Kitty, and
a second father to our children – though I cannot say I never
longed to hear his old royal bloody-mindedness break forth
again.

He died yesterday morning, deep in the sleep from which he
could never quite free himself any more. And if I open an old
wound it is only to let the bad blood flow out. He had long forgiven you, I am sure, for anything there was to forgive. Indeed,
we often caught him, Kitty and I, chuckling on the sly over some
piece of yours we had left in the garden or tucked beneath a
glass, for him to discover, accidentally of course. If he never
mentioned you again, it is not because you had wronged him,
but because you had seen him brought so low – a temper such
as his could brook that worse than any evil. So often we resent
not the slight itself, for which a friend might be blamed, but the
revelation that follows it, for which he should not.

I knew of your doubts, Phidy, they were clear enough to me
from the first, if not to Sam. I did not share them then and I do
not now; for even as we laid the turf above him, this cold after-

noon, I thought, Some good will yet come of this, some chance stone will strike his fine metal and even now kindle to life and light. He was busy till the end, it may surprise you, revisiting those lost worlds of his imagination ('engaged' as usual 'upon certain calculations, etc.'); and may rise up when we ourselves are buried with him and forgotten. Perhaps we may catch the after-glow from him even then.

I scribble and scribble and Kitty (now a fine, silver-haired grandmama) cries, 'Come to the point, Tom, there will be time enough for all this nonsense when we see his face.' So come to the point I will – come see us soon, Phidy, now that all is over though not forgotten. We have a bed laid out for you (his old bed!), and a good stout lock upon it to keep the grandchildren out. And you must meet our sons, who, from his long company, bear more than a touch about them of their sweet 'uncle', and, of course, your old friends,

Tom & Kitty

P.S. Come at once. Kitty

Well, he never did come; though he got as far as Paris, and scribbled that strange rant we discovered plastered to the eaves of Inge Muller's bedroom wall. Before he got up the courage – with Phidy, as we know, a process involving years – Tom had died, too. I heard Susie calling me from the kitchen, once, twice; we danced the inevitable dance. I did not answer. Silence for a minute or so, and then the door pressed open, slurring the wall-to-wall; her head peered round it. She told me to eat, and I would not eat. Then she said, 'At least come and sit with the boys while they have lunch,' and I said, 'In a minute.' She lingered a minute, looking on, without comment; then roughed the carpet as she shut the door behind her. And left me to pore over an account of Tom's death, a copy of which Karding had sent me – that curious contrast of Xerox and fresh paper glossing the yellow brittleness of age; Kitty's pretty missive pasted to a page of Phidy's Parisian journal.

The letter came today, this first full morning of summer.

The trees shake the dew from their backs and sigh with the warm breath of returning life, and the girls, even before the flowers, smack the dust off their summer frocks, and, casting a hopeful eye above, parade in their fresh colours. Tom is dead, and my last link to the New World dies with him.

All these years I had been on the edge of returning, our sweet reconciliation on the tip of my tongue, like a word so plain and simple, the busy brain forgets to find it, trusting that it is understood. On Friday mornings I used to glance down the list of ships in the paper, note their destinations, the times of arrival and departure, their captains, their cargo, their quaint names – thinking, One of these will take me there, some day. I suppose it is more to be wondered at, not that I never returned, but that I ever set forth in the first place. But idleness, which at last pricks the young on to their feet and away, draws the old deeper and deeper within, until such time they have not the strength to go.

He died [says Kitty] quite happy, as he lived, and careful to cause as little bother as he might, to those who survived him. He knew it as it came, you see – you know, Phidy, what a great one he was for arranging things . . . The burial, an orderly affair, was presided over by a Mr Connaught, an indolent young man, more attentive perhaps to some of his prettier sheep than is quite good for a shepherd . . . yet he is idle enough that it was all over quickly, thank God. Mr Connaught, you see, succeeded in his place Tom's father, at whose grassy feet Tom himself now lies. Despite everything, you know, Tom had a great respect for proprieties and old ways.

He mentions you kindly, Phidy, in his will – I'm afraid he had not much more than kindness to bequeath. Yet he wished you should keep a copy of that old thing, the *New Platonist*, now alas quite bent at the spine, and somewhat ravaged by time and children. It used to sit on top of our piano under a glass of flowers. I hope the post don't ruin it more. You see, Sam himself had writ his name inside the cover – that little blotch of ink with the two hills. Say he addressed it to you, Phidy, and you will not be far wrong . . .

Dear, dear Kitty – practical, and sweet, and blasphemous to the end. 'A sweet bun,' she was and seems to have remained. And there it sits, upon my sunning lap, our proud firstborn, the *New Platonist*. How it hurts my heart now to note Tom's name missing from the front page, there, beneath my own, a gap of white, as humble as himself, as free from stain.

I am going home. The fact is that I have known some time now that I am dying. 'He knew it as it came, you see,' Kitty wrote and so do I. The red clot at the bottom of my morning's bowl announces it. And I will not die here, among these people. Even Tom's death has cut a string in my mind, which had bound me by some strange logic, to this city – a reminder perhaps of my second setting forth, a reminder that I had only stopped, midway, upon a journey that I shall not now complete. And when I die, I suppose, that will be the end of it at last. We will all have found the only hollow space below there ever was, a square of earth five feet deep, soon to be filled again. No one will remember our great revolution, our wandering summer, nor think again of those shining spheres, revolving always and endlessly beneath us (and so quietly).

Perhaps an hour has passed. I heard the boys clatter out of the front door, letting the screen clap to behind; then saw them, football in hand, make their way to a corner of the park, and begin to toss, looping the ball high, as if its mid-air ease and idleness expressed their own. Then Susie came in with a plate of Swiss cheese, and a stack of digestive biscuits left over from my English sojourn. She set it by the keyboard and pressed her palm to the side of my face. 'I don't mind if you don't come to lunch. I don't mind if you say you will and you don't.'

'I'm working,' I cut in, and perplexed my brow, in earnest approximation of the act, staring at the green screen.

461

'I *do* mind', she added, 'that you don't eat. Look how thin you've got, hanging off your own bones. The deal', she said, 'has always been that we stay plump together. Much cosier,' she said. 'So I brought you crackers –'

'They don't call them crackers. Biscuits.'

'And I want you to eat them; even if you are worried sick about Monday.'

So I mumbled crumbly biscuits and hard cheese, as the long and sticky afternoon slipped by jerks into the late twilight. Around four o'clock I turned on the air-conditioning unit propped in our bedroom window, simply to drive out the wet; and sat, in shirt-sleeves, increasingly chilled, in front of the computer screen, too cold to mind the goose-pimples running up my arm. Wrapped in that cocoon of solitude in which we never age, I pored over the last lines Müller ever wrote, the final piece of the jigsaw puzzle, at which the picture grows clear: Syme, Wegener, Karding, Pitt standing arm in arm in arm over a battered broken globe. For there is never an end, *pace* Phidy. Hutton was right: only endless modifications of the middle. As perhaps even Müller realized, subconsciously, when he scribbled this note on the back of the only sheets he had to hand, the Syme Papers, on his final journey.

> I have just had a most unusual and unsuspected encounter, which has left me in a flutter of nervous spirits and quite incapable of sleep. Passing on my return through Hamburg, a short day's travel from home, I dashed into a roadside inn to avoid a violent shower of summer rain. It had been threatening all afternoon, from a black, lowering, miserable sky, the air so thick it could scarce be breathed. Thus, drenched to the bones, I undraped before the warm fire and called for a glass of hot rum to chase the cough out of my lungs. Spreading these papers on the table before me to dry – the rain had come so sudden and so fierce that even my portmanteau, clutched beneath my cloak, grew wet as a rat – I turned again to that long-ago morning, the day of the great eclipse, when even I the doubter half-hoped, half-

feared we stood on the verge of something grand. Busily poring over the dripping pages, I did not look up, when the hot dose was set at my elbow with a sharp rap.

'I see you are an author,' said a voice, in the high, uncertain, fluting tones of old age, far too elegant to have fallen from the lips of a mere servant. I glanced up to see who had addressed me, whereupon I found his voice belied my interlocutor, for the fellow at my elbow, dressed in soaking yellow breeches and a pink cravat, was quite a young man still, scarce thirty. He possessed one of those eternally youthful countenances (and voices) which suggest such wonderful innocence and promise in a boy, and such idleness and neglected fortunes in a man: pink cheeks, a little puffed with exertion, startling blue eyes, dim almost as glass, golden, thinning hair pulled back from his forehead, a dirty neck.

'I was once an author,' I replied, 'but these' – I gestured over the drying pages – 'belong to a private matter.'

'Memoirs?' he queried, drawing up a chair and burying his nose in his own glass of hot grog. 'Forgive me,' he said, mopping a drop of the brew from his pink nose, 'I have had a cold these . . . three years,' he added, 'and this is purely medicinal.'

'Memoirs of a kind, besides an old journal, a recent inheritance,' I answered, to my own surprise; for had I not kept these things under such lock and key, that even now I felt the blood flutter in my veins to speak of them again, and blinked, as though unaccustomed to the light? 'They refer rather to a matter of science.'

'Ah,' he said, drinking another long draught and summoning more. 'Now we come upon my particular province. Peter Wegener,' he added, stretching forth his hand, 'Inventor.'

'Phidy – Friedrich Müller,' I replied, and cast a querying glance at him. 'Might I have come across any of your devices, do you think?'

'Not likely,' he said, tapping his forehead. 'I'm no such fool. Keep them locked up, in here. Now,' he added, rolling up his sleeves and setting his elbows on the table, 'let's hear the business.'

Why did I not turn him away at once? For I had reckoned now what manner of man he was. I had seen them before, in my time. A younger son, perhaps, supporting a meagre income with some grand illusion, some wonderful ambition, never realized, never attempted, yet colourful enough to accompany him on his travels. Too poor to marry, too idle to get on, they spend a perpetual youth on one hopeless goose-chase after the next; and die, as like as not, in the Debtors' Prison, among a class of men they have had every chance to grow accustomed to. Often quite clever gentlemen, more's the pity, only lacking the necessary fire.

This particular specimen of the breed, I soon discovered, was quite exceptionally clever – quick as a terrier on his wits' feet, he nipped at my heels through the long, dark afternoon, and would not let an old man sleep. And before I could say yea or nay I had begun the whole mad thing from the first. Would you credit it, the half-forgotten thoughts – ideas I had believed long rusted and out of use – flew from my lips as bright as the day they were coined, made of such shadowy stuff time could not touch them? Sam himself could not have explained them better; his words had such a renaissance in my heart, I almost wept, an old foolish man, at the recollections they aroused.

'It all began', I said for the hundredth time, but the first in nearly half a century, 'with a question of mass.' And the sad fool called for quill and paper and quibbled and scribbled through all that dark, thunderous afternoon, pausing only to wet his lips and call for more grog. Only once Herr Wegener stopped, pointing with childish delicacy and delight, to a small robin, much bedraggled, so dirty with rain and weather his breast scarce blushed, who had hopped on a broken leg through the door as a traveller swept past him towards the fire. 'Now, now,' said the landlord, a short, squat gentleman with a great head of hair, 'we'll have none of you,' and plucked him from the ground and, cupping the delicate bird in his great hands, tossed him light as ashes into the windy night, where we saw him flutter up against the lines of rain and away.

And so through supper we threshed the matter out, gesticulating bone in hand and diagramming wildly in butter, setting the salt here and the pepper there, explaining the world away with potatoes and a sliced fresh onion we called for from the landlord. Deep into the night, as drunk as lords we talked, until the flushed pink face before me gave way in my mind's eye to other faces in other times; and the landlord sent us up to bed at last, lest we demand our breakfast next. And here I am, a drunk old man on his knees in bed, with a foolish fire in his heart, searching desperate and happy through a white and crackling world of loose pages.

There is nothing reminds a man of his age so much as sudden happiness. For it begets in him a kind of worry, a feeble trepidation, a weakness of heart and knee, a sleeplessness, an ache, the whole condition as much like joy, as a young man's longing resembles love. All this wants thinking on.

And so the morning comes, and, as I have a thousand times in youth, I wonder at my foolishness of the night before. My head rings like a cracked bell; my eyes blink aching against the sun which shines bright as new in the forgiving heavens; and the pain in my stomach is such that twice this morning I could not breathe for as long as a boy might count to fifty, the air comes in so sharp and bitterly. It took me the best part of an hour to collect these scattered pages, and only then did I realize my great loss.

I summoned the landlord at once, and tried to keep an old man's petulance from my voice. 'I possessed, you see, a certain journal, an old battered thing, a keepsake, title of *New Platonist*, with a man's name scribbled inside. Not my own. It was of no earthly use to any man living apart from myself; but I would like it back. I would very much like it back.' How I hated the quaver, high pitched, fretful and lost, which echoed in my ears like the voice of a stranger, a tiresome, meddlesome stranger, who will not keep quiet and will not leave.

'Who do you suspect took . . . it?' the landlord asked, grimacing at the end, nodding his great head on his short neck, and leaning conspiratorially forwards. He had a terrible habit of keeping the last word back and using it only when nothing else would do, as some men save the icing of a chocolate cake for the final bite.

'Why, man,' I answered, already in a temper, 'I should have thought that was plain. That inventor fellow, I mean the young man, Wegener, who kept us up so late. I wish you to summon him at once.'

The landlord nodded his great head again. 'That', he said, 'is where you and I . . . agree. That's precisely what I wish, too. The fact is', he added, as one considering a delicate matter, 'THAT man has Took Off. Without paying neither. Which roughly puts you and me, sir, in one and the same . . . boat.'

So there was nothing I could do but settle the bill and have him bring my luggage to the door. I cannot think what such a fellow would want with such a thing. I suppose men like that get in a habit of stealing, as certain birds are said to lard their nests with food they will never touch. They take what comes their way, never guessing what will serve their purpose in the end, they have such wandering intentions. Pinch it for luck, they say to themselves; and like as not forget it at once, or discard their prize, acquired at such risk, negligently by the road, whenever their burden becomes too heavy. Else it lingers so long with them, tucked in some out-of-the-way pocket, they cannot bear to part with it at last; and keep the thing, forgetful of the day they stole it or the reason therefore – as a kind of charm.

Sam you are dead now indeed, when such a man as he has got you in his hands. And now the last journey home.

A bit of luck, you say, for Wegener and geognosy. Well, perhaps, seen back to front. (How easily, you see, we slip into belief, simply because a pattern holds!) But by an irony of fate, the theft that drew Syme into the great evolution of intellectual history robbed me of that vital piece of evidence, the last *New Platonist*, necessary to prove my . . . to prove *his* case (and win my tenure?). What struck me, however, as I sat in the blow of the vent, was that Phidy, regardless of all that nonsense my son discovered – 'you are wrong, you are wrong, it is all absurd, you are wrong' – at the very end, could not quite bring himself to . . . *disbelieve* entirely: 'the half-forgotten thoughts flew from my lips as bright as the day they were coined, made of such shadowy stuff time could not touch them'. We would soon learn what time could touch, however – when the tenure committee sat to decide my future and their past. Sam, you will be dead indeed if they turn me down.

Pitt did not lie easy in bed that night; and Susie held him, in the warm stink of her arm, until she slept; but he could not.

It seemed the best thing I could do – on a bright Monday morning utterly forgetful of the night's sweats – was to *press on*, as the English say. Joe was stuck at the office all day (teaching, or some such lark), and set in the evening to attend the Promotion and Tenure Committee, as it sat in judgement over Pitt. But I had the key to Joe's garage. (Keep busy, boy.) 'Run out the boat, my broken comrades,' Pitt murmured to himself and the shades of Syme and Phidy, in that dry-grass whisper of Dr Edith Karpenhammer. 'For the last embarkation of feckless men, let every adverse force converge: here we must needs embark again.'

I drove on a sparkling March day towards the hill-country where Joe lived, north and west with the sun blinking off the mirror, as I chased my own shadow up the Missouri Pacific Highway. The city flew by me on either side, white clapboard neighbourhoods nesting somewhere behind the outlet malls and cineplexes looking over the road. A freight train, burned with rust, followed me slowly at one stretch, running clear against the low scrub of the flat land, towards, it seemed, the comforting illusion of the Nothing and Nowhere that lay all around us. Telephone wires dangled and glinted blackly in the sunshine. I wondered if Susie wanted me to fail.

Pioneering, Pitt thought, carrying on an argument well rehearsed, is the only way to set up shop and family. We must begin in Nowhere, stripped of accustomed props, to see how we Get On. I have always – and this is my proper boast – freed myself from the familiar, and then set forth. (If only Susie would follow, uncomplaining.) The burden of old errors is too great for little lovers to share: the unraked harvest of the family tree, rotting, mulching its acid into the soil. (Pitt, if he knows anything, knows about the burden of old errors.) It is best to begin from scratch. Scratch away until you get to scratch. Texas is it: *scratch* itself, a dry, prickly country, big enough for any number of beginnings. In short, I had little desire to go 'home' to New York.

Turning off MoPac, I entered green and shadowy streets, heaped upon one another, rising, along the thrust of rock beneath the wheels. There were no shops or sidewalks here, only the broad asphalt trembling like a butterfly in the sunshine that got through the sharp, dark sycamore leaves. Much of the faculty lived round-abouts, in houses they designed themselves, to suit an outcrop of the hill and catch the view – long, high views over the Nothing and Nowhere below. Curious, Pitt thought, how similar our imaginations run when left to themselves: for most of the houses looked as like as two hands, belonging perhaps to different men but built along the same lines. Maybe the Pitts would move round here, given time and fortune. I pulled, crackling over pebbles, into Joe's drive.

It took me much of the afternoon just to set up the thing. Phidy, of course, had come upon the middle of the experiment, and could not help me. Joe had got together a bucket of shavings – nickel and iron ore; he worried the scraps might choke the fire, but he figured they'd melt quicker, and start to run among the coals, which is what we wanted. Joe, pushing his tongue against a corner of his cheek, and scratching the stubble of the skin, had expressed certain doubts regarding the 'upshot' of the experiment. 'Seems likely to me', he'd said, 'Syme meant it for show, mostly. Smoke and lights, fifty cents a pop, as you say. Can't imagine he had much hopes for it, beyond that.'

Pitt also had his doubts, especially as he came to lay the coal in the bottom of the clay globe – cut open at the half, and connected each way by a peg-and-hole system. He nested several layers of coal with a sprinkle of shavings, and hoped that the bump and grind of the spinning planet would cast together the elements. Creation, at its best, would prove to be a very messy affair: a gunge of smelted ash caking the clay sides in various configurations (which exactly, Pitt presumed, Syme hoped to discover). At its worst, Pitt feared, he would open a smoking globe only to find a heap of burned coal, occasionally interspersed with slightly glowing fingernail-clippings of iron and nickel. He rummaged through Joe's junk to find some fire-lighter, and came across all sorts (including a rather remarkable collection of mustard jars), before discovering a box of the shiny white sticks. These he crumbled into the opened world.

Yes, as Pitt surveyed the 'crazy-thing' (Fräulein's word) – their careful handiwork – doubts beset him. (How clever doubts are, and far-reaching – much more insinuating, intricate and complete, in their way, than hopes. Hopes at least have ends and beginnings; whereas doubts eat everything, even the ground beneath our feet, even the space through which we fall.) Such a silly little planet, stuck with handlebars for spinning, pricked through with holes.

Those mad legs, resting quietly; the single whirling arm, flung high, clutching the globe, quite still now, time stopped. I was reminded of Phidy's reaction to the double-compression piston (would that be next, on my spiralling career?). Phidy had said:

I felt somehow as if I had stumbled upon a former field of battle, which by its very stillness evoked some measure of the storm that had led to such a calm. At the same time the fantastical device smacked of a more intimate and solitary defeat, suggested in some indescribable fashion the mechanical workings of a most particular imagination, which had overreached itself and become entangled in its own proliferation.

(The trouble was, as Syme had said, that it could not – rather, that I could not – *swallow* myself.)

Yet Sam himself seemed to set some store by the 'experiment of creation', unless it was merely the wilfulness of temper that turned him against Tom, as his associate cleared up the harmless remains of the broken world:

'Stop at once,' he cried. 'What act of ignorance – of wanton waste and destruction – are you about to commit? Answer me, Tom. Indeed, there is no fool like a happy fool; and all you can do is stand there, grinning idly. Give that to me directly.' And he snatched the parcel from Tom's hand, and spread it over the flagstones before the hearth, adding the small piece in his palm to the suddenly precious collection.

Perhaps the pieces held some clue to the 'mechanical workings of a most particular imagination'; proving like dreams to be fragments and emblems of a deeper preoccupation.

It was around teatime that the *Fräulein*, knocking timidly from the inside of the house, came in, bearing tea. A pretty girl, I must say for Joe – too thin for Pitt's taste, lightly freckled around the eyes, straight in figure under cropped sandy hair.

'Thank you, my dear,' Pitt said, taking a mug, and raising it to his face to inhale the brown heat. 'Much needed.' And Pitt stood with his eyes shut against the comfort of steam.

'Joe said I mustn't show you this,' the *Fräulein* murmured through thin lips, lifting a crumple of paper from the back pocket of her skinny jeans. 'But I thought – it is only fair – to know. It is always fair – to know.'

I took it from her freckled hand, which hung idly, its duty done, by the *Fräulein*'s hip, too still for comfort. Then she clasped the fingers in her other hand, and held them both against her belly; released them, conscious of her fidgeting, and stood painfully quiet – a wrinkle trying to smooth herself away. But she did not go. She waited for Pitt to read.

Memo: from Dr Sal Bunyon, Dean of History
To: The Promotion and Tenure Committee
Regarding: Dr Douglas Pitt

Forgive informal nature of note but I'm off to Paris tomorrow to chair conference on the Politics of Food so shan't be around for Doug's tribunal. A few jottings then as I'm the man that brought him in and should answer for him.

Facts. He hasn't written. (Except for a little piece blasting me on Trinitarian thought which I took in good part though he played the man and not the ball as far as that went and kicked him in the shins. This isn't the place for my reply.) As for his teaching, he hasn't, much. We don't mind folks trotting off to London God knows but they gotta show something for it and he hasn't shown. Most of the kids here think he's nuts except for the kids who *are* nuts and I suspect we split along the same lines. There are stories which I won't get into now about his 'classroom antics' (involving some species of broken lantern and a swimming trip to Barton Springs) but what worries me more are his classroom *absences*. The truth is this year he's let himself go. The best thing we can do for him is to get him to stop.

Regarding *magnum opus*. This happens to be my line of work so I don't mind saying a few words. Syme was a crank; a deluded crank who died in deserved obscurity – either drunk or mad and I don't much care which, to be

471

honest. We know about him. He came to be a figure of fun in Richmond Society; and as late as the 1880s we find references to the 'Professor' – a child's bugaboo and a promise of Doomsday, if you stole apples from the neighbor's yard. That kind of thing. 'Sent to the Professor' was short for 'the earth would swallow you'. Author and illustrator Howard Pyle picked up the phrase in Virginia and borrowed it for Pepper & Salt in 1886. There's even a very pretty picture that goes along with it, if you can get your hands on a first edition: shows Syme, shod in sandals, smoking a pipe, grinning broadly as the ground opens to eat him. I don't mind that but Pitt's turning into something worse: a crank chasing a crank.

As for the Syme Papers itself, the missing *New Platonist*, and the supposed connection to Alfred Wegener: a series of improbabilities founded upon inaccuracies, and the rest of it plagiarized, I regret to say. A great shame, for Pitt is a genial little goblin, and I wish him well.

'Joe said I shouldn't show you,' the *Fräulein* repeated, when I was through. 'But I thought it's only fair. *Es tut mir leid*,' she said, turning to the gentleness of her mother tongue for comfort. 'I'm very sorry.'

Pitt, curious as ever and quite particular, asked only, 'Had Joe seen – this', clutching the memo, 'before we made – this?' waving his arm at the Headless Bicycle, Joe's nickname for that 'fantastical device' proliferated from the collective imaginations of Syme and self.

'We both had,' the *Fräulein* answered, resting her hand on the seat.

'You are – very kind,' Pitt said, sweating, flushed perfectly crimson from chin to pate. 'Very kind,' he insisted, as he walked into the bright shadows of the street and left her there – in the open garage, staring after him.

The pebbles ground and scattered as he backed into the road, swung outwards, and then – breathing stertorous calm – drove slowly off. Pitt fled the rich hills and green-canopied streets. The sun came out over the highway again, as he turned south and home. Towards Susie and failure. He recalled another sunny occasion, many years before, on which his father had taken young Pitt 'on the job' one summer morning over the school holidays. The boy did not know what to expect, he had heard so much of his father's innovations. 'Did Dad make this?' he asked, fingering a jointed gasket. 'Or this?'

'Your dad?' the man said, a barrel-chested figure with hanging arms, stooped against a board to tie his boots. 'Which one is he?'

Pitt pointed below.

'Him? I don't really know what he does. Orders parts, I think. I never see him up here.'

How my face burned at that, grew hot to touch! Fitting, I think: for shame runs in the blood, as deep as love, and just as old. Pitts, I believe, have always been laughed at.

'Have you heard?' Susie said, as Pitt strode in the door.

'What? Heard what? What's there to hear?'

'I don't know. I was asking.'

'Don't ask. How should I know? They've only just started.'

She lay upon the couch in sweet collapse, under a feather-bed, watching TV – the boys hidden about her person, only their heads appearing. Spring break must have begun, Pitt thought, on the quiet. 'I brought the bed in here,' she said. 'Three little slobs. Shameful.'

'You should be – out and about. We should all be out and about. This is crazy. Sun shining. Everything.'

'Heard what?' Ben said – quick child, attentive to all elision, stubborn in ignorance.

'We're cold,' Aaron added. 'And I'm trying to watch.'

'Do you want us to burn things?' Ben said. 'For science?'

Pitt turned off the TV. 'Come on,' Pitt declared, making a fist of the cover, and beginning to pull. 'Come on. Come on.'

'Leave it, Doug. Everyone's snug and happy. Why do you want to spoil it?'

473

Pitt thought of reasons; then picked one. 'I'm going to bed,' he said. 'I need the duvet. Come on.'

'You should treasure such a sight,' Susie said, wrinkling her nose, resisting. 'Wife and babes, in arms.'

How sweet and clear is anger! A bell ringing, summoning old strength. He pulled the feather-bed free, and wrapped himself round – like a bear in snow. 'Good night!' he said. 'Good night!' (My mind had not been so . . . lucid . . . in months. Utterly empty, spick and span, picked clean. Then filled with light. A perfect treat – pristine. Pure and simple as a glass of water.)

'Why do you spoil everything?' Susie cried, sitting up, and – from some compulsion – beginning to tie on her tennis shoes. 'Just when we're happy? You hate it when anyone's happy except for you.'

'Good night,' Pitt said, and closed the bedroom door.

Then another door banged shut; and the screen followed lightly behind it.

Pitt awoke from a deep sleep at dusk. *Courage, he said, and pointed towards the shore.* Lines drifted at the edge of his thoughts like loose wood on a slack tide. Outside his window, the yard lay brown, becoming black. The neighbour's kitchen glowed in the soft air; someone stooped below the counter. Disappeared. Pitt had turned away before she rose again; a hand, perhaps, against her aproned back. Sleep like cotton filled his head: a muffling. He stood quite naked, to his surprise – he did not remember undressing. Then he stepped into the bathroom on cool feet and peed. A bright stream; the sweet stink of it rose into his breath. Afterwards, he dipped behind the shower-curtain, wetting his bare shoulders, and switched on the tap; waited quietly till the hot began to spit and sing against the tiles, then slid in. '*Du mußt dein Leben ändern,*' he muttered into the thresh of water. I feel a new man, he thought; only worse.

When he walked into the living room, Susie had a cup in her hand, and poured it trickling into the potted tree beneath the window. 'The boys are getting changed for the dance,' she said. 'Joe called, with a heavy cold, poor man. The committee have decided. I told him you were asleep.'

'Yes?' Pitt asked.

'No,' she sighed.

She drank the rest of the mug, and set it on the television. 'It doesn't matter so much, Doug.'

'I suppose you're pleased?'

Susie considered, holding her mouth in the palm of her hand. 'At this point, I'm relieved. The way you were going. I'll be glad of a – change of pace. We can go home now; no reason not to; in the summer.'

'It was Bunyon, you know,' Pitt said. 'I got done.'

'Among other things. Boys!' she called out. 'It's almost time.' Then 'No, no, no,' she cut in quieter, squeezing her eyes shut and shaking her head, 'I'm not a bit pleased or relieved, only miserable that you have suffered disappointment, which I would keep from you for all the world, though I can't.'

Pitt, in the sweet dew of his wife's pity, began to revive. 'Only a temporary disappointment,' he said, scratching his nose, pinching it, sniffing, in the restless flow of thought. 'A step – or, rather, a stumble – along the way. Syme had dozens like it – and kept going. Worse, indeed: a mother's death; a friend's betrayal; a lover's faithlessness. There are always Bunyons and Ben Sillimans in the path of – well, there's no harm in saying it – of *inspiration*. That's how we know her when she comes: a breath of sharp air that makes us suddenly feel *that everyone else is wrong*. Naturally, the *uninspired* put a kink in the works when they can. But it's our job, to –'

'When is it my turn to do what I want?' Susie said, in a voice as flat as counting to ten. She has round cheeks, my wife, flushed slightly in the heat of her insistence; a strong, short nose, blue eyes, and these she turned on me, sharp as broken glass.

'What do you want?'

'I want you to give up,' she said.

'That isn't in the power of your wanting.'

'I want to go home,' she answered. '*That* is. I want – no, there is too much wanting – *I would like* to move back to Yorkville, to a long flat on a side-street with a tree in the window and leaves on the fire-escape, not far from Carl Schurz Park; to catch the yellow school-bus to the Bronx again, every morning with the boys. *And you* – at a proper job – that doesn't swallow your life – *our* lives. (Somewhere you haven't failed.) They'll take us back, you know. They said as much when we left. I would like in time to take time out: for a girl, perhaps, or for me, painting again. Both, perhaps; and leave her at Na-na's while I set up an easel in the kitchen; and on sunny days in the Socrates Gardens. You have had your years now: five at NYU, three in Texas, one in London. You've used them up. I – would like mine.'

'I don't think you understand,' Pitt said. 'There is an – evolution. No, let me finish. There is a kind of evolution at work, and I'm a part of it. In the long view, this is all that matters, the only thing. Above the common run of the generations, there is another, much rarer, accumulation: of *knowledge*.' ('Don't talk to me like this,' Susie said, shaking her head. 'In this *manner*.' Pitt continued, *declaring*, showing his hand at last.) 'A higher natural selection, if you like, survival of what's true at the expense of what isn't. You have no idea how little of what we do proves . . . collectable, afterwards.'

'I'm not *a little girl*,' she said, in the pink of fury.

'Syme had a single idea, just one, that – slipped past the censors, the judges of oblivion. *That the shell of the earth was full of cracks, and the continents split along them.* This thought, the echoes of it, inspired a young German scientist invalided from the war to a true picture of the world. A *first-edition* true picture of the world – very rare. Pitt, in his small way, hopes –'

'Pitt,' she said, 'always Pitt.'

'Hopes to add his pinch of truth to the history of the universe, by proving Syme's part in Wegener's discovery; hopes, in his small way, to take his place in the great evolution, the only thing that matters in the end.'

She stared at me, her great eyes wide, as if I were mad; and, worse still, unfamiliar to her in my madness, a strange, unpleasant creature that had scuttled through the door of her home. 'I suppose', she said at last, 'that I have no part in this evolution?'

There was nothing I could answer.

We heard the clatter of the boys in their room, the intimate babble of their brotherhood, such as I never knew. Something fell over, a chair perhaps, with a jacket round it. It could not be lifted again, it seemed, without a great discussion, a settlement of fault, restitution to the injured party. Yet only the injured party seemed concerned; and Ben's voice rose shrill above his brother's. I thought of cutting in but kept quiet; then they fell quiet, too. A cat scratched at the screen door outside, began to pick at the thin wires, tearing them wider. 'Go away,' Susie said. 'Go away.' It did not. Susie opened the door and looked at the long-starved tabby, stretching itself, arching up the screen, and plucking. Suddenly she hissed at it, and the cat scrambled yowling into the yard and slunk away along the low kerb of the street.

'Well, regardless,' Susie began, turning round – quite calm, in fact. 'This summer the boys and I are going back to New York. You can do what you like.'

'I thought you loved me for my – arrogance, *uncompromising* arrogance,' Pitt answered at last her earlier question. 'I thought you loved me for that.'

'I thought you were funny,' she said. 'At first, if you must know. A funny failure. Not so funny any more.'

'Don't you see', Pitt urged, in gentle undertone, 'that nothing is settled yet? They voted –'

'Twenty-five to three, against.'

'Against granting me tenure; well and good. But I might be able to stick around another year, as an assistant. Bunyon stepped over the line – he knows that. There are complaints to be made, through a variety of channels. The charge of plagiarism, for example – here, let me show you what he wrote –'

'Hush, now,' she said, softening; the more I talked, the less she listened. 'Hush.' And squeezed me in her rounded arms, so that my elbows pressed against my ribs. (How unhappy I suddenly felt in her comfort!)

'I have *evidence*,' Pitt insisted, his voice rising, 'evidence that Bunyon poisoned my chances from the start. I'd confront him – if

477

he hadn't run away. Quite apart from the fact that the final proof of Syme's genius is only a piece of good luck away. An experiment, a discovery, that will make good my name. Sitting in Joe Schapiro's garage as we speak is a wonderful contraption, invented by Syme himself, to test the cooling of the earth in its first creation. A kind of bicycle with a spinning head attached – a clay globe, pricked with openings, and full of coal, which, once set alight, will melt the shavings of iron and nickel scattered among them, and approximate the formation of the planet itself. Whereupon –'

'For God's sake, Doug,' she said, pressing harder, 'don't make yourself ridiculous.'

Pitt loosened himself from her grasp. He wasn't a coward much – as Dr Edith Karpenhammer once declared – 'but *stuck*, while things like pity were thinning.' Susie breathed deep, hiding her mouth, holding her nose between thumb and forefinger, at her wit's end; sat down. Pitt walked into the kitchen, stooped and took a bucket from under the sink. Then he opened the freezer and lifted the ice-tray, crackling with cold, and began to bang it loose into the bucket. Some cubes skittled across the linoleum floor, and he bent on hands and knees to gather them up. After that, his fingers crawled among the stuck ice to pick off the last ones; before he pushed the tray in place, and raised the bucket to the sink. The ice clicked and cracked in the cold water as it rose between the gaps. Then the bucket swayed as he lowered it and set it on the lino tiles.

Ben came in, wearing a green jacket and a green tie tied much too long and hanging below his belt. 'Are we freezing things now, Dad?' he said, seeing his father bent over the ice. 'What are we freezing?'

'Let me do that,' Susie said, rough-handling her boy, and loosening the knot at his neck. 'Aaron!' she called through the closed door. 'Betty and Mrs Liebowitz are on the way. It's time.'

'What goddamned dance?' Pitt asked at last, rising, a piece of his thought clicking in place as the wheel of his family turned round and round.

'Purim Prom,' Ben said. 'For little Jews.'

'I'm not going!' Aaron cried, mysteriously muffled, through the bedroom door.

'For God's sake, Susan.'

'I like getting dressed up,' Ben confided in a stage-whisper to his father. 'I want to go.'

'I've sprained my neck.' (Aaron again.)

A car-horn tooted in the dark of the neighbourhood, and a door slammed shut.

'The Liebowitzes are here!' Susan cried to no one in particular, some imagined clerk recording all household facts in tireless shorthand, for future reference.

Pitt, in sudden inspiration, an irresistible overflow of revived spirits, declared, 'He's not going. He's coming with me. Aaron!' (Louder.) 'You're not going! You're coming with me!'

'Doug!' Susie, vexed, her hands akimbo on her sweet plump hips. And then, in shadowy signification, speaking in capitals. 'We Have Things To Talk About.'

The doorbell tinkled, twice, as if a thick thumb pressed it, and stuck, then fell away.

'Just a sec, Betty,' Susie cried. 'They're coming.'

Aaron emerged, a jacket hung loose from his forehead, a tie vaguely noosed about his neck; shirt-buttons buttoned awry along his ribbed chest; sleeves rolled up to the elbow, in manly show of disinterest at his sartorial dismay.

'I sprained my neck,' he said, quietly. 'And I can't go.'

'You're coming with me. I need you – a little experiment – creation of the world.'

'Doug! Not now. Not like this.'

Perhaps Pitt did shame himself a little, to fight for his son in such a fashion, and split the boys between father and mother. But the battle – thank God! – was back in his blood, and nothing could quell it. There is no 'serpent', Phidy well knew, as insidious as our own high spirits, so seeming-innocent a tempter.

'OK,' Aaron said, turning to the door. 'So long as you know, Dad, this is only to get out of the Purim Prom.' Pitt took the bucket of ice in hand.

'Say, *Hello, Betty*,' he told his son, as they passed in the doorway a girl in pink, bobbing up and down on unaccustomed high heels.

'Hello, Dr Pitt!' Betty cried, scratching awkwardly at a run in her tights.

'Say, *Goodbye, Betty*,' Pitt said, as they strode into the cool of the spring night.

'Aaron?' the girl said, lifting a corner of her mouth into a corner of a smile.

'Goodbye, Betty,' Aaron dutifully replied.

A blinking, pink and longing look followed the boy as he followed his father, into the Volvo. Then more scratching.

'Doug!' A last, forsaken cry from the doorway.

Pitt honked, a little tootle, in answer to his wife; then waved goodbye to Liebowitzes, Peggy and Betty both; backed into the quiet of the road, and turned into the tree-spanned peace of the neighbourhood side-streets. They drove past the lit blue of the public pools and crossed towards Guadalupe; approached the green wire-fenced expanse of the Home for the Blind, and turned left, on to the strip mall, in a glitter of lights. He said nothing to his son till they slipped on to the bright smooth of the highway, driving west.

'Where are we going?' Aaron enquired at last. 'Where are we going?' he said again.

'To finish an experiment,' his father answered.

Joe was out when they rolled on to the pebbles – engine in neutral, drifting quiet – of his drive. Joe and the *Fräulein* both. At least the house stood curtained and dark; and no one stirred when Pitt muddled with the garage key, clicked and rumbled the iron shutters into the roof at last.

'Should we be doing this?' Aaron asked, brave enough in his way, but naturally respectful of property and propriety.

Pitt stopped short, considered the question. 'What do you think?'

'I don't think we should be doing this.'

(Pitt should disabuse his son of such conventions. Though, I must confess, he felt like a thief in the night himself – from a different guilt, however, obscure to him then, but growing clearer by the minute.)

'No, probably not,' he said. 'Let's go.'

He set the tub of ice – a fine sluggish slush now, slow to sway in the sway of the bucket, tinkling and crunching lightly – in the shadow of the Headless Bicycle cast by the street-lamp. Then he rummaged for the light-switch, found it, and blinked in the sudden illumination that filled the garage.

'What the –' Aaron muttered, 'what the –' as the full wonder of 'the fantastical device' struck his gaze. He stared at it, sucking the knuckle of his thumb between pressed lips (a family gesture), emitting faint windy squeaks of perplexity. 'You know what,' he declared at last, his mind made up. 'I think I'll stop asking questions.'

'Syme made it,' his father answered, somewhat hurt – that particular guilt from which he suffered now welling up, growing clearer all the time. 'Two hundred years ago, nearly. To test how the world was made. Don't you see, Son? *He tried to make the world himself*. Such splendid –'

'Delusion.'

'Ambition, I would have said. Come on; help me get the fire going.'

Aaron found the matches at last under a brow-stained baseball cap, which also covered a sandwich bag full of dry and wrinkled grass. The boy kept mum – a child can learn too much at once about how a father lives. Pitt opened the lid of the world, struck the matches on the rough clay side, and dropped them burning in. The crumbled white sticks caught first, glowing furtively along their shiny edges – a low, faint flame like the bright shadow of true fire. Strange how great, how various, the degrees of conflagration are! Burning is never burning simply. The act must always be qualified by the *heat* involved: like the human passions (like inspiration), brightest when forcibly compressed, over time. He shut the lid; and waited for the glow to swell.

There was nowhere to sit, except the Headless Bicycle, and the boy perched there, in a collared open shirt, forgetful of the tie around his neck, letting his legs dangle. He looked silly and touching upon it; or, rather, the crazy-thing appeared to be an overgrown toy between Aaron's bony knees, a boy's device, simply multiplied in scale to suit adulthood. Once he stretched to reach the pedals, half-slipping from his seat, and spun them, again, again, rising on his haunches to muster weight. The world shuddered briefly and began to whirl, swinging a long loop towards his father's head; but a sharp word from Pitt cut short boy and world. Still, Aaron looked upon the strange machine with some slight . . . curiosity, afterwards; as if his father, for once, had invented a game worth playing.

You could almost *hear* the fire when it began to tell – a rich concentration of silence that drew the ear to it. The artificial glare of the garage grew imperceptibly softer, bleached of colour, as the slow smoke filled the space. Pitt lifted the lid on the globe and saw the beginnings of inferno: a churning mash of coal, orange valleys streaked by translucence amid black hills of unconsumed lumps. He shut the globe again by its wooden handle, and touched a finger to his plump, sweating cheek to feel its heat.

'Come on, boy,' he said. 'Let me get up there and take a turn at the wheel.'

Aaron scrambled off, a figure of comic dishevelment, opennecked, shirt-tails hanging free – a miniature of after-work ease.

'Watch your head,' his father said. Pitt struggled up and began to pump, slowly at first, already sucking wind. (Was it nerves only, or the first blows of failure – Susie's sudden 'for God's sake' – hitting home at last, in the belly?) The arm creaked awkwardly round. 'Watch your head,' he said again, so Aaron squatted, lay back (how lightly children touch bottom!), resting his head against the concrete floor, while the smoking planet swung above him, once, twice, in great elaborate arcs.

'No, no,' Pitt said. 'I need you. Don't get up. I said don't get up NOW. Roll out of the way first. That's it. ALL the way out. What I want you to do. Is this. Push the wooden bar as the world comes round. Just enough to set it spinning. That's it. Lightly. We don't want it toppling on your head. Just enough. To set it. Spinning.'

The world swung easier now with the weight of its speed. (Pitt should know, the first revolution is always the hardest!) It trailed a flag of smoke behind it, which tore into strips when Aaron touched the bar, spinning, just at the height of his eye. Pitt's legs pulled swifter now, stronger; he rose on his hams to bring the last ounce of his vital mass to bear upon the pedals. There is joy in the mere fact of *pace*, in the brisk flow of things; and Pitt tasted some of it, in the thrust of his blood, in the sweep of the planet. Such swift years passed around his head! Decades flew by in minutes. Centuries spun round in the hot wind like a weather-cock in spring gusts.

How short the space of time since Sam himself strode the world along its orbit, since Tom touched it into night and day, dressed, like Pitt's son, in neglected finery. Aaron, for his part, seemed to have entered into the spirit of the thing (and that spirit was joy!):

He performed this task with great nonchalance, standing idly by in his black suit, only touching from time to time, with the tip of his finger, the flying handle . . . Fresh gasps of fear attended the perilous launch – it is the only appropriate image – of each new day. In short, all was confusion and terror and delight – and none of us could suppress a powerful sense of imminent and enormous and wonderful disaster, of conflagration and world's end.

Pitt saw the beam of a car's lights swing into the road, heard the hum of an engine easing home. Then the light drifted by and the noise faded. He wished to make an end of things before Joe got back and – saw him, thus. It occurred to Pitt then that Joe might read a certain *desperation* into the experiment; and the word itself arrested his thoughts (though never his legs). Not so much for the misery of it, but the shadow of some former hope the word suggested. Sat upon that strange device, sweating and pumping away, Pitt – more curious than anything – could not for the life of him recall what he had hoped at first to prove. Well, the reason would come back to him, no doubt – only a momentary blank. Strange, he thought, how much of what we manage to do involves forgetfulness.

'Now,' he told the boy, 'I want you to get the bucket of ice.'

Fact is – and I see that now – Aaron was just too small to lift it. So much came light and easy to the boy, Pitt had forgotten he was only nine: a strapping nine, king among his classmates, broad-shouldered and long-armed, but unfleshed by age, a creature getting by on bones and sugar. 'Tip it over the world,' Pitt said, slowing slightly, 'as it comes by. Lift it over your head – high as she goes. And tip.' (Of course, Pitt thought suddenly: the cooling of the earth. Syme posited an end to the perpetual modifications of Hutton's internal fires. He wished to test the *shape* of it. That's what this is all about.)

The shock of what happened obscured – for a minute perhaps, or a second – what happened. In the smoke and hiss of warring Nature, Pluto and Neptune set at odds again, I could not distinguish bad from worst. Aaron had staggered, stoop-shouldered, into the path of the world. Globe struck bucket balanced on head, and both (though not, thank God, all three) tumbled down, a furious spitting explosion of ice and fire. The clay split and shattered across the concrete floor. A loose burning shard caught Aaron in the smooth of his cheek, raising a puffed, hot inch of skin – perhaps the lightest scar he would bear from his father's obsessions. (Pitt crying out meanwhile the familiar declension – you go too far, you have gone too far, you are too far gone.) Sodden smouldering ash lay everywhere in ruins, among glowing splinters of shaved iron and nickel. Icy waters slopped over the floor, soaking the poor boy's shiny best shoes.

He began to cry; mostly at the fright of it, no doubt, and the noise – only now the coal unclenched its teeth, and the hissing sighed away – and the smoke, so thick that our eyes ran anyway. Partly, I suppose, at the disappointment of his father. At having failed. Pitt wept, too; first at the sting of fumes; then freely, as he climbed off the crazy-thing and shuffled through the burning slush into the clear night, holding his boy. His guilt grew clear at last, welling up; the obscure sense of wrongdoing that had troubled him: the guilt of someone who chases his solitary imagination and begins to . . . bump into others along the way, bruising what he cannot see, and stumbling on. ('Not though I have Truth on my side,' Syme said, 'never doubt that, either. Never doubt it, Tom. But we haven't such right to it as we pretend.')

'Let's go home,' Pitt called gently, from his miserable depths.

'Should we clear this up?' Aaron snuffed his nose on the palm of his hand.

Pitt looked at the mess, a scattering of damp grey, only a few glints of the old fire remaining. In his hurry, he had tipped over the Headless Bicycle, which now lay awkwardly on the floor, resting on a cracked arm. 'Whatever you do,' my father told me, 'make things that last. That's the great trick. *Sticking*.' It could take an hour or more to sweep what I had made clean. Joe might come upon them, in Pitt's shame. 'Look,' Aaron said, lifting the shard that struck his cheek from the ice and ash at his feet. 'Like Texas.' So it was – that inimitable shape, a slight protrusion from a ragged triangle, unevenly split.

'Keep that,' Pitt said. (If only he had guessed it: the final clue.) 'We'll leave the rest for Joe.'

And then Joe appeared. It needed only that. Woken no doubt by the crash, he came from the back door, stood in the light of his laundry room, blinking, his face blurred from an early sleep, his eyes pinched, his nose thick with 'flu. He looked at the litter of ice and ash; the toppled contraption propped on a broken arm; the smoke; the wet stink; the crying boy and man. Gingerly, he stepped into the mess, wearing loose moccasins; stood in the middle of the garage, surveying the ruins of his workshop.

'Seems', Joe said, shaking his head awake, 'that history does – repeat itself.' (The hollow spheres keep spinning, the cracks overlap, producing: disaster.) Bianca peered round the door-frame, gangly in her long T-shirt, all arms and legs – astonishingly young. She looked at me, at Aaron, hiding from his father's humiliation in his father's arms. '*Na ja*,' she muttered. 'I see it did not come off, as they say. It came off so it did not come off. As they say.'

Pitt, for once, had no answer for her quibblings.

I had made myself ridiculous enough.

PART V

·The·Great·Eclipse·

So we came to Philadelphia, a red town in a green valley, and the sun tipped its hat over the trees in setting as our carriage rattled on to Chestnut Street. Stiff of knee and heart, we emerged, and propped our backs on our hands and looked up at the great clock tower, calm with time, of Independence Hall.

'Come,' said Tom. 'Tomorrow is our great day. A bite of one thing and a swallow of something else and then bed. Sam needs his sleep.' He took Sam's bag and his own, and strode towards the Liberty Hotel under the fat green leaves. The Liberty was a fine, square-cut Georgian establishment, with tall, bright windows rounded at the top, scattering the chestnut trees in their shimmering glass. This was the smartest roof I had known in the New World.

Sam followed without a word, through the great doors.

I slept like a king in a deep bed and could not prevent curiosity and joy, those sly tempters, from stirring in my blood as I awoke. I walked to the window, pushed it open with elbows scraping the sill, and looked out. The sweet air was too thick to come in, and I must needs poke my head and naked shoulders into the street to snuff it. I looked at the great red forehead of Independence Hall and thought of those sweating men, almost a half-century before, dropping blood with ink, and spelling a new country with the compound. Now a different revolution would be born within its halls. Who could not hope there, where so much had been hoped for and won? For all my earnest, decent protestations to the contrary, THIS, I thought, was too rare a chance to have missed – to see Sam dressed in clothes as grand as himself, walking upon rich carpets, under high ceilings. I had come for this, not the squalor of race-tracks and barns and agricultural lectures.

I dressed and ran to breakfast.

In the morning, Sam sat for Charles Peale, the painter, and a naturalist in his own right. 'What do you think of my museum?' he asked proudly, in his thin, strained voice, like a reed in sand. I visited the museum, too; an odd collection of devices, natural and artificial, shells and telescopes, on the second floor. 'If I had such a library,' Sam said, 'I should not look for books.' That always surprised me in Sam, that he could flatter when he pleased and when it suited. Indeed, it suited now; for he owed his engagement at the hall to Peale, a generous and curious man, as well as just and proud, who had founded his Museum of Natural History and Technologies some years before.

He was past eighty then – the famous dry face and leather hands. 'I have only got the patience for a sketch,' he said, drawing forth a case of pencils. 'I do not like to start anything I can't finish, and at this age, I have no faith in finishing anything.' I watched them, painter's hand and Sam's face, as the former drew the latter to itself, in lines as sharp and bare as the green veins over its knuckles. The delicate temples and too big eyes, the face sad, inward, except for the butting, jutting chin, stubborn and strong above the white cravat; the hair thinning over the large forehead. Later, he added colours, and the tip of a brush darkened the eye with blue and the cheek with red. But the sketch was truer; and caught without keeping, as only a pencil can that does not hide her strokes, the face in time, fluid, aware that the next stroke or moment could mean another line, an altered look.

In the afternoon came the speech in the great hall. The mayor was there, a pink man in a green suit, along with the lady mayoress, taller, with a sharp nose. A geologist from Harvard had come down, quite a young man, with tiny, restless feet. Name of Potts, I believe – he mentioned it often enough in shame-faced asides, 'poor Potts', 'foolish Potts', 'hopeless Potts', and the like. He hopped about like a wren, looking perhaps to pick up scraps of preferment round the feet of the great Dr Benjamin Silliman himself – a proud, pompous creature he proved to be, fat-cheeked, red-breasted in a silken waistcoat, fonder of politics than geology, it seemed, and a 'particular friend' of the lady mayoress. Then another specimen from Yale, tall and loud, with swinging elbows and a sharp cane, Mr Polidori. His tongue *stuck in his cheek as he spoke, his words came out half-chewed. He could be heard lecturing over a circle of littler men. The Pennsylvania University had sent its delegates, too, a row of comfortable old locals, sitting down from the first, gossiping. The elegance of Philadelphia was also on hand – gentlemen in black leading a perfect rainbow of ladies. The hall rang with well-bred echoes; chairs scraped the floor in a hushed tone. The sun still shone through broad windows, flung open against the thick air. Its beams were stopped short, here and there, caught by necklaces and diamond studs, trapped in the flat silver of watches, glittering in the dust of shining shoes.*

A different species lined the galleries at the back. Shy youths, the sons of mechanical men, came with notepads and blunt quills, cut too often. For them this was not only an Occasion, but a lecture 'On the Structure & Composition of the Earth's Core – a New Answer to an Old Question', advertised in the Inquirer. *Wives with scraped thick-fingered hands had come from their chores, perhaps for the relief of a spare afternoon in the shade, but Sam's 'news' had a deeper spell as well. 'The Earth is Hollow! The Earth is Hollow!' the newspaper cried, mostly in mockery, as it announced Sam's visit today on the front page. 'The Seas are seeping through. We must arrive in Boats to the Lecture!' Some had come hoping for a hoax, to be sure; but there were others, and many indeed among the jokers, who had come because a man stood there telling us that we were all wrong, and somewhere we desire this to be true, and partly believe it as well. Lastly, as always, came the Doomsday set, hoping for any kind of hopelessness, believing that an empty earth would do as well as anything. I had long grown accustomed to them, and saddened that such flies buzzed about my Sam, louder, more faithful, than any other. For once there were brighter creatures to obscure them. Sam rose up to speak, with a sheaf of notes clasped between elbow and rib.*

O Sam! My heart dwelt in his fingertips, lest he should drop those papers, and my heart fluttered with the papers, too. Tom gossiped with a gaggle of newspapermen, old friends, from the Inquirer, *but I could scarcely look up.*

491

'I have often wondered', he began, in a voice slower and lighter than usual, but broken up into his familiar staccatos, 'why we place such trust in our feet.' No one had expected this, and there was a great shuffle of the appendage in question, and the vast settling sigh of a mass of mankind.

'We question every matter of this', he continued, touching his heart, 'and that,' touching his head. 'Whatever flies above us – puzzles us to perplexity. We stare and stare. Stars, moons, suns, involve us in fierce disputes, fiery faiths, passionate doubts. We argue for centuries.

'We spend lifetimes of love and doubt – on what lies before us and behind us. We turn and turn to catch – what flees behind our backs – tiptoeing years; and yearn forwards – gazing to know what some cloud portends for the next day.

'But we never question what lies beneath our feet. That at least, we seem to say, is sure. There is nothing there to trouble us. So we move onward, look upward, curious – indeed, we mock the downward gazers – hunched old men and babies with their faces to the floor.

'Yet it has always seemed to me – that theirs is the most practical curiosity. We have slight hopes of prying into the stars. The past behind us is – too tight – for our clever fingers; nothing lies ahead but what we put there. Yet the ground beneath our feet awaits our consideration. I have always been puzzled by the story of Babel. Why did they wish for a tower? A curious race, I believe, would have looked below – and dug a great pit towards the heart of God – for there at least lay hopes of an answer.

'So I ask you now – to suspend your faith an hour – and dig with me some ways below our feet.'

They were caught; that light hook that pulls us by the ear and thought deep into another man's mysteries had stuck, though slight, and drew us towards him.

I knew the argument well, that question of mass ('I shall begin with a calculation – an error no greater than a man's hand . . . '), the list of possibilities, dismissed one by one. I knew it well, but I had never heard him speak so . . . lovingly before. He had changed: the massive, restless strength was gone, but something sweeter had

492

replaced it. That great energy, for which I loved him, had ebbed with grief, but left behind to my surprise a surer faith. He knew – this fact never struck me more forcibly – he knew that he was right. And so he spoke with less bluster. He marshalled his arguments one by one, slowly, inevitably – he did not circle his audience with a restless swarm of proofs and considerations. He left things out – trusting the main path, as though he walked a familiar way again, noting the points of interest to himself, secure in the faith that we would follow. We did.

There was something else. It seemed as though some pent-up joy had been loosened by his mourning, and that he now tasted it again. We tasted it too. The cook came in at one point (a great supper was laid on for the elect). Some usher must have alerted him – of what, I can only guess: 'Believe him, believe him; it's all true!' I saw him in the doorway, wiping his great farmer's hands on his knees. He listened unmoving for a while, then began to nod, slowly at first, then longer, happier, great sweeps of his great head up and down, as though he said, Now you see, this is what I have been trying to prove all along, with my duck . . . and my lobster salad . . . and particularly my marzipan torte!

I guessed then (wrongly, alas!) that Sam would not come this way again. This was the end. He talked slow and long because it was the last time. I wondered what had settled him, as he laid each familiar thought glowing to rest one by one. His mother's death? He was a young man, remember. We were all young men. He stopped short at her death, as an older son might not have, turning to look at that great gap behind him, forever empty, unfilled, unfillable. He would turn back home, I knew, at least for a time.

Another thought occurred to me, less kind, more jealous. I am suspicious of this thought myself. He was quits because of Tom, that pure man, selfless in the cause. Sam wished to be free of Tom, his tireless shadow, striding always a pace before. I turned to look for Tom. He sat by the great door, with the cook smiling and nodding beside him. Tom's chin propped upon his hands, his hands buttressed by his elbows, his elbows laid upon his knees. He was half-asleep, but he waited there to greet the men 'who might be of some use, perhaps, in your business, Sam', as they walked out. Then he looked up for the sweet close to Sam's valediction. The proof was over.

'There are further questions to be asked,' Sam said, and paused, putting aside his notes. Five hundred feet shuffled and resettled, and you may be sure their owners stared at them now, and beneath them. There was a quick shower of coughs and sneezes, and Sam gathered himself for the end. 'We have begun to stop at the answers – a great mistake – one which the churchmen do not make. The answers are our harbours. From there, the lesson begins. We have a page before us – richer than all our books. It is written in a thousand languages – in water and leaf – in finger-prints and firmaments. One might puzzle over it for centuries. But it is only the first page.

'We should take our thoughts in earnest – and accept the coin of our intellects at the market-place of ordinary life. I will have no half-measures – none of the legerdemain of our own philosophical consti-tutions – that can propose with our pen and tongue – what we reject with our hearts and our stomachs. Let us not turn as Hume did – to the light of day and breakfast – and forget the dark book on which we spent our nights. What can we learn from this hollow earth?

'I draw two lessons – that touch me deeper – puzzle me more pro-foundly every day. I wonder ever more at the wisdom of such an Architect. The first is this – that God delights in device. Spheres under our feet – hurl themselves – in endless rotations – below. They shine only in dark air – but they shine. These spheres are built for Beauty, sure – and Size – and Sweep – but also for sheer, bloody-minded, heart-breaking Complexity. The Architect delights in shapes – in speed – in gambits. There is a rush to these inner spheres – that must please him – as a sharp wind and a flying sea delight a sailor – who understands that such tides – such bouts of breeze – require this course – these sails – set hard and sharp at just such an angle. I marvel each minute that the heavens below us do not break apart – that the Creator who watches over His work trusts and revels in His nice eye.

'The second lesson moves me less to wonder – more to Grudge. We do not stand on rocks – but fleeting, turning, HOLLOW balls.

There is no core – no anchor – no Bone set fast below – but layer upon layer, and at the Heart, a gap. Imagine an onion – as rich and revealing at the first sharp cut below the skin as at the last. This troubles me – we are scientists – would like a final resolution. When Galileo argued that the sun – not this slight satellite – lay at the centre of things – the churchmen, appalled, knew well what stood at stake. Light and Heat and Mass lie at the heart of this Space – not we. A great lesson. WE cower in the distant shadows. They were right to imprison him. They understood him and took him at his word. What shall I say to you – as I propose – that the earth beneath is hollow? Where is the hope or the lesson in that?

'The core haunts me, I tell you,' he said, brisker now, rubbing his hands. 'It troubles my sleep – like a deed undone or a lost love. The core of cores – the seed at the heart of the fruit. If nothing is there? Nothing at all, at the centre? Tap your foot, again, again – imagine the echo in that space.

'Slow and stubborn I learn its lesson – the lesson of the onion: to go deeper in time or thought is only to go on. We touch no core – no heart – where the proof lies. We simply continue – as we must – but with this in mind. Do not look for final answers. There are no mysteries or veils – only layers – followed by others like themselves. I do not know if there is any consolation in this. And I dwell – as little as I may – on that appalling gap where the root should be.'

Silence followed, long enough for the first chill air of the evening to come with a shadow through the window. And then they stood, in ragged and then swelling numbers, to applaud; a lady holding the lap of a pink dress in one hand, cheering with the flutter of a fan; farmers beating thick palms, red as beets; Tom for sheer delight dancing like a puppet, strung against the back wall; the cook's face breaking apart at the cheekbone in his smile; the scientists from Pennsylvania tapping a smart pace with their rolled notes; the little man from Harvard standing on tiptoe to see above a great green lady caught in her chair and positively roaring; even Ben Silliman striking a brisk palm against the back of the hand that held his pocket watch as he checked the time; and Dr Polidori, rising above the rest, spitting out half-chewed 'bravos!' and conducting the assembly with long arms; and I, loving and happy, while the echoes of his praise doubled and redoubled in my heart.

And yet and yet and yet – did I believe him? Now is not the time, Phidy, I thought – though never did my doubts oppress me as then, in that great applause, in my high joy. It is over, Phidy; give it peace. No good can come of it; and yet and yet, some harm came – Tell him! 'I doubt, Sam. I am uncertain . . . '– you have, Phidy, ten times told him, in your way – no, tell him plain: 'The path is wrong, perhaps the path is wrong.' Did I owe him such sheer honesty, that no lies or love or joy could grow on the face of it? On his great day, when Independence Hall ran over with his praise? Perhaps, but there is more blame to come, and greater. And then the noise died and the people fled and it was an ordinary late afternoon among rows of scattered chairs. And by nightfall it did not seem to matter any more.

We left Sam to his devices that afternoon. He went up to his room to nap, and Tom and I sought out some local tavern and drowned our joy in a nut-brown liquid very much like it. Then, just before the great supper, as night fell black and flat on Chestnut Street and our heads rang with the faint echoes of an afternoon drink, we sought him out. Arm in arm, we rumbled up the stairs of the Liberty and burst upon his room. Sam was in bed. 'Come on, man,' I cried, kicking the foot of the bed and lighting a candle. 'The best is to come!'

'Come on, philosopher,' added Tom, softer. 'You have a reputation to make.'

'I shan't come down,' Sam said. He lay with his head against the bedboard, propped on cushions, and rubbed his palms together slow and thoughtless, with the dry swish of skin. The room stank of grief, the dull sweat of crying. But there was no trace of that left in him and his eyes were clear as bells.

'Go on, Tom – go yourself, you have earned the dinner, and Phidy too. This is your occasion. I have done with it.'

Tom sat down in the stiff low chair by the door. Perhaps because I had expected something of this, I spoke out first. 'Come on, Sam, *don't be a fool. Throw something on and come down. The hard part is done. The mayor is expected, the dean of Pennsylvania College, Dr Silliman from the* Journal of American Science, *besides a dozen wealthy young men looking for a cause . . . This is your great debut – your dance-card is full.'*

'Sam,' Tom said at last, then paused. 'You owe me this at least.' Syme *had no answer for that, and I felt again suddenly how small my part was in this play. 'This is your great chance.'*

'My chance for what, Tom? A lectureship? The ear of the mayor – somewhat red and hairy, it must be admitted. A long article in the Inquirer, *perhaps even the* Journal of American Science *itself? A hundred subscriptions? I doubt even that many would sign, and we need twice that.'*

'To prove that you are right,' Tom said, answering Sam's first question. 'This is your chance to prove that you are right.'

'I know that I am right. That is the only satisfaction I desire.'

'NO, IT IS NOT!' Tom roared, with his blood up at last. 'Else what have I to do here, Sam? These two years?'

'I am sorry, Tom.' Sam for once was the calmer of the two. I looked for somewhere to sit down, could not find it, and leaned against the window sill. I was – curious.

'Among other things, this is a chance to mix with your own, Sam. Not a dim but hopelessly enthusiastic young newspaperman and a German country doctor sent away by his pa. These men are your kind. You belong among 'em.'

'I belong at home with my own pa. I belong with bargemen – farmers – clerks – trinket-shop ladies. All men whose belief is not a faculty of their wit, but their faith and thoughtfulness. I assure you that I will not find such men at that dinner.'

'Is that why you left the university and pursued your career with the army? And then left the army to join us? To escape men of wit?'

'You know the story behind that. This is unkind of you, unlike you.'

'Do you fear these little men so much, that they will find you out?'

'I have found them out,' Sam cried, stirred up at last. 'What have I to win?'

'A lectureship, influence, commissions, companions, subscriptions.

A chance to pursue this thought you have had and broadcast it from an appropriate height. To prove it to the World, and, Sam, you know as well as I that the world does not reckon much of the faith of bargemen, farmers, clerks and trinket-shop owners.'

'Tom, I am sick at heart and wish to leave this business. At least for a time. I do not like these occasions – not in this disposition you see me in. I have not stirred through the hours, nor slept. I only stared at the door and waited for you to come in – to put the bellows to me as I knew – and now I wait until you leave me so I can sleep. I have proved this thing to myself and there is no other judge so hard and grudging – nor yet so generous when satisfied of the case. I am satisfied. Today I was satisfied.'

'I know you better, Sam. You have never been happy alone. You will dry up in a month, then burn away. Phidy, have you nothing to say?'

What had I to say? I could as well leave a great blank gap to the bottom of the page, then scatter a thousand inky thoughts upon it, running over one another in every direction, till not a single one was clear enough to read. What could I say? Only that afternoon, in the roaring middle of Sam's greatest applause, I had felt that awkward, terrible wriggle of doubt that runs through and rots our dearest loves and faiths. And turns us from our friends.

'Tom, let's leave him for a night. He has done his work, let us do ours. We can consider it again in the morning. He is not fit to come down now. We may do our griefs as well as our loves mischief with false good humour. He has no heart left for a feast.'

I would like to say that I gave that answer because the one clear thing I knew was that Sam's magical theories were wrong. That I answered as I did because I hoped to protect him from the great, heart-breaking disappointment that would come of pursuing his calculations. There seemed little point in telling him my doubts then, and for that night at least I may be pardoned this dishonesty. But this doubt had nothing to do with my answer, as I came to understand clearly in the months to come. I think that even then I guessed the real root of it. I saw perhaps that Sam's failure was my chance – my chance to beat out Tom for the watchpost at Sam's side.

'Do you know?' Sam began quietly, mostly to Tom, as we prepared our dress for dinner. 'Ben Silliman took my hand – in both his
– as I left the lecture. Apologized – that was his word – for our mis-
understandings; said he hoped to bring me round the office of the
Journal – some day. Have a chat. There was time enough at dinner
– he promised – for all we had to say to each other. His very words:
"all we have to say to each other" . I never guessed – success –
meant joining Ben Silliman, and his kind.'

'I shouldn't worry about that,' Tom said, looking him in the eye.
'This is the end of it. I will have nothing to do with this theory
again.' Sam caught his gaze and held it; said nothing, pressing his
knuckle to his lip, a countenance neither in sorrow nor in anger,
though he would not budge until Tom turned first aside, blinking
sharply and pinching the sniff in his nose, to clatter out.

I followed Tom down the stairs to the great dinner. 'Why Ben
Silliman?' I whispered to him, closing the door behind me.

'Sam could never abide', Tom answered, in plain matter of fact,
'the favour of lesser men. Condescension, he would say. Why do
you suppose we found him where he was – where he will remain.'

Why Sam stopped short there I can only guess. I have touched on
this before – the natural desire of the great man to turn aside from
triumph, at the last minute, the battle won. The need for failure
itself, a fitting injustice. Perhaps that, and a son's grief, and a long
day, and a tired heart. (Alas, that this was only a postponement.)

We still had the dinner to endure. Our first apologies for Sam's
'present indisposition' were met with great cries of 'Shame!
Shame!' and 'Fetch him! Drag him out!' but those soon gave way
to other shouts: 'More wine! The red stuff! Another dish of potatoes!' Tom sat among his cronies from the Inquirer, and with his
great gift for happiness laughed and drank as merry as a schoolboy
sipping his first punch. He had some spell with which he could
suspend a thought, wingless, rootless, fluttering just above his
head, until he called it down, and considered it, and engaged it.
Perhaps that was the halo about his head, a ring of worries, put
off, smoothed out, balanced so delicate he must keep still.

I remember chiefly from this occasion the bright glitter of silver,

499

the smoking lamps, and the headache raging like a lost child at the foot of my skull. It must have been the effects of the afternoon's ale. I sat with Dr Polidori – Pollydolly, as Sam once called him – who spoke at great length of arms, and with much mastication of vowels, of the Astounding Prospects of Mr Syme. 'He might do something, Dr Müller, he might reach an eminence . . .' – and here he sketched the eminence in question with a flourish of forks, and placed it somewhere just above the boiled chicken – 'if he would let himself be taken in . . .' He never explained to me what was meant by this taking in, though he implied that he had in mind about an inch and a half in the length of sleeve. I did not ask him – for though I mocked dear Pollydolly, I could not help but – no, I shall not write 'agree'. For I remember this too from the dinner, for I had seen it a hundred times before: I remember how the first flush of delighted belief that greeted Sam's oratory at its height gave way (in a minute or an afternoon) to admiration. And how short a step it was from admiration to affection; and from there, by a natural and inevitable process, that shining vision of an unguessed world gave way to a good piece of advice.

The saddest effect that followed Sam's Cause was not disbelief nor even mockery, but the complacent concern of lesser men – my own, I am rather afraid, included. How often did I see proud Ben Silliman glance at the time and look about him, unused to disappointment; as if Sam, like a wooden cuckoo, would appear upon the hour. Whenever his glass emptied of sweet red, or his companion, the lady mayoress herself in a green gown, began to pall, he lifted the thick gold watch from his fob and pinched his florid nose, wrinkling his brow in a very public show of private concern. Shook the device, pressed it to his ear, to hear the seconds ticking over, proving time passed at its usual rate. Then returned the watch to some silk recess of his girth, shaking his head now as if to say that the usual rate left little time for such men as Sam to squander his own.

I do not think Sam slept; shadows from his guttering lamp played beneath his door as I returned, drunker and unhappier still, to my own bed at last.

*

*A coach was ready in the morning, the horses steaming in the brisk
dawn air, and I had only to stumble out of bed into a travelling
sleep. A cold ache and a crooked neck awoke me at lunchtime. Then
the coach rambled south through the soft afternoon, making the only
stir in that windless perfect blue air. We spent the night with
Cousin James – arriving in the thick, crackling evening, too sleepy
to talk, or do anything but swallow crusts of old bread with fresh
milk still warm from the long sun; leaving in the drenched morning,
too sleepy to talk. James stood in the middle of the empty Main
Street, neither waving nor moving till we were out of sight.*

*The bright lake opened through a gap in the trees and vanished
again, as the coach rumbled on. Sam brought his right hand to his
snuffling nose and drew Tom to him with his left. 'I heard your
protestations, remember that,' he said kindly. 'Do not think yourself
ill-used – or ill-loved – simply because I abuse my own prospects.
There is nothing more you can do for me – that's what grieves you.
And that you seemed to plead the more heartless cause. No one
doubts your good heart. If I no longer need your good offices – it is
not they that failed me – but I who failed them. We give ourselves to
Ideas – as if they were not ours – and we serve them and sacrifice
others to them – as we would be ashamed to do in our own cause. I
have done as much for you. I would not add my mother (or my
father even, rot him) to the list of my neglect. Not though I have
Truth on my side – never doubt that, either. Never doubt it, Tom.
But we haven't such right to it as we pretend.'*

*He drew Tom's head beneath his own and kissed his hair. His
own face was still thick and gentle with tears, and I have never seen
such a tender paw for comfort as his hand. Tom said nothing,
though I saw later that he wept. O comfort me, I thought. Sweet
Sam, smelling of shaved wood and misery, comfort Phidy in your
round arms. But he straightened again in the coach, snuffed his nose
with a blue handkerchief and said, 'If I talk fooleries, I am not myself
now. 'Tis only pomp that holds me up.'*

*Days can be slow work. But my mind slipped its moorings and
floated easy and unmoving over the passing hours like an idle boat
letting the waves run beneath it. A night passed, and then a*

501

morning, and still we scarcely spoke with our heavy-desired home-
coming. I feared an end, for my father called me home as Sam's had
done. I could see no cause to keep me. Sam's ambition had dried up,
our coffers were empty, and our company rode towards disband-
ment. I had no choice but to sail . . . have I not said home already,
and can I in the space of a few lines use the word for so distant and
different a destination? We did not ask what was to become of Sam.

At length the low hills of Baltimore came into sight, and in their
uninterested shadow we reached the town. Our long-hated, travel-
ling, unchanging, cramped abode grew suddenly dear to us. What
strange reluctance we felt to leave those indifferent quarters. For
how many times on the long road had we thought of a quiet,
unmoving day, with the freedom to walk ten paces to the left if we
chose in the morning? We did not want it now it came, and sat in
the still carriage while the horses sweated in harness. 'A word before
we go,' Tom said. He looked at Sam and then at me and descended
for once from his high perch. 'Kitty and I are going
to be married. She has accepted me.' He held up a letter from the
same pile that brought Sam's darker news. 'As this business seems
finished, I may return to the Southern Courier *in the fall.'*

Then the driver cried, 'Get off with you, lads, the horses need
tending.' Our long, companionable, silent journey was broken up.
We stretched our stiff knees and propped our hands beneath our
backsides and yawned.

'I am pleased for you, Tom,' Sam said gallantly. 'She is a sweet
bun.'

Edward greeted us in tears. He embraced Sam long and silently, but
even in his son's arms peered across his shoulder and saw
company. He was led astray by his charm as a child is led by the ear.
'I am sorry to intrude a private grief on your welcome,' he said,
stretching his arm from Sam's clasp and taking Tom by the hand.
'But I have only one son.' He smiled sweetly, but I should have
preferred a ruder, warmer greeting.

They were slow weeks that followed. Though we were often idle
that summer, it had been an ever-shifting idleness, of travel or talk,

company or scenery. Suddenly there was nothing to do. I stayed with Sam in Baltimore for a time, at a loose end. Tom left for Pactaw to see Kitty and arrange his affairs with the Southern Courier. Our enterprise had spent its force. I do not know how much I was to blame, if blame can be assigned to a shift in intimacies. I believe it can. At least I had done myself little good. I had no employment, no home, no purpose.

Yet I was reluctant to leave. Home was a changed prospect to me now. My thoughts of Neuburg had grown weak indeed. Only a duty called me back. A grave duty, true, towards a much-loved, worthy father, imprisoned in the Prince's wine cellar, awaiting trial. But I was young, and Sam was a much-loved, worthy friend, in equal need. He stood at hand, in plain colours, in full form and flesh. He did not call to me from those thin bones, dressed in niggardly black ink, lying in that bare graveyard of the page, rattling, 'Come.' So I trailed the coats of Sam's grief and found in it a most welcome misery.

I have always been drawn to the first flush of grief, like the fall of a storm. That great ranting and breaking calleth to me. Look, look, I cry, like a child at lightning. The sudden landscape of night is illuminated and dark things like love and misery grow clear as day, but without the bustle of activity that hides them then. Grief calls to me. But I have never been able to abide its duration. I have no ship for those seas, only a skiff that seeks the harbour after the first great wind. Heavy fortune, like a heavy sky, soon palls unless it lightens and flickers.

Sam's own misery grew hard to watch. He moved meekly about the house in his father's shadow. For the first weeks, at least, even his temper deserted him. We awoke late most mornings and sat long over breakfast. Then Sam and I took it in turns to bring the day another hour or so along. We visited the church where Anne was buried, and forgot the flowers Sam wished to strew on her grave. So we sought out some wild bunch, a good hour spent among the woods. Even as we laid those plucked stems down, brittle against her gravestone, in spite of his true grief the thought rose up, What shall we do next? Sam had no answer.

A week passed and another. Edward was chastened by Anne's

death. But he had not the stomach for hard grief and ate only the sweets of it. Sam bent under the load. He wished to spend more and more time alone. He slept much of the day and read much of the night, perched in the consoling hollow of a lamp's light, bright as a star in the general darkness. Yet he was gentler in company than before, with a sweet tongue and a listening ear. In the first flush of humility, he grew attentive, if not loving, to his father. Edward had seen Anne die, and he was rich in circumstances, like a soldier on St Crispin's Day. At first, Sam urged me to his company, as an excuse perhaps for his solitary grief. 'Make a note of him,' he said, knowing I kept a journal. 'He is worth the study.'

School had not yet returned to session, and Edward and I spent much of our days together. At first we talked of Sam, but he led us, even in absence, to a broader intimacy. Edward had an attentive nature and asked after my travels and plans, with a curiosity that was beneath his son. We explored Baltimore together, and Edward showed me its humble beauties – poky cobbled side-streets, running betwixt sweet red brick – with a mixed pride. 'A country of barbarians,' he said, 'in a palace of Nature.' We walked around the harbour, climbed the low hill on which MacPherson stood his ground in 1812, swept our eyes along the throat of the Chesapeake, stretching forth towards the Atlantic; visited the Indian ruins near by. Then he took me to his school, a white-boarded house with three rooms. I sat on one of the tiny stools in his classroom, dusty with summer, and looked out, feeling like a boy again, wondering at and waiting for the world. Trees waved and scratched a blue sky.

When sorrows come they come not single spies, but brothers. If I spent so much of my time in Edward's company, my fears for my own father may have led me to look kindly on Sam's. The trial was fixed for the new year – Prussian agents wished to track the flood of revolution to its source, before determining my father's fate. They would not credit the fountainhead poured from a smoky basement in Fischersallee, where an old bureaucrat entertained such students and soldiers who liked to talk fantasies and prophecies in their cups. The time for decision was at hand. My official purpose in America had been over since the spring. The burst of activity that followed through the summer had also finished. I would have to go.

I planned to sail as soon as Tom married, a final celebration to send me to my old life again. 'You may have Bubbles' room in the meantime,' Edward said.

'It may be as long as two months.'

'All the better. I need footsteps in the house, you see.'

I grew close to Edward then, as Sam had wished. He was a charming man, attentive to all guests. And I was a gentleman from the Old World, the 'little minister', with an accent and occupation that ennobled me in the eyes of an outcast Englishman.

The home I dwelt in had changed greatly since my first visit. Edward had the run of it now and hired a cook, Mary Quinn, a big, young girl with plain tastes. She loved a clean house and often chased Edward's dusty shoes from the kitchen. 'Peace, Mary,' he cried, fleeing her dust-pan and laughing. 'I will not endure it. I hide in fear in my own house and tiptoe through the very door.' She was an indifferent cook, who burned the meat and left potatoes hard as apples in the pot. But she had a gift for cakes, and Edward loved her company, though she was a big-boned lady, as Anne had been. Bubbles took to her at once, and the two often spent the afternoon baking and sweating themselves into a state. Plum-cakes and custard-tarts and cherry-pies, sprinkled with cinnamon, were forged in that great furnace of a kitchen, and emerged bright with juice and steaming for our tea.

Sam could not abide her. He had changed. His mourning entered a new season, and he found his temper. Edward took the brunt of it, after his brief grace. 'I will not stay to hear you giggling with Mary, a week after Mother was put in the ground. We did not have cakes when she could eat them.'

'She did not make them, Sam,' Edward cried.

'Two months have passed, Sam,' I added. 'We cannot live in a church.' Perhaps I should have kept my tongue.

'He would not call a doctor till the end, Phidy. Bubbles told me. Even then, he wished to bring the apothecary's son, fussing with some nonsense of a root called pipsissiway, till she stopped him.

"He's a clever lad," he said, "who studies hard. We are not such who can afford to be bled for the head-ache." Though all the while he thinks himself the King of England, I suppose, with his air and his education and damned refinements in this "barbarous" land. Have you not marked, Phidy, that his speech grows daintier with each passing day as he hears you speak it . . .' I turned my head in shame. Edward could not see for tears. Great fearless Mary hid her face in her apron. Sam was the only one she heeded. Even she looked bright when the 'young master' came into the room, if he did not glare at her.

I turned from him a little in those weeks, when perhaps he needed my companionship the most. But he abused it when he had it. Perhaps he desired my loyalty to run so deep that it would not split nor turn aside, break and chafe it as he would. I do not think I owed him that debt. He wished to have things sure 'despite all considerations'. He was suspicious of Edward now and desired me to 'be wary of him', with an eye long practised in its jealousy. He all but desired me to avoid him. Then he did desire it. I would not. 'Despite all considerations' he wished us to love him, considerations such as his kindness or the virtue of his enterprise or his deserts. He had no right to it.

After the first few weeks, Sam spent more and more time in Pactaw, visiting Tom and Mrs Simmons. To my surprise, I did not wish to join them. I was happy in Baltimore and had no part in their lovers' lives. I had grown tired of the company of young men, too, was glad to return to a fixed home and ordinary prospects. 'Will you come for once?' Sam said, when the first north wind blew upon us in October. 'Tom misses you sorely, he says, fears some coldness lies between you.'

'I have no business there, Sam.'

'You have none here,' he said, smiling, and smiles were rare between us then.

'I am a cuckoo in your nest. Your father grows lonely without you.'

'I will answer to my own father, Phidy, as you may to yours. I did not think you would forget my wishes so soon.'

'Sam, you thrust us together. "Make a note of him," you said, "if you love me. He holds a key to my heart, and you may peer in the hole."'

'He has lost it, Phidy. Come once with me,' he said, in a gentler tone, 'bring all the old band together. Tom is to be married soon.'

No, I said again, for I could be as stubborn as Sam. I could not fathom my own reluctance, but my blood was up and I would not give in. This was my first betrayal of Sam. A small one, but just of the kind that rankles: that I gave his father so much of my time and talk.

Much of the time I spent reading, alone, and slept in the shortening afternoons. I finished Waverley at last, one crisp evening, then stared at the growing dark. A single bell tolled. Edward stood always on the balls of his feet, and so he entered now, lightly, with something under his arm. He flung his coat beside me on the settee, then perched on the piano stool with his back to the keys. I had to turn my head to look at him, but he was gone again. 'A moment, sir,' he cried and left for the kitchen. 'Aren't they lovely,' I heard Mary say, then someone clattered outdoors and the creak and clang of the pump began. What could he be about, I wondered?

He came in slowly now, with a brown jug held between his hands from which flowers bloomed. Two roses and a sprig of white buds scattered like stars around their heavier planets. 'I filled it too high,' he said. 'It is a task for the girls, d'you see, but they must have their drink.' I saw the source of Sam's impracticality, whose deficiencies Tom had worked so hard to supply. The water trembled at the jug's rim and he set it down on the polished top of the piano. He quickly saw his error and took a sheaf of songs from the stand and now set the jug upon it. The water lipped over and darkened a patch of music. I laughed and rose to help him, stooped and drank quickly from the jug, to both our surprise, then lifted it slowly and left. 'He is a child,' Mary said when she saw me. I poured half out of the kitchen window, then returned and set it on a newspaper. I joined Edward on the settee.

'I bought the vase over lunch,' he said. 'Gypsies came round the school with bits and bobs for the children and I took this for myself. Anne liked flowers, you see. I set young Timothy to pick some for me after school. He sleeps, poor dim child, and does not attend, but it is cruel to punish him sorely. The other boys don't take to it either, though you would not credit it. He is their pet, poor lamb, but he won't learn; nor can he, I fear. Still, we can make his school days gentle. They are lovely, no?'

Anne had died just over two months earlier. He mourned her still, but with a light heart. His was a pretty grief. 'Anne liked pretty things, and flowers, roses especially, and the piano. So there we have them all together for her sake.'

'Sam cannot take it so lightly, sir. I fear for him. He does not attend to me, which I don't take amiss at such a time. But he neglects himself and that grieves me. He needs some occupation, or purpose at least, something beyond mourning.' We are never proud of the tone we take with our elders, but my worries were real enough.

'Has he not these theories he attends to? Don't that occupy him? I recall he made much of certain calculations concerning masses and orbits and so on, though they don't signify to me. Sam is cleverer than his father, Phidy, I'm afraid. But won't they serve?'

'Has he not said? He broke off his last engagement to return home, as much for you, I think, as Anne. Besides, he was in no state to continue. I could not say what he plans now. All that seems to be over, though he gave so much of himself to the cause, that's so.'

'What do you consider he should do, Phidy? What do you make of these theories?'

Before I could reply, Edward broke in, and on hearing him my answer swiftly changed. 'It has always seemed to me', he said, 'a madcap business. Hollows and spheres and gases, conjured out of . . . He's a bright boy, Phidy, but a strange one. Scarce another man thinks as he does. There is something else, too.' He paused to consider.

'Were I to tell a story, I should put more faces in it. Were I to explain what goes on below, like a myth, I should have people in it for a start and maybe caves. All these implosions and numbers and rotations seem dry to me. They smell of the abacus and the lecture hall and great big dusty geometrical tomes with cracked spines. One needs one's spectacles to see them.' He was joking partly, but he meant it, too. 'I should have a bit of colour down there. Goblins and

spooks and little dancing creatures. Fires and smells, you understand. Great stony monsters beating away with great hammers, and
sparks all ahoo, and a dreadful noise. And sinners repenting their
sins, or being boiled to pieces. And lots of shadows. Creatures with
huge hands and tiny faces, girls with deep voices. Men and women
confused and monsters with two heads. And dainty things, like tea
and tables, stretched and pinched as if you saw them in a spoon. A
horror of a place, to be sure. But with some life in it, a few faces.
I could not give myself to all those numbers without a few shapes I
knew what to make of. Though I dare say I'm talking hocus-pocus
and my son all the time a perfect Newton. Still, I shouldn't have
spent so much time on it without faces.'

What could I answer, when he said what I knew in my own heart
to be true? Had I not stayed for the faces, for Sam's principally, and
Tom's, Edward's, Mrs Simmons'? Had that not become my own
creed? Yet I felt Sam was right. 'Without considerations', he had
argued. My gorge rose as much at my own doubts as Edward's
naming of them. Then I recalled Sam's speech in Perkins. A bit of
his father's chicanery, Sam said, that story of elephants and eagles.
Sam was right, but his father's vision was less kind. Did not Anne
have big hands and a face upon a face? Her large bones appalled
him, and, in her need, he shrank from her blood and inarticulate
clamour. These were not idle pictures. Edward had raised the flag of
his imagination. Though he won my sympathy and my belief, as a
man of such niceties, I could not let him win my heart. So I
answered him.

'I once thought as you. As a story, I said to myself, to say nothing
of the science, I should have chosen another scene, a different subject
for my brush. Speaking as an artist, I mean, and I believe Sam wishes to be judged, at least in part, according to their fashion. The stars,
their extent and nature, should have drawn me first. Barring that,
perhaps creation itself, the processes of human life. As a doctor, I
have seen such mysteries first hand. There is much to be delved into.
I often find that narrow corners offer wider prospects of discovery
than open spaces.

'But there is a something in Sam I cannot quite shake from me.

509

You, sir, seem blessed with a bedevilled imagination. My own thoughts are often tempted by freaks and frolics. To us, Sam's improbable images seem cold, his conceptions smooth and lifeless. And yet . . . there is great consolation in numbers. Do you know, sir, I have often consoled myself with the drudgery of Sam's theories, their attention to calculation and detail. Perhaps because the charlatan binds half-truths lightly and would not cement them with such hard mortar and impractical falsehoods (as they once seemed to me). As I came to love him, sir, I wished him an honest man and misguided, rather than a cheat. Even though the latter is a happier trade. And yet . . .

'The more I think on these hollowed spheres beneath us, revolving endlessly in measured patterns; the brief coincidence of their faults, the eclipse of vacuii. Coincidences, I say, though Sam believes he will learn their seasons in time. These eclipses in their course breed storms, stir volcanoes, toss seas, ruin crops, burn cities, swallow ships, that in turn desolate nations and leave widowed wives and orphaned children, that in turn . . . you follow me, sir? Sam once said to me that precision is only one kind of abundance. He loves it for that reason. And his is an abundant world, more intricate than our fevered imaginations of gargoyles and ghasts; richer, too. Those shining revolutions . . . bright overlapping metals . . . bursting and colliding suns. The tale of disasters to be spun from such thread, of Pompeii and Sodom. You and I are drawn to deviations, freaks, things that suffer no explanation. But your son has made a muse of inevitability. It calls to him as beautifully as chance to us. It is a being full of light and colour in his eyes. Is not his the nobler faith?'

There was a clatter at the door and the thud of a dropped pack. Sam walked in. 'I have come a day early, as you see. I missed my Phidy,' he said, 'and knew we should return for Tom's wedding soon. And now your news?' He greeted us both easily, enquired after our healths. He was too much at ease for anything but happiness to sit smiling at his heart. He had overheard me, of that I am sure. I was moved to see how calm and content even my poor fervent admiration could make him. He was, though I had not suspected it before, a creature of loves. That night, Sam and I resumed all our old habits of intimacy.

In a week, we left for Pactaw and Tom's wedding. I said farewell to Edward at the door. He was ever gracious, especially in farewell. We two were closer kinned in nature than Sam and I. But I walked with his son down the garden path, linked arm in arm.

I slept through most of the journey to Pactaw and awoke with my thick head in the crook of Sam's elbow. Eyes shut, I breathed the odour of his side, rich and warm as baking bread in the sunshine trapped by the carriage window. His eyes were open, but he did not mark me until I sat up and said, 'A summer is not so long, after all.'

'No,' he answered absent-mindedly, 'but coming home always steals time.'

I began to note the first signs of Pactaw. The road dipped into the valley and ran beside the river for a space. The Apple Cart flew by us on the left, and I thought of that colder day when all our prospects lay clean as snow before us. Now the land was brown and green and cut across by rows of fallen trees (tipped over by the great storm, I suppose), whose roots reached from the dry earth like buried hands. Then we passed along the Dewdrop in a slower canter (old Barnaby sunned himself upon the stoop), and the town surrounded me, with a homecoming whose joy caught me by surprise. I had come a year before, a stranger to the place. Now I rode to Pactaw for a wedding and farewells.

My familiar eye tallied every street and house and tree. The market square, half-empty in declining day, a clutter of trampled greens underfoot. I looked long at the Boathouse across the water, gleaming under a lick of fresh paint; the fresh-built jetty below thronged by pleasure-boats, a thick fire smoking from the chimney. Even the crickets scraped a native air on their dry legs. The eucalyptus trees, with flowers in their hair, filled my breath. I know the song the sirens sing, and it is this: rest a while, you have been here before. A while, I thought, but I cannot stay.

My feet led me of their own sweet will back down Main Street towards the Dewdrop Inn. 'Shall we sup here?' I cried to Sam, lagging behind.

'If you please. Tom will take a glass of wine with us later, but he dines with his father-to-be. I would never believe it,' he said, coming up, 'I am out of breath. Grief has made me fat.'

A small boy, barefoot and sprouted from his leggings, stood at the post by the door on whose step old Barnaby sat. 'Your kind never do have horses,' the lad remarked sarcastically, spinning a coin in the air.

'What kind is that?' I asked him.

'Layabouts,' he answered, which pleased us somehow, and I gave him a penny for luck. 'It won't buy you that,' he said. 'But it might buy me something.'

'Hush now,' Barnaby cried, in his slow rasp. 'My niece's boy, a vicious creature. Ah, 'tis the Boxer himself,' he said, squinting against the last of the sun and addressing Sam. 'You should have gone far, sir, in that noble science, I believe.'

'Too late,' came the answer. 'For I have got fat and scant of breath. And wish to grow fatter.'

Sam and I ate our two great chops in hunger and silence. He was as common as a brother to me now, and time lay so light in our hands we could bear it between us without a word said. Sam was unhappy and quiet. I was only quiet. Then Tom came and spurred our spirits to a quicker gait. We sat for hours over glasses of ale at the Dewdrop, talking comfortably. Though afflicted by such separate and lonely considerations, we had each hoarded sufficient mirth to pay for one happy evening together.

'O Tom, what shall I do without you?' Sam said at last. 'At least I have my widow to turn to.' I had never heard him call Mrs Simmons by that name, as if she were a badge of middle age. Then the church-bell rang its ten slow steps into the night. Sam rose and said, 'They call me to her, gentlemen. Bless you, Tom. Kitty is a sweet lass. But there is much to be said – for widows with heavy purses. Remember the proverb – "For blood grows old and cold, and so (thank God) does gold." The round is yours Phidy. Good night.'

'He jests only from a heavy heart,' Tom said, after Sam had gone.

'It is something else, Tom. He grows gentle slowly. Another glass with you?'

'No, thank you, Phidy.' He rose to leave. Even now I wished to linger beside them, when they turned to their own purposes. 'You sleep with me tonight, I believe?' Tom said. 'I have taken a room on Seymour Lane.' Then he added, as if someone had just brought the news, 'I am to be wed tomorrow.'

We lingered at the lamp-post outside his gate. Tom, whose body had grown more eloquent than his tongue, twined himself about it and about, supple with sadness. 'I suppose, Phidy,' he began, then paused. I had known him for a year, and still I sought some peep-hole to his thoughts – a sweet creature, easy in joy and easily upset, occasionally peevish, tireless and faithful in love. He would be married on the morrow, and I hoped perhaps to gossip my way into his affections. 'I suppose', he resumed at last, 'you won him after all. In the end – you understand me.' Even then he could not turn the talk to his own life, or would not, though I desired with all my heart for some speech touching the matter nearest Tom's own. 'You won him after all.' He had a guilty air, too, as if he confessed a secret. 'Too late, however, I suppose. It is all the same now,' he said.

What is? I thought. But he had gone to the door and slipped inside with a finger on his lips. We tiptoed to the second floor and undressed in silence. 'Kitty,' he called me, joking, as we lay side by side in bed. 'Tomorrow Kitty will lie there.' He soon fell asleep, more easily than I.

The wedding day dawned in a brisk hurry of clouds. We ran into the church with our heads bent under a quick shower of rain. The church filled with people and noise and the smell of wet clothes. (Pactaw had gone to great lengths to prove its finery. I observed with a secret smile the red necks of unfamiliar collars; the pinched bosoms of outgrown frocks; not to mention sly snifflings snuffed in the damask folds of best shawls.) Tom's father, a vicar himself, presided with efficient cheerfulness.

'As this is not my church, I don't mind SHOUTING to keep order. Jeb, keep young Tommy tight on your LAP, even if he is dirty and bites. I won't have him throwing hats at the choir. The good Reverend Docket has been kind enough to let me borrow his church for an afternoon, for he only lets it from the Lord, and he may, I hope, sub-lease it as he wishes. We are all cousins in the eyes of God

*(no nearer, praise Him). As most of you know, I have come to seal
my son and Kitty Thomas in eternal happiness. If the rest of you
would be quiet for a moment, the choir might have their sing, and
we can translate the pair into holy bliss as soon as possible.'*

The makeshift scenery of marriage was set in place, the props and
actors of the stage. The citizens gathered below, the heroine stood in
splendid array, and the music played. There was much gold and fine
cloth and a great sweat. The two lovers entered stage left and marched
to the head of the platform. They gave their lines beautifully, too clear
and loud for life, and even Kitty's whispers echoed in the silent hall.
There was a shout and tears and the play was over and the crowd fled
in great spirits and noise and the scenery was taken down and the
actors left wondering which life to turn to. But then the party began
and they were led triumphant from the theatre, in a carriage with
white horses down the street through a river of men. Someone had
brought a trumpet on the way and tooted hymns above the cantering
hoofs. Even the fathers sang. All the way to the house of Pa Thomas,
the prosperous baker, who had put a tent in his garden and more cake
and food than the Pied Piper's crew could eat at once.

By the afternoon a great wind had swept the clouds from the sky.
We were shouting like sailors across the tables. Pa Thomas sent
forth his servants and hushed us with bottles of champagne. At last
we each sparkled with a glass and looked up, waiting. Sam rose to a
speech, with a voice to carry across the busy winds.

'I feel indeed as if I have given – my own bride away to marriage,'
he called. *'Tom has been my dearest friend – my most faithful
comrade for many years. He has worked tirelessly for our cause.
And if at times I have been mean in thanks – it is only because I had
not the heart to bear our disappointments – and I knew he could. I
cannot imagine a truer friend. I know that some among you – all
good and sensible people – have wondered at his dedication. He
wastes himself – you thought – on a blind faith. I know the gossip. I
may be mad – but I am not deaf.'* A few people laughed, and I knew
then I could never hide from him.

*'Blind faith. What a strange phrase that is. Tom is blind and deaf
to doubt – for he does not trust his eyes or head – but he will grapple*

514

you to his heart with hoops of steel. Which is the wiser, I ask: an intimate hand or a spectacled curiosity? Tom does not look to either side of him. So he neither swerves from his purpose – nor turns from his love. A skill, I think, that will serve a wife as well as a scientist. Kitty, I could not wish you a truer husband. The gossip may cease now, I believe. Tom has joined the race of respectable men.' The laughter was now general. 'If I were a young lady, Kitty . . . I should have fought you tooth and nail for his hand. But I yield to a fairer rival – and wish you both the joy that is Tom's peculiar gift.' Kitty went to him and kissed him on the cheek, and everyone else began to eat.

There was a great crowd, of penguins and peacocks, the men in black and white and the women bright as feathers in their summer dresses. Nobody looked at ease. The peacocks talked among themselves, with a penguin between them. Mothers and grandmothers stood with children flapping unobserved around their knees. The wind puffed to burst its cheeks. It blew the dresses right round, wrapping the ladies like fish in newspaper. 'Come under the marquee,' cried Pa Thomas, 'come under the marquee!' So we huddled like birds on a sandbank, and there were great cries of 'Pardon me, madam' and 'Is that your foot?' I wondered if the gulls had similar calls. But the tent served little purpose, except to bring us to the tables of cake and champagne.

Then there was a crack and a flap and a thud and the canvas sky came falling about our ears. The ladies screamed as if lightning had struck. Two old men were rolled like a sausage in the fallen pavilion. A pole knocked me on the head and a table tipped over in the scurry. We all cheered, drunk and laughing, but did not venture beneath it when the tent was propped up. Squashed cake lay like leftover snow in the grass. 'Heaven has fallen,' said Jeb gallantly to a pretty girl, 'and risen again.'

I have not told the real issue of Tom's wedding, nor described its most important guest. Joy, like sorrow, comes in brotherhood. And the day that sealed the course of Tom's life ushered a new season in Sam's, a season that brought with it such fruition as we had all desired until perhaps it came. Sam was dressed in his finest sorrow for the marriage, and spoke with such kind love as I had never known in him. He had the air of a summer day whose heavy atmosphere has been lightened by a swift storm, and all is still and the breath sweet though cold for an hour or two perhaps, until the old heaviness comes down again.

The bells rang out six o'clock and our spirits began to flag, happily, like the light-filled sails that bring a boat to shore with the land-breeze at sunset. We grew quiet and watchful. The wind blew a flap of the tent against a table and its bottle of champagne, but ever failed to knock it down. The children sat in a heap on Tom's mother. Even Kitty failed to keep her sharp tongue, grew silent with her arm around Tom and did not attend to the slight talk around her, nor to her husband indeed. Her eyes twitched when she saw a stranger at the garden gate, blown open by the wind and clanging to and fro against its post. My eyes followed hers, for I had made her my study of the afternoon. A gentleman pushed the gate open and closed it carefully behind him, though the latch refused to stick and he abandoned it at last. He waved at all of us, though we did not know him, and came towards us.

He was a tall, pink man with moist hands, as I found from his soft handshake. But he had not a nervous temperament, and stood surprisingly at ease in our small company, for an intruder. He could not have been much older than thirty.

'I am sorry to disturb you on such an occasion, but I have come lately from Baltimore where your father directed me, Dr Syme – a most hospitable man. I seem to have arrived at the feast.' He smiled. He gave the impression of having a great deal of time, though he understood that others around him were less blessed than he in that particular. 'Perhaps you don't remember me, Tom. My name's Ezekiel. Harcourt.'

Tom was instantly attentive, as always, to someone who could do Sam a bit of good. 'Of course, sir, I recall: that foul day at Perkins and the miserable Mr Cooling. What business could have brought you there I can't imagine, but it was kind of you to attend, though Sam was sickening a little that day . . .' Tom protested too much.

His offices were over, and I watched for a sharp look from Kitty, but none came.

'Indeed it was my pleasure, Tom, a welcome respite from the business that brought me there. Sir,' he turned to Sam, 'I was interested, a great word with me. Rarely do I have the occasion to apply it. That other business came to no purpose, as it happens, so I would be glad if something good could be saved from a bad day . . . How much money, Sam, would you require for a magazine?'

'I would not have this – come upon your wedding for the world, Tom,' Sam answered. 'It is no longer your affair.'

'Kitty can spare me a minute? My sweet love, you do not mind?'

'A minute or two I can spare, Tom. I leave you gentlemen to your . . . business.' She walked through the happy wreckage of the wedding-party, towards a wilful boy, hanging and banging on the gate.

'I am sorry, gentlemen. I did not guess I had dug up a bone of contention.'

'There is no contention, sir. Only Tom has just accepted a post at the Southern Courier, and my German friend is called home. Alas, I am not their only duty. But they were my props and I wonder whether I can walk without them.' There was a silence, broken only by the flaps and freaks of the marquee, loud as whips.

'I might stay,' I said at last.

'Think, Phidy,' Tom said. 'You must be certain.'

'I have often acted as secretary to my father. They called me the little minister in the court. I think', I said, looking straight at Tom, 'I know what your duties were.'

'That is settled then,' said Mr Harcourt. 'I will not intrude my business on the marriage feast. Indeed, I am sorry now to have come at all.' He paused, and added with an odious air, 'Though I hope you are not.'

'No, indeed, Mr Harcourt,' I said quickly, taking him by the arm. 'I will show you to the gate. We hope to hear from you shortly. A note at the Dewdrop Inn will find me for the time. I'm afraid you will think us a band of gypsies, but the truth is, another week would have found me under sail. I am glad of the chance to stay, however. Even in Pactaw of Pactaw County. That is the blessing of this coun-

517

try. There is no one like Sam in all the courts of Europe, and here we find him in a corner by himself.'

'That is what I hope to change, Phidy. May I call you that?' he inquired smilingly and took his leave.

'There,' I said proudly, rejoining my friends. 'Tom could not have done better.'

'What do you think of old Easy Harcourt?' Tom said.

'Is that what we call him? "Easy" is good. He had me by the "Phidy" before we reached the gate. A foul man, though wealthy, you say? All honey till he sticks to your hands, though I should not think he is sweet, when crossed.'

'Phidy,' Sam broke in, 'are you sure of this?'

'Of what?'

'Have you the heart to stay?'

'I did not think twice before I answered "yes". But if asked twice, I will answer "yes" again.'

'Do not answer me tonight, Phidy,' Sam said. 'Your own father needs you. Easy has offered us no postponement. This is the sticking-point. If you say "yes", who knows when you will turn home again or what you will find there?'

'I will think on it, if you wish, Sam.' Yet in my heart, did I not know it was a postponement, a season prolonged? 'But you know my love for you, and that has only one answer.'

'Sam,' Tom said. 'May I speak with Phidy alone for a moment?'

'I will find Kitty,' he said, 'and quiet her fears.'

'Phidy.' He turned to me with an air I could not read, a kind of remorse. 'You do not owe him this. I may follow his fortune if I abided his defeats.'

'You cannot, Tom; look about you. Sam himself said it. You have joined the race of respectable men. The paper awaits you. Your new father stares at us. Kitty weeps in Sam's arms, but he cannot comfort her. These are games for young men, and you have other duties now.' I could not help adding, 'I have won – you said as much yourself.'

'Oh, I would love to stay for his triumph, just that long. To see all those little mocking men scrambling in his shadows.'

'You must leave him some time. That much is clear for all of us.

It is only a question of the occasion. I hope mine will be as happy.'

'Perhaps you're right, Phidy. Well, I must see to my new wife.'

As I watched him cross the garden to Kitty, I could not help but mutter, 'Tom, oh Tom, I do not have your faith.'

Then Sam took me by the elbow and said, 'A magazine, Phidy. Our very own, after all. Just the thing to give old Ben Silliman and his kind – a kick in the breeches.'

Tom and Kitty left that night for their honeymoon, by river-boat towards Norfolk along the Potomac. 'I have a fancy to see New York again,' Tom said, 'before we settle in Richmond by the Courier.'

'I thank you most of all, Phidy,' Kitty said. 'Tom would not trust that great baby to anyone else's care.'

'I will have my eye on you, Herr Mooler, never forget it,' Tom said, and I waited for a smile but none came. 'Perhaps I will ride to Pactaw some time to see how you get along.'

'Kitty, see that he thinks of something other than Sam's great theories for a week or two. It will do him good.'

'I think so too, Phidy. I will do my best.'

They had a full moon for their river journey, and I was lonelier when they left.

Sam and I slept at the Dewdrop that night, and stayed a while over our last glass of ale.

'It is some destiny, Sam,' I said, half-joking, 'that Easy should come just as we gave up hope. I look on it as proof of our triumphant fate.'

'On the contrary, it is a proof of my theories, of mathematics. In all justice, I lost my right to success when I turned from Philadelphia. But life is only a question of conjunctions, and the seasons they usher in.'

He was right, too, and the season that followed ended in another conjunction, of men and circumstances, that yielded a rare and great eclipse.

'What are you thinking, Sam?'

'That I shall miss Tom. And that I have always envied him.' Then, after a pause, 'Remember what I said. Think on it tonight, Phidy, and do only as you please.'

'I will.'

'Then drink up. There is work to be done in the morning, of one kind or another.'

I had a task that night and sat at the table by my bed, writing another letter to my father. How lightly I dropped a fine coat upon the floor now; left a cravat dangling loosely over the back of a chair. My hair unkempt – those fine brown locks falling at their own sweet will about my face, so that I knuckled them from my brow, more than once, before the letter was done. Some ease at least had been learned; a certain primness forgotten. Did I stay because I could not bear to lose such changes I had rung upon myself? Did I fear my father's anger at my delay, and so delay the more? Did I remain because I mistrusted the vicissitudes of my own home more than Sam's? 'My dear Sir,' I began. 'I am sorry to write you only with news of another postponement, though it may be a happy one, I hope, and find both our circumstances improved on my return . . .'

Or did I linger simply because I could not part from Sam – yet.

The first order of the day was to secure lodgings. Easy found us a house on Whippet Lane, in a formerly grand though never genteel neighbourhood of Pactaw, away from the river, towards the low hills in the west. The lane once led to the racetrack. But Pactaw had suffered greatly in the last decade from enthusiasm, which had drowned out those loose games in the tide begun twenty years before with the sermons at Cane Ridge. Church End had become the fashionable quarter. The track now was simply a round brown field that grew out of the end of the street and then fell away into trees.

Hotels and taverns had lined the street in its heyday, when Pactaw was an English town, a drunken night's rest for merchants sailing up the Potomac, or farmers bringing their goods to Norfolk, and thence the world. The buildings were still grand, though somewhat fallen in. All the business had shut down. A distant rumour of a man, Mr Talbot from New York, had bought up much of the lane, and split the great houses into apartments and let them, mostly to large families whose parents had known better lives: schoolteachers and newspapermen, and in one case the large and

shouting brood of a theatrical match. Ours, once the least and
darkest of the inns, had been left to itself, and now, by revolution,
had become the smartest house by 'the Races', as we all still called
the muddy field at the bottom, where torn papers and bedraggled
pamphlets among the leaves announced its old and busier purpose.
It was a draughty, ghostly, windy, cold place, gone in the tooth. The
cheap glass in the window panes had grown fat and cloudy at the
bottom, so Sam and I saw the world through a Hamburg fog, except
for the sky, which shone through the thin pane on top, clear as winter air. We had no need of a cook and turned the kitchen into our
parlour; spent divers afternoons by the great iron stove, smoking our
pipes and warming our hands flat on the sour metal, saying little
or nothing, happy in our common cause against the cold. It was so
cold when we first moved in that we burned the chairs.

I missed the Boathouse, sure. Sam had a taste for dilapidation;
this, I argued, was taking things too far. Yet I was never happier in
America (which means never happier in the world) than by the
Races – where I got Sam to myself at last.

The second order of business was to see Easy's father. We set off
one dark November morning west from the Potomac for a visit of a
few days. An oriole woke Sam and me at black dawn, and then Easy
called for us in his carriage. The bird's call ran through my sleepy
head to the tune of the horses' hoofs all the six-hour journey, across
the Rappahannock River, even to the long avenue of black elms
cutting through the plantations towards the Harcourt mansion. The
song ceased only as we sat down to lunch.

Easy grew silent in his father's shadow. He bent his eyes to his
plate and hid his hands as well, as if they might reveal him. I marvelled to see Sam deferential.

'Superior grounds,' Sam said, 'and such magnificent sentinels,
those great black elms.' And even, 'Mr Harcourt, your son I mean,
sir, has boasted of your facility – shall I call it that? – in the last war
. . . I would be delighted to hear the particulars.'

It hurt my heart to see it, for Sam was truly a great man, and Mr
Harcourt a mere bull, with the cleverness only of sharp horns. He
was a bull in shape too, with a barrel chest, and heavy dark brows

and a red face. His back ran straight as a pike but his arms hung curiously loose and idle, as they do in men whose strength lies in their ribs. The exploits Sam enquired after proved to be no soldier's stories, but the commercial rogueries of a man who made a treasure in the late war with England. (In which Sam risked a great deal more than a fortune.) Sam always hated 'money tricks', as he called them. He left such to Tom, and I felt a sudden shame to hear him ask after Harcourt's 'facility'.

I wondered at Sam's desire to please and reflected that a rich man can draw honey from the voice even of a stubborn old soldier like Sam, who hated common proprieties. I heard money in Sam's accent, the sad, tinny sound cluttered his true note – like a groschen rattling on a piano string. But then I thought more kindly and considered that even a noble hope – especially a noble hope – can put a false catch in the throat of a man an inch from his purpose. How many ways our own desires deceive us.

My shyness and a glass of claret, I'm afraid, had led me to a rather superior silence. I watched Jeb Harcourt's thick wrists tear bread, while he talked on. 'The rotten – quite literally, mind you – rotten English harvest in the year eleven . . . simply a question of knowing the ports – and the captains . . . as to pretended embargoes . . .' and so on. To be fair to Bull Harcourt, he spoke honestly and without fuss, though indeed he did pride himself on just those qualities. The thought struck me then, how just such a creature as Syme (even without any hope of advantage) might fall under the spell of someone like Harcourt – a man of good parts who knows the world and his trade in it. And being ashamed to call it envy, he might call it something else. 'Do not be deceived,' Sam told me afterwards, 'Harcourt is more than just shrewd, for all his bluster.'

We ate snow-goose for dinner. And the claret was very good.

For a day and a half Easy and I were thrust upon each other's company. Mr Harcourt assumed that Sam was the only man of substance and business among us. Sam was flattered, and, with manners borrowed from his father, quickly dressed himself as a man of the world. Easy was accustomed to this neglect. And oddly, in that grand house, with the long, flat fields all round, I felt for-

eign as well as strange. My accent hung in the air like oversweet tobacco.

Ezekiel was not an Easy companion. He was too tall to be quiet – his eye peered down an inch, even, above my own – and yet he was quiet, made a man feel awkward. His character grew clear to me in that house. His father, strong and practical and rich, had left his son to his own fancies. At thirty, Easy was still frightened of him. But he fell in naturally with clever, ineffectual men, who talked philosophy and art, topics his father knew little about and cared less for. So Easy had something to say. At the foothills of middle age, he had learned to dress well and amuse men who prided themselves on their nice sense of amusement. And then I thought, This is how he has fallen in with us.

But for once he had found a pursuit with hard science behind it, or at least something like it. So he brought the protégé to see his father, who liked what he saw and took it to himself. This left the two of us together. We went for a ride that afternoon in the early dusk, well wrapped about, to the chatter of brisk hoofs. It grew dark early but it was too cold to talk, so the dark suited us. We returned to a bright fire and a glass of brandy glowing in it. I could hear Sam above us, in the map room, intoning a familiar lecture to Mr Harcourt. At last he sounded sensible and himself. The warm sting of the brandy brought the sense back to my hands and heart. Now I was happy, hearing our prospects argued in such sure and assuring tones above. Then Easy turned to me, and said something that clouded my comfort, though I liked him better for the confession.

'Shall I tell you my secret, Phidy.' He held his shy damp hands before the fire. 'It is that I like other people overmuch.' My heart went to him, though I found nothing to say. Soon after we sat down to supper.

That evening, after Mr Harcourt had retired to his study and Easy had gone to bed, I came to Sam's rooms. Half a moon shone through his black window and lay on the floor at our feet. Sam could not keep silent for excitement and talked like a swarm of bees.

'I could have wished you to see more of Mr Harcourt this afternoon,' Sam said, 'for he makes an interesting study – and is no fool neither. For one, he has read more deeply in Greek than either you or I. I began my little tale of creation, hey Phaedon, etc. – and he completed it for me in sonorous tones – much pleased with himself, to be sure. And then he is the acquaintance – and often more than friend – of the chief American literary figures of our day. Last week that fellow Cullen Bryant slept on this bed. Harcourt says he has dined out with Irving. I tell you what it is, Phidy – he is a true American – of a species just now beginning to flourish. There was a different breed in old revolutionary days – Jeffersons and Frenchified folk – some more English than the English. I should know, my father was among them. But this Jackson has set up a new flag – and he is finding the men to raise it . . .'

There was more in that vein. He was happy as a schoolboy with a brand-new teacher. I saw only then how discouraged he had become in this past year and how much he had shrunk in his own esteem.

Perhaps he saw this for himself, for his spirits ebbed and he sat on his bed, with his large hands on the large knees of his short legs, and rocked somewhat to and fro. Then he said, 'I am frightened, Phidy,' and I knew his meaning, but he went on. 'What if I should not deserve his faith?' Then he undressed and I stayed, though we both were exhausted of speech. I sat on the green-backed chair by the basin and lingered until he was content and breathed happily, and then I snuffed the lamp and retired to my own cold room and bed.

The next evening, after supper, the Bull called us to the drawing room. We sat down and he talked. 'I shall get to the nub of it quickly. You tell me, Mr Syme, that you are right and that everybody else is wrong. Fine. I am no judge of that. I know enough of history and the masses to have no great respect for either. Nothing to me seems more likely than that we are all blundering about on an eggshell. For me the question has always been: Can I guess what way the blundering will go? And where the shell will crack? I am a lawyer and a landowner, not a scientist. But I am also a citizen with an eye to our country's honour. Don't let that put you out, Mr Miller. I have money and don't mind spending it on what my son calls "the Questions". You tell me, Mr Syme, that your theories could christen a new American Science. That's the line I like. Stick to it.

'I don't know what you came here expecting but this is what you'll get. I want those ideas to get about. I never saw the use of burrowing away in a library so you could stick another book on the shelves when you've finished. One thing I know about is business. I will buy you a magazine. My son tells me that you live on Whippet Lane. You know about the Tracks then. Two streets away is the old office of the Pactaw Racing Times. That closed down with the Races. Nobody's there, but upstairs the old press still stands. That's yours. I have agents from Williamsburg to Baltimore to see that what you print gets around. I think in terms of twelve months. I want six magazines to come out in that time. If you can, contract articles from other scientists. Remember, this is to be the forum for the new American Science. That's the line. Call it what you like, just make sure it says "New American Science" big and black underneath it on the cover. As for the rest, how to live and such, I'll see you men taken care of.'

He smiled then, big as a cigar. Which in turn he handed out, and Easy opened a bottle of champagne, which tasted very cold in front of the fire and brought us back to ourselves. We smoked the cigars and drank another bottle, four grown men happy and standing straight. We did not know what to say to one another, but Sam took each of our hands in turn and shook them. The Bull laughed, and smiled as big as a glass of brandy, which in turn he handed out. I remember mainly how quiet we all were.

In the morning we rode back to Pactaw and began work.

The next month was among the happiest of my stay, a renaissance of the joy of my arrival. Sam took to prosperity like a duck in water. He preened himself and glistened in it and swam lightly. I could not then have guessed how soon I should be going.

Sam and I slept, ate, read, worked and wrote together, often side by side on the long table in the attic with his strong left arm flat on the wood and his cheek in his hand. The sour-sweet smell of his pipe *hung in a cloud above us. Snow fell in heaps that week, stuck and froze. Children cluttered the track with makeshift sleds, falling and pulling one another till the rope cut and burned their hands in the cold. Once again that round field was streaked with races.*

'The cold is good for business,' said Sam, with the warm stem of his pipe in his mouth, but the smoke cold and sweet. 'Can you not hear – the prickings and stirring of the gases underground – caught in snow piles and the frozen channels of stiff roots? A great eclipse is coming – very near indeed. I had not mentioned it before, Phidy, when my purpose seemed dying. No volcano, to be sure. We could hardly hope for such in Virginia. But still a great eclipse near Pactaw, the biggest in my time – so that a man well placed and well informed – might with a little digging – have a glimpse inside.'

Our magazine was to be called the New Platonist. *Sam settled on that. He wished at first to call it the* Phaedon, *'to please you, Friedrich', he said. My cheek burned and my heart glowed but I declined. So it became the* New Platonist. *The first issue was to be a declaration of our intentions, and Sam had got up the high phrases in which to ring it out. 'A new Science, like a discovered Ocean, has "swum into our ken" and so on – only, Phidy, be sure to call it a* new American Science . . .' *And all the time the snow fell as though the tender lips of God blew white glass, shattering and remoulding it, as He had in the month of my first arrival. Only now there was no Tom.*

Though he did come for a weekend to help us with the press. The four of us, Tom, Easy, Sam and I, played Atlas and hauled that little world up to the attic in Whippet Lane. Sam and Easy had business afterwards, over Mr Harcourt's accounts, so Tom and I took ourselves to the Dewdrop for a glass or two. He had grown as distant as the Pole, for now that we had no business together, I could scarce touch him where he lived. I did ask after Kitty and 'your translation to conjugal bliss, Tom' and he smiled and I knew him happy, as I know that a fish is cold. He returned that night to Richmond, but said before going, 'Be careful of Sam, Phidy, will you? As I can't, any longer' – which I forgot and only remembered afterwards.

Fearing that Sam and Easy would still be huddled over their papers, I paid a visit to Mrs Simmons. I stood at her shop-window a few minutes before knocking at the green door beside it. I was half-fearful, or perhaps only shy, for we had neglected her of late, but I still could not account for my hesitation. I nearly turned away. The brass and glass of her instruments lay in shadow and I watched them for some time, then knocked and made to go, before I saw the slow light of her lantern answered by their gleams. The door opened and she stood in the doorway, wrapped in a shawl red as wine.

'Guten Abend, Frau Simmons, I am sorry to call on you so late.'

'Nonsense, Friedrich, it's just gone eight. It's too cold to stand fussing, so come in.'

I followed her slow steps through the shop to the back room where she lived. She moved always with such deliberation that she required the courtesy we give usually to the old or beautiful, though strictly speaking she was neither. I counted her steps to the door, then stooped into a green room with a cold fire in it.

'Sit down,' she said, but I stood, from that damn shyness, and looked at the pictures on her walls. 'Mr Simmons painted them,' she said, 'he was in the shipping trade.' Most were of storms and ships, the usual scenes. But one, above the fire, was the picture of a ship's deck, cluttered with cargo, without men. 'Yes, that is my favourite too,' said Mrs Simmons. 'His business was goods and he knew it best.' She came to me with a glass of sherry in her hand and then I took it and sat down.

'We have always talked in the shop,' I said, 'I cannot recall being in your back room without Sam, and then I am mostly silent.'

'Nonsense again, Phidy,' she said, 'I have never known someone with such a clattering tongue as yours.' She laughed and we were away. I thought then how our laughter grows old before us. It often surprises us into a new reckoning of our age. Hers was deep and foolish, unlike her, and I loved her for it.

I sat on a stool by the fire with a third glass of sherry, dry as wood, in my hand, and wondered what had brought me there. Envy for Ezekiel perhaps, deep in business with Sam. His father had supplanted mine as financier, only on a much grander scale,

and that brought with it other sad reflections. Sadness also at see-
ing Tom, who had delighted me so often, go. His faith in Sam had
been so great that I felt lonely now without it. Yet he had married
and found a proper business to engage in, while I, a half-believer
only, remained. No, I was more than that, for had not the tide of
Sam's fortunes turned, and had not . . .? Perhaps I was a little
drunk, and only sick for home. And Mrs Simmons knew the lan-
guage of it.

When I steered myself home at last, I found Sam and Easy on the
doorstep. To my surprise, there were tears in Easy's eyes and his
face looked puffed. I did not like the man, but for that, his grief
touched me more nearly. It was so unexpected. He shaded his wet
eyes with his damp hand as I walked past into the house. I did not
greet them. Sam followed me soon after into the parlour. He looked
at the clock. It was midnight. 'Tom will not be back tonight,' he
said. 'Kitty won't like it.' I said nothing and we both went to bed.

The following morning, with the press installed, Sam and I
could scarce leave the house for happiness. Tom had explained its
workings to us, but we could not recall his instructions and were
compelled to experiment. All day we spent in drafting and printing
nonsense then scuttling out in the cold and pasting them broadsheet
at every convenient post in Pactaw:

The Races Have Returned!
Two Year Old Mares
Two O'clock
The End of Whippet Lane

But we grew tired of jokes. And by the close of the short afternoon
we printed again and again, with growing fear and excitement of
spirits:

The New Platonist

———— •• ————

A journal establishing the
REVOLUTIONARY AMERICAN SCIENCE
It may change the Course of History

COMING SOON

Edited by
Professor Samuel Syme

❧

I recall looking out of our high window at the end of the light and seeing two old men in cloth caps, one with a stick in hand, the other with a single sheet of paper, walking slowly to the tracks down Whippet Lane. They seemed not at all puzzled by the silence around them. And though I lingered by the cold window to mark their return, they lingered longer, and I did not see them come back.

The next fortnight was spent in a fever of work. We rose early in the heavy dark before dawn, flu' in hand, to catch the faint emissions through the snow pricked by the first sun. It was a cold and miserable business, but it gave us an appetite for breakfast, gobbled quickly, from frozen hand to mouth. Then I remained in the parlour with its steaming windows and wrote down the morning's findings in the fat book, while Sam scrambled like a boy upstairs to run himself warm, before he sat down at the long table to write in that cold room. I often heard his large feet above me, jumping to keep the blood flowing, but he said the cold kept his brain sharp and I believe it did. He spent day and night over some 'fresh speculation', as he called it – begun that foul day in Perkins, when Tom fell sick. 'A gesture only', he said, 'at a wonderful possibility.' In the afternoons I turned to my own composition, 'On the Use of Hot Wax in Bandaging Opened Wounds', which Sam promised me would sit in pride of place at the end of the first issue. Sam wrote and wrote.

It was at this time that I noted the first signs of nervous disorder in my companion. He himself called me in to view his discharges, flecked with bright pink spots of blood. His hair had thinned as well, and I often found evidence of this on my own clothes. I would brush them with my thumb over my fingers into the wood stove's fire and watch them suddenly change colour and glow and rise like a strand of smoke. He cut easily in that time as well, though this owed in part to his dry hands, chapped from the cold. But often, on fumbling with a key or bringing wood for the fire, he would turn his palm up to me, showing a beautiful bright spot of red.

These were the tokens of nervous joy as well as fear. The day of the first printing approached quickly. We had become inseparable. That morning when the first thaw came, and a frozen world cracked and dripped around us, he tumbled downstairs to read me 'Our Declaration'. There was a great deal of pomp and bluster in it: 'a new planet has swum into our ken; it is our own . . . , plain as the ground beneath our feet; a new science, an American science . . .'

Sam read it to me breathless from first to last. Outside tinkled the happy torrents of a melting winter. My heart lightened and I laughed at the last stroke.

'Bull Harcourt will be pleased!'

'A piece of my father's chicanery!'

We printed it directly and posted it all over the house, on the front door, at our bedside windows. We rushed into the running streets and nailed it to wet trees and benches. We came back to the steaming parlour red-faced and hungry. 'We have our declaration,' I said. Only a worm of doubt in the fresh apple stirred its head. What would be the end of such games? I wondered, and Sam felt it nibble at him, too. 'There is a grain of truth in it, too,' he said to me after we had eaten. 'More than a grain?' he asked me.

I nodded; and then at last declared what had cluttered my thoughts and burdened my conscience since that first long-ago morning in the snow when Sam explained the world to me. At last I gave a voice (plaintive and hesitant, too weak to carry doubt, which needs a stronger, subtler tone than conviction) to my heavy fears; perhaps only when it was all too late, and our course set. 'Sam,' I said, taking him by the hand, 'perhaps . . .'

'Yes?' he answered, withdrawing, leaning against the edge of the table and waiting patiently.

'I speak out of love, not doubt. You see . . .' I paused again, puzzled to proceed, until my tongue found its thought, and poured forth a year's worth of hesitations in a single torrent. 'You see . . . there is such force to your early calculations, the question of mass, I mean, the doubts you cast, rather than the . . . rather than the . . . which are only after all speculations . . .'

'Faint heart,' he said, looking me full in the face.

'Not at all, not at all,' I answered, perhaps too quickly, my heart on my lips, and I uncertain whether my loves or my doubts would come tumbling forth. 'There is such virtue in clearing the ground, razing old errors and letting the grass grow beneath them again. You have done that, Sam, brilliantly; we need not supply their place.'

'You are a critic,' Sam replied, in a precise, cold voice, 'by trade and inclination. You delight in pruning, Phidy.' And then he smiled and said with the sweet breath that replenishes a sigh, 'I grow and grow and grow – and time will sort the ruins.'

'Not at all, not at all,' I stammered again, to nothing and everything at once. 'Only . . .' But 'only' died on my lips, for then an extraordinary thing began to happen. Sam began to dance, an odd jig beginning at the feet, shivering from his knees to his elbows, strangely slow and moving and wonderfully happy, in time to nothing and no one but the flaws and starts of his own delight.

'In for a penny,' he chanted, smiling, lifting his knee to his elbow, again, again, 'in for a pound.' I could not help but smile back at him, warmed by the fire of his own joy, delighted at the sudden conflagration. 'Hanged for a horse as a . . .'

'Sheep,' I answered, joining in, fetching his hands again and swinging together across the ice-cold parlour, upsetting chairs and rattling the pots on their hooks, making such music as if the spheres themselves sang fitfully to our dance.

531

'We go to press,' he declared at last, resting his hands on his hips and gasping forth white, chill air.

Yes, I thought, we will set down in stone such gossamer tissues that one strong gust will see them dispersed to the winds.

Tom came to town to see it done. The business took all Saturday, and we grew smudged and inky ourselves, like characters running on a wet page. Sam had a smear of black under one eye that made him look more than ever like a navvy. Fifty pages lay in a fresh heap on the long table, with the ink still shining like molasses and looking just as sweet. 'The New Platonist: an American Science' stood big and black on the first page. Edited by Professor Samuel Highgate Syme, for Sam was proud of his middle name, a rare gift from his father. I turned the page, delicate as china, and there stood the declaration in pride of place. It looked to me now, after printing, like a jumble of letters, all correct but without sense, like the bright black spots on lucky dice:

Contents

Our special Appreciation to Mr Harcourt, Esq. of Richmond, Virginia, who may properly be termed the Medici of the New Science, our Prince and Patron

Not a word in it to Tom Jenkyns who now stands above the soft pile and takes Easy by the hand and says, 'Come, I believe you owe us supper!'

It was a famous night. The three of us were together once more, and though Easy stood somewhat in the shade, he seemed content there; at least he did not murmur. He ordered champagne for us at the grand new Boathouse Hotel, and we poured it down cold as rain with our heads in the cloud. Chops followed, and, bone in hand, Sam was at his finest, at bay against the three of us, keen in dispute. The contest was over Faith and Knowledge, and Sam (to my surprise) took the part of the former, crying out, 'Faith! I will buckler thee against a million!' For once Tom stood against him, but we were no match for Sam in his heyday, and we fled the field in ruins. In my youth, before the shyness set in, I used to clamber up behind the farmers' carts, full of apples or pigs, going to market. Some of the farmers took a stick to me, but I remember only the swaying and the shouts and bumps and laughter. That night we were drunk as lords and I remember the same scrambling joy. Only when Tom – of all people you, Tom! – said, 'What follows, Sam?' did we fall quiet, and then Easy, stout-hearted, raised a meek voice and piped, 'Another,' and then Sam said, 'Another!' and I cried, 'ANOTHER!' and soon we were chanting, and another bottle came. Tom left soon after, almost sober, tenderly dislodging himself from our embraces, and I never saw him again. Easy followed behind, and then Sam and I, blind drunk, staggered home, across the familiar footbridge and the roaring wintry river.

'Faith and Knowledge' was still the cry as we walked arm in arm up the porch-steps. I was in a happy rage. To prove his point, Sam proposed an experiment. The house opened into a narrow hallway that led to the staircase, with a door to the parlour left of the stairs. A low lamp hung from the hall ceiling. We often struck our skulls against the bright brass, until we learned the habit of sailing past, like a ship on a leeward tack, leaning. Sam ran to the parlour and came back with a thick cloth, which he asked me to bind around his temples, obscuring his eyes. I did so. His cheeks were hot with joy.

'Stand in the parlour,' he commanded. 'I will come in blindfolded and drunk. Mark if I hesitate – even the flutter of a step – before I reach the stairs.'

533

My high spirits had laughed at everything all night, and in their ebb I was apt to giggle long, and to myself. I giggled now, leaning against the parlour door. Sam opened the front door, stood in the entrance while a man might count to five, then with five straight, bold steps, ducking like a pope on the third beneath the bright brass lamp, he reached the stairs beside me and strode up them two at a time. As he reached the landing, he tore the blindfold from him, crying out in triumph, 'That is faith, Phidy.'

Then he danced on the stairs, kicking up his knees. I stood beneath him. He caught his breath and cried, 'Knowledge, viz. – that there are thirteen feet to the door – and six before you must stoop for the lamp – will only bring you on hands and knees to these steps.' I giggled again.

'Sheer luck,' I said when I stopped.

'Nonsense,' Sam declared, then he came down. 'Good fortune can look like knowledge – never like faith. With luck you could guess the number of steps – but never stride them. Now,' he said, throwing the warm cloth in my face, 'let's see the colour of your faith.'

So I stood in the opened doorway. A cloudy midnight had warmed the cold, clear day and I heard the snow drip down the porch-steps. I measured the distance stride for stride with my eyes open. I rehearsed the quick nod of the head in the middle beneath the lamp. But when Sam bound the cloth over my forehead and led me by hand to the front of the hall and directed me towards the stairs, I was at sea.

'Two steps, duck, then three more,' I repeated over and over, swaying drunk with the soft darkness in my eyes. I could not. I took a bold step forward, but my courage failed. Then a mincing half-step and I put forth a searching hand. I felt the heat of the lamp above me, but it seemed distant as the sun and I could not touch it. I swayed to the side, and caught at the wall, then edged forward, just past the lamp as I supposed, until I fell straight into Syme's arms, where he stood in the parlour door.

'Ha!' he shouted and I giggled again.

'Once more, once more,' I cried. And again he bound the cloth lovingly across my eyes and tied it at the back in my dank hair. This

time I took two bold steps with the blood pressing against my eyes and stopped dead. I edged forward with my head bowed low to the ground in exaggerated dignity. Then I strode ahead and heard the ring of the brass as it struck my skull before I felt the first hot pain. I fell back, more shocked than hurt, but Sam caught me and I brought him down and we lay on the bare floor in a tender heap, crying with laughter.

'Oh, oh,' I hooted, still blind, feeling for the angry line the brass had cut in my scalp.

'You fool,' Sam said, 'you faithless fool.'

I lay across Sam's legs and he lay on his back. The hairs of his neck stood on end where my hand held him. The wine on his sweet breath stunk to my very eyes.

'Enough,' he said, as I looked into his – blue and bright, as his pupils shrunk against the lamplight. I still looked – my lips parted to let the breath ease in and out – until his eyes blurred into a blue shimmer, and his face grew hot and red to the touch of my hand. 'Enough,' he said again, sighing.

Of what? He did not mean, I think, another stroll beneath the hanging lamp, but a different exercise, also of faith, perhaps.

A famous night. But in the morning my bruised head could not but fear the touch of madness in our game, like the liquor in old honey. In his blind high spirits, Sam would have walked against a wall to boast his wit. For a few weeks thereafter, I drifted leeward of him. We spent less time together, for he was busy in Easy's company, talking of sales and critics and his father's money. It was a happy night, but happiness may make men shy as well as anything.

Doldrums followed the grand excitement of our first issue. A heap of the New Platonist lay stacked in the hallway – Bull Harcourt wished to glance one over, before his men collected them and sent them to 'every corner of the republic'. Easy left a few around Pactaw, for the locals to stare at – in ale-houses and inns, even the white church north of Main Street. The weather grew warmer, and the snow that had come to us in clouds left us in streams and puddles. Sam now took Easy with him on his early expeditions with the fluvia. He wished to become 'better acquainted with the business from every angle'. I felt a pang at first to see them go in the morning. I still woke at dawn and heard them clattering on the stairs and in the parlour. Easy often spent a hard night on Sam's floor before their forays. When I heard the front door bang, I rose and walked barefoot to the window, where I could see them, two dark figures with their heads bent from cold and lack of sleep. But the dawns were growing warmer, and I felt on my skin the first prick of spring and envied them their journey.

As I had stood in for Tom, now Easy did for me. Sam loved to explain, and Tom and I knew all his explanations. Still I would have followed him at dawn across field and fence to hear and help him. Or perhaps I would not, as I did not.

It was only later I discovered their true purpose. Sam had got in his head the thought that 'something might yet be made of that visionary device – of such promise, both to miner and geognosist – in short, the double-compression piston itself.' Easy himself had some training as an engineer, and the two of them spent many dark weeks locked in the barn behind the Boathouse tinkering with the irreparable, dabbling with the impossible, reconstructing that shapeless heap of disjunct and fantastical conceptions. And drinking whiskey, I believe, to keep warm. Somehow Sam knew this would upset me – as it had upset Tom – and so the pair of them snuck away before dawn and returned after moon set, to practise their secret, hopeless machinations. I can't say why the thought of that device made me despair. Something in the terrible proliferation of problem and solution it created – a joint here, broken, a wheel there, fixed – seemed to prove the futility of Sam's speculation; offered mechanical evidence of the fact that his thoughts could never escape the terrible cycle of inspiration and confutation.

But I never guessed their business till Sam came home one afternoon, early, as the low sun glittered off the frozen grass, and declared the double compression to be 'finally and fantastically – fixed and finished. Reborn. I – that is, Easy and I – have done it.' He stood swaying arm in arm with Easy on the windy porch, and I ushered them in, and boiled a pot of tea for their frozen fingers and parched throats; and we lifted hot mugs and drank a toast 'to Digging, as the farmer said'. But I didn't have the heart to test him, prove him right or wrong again – and did not guess and did not care which outcome would have disappointed me, pleased me more.

Meanwhile, I began to fall in with Mrs Simmons. Every Thursday evening I took her light-boned arm – the arm, where Youth and Beauty linger last and sweetest! – and walked her home, after a party of whist with Mr Fawlkes (a bookseller) and his mother. Sometimes we peered up and down the street, and I snuck in for a glass of sherry by her fire.

'Will Sam mind us, do you think?' I said to her one evening.

'Leaving him to his work? No, that's the best of him.'

'No, that is not what I meant, I think.'

'He is not a passionate man. Does that surprise you, Phidy?' she answered, considering. 'And a woman of . . . forty or so needs company. A young man is always pleasant. Sam and I are like in that as well, taking young men to us. There was an Alcibiades before you, but he was a mouthful so we called him Alley.'

'Tom has always been Tom.'

'And now there is Easy,' she said. 'Though he is a sad young man, and I should not have chosen him. Easy is a sweet name for him, though cruel. Tom has a sharp tongue for all his courtesy and a name for everything. Such a lovely boy, but he never liked me, more's the pity.'

'Why not?'

'He thinks I draw Sam from his purpose. He is jealous, too.'

'Would it upset you if he stopped all this nonsense for you?'

'Why should it?'

'As a matter of principle.'

'You are a great one for asking questions, Phidy. You imagine yourself so shy and silent, but all the while no one can hush you for love or money. If it comes to that, I have my own principles.'

'What are they, if you will pardon another question?'

'That everyone can find a reason to be unhappy and that most can find a reason to be happy. That should answer you as far as Sam

goes. It has got me across an ocean and through the death of poor
Mr Simmons – and pushes me out of bed in the morning, when I
would much rather sleep.'

'Would you like to sleep now?' I asked, hopeful and afraid.

'Not quite,' she said, laughing at me in her eyes, with such
shyness as looks like daring.

Then I stood up and heard my knees creak; they hurt me as I knelt
with my elbow against the armrest of her chair. I stooped to her dry,
soft lips and my blood raced, with two thoughts. With the intimate
thick thought of her before me, and the second tiny whisper in my
head that I was following Sam. We kissed, gently and then longer.
Then she sat back, content and not at all surprised. She was too
comfortable in her soul to deny me a resting-place there, though I
knew Sam was her great and only love. 'A young man is always
pleasant' echoed in my thoughts, but in fact she said, 'You make a
lady wait.'

Here I dwell, I thought, even in the house of your love. Mrs
Simmons held the key to his back door, and I might come with her to
his very heart of hearts, when he would turn me from the parlour on
my own. 'Enough,' he said to me that night, and left me with a
breast overcharged with his love. Is it any wonder I should give it to
the heart closest his own?

But if Sam stood behind my thoughts, Mrs Simmons lay before
my eyes. She had nursed me in the spring, and time passed easily
with us. Even the slight wrinkles of her neck gathered sweetness in
them, as the veins of a leaf drink dew. Her hair was thin and old,
but the tenderer for it; and her eyes were cut from a wonderful blue
stone time could not touch. She had her own charms: long, thin
arms and a curving side.

It was well past midnight before I turned to my own bed.

The doldrums gave way to a hurricane. I returned one night late
from Mrs Simmons to find Easy in our parlour and a great fuss in
the air. Easy shook a letter in his hand with furious indignation. He
turned to me as I entered. 'Bull Harcourt, as you call him, Phidy,'
he said, 'is a bull, a bull-headed, thick-skulled tyrant with all the

fineness and sensitivity of a butcher. He is a bully, a bull.'

Sam laughed, 'Don't take on so, Easy. He is plum right.'

I had never seen Easy in such a state. His blood boiled and his hair stood on end and he paced up and down in a storm. Sam was calm as cream beside him, but had he known what was to come, he should have burned that letter and never spoken of it again.

'Settle yourself, Easy, and tell me what's the matter,' I said.

'"Dear Dr Syme,"' he read in a squeak and squall. '"I have lately had the pleasure of looking over your first instalment, the outcome of our association." Pompous fool, it is the outcome of his genius and your bullion, you bull, butcher.'

'Carry on,' I said, and Sam and I looked at each other, smiling.

'There is more of such stuff, but I pass over it. Here, no, here, he says, yes, here it is. "I am a practical-minded man. As you no doubt recall from our discussion, among the conditions to our arrangement, was the agreement that you justify your discoveries, either with the acknowledgement of a community of scientists, or with the dramatic proof of a demonstration of some kind. Though Mesmer was turned out of Paris, he had a crowd of witnesses behind him. You have two, an outcast German physician" – I am sorry Phidy – "and my son."'

'He knows nothing of Tom,' I said.

'A down-at-heels newspaperman,' said Sam, laughing.

'Is there more?' I asked.

'Is that not enough?' said Easy.

'No, there is more,' said Sam. 'Read it.'

'"In case I appear an insensitive critic, my dear Doctor, let me observe that, towards the end of your essay 'What it Means to Pactaw', you furnish ample material for such a demonstration. Unless I am mistaken, the calculations on page thirty-seven reveal that no less than a triple eclipse is predicted within the next month not thirty miles from Pactaw itself."'

'Is this true?' I asked, of a sudden fearful. That word 'calculations' had rung a bell in my memory. Tom had dreaded the proof of certain 'calculations' before me. Now I had inherited Tom's . . . hesitations.

539

'I have looked at it and it is.'

'Had you known it?'

'Perhaps I had.'

'What does Mr Harcourt say to it?'

'There is not much left. Finish reading, Easy.'

'"Surely such an event would proclaim itself in some dramatic, or at the least observable, fashion. Could not a crowd surround the spot, as at some entertainment? Or, if that is impractical, a few fellow geonomists could be alerted and brought to witness. As I have said, I am a practical man, and you may rely on me for any assistance you require to bring it off. Your servant, Bull Harcourt."'

Easy had grown quiet and dull and the joke fell flat. Again his father had trod upon his toy, and he feared it would not mend. Sam said nothing, though he cocked a cheerful and enquiring eye at me.

I could still hear him in my head, loud as on that happy night, 'You faithless fool.'

My last month in America was upon me. We stared at Sam's calculations night after night to be sure of them, until the numbers grew like leaves in our eyes, scattered at hazard in a storm, and we could as little understand their order. Seventy-seven degrees nine minutes thirty-three seconds west of Greenwich, thirty-eight degrees twenty-two minutes fifty-seven seconds north of the Meridian.

Sam had a friend in Richmond from army days, Tippy Adams. He was a surveyor still in the 53rd Infantry. So we set off for Richmond one day, over a landscape the sharp snow had scraped dark and bare as it retreated. The army offices were bright red brick with a high, bright flag stuck from a pole above the entrance in a happy flutter of nerves. The sky was thinnest blue at lunchtime, but all else was brown and slop, the grass outside deep in mud and the hallways streaked with it and smelling of the stables.

Tippy was a mild, tall man with iron-coloured hair and a plain face that had been handsomer and happier in his youth. He wore spectacles that glinted over the pupils of his eyes, and he had grown fat round the middle for the first time in his life. He looked as if he knew his dry business; and he loved Sam.

He laughed to see him and then stood blinking at us. 'Come to lunch with the boys,' he said at last. So we followed him into the mess hall where the tinkle and roar of a hundred voices and the sour smell of boiled water reminded me of my own days at Werner's academy. 'Fellas!' he shouted, as we came in. 'Look what I've brought!' And a hundred faces turned to Sam who smiled like a pumpkin and I heard cries of 'Moonie!' and 'Old Moon-Eyes!' and the slap of a dozen hands on his strong back. He was at home as I had never seen him, and when we sat down with stiff straight backs at the end of the low bench, Tippy said, 'So, Doctor, are you still poking for holes?'

'I've got a rag out,' said Sam.

'Hell,' said Tippy, smiling.

'The New Platonist. I'm here on business, really.'

'Let's eat and then talk,' said Tippy, and that's what we did. For dinner came and Tippy ate and said not a dozen words between mouthfuls. He had a thick jaw and looked at us and smiled each time he brought a napkin across his thin mouth. He was like a schoolboy gone grey and still gobbled.

After dinner Tippy took us to the officers' room, with a brown carpet underfoot, and brown chairs and odd brown tables, and brown paintings of men from the 53rd with white faces at their brown oars on the brown Potomac against the brown walls. The brass grate was slick as honey and the fire glowed orange on it and the sky outside the cold window was blue and thin as blown glass and empty for the wind to play in. We could hear it down the chimney deep in our brown chairs.

'What's this business then?' said Tippy.

'I'm at my old loons,' said Sam, in a voice I scarcely recognized – rough, quick, utterly at ease. 'Fella I know put up some money for a magazine. But he is a thick-sighted old mole – would doubt a rock till it had struck him in the nose. As it happens, I know where the rock is, but I need a map.' Sam had fallen into his old gait.

'Where away?'

'Pactaw County. Can you help us?'

Tippy laughed, quiet and at the back of his throat, nothing so like the sound of someone chewing nuts. 'Did you know Perry?' he said. Sam shook his head. 'Literary fella. Wrote jokes about us, rhyming things, you know, like "gun" and "fun". He had a girl – "yellow-haired nymph" was her name, I think – in Pactaw. He says to me, "Ain't there something to do in Pactaw? Shoot Injuns or something?" No Indians in Pactaw, but I let him chart the place. So I do have a map, if that's what you want.'

'It is.'

'Stay put. I'll rummage later.'

He said nothing and I was quiet as a mouse. Sam's thoughts were all on the map, but then he did turn and ask Tippy how he was keeping.

'Well stuck in, you know me' was all the answer, but he had waited for this question and grew content; and soon after he rose on stiff knees with his right hand on his new belly and took us to the chart room. We spread the map flat on a table in a rustle of paper like the slap of sails, and in an instant we had tacked down the Potomac to Pactaw County with its low hills pricked with thin ink. Bull Harcourt was right. The spot lay in 'Tyler's Farm', not fifteen miles from the Races.

Tippy gave us the map and said, 'Bring it back when you come and see me.'

'I will, Tippy.'

'You would have been captain by now, do you think of that?' He looked at me then, as if I had the same sad thought at my heart, which I did.

'I was an old hothead,' Sam said. 'Should've got killed somehow or other – long before now.' Perhaps it was true.

'What happened to the nymph?' I shouted as we left.

'They were married,' Tippy called across the windy day.

The visit to Tyler's Farm was the last happy piece of nonsense I met in America. It rained like the great flood so Easy came with us and we took his carriage. The rain shouted at us all the way, and the close air under the trembling roof tasted sour on the tongue, like metal. Our spirits were electric and the three of us could scarcely speak for wonder and joy at all the banging.

'Mr Tyler's Farm' proved to be a brown, bedraggled hump of a hill with a bright cloud behind it and sparks of rain above it. It ran over to the valley under that cloud, and there our business lay, before the copse at the foot of the hill. There was a small building marked 'Shed' on the map near the magic spot, though we later found it to be a tiny chapel. It had a single pew in front of our crumbling Saviour, with an odd iron tree of candles before it, with cracked black paint. We also found a game of draughts under the pew and a child's collection of rocks, with one dead mouse among them. The Tylers were Catholics.

The farmhouse was low and wooden, though backed against the sky by taller barns. The long drive up to the farm had dissolved into a stream, and the stones in the road glinted clean and shining in its current. They cracked and crunched under our wheels, and we left a path of brown mud behind us. The yard was a black puddle with two chickens in it, and a rusted plough and a heap of flat rocks in a corner for building walls. The hour had just gone two but the day was dark as suppertime except for the big, bright cloud over the hill. I knocked with a heavy fist against all the noise.

A tiny staring woman opened the door. 'Is it te Inglish?' she asked.

'No, Mrs Tyler . . .' Sam began.

'Where has they got to?'

'No, Mrs Tyler. May we come in? We are all wet as fish out here.'

'Henrik!' she called. 'They are coming in!' Her head was cocked up to see us, like a wren's. Her nose was red, and she took a handkerchief and pinched the end of it. 'Take off your boots!' she said. 'You want tea, I guess, if it's te Inglish?'

We sat with Mr Tyler around the kitchen table. He sat by the stove with his boots off and leaned back against the wall with his feet in wet wool socks against the stove. 'Ah!' he said, and snatched them away and came down in a clatter. He rubbed his toes then leaned back again carefully and put his feet back on the hot iron. 'I just come from the bottom of the hill,' he said. 'Wet.'

'We have come on rather odd business, I fear,' Sam said.

'Just say what it is, but all we got right now is chickens,' said the man.

'No,' Sam said. 'We don't want chickens.'

We all sat silent, puzzled how to begin. 'Leepshen,' said Mrs Tyler from the kettle, 'haben zee vat im Kopf?' The kettle whistled and she brought us tea and we held our red hands around the mugs. They were Germans, but I kept my tongue, for I did not wish to explain.

'I am a scientist,' said Sam. 'A doctor.'

'Ah,' said Mr Tyler. 'No doctor.'

'And I wish . . .' Sam said, and began tapping on the table with his thumb.

'I am not a doctor!' said the farmer. 'Er denkt ick bin ahn Ars oder vat?'

Easy looked shocked.

'I want to poke a hole in your field to see if there is something there,' Sam said quickly.

'What you looking for?'

'I just want to make a hole,' said Sam, avoiding the question.

'What you want to find?' said Mr Tyler in a big voice.

Sam hesitated. 'I have an idea the earth is hollow, you see. That there is nothing there.' He looked downcast and sheepish.

Mr Tyler looked at his wife. 'Er denkt da ist gahnit da.'

'No,' he said in Sam's ear. 'Is mud. All the way down is mud.'

Easy grew red in the face. 'This has nothing to do with mud,' he said. 'It is a theory.'

I was suddenly sad and sick at heart and wanted to go.

Then Sam took Mrs Tyler's hands in his own. 'Please,' he said, and made a cup of them. 'It is hard, you see. Nothing can get through.' Then he put his little finger in the crack between her thumbs. 'But inside there is nothing there.' Mrs Tyler was shy and pleased and kept her hands together even when Sam let them go. 'Do you have an egg?' he said. She rose quickly and brought him one and put it on the table, where it made a rolling echo. 'Can you break it?' he said and she laughed. 'No, but like this,' and he opened her palm and put it in her fist. She squeezed her eyes as she squeezed her hand but she could not.

'Mostly, the ground is like an egg,' Sam said. 'There are no holes in it and nothing comes out.' Then he took her hands again and cupped them. And he smoothed out the dark fingers of her husband's big hands and laid them in a cup around her own. 'Underneath,' he said, 'there is not one circle, but many. Like an egg around an egg around an egg, and so on, all turning different ways.' Husband and wife sat hands in hands beside him. 'The circles have holes in them – but since they don't overlap, nothing comes out.' He poked a finger through a gap in Mr Tyler's hands and ran into the back of her hand. 'But sometimes the holes come together,' and he shifted their hands so their thumbs lay over each other, then wriggled his small finger through the gap and tickled Mrs Tyler till she laughed. 'That is what will happen at the bottom of your hill.'

'How do you know?' said Mr Tyler.

'Because inside the shells there is a special air – quite unlike what we breathe. Do you have any salt, Mrs Tyler?' She got up in a bustle and brought him a small dish of it with a little spoon. 'When the holes come together – the air leaks out and burns blue if you light it. Like this.' He opened the stove door and threw a pinch on the fire, which cracked and hissed in blue spurts. Mrs Tyler flinched when she saw it, then took a whole spoonful and threw it in the oven and stood back grinning.

'I know this,' she said. 'We did this for games on Christmas Day.'

A girl came to the kitchen door with a wooden spoon in her hand. 'Can I have honey?' she said.

'This is business,' said Mrs Tyler.

'Oh, business,' said the girl and went away.

'What will be when the holes come together?' said Mrs Tyler. 'Will we fall in?'

'I don't know,' said Sam. 'That's what we'd like to discover.'

Husband and wife looked at each other. Not much made sense to them in this strange land. One more thing could do no harm. Herr Tyler scratched heftily at his ear and observed the results. 'Na ja,' he said at last. 'We don't mind.'

His wife cut in quickly, shyly. 'We like a show, you see.'

So we came back the next day – blue and wet after the storm – and found the chapel. Frau Tyler wrapped herself in her husband's greatcoat and carried a stool to the top of the hill. There, as we began to take our measurements, she sat watching: a curious bundle of cowhide and thick wool that grew dark when the sun set behind her. That was Tuesday – the eclipse was two weeks away.

Every morning we set off for Tyler's Farm, flu' in hand. Frau Tyler gave us breakfast, which we gobbled in the dark. Herr Tyler had found his shoes again and teased us. 'Did you find gold yesterday?' he called out, before he closed the back door behind us, bent on his ordinary tasks. The snow had gone and he was right before. We found only mud.

77°9'33" W by 38°22'57" N. We took fallen branches and cut them down and stuck them in the ground to mark the spot. A second measures about thirty yards. Then we borrowed rope from Mr Tyler and tied it around the posts to make a square, thirty yards by thirty yards. The chapel stood inside it.

At first the size of the ground daunted us, I confess. We could not possibly dig up nine hundred square yards at the hard foot of a hill. Unless, of course, we applied the mechanical vigour of the double-compression piston, that treasure of Sam's heart – though the puzzle of how to haul that impossible beast fifteen miles up and down the hills appeared insoluble. The cordon itself proved to be a great comfort. Each time we stepped inside the hole (as we came to call it, though it was none) we must raise our foot over a taut line of dirty, dripping hemp. The square grew fixed in our imaginations: the ground a foot outside the line and just within seemed seas apart. Inside the land was magicked and in our thoughts burned blue.

Yet – as Sam repeatedly reminded us – his measurements were rough and all our faith in the map of Perry, a surveyor with his eye fixed on a brighter, warmer star than the heavens possessed, yellow-haired withal and somewhat nearer the ground. I borrowed a sextant from Mrs Simmons one day and Sam took a sighting at noon. The numbers tallied near enough, though they told us only the distance north. None of us cared much for the result, either way, and we did

not check again. Having ventured so deep, we had resigned ourselves to faith.

And trusted to the flu', for we had never known such fervent and
blue indications. Day after day the lamp burned with a throbbing
flame as clear and bright as dawn. The readings proved strongest at
the heart of the hole, a patch of ground three yards from the chapel
door. The flu' cast a blue glow at our feet that shimmered and shifted
like the azure flutter of a hummingbird's wing.

We had reached the middle of March and the air was pricked with
spring – as if the sun could lay its seeds, those first shoots of summer warmth, in that sweet transparency. A letter came from my
father, brimming with extraordinary good news. It seemed
to bless our own enterprise and usher in a season of general prosperity by one of those strange conjunctions to whose power Sam
attributed all luck.

My dear boy [my father wrote],

I hardly know where to begin, and shall doubtless forget where to
conclude, so drunk on good fortune am I (and a glass or two of
brandy I confess, lifted in honour of our new republic, but I outrun
myself). Two nights ago, I lay on my dank pallet in the Prince's
cursed, miasmal, rheumatic, calciferous cellar, waiting for the day
of my trial – endlessly delayed, as the fools from Berlin sought to
trace a great web of Liberal menace from that poor spider, your
father, whose only fault had been a curious intellect, a free table, an
attentive ear, and perhaps – there seems no harm in writing it, now
that all's well – a loose tongue, and, upon occasion, a spirit of generosity not confined shall we say by its own resources.

When morn and even pass undistinguished from each other
(believe me, my boy), days, weeks, months slip unnoticed into the
general sea of time – a great flat gleaming wasteland, unruffled by
nows and thens, an endless becalmed never and for ever, at
once. (A touch of the headache is ringing at my temple now, a
faint bell, an almost delicious echo of the night's joy. Excuse, in
short, the purple in my prose – a happy stain from the flow of

Burgundy in my blood.) I cannot tell you if the clamour awoke me – if I had been sleeping or daydreaming – or merely thinking, so little separates these three occupations in the prisoner's mind – when the dull rumour of crowds and song and trampling feet met my ear. Perhaps an hour passed, or only a few minutes. The clamour grew loud and soft by turns, but louder, and louder in the general run of time. And I saw, through the keyhole, against the walls of the corridor outside, the flicker of torchlight in procession.

Certain it is that when the tread of feet echoed along the passage outside my door, when the key jingled on the chain and scraped into the rusted lock, and began to turn; when the door swung open – I had the sense of being woken, of rising from a heavy sleep, that thicks the eyes with remembered clouds of dreams. I could scarce speak or stand or listen to the kind men, my confidants and conspirators, who took me by shoulder and arm and led me out, trembling in heart and step, out, out, along the dark passages, glittering in the torchlight, and up the narrow stairs, to the kitchens and thence, issuing, it seemed, like a growing river, to the courtyards thronging with our happy countrymen, who sang and danced and drank, to my release. Below us, along the river, armadas of little burning boats (newspaper hats, no doubt, upturned) streamed over the water, a pretty scattering of dying glows, in honour of our new republic, the great state of Neuburg-on-the-Elbe!

Ushered from the press of drunken happiness towards the Prince's balcony, I stood in the brisk spring night – so sweet to my liberated nose, long clotted by damp and the chalk of the cellar – to address the crowds, who, to be fair, seemed too much overjoyed by the great events to attend any discourse on their significance, so I contented myself with raising a rabbling cry of 'Freedom, Faith, Fraternity', which a chorus of revellers took up, and on the sweet tide of that song I came in triumph down the hill to my own dear town and my own dear street and the tender embrace of my own dear daughter again.

Of course, there is a great deal to be done – a great deal of plain hard work. For even liberty – especially liberty, perhaps – requires a certain attention to tedious detail. The widest freedoms depend on precisions of the law. A great deal has been done. The Prince, Hespe, a handful of faithful retainers, as I believe the phrase is, have been locked up – in the very cellars where I lay so long confined. No harm shall come to them, of course, barring a fright, and such reprisals as they commit upon one another. I have not slept these two days. I would not sleep, I could not sleep, for the world. I have lain long enough in slumber, at various times, of various kinds – and have never felt so bright and wide awake, almost painfully conscious, indeed, of the passing minutes, and the honour of our opportunities. For we have begun to draft – that great thing – a Constitution – sat up late in the palace dining room, over coffee and cognac and cigars, squabbling, quibbling, screaming at one another; for liberty is almost an angry delight, and one cannot raise republics, fashion parliaments, without a certain bloodshed of ideas.

The great thing – our abiding hope – is that our little town proves too slight for troubling over; that no bully from Berlin or Vienna will come to restore a throne he hardly knew existed; that we shall be given leave – to experiment – with Freedom; and might succeed in a small way, where we could not on the grand scale. Come home, Son, soon – surely to have a hand in such beginnings is worth the sacrifice of any speculative enterprise. We shall talk politics as the evenings stretch away, and awake to find our lightest thought made Fact.

Your free & loving –
Father

I wept, little guessing till then how much my father's fate had oppressed my heart; I wept, simply at the thought of home and plum brandy on the long, flat nights of a northern summer; and I longed to return. Even the excitement at hand, the triple eclipse, heralded *an ending of a kind, and the months after 23 March, that famous day, were an empty space. I trusted at once to these conflicting thoughts: that Sam would triumph and need me no longer; and that he would fail and his cause would be lost. Both convictions with an equal weight pulled me home (the push had come when Sam declared, 'Enough'). My hopes lay at odds and ends. I had come over a year before to test a geognostic revolutionary. And then he had won my love but never my faith. Now we stood at the edge of a discovery – a small one about a man or a great one about a world. I felt as one might at the foot of a lover's grave, wishing for a miraculous rebirth and fearful at the same time of the rending and terror of that transformation.*

I feared for the first time: what if it all were true?

Sam was an April day of changing weather. At work he was sunny and brisk with a head for a thousand things at once and hands that could attend to each in its turn. But at other times a blue funk would fall upon him, like a cold drenching, and he would sit and be miserable, his fire doused and nothing left but a stinking smoke. Then he could turn savage and I learned to fly to Mrs Simmons when the first cloud appeared.

A boil came up in the middle of his back and he was always at a stretch to rub it. Without heeding, he often twisted awry to get at it. This grew into a familiar posture, his thick shoulders bunched together and his strong hand searching blind for the spot. I offered to treat it and every night he sat shirtless in the parlour with his back to the stove, while I dropped hot wax upon it. He never flinched or cried out. It was an ugly red welt on his mottled skin, but it grew hard and black. Then I rubbed an ointment on his back which steamed against the fire. We talked little enough in those weeks with one thought in our heads and still less at those times when I stood above him with my left side hot against the stove. But his back and my hands grew companionable, like children who get along quite happily when their mother and father cannot think what to say to each other.

By some miracle of invention we got Sam's beloved double-compression piston to the spot at last – the dank, sweaty, bruising labour of two days and nights. He had the notion of transporting the great beast by water – a slender, leaf-choked tributary of the Potomac ran from the foot of the Boathouse to within a mile of Tyler's Farm. 'The secret of every enterprise', Sam declared, on setting forth, 'lies in beginning – stopping when you can't go on – then beginning again – when you can.' I'm afraid poor Easy and I suffered most of the beginnings. It took four horses, heavy-flanked, whip-sore brutes, simply to drag the device to the river's edge. We hired a river-boat, broad at the beam and shallow-bottomed, which lay slapping lightly against the banks for five hours, as the dark grew round us, and Sam tried to rig up a winch to lower the iron darling of his imagination to the water. It got so we could not bear the bang-bang-bang of the prow against the water, and the flap of the mooring against the post; so we paid a boy just to take the rope in hand and hold the vessel quiet. The sun set behind him and it got so cold we could hear his shivering, sneezing at last, a short blue figure stuck in the muddy bank, never daring to move. A dollar seemed cheap for such dedication; and you may guess we heard an earful from his mother, Mrs Scutching, who kept the Boathouse Saloon, in the morning.

The best I can say for the river journey is this: we did not drown. The Potomac drifts into flat rocky stretches, the current encumbered by weeds and broken trees, and though the winter swelling eased our passage, several times we stood thigh-deep in icy waters, shifting rocks, lifting and pushing and wheezing, kicking and cursing that damned machine, till our hands grew too cold and numb to mind the cut of rock and splinter of wood, and we heaved the vessel into the next deep flood at last. Only at moonrise did the nose of that stubborn boat nudge the spruce tree at the bank below Tyler's Farm; and we left boat and mechanical beast alone together, to sink or rust or rot as they desired, and slept among the hay of Tyler's barn. Good Frau Tyler roused us at noon the next day, sleepless, stiff in back and neck, filthy and stinking and scratching loose stalks of hay from our collars, for a late breakfast, hot cups of coffee and chops fried in onions; and thus fortified we tackled the weight of Sam's tireless imagination once again.

We hauled it out at last and up – behind four horses strapped to their burden by a contraption rigged from the harness of a plough. The beast had wheels, of a fashion, I confess; though we cursed these most of all, as they seem determined always on returning whence they came, and never adventuring, in true pioneer spirit, across fresh woods and pastures new. In short, they liked the bottom of every hill, the rut of every track, the ditch of every field; and Easy and I scrambled desperately behind, to prop the wheels with logs, whenever the horses, steaming, foaming in the cold, began to slip in the mud; or sat back on their haunches, in equine protest, utterly spent. Sam drove on before; and I'm afraid the pair of us behind looked somewhat ungratefully upon his inspirations – both mechanical and oratorical – as he urged us on.

Easy indeed lost his temper at last. The long-boat we (or, rather, his father) had hired, while not entirely sunk by our exertions, required certain decorative improvements – in the manner of cross-benches, tiller-ropes, rowlocks and such – before we could return it; and Easy resented for once the imposition upon his father's generosity. The fact was Easy was an indolent young man, unaccustomed to the pure drudgery of geognostic exploration, and grew, as well he might, peevish and snappish at the cold and the muck, at our chapped and bloodied hands, bruised and aching knees, wet feet, dry throats, sore heads. 'Haul the damn'd thing yourself!' he cried once, when Sam called one of our brief respites to an end. 'When you know yourself, as a matter of fact,' he muttered on, 'that she can't dig deeper than a grave, without exploding, in mud and fire.' I, for one, felt glad of his outburst, relieving as it did my own pent-up frustrations, and drawing, as I guessed it would, Sam closer to me again.

Well, we got the beast up in the end, as the sun set over the hill; and even found time and spirit enough to rumble a barrowful of Tyler's coal to the spot – which we stored inside the chapel door, in case we wanted it on the great day, to clear whatever passage to the earth's core Nature and that eclipse of the internal spheres would quarry out. The journey home, in a leaky, knock-about way, passed astonishingly swift; the moon glittered over

the water, and we pulled ourselves along its bright chain, till the
boat eased against the low pier beneath the Boathouse at the
stroke of ten – just in time for us to stagger up the bank and swallow a hot, sharp glass of grog, as we stared out of the familiar bay
window, before turning to bed. We were too tired for hope or misery or any such luxuries of the human heart; too tired even to
recall the labour that exhausted our limbs and emptied our
thoughts; too tired to dream of those whistling internal spheres,
spinning away below us, towards terrible conjunction in a day
and a half.

Sam was in a black rage on the eve of the eclipse and I'm afraid
poor Easy suffered for it. The nights were still cold and the moon
promised frost – round and bright as a brass gong with a mist at the
edges – when Sam lit his pipe after supper.

'Is anyone to come tomorrow?' Easy asked. 'You know, as my
father said.'

'No.'

'I do not mean a crowd and toffee apples . . .' Easy went on,
though I wished he would not.

'It is not a circus.'

'Exactly, but I thought perhaps your old Professor Silliman; or
that man from the museum in Philadelphia – of natural histories
and technologies and such – who mentioned you kindly.'

'I never guessed I was a cause for charity.'

'No, of course not, but as the Bull says, a community of . . .'

'Because Mr Harcourt pays the bills, does not mean I must attend
to each whim of his son.'

'That was unkindly said,' replied Easy, for I kept silent, though I
should not have.

'I did wish to say, though, Easy,' Sam continued in a cold voice,
'that I don't expect you to bother with us tomorrow. There should be
little to do – and much of it may be long and dull.'

'I should like to come.'

'I would prefer you did not.'

Easy was silent a moment, then he said, 'I may look a fool to you.
And you call me Easy though I am not. A year ago, Phidy, you were

553

just such a one as I and Tom before us no doubt, though he had the sense to leave in time. Does it concern you, Professor, that you attract only hopeless young men with little else to do?' He could be small when he chose. Sam was only cold and quiet. Easy then left without a 'good night' or 'good luck'.

He had left us the carriage, though, and his boy had the horses ready before dawn. Sam was in sunny spirits in the dark morning and said, as the horses jostled in the quiet, 'It is a shame about Easy, though. It is only that he is so awkward – and then everything is such a bore.' My eyes were gummed with sleep and my tongue thick in my mouth, so I said nothing. But Sam would talk. 'It is a queer thought – but we may be riding quite happily towards some disaster. Some fire or great trembling, perhaps, and fallen trees. I really cannot guess.' I was again silent, then he said: 'I should expect at least a strange fog.' He mused for a while at that and then the dawn broke on a pale blue day and my heart rose happily beside his.

Mrs Tyler had tea ready for us at the farmhouse. She knew it was the Great Morning. Her poor hands, thick and brown for such a tiny woman, trembled as she poured. 'It will be all right, Herr Müller?' she said to me in German.

I looked at her, queerly – curiously pleased. 'I really couldn't say.' Even my doubt partly comforted her.

The ground had frozen overnight in dry cracks and the grass crackled underfoot as we walked down to the hole. The morning began ordinary enough. We waited till the sun rose over the low wood and the mists came. Then we tested the softening earth in the flu', which again burned bright and blue, and brightest just before the chapel. Then we waited. The sun burned away the mists and then the dew.

At noon Mr Tyler came with bread and hard cheese and I ate, though Sam could not. He asked us happily, 'Any gold yet?' but we did not answer. We saw Mrs Tyler come down the hill with a flask of tea in her hand, but she would not approach and stood and looked at us thirty feet from the rope. 'Is it all right yet?' she called, and I thought the question hurt Sam so I fetched it from her. 'Is it all right?' she asked again.

554

'Not yet,' I said and took the tea.

I explored the wood for a time and came back and found that Sam had not stirred. It was a beautiful day, the air trembling with spring and birdsong and the sky flushed deep blue. The heavens had none of that winter pallor, like thin milk. Sam sat at the foot of the woods on a fallen trunk. I took his hand and he let me and it was cold as stone. 'Come,' I said, 'let's rummage about the chapel.' He said nothing but he did follow.

It was still colder in there, but I lit some of the candles in front of the crumbling Christ and we warmed our hands on them. There was a nest at His neck, of jay or titmouse perhaps, and though it was muddy there was something tender in it, crackling, stirring softly. I pried at it gently with a stick, simply to pass the time before apocalypse; then desisted, having lost the heart for such cruel meddling, in sympathy with Sam, utterly at the mercy of those tremendous powers, who tease our senses with intimations of the universe. We had seen the child's tin of rocks before, and the mouse; and there was nothing else except the game of draughts so we sat on the pew and played that.

It was five o'clock before we began to dig.

This was next to impossible for the ground was still hard after a muddy foot and anyhow there was far too much of it. Sam began at the north rope and when he could not any more I dug. Soon there was a soft heap of earth along the cordon, no bigger than a mole might make. That took us over an hour. Sam began digging at random in the middle and along the chapel walls. He dug a foot or two and then turned to the next patch, as one might dig for potatoes. I helped for a time, then gave up and sat down, but I grew too cold so I joined him again, all the while saying, 'Sam, there is nothing,' though he did not heed me. Then I gave up again and went for a walk and when I came back he was still digging. 'Sam, there is nothing.'

And yet he did not touch that patch ten feet from the chapel door where the flame had burned bluest. Like a loose brick discovered by a child for hiding secrets, he kept it to himself. I sat and waited, too cold to care. There were small heaps of earth all about like draughts on a board. Only when the sun had set and the moon risen, just waned from the full, though I had to look twice to be sure – only then did he turn his caked spade to that lucky ground. We had not lit a lantern for Sam did not wish to concede the day was spent. I could scarcely see him in the twilight, saw only a dark glow, but I heard his cry of joy as the spade struck something and I ran towards him. He dug deeper in great chunks and already a heavy mass lay at his feet. Then the earth loosened and fell away and the spade cut more easily in the soft ground.

My heart caught in my throat; I could scarce breathe. And yet, and yet, the thought formed, half-finished, echoing in my head, the silly great man has been been Spot On first to last – first to last. The old mad tingling fluttered up my legs, the blood of joy. The ground opened up at a great rate; he stood already knee-deep. Sam was clear – the strange word rang in my thoughts like a touched glass; no crack ran through him after all. Then the spade struck a soft hump in the earth and we looked down.

It was a litter of drowned kittens, slumped all ahoo in the early moonshine, and they stank of the grave.

I lost all hope. (It is worth remembering that our doubts are often as whimsical as our faiths. We dote on such slight evidence, such poor proofs, to found our unbelief.) Sam himself stood wrinkling his eyes against the stink; the poor creatures lay blind as worms entangled upon each other, lightly furred by streaks of mud and crumbled earth; their poor pink snouts mischievously suggesting the urge to sneeze, by the black dust that trembled on their whiskers; their eyes shut tightly against the great black world that had devoured their senses.

'They belonged to the girl, I suppose,' I said.

'Yes.' Then he added, in a curious turn of phrase, 'Can't be helped. Come on, Phidy – bear a hand with the compression piston.'

I did not mean to ignore him; only I had got so cold, grown so weary of the battle of faith and doubt, that in its sudden silence I could barely stir; stood stock still, observing the scene as if from a great distance. Sam's face was muffled by the dark: the broad chin a shadow of stubbornness, his cheeks a rounded silhouette, empty of feature, his noble brow blank, cipher of a thousand thoughts; only his eyes sharp, slight as the glint off a penny.

'Come on, Phidy,' Sam repeated, then bent his back to the beast himself.

I can give no clearer conception of the simple hunger of Sam's faith than by the image of his darkened shape heaving the metal brute from its muddy birth, and shifting it, perhaps an inch, from its sucking bed, downhill towards the hole left by the cats' grave – what had taken four horses to drag up the slope. 'Come on!' he roared now, in the brute anger of physical frustration. 'Phidy! Come on!' And, shaken at last from my reverie, I stumbled to help beside him, pressing my shoulder against his, and breathing the steam of his sour sweat, as we laboured together.

The first inch proved to be the hardest. Gathering reluctant speed, the jolting iron engine shuddered slowly towards the grave; and when at last the edge of the wheel rucked into the dip of Sam's spade-work, it was all we could do to keep the rest of the machine from toppling over after it. We stood now, with our hands propped against our knees, heaving sighs whose cold gusts pinched our lungs at every breath. And Sam looked up, sharp at me, with a white grin in the dark.

At first, I confess, I was grateful for the warmth. Sam hauled a shovel of coal from the chapel doorway, and fed the clattering mouth of the black machine. He huddled over to strike a flame, then lit a handful of loose twigs and broke them over the coals. For the first time in hours, I could see his face by the uneven light: black with dirt, and streaked by sweat run dry and cold against his skin. I had never seen him so fatigued; his eyes wore that wrinkled, crackling look that speaks of an anxiety that cannot exhaust itself. No doubt I looked his brother. And we fed the blaze and fanned our hands against it, a minute or two or ten, simply to rouse the cold blood stopped inside our veins, until our numb fingers blushed and loosened in the heat.

Perhaps a half-hour passed thus – while we built the flame to a crashing roar, and fanned ourselves against the wave of heat and shimmering light that issued from the black gut of the machine.

'Shall we make a beginning?' Sam said, never turning his fine countenance, browned by the hot beams, from the glare of the furnace. How sweet, I thought, even the calm before imminent catastrophe stretches away! I would not break its spell for the world – such companionable warmth we shared in the sharpening starlight, two old friends huddled together by a smoking stove after a bitter-cold day, before a bitter night. A lesson – that the great gift of man lies in postponements, delays, prevarications, in that tireless spirit of neglect of our irremediable fate that sweetens our journey to the grave. Another quarter-hour passed peacefully, though the dead kittens lay soft-backed at our feet, almost squinting it seemed against the unaccustomed light. 'Shall we make a beginning?' Sam said again, and again I did not answer him.

'Come then,' he said (being a brave man), waking suddenly to a sense of his decision, in the abrupt way a fellow lifts his first foot out of bed in the morning, rousing himself. I stepped back instinctively as Sam pressed a lever beside the great iron wheel circling the piston above the furnace; a cog slipped into place and the black dragon cracked and creaked into life at last, a slumbering, shuddering, rough mechanical awakening. Sam paused beside it a moment, to observe the free action of its parts: the piston pumped happily now, shining in the reflected glow of its own heart, in the fire that powered it; the wheel, gathering pace, spun sweet and sweeter, as the force of habit acquired a smoother flow. The racking groan of its inception gave way to a low whistling hum, like the cry of wind in the rigging of a flying ship.

'Come now,' Sam cried, striking his hands together – so true it is that the exercise of force, simply and of itself, begets delight. Even I stood roused – if not to hope then to a pleasure near allied – at the burning spectacle of Sam's imagination thus embodied: a powerful compressed explosion of inner heat driving a swift and shining complexity of interlocking outward parts. Perhaps, I thought, it was merely the long cold that had sapped our spirits; a touch of fire only was required to quicken the blood. 'Shall we have a look', Sam said, 'below?' and dipped another lever, till a cog shifted, and a second wheel began to spin.

On the instant, a kind of drill or spear thumped into the cold turf, raising a shock of dust, and echoing against the low hill in the clear night. Boom – boom – boom, rang out to the stars, as Sam attempted to batter his way to the planet's heart. The drill retracted as the wheel came round, lingered at the top when the joint spun through the flat of its arc, then shot to ground, producing a violent percussion of iron upon earth, as that strange hammer of human conception struck the immutable anvil of the world.

It is true, some progress resulted, a certain degree of excavation, as the turf softened at these repeated blows and dissolved into a thick black cloud that surged around the double-compression piston, sputtered as it drifted into the open furnace, and enveloped Sam himself in a smoking pall.

By this point, I had retreated some way up the rise of the hill, where the fumes of his experiment could not choke the sweet spring air. Sam shifted like a blackened shadow against the glow of the fire, as he fed the red heart of the machine with scraping shovelfuls of coal from the heap in the chapel doorway. 'Sam,' I cried, above the roar of combustion and the banging of that earthen drum, 'Sam!' – calling out for no other reason than an awful sense of overpowering futility. But Sam could not or would not hear; and when the spitting blaze began to overflow its iron cell, torn to red rags in the wind of its own creation, he pressed a third and final lever, releasing within the hollow of the pounding drill another, sharper auger – as if, in Sam's wonderful phrase, the device had managed to 'swallow itself', and thereby perpetuated its downward assault upon the world.

Easy was right – he could dig no deeper than a grave, six feet perhaps of fractured soil, before the battering instrument began to turn upon itself. Or rather, it seemed to my smarting eye – as the thick compound of smoke, ash and dust began to drift across the fields – that the double-compression piston itself sought to bury its body in the reluctant ground. The shuddering machine heaved its full frame against the stubborn turf, as if the drill were only a hook by which it hoped to reel itself earthwards at last, consumed by the mass it strove to penetrate. Sam had passed the point of all his purposes. The furnace lit his streaked and blackened face, shining in the heat of his exertion. There was a kind of frantic joy to his desperation, as if the fury of failure itself offered some violent relief to his great disappointments; as if disaster proved its own reward in the end. 'Sam!' I cried again, pushing through the black cloud to seize him by the arm. He shouldered me away and fed another clatter of coals into the fire, which consumed them at once, unsatisfied, and roared for more. I took his head fiercely in my hands, by the ash and sweat of his blackened hair, and screamed into his blinking eye. The machine had begun to break itself apart, inwardly consumed, outwardly dissipated, by its own desires. The wheels caught and slipped in the violence of their endeavours; drill and auger jolted and shook as they struck home, stuck in bedrock, and could not shake free. The body of the whole began to heave and shudder as if it sought relief from its own intentions. Sam broke free of my hand and scooped another bellyful of coal into the fire.

'Sam,' I cried again, past all patience (and faith, at last), 'for God's sake, Sam; don't make yourself ridiculous!'

This, as I well knew, was the charge, the choice of word, for which he could never forgive me; but it brought us free at last, into the higher air, and the ordinary chill of a spring night, while our ambitions slowly consumed themselves away below us and without us.

It was ten at night before we reached home. Easy waited for us in the parlour. He stood up quickly when he saw us and his hands sweated so he put them in his pockets. He could not think what to say so he said, 'I heard nothing here. You cannot think how jealous I have been. Was it grand – was it very grand?'

'No,' said Sam, 'no,' and pushed past him up the stairs.

'We are only very cold, Easy,' I said, 'and it has been such a long and dull disappointment.' Then I whispered in his ear, 'He is sorry for what he said, Easy. Can you manage him? I fear I angered him today.'

And in truth Sam had little heart to face the friend who had called his 'ridiculous' endeavours to an end.

I fled to Mrs Simmons. She fed me soup before the fire, and then I crouched on my knees at the foot of it, for I was cold to the bone and in the heart. I looked at her husband's painting of the laden ship and said, 'A trade is best. I love your markets. None of this lonely digging.'

'What happened?' she asked.

'Very little. Only we waited a long time and did not talk. And then Sam brought some strange device to bear – on which he had spent his life – fired it and watched it break apart.'

'Is it for the best?' she asked, holding a glass of sherry to her lips, and pausing.

'I could not say. Do you think it is for the best?'

'Yes,' she said, drinking. 'No.'

Then, later, she asked, 'Do you admire him less?'

I thought a minute – a good long minute, chin in hand – biting, kissing my finger in gentle abstraction. But nothing came to mind, nothing at all. 'Yes,' I said, at last, in such careless fashion I knew it to be true.

'Just as well,' she whispered, 'fool.' But it made her unhappy.

We were both so cold at heart that passion itself could give us but a dim light and warmth, as a candle cupped from the wind glows through the red blood. Even such warmth was good to us and eased us into sleep.

At midnight we heard a step. Sam came in and there we lay broad to see, our crimes flush to heaven and to him. 'Oh, oh, oh, oh, my only love,' cried Mrs Simmons, staring and rising, half-held by a dream. She did not mean me, I know, but that other One, the great and mystical and everlasting Sam Syme, the cold, the beautiful, the brilliant, the heartless, the geonometrical, the falling Samuel Highgate Syme, where all our consolation lay. She did not mean me, I know, though, hoping, I turned to her, but her eyes were gone, fled to Sam, hidden with her face in a crook of his arm and her dim hair falling down to his elbows and all her pink-grey back hiding him from me.

But Sam's gaze was mine and how could I answer it? I would have been thine at a word, I thought, but thy word was 'enough'. Yet I knew then that my betrayal had cut him the crueller. Mrs Simmons he comforted with his endless gift for solace – his left arm *pushed her head against his ribs. There she stood blind but full of his smell and rhythm. He looked at me.*

Say 'faithless' to me and I may answer, My love will come to your call for faith. (You did not desire my love, though.) Even your anger would suffice me. Cry treason and lost brotherhood and forsaken friendship. Speak even of the cold bad day, our prospects buried in the gravebed of a heap of kittens, and ask me how I could turn from you at this sore pass.

You did not desire my love, though, only my faith. (I wondered which stung you more: that I saw you brought so low this bitter evening, or stole into your mistress's bed?) Tom was blind to you, a disciple by trade. I was a scientist, with a faith worth winning; but you could not and you knew it — at least you knew it then, as I scrambled into my clothes at the foot of the bed, my rich blue coat, somewhat stained by soot and ash; my yellow breeches, lately much bedraggled; my cream cravat, bound tight to warm my neck, a dirty yellow; my scuffed and filthy shoes. I would have given you such love, a thousand faiths could not make the sum of it. You did not want it.

'I know you,' said Sam, looking down at me, and, truth to tell, I cut a shabby figure. 'I know you now — and what you will become.'

Sam, you are heartless and cruel, and turn only inwards and there is nothing there, when a world lies before thee, bowing.

'She fed me soup,' I answered miserably, 'because I was cold,' and left them together.

Easy was a squall of misery on my return. His nose was wet and shone and his eyes were smeared with the fat of his hand. 'He would not talk to me,' he blubbed. 'He had not a word for me.' My own misery had got tired and slept and would wake in the morning.

'It was only an experiment that failed.'

'That's it,' said Easy, 'a squib,' and the word cheered him, 'a damp squib.'

'Only a very dull day,' I said, and thought, He is more faithful than I.

'I gave him tea and put a rug over his knees for he was so cold and I asked him what he found. He said "dead cats".'

'Oh,' I said. 'We forgot to bury them again.'

'That's what he said. Is it a little funny? I shall use that word in the morning – a squib.'

'Yes, a squib. Not damp; quite – burned away, in fact. Burned up. Excuse me, Easy, if I talk nonsense at you. I'm for bed.'

As I lay down to sleep, I had a new image of Syme. He was like a tall tree, towering and graceful. Yet everyone sought to cut their names in him. And in his shade, all kinds of unclean things were done and left their mark. So that, upon a closer look, we saw only other people's scars and other people's dirt. Nothing kept me there any more, certainly not my faith or my courage.

In two weeks I was gone. Sam was in such a low hole that he would speak to no one, certainly not myself. In the end, Easy sent for Tom and the two of them spirited him off to Tom's own home, where Kitty I believe nursed him tenderly. In an odd turn of events, I retired to Baltimore and Sam's father, from whence to take my journey home.

Mr Syme embraced me warmly and fussed over my things. 'Perhaps', he said to me on the stairs, with my bag in hand to lead me to my bed in Sam's old room, 'my son will come back to me now.' He was sad and pleased.

I thought often of that long day, frightened of my own faithlessness. The steady accumulation of belief, stuck on me and hardened by habit, had been dislodged by that blow, easy as snow from a green tree. They all seemed madmen, each one. Sam with his opium theories – a hollow earth! concentric spheres! fluvia!; Ezekiel with his damp enthusiasm; even Tom, indefatigable in the cause, had something crazy and cold about him. I was no better. Now my father urged me home, by his triumph not disaster, so I left.

To collect my things, I stopped at Pactaw one last time. I did not dare call on Mrs Simmons, but she met me at the coach station, and helped me with my box. She wore a blue jacket, bright as a butterfly's wings against her silvered hair, and a green skirt that swept the ground like a willow. She had strong hands, as I discovered,

563

when she clasped the iron handle above my own, and pressed my finger to the bone, setting down the trunk.

'I heard you were going,' she said. 'Tom sent me this to give to you.' It was a letter. I took it through the carriage door, and then urged suddenly, 'Come home with me. We have no place in this New World. I will find you a berth on my ship and in a month you will be in Germany.'

Before I could think what I had asked, she began to weep. 'Sam sleeps like a baby now,' she said. 'Before he could never endure the night. He comes to me now more often, even more than at first. So I am grateful to the cats for that at least. Sam is my only love and a great man, and I would rather be miserable with him than happy with another. He is grand and fine, and everything around him matters wonderfully – the least thing, like me. I wish Tom had been beside him that night, for Tom is such a happy fool, he would have found some trick.'

'Then there is nothing to be said,' I answered, turning away. And the coachman struck his whip and the horses began to move. I watched her shrink behind me, as blue as a stone.

'Sam will miss you,' she called after me, from her own heart perhaps or to leaven her hard words.

We rode past the Dewdrop Inn and I took my last look of Pactaw, before we reached the river and turned north. The two low hills burned green with spring, and even the wind had a new air. The last patches of snow had gone and the streets were ordinary brown streets and the houses were ordinary white houses. There was nothing to keep me. I tore open Tom's letter and read.

Dear Phidy,

They tell me 'tis decided you depart. I would have wished to make a warmer farewell, a flesh-and-blood goodbye, you know, and taken your hand; but Kitty can't spare me now, being six months gone, and Sam won't spare me now, certainly not, he says, to visit you. I don't know what's come to pass between you – Sam won't tell me, nor breathe a word of that long day – but I can *guess,* having *guessed, long before now, that it* would. *I trust this letter reaches you through Mrs Simmons.*

Well, we have burned the last of the New Platonists, *whatever we could lay our hands on. Sam says he couldn't bear the thought of Harcourt reading them; and so we heaped the lot of them in the yard, rolled one up and lit it at the lantern flame, and tossed it burning on the pile. A pretty little blaze it made, too – to think how quickly words may be consumed, what take such a weight of thought and time and even* iron *to bring to press. Thin ash scattered to the heavens like crows at dusk, and for weeks afterwards, they say, little black feathers, as it were, of the great American geognostic journal, lay scattered about the streets of Pactaw, till some footstep trod them into dust. But we were gone by then.*

You won him, Phidy, I told you, in the end. Perhaps I should not have given him over so easy; and for this I blame myself, knowing as I did that some deeds cannot be ventured without faith, a full faith, that is, which shall not crack along the line of doubt at the first touch. I shall not give him over again, I think; and Sam for one no longer has the heart to cast about him.

Your faithful, etc.
Tom Jenkyns

Farewells are always the swiftest of occasions – how soon the day of my departure came. Reuben brought his coach to the door and lifted my trunk as light as a bundle of hay in his great hands. 'Are you coming along, Barbara? We get on pretty well at the shop,' he said to me, confidentially. 'Ain't they fine horses?'

Edward embraced me warmly on the steps and kissed my hair. 'I have forgotten Ezekiel,' I cried suddenly. 'I borrowed Easy's chronometer on . . . to mark the time on that bitter day . . . when the earth opened up. I pray you return it.'

'Never mind, Phidy,' Edward said, standing outside in his shirt-sleeves. 'He can spare one, the fop. You must take something back

565

with you, after all, to remember my son. There, now you're off. You are much better out of this business, you know.'

That hurt me deeply, for it made my allegiances suddenly clear. I knew even then Sam had dry years ahead, and that we can resign ourselves to unhappiness is as much a miracle to me as faith. (The clock now lies ticking on the table where I write.)

So on that bright spring afternoon I stood with my trunks around me at the pier. Bubbles saw them on to the boat and gave me a quick kiss on either cheek. 'I hope we have not disappointed you,' she said.

I thought of Tom's greetings, on that colder, more hopeful day just over a year before: 'You're almost too late. Have you brought fifty cents? Oh, never mind, come in. We'll see about that later. Come on!' I cried into the spray as they rowed me to the ship.

I dreamed a strange dream the first night on board, which has come to me often since. It was born perhaps out of my shifting bed and the clank and hiss of water and wind, and my uneasy sleep. There is something comic to it, though it troubled me sorely and I woke weeping. I dreamed that I spotted Sam on some crowded street, I could not say where. I saw him clearly among all the people, for he was a head above them, and when I found him he looked down on me, though I am taller. There was some great fear in his face, but I could not reach him and the dream shifted. A few weeks had passed and again I saw him in a crowd, and now he had to stoop for we were in a room. What I first thought was fear was sadness now, and I knew, without a word said, that he was growing and could not help himself, unfit for company, taller and thinner and more remote. It was the certainty that appalled me. He knew what would happen and could not stop. When I saw him again, a month later, he had reached such a height I could no longer make out his face.

·Epilogue·

THE GREAT TRICK, IT SEEMS TO ME, in teaching high school lies in becoming *characteristic* – of oneself, it goes without saying, though it does not always go without *acting*. 'And me so deeply *me*,' good Dr Karpenhammer warbled at us at one particularly drunken convocation of the Blue-stocking Society . . . oh, many years ago now I am sure. (We have come upon the final revision of my professional ambitions.) Children believe, naturally, in the power of personality: the broad gestures, declaring, *here am I and this is what I'm like*. Hier steh ich, as Luther cried, ich kann nicht anders. Though we proclaim instead, Here stand I, and I can and will *repeat myself* – and continue to repeat, that is, until you understand *me*, and through such understanding, the world – or whatever particular chapter of its history we hope to sell to a rabble of eleventh graders, on a dark Thursday morning in November, when the electric lights flicker in their wire cages against the stippled ceiling-tiles, unless it is only the teacher's hangover *blinking*. In short, characteristically, I have begun to affect a pipe.

You can see me, if you wish – and since I have begun with a blank, dripping day in November, I may as well continue – huddled in the half-cold in the wet parking lot, at the exit ramp, standing by Ralph, the security guard. Chatting occasionally, as I stuff the pipe-bowl with Old Virginia, and try to set the flicker a-glow – while the seniors amble 'down the hill' towards the subway joint, or the pizza parlour, or the tattoo parlour, for all I care, or the Irish bar hidden behind the iron stairs and stanchions of the number 9 train, on 242nd Street. Where the bums sleep over the road on the benches by the park – that flat green stretch of drizzling nowhere on which the eye lingers and for which the heart yearns from the corner window of the history office on the third floor, between the copy machine and the stack of empty water-butt jugs, unreplaced.

Of course, it takes more than a pipe to run the History Department. A pinch of gravitas, lightly sprinkled, as the salt in the pepper of my new beard; a tongue sharp or sweet as the occasion demands. And a clear access, free pipeline, to our enthusiasm – that *fuel* undiminished with age, by which *we* light the world, kindle and rise to Her, when she feeds us a fresh intimation of her nature; while keeping a sufficiency of old ardour in reserve, which (like the oil of Judas Macabee) burns brightly between these rare replenishings. (I have become a Jew, you see, at last; finally persuaded by Susie's insistence 'that most of us live by faiths we don't believe in' – quite happily, as it happens, she neglected to add, and to the benefit of our children.) A certain clutter helps, too. A dishevelment of the classroom and the person, the rumour of a mind on higher things, bruited through frequent inattentions, slips of the tongue and 'soft, abstracted airs' – not to mention the irremediable *rummage* of books, confusion of papers, curious objets d'art, ornaments, heirlooms, keepsakes, cartographical records and obsolete instruments, upon desk and shelf. To this end, if no other, Syme has proved a great resource. A copy of Phidy's manuscript lies under a heavy round stone (painted over with ships) within my office cubicle. The magnesium flu', that magic lantern Joe constructed, hangs from a hook in the ceiling. And the last and final proof of his genius lies in the small, wooden, glass-panelled box Tom Jenkyns built for him, before he died – which sits, under a pot of dried heather, on the top shelf of my classroom bookcase, next to the dusty and unused VCR. But I outrun myself, as ever.

Susie, as they say, doesn't work here any more. She stopped, when Kitty (named to please me) came along, now five years old. That's when we moved to Astoria (so Na-na could help with the baby girl), in a sweet, brick-fronted, child's sketch of a row-house on 34th Street, with half a back garden – now flowering over, after the tireless application of Susie's sturdy green thumb, with roses, primroses, daffodils, pinks and even a small chunky patch of potato plants and cabbages. Not to mention two bicycles, belonging to the boys, and Kitty's tiny two-wheeler with safety wheels still screwed on, leaning awkwardly together against the fence, on good days, and spinning among the flowers, on bad. And Susie's pine shed in the corner, looking over the garden through a broad single pane of glass, flecked with colours from the spattering of her palette – her studio.

She took up painting again when Kitty was born – idly, at first, between bouts of damp exhaustion, simply to dabble her fingers in colour again, delightful in itself – especially with her sense and flesh keened to such a pitch, the lightest touch could set her quivering. But then, as the girl grew (and began to sleep, upon occasion), the old passion consumed her – for precision, that intricate *abundance* of lines and angles that composes our vaguest shapes, sights and insights. We lived, still, cramped in a railroad flat on 89th and 2nd, just above a bar – a shady, ramshackle watering-hole, with high windows opening on to the dusty street in summer, and broken-footed chaise-longues, brocaded settees and unstuffed vermilion armchairs, cluttering the wood floors. Susie looked out the kitchen window and she painted fire-escapes, in reds that rusted like the iron ladders, and greens and coppers where the mildew caught, and shining browns where the rust and paint scabbed and scraped away. Clever and plain escapes, some with loose straggles from plant-pots clambering over and through the ironwork; occasional pieces of washing (rare); occasional misfits sitting and smoking on the steps into their opened windows; occasionally joined by company (rarer still).

I would like, from sheer romance, to say that Susie was discovered 'by accident' – coming home, as may be, after a long afternoon on a neighbouring side-street (further west perhaps, towards Park Avenue), where she painted the ornate escapes of single, stony family homes, covered in plants. By the barman, perhaps, who saw her clutching a wet canvas in the entryway, and offered to buy it for the long, exposed brick wall above the fireplace. The truth is, Father and Mother Pitt in the hot summer nights used to 'retire below', as we told the boys, permitted for once to watch TV while they kept an eye on Baby-Kitty. While we, of course, drank lemony gins and tonics in the opened window of the bar, talking amid the tap-tap, tap-tap-tap of an evening rain, which spat dusty drops on the sidewalk between the trees. It was I, in fact, who approached the barman, over Susie's blushing, anxious protestations, somewhat puckered by the lemon rind she twisted in her mouth, and persuaded him to hang a series of oils, by a local artist, recording the 'quiet façades of neighbourhood life'.

In truth, she needed little discovery, possessing as she did *a mother in the trade*. As Susie declared to me, her early shyness overcome, plugging the corner of her mouth with an imaginary cigar, 'I got my peoples here about me.' So she did. And made a quiet, unsteady income, on top of my promotion to 'Department Head' (a strange, unflattering title, I maintain), sufficient to support the purchase of a house in Queens, on another, more permanent, mortgage of our loves and lives. (If I tell you that we now drive 'the family car', *finely tuned*, as the family insisted, and riding sweetly on four 'perfectly acceptable' tyres, I believe you will understand that I have said all I need to say upon the subject of our settling *in* and *down*.)

Then, two years ago, my father died. On the quiet, as usual. Or, rather, in such characteristic solitude that nobody could have heard him had he shouted. The maid, Florinda, who came on Tuesdays, found him in the bathroom, slumped back against the cistern with his head on one side. He was one of those old men who got thin against the grain, skinny as he never was in youth. (Pitt, like his son, was born plump.) His neck lay curiously exposed, bristling slightly, fine enough for a single hand to curl about it, as they lifted him from the spot. Florinda, of course, never touched him; but a career spent among the dirty corners of people's lives had prepared her for the corner in which she found him dead. She called me first, and – since sweet summer had come, greening and thickening and dusting the city – caught me at home, in a dressing-gown at one in the afternoon, watching cartoons with Kitty. 'There was nothing in the pot,' she said, 'Dr Pitt. He did not even go.'

By some sleight of grief, I thought at first only of my own long dallying in that smallest room, where I keep a stash of books above the cistern on a shelf and bring the papers on Saturday morning, to hide from the swell and clamour of my family rousing and breakfasting outside. Inside, the world crumples and spreads out at my unclipped toes. Outside, it chatters along without me. And I thought, He probably wanted a minute's quiet to himself, retiring as he had without a particular urge in that direction, before I recalled the old house hushed and empty beyond that little room.

I decided to drive to the funeral, fixed for the Wednesday following; and set off the next morning, under a cloud of Susie's sympathies and tender reproaches – for shrinking from her just when she wished to comfort me, and barring her company on what she called my 'trip'. But this seemed to me a matter of family business; and the family business, as we know, was Islands – and they are not easy to . . . desert. Besides, I had other duties to attend to, as an only child; and expected to be gone several weeks, clearing up my boyhood home and keeping what I liked, and selling the rest. My children did not know their grandfather well; and perhaps I desired as much, from a cause split two ways. Partly, he shamed me, in his brisk, misplaced enthusiasms and well-meaning ill manners; there was something low class about him, I could not deny, and he brought it out in me as well. 'Ask and you'll get on; that's what I do; always asking, me. But make a name for yourself, my boy – stick out a little, unlike your old man – a name that lasts is the only thing that counts.' Partly, I desired some respite from the world I had joined – Susie's world, it seemed, to which our children belonged. I desired a familiar refuge *from* the life I had made, *out of reach* of the life I had made, untouched and undiminished by it.

Hers was the only cloud I struck until New Mexico – a blissful scorching run of summer days. The sun stripped layer upon layer of blue from the shimmering skies, peeling the old paint to get to the first wash. The nights rang clear as a bell, and that bell was the moon – trembling in the heat and bright as brass. I stopped whenever I could off the highways. The towns, even those slight clusters around a church or a park or an outlet mall, in Pennsylvania, Indiana, Missouri, Oklahoma, oppressed me with a sense of lives

573

lived. Only the solace of Nowhere, off the interstate, offered such suspension of accustomed laws as I desired. I swam in the lit pools before going to bed, and lay, it seemed, always in the same sheets, watching the same box, eating the same pancakes in the morning, and growing fat and spotty as a boy again.

In New Mexico the storms began. Lightning split, suggesting a run of cracks in the delicate, invisible shell of the sky – flaws briefly illuminated, before our eyes lost the trace of them again and thankfully forgot such evidence of the hollow, imperfect spheres in which we lived. God sifted sugar of light between cloudy hands. The heat thickened, grew heavy. Even the plants, such as they were, started to sweat. The land began to grow familiar as I entered the littered deserts of Arizona – scrub and dirt and nothing to look at except for the nothing to look at, mile after mile, and the glitter of low towns in the distance before the road passed them by. At last, the vistas grew green again, under the tireless sprinklers, as I turned on to the 'happy highways' of my youth on a low-muttering Tuesday afternoon. And drove through the hot dusk into San Diego – 'land of my birth,' as I once wrote, 'under that synthetic sky, a creation of God's akin to an architect's model, clean, unchipped, constructed for tiny men' – coming home to bury my father.

The funeral itself passed easily enough. Time is wonderful in its persistence; and I knew at the Eternal Home Crematorium (EHC Ltd) it was only a matter of time before the service finished, and the few mourners, dressed in khaki (the Californian black) or flowered prints, muttered at me and departed. My father was the kind of man who had a friend at the garage, and a friend at the deli, and a friend at the library, and the hardware store, and – yes, even at the hospital where my mother lay dying, at the front desk, where he delayed his visits. At work, he boasted a number of 'buddies', but no one by name. He used to know 'a couple kids' in reception, and acknowledged several 'friends' in the secretary pool at admin. Few of them survived his retirement. He thrived at . . . passing compliments; and so passed ordinary, enduring friendships by. There were always a few 'gangs' on the go, in my childhood, for *evenings on the town*, as he said – groups large enough, that is, to get by without intimacy. My father loved games – these also kept acquaintances at arm's length. I believe he prompted several fads himself. But then the passion for the particular game – bowling, Scrabbling, charades – died out, and the gang died with it, and its members dispersed. A few were left over for the funeral, and I knew them vaguely, and they made things worse.

In the end, I took only Florinda for a cup of coffee afterwards, at a diner whose air conditioner proved to be on the fritz. A hot, fussy day about to break in clouds above us. We settled accounts, and she wept slightly and tenderly into a paper napkin unwrapped from an unused fork and knife as I paid the bill. Our bottoms sweated and stuck to the vinyl seats when we stood up to go.

I used to dream of his death, from time to time, before it happened, you see – sob in my sleep, sharp sucking breaths that woke Susie, who woke me, who woke weeping. And then a day or two might pass before the muddling misery dried up again, and the shadows of mourning faded into ordinary day. I was prepared, you see – that's what I mean to say. And the great resource of dreams did not diminish after his death; and he died to me, again, again, years afterwards, only now I woke curiously comforted, by the freshness of his image in my heart. And there I consigned him, to these shadows, where I knew he would keep long and well, untouchable by time as well as me. The funeral itself mattered less; like my father, I have no stomach for the details of decay, the blood and ash. I prefer the leftovers – the letters, books, clutter our lives leave behind us – to the evidence and etiquette of death.

It took me two weeks to go through the house. 'Have you ever', I once asked, on a much happier occasion:

> stood in the dust of a dead man's house, opened creaking
> the closet of his clothes – racked neatly still, the jackets set-
> tled loosely over the thin shoulders of the wire hangers, the
> trousers pressed and dangling in even rows; explored the
> larder, the tins of uneaten soup, the packets of spaghetti,

the undrunk wine; and *then*, slipped on the jacket, and eaten the soup, and drunk the wine, alone, in the quiet of his absence? Have you ever tracked a dead man's thought down the gloomy corridors of the mind, your comprehension lit by the same shower of synapses that illuminated the passages of his brain . . . spark for spark? Have you ever done all this, and then *tidied up* what you found?

This, however, proved slow and mournful work; much of it unbearably finicky and tedious; all of it unmentionably . . . well, I would say 'soul-destroying', but it seemed simpler than that and less dramatic. 'Defeatist' is perhaps the better word, or 'defeated' – though neither seems quite right. (I had ample – I would not say, *leisure*, to choose the word for what was happening to me in those two weeks. I picked and pored over it, as I packed and unpacked and repacked; and sold and threw out. But having said it was unmentionable, I will not mention it any more.) Let me say only that he left a great many . . . worthless papers behind; and I recognized my inheritance.

Among them (and after this, I will let the matter . . . rest), I discovered a rather surprising collection of notes, photocopies and clippings, from the period leading up to my mother's death. He used, as I said, to spend his Sunday evenings at the public library – shoulder to shoulder with the bums and the drunks and the kooks and the pill-poppers and the needle-pushers and the out of work and the washed-up pensioners in threadbare suits who frequent such honourable institutions – researching his great treatise on the history of falsework: 'the temporary structure which enables the permanent structure to be constructed, and which must be retained until the permanent structure is self-supporting'. Only he wasn't, you see. I found instead a notebook, meticulously dated and annotated, carefully pasted over with newspaper accounts of miraculous recoveries.

From *cancer* – and there are countless such; it is a strange, proliferating disease that yields almost as many opportunities for new hope as for sudden despair. (*Sure as blackthorn bursts with snow*, the words echoed in the hollow of my thoughts, *cancer in some of us will grow*.) Some of them dated as far back as the death of Syme's own mother, after that terrible storm, so many summers ago. My finger paused over the crinkled, glued-on, yellowing paper, to find that father and son had, in their separate pursuits, stumbled across the same jumbled account:

> Having heard rumour of that wonderful leaf, pipsissiway, in curing cancers; in the meantime, several tumours appeared and daily enlarged. Her physician, an eminent practitioner, advised a sudden use of the knife, but her friends dissuaded her from the operation, believing it would be undergoing severe pain without the smallest hope of relief. The herb being near at hand was immediately procured and used as directed, and I rejoice to add that the tumours have been completely removed, her general health much improved, and there is every prospect of her recovery. I have set this for publication, without waiting her perfect restoration, that others may avail themselves of the same means as early as possible. The plant is an evergreen, and sometimes called winter green; the mode of using it simply to drink of the tea, and wash the part frequently with a strong decoction. I hope your brother editors through the country will give this a place in their Gazettes.

Somehow, this hidden treasure of my father's fears (and hopes) only saddened me. I could abide the fact that he neglected my mother from an *absence of love* – fled to the library in the evening while she suffered that 'severe pain without the smallest hope of relief'. (Mother and son watched the *Sunday Night Movie* together; I dreaded school in the morning; she, chemotherapy.) Marriage teaches many things, among them indifference and its attendant desire – for honesty and the solitude necessary to its practice. It was, no doubt, foolish of God to invent a species of creature whose heart is corrupted by even the kindest dishonesties; and whose life cannot pass without them. Yet I did not mind the way he escaped her suffering, until I saw that he neglected her *out of love*. And such a strange, curious, burrowing love, that sought relief of fear in books and newspapers and his own crazy speculations – pipsissiway, for God's sake – and never in his wife or son. That leakage in all of us whose flow may only be staunched by a human touch had been *plugged up* in him, till I had no news within, to judge whether he rotted or dried up. 'And I became conscious', in Phidy's words,

that some vital appetite had died, some necessary joy, leaving behind it, dried and choked, the most indispensable well-spring of the soul and source of continual replenishment – curiosity in the workings of the human heart.

You must remember that I was sleeping in my boyhood bed at this time, in a house emptied of father and mother; and Dad had changed little since she died and I left; only disorder and disrepair had accumulated since. I should be forgiven a certain indulgence in morbid thoughts. I thought to call Susie but could not and did not, shrunk into solitude till my voice squeaked at the touch of air. (Strange how quick we grow unaccustomed to company; how deep the current of loneliness runs within us, if we let it.) I sat up, sleepless, through the loud summer nights, going over the father's old papers in the son's old room, drinking up whatever he had left in the house: foul blackberry wines and flat beers; mini-bottles of gin and vodka, carried off a plane; an untouched bottle of Christmas port.

I discovered, before closing his affairs and turning home, one curious account, unlike the mass of miraculous recoveries he pasted in the book. It struck me at once – it was the only story that ended in the sufferer's death. The article, which appeared in the *San Diego Chronicle* shortly after my mother's diagnosis, described the slow and inexplicable decline of a 'young man, newly married and the father of a baby-girl' thirty years before. He had simply begun to 'shut down' – that was the phrase – in his late twenties, complaining at first of a slight nausea, general lethargy, tingling in the legs and hands. He grew fat, unpleasantly, awkwardly fat, despite a general loss of appetite; he was confined first to his armchair and then to his bed; in the end, he lacked the energy even to relieve himself, and a full-time nurse was installed to shift him periodically and induce the necessary evacuations. His wife moved into the spare room as she awaited his recovery. He never recovered; the doctors despaired; first, second, third opinions retired perplexed. The man hovered at last at the edge of coma, without slipping under – he could just about manage a grunt to acknowledge some passing relief from the tireless monotony of his life. In an almost equally astonishing triumph of lethargy (and love), the wife never shifted from her temporary sleeping accommodations; turned every night to the same small bed beside an office filing-cabinet; hoped her husband would 'feel better' in the morning. (A lesson in the subtlety of time.) Thirty years passed.

Then a new doctor, alerted perhaps by a gossiping nurse, desired to inspect the patient. By this time, the baby-girl had escaped to Seattle, as far away as she could drive up the coast of the Pacific; the wife was grey-haired, somewhat delicate. The trouble, the young man concluded, was that her husband's metabolism – for whatever reason – had simply 'switched off' (this was the phrase). 'That's why he just kind of slowed down,' he said. A new procedure, lately developed, might just 'turn the switch back on again'. Mother and daughter didn't know whether to hope or fear – *what* to hope for or what to fear. But they accepted the experiment, and watched astonished as the old man rose to life again, awkwardly, miserably, hungry and sharp. By the end of one month, he could walk about the house, resting each hand on a shoulder (the daughter had returned) – how he talked, gazed at the television, gobbled his grub again! By the end of two, he could venture into the front yard and stare at the passing traffic of the street – immeasurably saddened by such excess and exhaust of energy, endlessly repeated. By the end of three, he was dead – from cancer of the liver, which had been arrested by his general decline and lain dormant in him through his long dormancy. His body had sunk instinctively to such low ebb that the barest breath of life remained and the cancer starved. Now it revived again in his general revival, and killed him. The article did not say for better or worse – though clearly the body itself had sought to live, even at the lowest rate.

What made my father paste this terrible story into the book? What faith or doubt did it inspire? Of whom did it remind him? My mother, in her ageless skinniness, fearful of any change? My father himself, retreating for survival so deep into his own resources, and slowly freezing over? And yet to my mind it suggested nothing so clearly as Syme: happily buried in the ice of his obscurity, until my intemperate revival dragged him to the heat and light of day again, where he began to rot and stink, and required a second burial.

You may guess I turned from my home in some relief, and settled to the long road quite happily, despite the close air of hot old leather and the broken seat-springs in the family Cadillac.

I took the southern route home again. 'Have I not said home already,' Phidy once asked, 'and can I in the space of a few lines use the word for so distant and different a destination?' *Yes*, is the only answer – and I drove six thousand miles, and forty years, as it were, from my childhood to my middle age. I passed through the dry breadth of Texas – along the shoulders of that great state, across the neck – and tinkered with the thought of turning south to Austin at its heart. Over the long, flat road I imagined several pithy conversations between myself and Bunyon, happily reunited, shall we say – in which through various feints and false lunges, misdirections mischievously applied, I managed to turn the talk (and tables) upon him at last, to utter a clinching come-uppance to the phrase I am sure he had forgotten long ago: 'Pitt is a genial little goblin, and I wish him well.' But such is the stubbornness of our fancy, composed as she is of a logic older than and independent of ourselves, that she baulked where I would bend her and refused – granting instead even in *my mind's ear* the last word to Bunyon. 'You'll thank me, Pitt,' he said, almost whistling through the exposed brickwork of his grin, 'in the end.' Knowing, as I did, that he was right – I was better off going where I was going, and doing what I was doing, in a small way; so I did not stop at Lubbock, nor turn south, but headed straight to Dallas, thence to Arkansas, before nudging gently to the north.

Only coming through Virginia on a burning, stinking summer day, with a black cloud hanging over the road, which declined to budge or shake into rain at last, did I consider, *A quick look couldn't hurt*. The air conditioner on the family car had broken down in 1973, and a sweet, hot handful of sweat ran down my spine, and stuck against the leather seat. So I stopped at a diner outside Richmond, ordered the home-brew ice-tea and asked the waitress, a round-faced high-school girl with a nose-ring and a summer cold, if they had a phonebook I could borrow? Pactaw itself I knew had long gone the way of all flesh (and wood). Union Pacific bought the land in the 1870s and tore down the village to lay a track (itself now defunct) from DC to Richmond, across a narrow pass of the Potomac. But the family Jenkyns, along with Syme himself, had moved to Richmond after Phidy's disastrous departure in 1827.

There were no Symes in the phonebook, and I expected none; the enduring convalescence of his later life produced, as I had supposed, no heir. And 'Syme' itself is an uncommonly uncommon name, for such an ordinary conjunction of the alphabet. It is the 'y', I believe, that bears such rare distinction. Of Jenkinses and Jenkynses (the strange 'y' notwithstanding) there proved to be a greater selection, five or six perhaps of the latter, though I knew my man at once: the Reverend Thomas, of 17 Kendal Place. 'Called to the Church by family tradition,' Phidy wrote of Jebediah – a tradition which, I hoped, had survived these hundred and thirty-odd years since Tom died and I came to look for his descendant. Odd how deeply this living instance of the familiar name moved me, to a recollection of those passionate and solitary two years I spent attempting to restore Syme's withered glory, when I had leave, in his phrase, 'to go over even old ground with a fresh hand, a clear head, and a curious heart'.

I ignored the telephone number along the dotted line, determined to venture everything upon the luck and courage of the moment. 'These', I said, returning the heavy tome to the snuffling waitress, 'are wonderful – *historical* – records. If I could begin', I declared to her, to brighten her middling afternoon, 'my career from scratch, I should choose to study that rich ground on which genealogy and geography overlap. In short, phonebooks and graveyards – scenes of the heartbreaking juxtaposition of *name* and *place*. Now, my dear girl – might I trouble you for a map?'

Borne on the flood of forgotten high spirits, I soon discovered Kendal Place, at the southern tip of Highland Park, a broad green neighbourhood of bluish clapboard houses set amid unfenced lawns. Sagging inflatable baby-pools, dirty with green water, lay in the front yards, next to kicked-over tricycles and flat footballs; minivans and Volvos gleamed in the open drives. Kendal Place itself proved to be a short, kerbless dead-end, running into a green bank of wood, which fell to a creek littered with orange peels, candy wrappers and beer-cans. A yellow truck had pulled in front of number seventeen. The Jenkynses were home, it seemed; and *moving home*, as the phrase is. A long white couch sat, implausibly and imperturbably, in the front yard; two small boys perched upon it, stretching their legs straight out, too short to touch the ground. They stared disconsolately at the clutter in the front yard – television sets, two; a refrigerator on its back; several boxes in various states of disrepair; a tumble of books spilling out of one; a glass case, empty, it seemed, antique, beside the sofa; loose heaps of clothes – waiting, as boys do, for the world to bear them along wherever it would.

I supposed the Reverend Thomas to be that exasperated gentleman, at his wits' end – he seemed, to be fair, quite comfortable there, and accustomed to it – standing on the doorstep and directing a traffic of box and bag from house to truck. He was an affable, fattening young man, fair-haired, dressed in a plaid shirt and a pair of outgrown corduroys that exposed, above the slackening tube-socks, an inch of honey-coloured ankle. No one listened to him – not wife, not labourer, as they dismantled, in Phidy's phrase, their

home on the river until a houseful of things had shrunk squarely into three large wooden boxes and two trunks, my own among them.

Afterwards, Sam perched on top of one of the boxes with dirty hands
and dusty knees and remarked in a rare flight of whimsy, 'It is like
sitting on top of a year – a very small year.'

The Reverend Thomas, however, had accumulated a greater *quantity* of years, it seemed, than Syme had – or an equal number of *larger* years, perhaps. In any case, they refused to fit in a yellow Leviathan of a rental truck, never mind a few boxes and trunks. So I approached him gently, gingerly, with all the deference at my disposal. 'Reverend Jenkyns, sir!' I cried, running across the yard. 'Thomas Jenkyns, I believe – a minute of your time,' huffing as I strode to take his hand.

Phidy's description, I discovered on a closer view, of Tom's beloved cousin had come to life before me. The Reverend Thomas seemed the *Word itself made flesh* (several generations along the line):

James greeted us mopping a wet brow with a wet handkerchief, and
extending a newly dried hand. A fine light sweat still pricked from
the skin . . . He was a kindly, sweating man. His hair was always
moist and his hand always damp. He ran to fat, too, like Jeb; but
James's spreading waist seemed accretions of hesitant contentment,
too polite to form actions or words. He was still a young man,
though he would not be long.

I knew at once that I had found my man, so sure a stamp is genealogy (pity my poor boys).

'Of course, of course,' he said, with the faintest echo of slow Virginia in his voice. 'Take a minute. Take as much as you like. I'll tell you a secret, Mr –'

'*Doctor*. Doug Pitt, from the University of – of . . .'

Tom spared my shame, stooped to my ear and whispered, 'No one heeds me, anyway. Pull up a chair – a temporary blessing of moving house – somewhere to sit in the front yard.' He lay back heavily in a leather armchair, lifting his eyes to the heavens, and arching his neck till the knuckles of it cracked. 'Oh,' he sighed. Pitt sat at the edge of a kitchen stool – Tom was a man who took his own pleasures, and expected the rest of the world to do the same. 'If my wife asks,' he said, 'this is parish business. Now, what can I do for you?'

A great deal, as it turned out. I feared at first a certain *hacking* might be required, to get my question across – and launched at once (abandoning metaphor and misgiving at once) upon the high seas of my old passion, hoping to carry him along:

> And before I could say yea or nay I had begun the whole mad thing from the first. Would you credit it, the half-forgotten thoughts – ideas I had believed long rusted and out of use – flew from my lips as bright as the day they were coined, made of such shadowy stuff time could not touch them? Sam himself could not have explained them better, his words had such a renaissance in my heart, I almost wept, an old foolish man, at the recollections they aroused.

Only the Reverend Thomas cut me off at once. 'Oh God,' he said, smiting his hefty flanks and sitting up. 'You've come about Syme, haven't you? *Edith*,' he called out, loud and idly at once. 'A fella's come about Syme!'

'Does it happen all the time?'

'Heavens, no. Only my father always said some day somebody would.'

It took a good half-hour to dig up the relevant box. By some mischance, the thing had gone first into the back of the truck; but Reverend Thomas, on an ancestral quest, clambered into the hold and only blinked smiling when the movers told him angrily it couldn't be got at. The piano had to be shifted. The piano *couldn't* be shifted. The piano *was* shifted, at last; and the precious wooden crate – a grapefruit box, filled with papers, home once of Florida's finest – scraped along the steel bottom into the clouded sunshine again, into the clutch of Pitt's greedy fingers and the gaze of his greedier eyes. I hauled it back to the leather armchair in the grass, heaved it down at my feet, and dried my sweating paws upon my jeans, before tenderly lifting the first sheet to my lap. I almost wept, in Phidy's phrase, at the recollections they aroused.

The great thing, of course, would be to find a copy of that elusive rag, the *New Platonist* itself – final proof of Syme's genius, of his place in the wonderful evolution of thought that led to Wegener's breakthrough at last. But I have spent a lifetime holding back the highest joys until the end, to sharpen the sweet appetite – and did so now, working meticulously through the heap of papers (letters, fliers, journals, books, etc.) before me, as the dark sun spun slowly round the heavens, and first the clutter of the house behind me and then the jumble of the yard around me emptied into the back of that yellow truck. (Pitt never begins with 'the great thing'.) I discovered, of course:

* a gross of fascinating but irrelevant detail – love-notes (passed between Tom and Kitty), then bankers' bills, household receipts, even recipes (for shepherd's pie), from the period following their 'translation to conjugal bliss';
* a leaven of familiar material – a draft of the note Tom sent to Phidy at his final parting, scribbled over with some tender and some bitter emendations;
* and a spice of novelties, including the heartbreakingly hopeful letter (fluttering out of the old Reverend Jenkyns's Bible), which I quoted earlier and out of sequence, from Tom to his father, introducing that

> German gentleman, a certain Dr Müller, and once a protégé of the great Werner himself [, who] has arrived, to look into the question of Syme's theories, and adapt them it may be to the service and renown of his own country.

(This I folded and tucked on the sly into my left sock against the flat of my calf, and rolled the jeans down over it.)

But when the sun set in black and yellow through the trees, and two men lifted the sofa (empty of boys) into the back of the truck; when the yard lay green about me again, undecorated by the sitting room; when Granma had come to gather boys and *Edith* to supper, as the household was shifted several neighbourhoods south to Church Hill, and only the Reverend Thomas remained, insisting as he did on *overseeing the men*, hoping in fact to catch the baseball on the radio; when I had lifted the last sermon from the heap – William Jenkyns's eulogy, as it happens, 'upon the death of a Mr Seaborn' (Syme himself), which caused such a 'stir among the American clergy in 1850, occasioning a flurry of correspondence and a distinctly chilly ecclesiastical *air*' – and no revolutionary 'journal of the new American science' lay beneath, I was forced (in some relief) to confess that my quest had died once again, stillborn, at its *rebirth*.

Fitting, it seemed, to read over old William Jenkyns's eulogy of Sam, before the men claimed and pinched the leather armchair from my bottom, and left me alone with my thoughts in northeast Richmond:

> I read Mr Seaborn's account of those Remarkable Journeys with amusement, and a pleasing modicum of instruction. And the Great Dig, my own son's particular Holy Grail, and on which Syme himself spent the best of his life and indeed a portion of the *last* and *worst*, I believe, summoning a lost enthusiasm for the project only a month before his death, in the pursuit of which, as I had warned him before, he forgot to keep his eye on the dinner-plate, and died of a general weakness and agitation – the attempt to burrow one's way into the heart of the matter, or, rather, the matter of the earth's heart, with great drenching and plowing, and tunneling, and occasional Explosions – the great dig, as I say, has a noble ring to it, though I have always thought of it as the Big Dig, which, I cannot deny, sounds less well . . .

I had just come to that bit, scarce heeded before now, regarding the lost *enthusiasm* summoned *a month before his death*, 'in the pursuit of which . . . he forgot to keep his eye on the dinner-plate', when the Reverend Thomas tutted at my ear and sat in the grass at my feet.

'How are you getting along?' he said, rubbing his brow with the flat of his palm to relieve a tickle or itch from the sweat of the air. 'I'll need those, of course,' he apologized, 'Grandfather's papers, you know, somewhere along the line. Going now,' he added. 'Only –' he began, struck by a sudden thought. 'Edith would be *thrilled*, I'll say that much. I can't say I'd mind, either – it gets to be a bit of a burden, all this *history* – don't you think? – and you never know why, or what it was all about in the first place. The papers are straightforward enough, and sometimes I borrow something for a sermon – keep it in the family way, you see, I like that. But then there's the matter of *the second-best bed*. You wouldn't want to take it off our hands, by any chance? The glass would likely break in the truck regardless – of course, it's nothing but *bits* to begin with, and I never could see the point. The case is fine enough – a Jenkyns made it. It's just the junk inside. Filled with clay-dust when I got it, so we cleaned it up – not that it helped, the rest is clay-dust, too. I see you're staring, Professor. *The second-best bed*'s just what we call it – you know, the short straw of an inheritance. (That's me all round, I'm afraid.) Here – I'll get it.'

He roused himself from the grass with his hand on his knee, sighing, and made his way to the truck. Rummaged briefly and returned, carrying *a small, wooden, glass-panelled box* in one arm, filled with grey fragments of some kind. 'Well,' he said, setting it down at my feet. 'That's it. Take it or leave it. (I'm afraid to say, we need the armchair now.)'

I could not leave it, quite; I am not so heartless or hopeless, after all.

It took me some time (half an hour, perhaps, sitting beside it in the close, hot car) to realize what I'd got. My hands were thick and clumsy, filled with blood and sticky, as I lifted the first shard from the case and laid it across my lap. Clay, delicate, fragment perhaps from some kind of shell, curving, as it did, gently inwards. Very brittle, dusty to the touch, and carefully rounded at the edges, along which a smattering of numbers and letters (and occasional words) had been scratched by a sharp point. It seemed curiously familiar, as if I had seen it before, or suspected something like it. And then the words came back to me:

Tom picked up the broom again and formed a small heap from the broken shards of the globe in the centre of the floor, which resembled nothing so much as the remains of a great grey egg, from which the chick had escaped.

And I remembered, if not the letter, then the *matter* of the story that followed:

'Stop at once,' [Sam cried, as Tom moved to dispose the fragments out the window]. 'What act of ignorance – of wanton waste and destruction – are you about to commit? Answer me, Tom. Indeed, there is no fool like a happy fool; and all you can do is stand there, grinning idly. Give that to me directly.' And he snatched the parcel from Tom's hand, and spread it over the flagstones before the hearth, adding the small piece in his palm to the suddenly precious collection. 'It is not enough', he continued, bitterly, 'that my experiments are botched – by his clumsiness – my studies interrupted by his circus antics – but that his ignorance – his really rather astonishing ignorance – don't you agree, sir? – must be watched, constantly, like a young dog – lest it foul this or that on its way.'

And yet the ignorant dog had kept them safe so many years, and bequeathed them, an awkward burden, like the second-best bed of Shakespeare's will, from generation to generation of puzzled Jenkynses. I knew then, with such certainty as proves delightful in itself, like a bell rung clearly, that I had scattered across my lap those 'clay fragments of the world' that had moved Sam to such anger and curiosity a hundred and eighty years before. Pitt, after all, was familiar with such ruins himself; having kept, as brittle paperweight, the clay fragment of his own disaster, which scarred his son – 'that inimitable shape, a slight protrusion from a ragged triangle, unevenly split' – to remind him of Texas, and the danger of his enthusiasms.

It struck me suddenly why the shapes seemed so familiar. Some tender, meticulous hand had smoothed them into recognition. (Could I doubt that it was Syme's?) Here, a top-heavy piece of clay stood on a single toe, the belly hollowed into the form of

588

Africa; there, a delicate finger stretched forth from the main, where Florida jutted into the Atlantic; the breast of South America puffed sharp and proud into some imagined sea; the western coast of Greenland softened to a long bay. Was this strange loving duty of *precision* to those shattered fragments of the world 'the lost enthusiasm' that occupied his final month, 'in the pursuit of which . . . he forgot to keep his eye on the dinner-plate'? And then, of course, foolish Pitt, the numbers tallied at last in my thoughts, and my fingers found their echoes in one another. The proud breast of South America (3π), sought comfort in the belly of Africa ($3\emptyset$). The broad shoulder of Africa ($2\text{\ss}$), let Florida (2μ) tickle it with a gentle finger, running along. I got out of the car and squatted, in the low heat of dusk, against the kerb; spread the fragments across the leather seat in the dull light of the car door. Slowly the pieces of the world came together. Only consider, Pitt! I thought, the implications of the experiment as a whole: a molten, spinning core enveloped in a hardened, fragmented shell, splitting apart. And there, across the end of Africa, the back of Australia and the foot of India (nestled together), he had scratched the faintest of bold triumphs: 'THIS WAS TO BE SHOWN'.

Ten (long!) years before, I had written:

> For Syme, that moment, had had *the* thought – the shadow of a door fell on him from a house yet to be built. 'Fragments' drifted at last over the sea of his speculation into those famous 'segments of the earth's crust which float on the revolving core', to which Wegener himself alluded in that careful introduction to his ground-breaking work *On the Origin of Continents and Oceans*. Syme for an instant suspected the truth: the *outside* sphere was the only one that mattered; it had cracked and pushed the continents with it.

And just before his death, Syme discovered this fragmented evidence of his ground-breaking suspicion – first aired, I still maintain, in the final, suggestively titled article of the *New Platonist* ('Speculations: a curious coincidence'), which fell into Wegener's hands at last, from the lap of a no-good uncle. 'And Syme's suspicion', as I once declared (how proudly!), 'grew into Wegener's half-certainty, which Wegener gave his life to prove *utterly* certain. I have no doubt of this any more; I would stake my reputation on it, my academic career. I *have* staked my reputation on it and my academic career.'

You may suppose for yourself the fantasies I constructed from thin air on the rest of the journey from Richmond to New York. Such conferences I chaired and such papers I published! The branch of Syme Studies I opened at NYU, a department of the History Faculty devoted entirely to 'errors of science, redeemed by their place in history'. The word *Symist* itself became a commonplace of modern discourse, signifying a certain honour attached to solitary speculation and solitary speculators, distinct and distinguished from the grey mass of ordinary thought and ordinary thinkers – coined eventually in the mintage of the *Oxford English Dictionary*, proving once again my old suspicion that we can only be right *alone*. I drove deep through the night, in that vast landscape of the mind's eye presented by the unchanging unrolling of the highway under the road lights, until the summer storm broke over Philadelphia, and I turned at last to a cheap bed to sleep it off.

It proved to be more than road-weariness. I had learned to fear my enthusiasms – not only for the loneliness they produced, but the blindness in them. Like a sudden shower, they deepened the colours of the world; even the sidewalks grew rich and shining in the wet. But they drove everyone else inside. And when the sun returns, as it did, flickering through the bent blinds of my motel window, and the drunkenness of inspiration dries up, the colours fade, and solitude seems more desperate and unsure. 'And so the morning comes,' Phidy wrote shortly before he died, 'and as I have a thousand times in youth, I wonder at my foolishness of the night before.' And certainly my mission seemed less grand in the late afternoon, as I drove clanking from the parking-lot of the all-day-breakfast diner with a heap of dust and broken clay in a glass box on the seat beside me. 'My head rings like a cracked bell,' he muttered, and 'my eyes blink aching against the sun which shines bright as new in the forgiving heavens.' I was coming home. Inspirations, like shadows and nightmares – thankfully! – often vanish in the afternoon.

I crossed into Queens at dusk. The first of the car-lights glowed in the dusty summer. And after a clutter of traffic on the Avenue – amid late Sunday shoppers, and young men drinking the first drink of the early evening – I turned at the glass front of the Greek Café into poky 34th Street, eased between rows of parked cars to the pretty house with the false-brick facade, and the familiar shapes at supper within it. Familiar shapes – our solace lies in familiar shapes. (One of which just opened the front door, smelling of paints and tomato sauce.) The broad warm round of Susie's cheeks; the tender hoops of her ribs; the soft shallow of waist between the last rib and the sharp of her hip, gathered in my hand. How passionately I turned at last to *her* in the hollow of my father's death! Somehow the tide of my enthusiasms, old and revived, had begun to ebb again; and left behind its soft retreat something that looked very much like – happiness. (Love or happiness, take your pick; equally forgettable in the long run, but sweet none the less.) I was built for nothing better; and comforted myself (falsely perhaps) with Phidy's assurance that 'even Syme came, as we all do, like a lover to his insignificance'.